Master
of
the
World

Master of the World

COTHBURN O'NEAL

CROWN PUBLISHERS, INC.   NEW YORK

FOREWORD

This is the story of Timur, the invincible Tatar known to the Western world as Tamerlane. In Timur's own time the story was told by Sherif ad-Din and Ahmed ibn Arabshah and scores of other men who followed Timur or fled before him. It is reflected in Russian histories and Persian chronicles and in the literatures of India and China.

Clavijo of Spain, Perondino of Italy, Froissart of France, Schiltberger of Germany—these are but a few of the writers who have spread parts of the tale through continental Europe. And, in England, Timur was the subject of Marlowe's magnificent two-part tragedy *Tamburlaine the Great* and the model for Milton's Satan in *Paradise Lost*.

So great a story is timeless, and can be retold as time gives it new meaning. Although I have taken few liberties with significant material, some readers steeped in Western culture are sure to find parts of my narrative unbelievable; others, in the light of recent developments in the Timur country, will be quick to brand some parts *pat* or *contrived*. I can only ask those readers to suspend judgment until they have checked the offending passages against authoritative documents covering the times and places and peoples with which I deal. As I worked on my sources, I, too, was dismayed by their implications. And on rereading my script, I find it difficult to tell where factual history leaves off and fiction begins.

Perhaps it is true after all that there is nothing new under the sun. Certainly there is nothing new in Asia, not even a new story. So I retell an old one in a new idiom—the story of Timur, in contemporary American English. Timur might have told it in much the same way to his son, N'il Mahdi-Soun, who writes, as a preface to his version: *Despite his informal approach to his life story, my father was deeply sincere in his mission and firm in the conviction that he, and perhaps only one other man in his lifetime, understood the true meaning of these words of Moses as handed down to us by the Prophet Mohammed:*

> *So He drove out the man; and He placed at the east of Paradise Cherubim, and a Flaming Sword which turned every way to keep the Way of the Tree of Life.*

N'il Mahdi-Soun's story bears out that belief. Read on and see.

CHAPTER 1

My name is Timur. I am the son of Taragai, Amir of Shehri-Sebz; and in my own right I am Prince of Samarkand, Protector of the Faith, Master of the World, because I have kept the Way of the Tree of Life. I found the way I should follow on the last day of the fast month of Ramadan in the nineteenth year of my life—the seven hundred and fifty-fifth year after the Hejira.

Together with my young servant, Abdullah, and a dozen or more residents of Shehri-Sebz, I sat that morning in the chill of the mosque, which was still half darkened by the shadows of the mountains rising higher and higher, eastward toward the Pamirs. My father, attired as a monk, sat at the right hand of the old sayyid as Zain ad-Din read to us from the Koran. He smiled comfortably at my concentration on the mollah's words and frowned at Abdullah when the boy grew restless behind me.

My father was confident that I, too, would enter the monastery, since I had finished my four years of study. But although my gaze rested on the face of the sayyid, and my eyes followed the first rays of the sun as they filtered through the latticed windows and played on the jewels in the green turban which marked Zain's lineal descent from the Prophet, my thoughts were not on the sura being read. I was thinking more of the polo field, the archery range, and the arms pavilion than of the cloister and the minaret.

For Elchi Bahatur, in command of the pitiable little garrison encamped across the river, was also my mentor. I had not given up chess and polo and archery and swordsmanship, as my father had suggested, while I was studying with Zain ad-Din. Especially during the last year, under Elchi's tutelage, I had made much more progress and acquired far more skill in horsemanship and arms during my afternoons spent at the camp than I had in theology and letters during the morning sessions held in the quiet sanctuary of the mosque.

Underneath my robe I clasped my hand and felt in memory the hilt of a sword, and my arm muscles thrilled as I remembered the tension required to draw a bowstring taut. Inside, too, I felt a surge of anger when I heard again the taunts flung at me by the younger warriors—gibes which reflected on my father's gentle nature and on my own regular attendance at the mosque. But I knew that the young men's derision was only a cover to hide their envy of my superior strength and skills.

I must have frowned, because my father, probably thinking that I had taken exception to something in the Koran, frowned back at me and slowly shook his head in mild rebuke. So I centered my gaze on the monotonous movement of the sayyid's lips and tried to concentrate on the sura, which I already knew, for I could read the Koran for myself. I could not, however, drive from my mind the thought that I was the only man of the military caste in Shehri-Sebz who had not been called by Kurgan or had not joined my uncle Hadji Barlas at the clan sarai farther up the valley.

When the reading was over, Zain ad-Din dismissed us, and my father nodded farewell to me, and went into the inner cloister. Abdullah and I went into the outer court, stepped into our sandals, and walked out into the glare of the sun, which was then well clear of the mountains.

"Are we going across the river now, Amir?" asked Abdullah.

I looked down at my robe and sandals. They were not the garb of the warrior.

"I think we had better stop by the house and put on our boots," I replied.

"Yes, Amir," agreed Abdullah. "And get our horses?"

"No," I said. I was ashamed of the shaggy mountain ponies which were all that Hadji had left us when he took the Barlas clan up the river. I was as loath to walk as was Abdullah, but I had pride, which one should not expect in a servant.

"No," I repeated. "We'll walk." And I led the way through the almost empty streets.

"We'll need boots, though, Amir," said Abdullah. "Part of the way *is* pretty rocky." But I was sure that my servant was as well aware of my reason for changing to more manly attire as I was myself.

Abdullah fell into step a pace or two behind me and followed along in silence. Most of the low clay houses along the street were empty. The profusion of fig and apricot trees by the way sprawled untended and hung over the garden walls or overran the flat roofs of the houses. Since the Barlas had left, there remained only the Iranian peasants who tilled the irrigated fields by the river and the few farmers who could earn a living by trading with the peasants and catering to the hundred soldiers quartered across the river.

As we threaded our way through the center of town, past the dreary bazaars and food stalls, the idle merchants spoke to me respectfully but unenthusiastically. Such of the women in the brothels as were up at midmorning showed no more enthusiasm. They knew that neither I nor my servant had any money.

"Old bags," Abdullah snorted behind me.

They *were* a sorry lot. What could one expect in a rundown city with a garrison of one skeleton squadron? Shehri-Sebz could not even attract a passable whore. Such was the state to which the capital of the Barlas clan had sunk since my father's abdication as chieftain.

4

Farther out, where the streets were wider and the winter palaces of the Persian nobles from Samarkand were spaced farther apart, Abdullah drew up closer behind me.

"Let's not let Mamma see us, Amir," he suggested. "She'll make us stay at home and fast until sunset. I'd like to go on now and eat with the soldiers."

"I would, too," I agreed. "We'll go in the side way."

So, instead of following the street, we cut through a grove of mulberry trees and followed the wall around Ak Sarai until we came to a place where the wall had crumbled. Climbing through the breach, we came out into the grounds of Ak Sarai, the white clay palace which had been the seat of the Barlas clan. Once the showplace of Shehri-Sebz, it was now faded and rundown. The garden was overgrown with weeds, the trees and shrubs untended, and the pools empty or stagnant.

No one lived in the palace. But Abdullah's mother, who had stayed on to look after me and her son, kept open one of the servants' houses, which was always neat and clean and still reasonably well preserved. Abdullah and I stole around to a side door of the building and went to our rooms. I could hear her in the kitchen, rattling pans and humming an old Tatar lullaby to herself. The tune was familiar—the old servant had often sung it to me when I was a child, for she was the only mother I ever knew. But she was imperious, and after all only a servant; so I preferred to change my clothes and leave without her knowing it rather than to respect her wishes in the matter of observing the fast of Ramadan.

Abdullah joined me in the hall, and we went out the same way we had come. We hurried through the breach in the wall and skirted the town and crossed the dry moat to the bridge where the Samarkand Road crossed the river.

The road was much busier than the main streets of Shehri-Sebz. Merchants, singly or in groups of two or three, passed up and down the road with their pack animals, for the country from the Iron Gate to Samarkand was well protected and there was no fear of robber bands. Some outriders of a caravan were already making preliminary preparations for an overnight camp by the river.

"Which way are you going?" Abdullah asked one of the guards.

"North," the man replied, "to Samarkand."

"Where from?"

"Kunduz. Some from Herat, some from Kabul."

"Big?" asked Abdullah. Although I would not have spoken to the guard, I stopped to hear his reply.

"Big, I'll say," he answered. "Fifty camels and two hundred horses. Rich, too. Lots of girls." He leered at Abdullah.

5

"Going to break fast here?"

"Yes—and I'll bet it's some festival. I'd like to get to Samarkand to-night, but the slavers are afraid to go on in," the guard continued. "Afraid they might never get their girls to the market. Much of a garrison here?"

"About a hundred," Abdullah told him.

I started on across the bridge, and Abdullah turned and followed me to the camp. Some of the soldiers had already quit work for their midday meal. Others were finishing up odd jobs around their tents. Some were tending the fires under cooking pots which gave off savory vapors of stew and pilaf.

Abdullah stopped and joined some young soldiers whose tent was pitched near the picket line along the river. I went on upstream toward the more pretentious kibitkas near headquarters.

Before I came within speaking distance, I saw Elchi, the bahatur, seated under an awning in front of his tent. With him were several strangers, whom I took to be the new commandant and his aides. I pretended that I was not seeking Elchi and started to pass on by; but he hailed me, and the men rose, signifying that the conference was at an end.

"This is Ulatai Bahatur, my successor," Elchi said to me, as I came up. "Timur Barlas, son of Taragai, Amir of Shehri-Sebz."

Elchi, not of a chieftain's family himself, took pride in being the friend and mentor of the nobility.

Ulatai acknowledged the introduction, but seemed unimpressed by my title and showed no sign of ever having heard of my father. One of his aides, however—a young Hindu or Persian, he seemed to be, because he was too dark for a Tatar—twisted his lips into a sneer and spat when he heard the name. Although I was a head taller than the boy, I was unarmed and dressed in town clothes; and I felt helpless and inferior as he looked me over insolently and fingered the hilt of a Ghurka knife at his belt.

I stared the boy down, though I envied him the steel chain mail he wore under his striped silk surcoat, and the richly inlaid sheath of the yataghan which he sported on his belt. So he knew of my father and of me—but he would have heard of me through the envious younger soldiers and could not have gained a true estimate of my skill with the sword. I would have liked to challenge the arrogant southerner then and there. I felt only impotence and resentment—perhaps I should have returned to the monastery.

Elchi and Ulatai dismissed their tavachis, and the hateful youth turned and left with the rest.

6

"Join us at lunch, won't you, Amir?" invited Elchi.

"I had intended to," I answered frankly. "Anyway, I wanted to see you again before you left."

"Good. You and Ulatai sit down here and I'll see what Gaza has cooked up. My women have gone on to Sali Sarai," he explained to Ulatai, and went around the corner of his pavilion.

"Have you just come from Kurgan's ordu?" I asked, after Ulatai and I had sat down on the rug under the awning.

"Yes," said Ulatai. "Four days ago."

"How are things up that way?" I tried to be casual and perhaps leave the impression that I had served with Kurgan's forces somewhere.

"About as usual. Some trouble up around Badakshan, which Kurgan is trying to clean up before winter. A few Persian raiders along the Amu-Darya. Pretty quiet—nothing serious." Ulatai was more talkative than the general run of Tatars. He was telling nothing new, however.

Elchi Bahatur returned, followed by his servant, who brought a pot of stew, some barley cakes, and a crock of metheglin. Elchi sat down facing us, and Gaza set the food before him. We took bread and dipped stew from the pot. Elchi passed the crock of liquor around, and such suspicion and tension as existed between the officers—and I was sure that there was some rivalry there—was soon dissipated. The more or less formal military talk, in which Elchi was careful to include me, eased into friendly give and take.

"Who's your wild boy, Ulatai?" asked Elchi.

"Nihmu, the Ghurka? Oh, he's a fugitive from Sheik al-Jabal," replied Ulatai. "Seems that he discovered the secret of the old man's false paradise and tried sneaking into the seraglio without permission."

The story of the Old Man of the Mountain was a familiar one.

"What does he say about it?" asked Elchi, his eyes brightening at the prospect of an authentic account. "I mean, are the girls as luscious as they say, and is it true that milk and honey and wine are piped to silver taps all over the place?"

"I guess so. Nihmu won't talk much—just scowls and spits—but from what I've gathered, it must be so. Anyway, the boy liked it so well that he risked his neck. He was already used to hashish dreams—been on the stuff for a long time—and the paradise business just didn't make sense; so he started looking around while he was awake, and sure enough he found the place—and got caught. Escaped by the skin of his teeth."

"Where did you pick him up?" asked Elchi.

"He drifted into camp—started causing some trouble in the bachelors' pavilion, and Kurgan assigned him to me so I could keep an eye on him.

He's a bad one, all right, but he may come in handy some day. When he's drugged, he'll try anything."

"He'd better not try Amir Timur here." Elchi grinned. "I saw him sneering at the city clothes."

Ulatai looked me over. I was more conscious than ever of being unarmed and dressed more like a monk than a bahatur.

"Don't you be fooled either, Ulatai," Elchi continued. "The young amir"—Elchi and Ulatai were no more than thirty themselves—"has trained with my boys regularly for a year, and he's as sharp as the best of them, including me."

I knew that the words were true, but I was embarrassed at Elchi's having to make what amounted to an apology for me. I wished Nihmu would come back and insult me again so I could prove to Ulatai that I was no milksop. For I could see that things would be different under the new commandant. He gave polite heed to Elchi's words, but seemed to discount them and to share Nihmu's more open contempt for the non-military. Yes, I knew that Ulatai's coming had just about closed the Way of the Sword to me, and that left only the monastery.

After lunch I left the two officers to transact their business, and wandered over to the arms pavilion. I made the rounds of the weapons cases, trying the strength of the bows, sighting down the straight shafts of the arrows, and testing the mettle of a talwar or yataghan here and there. Best of all, I liked the ring of the swords as I flicked their keen edges with my thumb, and the swish of their blades as I swung them, Tatar fashion, in long full-arm slashes.

Other men, finished with their meal, began to drift into the pavilion. Happy to be relieved of duty until time for retreat, the warriors spoke to me jovially, and went about their business of cleaning weapons, polishing lance heads, and furbishing up the platoon guidons. Some of the older men settled down to games of chess, backgammon, or fan-tan, and it was the company of these that I sought when the tent became crowded.

"There's a caravan camping by the bridge tonight," I said, by way of opening a conversation.

"Where's it from?" asked Nihmu, who had come up with some of Ulatai's men.

"South," I answered, trying to appear as though I resented having to answer the insignificant southerner. "Kunduz, Herat, Kabul."

"Kabul?" repeated Nihmu.

"That's what the amir said," answered one of the boy's companions. "Some of them will have a little hemp." His voice was insolently suggestive.

8

Nihmu glared at the older man and grasped the hilt of the kukri in his belt, but turned slowly away, spat into the dust, and walked off toward Ulatai's pavilion.

"Tough," observed an older officer.

"He thinks so," said the newcomer. "And he's even worse with a chew of hemp in his jaw. He'll back down before most of us, but he may kill one of these boys, if we don't watch him."

"Why does Ulatai put up with him?"

I wondered the same thing.

"Kurgan seems to be salting him away for some reason. The old man has aged a lot in the last year. He's not what he used to be."

"Who's going to take his place when he dies?" asked an aide.

"Ladakh is in line for it, but he's too weak. Hussayn is making a bid, but he's too hot-headed. I don't know. I think somebody strong could easily topple either of them."

"When old Kurgan goes, hell will break loose in Tatary," said a pessimist. "The Kha Khan will probably come down from Almalyk and try to make that silly son of his the ruler of Samarkand in fact as well as in name."

We all knew of the old agreement, engraved on steel tablets, by which the descendants of Kabul—the house of Genghis Khan and Kublai Khan—should rule as khans, and the descendants of Kayouli—of which Kurgan and my own father were members—should be generals of the army and protectors of the khans. We knew, too, that Ilias Khan of Samarkand was vain and impotent, a willing puppet who served Kurgan's ends as well as the ambitions of the Kha Khan. And we doubted that Tugluk the Kha Khan, who had been soundly trounced by Kurgan, would accept a new protector without another full-scale war.

Further conversation was cut short by the high voice of a muezzin calling afternoon prayers. The Mohammedans bowed, knelt, and prostrated themselves. A few men who came from far-off Khitai and still followed the law of Genghis Khan continued their fan-tan game uninterrupted.

After prayers the camp was a beehive. I moved about and watched the horses being groomed, bridled, and saddled; the weapons and standards given their final touches. While the platoon commanders inspected the men in their own areas, I went to the parade ground and joined Abdullah, who stood with a crowd of camp followers near the reviewing stand.

Soon the trumpets and drums sounded adjutant's call and played the troops into line. As the squadron first formed, the bright armor and brighter surcoats of the soldiers, the brilliantly dyed horsetail standards,

9

the colorfully caparisoned mounts, all caused a warm feeling to rise in my breast; but still the garrison seemed pitiably small to me, for I remembered my boyhood, when my father had reviewed his thousand men on this same plain.

My heart sank steadily as Elchi reviewed the troops and the squadron re-formed to stand retreat and pass in review again with Ulatai in the place of honor. I contrasted the pageantry of even this small ceremony with the quiet of the monastery. My father, the great Taragai, had known both and had chosen to live out his years in the cloister. And he was a wise man, and a brave man. Why? I asked myself. How was a man to be sure of the Way?

Saddened by the realization that Elchi Bahatur's tour of duty at Shehri-Sebz had ended, and disturbed in my soul by the problem that filled my thoughts, I turned from the parade ground and dragged my feet toward the caravan to see what it had to offer when sunset marked the end of Ramadan.

The outrider had not overstated the size or the wealth of the caravan. Even though the sun had long been dimmed by the mountains to the west and the only bright light came through the gorge cut by the river far downstream, the bright stripes of the luxurious Persian tents seemed fairly to glisten along the bank of the river. The sense of restrained excitement which animated the travelers was infectious. My spirits rose as I passed among the tents and savored the aroma of steaming pots of pilaf and the long skewers of shashlyk roasting over the open fires.

Iranian peasants, who had come to hawk fresh fruits and melons among the pavilions, stepped respectfully aside as I approached. Their references to me as *amir* established my local standing in the minds of the travelers, and consequently I had many invitations to share salt and to dine with the merchants as soon as evening prayers broke the fast of Ramadan. I read invitations also in the coy glances of the peasant girls carrying their baskets of fruit, but I had found that they did not always adhere to the letter of the Koran regarding cleanliness of person and of garments. I could tell, however, that Abdullah, who was trailing along behind me as usual, was less fastidious, because I caught the answering smiles of the girls as they shifted their eyes to my servant.

Several of the merchants had set up temporary stalls in which to display their wares. As if drawn by a magnet, I ultimately stopped before the stall of a Persian armorer who was arranging his weapons to show to the local garrison. With the sun only a few minutes high in the gorge, the merchant had lighted his stall with naphtha flares, whose flames were reflected in the polished blades of the swords—talwars, sabers, yataghans, and scimitars of all kinds—and in the lapis-lazuli and turquoise designs worked into the silver-and-leather scabbards.

Almost immediately I espied it—the finest talwar I had ever seen, the only sword in the world for me, with a beautiful jeweled hilt and a sheath ornamented with the greatest cunning of the Persian craftsmen—much silver and many stones worked into designs of fascinating intricacy. And the merchant sensed my eagerness at once. Recognizing me as nobility— Abdullah seldom left my status in doubt for long—the armorer insisted that I handle the talwar at once.

I grasped the comfortable hilt, which seemed to have been custom fashioned to fit my hand, and flicked the blade with my thumb. The musical ring attested the truest steel in the world; and when I backed away and swung and whipped the talwar through the military cuts, I knew for the first time what real balance in a sword was.

"Just the weapon for you, Amir," the merchant urged. "Look at the sheath, too. Truly a thing to wear before the Khan."

"How much?" I asked. No matter what the price, I could not buy the sword.

"One thousand dinars." He eyed me speculatively, as though he expected me to haggle.

"Too much," I said. As long as I haggled I could hold the talwar and feel its excellence.

"For the Amir of Shehri-Sebz"—the merchant looked to Abdullah for confirmation and, of course, got it—"maybe eight-fifty."

"No," I said, "I can't pay eight-fifty."

"Eight hundred, but I'm losing money." He shrugged his shoulders and looked pitiably cheated at the very quotation of so low a price.

"Let me think it over," I said, "and bring my friend, the tuk-bashi, to look at it."

I reluctantly put the talwar down and turned to leave the stall.

"Here," insisted the merchant, suddenly eager again, "first a gift."

He hastily produced a curved Persian dagger of no great value and pressed it on me as a present.

"Think it over and come back after prayers," he urged. "Maybe I could consider seven-fifty, if the tuk-bashi likes the talwar." He almost wept.

In a few minutes the sun set at the end of the canyon, and again the muezzin's voice sang out into the cool evening air. Hastily the Faithful bowed down and intoned their prayers. Some of the wealthy Persian merchants knelt on luxurious prayer rugs before their pavilions, but the drivers and guards buried their faces in the trampled grass of the campground. I spread my cloak, and Abdullah shared a head scarf with a plump little peasant girl. I wondered to whom my servant was addressing his most earnest pleas, for I could have sworn that I heard a muffled giggle between the first and second "come to salvation."

As soon as propriety would permit, the turbaned southerners and the helmeted guards from north of the Amu-Darya rose and scurried to their campfires to break the fast of Ramadan. The orthodox believers, in token observance of the law, heated their wine, called it by another name, and poured mugs full to wash down their feast meal. Members of schismatic sects, making no such pretense, opened jugs of date wine, mixed in more potent spirits, and started the celebration in earnest.

I lost Abdullah completely, but I had no doubt that he was faring very well. For my part, I moved freely among the pavilions, accepting a skewer of shashlyk here, a bowl of pilaf there, and a cup of wine almost everywhere. I shared salt with all who asked me, but primarily I managed to pass the armorer's tent again and again to admire the magnificent talwar and make sure that it was still there, at least until Elchi arrived and gave me another excuse for handling the weapon.

In memory I clasped the hilt again and listened to the clear ring of the blade. Childishly I wished that since I could not have the sword no one might ever use it. I even considered stealing it, but the merchant sat cross-legged before his stall, dipping into his pot of pilaf and smiling at me as I passed.

At last Elchi and Ulatai rode up together and tethered their horses by the bridge. I met the two bahaturs at the first line of torches and led them to the armorer's stall.

"Isn't that the finest talwar you ever saw, Elchi?" I asked, as I pointed it out to him.

"It's a beauty, all right," he said solemnly, and took the sword from the merchant.

Elchi flicked the blade and listened to it appreciatively. Then he backed away for room, and I watched his face as he swung the talwar full-arm from the shoulder—over, down, across, backhand, and forethrust. By the look of complete satisfaction that spread over his countenance, I knew that he, too, considered that weapon the sword of swords.

Ulatai stood by impatiently until Elchi nodded and tossed the weapon, hilt first, toward him. Ulatai judged the throw, stepped nimbly to his left and caught the talwar deftly by the hilt and let the blade swing clear of his body. Then he duplicated Elchi's performance in testing the sword.

"Perfect balance!" he exclaimed, and after waiting for a nod from Elchi to confirm my competence, he turned toward me and tossed the talwar in my direction.

I followed the flight of the sword and caught it with the same flair Ulatai had exhibited—I hoped. I, too, went through the testing procedure and finished up with a full manual of the saber, as Elchi had taught me.

A sizable group of Elchi's men had formed a semicircle in front of the stall and were looking on admiringly. To feed his vanity and my own, Elchi picked up a short piece of willow and held it out at arm's length. I swung a full high forehand and sliced off the tip of the branch. Then Elchi held the branch at different angles and let me make all the standard cuts until a scant inch of the willow extended beyond his finger tips. In one final bit of bravado, Elchi held the stick just clear of the horsetail tuft on his helmet. I swung the talwar in a wide circular backhand over my own head and cut a clean half inch from the stub left in Elchi's hand.

The bahatur dropped the butt on the ground and counted his fingers in mock surprise. Then, with an elaborate sigh of relief, he grinned and said to Ulatai, "Just lucky, I guess."

"Sure, just lucky," agreed Ulatai, but I was pleased to note that he reappraised me with the same intense scrutiny he had subjected me to at lunch. I saw a new respect in his eyes—whether it was friendly or not, I could not tell.

I was saved the embarrassment of having to admit again that I could not afford to buy the talwar by the soldiers' crowding around to admire the wonderful weapon. During the confusion, which demanded all of the merchant's attention, the two bahaturs and I moved on down the row of tents. I was ruefully aware that I had probably handled the great sword for the last time, but I tried to hide my disappointment from my two companions. It was a childish feeling for me to indulge in, and I was a bit ashamed, because, except for the tufted helmets, I was taller than either of the tuk-bashis by two or three inches.

Guided by the thin reedy whine of an hautboy and the rhythmic clatter of tambourines and drums, we found our way to a torchlit circle of squatting men ringed before a slaver's tent. Inside the circle two Persian slave girls, naked except for veils covering the lower parts of their faces, writhed in a sensual nautch dance.

I scanned the circle for familiar faces—my father objected to my hanging around caravans—before we joined the spectators. Across the lighted space I saw Nihmu the Ghurka lost in his intense absorption in the dance. When the torches flared up, I could make out the bulge of the cud in Nihmu's cheek and the trickle of hemp juice slavering over his chin. Then we sat down in the front row, in a space cleared by Elchi's order, and I, too, became engrossed in the enticing movements of the dancers' smooth bellies and loins.

The men around me made little catcalls and laughed salaciously at softly spoken obscenities. They tossed money and cheap jewelry into the ring as the girls passed near and flaunted their musk-scented torsos in the men's faces. The women were allowed to keep the trinkets and small coins thrown into the ring, but the slavers who owned them got revenue from their bodies; so, as the dance drew to a close, several men rose and went to haggle with the slaver standing near the door of his pavilion. When the dance was over, the high bidders claimed their prizes and each, accompanied by a fat eunuch guard, led his girl to one of the slaver's smaller tents. Again I felt the sting of poverty—I could no more afford one of the women than I could afford the talwar. All prizes were denied me.

With the disappearance of the first dancers the spectators clamored for more, and the slaver went inside his own pavilion and returned pushing another girl before him. She was unveiled, probably a captive from one of the mountain tribes north of Badakshan; and as she walked timidly into the ring, trying to hide herself with her hands, she appeared to be a mere child—not over fourteen at the most.

At a curt command from her master, she reluctantly raised her arms over her head and began to imitate the motions of the older girls; but she was awkward and unsure, and her immature breasts and thin buttocks gave an angular quality to her dancing which contrasted sharply with the sinuous grace of the harem-trained houris.

The girl knew, however, what was expected of her and twisted her small body into grotesque contortions as she paraded herself around before the circle of men. They were strangely considerate; but no one save Nihmu, who by some perversity seemed to be fascinated by the creature, tossed coins to her; and no one rose to bid for her body. Nihmu followed her with the look of one transported and threw money at her feet every time she passed his way, and finally took off his own ring and cast it before her.

Seemingly frightened by the wildness in his eyes and perhaps recognizing the hashish stains on his chin, the dancer began to avoid him and, for some reason, to devote her entire attention to me. She paused before me and writhed in a travesty of the nautch dance. The scented oils on her body filled my nostrils with perfume, and when she bent low over me, her hard young bosom brushed my forehead. And I, too, began to want her—the ache in my groin rivaled the ache in my heart at the loss of the talwar. But I could ease neither.

The girl's attentions to me, heightened by the partisan gibes of the spectators who had joined her in urging me to bid on her, fanned Nihmu's desire into a vicious fit of jealousy. Before I knew what was happening, the enraged Ghurka had drawn his kukri in his left hand and rushed across the circle of light. I saw him grasp the girl's wrist and jerk her to one side.

"Don't waste your time on this priest-licker," he screamed, and slashed at my throat with the kukri.

Only the girl, panic-stricken at having been caught from behind, saved my life by pulling away and throwing the berserk Ghurka off balance.

The knife barely passed over my head. I felt another man's knees in my back; so I doubled up and somersaulted under Nihmu's arm and scrambled to my feet in the middle of the ring with my dagger drawn.

Nihmu wheeled to face me; and seeing the dagger in my hand, he let go of the girl and quickly drew his yataghan with his right hand.

"Talwar, catch!" Elchi barked from where he was standing—all the men were on their feet by that time.

I glanced toward Elchi just long enough to judge the distance and see him hook his thumb below the guard of his talwar, flip the weapon out of its sheath, and send it flying toward me.

I dropped my dagger and faced Nihmu as I watched the path of the talwar out of the corner of my eye. I sensed that the Ghurka expected me to lean forward for the catch. Instead I took one more step back and caught the hilt of the sword when it swished by my waist. Nihmu's blade slashed where I would have been had I leaned forward. But the Ghurka still had the advantage, for I was forced off balance and had no opportunity to take a positive stance or to bring my talwar into play for anything like an orthodox thrust.

Nihmu recovered quickly from his wild swing and pressed forward, bringing his left arm across his chest to ward off my first blow with the curved blade of his dagger and so leave his sword-arm free to plunge the yataghan into my heart. Feeling strangely calm in the face of the boy's terrible rage, I recognized his move, for it was part of the training of all Ghurkas.

Still, all I could do was to keep moving backward and allow my talwar to swing through the full arc begun with my catch. I dared not sidestep while my sword was in motion, but I did turn the hilt so the cutting edge of my blade would be forward at the completion of my swing. When my sword was high over my head, I saw Nihmu shift his left arm to parry my blow. The curving blade of the dagger flashed for a moment in the firelight, but Nihmu's timing was slow. The tip of my talwar went beyond the blade, even the hilt of the knife, and slashed cleanly through the Ghurka's wrist, severing the hand, which fell to the ground and tumbled erratically in the dust.

I stepped quickly to my right to avoid the blade of the yataghan, and then drew away from Nihmu. A cheer went up all around me, but I was filled with a feeling of dismay. I had done far more harm than I intended. I also felt relieved. I thought the duel was over. But the hashish-crazed youth seemed insensitive to pain, unaware of the loss of his hand. He wheeled and faced me, more cautiously than before, for now I had regained my balance.

He forced me to put up my guard. When he unconsciously drew his left arm across his chest he saw the bleeding stump for the first time. Stunned, he looked dully at me and then around at the circle of men who had witnessed his defeat. His eyes stopped on the little slave girl, who, unable to break through the ring of spectators, crouched shivering on the ground where she had fallen on breaking away from Nihmu.

The Ghurka seemed to go completely insane at the sight of her. He screamed shrilly and lunged toward her. I was the only one who could have stopped him, and he was almost out of my reach. I ran to intercept him and brought my talwar down flat on his sword-arm. Contrary to stories which spread, I did not cut off his other hand—I was careful of that—but I did break his forearm and deflect the yataghan pointed at the girl.

Nihmu lay where he fell. He began to whimper softly, then to cry in deep chest-ripping sobs—and crumpled unconscious in the dust.

Ulatai broke from the circle of spectators and ran to his fallen tavachi. Then he faced me angrily and grasped the hilt of his sword, but two of Elchi's men had already taken a stand beside me with drawn swords.

Elchi rushed to Ulatai and grasped the angry bahatur's arm.

"Hold it now, Ulatai," he said. "You have no use for a man who can't defend himself. The boy asked for it."

Ulatai slowly relaxed his grip on his sword and called some of his men to help him with Nihmu. Elchi took his own talwar from me, and my three friends escorted me through the excited mob.

"Better lie low for a while," Elchi cautioned me on the way to the bridge. "Take to the hills until I make peace with Kurgan. I don't know what Ulatai will do, but we can assure you a headstart."

I said nothing. As we passed the armorer's tent, I looked for the talwar. It was gone, as was the merchant himself. I wondered whether someone had bought the wonderful weapon or the armorer had simply put it away. I was depressed, disappointed over the loss of the sword. As for Nihmu, I did not know how I felt about him, but I did know that I was irrevocably committed to the Way of the Sword. It had not been a voluntary choice. Perhaps no man ever willingly draws his first blood.

Elchi untied his horse at the bridge and borrowed a mount for me to ride to Ak Sarai. On the way home he gave me more advice on hiding out in the hills. He did not tarry long at Ak Sarai, and I went to my room to collect the gear I would need on the flight.

I heard Abdullah come in later and start rummaging around in his room. In a few minutes he whistled at my window.

"I'll get the horses ready, Amir, and meet you in the mulberry grove," he whispered, and went off toward the stables.

CHAPTER 2

By daybreak Abdullah and I were far up in the mountains to the north of the river. The sharp air of the first Shawwal morning carried the smell of autumn in it, and the exhilaration coming with the higher altitude did much to drive off the feeling of depression which had dogged me through the night. Even our shaggy mounts and pack ponies seemed to catch the spirit of the morning and to welcome the challenge of the rugged trails and steep inclines. They shied less frequently at the wisps of mist that drifted up from deep fog pockets in the narrow defiles dropping off below the ledges we traveled.

The piney odor of larches welled up around us as the ponies trampled cones and fascicles under their feet. The horses, guided by a keener sense than ours, smelled forage ahead and pushed forward eagerly and, just after sunrise, brought us out onto a meadowlike plateau covered with lush grass just turning yellow in the first chill of autumn.

We reined up and dismounted in the cover of tall birches which ringed the meadow.

"I'm hungry, Amir," said Abdullah.

"So am I, and so are the horses," I said. "Take off the saddles and packs while I see what I can find for breakfast."

I took my saddle bow and chose some double-headed arrows for my quiver and started skirting the edges of the meadow. As I had suspected, the plain abounded in quail and partridge. Since I had not brought a falcon with me, I hunted by tossing stones into likely-looking coverts. On my third try, I flushed a covey of quail and brought down a bird with my first arrow.

In a few minutes I had enough game for breakfast and returned to find Abdullah with a good fire going and barley cakes warming on a stone beside it. Abdullah slept while I cleaned the birds and cooked them. After breakfast I took a short nap while he buried the evidence of our camp and watered and repacked the horses. Then he woke me and we set out on the trail again.

We continued the flight for a week, roughly paralleling the river valley. The days were much the same, the nights colder and colder as the Shawwal days grew shorter and the average altitude of the terrain higher. For the first few days we stopped frequently and listened for pursuers. We used little fire, until we lost a horse to panthers—after that we kept a flame going all night.

On the fifth day, while we were climbing a tortuous trail along a narrow ledge on the face of a sheer precipice, we were showered by rocks falling from a hairpin turn above us. We could not turn back, although we were afraid to meet the party above us, since we had no way of knowing how many men were in it. Our only course was to push ahead cautiously and trust to luck.

The narrow defile seemed to be walled by solid rock all the way, and there was no cover of any kind, nor did the ledge get any wider. And mountain men are loath to give right of way to anyone—besides, most of the tribes would consider our horses well worth the lives of two strangers.

I drew my saddle bow and hoped for the best. Edging along cautiously, we finally came to a crack in the wall, a gorge scarcely wider than a horse pack, opening off to our left. I sent Abdullah far into the gorge with the horses and took up a position above, which commanded a view of both the trail and the mouth of the canyon.

A few minutes later I heard the voices of men and the clatter of stones as the horses eased stiff-legged down the treacherous incline. Finally the leader came into view and I recognized the dialect of the laughing men as that of a Tibetan tribe from far across the Pamirs. The men, fifteen in all, with an equal number of pack horses, passed below me in single file.

Only the youngster bringing up the rear showed any curiosity concerning the canyon. He reined up at its mouth and peered into the shadows. I drew my longbow taut, until the feathers on the arrow tickled my ear. I aimed at the boy's throat, so I could destroy him without an outcry, although his companions could not have turned around on the narrow trail, or even have dismounted and made their way back to his aid.

Probably fearing that he could not get back out of the canyon, the Tibetan guided his horse back onto the ledge and followed his leader down the trail. I relaxed the tension on my bow and leaned back against the rock wall of my hiding place. After the sound of the horses died out, I called to Abdullah and we went on our way.

After that close encounter we followed trails nearer the valley and finally worked our way to a ridge which commanded a view of the river. Then I could watch the valley for parties heading toward Hadji's camp

18

and also stay in a position to make a run for the protection of my own people if we were surprised from the mountain side of the trail.

About noon one day we sighted the camp. The busy tent city spread out far below us. The gray-white felt domes of the Tatar kibitkas were brightened here and there by the more colorful pavilions of the Barlas who had intermarried with Persians and adopted the striped canvases of their wives' people. The herds of cattle and horses which dotted the plain looked like colonies of ants, and the trails beaten to them appeared to be no more than ant paths in a garden.

My horses were eager to get at the grass on the plain, which was still green, well below the Shawwal frost line. Abdullah was tempted just as strongly by the smoke rising from the midday cooking fires, but I was too cautious to rush down to the camp. I knew too well Hadji's feeling toward me, and I was willing to risk asking his protection only after some preliminary contacts with other of my kinsmen.

So, keeping out of sight and being careful of our fires, we worked our way down to a lower ridge, affording a closer view of the camp, and set up a more or less permanent base. I watched the plain for several days, until I was sure that there was no unusual activity in the camp, and then began to make daily reconnaissance trips around the outlying herds in hopes that I might catch Jaku Barlas, my youngest uncle. Jaku was friendly toward me, and although sometimes openly opposed to Hadji, he still had considerable influence with the clan.

At last I saw his big Arabian horse cantering toward a herd of sheep which grazed near the edge of the plain. I broke cover and raced to intercept Jaku before he reached the shepherds' tents.

"Jaku," I called, holding my hands high over my head to show that I carried no weapons.

"Timur," he called back in recognition. "We've been expecting you."

"Yes? What's the word?" I asked, as I reined up beside him.

"Kurgan wants to see you."

"I was afraid he would."

"It's all right," Jaku said reassuringly. "Elchi got word to me personally that he had made peace with the old man. You've been cleared of all blame."

"Then, why—?" I began.

"According to Elchi, Kurgan feels that since you killed one of his promising young warriors, the least you can do is supply him with a better one."

Jaku grinned.

"Killed him?" I repeated.

"Ulatai let the Ghurka die. A soldier with one hand is not good for much."

We started on toward the shepherds' tents.

"How does Father feel about it? Have you heard?" I asked.

"Oh—kismet. You know, there is only one Way for a man—seems yours is the Way of the Sword. He's reconciled to it."

"And Zain ad-Din?"

"So is he. He may need a sword like yours one of these days. You must have done a neat piece of carving, from what I hear."

"How about Hadji?" I was still worried.

"Suspicious, as usual. You know how he feels about you—afraid you'll claim head of the tribe when you're old enough. He'd prefer to have you in the monastery; but, next, I think he'll feel safer with you in Kurgan's service. You might get killed, you know." Jaku turned in his saddle and grinned at me again.

"Yes, I might, at that," I agreed.

"Well, hold off awhile, for the sake of the clan. You're the youngsters' hero right now. The women's, too. You know, they're saying, 'Timur cut off the hands of a man who dared to touch his girl.' Tell me, boy, what was she like?"

"I don't know—just an awkward little slave girl," I admitted. "I never saw her before or after. It wasn't the girl. Nihmu was full of hashish, and he was trying to pick a fight with me."

"Well, don't disillusion the Barlas. They're proud of you right now. It irks Hadji painfully, and I must admit that I enjoy watching him fume."

We pulled up before the shepherds' tents and dismounted. Jaku talked with the herdsmen for a few minutes and sent two of them who knew Abdullah to break my camp and bring the gear into the sarai. Then he and I rode back to the clan headquarters.

As Jaku had predicted, I was heartily welcomed by my clan. Despite Hadji's sour attitude throughout my three-day sojourn in the camp, the men of the tribe insisted on outfitting me with a string of the best horses, suitable armor for me and Abdullah, and the finest bows and bowcases the armory afforded. They gave me also the best talwar in the camp; but as I tried it, I still remembered with regret the fine sword I had handled and missed at the caravanserai.

Jaku and several other men rode with me down the river to Shehri-Sebz. And again Jaku's predictions were true. My father merely gave me his blessing and some advice.

"There is only one way for a man," he said, "and every man must find the Way and recognize it when it comes. Even though your way is the Way of the Sword, be strengthened by the four pillars of the Church—

20

Law, Prayer, Fasting, and Pilgrimages and Alms. Respect the sayyids, listen to the mollahs and imams, and ask blessings of the dervishes. Follow Allah, the One God, and give heed to the Word of Mohammed, His Prophet."

Zain ad-Din went still further. He presented me with his own best robe and shawlgirdle and a sacred ring set with a carnelian. He even dipped into the coffers of the Church and gave me a bag of gold coins sufficient to last me a year at the ordu. Then he produced a richly jeweled medallion for me to present to Kurgan as my personal gift.

So it was that the second time I left Shehri-Sebz, it was not as a fugitive, but as a warrior attired and outfitted as an amir of the Barlas clan should have been. Abdullah and I traveled openly and proudly to the Iron Gate and threaded our way through that narrow defile walled in by six-hundred-foot rusty sandstone cliffs, where I could answer, "Timur, son of Taragai," to the challenge of archers stationed on ledges high above us and be allowed to pass freely, even sometimes encouraged by hearty words of recognition from the hidden guards.

We came out of the southwest end of the gorge a little before sunset and camped in the shade of some stunted oak trees that struggled for life among smooth granite boulders on the banks of an eroded gully. When Abdullah unpacked for the night, he handed me a case wrapped in one of his mother's old shawls.

"I think you'd better wear this tomorrow, Amir," he said.

I unfolded the shawl and there, glistening in the late afternoon sun, were the jewels in the hilt and sheath of the Sword of Swords.

"Where did you get this?" I asked.

"I stole it, Amir," he replied, "while you were battling Nihmu."

"For me?" I asked.

"Not exactly, Amir. I stole it for myself, if I should run away and join a leader—in case you entered the monastery."

"But you know I would trail you down and kill you," I said severely.

"Not if you became a monk—or if I killed you first and then ran away." He was unusually bold, I thought.

"Then surely someone would seek you out and kill you."

"I thought of that, Amir. I have given you the talwar. You shall be known, and so shall I. Now I can't pretend to be what I'm not. I think it is better not to run away." He returned to the cooking fire.

"I had never considered the possibility of your running away, Abdullah," I said to him, as I fondled the talwar. "But since you have mentioned it, I shall remember."

That night I kept the talwar under my blanket with me. It seemed to me in some way prophetic that Abdullah, a mere servant, a slave, had given me the weapon he had stolen for himself—the sword with which I might one day conquer the world.

CHAPTER 3

Beyond the Iron Gate we turned south and rode through the rough country toward the Amu-Darya. We saw few people except shepherds until the wild grazing land gave way to wheat and barley stubble and an occasional patch of melons or gourds turning yellow in the autumn sun.

At the river we turned upstream and traveled for another day along busy roads flanked by shady groves of mulberry trees and lush vineyards. We crossed many bridges over the irrigation canals flowing with yellow water dipped by giant water wheels. Then, as the water of the river became clearer and the current swifter, we came again into rugged mountain terrain and our horses tired more quickly on the steady climb toward the four-thousand-foot-high plateau on which Kurgan, the King Maker, had pitched his ordu outside the walls of Sali Sarai.

We reached the high plain one day about noon and could have made Sali Sarai well before sunset, but I chose to camp a few miles from the ordu and prepare for my entry. We camped by the river about mid-afternoon and washed our garments and bathed in the clear icy water. We grazed our horses and oiled and polished our bridles and saddles.

Before sunset we could hear the seven-foot kourrouns and the huge kettledrums sounding retreat, and I could imagine the tufted helmets and bright turbans of Kurgan's two thousand warriors passing in review. I could see the horsetail standards of the mountain men and the gay silk guidons of the desert tribes. Soon I would be a part of that pageantry.

Abdullah was excited, too, over the prospects of the adventurous life we were entering upon the next day. I wondered as I sensed his eagerness. Two years younger than I, he was strong and healthy and alert. And he had sat behind me in all my sessions with Zain ad-Din—he could read and write as well as I, and spoke as well. But for his birth, he, too, might have been a bahatur. And he had thought of himself as a warrior to the extent of stealing an expensive weapon. I thought such men as he must be of military value, if one only knew how to put them to use without recognizing them as aristocracy. Slaves did have a sort of courage and a strong sense of loyalty to their own caste.

So it was with mingled dreams of pageantry and slavery, of fighting men and working men, of yesterday and tomorrow, that I slept that last night before I reported to Kurgan, the King Maker.

With the first light of morning, we were up again, putting the final touches on our battle gear and preparing for our grand entry into Sali Sarai. We curried and brushed our horses to a high sheen, covered our saddles with saddle clothes of fine silk brocade from Khitai, and dressed in our court clothes. Abdullah helped me on with my boots of soft new shagreen and held my jeweled leather belt while I put on Jaku's horse-hide khalat with the broad shoulder straps favored by the kazaks of the Kirghis Steppe. Then I girded on my prize talwar and threw Zain ad-Din's rich silk cloak over my shoulders. With all of this topped off by my father's polished steel helmet, I mounted my horse and rode in splendor toward the ordu.

As we approached Sali Sarai, however, I forgot my own elegance. The camp, spreading out on the plain before us and overflowing into the wooded foothills around the walls of the city, was the most magnificent spectacle I had ever seen. Long, wide streets ran in front of the high-domed felt kibitkas of the Tatar amirs and the luxurious, heavily carpeted pavilions of the Persian nobles and Indian rajahs who had cast their lot with Kurgan.

The streets were crowded by tall, high-cheeked Tatars riding beside their hardy wives, who were dressed in fine northern woolens and Khitai silks, and hats with feathers which waved as high as the warriors' tufted helmets. No less brilliant were the Indian camel litters and Persian sedan chairs from which richly garbed princesses peered over their veils at us as we passed.

The surroundings dimmed the luster of my accoutrements; so I was proud to remember that I had the high forehead and wide-set eyes of my father and the fair skin and white teeth of my mother's people. I could hardly expect to match the wealth of Kurgan's officers. Only in things which could not be bought could I expect to merit the attention of these people—the finest warriors and fairest women in all Asia. Of course my horses were good, and I had so far to make no apologies for my weapons or my skill in arms. And the day would come when I would have the luxuries of the victorious.

Stalls and bazaars near the center of the camp were full of those luxuries—silks from Khitai, rugs from Baghdad, jewels from India, swords from Damascus, jade from the streams of Khotan, sweet-scented musk from Tibet, fresh young slave girls from Ungut—anything a man could want. But even then I felt that it was weak to buy the prizes which should be won by the sword and that money was only for the bribery and subversion of men when warfare seemed impractical. I was hardly aware of the bag of gold given me by Zain ad-Din.

At length I reached Kurgan's kibitka—a huge felt dome furnished, as

23

well as I could see, with all the elaborate trappings of the less functional Persian pavilion. The sidewalls of the antechamber had been rolled up, despite the chill in the air, and Kurgan, flanked by two readers of the law, sat on a low ebony-and-ivory throne and passed judgment on his erring subjects.

I dismounted and left my horses in the care of Abdullah. When I presented myself to the tavachi in charge of the guards stationed before the kibitka, I was told to wait until the end of the session. So I stood for an hour and watched the gray-bearded old patriarch hold court. In spite of the fact that he had lost one eye years ago in a battle on the high steppes, he seemed to see clearly through the fallacies and sophistries argued before him and to be entirely just—or expedient—in his decisions. Certainly no one questioned the verdicts once they had been voiced and recorded by the scribes, for there was no higher appeal.

When I was finally presented by two guards, who held my arms rigid and ushered me to the throne, I prostrated myself before the King Maker and identified myself.

"I am Timur, son of Taragai," I said, "come in answer to your summons."

Then, at Kurgan's command, I rose and the guards retired.

"I am glad to receive a son of my old friend Taragai," said the King Maker. "Come into my chamber and tell me about your father."

He rose and led the way through a heavily draped door into the most luxurious room I had ever entered. I followed him through the ankle-deep pile of the rug which covered the entire floor from tapestried wall to tapestried wall. Kurgan sat down on a brocaded ottoman beside a richly inlaid chess table and motioned me to a seat opposite him.

"Now, about Taragai, is he well?" he asked me.

"Yes, Amir. Well and happy."

"Happy?" mused Kurgan. "There are pleasures but no happiness. I remember well when Taragai and I campaigned together and enjoyed together the pleasure of victory—and the pains. He was with me when I caught a Jat arrow here." He pointed to the flap over his vacant eye socket.

I had hardly noticed the flap, so clear and penetrating was the gaze of the one good eye.

"I've seen him fight off four men in snow up to his horse's belly," the old man continued. "—And he has entered the monastery?"

"Yes, Amir," I said, uncertain whether to be proud or ashamed.

"And I understand he urged you to do the same. Otherwise I would have claimed you before now." Kurgan smiled at me, and I felt the intensity of his gaze as he studied my face.

24

"I would respect Taragai's wishes," he went on. "But Elchi's reports seem to rule out the monk's life for you—at least for a time."

I had no reply—if one were expected.

"I find it hard to believe all that Elchi tells me. You know how these junior officers are."

"Yes, sir." But I was not sure.

"He says that you are an eight-goal man at polo and the talwar champion of his pavilion. And he says that you can draw a twelve-strength bow until the feathers tickle your ear—and that you can take a saddle bow and put thirty arrows into a moving target while you are riding a distance of a thousand paces at full gallop. That's hard to believe. Can you do all this?"

"Not always, sir," I replied. I could not tell whether or not the old man was taking me seriously.

"But sometimes?"

"Yes, Amir," I answered, perhaps a little defiantly. "Sometimes I can do what Elchi says."

"Then you should go far—if you have the mind-set which goes with such skill." He seemed to be in earnest.

"Mind-set?" I asked.

"Yes, the mind-set that makes the difference between a mere warrior—many warriors can match your skill—and a conqueror."

"I don't believe I understand, Amir."

"No, but perhaps you can." Kurgan again scanned my face with his good eye. "I've had reports from Zain ad-Din, also. He says that you are alert, that you can read and write and grasp some of the subtleties of theology. I can see that you have learned much from Elchi and from Taragai. Your success depends on how well you can isolate and balance the things you have learned—and will learn—and feel."

"Isolate and balance," I repeated, half to myself, for Kurgan seemed to be animated by some urgency to communicate a secret, in some race against time.

"Man has a three-fold nature," he continued softly, but with the hint of necessity in his voice. "An Arab scholar I captured some years ago described it as a chariot drawn by a black horse and a white horse and guided by the charioteer—he quoted a Greek named Plato. I don't entirely agree with him—there is no black or white—but a man does have an intellectual, an emotional, and, perhaps, a spiritual side to his nature—"

Kurgan paused and looked away.

"I have found," he said, "that these must be sealed off from one another and kept out of conflict, or a man is lost.

25

"Each applies in its restricted area, and each carries its own measure of satisfaction. The intellectual area, for example, includes war, trade, and government—all dealings with men. No emotion, no spiritual consideration must ever enter into affairs among men. Any feeling of friendship or affection between men is as unnatural and debilitating as sodomy."

He looked directly at me.

"Do whatever you must do to a man, or for a man, without reference to any feeling for him. Friendship, hatred, jealousy—emotions of any sort—will hamper your efficiency in doing what is logical, expedient, and necessary. Do you understand me, Timur?"

"I am not sure," I said. "I am trying to follow you, sir."

"Wear your emotions out on women—that's the emotional area. Love them, hate them, caress them, torture them, but see that you use up all your passion on them and leave not one bit of feeling to influence you in any other field. Just as there is only one God and He is Allah, there is only one pleasure and she is woman. Wealth, fame, food, wine—all are but a prelude to the pleasure in a woman.

"Remember that—seek your pleasure in women and don't look for happiness in other things, not anywhere. Bribe stupid men with the illusion of happiness in wealth and power, but seek not joy for yourself in those things. Use them for trade and war. Do you follow me, Timur?"

Again he scanned my whole face and ended up looking straight into my eyes.

"Not too well, Amir," I replied. I searched for the meaning in his words and tried to divine his reason for saying them. I wanted to get absolutely clear in my mind everything he was saying. For I recognized the great importance of his statements. Through all the years of my life I have remembered his exact words and they have affected me vitally.

He relaxed somewhat and went on.

"And the spiritual side—the side that has blinded Taragai as the emotional side deludes my grandson, Hussayn—I don't know. Perhaps there's something to it, but it seems to me that religion covers the area of the riddle, of the absurd—things that are at best unproved if not really untrue, guesses at reality."

I had the feeling that Kurgan was no longer talking to me, but to himself, groping through an old, much-considered problem.

"So much stress on the unusual, the exceptional—holding on to the freakish rather than the normal. Moving mountains by faith—the virgin birth nonsense of the followers of Jesus. And the miraculous gift of the law to Moses, which Mohammed passed on to us—a law which prohibits the ten actions most natural to man. All wrong, all absurd."

26

He turned his attention back to me, as though he had still another point to make.

"Some parts of religion are functional—probably not spiritual matters at all, so use what you can turn to your own ends, but be careful to weed out the absurd. Delude men if you can but be not influenced by the myths of the mollahs. Always choose twelve strong men over the favor of Allah. Does that go against the teachings of old Zain ad-Din?"

He smiled quizzically at me.

"I'm afraid so, Amir," I answered.

"But not against his practices. He has been able to hold on to his serenity of spirit only by virtue of the keen edge of my sword. Protector of the Faith means guardian of the wealth amassed in the name of the Church, and I think Zain ad-Din sees that as clearly as I do."

Kurgan settled back onto the ottoman and rested his arm on the chess table.

"I'm relying on his estimate of you. I think the old sayyid is picking a Protector of the Faith. He's never picked a loser yet. And after Elchi's report, I am inclined to go along with Zain and give you your chance. That's why I have delivered this little lecture."

"Thank you, sir," I said, feeling that the interview was drawing to a close.

"Don't thank me yet. All I'm giving you is a chance and some advice. You may be merely a first-class bahatur, or you may be the King Maker. But I can't give it to you—you'll have to win it.

"My son Ladakh is in line for my place, and Hussayn is challenging him. But Ladakh can't learn—and Hussayn already knows everything. I'd keep an eye on him, if I were you. And I'll be watching all of you—remember that."

"Yes, sir," I said.

"Zain ad-Din says that you don't talk your head off," Kurgan said significantly as I rose at his gesture of dismissal.

"No, sir," I said.

"Report to Elchi Bahatur. I'm assigning you to him for the time being."

"Yes, sir," I said, well pleased with the assignment, and hurried away to join my friend's squadron.

CHAPTER

4

Already acquainted with Elchi Bahatur's personal followers, I found it easy to fit myself into the squadron. Again I was privileged to listen to those experienced warriors, to learn by the direction and example of my elders.

I was able to sift the grains of truth from the wild stories of the most boastful bahaturs; and my attention to their favorite tales, which some of them had begun to believe themselves, flattered them and earned their favor.

In the beginning, of course, some of the older men who had not been with Elchi at Shehri-Sebz were inclined to take advantage of my apparent naïveté. I resented their attitude, but I tried to follow Kurgan's advice not to let personal feelings affect my career.

When I asked Berca about the scar on his cheek—a question which was usually welcomed and answered in elaborate and fairly accurate detail by the battle-scarred warriors—I was forced to take action, however.

"This scar?" said Berca. "Oh, I got it in battle with a giant riding a unicorn."

I grinned at the absurdity and urged, "Do tell me about it."

"Well," he said, and winked at some of our companions. "It was far north in the Land of Shadows, beyond the Syr-Darya and the Ob, where the sun shines for half a year and is hidden for the other half."

I did not like the tone of ridicule in his voice when he began his story. Drunk though he was, I detected more than idle jesting in his intent.

"This giant appeared out of the northern lights and challenged me. So we fought from sunrise until sunset—let's see, that would be about six months, wouldn't it? Anyway, a few weeks before dark, my horse starved to death, and I had to continue the battle on foot.

"Well, I finally ran the giant through, but as he fell forward, I dodged to get out of the way of his body and snagged my cheek on the horn of the unicorn—you see, I'd forgotten that it wasn't a horse."

I laughed, as did the other soldiers, but I detected a note of mockery in their laughter which was directed at me instead of at Berca's story. Personal feelings aside, a warrior could not allow men to mock him.

"Now, tell me the truth," I said. "It ought to be good—maybe a slave carved you with a kitchen knife."

Berca scrambled to his feet, and the scar, which ran from his right eye to his chin, grew livid in the yellow light of the winter campfire.

"You doubt my story, kopeghi? I'll give you a scar and let you make up a story to match it."

I, too, rose and drew my talwar.

28

"I can never match your lies," I said, "but I'll give you a scar to match that one and frame your silly face."

At that Berca slashed at me, but I recognized the rage in my adversary and again felt the confidence of a clear head. I knew that I could kill the man, although he was a veteran of several severe campaigns. However, a living testament to my integrity was to be preferred, and so I merely parried his blow and enraged the bahatur even more.

He swung again at my throat, and I deliberately left my sword out of play and ducked under his arm. So wild was he that his swing spun him around, and I had a clear opening to sever his neck from behind. Instead of taking advantage of his position, I let him regain his balance and face me again.

"He's playing with you, Berca," jeered one of the spectators. "Your kopeghi is a fox."

I let him swing once more and then called, "Your left cheek, Berca," and stepped back as I swung so that only the point of my talwar sliced through his cheek and laid open a wound, which, when it had healed, was as near a match to his other scar as if I had carved it carefully with a surgeon's knife.

Thereafter no one mocked me, and even the most arrogant bahaturs answered my questions and told me straight stories. And when I was made tuk-bashi and put in command of my own troop, I had Berca assigned to me. He was a valiant officer, and his monkey-face, framed by the saber scars, was a fit warning to my men. I never had cause to question his loyalty or his respect for my sword.

I gradually became accustomed to the grandeur of the ordu—to the glitter of the winter sun on the snow before the fine pavilions, to the pageantry of the colorful troops in full dress passing in review and casting their brilliant reflection in the polished brass kettles of Kurgan's nine-foot nakaras, to the elaborate feasts to which the nobles brought the most beautiful women in the world. And to the easy informality of the long winter evenings around the campfire, the berserks crying-drunk on kumiss made from fermented mare's milk, the officers equally drunk on wine and spirits, the squabbles which brought the rivalries and weaknesses of the amirs out into the open. And to the night-long orgies in the tents of the Persians, where buxom houris and slender Hindu slave girls danced naked and passed among the guests with trays of sugared dates and wine.

I proved myself in battle, too, on raids with Elchi when he let my troop, under my own standard, lead the squadron into the field. And when the chieftains of distant tribes came in to pay tribute and to celebrate the

New Year, I was included in the councils held in Kurgan's tent. There I was allowed to sit in on the discussion of strategy and tactics for spring campaigns by the greatest warriors in all Tatary. There I began to learn about the peculiarities of the various tribes from the Sea of Abaku to the Pamirs, from the Kirghis Steppe to the Desht-i-Lut. And I began to appreciate the genius of Kurgan which had enabled him to hold those strange men together since his revolt against the Kha Khan.

It was during one of those meetings that I got my first assignment to lead an independent expedition. While the important amirs were deep in the discussion of weighty matters of the empire, a breathless courier broke into the council to report that a band of Persian raiders had crossed the Amu-Darya and stolen a herd of horses in addition to pillaging a number of peasant villages.

"Timur—Timur Barlas!" Kurgan called, and looked around the circle of seated officers.

"Here, Amir," I answered, and rose from my seat in a back row.

"Take a hundred men and bring back those horses," he commanded.

"Yes, sir," I said eagerly, and hurried self-consciously to the door. Hussayn or one of the other experienced leaders could have been chosen, but I felt that Kurgan was making a point of bringing me to the attention of the assembled chieftains, and I was doubly proud of the assignment.

I had my trumpets and drums sound assembly; and before midnight my troop, with my lieutenants Kaidu and Berca leading the second and third platoons, rode toward the Persian border. All night we raced through the light snow which lay smooth and glistening on the high plateau. In the early morning we passed through foothills, down to the lower plain country watered by the river.

We had no trouble in following the path of the raiders. Despondent men and weeping women everywhere pointed the way the Persians had gone after they had taken the most valuable property and the fairest girls and sturdiest boys from the peasant villages. For a whole day we trailed the raiders before we came to the place where they had forded the river and headed out into the desert to join the main body of their tribe.

The trail was clear in the moonlit desert sands; so we again rode all night and came upon the oasis where the tribe had been in camp. There we watered and rested our horses and slept for an hour or so. Then we galloped on into the desert. A little before noon we sighted the dust of the caravan several miles ahead of us in the floor of a dry riverbed flanked by windswept sandstone boulders.

I called a halt and summoned my lieutenants.

"Let's race for the train," suggested Kaidu eagerly.

"No," I said. "We shall first destroy the warriors who come to meet us. Then the drivers will flee and we can capture the train without further resistance."

"They might get away," objected Berca.

"We can catch them," I said confidently. "If we capture the train first, we shall be harried by the guards all the way back. First we destroy the fighting men—every one of them. Understand?"

"Yes," said my lieutenants.

"Now, Kaidu, you split your platoon," I directed. "Take half of your men to the left and send half to the right. Stay behind the boulders on either side—keep out of sight until I charge—then pour arrows into the enemy's flanks."

Kaidu split his forces according to plan and spread to the sandhills and rocks on either side of the river.

"Berca." I turned to my second officer. "Stay a hundred paces behind my men. Keep your platoon in reserve to run down stragglers and breakaways. When I charge, have your men take longbows and volley arrows over our heads until we engage the Persians. Understand?"

"Yes, Amir."

Berca returned to his platoon, and I led the troop forward again at an easy canter, to allow Kaidu to stay ahead of us on the more rugged terrain he had to cover.

A few minutes later, the Persians sighted us; and as we approached, I could see the warriors turn back from the caravan to meet us, as I had anticipated. I continued our gentle pace, stirring up as little dust as possible in order to give the impression of a small troop. When we were near enough to estimate strength, I saw that the enemy force was slightly smaller than my own company still in the valley.

The Persian chieftain, riding ahead on a white Arabian stallion, seemed to take heart from the apparent equality of forces, for he brandished his sword above his head and his men let out a battle shriek and charged. My trumpeter sounded "charge" at the same time, and I led my platoon into a gallop.

At the blast from the trumpet, Kaidu's men broke cover from the enemy's flanks and began shooting arrows from both sides. Berca's reserves, bringing up the rear at a slower pace, let go their volleys from the longbows.

Although the arrows disabled few horsemen, because the flowing robes of the desert men make blurred targets, the archers did confuse the enemy and tangle many of the robes so that they hampered the sword-arms of the Persians. Heading for the chieftain myself, I led my platoon straight through the ranks of the raiders, slashing at the enemy or parrying blows, as opportunity permitted, but not stopping to engage the enemy in prolonged combat.

I warded off a blow by the leader as I passed, but neither of us did any damage. With the fighting too close for archery, Kaidu's men closed in on the enemy's flanks and a section of Berca's reserves rode forward to break up the turn of the main Persian forces, so that by the time my platoon wheeled for the second charge the enemy was in a near rout. I sought out the leader again and found him engaged with one of my lancers. I rode hard for him, and swinging my talwar wide and high, I neatly severed his head from his shoulders before he ever knew of my attack.

Soon thereafter the battle was over. I counted forty enemy dead—none left wounded—and Berca reported that his reserves had slain the eight raiders who had tried to break away. I had lost eleven men dead, and six injured, none too badly to ride.

I instructed Abdullah to clean the chieftain's skull, which I planned to have lined with gold and made into a cup for Kurgan, and then led my own platoon to capture the train. As I had predicted, the drivers had fled into the hills and we met no opposition.

In addition to the stolen horses and captive peasant children, the train consisted of ten camels, eighty horses, twenty pavilions, several small tents, a big cache of food and loot from former raids, and some two dozen women, including the chieftain's eight wives and concubines.

It took us two days to sort the loot and return it to its rightful owners and to restore the captive girls and boys to their parents. I saw to it that Abdullah spread my name widely among Kurgan's subjects along the river so that I might be known as a savior to those simple grateful people.

Since the expedition was a swift movement of retaliation, I allowed no looting or raping, and I presented the remains of the Persian tribe intact before Kurgan's kibitka.

"Well done," said Kurgan, before the assembly of amirs. "We shall make your victory a part of the New Year's celebration. Come back after prayers for your reward."

Kurgan ordered the loot sorted and stacked, and sent the captive women to be bathed and perfumed. I dismissed my men and retired to my pavilion.

Sore and tired from the rigorous mission, I undressed, put on a heavy robe, and sought a banja. I found a vacant one with a stone already hot from hours over the roaring fire. I sat on a wooden bench while the attendant threw buckets of water on the stone and the tight little room filled with hissing steam. Then I lay down on the bench and slept for a while and let the heat penetrate deep into my body.

An hour later, the attendant awoke me, and I went into the next room, where he drenched me with cold clear water from the river and massaged my muscles back into tingling life. Then I returned to my pavilion and put on fresh linen and my finest khalat. Feeling fresh and relaxed, I made my way to Kurgan's kibitka for the New Year's feast. I went past fires over which whole sheep, haunches of camel, and quarters of horsemeat were roasting on revolving spits, and loaves of wheat and barley bread were baking in open-faced ovens. There was a festive air everywhere. Warriors and slaves alike toasted me as I went by. It was good to be the hero of the New Year.

The heavily carpeted chamber of Kurgan's tent was brilliantly lighted by naphtha torches and lamps placed on stands around the room and hung on golden chains from the lofty dome. Already the leaders of Tatary were assembled. They lay on rugs or divans or sat on pillows and ottomans scattered around the room beside charcoal braziers and low serving tables. The amirs cheered me when I entered, and Kurgan beckoned me to sit beside him on his royal couch.

"Hero of the hour!" He greeted me lightly and invited me to share his tray of food and wine. He talked easily to me as the nobles gorged themselves almost into insensibility.

Every known food, every dainty, every vintage of fine wine was passed at some time during the evening—caviar from the Sea of Abaku, dates from Bokhara, candied melons from Shehri-Sebz, dried figs and apricots from Samarkand—the best Tatary had to offer. And Kurgan kept a steady flow of gifts coming from his stores of wealth. Slave girls passed among the guests and sprinkled seed pearls on the turbans of the southerners and hung gold chains and jeweled pendants on the Tatars' helmets.

During the course of the evening Kurgan had the Persian chieftain's fast white horse led in and presented to me. He also ordered the leader's royal pavilion, complete with furnishings, set up for me during the banquet and sent word to Abdullah to move my personal belongings into it. Later he gave me jewels and stocked my new home with provisions from his own choice supplies.

And each time he gave me a gift, he passed out similar or lesser gifts to other amirs present. Only Hussayn seemed to resent Kurgan's attentions to me. It was his obvious envy that prompted me to ask more than I was due at the time.

"Now, you may ask a gift," said Kurgan, toward midnight. "What would you like?"

"Amir, this action was carried out under my own standard—the Barlas standard, with which I have led my troop into battle before. I would like a thousand men and command of Shehri-Sebz and my valley." Hussayn was the daroga of Kabul with his own regiment as its garrison.

"You *are* a pigeon cock, aren't you, Timur Barlas!" the old man said, and laughed indulgently. "Do you know what it costs to maintain a thousand men when you are not at war?"

"I could take Karshi," I said.

"Karshi is already controlled by my son Ladakh. I can't allow you to rob him."

"Or Balkh," I said. Balkh was rich, far richer than Sali Sarai. "With a thousand men I could sack Balkh."

He looked at me in astonishment.

"Balkh is subject to Shah Malik of Herat. Would you challenge Malik with a thousand men?" He eyed me narrowly. "Yes, I believe you would."

"Of course I would," I said eagerly.

"No. I can't risk any trouble with Shah Malik of Herat."

"The raiders I just killed were his subjects."

"Yes, Timur—but both Shah Malik and I must consider the raid and your retaliation as unofficial. Neither of us wants a war."

"But Malik would not discipline his raiders. I thought such actions caused war."

"No, nor will I discipline you—this is another kind of war, which you must learn. But back to your request—you can't afford a regiment yet, not unless there is a war. I'll give you a squadron—and something else." He summoned a tavachi and whispered a command.

Presently the musicians began to play, and the women captured from the Persians were ushered in. Dressed in their finest court clothes, the veiled women were paraded before the guests and then lined up before Kurgan.

"Show yourselves," he commanded.

Unabashed, the women stripped off their upper garments and stepped out of their sheer pleated bloomers.

"Dance," commanded Kurgan.

Naked, except for their veils, the women went into one of their native harem dances. Since the women knew that there would be no bidding as at a slave market, they danced beautifully and gracefully, bending and swaying their nude bodies in sinuous pirouettes instead of wriggling in the low nautch of the bazaars.

"Pick any two you want," Kurgan said to me.

"Two?" I asked.

"You wouldn't start on a long journey with only one mount, would you? Or perhaps you want more than two?" He laughed at the alternate possibility.

"No," I said, "two are all I can afford."

Although I was fascinated by the mature body of a beautiful houri who appeared to be several years my senior, I hesitated to choose her. Perhaps I was afraid of her, of her wider experience, and of *any* older woman's tendency to dominate. Anyway, I tore my gaze from her full breasts and wide comfortable hips, the pride of southern women. Instead I watched with growing admiration the seductive grace of two soft-eyed Persian girls, one about my age, I judged, and the other two or three years younger. Both were lithe and well formed and promised to develop into beautiful women; so I pointed them out to Kurgan.

He had them brought before us, and when a screen had been placed around them, he ordered, "Show your faces and tell your names to your new amir."

They removed their veils and stood before us, their faces as lovely as their young bodies.

"I'm Lillit," said the older one softly.

"Reba," said the younger.

Both addressed their answers to Kurgan.

"Not me—this young amir, the hero of the New Year," he said, and laughed in genuine amusement at the look of pleasure which spread over the girls' faces at being given to me instead of to a gray-bearded, one-eyed old man.

Kurgan had rich garments brought in, and as soon as the girls emerged fully dressed from behind the screen, he dismissed me and announced to the group, "The guest of honor is eager to be about his home life."

The amirs jeered at me as my women fell into step behind me and followed me to the door.

"Timur will not ride tomorrow," shouted one of the men.

"Not a horse, anyway," said another lewdly, and the whole company laughed.

I returned to my quarters to find the luxurious new pavilion in order and the sleeping chamber already warm from the heat of charcoal braziers which Abdullah had fired.

By the dim light of the coals I undressed and took my wives to bed. As the night wore on I found it difficult to decide in which I enjoyed the greatest delight. Lillit was more skilled in the arts of the harem, but Reba's fresh eagerness seemed to offset the older girl's longer experience. Both were as affectionate as little kittens, and I began to realize the truth of Kurgan's statement that there is only one pleasure and she is woman.

But, in the early morning hours, as the two smooth warm bodies snuggled quietly up to mine under the silken covers of my couch, I had an even fuller measure of satisfaction. I had a squadron of my own, fine horses, a royal pavilion luxuriously furnished, and two adoring wives—none of which had been bought. All had been won by my sword, as such things should be won.

CHAPTER 5

My new estate as a tuk-bashi of some consequence, as evidenced by my rich pavilion and my two beautiful wives, gave new zest to life in camp during the dull season when there was little military activity. I found life in my household different from anything I had known since I had been a child in my father's court.

Lillit made an excellent mistress of my pavilion. She was adept at haggling with merchants and food peddlers and efficient in handling Abdullah and the old serving woman I had added to my staff. Her sharp tongue, in marked contrast to her soft eyes and her obsequious manner toward me, kept our domestic life running smoothly and pleasantly.

And Reba made it her special duty to look after my personal comfort. She saw to it that I had the choicest food from our common tray and that my clothing and armor were always just as I would wish them.

Abdullah, of course, felt that Reba's solicitous care of my person invaded his rightful province, but I assured him that he should concentrate on learning how to serve me in the field. To absorb his leisure, I set him to visiting with the servants of other amirs and learning from them what would be required of him during spring campaigns. I found that he learned more about the private lives and failings of the amirs than he did about the duties of their servants, and I marked this down as being of some possible value in the future.

Although I began to want a true princess wife, one I could take with me to court functions, I never ceased to find delight in my affectionate slave girls. Both were accomplished musicians and singers, either solo or in duet, and equally pleasing in love play, either solo or in duet, as I learned when they taught me the harem game called Scheherazade. As we played it, it was a duet, but I was given to understand that with sufficient resources it could become a chorus game. The rules were that I should indulge in love play with one of the girls while the other sang one of the many long stanzas of the sensual *Love Song of Scheherazade*. At the end of a stanza I was to change girls unless my partner could hold me, either by main strength or seductive wiles. The girl who gave me final satisfaction received a gift—some jewel or bauble chosen beforehand.

We played the game many times during the short days and long nights we were snowbound in our pavilion. Although Lillit was both stronger and wiser in the tricks of the harem, I exercised sufficient control to see that the prizes were about evenly divided between her and Reba during the winter and so kept both of my wives happy and contented. All in all, the arrangement was highly satisfactory. And there were sufficient short raids and defensive expeditions to give me a chance to improve my squadron and my leadership in the field. I was still somewhat piqued by Kurgan's refusal to give me a regiment of my own, because Hussayn, even during the winter season, had continued to build up his power in Kabul. He had secured Badakshan and Kunduz and was admittedly the master of all the territory from Sali Sarai to the Khaibar Pass. For, despite his volatile nature, Hussayn was a first-rate warrior and field officer, for a man of twenty-five. And even then I felt that he was my chief rival in Tatary.

So I asked for the most difficult assignments available and tried hard to convince Kurgan of my ability. I continued to destroy completely all of the warriors in the small bands I attacked, as I had done with the Persian raiders, and to bring the property and women untouched into the ordu. Arabshah has written that I was unnecessarily ruthless and cruel, but he got his information only through hearsay. He did not know me until many years later. I was a callow youth then, and I did what I had to do to impress Kurgan. I was not then, nor have I ever been, ruthless or cruel. My actions have never been motivated by any urge toward cruelty or any other feeling—not even greed, for greed is the driving force in little men who do not understand the Way. What I did, what I have always done, was dictated by a rational understanding of what is required by the nature of the world and men.

I *was* noticed by Kurgan. One day in early spring he summoned me and took me into the private chamber where he had first received me into his service.

"Sit down, Timur," he invited. "I have been reviewing your service record."

I sat down before the old man and tried to read his face. I had not accomplished anything in recent weeks, and I could not suppress a faint feeling of apprehension. I might even lose my squadron before the real test came in the big campaigns. I had never been sure how much of the favor shown me at New Year had been given merely to add to the pageantry of the occasion. But Kurgan was inscrutable.

"Can you sum up the present situation of my domain, young man?" he asked, without any hint of friendliness in his voice.

"Perhaps," I said, "to some extent. Why?"

"You should be familiar with the campfire talk, unless your wives are distracting you." He smiled for the first time.

"They are sealed off, Amir," I said, adopting his own phrase.

"And your servant, Abdullah, moves around among the other officers' camps quite freely. Is that your idea?"

"I don't discourage his visiting, sir," I replied. I had no desire to be censured by Kurgan for spying among his men.

"You should have the picture," he continued. "Give it to me."

"Hussayn has consolidated his position in the south," I began.

"Will he be a threat to me?"

"Not unless you show weakness. He would prefer to help keep your holdings intact and succeed you." I was emboldened somewhat.

"Go ahead," he said, inscrutable again.

"Ladakh, your son at Karshi, is in firm control from Bokhara to Balkh. Old Saif ad-Din is a weak Protector of Samarkand, but his son, Nur ad-Din, can keep things quiet as far north as Tashkand and Otrar. Of the commanders of more far-flung garrisons, I know little. All this is common knowledge, Amir."

"Very good," he commented. "Did you know that Bayazid Jalair of Khojend, a chieftain of my own family, is plotting with your uncle Hadji Barlas to resist paying tribute this year? They held out some on me last time."

"No, Amir. I had no way of knowing that."

"What would you do about it?" he asked. I still could not tell whether he was mocking me or testing me.

"I would enlarge the garrison at Shehri-Sebz," I answered, risking Kurgan's disapproval of my presumptuousness. "And keep both tribes in the hills until they accepted my terms."

"With Amir Timur Barlas in command, I suppose?"

"Yes, sir," I answered, nettled by the old man's continued imperturbability. "That would split the Barlas, and the mere presence of the garrison ought to quell any uprising."

"I think perhaps you are right." Kurgan smiled again, ever so slightly. "You seem to be getting a grasp of things, and your record shows that you will do whatever an occasion demands."

"Yes, sir," I said, still a little defiantly.

"I may follow your ideas, but first you will need a princess of the palace and quite a bit more wealth than old Taragai has left."

My spirits fell. I knew no chieftain who would bestow his daughter on me, much as I wanted a noble consort.

"I have arranged for both," continued Kurgan. "On the first day of Jamada 1 you will marry my young granddaughter, Aljai. She is Hus-

38

sayn's sister, and I can assure her a dowry equal to all Hussayn has amassed."

"Thank you, Amir," I said eagerly.

"I want more than gratitude. Don't consider this a gesture of friendship toward you or your father. I shall demand the loyalty of a true kinsman—then I shall be flanked on the north and south by rulers from among my own grandchildren. I shall feel safe with you and Hussayn about equal in strength."

"And pitted against each other," I remarked, accepting Kurgan's cold-blooded appraisal of the situation and letting him know it.

"If you won't co-operate, yes. I can always throw enough power behind one of you to keep the other in line. I should prefer to see you friendly and mutually dependent. Hussayn is a reckless warrior; you are a calculating campaigner. You could use each other and I can use you both."

"I think I understand, sir, and I accept."

"You are beginning to learn," he said, and then added, "There was never any question of your acceptance. I am still the King Maker. Prepare for your wedding."

"Gladly, sir."

"And I might add," he said in a lighter tone, "that Aljai Agha is as beautiful as she is wealthy."

With that he dismissed me, and I returned to my pavilion to ponder the new turn in my career.

Lillit was the first to sense my detachment from things around me.

"My amir is troubled?" she asked, as I sat beside a chess table and toyed idly with the pieces.

"No, not really," I answered, and drew her down on my lap.

"Did Amir Kurgan have bad news?"

"I don't know. I am to marry his granddaughter, Aljai Agha, on the first day of Jamada 1."

I felt her stiffen on my lap and then relax just as suddenly.

"And my amir doesn't wish the agha to take my place as mistress of the household?" she said hopefully, and her big soft eyes grew moist.

I had not worried particularly about that possibility, but it cost me nothing to humor Lillit, and I knew the rewards would be pleasant.

"I shall never find a better mistress of the pavilion than you, Lillit," I said, and stroked her thighs, which were smooth and firm under the sheer bloomers. "Nor a lovelier one."

"Nor a more faithful one," she added, and burst into tears.

"But the word of Kurgan is law in all things," I said, and tried to reconcile her to the inevitable.

Throughout the preparations for my marriage Lillit alternated between spells of intense affection, in which she tried to please me in every way she could, and fits of despondency, marked sometimes by a frantic sadness in her attentions to me and sometimes by the same sharpness she exhibited in her dealings with the servants. Reba, on the other hand, probably feeling that she had nothing to lose—since she had never been mistress of the pavilion—and perhaps welcoming the prospect of being equal to Lillit under the new agha, never wavered in her minute ministrations to my personal well-being.

"The agha is rich?" she asked.

"Yes, as rich as any princess in Tatary," I replied.

"And we may live in a palace with pools and gardens?" she asked excitedly.

"I hope so," I said. "In Ak Sarai, my own palace at Shehri-Sebz."

"Is it beautiful?"

"It was once, and it shall be again," I answered, and went on to describe what Ak Sarai had been like in my childhood. And in some strange way, which I did not understand, Reba's excitement over the prospect of living in luxurious surroundings animated her body with a new eagerness and willingness which increased immeasurably the exquisite delight I found when I lay with her alone. It was not that she was mercenary or that she was insincere in her desire to please. It was a physical thing. She was genuinely stimulated to sexual desire by the idea of wealth. I began to see why men would fight like devils for luxuries with which to surround their women. And although I was not sure how soon Kurgan would put me in command of Shehri-Sebz, I found it well worth while to assure Reba that our removal to Ak Sarai was imminent.

Abdullah, too, was delighted at the thought of our return home. He must have pictured himself as a chamberlain at least, a man of importance in the eyes of the merchants who had formerly looked upon us both as penniless loiterers around their stalls. I had to caution him not to spread any information beyond the fact that I was to marry Kurgan's granddaughter. And he obeyed my orders, for no one knew the military significance of my alliance until the very day of the wedding.

Kurgan called in the chieftains from every tribe under his control. I knew that he was using the occasion of my marriage to make final plans for spring campaigns—or using my wedding to add color to the assembly, for he well understood the value of combining holiday and military functions; but I resented his motives not at all. Again I would be the center of attraction, this time at the councils of both the highest rulers and the most learned men of the empire.

So it was that the ordu before Sali Sarai bustled as busily and shone as brilliantly on the first day of Jamada 1 as it had on New Year's day, more

40

brilliantly because the young grass on the plain and the tender leaves of oaks and willows on the banks of the Amu-Darya added nature's contribution to the festive decorations. All day the guests moved about from one banquet spread to another in the shade of the trees and awnings or joined groups of lazy revelers who sprawled on the fresh grass and listened to the songs and stories of minstrels from all over the world.

In the morning I appeared alone before the judges of the Church to hear the marriage agreement read and to see my name and those of my bride and the witnesses recorded in the Church register. I had not seen Aljai. She was still in the care of her ladies, who spent the better part of the day preparing her for the ceremony.

In the late afternoon she appeared, and from that time on I saw no more of the pageantry around me. She emerged from her own pavilion and faced the long carpet leading to the throne set before Kurgan's tent, where I sat with the King Maker. The drummers began a thunderous roll on the six-foot nakaras and the trumpeters sounded a brilliant fanfare.

Slowly the princess began her procession down the avenue of tribal standards, each held by an amir of royal blood and guarded by an escort in full dress. She was dressed in a sleeveless gown of pomegranate red, embroidered with gold floral designs. Over the gown she wore a white silk robe with a high cloth-of-silver collar and a long train which was carried by six of her serving women. Her long black hair was adorned by a cloth-of-gold cap with heron plumes curling back to the nape of her neck.

By the time I could see the black jade pendants suspended from her ears, I had become so enraptured by the beauty of her face that the rest of the ceremony was a blur in my memory. She was truly a princess, but, as the years proved, had she been a slave, I would have considered her the loveliest woman Allah ever sent to comfort a man. She had the fair skin and high cheekbones of the northern people; and her eyes, though sharper and clearer than those of the Persian women, were not one whit less tender or inviting. And I watched every movement of her soft sensitive lips, so that I heard not one word of the ceremony except Zain ad-Din's blessing, "Upon these two be the favor and the peace of Allah, the one God," for those words marked the time when Aljai left me and returned to her pavilion alone.

After prayers, when torches and lanterns were lit and new banquets spread, Aljai came back to the festival. She had changed into a clinging gown of white silk and wore in her hair nothing but pearls. Truly she was as fair as the moon and as graceful as a willow that night as she moved among the guests and accepted their compliments.

I still had no time with her at the festival. Kurgan outdid himself in the gifts he presented to the guests—rich khalats, jeweled talwars and yataghans, elaborate girdles and shawls—and since many of the things were given in my name, I had to walk with the King Maker as he led his gift-laden slaves among the revelers.

Finally Kurgan had his kourrouns call the group to attention. Then his adjutant read the announcement of my promotion to ming-bashi and my assignment as commandant at Shehri-Sebz. The amirs cheered—some of them. Bayazid Jalair, who had brought Aljai down from the Jalair fortress at Khojend, and Hadji Barlas, who could not refuse the invitation to my wedding, were noticeably displeased—especially when the adjutant announced further that each should contribute a squadron to my regiment. And the assignment of Musa Jalair and Jaku Barlas as leaders of those squadrons merely fanned the flame of resentment, for Musa and Jaku were both known to be critical of their tribal chieftains.

Hussayn, too, showed his disapproval by grunting in disgust at the proclamation. I was standing near him, since he was a member of the bride's family and therefore had a place of honor on the platform.

"Hussayn," I said, "I pose no threat to you. I respect your seniority in age and military rank. Now that I am married to your sister I want only to be friends with you."

He was mollified somewhat, but still suspicious.

"It's true," he said, "that I've never heard of your speaking a word against me."

"Nor shall you," I said. "I wish to serve Amir Kurgan well, as must you also. We can serve together, brother."

"Brother," he said, and I felt that he accepted me. I hoped so, because I wanted no outsider sniping at me while I had Bayazid and Hadji to attend to in my own territory.

When the announcements were over, Abdullah led my prize white stallion, caparisoned in a silk cover which reached to the ground, up to the throne, and Aljai came and stood beside him. Trembling with excitement as I touched her body, I lifted her and set her in the saddle. Then I led the horse down the carpeted avenue toward my pavilion.

Before my tent the officers of my squadron stood facing each other with their swords drawn and pointed to form an archway to my door. I lifted Aljai down—I felt a tremor run through her body as I did so—and we walked through the archway together. Then my men saluted and marched away.

Inside, Aljai's women had already brought her things and perfumed the elaborate marriage bed given us by Kurgan. They prepared my bride for bed and left, taking Lillit and Reba with them, and I was alone with Aljai for the first time.

I entered the bedchamber and stood momentarily in awe of my princess—the only person or thing before which I ever stood in awe in my life. Whether it was the thought of her high lineage or the sheer majesty of her slender person I never knew; but I recognized that she was not as other women, and nothing she ever did spoiled that illusion during our life together. Although she was younger than I by four years and shorter by twice as many inches, I felt humble—as though I were looking up to her.

"Come in, Amir," she said timidly, too timidly for so royal a personage.

"Thank you, Agha," I said, and advanced into the room, my eyes still fixed on the vision before me.

"Am I pleasing to you?" she asked with more confidence—she could not have misread the adoration on my countenance.

"Overwhelmingly so, Princess," I replied haltingly. "As pleased as if I had chosen you from ten thousand women and wooed you for myself."

"Then don't call me *princess*. Call me Aljai—or wife," she said, and with her smile she became the companion of my youth as well as my first consort.

"I am pleased with you also, Amir, if you are too bashful to ask," she continued with a note of friendly mockery in her voice, as if she already held the advantage of knowing me better than I would ever know her— as indeed she did, for the mystery of her was the one thing I never quite fathomed, although we shared every intimacy, even of thought, in complete frankness while she lived.

And her royal blood was something physical, something which I felt every time I touched her body. Fairer of skin than any other woman I ever knew, with the exception of Ali Soun and perhaps Sevin Bey, she was as softly feminine as a nymph and yet as firm and strong as a mountain boy. Even her young breasts were like muscles in repose, and the pleasure I took from her body brought with it strength and power instead of weakening satiety.

So, later that night, after I had drawn that pleasure for the first time and she had asked, "Am I still pleasing to you, Amir—as pleasing as Lillit and Reba?" with the strongest show of anxiety I ever heard in her voice, I could only answer, "So utterly pleasing that I would never have thought of comparing you with any other woman."

"You're sweet, Timur, lover. That's the only answer," she said with obvious relief. She bit my ear playfully and dropped off to sleep in my arms.

And my reply had been true. Her complete naïveté and entirely instinctive response had obliterated from my memory the studied wiles of my concubines. So, too, had I forgotten that on my wedding day I had been the cynosure of all Tatary. And I had had no thought of my promotion to ming-bashi or of Aljai's dowry, which would make my regiment strong.

Such was the danger my bride brought into my pavilion on our wedding night. She brought with her what could have destroyed me as it has destroyed men since first the Flaming Sword blocked the east gate of Paradise. If she had lived, my life might have been different, my sword might never have furthered the will of Allah, for the love I bore Aljai would surely have blinded me to the Way.

CHAPTER

6

The first years of my reign at Shehri-Sebz were an idyllic illusion of happiness. So completely convincing was the mirage that I came near to accepting happiness as a goal— and the projection of goals is the worst sickness of man. It is the fallacy of ends—wealth, power, happiness, or even salvation—which turns men's minds from the nature of the world.

The tawdry goals which make up wealth, the puny exertions of control which impress men as power, the transitory pleasures which pass for happiness, even the frustrated yearnings which sublimate themselves into promises of salvation—all these are but the by-products of the Way. Just as a gardener follows the laws of Allah in fertilizing, watering, and cultivating the soil and is rewarded with a large sweet melon, so, too, is he who learns and follows the Way of Allah rewarded with the good things in Allah's garden. But he who sees only the prizes or the melons has no thought for the Way and cannot long prosper.

The Way was dimmed for me by the illusory joy I experienced in rebuilding and refitting Ak Sarai with Aljai by my side. I knew that each pleasure in a woman was short-lived, and I should have realized that the thrill I found in beginning life as Amir of Shehri-Sebz could not be a lasting one. Let it be said simply that I was young and that for a time I was deflected from the course of my destiny.

With the dowry Aljai brought to me and the gifts of Kurgan and his amirs, I restored my home to its former glory. Aljai and I saw the palace walls repaired and painted again in glistening white. We saw artisans from Samarkand and Herat bring the interior back to its old-time splendor. We saw the gardens bloom again and the white marble pools reflect the moonlight in their shimmering water. We created a paradise in two short years.

"And I'm mistress of it all," said Aljai, as the trees started turning again. "And, Timur, lover, all I feel is that I am me and you are you and the rest doesn't matter."

"But I couldn't be me, as I am now, and you couldn't be you, without all this," I said proudly.

"Great big master of Shehri-Sebz, with his fine horses and soldier boys," she said teasingly. "I'm proud of you, lover, but I'm not too impressed with your importance."

"After I've won all this with my sword?" I pretended to be offended, but Aljai's mockery was only flattering to me. "By my sword alone I have gained my jewel and set her in a mounting worthy of her beauty." I kissed her on the tip of her nose.

"You and your precious sword," she said, and wrinkled her nose, as if my kissing it had tickled her. "Well, Amir, with a more subtle blade you have started something now which only I can finish for you."

"And what is that?" I asked.

"A son, I hope," she said, and turned her back on me and walked casually toward the garden wall.

"A son? Already?" I asked, and hurried to catch up with her.

"Yes, your son and I have been keeping company since sometime in Shaaban, I believe."

"Why didn't you tell me sooner?" I asked eagerly.

"Oh, a woman has to be sure before she starts boasting. Anyway, you've been so busy reviewing your troops and waving your pretty flags that I felt I had better wait until I had something to show before I started parading my reserves. Do I show very much?" she suddenly asked, and stuck out her flat little belly.

"Not that I can see," I said, laughing at the picture she made.

"Will you still love me, Timur?" she asked. "We have some time left before—"

"Indeed I will," I replied, and took her into the palace.

Things went on as usual for a while. Aljai continued to ride on hunts with me in the hills and meadows, for she was an excellent horsewoman and huntress, and she trained and hunted her own falcons. But as her womb grew heavier and she lost her girlish slenderness, I spent less time in her presence, for I did not like to see her that way and I did not want her to know that she was any less attractive to me.

During the day I found business with Jaku, Musa, Elchi, and my other officers; and in the evening I often sought Lillit and Reba, whom I had neglected during the early months of my marriage to Aljai. Lillit, although Aljai let her have a free hand with the servants and tradesmen, was not the same. She fulfilled her duties to me and practiced the skills she had learned in the harem, but her spontaneity was gone, and in games of Scheherazade she hardly tried to hold my attention at all.

Reba, however, surrounded by the luxury she had dreamed of, was more responsive than ever, and if Aljai had not dulled the edge of my desire for any other woman, she would have given me the most exquisite satisfaction a man could know. As it was, Reba most frequently shared my bed during the long winter nights.

Many of the Barlas men, beyond the squadron required by Kurgan, joined my regiment; and the size of the garrison encamped across the river kept Bayazid Jalair and Hadji Barlas quiet. When New Year came around, both of them paid their tribute and even accompanied me to Sali Sarai for the festival.

Kurgan was pleased to learn of Aljai's condition, although he was disappointed at her inability to attend the New Year's celebration, as was I.

"So you have kept Bayazid and Hadji under control and exacted tribute from them," said Kurgan, when he had time to see me alone.

"Yes. They have caused no trouble at all. They *are* both kinsmen of mine now," I said somewhat apologetically, because I had engaged in no large-scale military action the second year of my command.

"And of mine," said Kurgan shrewdly, "but not the kind of kinsmen that I trust. Don't let down your guard—you are in the quietest part of my realm and you have a sizable garrison for so well-protected an area."

"I realize that, Amir. Nur ad-Din protects me on the north, and you, sir, secure my southern flank."

"And you've had no occasion to go outside your own valley this year," he said, in what might have been a mild rebuke.

"No, sir," I said evasively. It was true that I had spent nearly a year in no more strenuous duty than polo and routine training.

"You might have been more active along the border, although the Iron Gate does mark your boundary and I didn't ask your help. Last year you would have been champing at the bit. It isn't Aljai, is it?"

"Oh, no, sir." I felt that Kurgan had put me on the defensive. "It's just that I needed the time to consolidate my position and rebuild the city."

A moment before I had been proud of what I had done—but pride, too, can obscure the Way.

"It is a weakness of men," said Kurgan, focusing his eye directly on mine, "that they will fight much harder for something new, something they have never had, than they will for what they have once gained—especially if they have plenty."

46

"Yes, sir, many men become complacent when they're surrounded by wealth and security," I said uncomfortably.

"But not you, Timur." Kurgan's remark was sufficiently well pointed.

"No, sir, not me," I said, but I wondered.

"Even though you're wealthy now and have the security afforded by your position near the center of a farflung empire with turbulent borders? And there lies the only security—in the center of a kingdom protected on its borders by men who are kept alert by fears—or promises of gain from wars with their neighbors. And even such men can't protect a ruler from himself or from his women if he allows the softness of his wives to spill over into other fields."

"No, sir," I said.

I understood Kurgan, and I considered him wise. On my return to Shehri-Sebz, I began perfecting my weapon of offense by which I intended to prove to Kurgan that I merited the responsibilities he had given me. I put Jaku in command of my heavy cavalry. He was particularly adept at the use of the heavy, armor-piercing lance. I have seen him place the round iron butt of a lance against his shoulder and ride at full gallop and sink the lancehead halfway into a solid oak tree. And he trained his entire squadron of heavy mountain men to do almost as well.

Musa, exceptionally skillful in archery, commanded a squadron of light cavalry which I planned to use as my left flank unit. Daoud I put in command of the right flank. I myself chose the best swordsmen and horsemen for my own unit of flying cavalry which I trained to sally back and forth in lightning attacks through Jaku's heavy cavalry in the center. Elchi, whom I knew best and respected most, commanded my longbows and reserves and stayed in a position in the rear of Jaku's squadron, where he was immediately available to me when my light cavalry withdrew through the center ranks.

As my whole regiment maneuvered on the plain, with their plumes waving and their weapons clattering, it was as though I was once again on the field of battle. Day after day we drilled until my weapon became a precision instrument of invincible force. I brought Aljai, swollen with the body of my son, out onto the plain to watch the war games. I wanted the thrill of the mock combat to penetrate to the living body inside her, the Barlas heir. So was I misled by a false idea of what my weapon might do; for Aljai, sitting among her women in a pavilion or lumbering along the fringe of the maneuvers in a camel litter, thought more of wiping the sweat from my brow than ever she did of the tactics I was perfecting.

One day I rode up beside her litter after a particularly satisfactory charge and asked, "How was that for perfect co-ordination of forces, Aljai Khatun Agha?"

47

"Fine, Amir Timur, Ming-bashi," she replied in kind. "Bend down here—your helmet is on crooked."

I leaned toward her and studied her face, which had grown even prettier during her pregnancy, while she concentrated on my helmet. Then I noticed how large she was—only three months to go.

"I'll be glad when the little monkey gets here," I said in pretended mortification at her lack of appreciation of my regiment. "I'll bet his eyes will pop out at his papa's soldiers."

"I'll be glad, too," she said as she adjusted my chin strap. "I'll enjoy watching his papa's eyes pop out when my body is as slender again as—as Reba's." And she averted her eyes and became interested in a troop practicing fancy riding on the way to the barracks.

My look must have betrayed my feelings; and since I wanted not to offend Aljai ever in any way, I resolved then and there to take my regiment to the border and find a pretext for trying my strength against the Persians. In that way I would be away from Aljai for a while, and although I remembered Kurgan's warning against taking Balkh and causing trouble with Shah Malik, I was sure that some of the wealthy desert sheiks along the border would have property worth seizing.

And there would be new women for my men, who were becoming somewhat restive. Women are the chief prizes of the common soldier, whether taken willingly or raped or bought with sweetmeats and baubles, which the conquerors control in an occupied country. I found the prospect of new women or of loot with which to bribe their favorite women at home to be the strongest inducement in recruiting new men and arousing veterans for new campaigns. And this fact, together with the keen edge for battle to which I had whetted my officers, strengthened my conviction that I should depart for the border at once.

So on the way to Ak Sarai I said to Aljai, "There is a rumor of prospective trouble along the border. I think I'd better ride that way next week."

"I hadn't heard the rumor," she said unenthusiastically.

"But you don't have the sources of intelligence that I have," I said.

"Intelligence, humph!" she said haughtily. "I'm as smart as you are." And she grinned a challenge.

"You know what I mean—spies and the mysterious sentiency of the military."

"Sure, I know what you mean—the mysterious sentiency of a woman. I'm ugly, and you want to leave me." She smiled, however, and continued, "But go ahead—I understand, and I'll be here when you return. Only try to get back before there are two of me."

"Oh, I will be," I assured her.

"I am certain you will," she said with a strained attempt at levity. "I

48

have no doubt that you can begin or end this border trouble any time you wish."

So keen was Aljai's insight into my very thoughts that to avoid hurting her I spent all of my spare time with her, not even seeing Lillit or Reba, during the busy days of preparation for the campaign. My troops, to a man, were enthusiastic over my plans; and my equipment and mounts were never in better condition. I, too, soon became so deeply engrossed in organizing the expedition that I sometimes forgot what had first prompted me to march toward the border. I really believed that there were rumors of Persian raids across the river.

CHAPTER

7

Certainly, as we marched down the valley and through the Iron Gate and finally camped near the river some fifty miles northwest of Balkh, stories spread among my men and grew into long accounts of raids by thousands of men. So I pitched my camp in an abandoned vineyard, well screened on two sides by tall poplars, and maintained the tight security of a regiment under siege.

Daily I sent scouting parties up and down the river with instructions to search for raiders openly and to caution the peasants to be on their guard. Abdullah went along on some of the patrols and implanted the fear of impending raids in the minds of servants and slaves. Gradually the whole valley, for several miles each way, was worked up to a condition of apprehensive tension.

I learned of a large sarai about twenty miles south of the river. No one knew who the sheik was, but all reported elaborate pavilions and unusual horse activity; so the camp promised all that I had anticipated. But for days there were no signs of hostility, though I was sure that no one, not even the farmers, knew the full strength of my force. Presumably, my patrols were members of a small troop of Kurgan's border guards.

At last my scouts reported that a small band of Persians had crossed the river up the way toward Balkh and ridden into the foothills. That gave me my chance, and I dispatched Kaidu with a hundred men and instructions as to what to do.

A few hours later I got word that Kaidu had driven the raiders back across the river and chased them into the desert. I quickly assembled my regiment, and we rode toward the sarai under cover of darkness. We picked up Kaidu's trail and followed it until we came into sight of his camp and then I ordered my main force to take cover behind sandhills and camp for the night.

Following my instructions, Kaidu had chased the raiders to within a few miles of the sarai and then had killed only three of them and let the rest escape into the camp. I was sure that a large body of horsemen would ride out from the sarai to avenge their dead.

I was right. Just at dawn my scouts reported a force of some five hundred men riding north in a cloud of dust. My trumpets sounded reveille, and in a matter of minutes my regiment had assembled in battle formation. Musa and Daoud led their light cavalry squadrons on ahead to get into position for a pincer movement to flank the Persians on both sides before my center was near enough to be accurately judged as to strength.

By the time Jaku's heavy cavalry was near enough to the enemy to prepare for a charge, the archers on both flanks had begun to harry the enemy, and some of the Persians had fanned out to attack my light squadrons. The leader, however, realizing by that time that he was facing a full regiment, massed his main force to drive hard into Jaku's men, expecting to defeat the slower horse by fast maneuvers while his mounts were fresh, and then clean up the flanking squadrons.

Before the enemy could engage us, however, Jaku spread the front of his squadron and Elchi's longbows began volleying arrows over our heads and into the Persian ranks; and while the enemy was spreading to avoid envelopment by Jaku's wider front, I led my fast light cavalry through the ranks of the heavy horse in front of me and made a full-gallop charge toward the Persian center. Caught off guard by my surprise maneuver, the Persians had no time to alter their tactics aimed at heavy cavalry, and my men rode easily through their ranks, slaughtering twice the number of men usually destroyed on a first charge.

Unfortunately, I was faced by both the leader and one of his tavachis, and I had to slay the tavachi first. This I did; and the leader, wanting to take me as his personal prize, reined up sharply and blocked my own horse. Off balance from my blow which had knocked the tavachi from his saddle, I had no chance to get my talwar back into play, and I could only watch the Persian chieftain swing his yataghan at my head as my own horse reared.

Rather than risk exposing myself by trying to counter his blow with my talwar, I sat stiff in my saddle with my right arm limp at my side and raised the shield buckled on my left forearm. I got the shield over my head just in time—the yataghan clattered noisily against the steel disk and glanced off my shoulder. Then I saw the bright head of Jaku's heavy lance pass over my own horse's head and run straight through the Persian's chest. So powerful was Jaku's blow that the lance lifted the chieftain's body out of the saddle, and Jaku rode ahead carrying it before him like a guidon lowered for the charge.

50

Many others of the enemy who parried the slashing talwars of my men had ridden ahead, straight on to the lances of Jaku's heavy cavalry. Elchi's reserves and my two flanking squadrons had prevented breakaways; and in a few minutes the Persians left alive sat inert and bewildered in their saddles surrounded by my entire regiment, which had suffered fewer than thirty casualties. I was disappointed that I personally had accounted for only one of the enemy dead, but I drew great satisfaction from the knowledge that my weapon as a whole had functioned with the keen precision of an engraver's stylus.

We collected the prisoners and riderless mounts and rode on into the sarai. Powerful Jaku, still dangling the body of the commander, rode beside me. There were two hundred or more men left in the camp; but caught dismounted, and discouraged by the size of my force, they offered no resistance as Jaku and I rode up to the sheik's pavilion and dumped the leader's body before it.

A handsome, bearded Persian noble, accompanied by several attendants, came out of the pavilion and looked down at the blood-caked body on the sand.

"I am Timur Barlas, Amir of Shehri-Sebz," I said. "I am returning the body of your insolent menial who dared to attack my men for chasing some of your thieving raiders back across the Amu-Darya. I demand the property of this sarai as indemnity for damage done to the subjects of Kurgan of Sali Sarai, and I take you into custody as prisoner of my chieftain."

The man smiled a twisted sort of smile and answered me.

"I am Malik," he began, "Shah of Herat, Sultan of the Afghans, Protector of the Faith, and I'll listen to none of your silly prattle. I hereby order you and your troops interned until my friend Kurgan hears of this act of aggression, by which you have violated my borders, and makes suitable restitution. Throw down your arms and order your men to do likewise."

I was quite taken aback by this revelation of the identity of my captive. I was sure that I would bring the wrath of Kurgan down upon my head, but I had no immediate fear of Malik—not after the showing my regiment had just made—so I tried to hide my apprehensions.

"I extend greetings to the Shah Malik, Sultan of the Afghans," I said pompously, "but I am a ming-bashi in the service of Kurgan, protecting his borders as ordered, and it was your men who first violated his territory, as hundreds of his subjects and yours along the river will testify— they have been living in terror of these raids for some time. And I can see no power by which you expect to interne a regiment of the King Maker's army."

51

Malik seemed not at all perturbed by my bombast.

"There has been no raid," he continued, smiling his wry smile. "My court and I are on a royal hunt. If one of my hunting parties happened to chase an antelope across the border, I am sure that the estimable Kurgan would not consider such action a justification for the slaughter of half of my palace guard. Order your men to surrender. We will harm no one until my envoys discuss the matter with Kurgan."

I turned to Jaku.

"Place the entire sarai under arrest," I said. "Pass the word to my officers to take over every pavilion and surround the camp with guards. Let no one in or out."

Malik showed his annoyance, and I knew that he had been caught by surprise and that he had no hope of enforcing his orders. But I still had Kurgan to consider. I was afraid to do anything further until I had talked to him. I could not let Malik go, nor could I hold him and stir up all Persia in direct disobedience to Kurgan's expressed command.

I summoned Elchi and issued my next command to him.

"Have fresh horses brought for me and Shah Malik and pick an escort of a hundred men. We shall take our captive to Sali Sarai," I said. "And you, sir"—I addressed myself to Malik—"shall consider yourself my prisoner and prepare for your journey."

I left with my prisoner about noon and we rode steadily, changing horses at Kurgan's garrisons after we crossed the river, until we reached Sali Sarai the next day.

I took my prisoner directly to Kurgan's council chamber, where an assembly was in session.

"A prisoner, Amir," I announced, "who has been directing raids of thievery and destruction along your borders below Balkh."

Kurgan recognized my captive at once, and it was the only time I ever saw the old man aghast.

"Why, my good friend, Shah Malik of Herat." He collected his wits and continued shrewdly, "Surely my zealous ming-bashi has made a mistake."

"That is what I told him," said Malik blandly. "Merely a party from my royal hunt chasing an antelope across the river by mistake."

"Antelope are somewhat rare along the river below Balkh this time of year," observed Pir Ladakh, who had passed that way coming from Karshi.

Several other amirs, who were obviously pleased by my capture of Shah Malik, joined Ladakh in his objections.

"All the more reason why my men were so absorbed in the chase that they inadvertently trespassed on the soil of my good friend Kurgan," said Malik, and he smiled warmly at the King Maker.

52

"A royal hunt," said Kurgan with equal warmth. "An excellent idea—perhaps I should join you."

"Indeed you should. I was on the point of sending you an invitation when this regrettable border incident occurred," said Malik. "By all means return with me."

"Accepted," Kurgan said, and turned to the other nobles present. "Prepare a train immediately and accompany us to the camp of Shah Malik."

After the amirs had been dismissed, Kurgan invited me and my prisoner into the inner chamber.

"Shah Malik," he said, "we may speak freely before Amir Timur. I think perhaps he understands our position. You didn't intend to capture the Shah, did you?"

"No, Amir," I said. "I was merely joining his men in an antelope hunt when the regrettable incident occurred. I'm sure the Shah will overlook the misunderstanding between our hunting parties, as he did the New Year's affair year before last." I beamed as warmly at Malik as Kurgan had done. The Shah showed his surprise.

"I'm sure he will," said Kurgan firmly. "Isn't that so, Shah Malik? We've ignored these little altercations before."

Malik's crooked smile spread over his face again.

"Yes," the Shah said slowly, evaluating me with his shrewd eyes. "I see no particular significance in this. After all, the young ming-bashi slew only four hundred of my elite guard, the best Persian and Afghan warriors I have."

"A mere trifle," I said, for I wanted Malik to know that I was fully aware of the kind of game he and Kurgan were playing. Each was building up strength for the kill and neither was ready to risk a war at the moment. In fact, I felt suddenly superior to both; I had defied both of them and I could stand before, or between, them—the two strongest men in Asia—and join in their deadly smiling persiflage.

On the leisurely journey back to Malik's sarai, I sensed, too, that Kurgan and the Shah recognized my position and appreciated its full significance. Especially when we passed the scene of my attack and they had a chance to estimate with what ease and dispatch I had disposed of Malik's prize troops, did I see the advantage I held in this fiction of the royal hunt to which both rulers subscribed. Knowing that I held a military advantage at the sarai as well, because my troops far outnumbered both Malik's men and Kurgan's small escort and were still flushed from their recent success, I was emboldened to press my strength.

Kurgan could not very well discipline me for an attack on Malik which the Shah himself did not acknowledge as being of any consequence and which Kurgan's own amirs, who did not understand the game being played, welcomed as the heroic capture of their leader's chief rival. Similarly, Malik was committed to a position of denying that I had offended him and could hardly reverse himself and openly censure me without admitting sufficient provocation for a full-scale war. So, since I was coming through the affair without being punished, I probed to see what profit I might gain as well.

"My men are becoming a little restless," I said one evening, as I dined with the royal hunters. "Ignorant as they are of some kinds of war, they are expressing a little resentment at not being suitably rewarded for their recent brilliant victory."

"Indeed?" said Kurgan casually, but I noted that he put down a morsel of food which he had already started to raise to his mouth. "Perhaps you should explain the matter to them more fully."

"Perhaps I should. They think that the Shah is your military prisoner instead of your hunt companion," I said just as casually. "I hate to disillusion them, especially since they will be disappointed to learn that both their own chieftain and their captive prince consider their military success a mere fiasco. They expected women and wealth—and I have prohibited looting."

"I believe they have not been without women," Malik observed, "if rumors are true."

"Just favors freely bestowed by the slain warriors' wives, who I believe consider themselves fair prizes of war—although I realize that there is no war situation," I said. "But the men expect more."

I studied the faces of my two dinner companions.

"That does pose a problem, doesn't it?" remarked Kurgan, with a new note of respect in his voice. "I can hardly reward a regiment for an attack on my neighbor. Such a gesture would certainly suggest that I approved, and that would offend my good friend the Shah and all his subjects."

"Nor can I afford to pay ransom," said Malik, as though he were countering a move in a game of chess. "Then I would be admitting that I had been captured by my good friend to the north. My people would consider my capture ample justification for war—and all of us here want only peace."

Malik and Kurgan were giving me their entire attention by that time. I began to wonder whether or not I was playing the game or had myself become a pawn in the hands of these master strategists.

"I realize the delicate nature of the problem," I said. "That is why I am placing it before older and wiser men than I. I can hardly allow my men to take the third course—complete confiscation of this sarai. That would certainly bring the affair to the attention of all Tatary and all Persia. And

54

if both the King Maker and the Sultan should accidentally be killed by my regiment, I shudder at the confusion which might result."

I poured a glass of wine and chose a particularly tempting piece of candied melon rind. My companions stared at me in silence.

"I would find it embarrassing," I continued, "if in the confusion a number of tribal chieftains, not understanding the real situation, should rally to my standard as that of the commander of the conquering regiment. You know that this sarai is rather remote and communications have been cut off for nearly a week. Almost any kind of story might get out." I took a bite of melon rind.

"You *are* a pigeon cock!" Kurgan laughed in a mixture of dismay and admiration.

"Can't you control your own men?" asked Malik in sudden annoyance.

"I can," I said positively, and paused long enough to meet the gaze both men had leveled at me. "All I have to do is explain the true situation and let the amirs present meet in Kurultai with Amir Kurgan and decide what disposition to make of the Shah. My men will abide by the decision."

The attitude of the amirs who had accompanied Kurgan was quite apparent. They had their eyes on the wealth of Herat, and some of them had openly demanded the execution of Malik and the division of his property.

"I had hoped to avoid that solution, also," I added.

Kurgan laughed aloud, and Malik joined him. And strangely enough there was a faint note of genuine mirth in the laughter.

"So this young man married your granddaughter," Malik said to Kurgan.

"Yes," said Kurgan. "He's a kinsman of mine."

"A valuable one, I dare say," Malik observed. "If you were my enemy, I should fear a man like this on your side, bound to you by the gift of your granddaughter and her dowry."

I resented the reference to Aljai, although it was true.

"The greatest gift a man could bestow," I said. "I am forever indebted to Amir Kurgan—and forever loyal."

I watched the two men ponder my problem. I myself did not know what to expect. I had set no goal—I was merely exploiting the weaknesses of the men before me. Without realizing it, I was following the Way—adding pressure to the course of events, capitalizing on the confusion of men confounded by Allah. So well did I understand the game Kurgan and Malik were playing by that time that I could almost read their thoughts.

Kurgan had built me up as a foil to Hussayn. He considered me a bulwark to his forces, a possible successor. And Malik saw all this—me as a strong adversary, me as a potential King Maker. I had proved my efficiency in the field and then forced these two masters of strategy into a monstrous four-horned dilemma. They had to reckon with me from that time on, and they knew it. And their first decision had to be an immediate one, for they had no way of knowing what my thousand men might do within the next twelve hours.

I said no more as I watched the older men exchange dubious glances and study my face in an effort to learn my answer or at least my purpose. Presumably they thought I had the solution. They made the error of thinking a man must have a reason. Unconsciously I had discovered the secret of Allah—that reasons are futile, that acceptance of the Way is a passive planless state. I was following the Way of the Tree of Life, however blind I might have been.

For Malik's face began to twist into its smile again as the Shah saw a way to checkmate the King Maker.

"I think perhaps I understand the young fox's game," he said to Kurgan. "I believe he has learned of my daughter, Shereza Begum, the fairest descendant of Fatima and the wealthiest princess in all Asia."

I had heard of the Begum—she was a prize worth winning. Although no man had seen her to describe her beauty, her dowry was reported to be tremendous.

Kurgan frowned; he saw at once the tack Malik was taking.

"I hardly think my grandson came courting when he rode across the Amu-Darya," he said grimly.

"Ah, but he did," said Malik. "In a more subtle way than we oldsters would have conceived. Why else would he put us in a position which offers no other solution?"

"Is that right, Timur?" asked Kurgan.

"I merely posed a problem to my elders, Amir," I said. "I am interested in Shah Malik's solution. Please go on."

"I see it all perfectly now," continued Malik. "I bestow the Begum on this doughty young warrior, with rich gifts for each of his men and some beautiful women for their recreation. We end our hunt with the ceremony and then go our separate ways. Isn't that a perfect solution?"

"Indeed it is," I said. "My men can believe the beautiful Shereza Begum and her dowry and the rich wedding gifts are the ransom Kurgan exacted of his prisoner. Your people will know the wedding for what it is—a most generous gift by a most gracious monarch. Ideal, I should say."

"It *is* a solution," said Kurgan sourly.

"The only one," said Malik. "And to match the great boon you have bestowed on your grandson, I can do no less than add a thousand Persian troops under my youngest son, Sheik Ali, to Amir Timur's fine regiment."

Kurgan merely glowered. Malik was backing me as fully as he himself had done. But I felt more secure than ever. Neither of these men was likely to lose the stake he had in me without long consideration. While both lived I would be a bond between them, and when one died I would be a valuable ally for the other. Had Kurgan not resented the stationing of a thousand Afghan and Persian troops deep inside his territory, we should have all three been very happy over the prospect. Such are the fruits of the Tree of Life for one who follows the Way.

Shah Malik immediately began making plans for the wedding, subject to my approval.

"I shall send a courier to Herat tomorrow," he said, "to prepare for the wedding. Sheik Ali's regiment can be the Begum's escort and then go on from here with you."

"A hundred of Sheik Ali's men should be sufficient," I said. "I shall send a hundred of mine with your courier—to see that your instructions are properly delivered—and the Begum and her train should be well guarded by a hundred of my best and a hundred of your best, don't you think?"

"Ah, yes," agreed Malik. "That should do."

Perhaps he had no intention of resorting to trickery—I believe he thought the bargain was a favorable one, since he was gaining an advantage over Kurgan—but I certainly was not going to see my force matched by Malik's men in his own territory. Kurgan nodded his approval to my suggestion.

"Since we are agreed, then," Malik continued, "you may summon a scribe."

"I read and write Arabic proficiently," I reminded him. "You dictate and I shall be glad to prepare the paper for your signature."

Malik worked far into the night and, finally, after several alterations and additions made at my insistence, he completed plans for a very elaborate ceremony. The next morning he dispatched one of his nobles as courier, with a hundred of my best men under Elchi and Daoud, to Herat. We announced the wedding to all the sarai. Kurgan's amirs and my men considered the bargain a great victory for me; and I allowed Malik to assemble his remaining nobles and troops, in my presence, and tell them of the affair in his own way. And since Kurgan was not at the meeting of the Afghan nobles, I raised no objections when the Shah hinted broadly at the favorable military significance of the alliance.

CHAPTER

8

During the ensuing month—for although the courier's escort had ridden directly to Herat, the caravan bringing Shereza Begum and her party was to come back by way of Merve and the Khorassan Road, a distance of some four hundred miles—the sarai began to take on a festive air. After the vultures and jackals had picked the battleground clean, the wives of the slain warriors found complete solace in the attentions of my men; and the Afghan and Persian soldiers began to accept my troops as comrades instead of conquerors. I sent a troop back to my camp across the river for such things as we needed from there.

All of the time, however, I maintained siege security and kept all communications with the sarai cut off. Presumably the royal hunt was proceeding according to plan. I had seen to the wording of Malik's dispatch, and Daoud had instructions to see that the courier delivered the message as written. The courier himself, after delivering the message, was induced to show some of my officers around the fleshpots of Herat, and was killed by an unidentified assailant. My men defended him gallantly and reported the regrettable occurrence in a body. All of this was made known to me after the men returned.

I kept patrols out in all directions, and for several days before the caravan arrived it was under constant surveillance by my men. Fast-riding scouts informed me that the caravan was the richest they had ever seen and that the overnight camps were gay and carefree. There was no sign of any hostile force following the caravan or approaching the sarai from any direction. Elchi and Daoud assured my scouts who came into their camp at night that everything had gone according to plan. Sheik Ali and the entire party had accepted the Begum's marriage as a compact of peace between Malik and Kurgan, and a diplomatic triumph for the Shah.

Then one day the dust of the caravan appeared like a cloud in the west. I responded eagerly to the cry of "Dust to the west" and rewarded the man who first sighted the train. Then I stood for an hour with the other nobles and watched the cloud while my regiment assembled and formed into a welcoming guard before the sarai.

Escorted by Sheik Ali's elite guard, the camel bearing Shereza Begum's curtained litter led the caravan into camp and went directly to Malik's pavilion. For another half hour the train poured in from the desert amid the stench of the animals and dry burning dust which stung my nostrils. A hundred more camels followed the leader—more women in luxurious litters—bales of silks and rugs and furnishings for the Begum's wing at Ak Sarai. Then hundreds of pack animals—horses and hinnies and mules; asses, little kiangs and ghorkars—weighted down with jewels and gold and the more prosaic gear of pavilions and drivers' tents. So many animals that half of them had to be driven to the river for water after they had been unloaded, although my men had spent ten days digging additional wells near the sarai and protecting the seepage from the sun.

Tired though they were from their long journey, the men of the caravan worked with mine till dawn setting up the Begum's elaborate pavilion and the lesser tents of her court, so that the dust had hardly settled before the sun rose on the shimmering canvases which had mushroomed in the cool desert night. Indulging in one of the few passions I have allowed myself, I rode to a high windswept rock jutting out of the desert to the south and sat for an hour watching the pavilions catch the sunrise in their brilliant stripes and draw their long clean shadows hastily in from the west. I wondered if my bride would be half so beautiful.

So it was with a feeling of eager anticipation that I rode back to the sarai. Momentarily I lost sight of the true nature of my coup—I felt that the good fortune coming my way was the reward for a well-planned scheme of my own. How near I came that morning to falling into the same fallacy which had left at my mercy two of Asia's greatest strategists—reliance on their own strength rather than on the weakness of others. No man can maintain his strength forever, but the weaknesses of men are eternally present. So, too, is it impossible for one man to increase his own strength to the strength of three; yet he can undermine and weaken the strength of ten thousand to less than the force of one. That is the Way of the Tree of Life as ordained by Allah.

During the morning I appeared with Shah Malik before Mir Sayyid and the judges of the Church to sign the marriage contract and see my name written beside that of Shereza Begum in the register. Again I walked among the campfires, which sputtered with grease dripping from the meats of my wedding feast. Again I watched men gorge themselves on wines and sweetmeats in honor of me, but they ate and drank not for my sake but for the sake of their own bellies, because the food was rich and good—fresh casabas and cantaloupes and red-meated melons, candied figs and dates, fresh gamy antelope killed on the royal hunt. Again I drank toasts to a bride I had never seen. And as the desert sun grew hot and basted the faces and bodies of the revelers in sweat and oil, I remembered the cool majesty of Aljai as she first came to me in the shade of the oaks at Sali Sarai, and I wondered if the torpid, exhausting afternoon of my second wedding day could be in any way portentous.

Nor was I enlightened when Shereza Begum emerged from the door of her pavilion and made her first formal procession before the massed standards of the tribes present. Veiled and robed in the finery befitting a begum, she appeared little more than a bale of rich fabrics and jewels being pushed along by her serving women. She wore the voluminous pleated bloomers which Persian women affect to make their hips seem broader than they really are, for the older nobles, their wealthiest suitors, prefer the lush comfort afforded by large soft bodies in their beds.

When my bride came to me before the judges, I found that her eyes, which were all I could see of her face, were large and round and inviting. Her hands, when they showed, were small, with the skin drawn tight and smooth to the pointed tips of her fingers. And as I held her hand while Mir Sayyid pronounced Allah's blessing, I found it hot, but dry, and firm in its clinging grasp on mine.

After my bride had made her recession, I joined Malik in dispensing rich gifts to our guests. My men at last received their reward and were completely satisfied. Especially were the hundred girls, whom Malik had ordered to enliven the festival, welcomed by the men who had not already enjoyed the wives of the slain warriors, so that Shereza Begum's second progress around the banquet spreads was greeted by cheers and toasts on every hand. Sensing the desire of the guests to make the ceremony short so they could retire and share their women—an urge which I also felt, since I had been away from my wives for six weeks and had subscribed to the fiction of the royal hunt and respected Malik's women—I showed my own eagerness, which was in no way counterfeit, and Shereza rewarded me with an understanding glance and soon approached the dais to mount my white stallion.

As the first chill of the desert evening was spreading over the sarai, I led the horse down the avenue of lances and took the Begum into my own pavilion. After the dismissal of her women, Shereza, with none of the timidity Aljai had shown, disrobed immediately and stood before me.

"Don't you find my hips large and my bosom full?" she asked proudly.

"Indeed I do," I said, and I was never more honest in my life. Shereza, no taller than Aljai, was about my own age and already in the maturity which comes early to women in the southern climates.

"I've eaten little food and drunk much olive oil to make my hips large and keep my middle small," she continued, beaming at the compliment I had paid her. "My bosom is the bounteous gift of Allah. Do you doubt that I can bear you sturdy sons and nurse them well?"

"Not at all," I replied. "Surely you're all a man could want in a mother for his sons."

She turned slowly around to display all her charms and then came toward me, confidently, flattered by my obvious appreciation.

"Have you any sons already?" she asked, with a sudden show of anxiety. "No—not yet," I answered.

"Then perhaps I shall give you your first," she said, brightening again at the prospect, and in her round face shone a kind of beauty I had not seen there before.

Her skin, smooth and tight like the skin on her hands, had the same pleasant texture, nowhere clammy, covering flesh which was both yielding and resilient. The enveloping softness of her body, which caressed an enlarging area of sensation, held in it an outreaching insistency—a hungry grasping for new life—which filled me with rapture and yet left me feeling that I had both cheated and been cheated. It was as though some starving thing deep inside Shereza's body would have no peace and allow me none until my seed had given it a living organism to feed upon.

For Shereza Begum was thinking of her son. Man—or woman—is most godlike when giving or taking life, when assuming the highest prerogatives of Allah. The joy in the act of procreation is man's nearest approach to the divine ecstasy; and man's ingenuity reaches its height in the perfection of weapons with which to destroy himself. That man who discovers the way to give all life at once, or learns Allah's secrets to a machine which will destroy all mankind in one blow, shall share with Allah in the supreme power of all.

But men of all ages have seen only the lives they can give and the lives they can take. They have counted their sons and gloated over the number of their fallen enemies—blind to the Way which brought these things about. In my time I have brought life to hundreds and taken life from tens of thousands, but never once have I given first consideration to those lives. On my wedding night I knew only that there was something inside Shereza which would delight and plague both of us until it was satisfied. For her it was a false lure, for me the urge Allah had put into my loins to carry on His work.

When dawn broke, my bride and I were still awake—Shereza was going to miss no opportunity until she was sure of my seed, and I was not averse to her insistence. Tired though we were—my elbows raw and burned from shifting the weight of her body around on the silken sheets—we rose and dressed early so the camp could be struck and our trains started on their way.

Kurgan's party left first. The amirs who had come with him seemed disgruntled and anxious to be on their way. Their remarks showed that they were not satisfied with Kurgan's handling of the affair. They had seen Herat slip through their fingers, and they perhaps read weakness into Kurgan's failure to gain profit for himself. I had been most amply rewarded, and my men had no complaints. Even Malik, the captive, had got more out of the bargain than had the King Maker. So it was a dour group of horsemen who first set out from the sarai.

Next, the Begum's train, with most of my regiment and Sheik Ali's men as escort, started for my camp north of the river. I left Elchi and two hundred men to bolster Malik's depleted personal guard on the way back to Herat. I insisted that Sheik Ali accompany me, and he seemed eager to do so. Perhaps only Malik thought of his son as my hostage, but I felt safer.

Sheik Ali rode beside me at the head of the column, before his sister's camel. He was a year or two older than I, as finely developed in his own lean way as was his sister. His handsome face showed keen wit and reckless courage, which indeed he had already proved in battle. He would have made a formidable enemy. I hoped that he might become my friend.

"Well, how do you like Shereza?" he asked easily, as we rode along.

"I'm delighted with her," I said. "She's indeed a daughter of Fatima."

"I like her, too," he said. "Of course I haven't seen her much since she's been living in the women's quarters, but when we were little, I liked her a lot. She sort of looked after me then." He smiled at the memory, for Shereza was the younger.

"She's a prize for me," I said.

"Yes, I know," he said. "Father told me how all this came about."

I looked up at him in surprise but found him still smiling as he continued.

"Oh, don't be alarmed. Father is well pleased with the bargain."

"I'm not sure Kurgan is so happy about it," I said. I thought I might try matching Ali's frankness.

"That doesn't disturb Father. He believes Kurgan has picked you as his best man and is inclined to agree with him. You're the one he has his eye on, after the way you handled this affair."

"And how do you fit in?" I asked. "Leaving your own country and serving under your brother-in-law?"

Sheik Ali laughed.

"I thought you'd get around to asking that," he said. "Well, there are several reasons. First, I'd like to go along. Then Ghiath ad-Din *is* the eldest son."

"And Shah Malik wants no split in Herat," I observed.

"No—and I could never get very far with Ghiath ad-Din on the throne. Both Father and I think you may some day rule Tatary and, if I prove myself, I'll fare better under you."

"You might even win my place without stirring up your own people by destroying your brother." I eyed him suspiciously.

"Never," he said jovially. "I could hardly hold your throne, because

62

I'm not a Tatar. No—you may rely on me. I think it's to my advantage to play straight with you."

"Good," I said. "I believe we're going to get along all right together."

"I'm sure that we are."

After that we became better and better acquainted, and I was sure that I had gained a valuable commander. I felt more secure with his regiment joining mine at Shehri-Sebz, in case Kurgan, by some perversity, should decide to weaken my position in Tatary.

But that eventuality never came to pass. Just after we came in sight of my camp beyond the Amu-Darya, a member of Kurgan's party rode his winded horse to the head of my column and reported that two of the disgruntled amirs had slain the King Maker and taken to the hills east of Balkh. The other amirs had scattered to their own tribal fortresses in fear of what might happen after the death of the ruler of Tatary. The rider was heading for Karshi, to inform Ladakh, Kurgan's son, who should succeed to the kingship.

I summoned Musa and issued orders to lead the train on a forced march through the Iron Gate to the safety of Shehri-Sebz. Then I rode into my sarai and ordered my guards to break camp and follow the train. I chose five of Ali's men and ten of my own and secured fresh horses for all of us. Then Sheik Ali and I led our picked band at full gallop toward Balkh.

All night and all day we rode, across burning patches of desert which parched our throats and stopped up our nostrils with sand, down rock-strewn gullies which lamed our horses, through briars and brambles which rent our garments to shreds. Changing horses at every desert sarai or mountain village, we followed without letup the trail of the killers. Another night and another day, on beyond Kunduz, through the icy passes of the Hindu Kush—and finally we caught them, two shivering men huddled together in the snow, trying to draw the last bit of warmth from the bodies of the horses they had ridden to death.

Bitter, beaten, bedeviled, they offered almost no fight at all. I slew one, and Ali slew the other. Then I cut off their heads and dispatched horsemen to take one head to Ladakh and the other to Hussayn at Kabul, with notes saying that I had avenged Kurgan's death and expressing my regrets over the loss of the patriarch of their clan.

Then Sheik Ali and I set out for Shehri-Sebz.

CHAPTER

9

Upon my arrival in Shehri-Sebz, I found things in a turbulent condition, as were things in all Tatary for months to come. Ladakh had succeeded Kurgan and established his court at Samarkand, the strongest fortress in Tatary and seat of the puppet Khan. Tribal chieftains everywhere had begun the battle royal to decide who should ultimately be protector of the Khan, for no one expected Ladakh to hold out for long.

Bayazid Jalair and Hadji Barlas were reported to be planning an attack on Shehri-Sebz—and I had no way of knowing how many others had their eyes on my capital as the only fortified base of operations from which to attack Samarkand. While waiting for Elchi to arrive with Sheik Ali's regiment from Herat, I had to spread my own men thin. I sent Daoud and his squadron to the Iron Gate to protect me from the south, and Musa to the west to guard the approaches from Karshi and Bokhara. Jaku and the Barlas and one Afghan platoon under Mouva went up the river to protect my herds from Hadji's raiders in the hills. Sheik Ali stayed with me and held part of his men in reserve to plug up holes in our defenses and to help my personal guard hold the Samarkand Road.

I planned no offensive action other than an occasional raid to keep my men in loot and new women. I gave orders to keep these raids small and always to attack one tribe and leave a trail leading to a neighbor, so to precipitate wars between my potential enemies as well as secure loot and women for my men. It would be better to let the still strong leaders dissipate their strength fighting each other before I made a bid for power.

Conditions inside Ak Sarai were no less hectic or strenuous. When I returned from the Hindu Kush, I found Shereza Begum in the midst of decorating and furnishing her wing of the palace with the luxuries she had brought from Herat. She was greatly pleased at the new freedom she had in being mistress of her own court and having access to the entire palace—for at that time the seraglio as such had not been introduced into Tatary. She was, of course, less pleased with the advanced stage of pregnancy in which she found Aljai, a condition which she could hardly expect to equal for many months but which she was eager to try for immediately and persistently.

And Aljai Khatun Agha, for she would of course retain her precedence, was more irritable than she was at any other time in her life. She was civil toward the Begum and indeed soon exhausted herself helping Shereza get established, so that I found her in bed when I returned from my pursuit of her grandfather's killers.

"So you've gone and married yourself a Begum," she greeted me peevishly, "complete with the sacred green veil and an outsized bottom."

64

"An amir is entitled to four princess wives," I reminded her curtly, disappointed in my welcome home.

"Humph, old Begum-Bottom should add up to three," she continued, in the same vein, and then softened toward me. "Don't mind me—it's my condition. Come here, Timur, lover, and pet me a minute, if I'm not too ugly. I've missed you terribly this last month."

"You're never ugly to me," I said, as I knelt beside her couch and took her in my arms. It was true—something in Aljai was always beautiful, misshapen though her body might be and swollen and tear-stained her face. "I've missed you, too, my dear, more than you will believe."

"I believe you, Timur, lover. When you touch me, I know. Your love is in your hands." The pettishness had left her voice.

I held her away from me and brushed her fine soft hair back from her forehead. I liked to cup her cheek in my hand and feel the pulse in her temple with my finger tips. Yes, my love for her was in my hands—in my heart and in my head, as well as in my loins. She was not as other women. Given time, surely my feeling for her would have shut out all else and destroyed me, for love—sacred or profane—can weaken and kill as relentlessly as any other plague let loose by Allah.

"A few weeks more," she said, "and there will be room in my body for you. There's never room in a woman for three lives at once. When this is over, it will be we two again, lover, we two forever—no more."

"Yes," I said, "we'll ride again and hunt again and swim together in the river—"

"And love again—"

"Not again, still. I love you this minute more than I ever have before." And I was sincere.

"With the Begum and Lillit and Reba? All sharing with me?"

"My love for you," I assured her, "is like a roaring flame—it can light a thousand other torches and lose not one bit of its warmth for you."

"Then fire up old Begum-Bottom and get her confined by the time I'm well again," said Aljai lightly, and I knew that I was home again.

But a few days later a courier rode down the valley and reported that a band of Hadji's men had come out of the hills and raided some of my herds upstream. I left Sheik Ali in charge of Shehri-Sebz and led a squadron of reserves to the aid of Jaku, who was holding the valley until Elchi returned from Herat.

As I approached the pasture lands I had no trouble picking up the raiders' trail. It was pointed out at a distance by the vultures which circled overhead and dropped down to frighten away the wolves gnawing at the entrails of slain cattle where Hadji's men had slaughtered and dressed the animals to carry over pack trails to Hadji's stronghold.

I found where Jaku and Mouva had attacked the raiders also well marked, for there the bodies of men added to the carrion feast.

We did not let up in our chase for a moment but raced on toward the mountain pass toward which the trail led. We came upon Jaku and the remnants of his men a little way inside the pass. They were being held back by archers hidden in the brush on both sides of the narrow valley. I split my force and led one platoon up to the higher ridges on one side and sent Mouva with the rest to circle the rear of the snipers on the other.

In a half hour or so of tortuous maneuvering over rugged terrain through dense undergrowth we so diverted the attention of the archers that Jaku, reinforced by a small band of Persian reserves, was able to attack and force Hadji's men to seek positions on higher ground. As the snipers revealed themselves, my men and Mouva's rained arrows on them from above and by mid-afternoon we had cleaned out the snipers, even though we had lost the booty to the main body of raiders.

"This is one of your men, isn't it, Jaku?" I asked, when Jaku at last joined me to count the enemy dead.

"Yes," said Jaku glumly, "and he's not the only one who's gone over to Hadji."

"Why?" I asked in surprise. I thought I had won the complete loyalty of my men by my brilliant desert campaign.

"You ask why, boy?" Jaku looked at me squarely. "You should know the Barlas—you're one of us. Hadji promises more."

"More? More what? Haven't I rewarded them richly?"

"And yourself more so. Hadji is boasting that he will take Shehri-Sebz within the week and divide the Begum's dowry and all her women among his officers and men."

"I see," I said thoughtfully. "Very well. I'll be ready for him. Can you hold out up here until Elchi arrives with Sheik Ali's regiment?"

"I think so—Hadji's still recruiting and provisioning. He'll not risk too many men until he's ready. And I must say he has done very well on supplies." Jaku grinned wryly as we looked back at the circling vultures.

"Tell the herdsmen to start the cattle down toward Shehri-Sebz," I said. "I'm going back to get set for siege. Pull in your lines as the herds move down."

"All right," agreed Jaku. "I'll hold them off as long as I can. When do you expect Elchi?"

"Any day now," I said, and rode back down the valley.

So the preparations for the defense of Shehri-Sebz were added to the demands made on my attentions by Aljai and Shereza. Aljai grew steadily more fretful and discontented, and Shereza was no less demanding. As I wallowed deliciously in the vast softness of Shereza's body, the call of her womb became an obsession with me. I buried my face between her mothering breasts and strained every power in my body to answer the call, to force my way into her womb, to lose myself entirely in Shereza's son, deep inside the lush body of Fatima's daughter.

Then I would return to inspect a defense position, to discuss tactics with Sheik Ali, to send another rider to the Iron Gate for word of Elchi. And I would spend a soothing hour with Aljai and bring quiet to myself as I held her hand and brushed the hair back from her face and the fears from her mind.

And Hadji attacked. I had already drawn my forces inside the wall around the inner citadel of Ak Sarai and diverted water from the river to fill the moat. All day and all night, for a week, Hadji's men volleyed flaming arrows over the wall, starting fires and terrorizing my people. Secure behind battlements, my men returned the fire—sometimes the same flaming arrows quickly retrieved and sent back, still burning, into the ranks of the enemy.

When our ammunition ran so low that we had to pick our targets with care, Hadji's men bridged the moat and started raising scaffolds along the wall, which was not nearly so high or so well built as the walls of Karshi or Samarkand. We poured naphtha over the attackers and their structures and then set fire to them, so that on the sixth night Shehri-Sebz was a flaming circle surrounding scattered blazes inside.

And among the parties of Hadji's men who succeeded in scaling the walls we discovered Jalairs and knew that Bayazid had arrived to help Hadji deal the death blow. Fighting began in the streets, but my men—the best in Tatary—held their own, and not an enemy got within an arrow's flight of the palace on that night. But the end was in sight.

Word came to me at my post that Aljai had broken water and was in premature labor brought on by the fear and the strain. I put Sheik Ali in command and rushed to her bedchamber. I knew not the folly, the irony, of leaving the job of taking life to go help give life to a child. That is not the Way of Allah. So far did I depart from the Way that night that surely I deserved the fate Hadji and Bayazid had in mind for me.

I found Aljai in great pain, screaming and writhing in her canopied bed. My old nurse was heating water over charcoal braziers, and my father and Zain ad-Din, who had taken refuge in the palace, were holding Aljai in her spasm when I burst into the room. I rushed to the bed and tried to soothe her with my hands.

"This is the last time!" she screamed at me. "The very last time, Timur Barlas." And she pushed my hands away. "Don't touch me, you beast! You did this to me."

67

Her eyes were wild and feverish and her words shrill and harsh. I backed away angrily.

"She's out of her head," said my father kindly. "She doesn't mean it."

I approached her again, and again she screamed and scrambled to a sitting position on the corner of the bed farthest from me. She stared at me like a cornered mink—vicious and frightened.

Zain ad-Din quickly ran up behind her to keep her from falling off the bed.

"Don't you touch me, either," she shrilled, and turned to face him and scuttled back across the bed.

Then a labor pain struck her and she bent double and writhed in agony. The sayyid and my father grasped her shoulders and knees again and straightened her body out by main force. I stood by, frightened and offended.

"Your mother was like this," my father said, shaking his head at the sad memory.

And I remembered that she had died giving birth to me.

"And I killed her," I said in terror.

My father bit his lip.

"If Aljai dies—I, too, will die tonight," I said hopelessly.

"Nonsense," said Abdullah's mother calmly, as she returned from the kitchen. "She'll not die. She's coming along well. She's just a girl, and this is her first."

"And my last," said Aljai, calmer and saner after the spasm had passed. "Let old Begum-Bottom be your broodmare. She may like it—but not me— Oh!" And the pain hit her again.

And so for hours, while the battle raged and the bedroom windows glowed with flames of the fires outside, Aljai labored and screamed, and I stayed beside her, letting an enemy destroy my stronghold. Aljai never let me touch her, but when the final labor set in, I snatched a spear which held up the canopy of her bed and held the shaft while she grasped it and strained to give life to my son. Toward the end Aljai gained confidence and co-operated with all her strength and will. She even smiled weakly at me in my misery, but I felt that I had forever lost the tender love she once bore me.

When the first gray of dawn began to filter the yellow cast from the flames outside, the baby was delivered and Aljai sank into the sleep of complete exhaustion. Abdullah's mother bathed the little boy and presented him to Zain ad-Din for Allah's blessing.

"What will you name him?" asked my father as he stood admiring the red infant.

68

"Jahangir," I said unenthusiastically. The son was no compensation for the loss of Aljai's affection.

"Jahangir," repeated my father fondly, "World Gripper—a very ambitious name for a being no bigger than a dressed hare. But he'll grow up," he continued sadly. "Into this world—this golden vase filled with scorpions and serpents. But will he want to take it into his grip?"

The words drew me back to the present, to the world outside, and my capital besieged and burning around me. As if to herald my doom, a distant fanfare of strange trumpets sounded across the plain. I was terrified for a moment—I had never heard that music before. Then, suddenly, it came to me. These were Ali's trumpets, and more of his men were advancing toward Shehri-Sebz.

With only a hurried glance toward Aljai, who was resting—or dead —I ran from the room and raced to a vantage point on the highest parapet. The battle still raged inside the walls, but I could see that my men were losing no more ground. Ali was never my match in strategy, but he was certainly my peer in close-in tactics—it was he who kept things under control while I was neglecting my duty in my hour of weakness.

And outside the walls, everything had changed. Elchi's first squadrons had already encircled the city and Ali's troops were still streaming in from the plain across the river. Caught dismounted, and some even cut off from their horses altogether, the attacking Barlas and Jalairs were trampled and slashed to ribbons by the fast-charging Persian horsemen. As I stood on the battlements during the first half-hour after sunrise, I saw every enemy inside and outside my walls slain or driven headlong into the hills.

And then everything stopped at once. Fires were extinguished. Tired, worn soldiers slept where they were when the battle ended. Terrified civilians lost their terror and returned to their homes to rest. Taragai and Zain ad-Din went back to the monastery. And after a ten-minute council with my officers, I dismissed them and suddenly found myself in the midst of a contentless quiet.

But only the tumult outside had ceased. My spirit was as turbulent as ever. Gone was the drive of battle. Gone was Aljai's struggle, and with it the world she had meant to me. I went to her room—she was still sleeping, with the baby beside her, and Abdullah's mother shooed me out with the assurance that all was well.

All was well! With my capital in ruins, my body worn by seven days without rest or sleep, my mind too weary to know how to quit and relax, and my feelings numb—except for one.

The urgent ache to meet that elusive demand of Shereza's womb still haunted me. I went to Shereza at once and found her sleepily receptive.

69

She passively yielded to my embrace, and I resumed my pursuit of the tantalizing promise of nirvana which had teased me relentlessly for nearly a month. But it, too, was gone. Outwardly Shereza's body was the same luscious pleasure temple and Shereza herself was obliging and co-operative—she obviously enjoyed me and found complete satisfaction in me, but the all-consuming hunger was gone. Try as I would, by power, by surrender, by hard-pressing eagerness, or by teasing withdrawal, I could not arouse again the insatiable appetite. I was the feverish wanter —the unwanted. I had been cast out of the womb.

So it was no surprise to me that Shereza wanted to talk. "I, too, am going to bear you a son," she said proudly, as I lay inert by her side.

"Yes, some day," I said.

"No, I mean soon," she continued in her excitement. "He's on his way."

"How do you know?" I asked, not very interested in what she was saying.

"How do women know, silly? While you've been busy this last week with your war, I've found out. I'm almost positive."

"Yes, you must know," I said, realizing that I knew as well as she. My son was on his way, and I almost hated him, for he had stolen my refuge in the body of Fatima's daughter—and I never found it there again.

CHAPTER

10

Completely dejected, bereft of any reason for continuing my struggle against the scorpions and serpents in the world, I rose early from another sleepless night and climbed again to the heights of the battlements to survey the wreckage of all I had won by my sword. I walked around the catwalks on the walls, bloody and stinking with dead bodies which had not been removed. Living soldiers, in the sleep of exhaustion, still lay beside their putrefying comrades. Outside the walls the same sorry sight stretched toward the hills. Wolves insolently gnawed at the cold bodies of my kinsmen and slunk back into the gray shadows when the sun rose out of the Pamirs and the first morning vultures closed in for their breakfast.

From my height I could see into the courtyard of the mosque. I saw my father walking there, saying prayers for the dead or for his new living grandson. And across the river I could see Ali's gay tents, beautiful as they had been that morning in the desert. But that morning I had been the victor, the gainer of new wealth. I was victor again but I had lost even in victory, and I was soul-sick.

I looked back at my father in his somber monk's garb, which perhaps did enshroud a kind of peace, peace in surrender, peace in giving up the challenge and hiding in the ignominy of the weak who have nothing left for a warrior to attack. And I wondered. Why should I strive? No man cared. No woman. Not Aljai, not any more—for she hated me. Not Shereza, not any more—for she had new life in her womb. And I was tempted to retire to the monastery myself, as my father had wished.

But Sheik Ali's regiment stirred into life across the river and began the routine business of soldiers in garrison. And Shehri-Sebz awoke around me and began to prepare its dead for burial. I felt that I must go through the motions of a leader.

And so I went to my courtchamber and took over the direction of the rehabilitation of my people. All morning I answered questions, issued orders, heard complaints, and approved plans for temporary relief measures. But despite the misery of others I never shook off the sick feeling of my own loss. I longed to go to Aljai, and yet I feared to see her, feared again to hear her say, "Don't touch me, you beast! You did this to me."

My son meant little to me other than the pain he had brought to Aljai. He did, however, provide an excuse, and so late in the afternoon I left my throne and fearfully sought the sickroom.

"Come here, Timur, lover," Aljai said brightly, as I entered her room. "See what I've got."

Half joyous, half timorous, I went to her bedside. She was engrossed in the little blanket nestled in her arms.

"Isn't he sweet?" she asked, and uncovered the baby's face and arms.

"Yes," I said, as I peered down at the wrinkled bit of red life.

"Next to you, Timur, lover, I guess he's the sweetest thing in the world," she went on gently, still looking at Jahangir, and I was relieved immeasurably—it was Aljai again.

"But when he was born—" I began in pleasant surprise.

"I was hurting then—" Aljai began, and broke off what she had started to say. "Why, you poor thing, when have you slept?"

"I don't know." I suddenly felt deliciously sleepy.

"You're all dirty and tired and worn out," she continued, with a look of worried tenderness in her eyes. "You look sick. Here, lie down beside me—us—and go to sleep. There's plenty of room."

She moved over to one side of the bed and protected the baby with her arm. I lay down beside her.

"There's a smudge right there," she said, and wiped my forehead with the corner of the baby's blanket.

That was the last thing I heard for two nights and a day.

When I awoke, Abdullah's mother was bending over me shaking my shoulder.

"Wake up, sleepyhead," she grumbled happily. "Three in a bed, for an old woman like me to look after."

I rubbed my eyes and sat up. She set a tray in my lap with a bowl of steaming gruel and a cup of black fermented tea.

"Good morning, lover," greeted Aljai, who sat beside me with her tray already before her. "Sleep well?"

"Like a babe," I replied.

"Not like that one," she said, pointing at Jahangir's cradle. "He screamed his head off yesterday and you didn't even move." She laughed as happily as ever I heard her.

Restored by the gruel and Aljai's return to normal, I rose and sought the warmth of a banja. After a two-hour steaming and a thorough rub-down, I returned to my duties. As I walked through the halls of Ak Sarai, I took stock of what I had left—and it was practically everything. Not one luxury in the palace had been touched, not one wall scarred by the battle. And I had Aljai.

With the exhilaration of the long sleep and the steam bath still in my veins, I resolved to rebuild Shehri-Sebz and to hold it at any cost. Little did I know that the determination to hold what one has at any cost, even appeasement and vassalage, is as fatal a sickness as over-reaching greed. It is one of Allah's lures that man shall set his heart either upon what he has or upon what he wants and leave himself open to pain and despair at his losses.

Bayazid and Hadji, after their failure to take my city, recruited new forces and concentrated on the greater prize of Samarkand. They were joined by many other chieftains, and half of my own men went over to them. But, behind the protection Sheik Ali and his men provided me, I rebuilt in relative peace.

Late in Dulheggia, Samarkand fell. Bayazid and Hadji pillaged and raped the city, and for days refugees streamed down the Samarkand Road.

One night a messenger came to my room.

"A lady to see you, Amir," he announced. "She says she's an old friend."

Searching my memory for a clue, I put on a robe and went to my court-chamber. There, waiting for me, was a young woman, beautiful of face and rich in her garments.

"Amir Timur, Master of Shehri-Sebz," she said, and approached to kiss my hand.

"Yes," I answered, still perplexed.

"Don't you know me?" she asked, when I had shown her to an otto-man and seated myself on my throne.

"I'm afraid not," I said.

"I'm Karin al Raschid," she said. "You once cut a man's hand off for me."

"You!" I exclaimed. I remembered Nihmu and the little slave girl.

"Yes. Men used to call me Karin the Cursed, but I call myself Karin al Raschid—the Blessed."

"Karin the Cursed? Why?"

"Well, when the slaver got us to Samarkand, the story was already there—that any man who touched me would lose his hands. That was my curse—the slaver couldn't sell me. No man would buy a girl with such a curse on her."

"And so—?" I said.

"And so the slaver had worse and worse luck. He couldn't even give me away or make money on me in a brothel. Finally he turned me out into the streets."

"You don't seem to have fared so badly," I observed, noting her rich coat and jewels.

"No. I was so small I drew men to me by posing as a poor helpless virgin. Then I told them who I was and asked more money from them to lift the curse. After a while I was able to get established in luxury. Braver men heard of me and came to me for the double thrill of my body and the challenge the curse offered."

"I see. So you finally found a rich lover."

She smiled a peculiar little smile.

"There are several ways, Amir Timur. To find a lover with ten thousand dinars, or ten lovers with a thousand dinars each—or a thousand men with ten dinars."

"And what do you want of me?" I asked.

"Protection. You haven't even asked me to show myself."

"Very well, show yourself."

She rose and removed her coat. Then she slowly removed her other garments and turned around for my inspection. She had developed into a beautifully formed woman. Her awkward angles were all gone.

"Quite a change since I last saw you," I commented. I still did not know what she wanted—surely not to enter my household, although she was certainly attractive enough.

"I never did learn to dance," she said lightly, "but I'm really very good in bed."

"And you want to come to my bed?" I asked.

"I'd love to, Amir. You were my first protector. But I want more, too."

"What?"

"I now own twenty girls. They are with a caravan by the bridge—remember?"

I remembered, but surely Karin had romanticized our first meeting unduly.

"I bribed an officer to get us out of Samarkand," she continued. "The new protectors would have made slaves of us all. I want to go no farther. I want to take a house here under your protection. You may ask of me whatever you will. You befriended me once—please do so again."

"What are your girls like?"

"The most desirable in Samarkand, Amir. You will not be ashamed of us."

"Very well, Karin," I said. "I have the winter palace of a rich Persian who was killed during the siege. I'll let it to you."

I sent for Abdullah. As Karin put on her clothes, I felt a measure of saisfaction in the quality of whores Shehri-Sebz could now attract, and I remembered the sorry wenches who had kept cribs near the bazaars during my years of study in the mosque. I had need for Karin's girls at the moment, too. With my curtailment of offensive action, Ali's men had little chance of securing new women, and I felt that if the girls were half as delectable as Karin they would provide many hours of solace to the defensive garrison and so keep down unrest.

When Abdullah answered my summons, I gave him the keys to the Persian's palace and directed him to see that Karin was established there. Karin prostrated herself before me, as though I were the Khan, and kissed my hand again gratefully. Then she and Abdullah left together, and I did not see my chamberlain for a whole week.

The Samarkand Road, clear again of refugees, took on the appearance of a highway in a well-regulated kingdom. Bayazid and Hadji had sufficient trouble with rebellions elsewhere to keep them from attacking me; and when New Year's Day came around, I sent tribute to Samarkand, although I did not attend the celebration. I felt that the tribute I paid was a fair price for the life I was enjoying at Shehri-Sebz.

For life was good. Aljai was her old self again except for a tenseness when I lay with her. She was extremely fond of Jahangir, but I could tell that she lived in constant fear of having to go through the ordeal of childbirth again, and her fears lay in bed with us every time we took pleasure together. I missed her old-time eagerness, but again I was willing to make concessions for the joys I did have—and then Reba was always around, and her excitement over the luxury of Ak Sarai never diminished. Lillit, too, when she was in a good mood, provided me with almost the same kind of tenderness Aljai had once shown in her embrace.

And Shereza was obliging but no longer demanding, except of ec-

74

centric little attentions as her time approached. To avoid another trying experience, I sent for the chief physician of Samarkand to attend the Begum during her confinement. When he arrived, he examined Shereza and forecast no complications. And to my delight, he examined Aljai also and told us that she could never again conceive.

With the specter of pregnancy banished from our bed, we were once more the carefree lovers of that first night in Sali Sarai. And Aljai sparkled again with the gay wit of her girlhood. She even showered Shereza with sisterly attention and called her "Begum-Bottom" almost lovingly when we were alone together. There was just a hint of malice in her voice, however, when Shereza was in labor.

"I want to see this!" said Aljai gleefully. "I want to see how old Begum-Bottom manages these things."

We hurried to the west wing of the palace.

"I hope it hurts," whispered Aljai as we knocked on the bedroom door.

Then she added, "But not much—just a little."

When we reached the bedside, the physician was already spanking a husky baby boy. Then, to our consternation, the physician turned back to Shereza and called casually over his shoulder, "Help me, here, that's only the first one."

And by the time Zain ad-Din and my father arrived from the monastery, there were two young princes bathed, swaddled, and ready for Allah's blessing.

While all eyes were on the babies, Aljai sidled up to me and said, "She smiled, actually smiled, while we were delivering the second one—and both larger than Jahangir was."

But Shereza's smile was for only one. Instinctively she knew which was her firstborn, and throughout her life all her smiles were for him. Although I never had cause, while she was young, to complain of her as a wife—her body never lost its soft welcoming embrace—it was as Miran Shah's mother that she existed.

The other boy, Omar Sheik, looked like his uncle, as soon as he developed any distinguishing features, and indeed grew up to be an exact image of the valiant Sheik Ali. And I favored Omar Sheik as Shereza favored Miran Shah, for it was the Begum's firstborn who had cut off from me that powerful hunger I yearned to satisfy. But life was too good for me to fret.

Indeed Shehri-Sebz was a quiet oasis in a windblown desert. While men and whole tribes were destroyed all around us, my people prospered. The farmers grew rich while their fields were protected by my few men and Sheik Ali's strong regiment. Caravans camped by my river awaiting lulls in the fighting all around my peaceful valley, and merchants enjoyed their best trade in years. Zain ad-Din waxed fat and complacent, for the Church prospered, too, and its coffers were filled.

I felt that I had learned the secret of happiness, despite Kurgan's denial that there was such a state. My father, Taragai, shared in the peace of my isolation. He came often from the monastery to watch his grandsons grow fat and smiling in the valley of plenty. He suggested that I hold a feast on Jahangir's first birthday, since I had not celebrated his birth because of the siege. It was my father's way of reminding the Barlas that Jahangir was an heir to the headship, for Hadji had not claimed title and the old men of the clan still respected Taragai. I suspected, too, that my father wanted others to see the peace of Shehri-Sebz and seek it for themselves, as he had done in the monastery.

So I sent riders to the Barlas and the Jalairs and other of our kinsmen. Bayazid and Hadji both declined, but many of the Barlas clansmen brought their families, and chieftains who had served Aljai's father at Khojend rode in with their wild mountain tribes.

They brought with them their music, and for three days and nights we reveled in feasting and song. Troubadours made up new ballads honoring the toddling prince. Young men and women danced the wild saber dance to spirited music of trumpets and drums, and sang love songs to strumming guitars and balalaikas. The old men recounted brave experiences of our valiant ancestors and told of fair princesses of Khitai who had lived in the snow with our forefathers.

Then the guests went home and the wheat ripened into a bounteous harvest. My sons continued to grow with the seasons. But with the first snow, Taragai took sick in the monastery. I spent much time with him; we played chess for hours on end, and he counseled me on the ways of the world.

"I have lived to see you find peace in your youth," he said to me. "I was an old man before I learned what you know."

"It was your precept, Father," I said.

"Continue your kindness toward your people," he went on, "and listen to the counsel of the mollahs."

"Indeed I shall. This is truly the good life."

"You have shown that if you seek not to rob others, you may keep what you have. You have strengthened my faith during the last two years—the world has lost much of its sting."

"I find it all pleasant," I said.

"Surely Allah has blessed you. He will protect your valley as long as you follow His way. I can die happy, knowing that I leave you and my grandsons in His favor."

And within the week Taragai died.

Again my kinsmen flocked into Shehri-Sebz. Even Hadji came, and Bayazid, with an elaborate retinue from Samarkand. They complimented me highly on the state of my valley and the wealth of my capital. They were impressed, too, by the graciousness of my princess wives and the luxurious hospitality of Ak Sarai.

Then in the cold shadows of the mosque Zain ad-Din said the funeral service over my father, and eight princes of royal blood carried him to his grave in the holy ground of the monastery. And with him died all peace in the world, for it was not Allah, but Sheik Ali, who protected my valley.

CHAPTER

11

I sent tribute to Samarkand but did not attend Hadji's festival; so it was by report that I learned of the proclamation in which my uncle claimed titular head of the Barlas clan. I knew what that meant—I remembered the greed in Hadji's eyes when I had shown my capital so proudly before my father's funeral. I was jerked back quickly to the realization that the world is not many, but one. There can be no peace in one valley with war all around.

By spring there were rumblings in the north. Tugluk, the Kha Khan, was on the march toward Samarkand; my most immediate danger was not from Hadji, but from the Mongol hordes from the frozen desert. Tugluk led the same wild nomads who had sired the most valiant warriors among our own ancestors—the original followers of Genghis and Kublai.

When the full strength of Tugluk's forces, twelve thousand men, was made known, Hadji and Bayazid decided not to resist. Bayazid took his men and returned to Khojend, which was the northern gateway of Tatary, and gave gifts and swore allegiance to the Kha Khan. Hadji called in all the Barlas and sent word to me that he was taking the clan south of the Amu-Darya. He asked me to be ready to join him when he passed through Shehri-Sebz. I surveyed my own position. Now that both Kurgan and my father were dead I owed personal fealty to no man. There was, of course, the historic claim of the Kha Khan, Tugluk, for my allegiance and support—but historic claims are no stronger at any given time than the power to enforce them.

Of Kurgan's two heirs, one was already dead, and Aljai's brother Hussayn could not be counted an enemy for the time being—our conflict was yet to come. My uncle Hadji, however, was bound to regard me as a rival contestant for the leadership of the Barlas. But my other uncle, Jaku, a stout warrior with no plots of his own, had been my father's trusted friend and would be mine. And Sheik Ali, Shereza's brother, was a far more useful relative by marriage than was Hussayn.

Now under the shadow of Tugluk would come the test of strength, between men rather than between their followers. My uncle Hadji had been able to combine the Barlas with Bayazid's Jalairs to overthrow Kurgan's weak son at Samarkand, but standing up against the Kha Khan himself was another matter. I called my officers together and told them how conditions were.

"I plan to stay here," I said.

"I'm with you," said Elchi. "We can hold out as we have before."

"I'll stay, too," Jaku chimed in. "I know that many of the Barlas would prefer to stay here, even some who are now with Hadji."

"Can we trust them?" I asked.

"Trust them?" said Jaku. "No, but we can use them, once they are inside the walls."

"I can't use such people now," I objected. "I must have men who are loyal, not men who are desperately clinging to a little property."

"Then send them on with Hadji," Jaku advised me.

"What about you, Sheik Ali?" I asked.

"Well, Timur, I'm personally loyal to you—but I think I had better take my men back to Herat."

My heart sank. I had lived in the strength of Kurgan, and he was dead. And for two years Ali had made my life secure—now he was leaving. I was beginning to learn that a man can rely only on himself.

"Why?" I asked, perhaps a little peevishly.

"My father fears Tugluk and has asked me to come to his aid. We can't risk my men against twelve thousand Mongols—and we can't afford to allow them to join the Khan." Ali looked directly into my eyes, as though he could read my thoughts.

"Do you think I should go with you?" I asked, for I respected Ali's judgment.

"No," he said, and smiled. "Nor does Shah Malik. He remembers your skill in diplomacy and thinks you will make out. So do I."

"Will you stay until Hadji passes through?" I asked.

"Yes. I'll see you that far."

"And will you return?"

"When you need me and have an even chance, yes."

"Thanks. I'll call on you," I said confidently. "Now you, Musa."

"I think I see your plan shaping up," said Musa shrewdly. "I feel that I can do better by joining forces with Hussayn, who is coming up from Kabul. We can hold out around Sali Sarai until we see how you come out. Then, like Ali, I believe we can give help when you need it."

"Very well," I said, for I had no choice. "With Jaku and Elchi, I can make a stand. I'll send Shereza Begum and her property with Ali, and Aljai with Musa to Hussayn."

So I began preparations for the evacuation of my family. I had Ak Sarai stripped, except for the main hall and a few adjoining rooms, and my wives' property packed for the journey south. Sheik Ali and Musa loaded their trains also, but we kept everything hidden until word came that Hadji had left Samarkand. Then I lined up all my men for battle along the Samarkand Road.

I met Hadji at the head of his column a few miles north of Shehri-Sebz.

"All ready to go?" he asked, when he reined up before me.

"No," I said boldly. "I'm not going."

"As head of the Barlas clan, I command you to pool your property with your kinsmen and join us in our withdrawal," he said.

I measured his strength, which was less than I had expected, and watched him look nervously down the gauntlet of my forces which extended far along the road. Several of his officers, lightly armed for guard duty, drew up abreast of him. Jaku and Elchi brought a larger force of battle-ready warriors to my position, and I decided to try Hadji.

"I, Timur, son of Taragai, Chief of the Barlas, demand that you surrender all tribal property to me for safekeeping in the capital of the clan," I called loudly and arrogantly, so that my words carried far down the column. "Such cowardly kinsmen of mine as prefer to run away with a usurping weakling may do so, but it is my duty to see that tribal property is not wasted in a foolish flight into the desert."

Hadji was taken by complete surprise. He started to bluster uncertainly.

"Nonsense, you little puppy, I command—"

"Jaku, ride down the line and give orders to draw swords," I barked over my shoulder, and Jaku galloped toward Shehri-Sebz, bellowing commands.

Hadji collapsed completely. He remembered the drubbing Sheik Ali had given him in breaking the siege of my capital.

"Let's talk this over," he began. "Surely you wouldn't rob your own people."

"No. Every man may keep his own property—except what I shall require as a fee for furnishing protection for your train to the Iron

Gate, but all tribal wealth, which I am sure is in the hands of the present usurper, must be surrendered to me."

Then came my turn to be surprised. Hadji agreed, so eager was he to be on his way, and I took over all his pack animals and sent them into Shehri-Sebz. I further exacted twenty gold dinars from all who had money and detached four hundred of Ali's men under Mouva to escort the caravan to the Iron Gate.

Such an impression did my apparent confidence and show of military force make that half of Hadji's people wanted to remain with me. Remembering Jaku's advice, however, I haughtily refused to accept their cowardly services and hurried the procession on its way. Some of my men, too, recognizing my bluff but not giving me away, chose to join Hadji; and so when the train had passed through Shehri-Sebz, I had a scant two hundred men left besides those who were going with Sheik Ali and Musa.

On the following day Sheik Ali broke camp and set out to join the advance force which had been instructed to wait for him at the Iron Gate after Hadji's party had passed through. Shereza Begum was eager to return to Herat. She tearfully begged me to go along; but when I assured her that my duty lay in Shehri-Sebz, she soon forgot her grief and thought only of the safety of her babies.

Aljai offered stronger resistance.

"I fear nothing you don't fear," she argued.

"I am not afraid of anything," I said. "But this will be no place for you and Jahangir until the looting stops."

"Then may I come back?" she asked anxiously.

"Just as soon as things settle down."

"And another thing—" she began haltingly. "Hadn't you better let me take Lillit and Reba?"

I laughed at her concern.

"Certainly, if you'll feel safer."

"I'll feel safer," she said positively. "I've overcome their original lead, and I don't intend to let anyone else be mistress of your household while I live."

"What about Abdullah's mother?" I asked teasingly.

"She's all right." Aljai was easy again. "Let her run Ak Sarai—as she always has, since I've thought about it." She grinned at the memory.

So Musa and his men, with my wives, set out with Sheik Ali's train. I was left behind with only my personal squadron and the loot I had taken from Hadji.

I issued orders that life was to go on as usual and that no special guard was to be posted. I wanted Shehri-Sebz to appear as normal and peaceful as it would if there was no threat of invasion. Nor did I want Ak Sarai to seem deserted; so I called on Karin the first evening after the train had departed.

Her palace, though much smaller than Ak Sarai, was luxuriously and tastefully furnished. She met me in her main hall and showed great relief when she saw who her guest was.

"Oh, Amir Timur," she said. "I knew you wouldn't fail me. With the men all gone I don't know what I shall do."

"How would you like to be the Khatun Agha for a while?"

"I'd like to be the Khatun Agha forever," she said, but I could not tell just how sincere her smile was. "Come into my own chamber."

"No, I want you to come to Ak Sarai," I said, "and bring your girls and everything."

"You really mean it?" she asked, and her eyes grew moist. "You are really asking me to come into your household?"

"You and your girls will *be* my household."

"So your princesses have run out on you," she said with considerable satisfaction, and rushed into my arms. "Of course we'll come— after so long, you've asked me."

I saw no reason for correcting her misunderstanding, and I was well rewarded for my silence. Karin moved into Ak Sarai that night and brought with her as lovely a harem as any man ever owned. I sometimes wished that I could have kept the girls permanently, but since the women had free run of the palace and sat at meals with the master in those days, someone would have recognized my wives in later years, and I could not have allowed myself to be so ridiculed.

For the next week, at least, I was a multiple bridegroom again. I never asked Karin to dance, but I found that she had not overstated her prowess in bed.

"I'm glad now, we had to wait," she said. "I was so skinny and awkward when you first saw me, and I knew so little. I can please you better now."

And indeed it was hard to believe that her fine, expert body had grown out of the shy little slave girl who had so excited Nihmu the Ghurka. Her hard small breasts were now melon halves of rare texture and her angular buttocks the skillful curved cushions of a nymph. Yes, she could please me better. And so could her girls, who vied for my favor both singly and collectively in lively games of Scheherazade. In fact, I frequently forgot my real purpose in establishing my false household.

But every day I remembered again, as the steady stream of refugees poured down the road from Samarkand. Warriors, merchants, nobles, with their finest horses and favorite wives and their wealth in gold and jewels, passed through my valley. I dressed my only remaining soldiers in their finest uniforms, as though they were only my palace guard; and if anyone asked, he was told that my troops were guarding my frontiers and that we feared no one.

I exacted no toll from the travelers, and many of them sought me out and asked me to let them stay in my peaceful valley. But I was adamant. I haughtily refused to accept men who fled before the Kha Khan, and they left my palace, looking back longingly at the serene faces of my beautiful wives and the luxury of the one room they had seen. And they rode away sadly, through fields being tilled by unruffled peasants. Only I knew how false the scene was, and I wondered if Shehri-Sebz at its height had been any less false, if my paradise had ever been real.

And then the traffic stopped on the Samarkand Road. Not one strange horseman stirred up dust from the north. A mosquelike quiet settled over my entire valley. Peasants paused in their field work and looked over waving ripe grain toward the highway. Merchants left their bazaars and walked out into the street for a look to the north. And women climbed up on the flat roofs and scanned the horizon fearfully. Everyone grew tense in the unnatural calm.

I sought Zain ad-Din for some final advice.

"Am I right?" I asked the old priest.

"I think you are," he said. "Surely the Church and the city have prospered under your rule."

"But Kurgan—and my father, until recently—counseled against bowing to the Kha Khan. I can still flee and return later with larger forces."

"No," advised Zain ad-Din. "That isn't like you. Your city will be raped and the Church pillaged."

"I can regain it all later," I said, wavering in my first resolve.

"You can't restore the virtue of our women nor bring back the dead. You have paid tribute to other masters, to Kurgan and Hadji. You can serve still another."

"Tugluk is different," I said.

"I know. He believes not in the Prophet, but follows the law of Genghis Khan. If you leave now his men will sack Shehri-Sebz and rob the monastery."

"And if I stay?"

"Surely no man can harm a host who welcomes him and gives him rich gifts."

"Then I will try," I said, for I wanted to believe my old tutor. "That was my plan, as you know, to keep Shehri-Sebz as it is. I'll pay all I have left."

"And more," said Zain ad-Din. "I'll open the coffers of the Church to you. Together we can appease the Kha Khan and save our city by peaceful means."

True to his word, the old mollah opened the vaults of the monastery, and all night long a squad of trustworthy men carried bags of gold and jewels and rich ornaments from the Church to Ak Sarai. I hid much of the wealth but kept gold and jewels handy for bribing the first wave of Tugluk's forces.

The next morning I sent a courier to the Kha Khan's ordu, with a message that I offered homage and waited for an invitation to his court. I vowed loyalty and assured him that all I had was his by the right of fealty. Technically that was true, for he was a descendant of Kabul and I of Kayouli; but the old compact had received only token compliance for several generations.

I sent out a few scouts also and prepared to receive guests. And they came—suddenly—a force of some two hundred Jat raiders, their pack ponies loaded with loot and their saddle horses fat from feeding on the ripe grain in the fields by the way. My scouts reported them two hours before they came in sight, and when they reached the outskirts of town, I already had meats roasting for a feast and my retainers dressed in gay party garb.

My guards at the gates drew no swords but saluted the Jats and welcomed them to Shehri-Sebz. Fearing a trap, the leader placed his main force on my walls and brought a dozen picked officers cautiously up to the palace. I greeted them heartily at the gate to the inner wall.

"Brothers," I said. "Welcome to Ak Sarai. I've been expecting the envoys of my Father, the Kha Khan, my beloved Amir and Master. I am Timur, Chief of the Barlas, Amir of Shehri-Sebz. Enter into my palace garden."

Completely bewildered by my hospitality, the Jat commander rode dumbly beside me to the door of the palace. Karin's girls were waiting with crocks of cool kumiss and salty caviar.

"Share salt with me and refresh yourselves after your long dusty ride," I invited, and the girls handed drinks to all the men even before they dismounted.

"The Kha Khan sends his compliments to the Amir of Shehri-Sebz," lied the leader, at last finding his tongue but showing poor grace in his patent disappointment at being put into the position of a guest and denied the chance to pillage the city. "I, Ibiku, the Kha Khan's ming-bashi drink to my Amir."

"To the Kha Khan," I said, and drained my cup. "Another to Ibiku, servant of the Kha Khan."

"And to Timur, the Kha Khan's gracious subject," Ibiku said and tilted his third cup.

"Call in your men and join us in this great holiday," I suggested.

"Where is your army?" he asked warily, looking over the hundred palace guards drawn up at attention before Ak Sarai.

"Protecting the Kha Khan's southern frontier," I said boldly. "I have only my elite guard with me, since I have nothing to fear from the north, where the great Tugluk provides my protection."

"Your city *is* peaceful," he said.

"Peaceful under the good rule of Tugluk. Invite your men to the merrymaking. We have plenty for all."

I waved my hand toward the spacious gardens, where cooking fires sputtered under many roasting carcasses. The Jats licked their lips, and the leader finally sent a tavachi to bring his men down from the walls.

"Now, come with me into my banquet hall," I invited him, and called attendants to take the Jats' horses.

Still skeptical, Ibiku led his men cautiously into my courtchamber, where my temporary wives again met them with trays of wine and sweetmeats. The girls made as charming a corps of hostesses as ever graced a khan's court; and soon Ibiku and his officers and my own staff, including Jaku and Elchi, were comfortable and relaxed beside serving tables placed about the room.

"Now, for my gifts to the Kha Khan's brave warriors," I said, and clapped my hands for Abdullah.

My chamberlain, frowning dourly, led in a procession of servants laden with gifts taken from Hadji's packs. I hardly knew what to expect, myself, but I found khalats and saddles and weapons for all the men present. Then I gave each a bag of gold and sent five gold dinars to each of the common soldiers feasting outside. For Ibiku I had some fine jewels as well.

I watched the commander closely. As he drank more and more of my wine, his Mongoloid eye flaps closed to a slit, and I knew that he still was not satisfied. He gorged himself further and accepted more gifts, but still his thin straggling moustache drooped over the corners of unsmiling lips. His expression became greedier and greedier, and I watched his narrow eyes as the girls walked among the guests with serving trays. Even Karin, who sat in the seat of the Khatun Agha, could not bring a smile to his lips with all her gay chatter. He wanted more.

Finally he clapped his hands and called, "A dance for the guests, a dance."

The girls stopped where they were and looked at me. I nodded, and they formed into a circle and began a modest nautch dance to the music of my court band.

Ibiku followed their prim movements with an even more pronounced leer.

"Show yourselves," he shouted, and I knew that he expected everything.

"Is that customary?" I objected, as I thought I should.

"That's customary," he said flatly.

"A man does not show his wives in our land," I said. "But I've heard that some of the northern tribes do share their women—and if that's true—" I hesitated.

"It's true. We are of those tribes."

"Very well," I said reluctantly, and faced the girls. "Show yourselves."

The dancers quickly divested themselves of all garments, and I was sure the Jats had never had such a treat before.

"You, too," Ibiku said viciously, and pointed to Karin, who sat by my side.

"Not the Khatun Agha!" she said in a voice of shocked modesty which would have been a credit to Aljai herself.

"The Amir of Shehri-Sebz would not deny his guests the fairest prize of all, I'm sure." Ibiku looked threateningly at me.

"Must I?" asked Karin in a hurt, pleading voice. I never really knew how deeply hurt she was. There was no way of telling about Karin.

"Yes, dear," I said. "If that's the Kha Khan's custom."

Whatever her feelings, she did not let me down. She rose from her seat and joined the girls in the center of the room. Then, as daintily and modestly as a true princess, she began to disrobe. She handed her veil to one girl. Hesitantly she unbound her bosom, showing first one plump dark-nippled breast and then pausing as though having trouble with a clasp before exposing the other. Fascinated though I was by her performance, in which I began to suspect practiced artfulness, I glanced at Ibiku to see him straining to help her along and licking his slack lower lip when she turned profile for a moment.

Then Karin began to fumble with the scarf which hung from her waist. First one smooth hip flashed, to disappear again and to reappear after Karin tugged gently at the skirt. Finally the recalcitrant garment was conquered, and Karin laid back a fold and revealed the clean straight line formed by the meeting of her inside thighs. She dropped one corner of the cloth, and the sheer silk slid around her body and hung before her and hid her again. When one of her girls took the scarf from her, in what I knew was a well-rehearsed act, Karin had shifted her weight to one foot and let the other knee bend forward and in. She lowered her chin and looked at the floor in a pose of such innocent abashment that I regretted for a moment that I had let her in for the ordeal. But that had been my plan from the beginning.

And I was immediately relieved of all responsibility of entertaining my guests for the rest of the night. Jaku and Elchi, who knew the girls, could hardly hold in their laughter as the Jat officers scurried out with my wives. My chief fear was that the Kha Khan's men might discover how few of the rooms in the palace were furnished. I doubted, however, that the men would be at all conscious of their surroundings, for I knew what the girls had to offer. I even felt a twinge of jealousy toward Ibiku, who of course made off with Karin immediately.

The next morning I had everything ready for my visit to Tugluk's ordu by the time my guests had pulled themselves away from their paramours, who, by the way, got back for themselves the jewels and most of the gold I had given the Jats. With a clearer head than my enemies could muster after their night of carousing, I hustled them out of Shehri-Sebz soon after sunrise. They really believed by that time that they had been sent to escort me to the Kha Khan; and as they rode along beside my hundred handsomely outfitted personal guards and protected my packs of gifts for Tugluk, it was hard to tell who was in command, Ibiku or I.

The Jat officers smirked at me as a cuckolded husband, and my men smirked back at them for the trick I had played on them. Later, at the ordu, Elchi spread the story of my hospitality, and Ibiku's staff became the laughingstock of their fellow officers. But as my train moved nearer Samarkand, I was not in a laughing mood, for there were still unknown difficulties ahead.

At the Zaravshan River just below Samarkand, I was halted by two ming-bashis with full regiments.

"No Tatars are allowed beyond this point," said one of the officers.

"But I am Timur, Chief of the Barlas, summoned by the Kha Khan himself, and escorted by my good friend Ibiku," I said.

Ibiku merely looked stupid, but I saw that the officers recognized him.

"And I bear rich gifts for the great Tugluk, my Father."

86

The ming-bashis were not fully convinced, but I noticed their expressions when I mentioned the gifts.

"—and for his valiant commanders," I added, and hastily summoned Abdullah, who produced two heavy bags of gold.

I gave to each of the Jats a bag which contained far more gold than he would have been allowed to keep if he had captured my train for the Kha Khan. While all three ming-bashis, including Ibiku, were still amazed by the gifts, I boldly ordered my column forward and passed on toward Tugluk's camp. A few hours later we saw the huge tent city, surrounded by herds of sheep, cattle, and horses.

For a mile we rode through the dung-laden dust of the main street between rows of white felt kibitkas. Squadron after squadron was marked by its horsetail standard and its armory filled with the horn-and-wood bows and the long tufted lances of the nomads. I saluted the Jat warriors in their fine court clothes—flowered Khitai satins, and gold embroidered boots of soft kiang shagreen—and no man challenged me, because my men's silver mail and rich garments proclaimed me a great ruler, and I had Ibiku's men for escort.

I approached the Kha Khan, seated before his pavilion with a circle of nobles, as though I were expected. Boldly I dismounted and prostrated myself before Tugluk and repeated the court karnash.

"Oh, Father, my Kha Khan, Master of the World, I am Timur, Son of Taragai, Chieftain of the Barlas. I come to pay homage and bring gifts to the great Tugluk."

Waiting only for a nod to rise, I had my men open the packs and lay the wealth of the Church and the rest of Hadji's loot before the Kha Khan. The gifts were really quite elaborate. Tugluk stared in open-mouthed amazement at the rich prizes.

"I would have had more to present to you, but this dog Ibiku robbed my palace, even to violating my wives," I continued, and turned viciously on Ibiku, "and your thieving ming-bashis at the Zaravshan river took my two heaviest bags of gold."

I spat contemptuously into the dust.

"Such dogs to serve so great a master, I never expected," I went on venomously.

The fat-faced old Mongol raised his greedy eyes from my gifts and looked at me unsteadily. He pushed a strand of his thin moustache out of the corner of his mouth and spoke for the first time.

"You are right, Timur, my son. They are thieving dogs, thorns in my flesh, and I am grateful to you for exposing them—and for your rich gifts."

He clapped his hands, and six nobles came to attention before him. "Strip Ibiku of his rank. Take all the loot from his packs and return it to the Barlas clan." He eyed me shrewdly, and continued. "Send it all quickly to the body of the clan now with Hadji, young Timur's second in command."

I read the Kha Khan's purpose. After accepting my gifts, he could not keep the loot also. But by returning it to Hadji, who was fleeing from him, he could claim it again as fair booty when he defeated Hadji in battle. I could only admire the Kha Khan, and I felt confident of winning his respect by aping his tactics.

"Relieve the ming-bashis of their command and bring them here to me," he continued. "They shall return the Barlas gold to my faithful subject, Timur."

"I only want the gold given to my Father, the Kha Khan," I objected. "All things are his. I am merely his steward."

"No, what you have been robbed of shall be returned unto you. Your gifts are generous—you have given your all."

Formally friendly though the words were, I knew they were hollow and false. But I took heart in the shrewd way the Kha Khan studied my face, for I saw respect growing as he cunningly weighed the measure of my own deceit. It was the same sort of appraisal that had prompted Kurgan to give me my start.

Clapping his hands again, Tugluk thundered out another command.

"I order a feast to honor my faithful son, Timur. Tonight we all welcome him. All men shall call him brother."

And Tugluk's lackeys sped off to proclaim the festival and set cooks and entertainers to work. By nightfall the camp blazed with flares and gay paper lanterns. I sat beside the Kha Khan and shared his feast tray while tumblers performed before us and agile little men from the islands off Khitai balanced themselves on tight ropes high above, their twirling paper parasols reflecting the campfires in bright lacquered patterns.

For two days we feasted, and Tugluk's nobles took me into their circle. Jaku and Elchi whispered stories of my cunning to the appreciative Jats, who loved intrigue above all things. So I grew in stature as the men laughed at Ibiku's officers and roared at the coup by which I had won my Begum from the wily Shah Malik. Tugluk took note of my acceptance by the bahaturs and I gained more of his favor also.

Then word came that the ming-bashis at the Zaravshan had resisted arrest and taken their regiments back toward Almalyk, pillaging and wasting the country in their path. Ibiku and his men fled in the night to join them, and the whole camp was astir.

Tugluk moved his court into the fortified city of Samarkand and sent half his men after the deserters. He took me and my men with him and honored us by making the Shehri-Sebz Corps his palace guard, with me in command. Throughout the summer and on into autumn I enjoyed such luxury in Samarkand as I never knew existed. The palace was fitted with the most gorgeous creations of the world's finest artists, truly a place of infinite beauty.

I longed for Aljai to walk with me through the tapestry-hung halls, to lie with me on silk-canopied couches perfumed with the sweetest musk from Tibet, to exclaim with me over the cunning of eastern craftsmen. And I would have been proud to escort my princess to the royal banquets where the tall Tatar aghas vied for men's compliments with the fragile doll-women from Khitai. The court lacked only my Aljai to be paradise, and I resolved one day to make it so.

For I thought that I was again on the Way. But I was set on the prizes of cunning and war rather than on the processes themselves. And my delusion was strengthened by the rewards which came later.

The rebellious Jats in the north had recruited large forces and were threatening Tugluk's capital. Before the first snow, the Kha Khan became worried and called his council into session.

"We have trouble at home," he announced. "I seek the counsel of you, my wise men and brave warriors."

"Let us return before the snow falls," said an old amir who had grown dreamy-eyed at the mention of home. "Ilias can rule here, as he has done in the past."

"And for a protector—" began the Kha Khan, and looked around for suggestions.

"Surely Timur is the man," said Khitai Bahatur, a wiry little man from inside the Great Wall. "He alone has remained true and steadfast while all other princes of Samarkand have scattered like quail in the shadow of a hawk."

"Yes, Timur has proved himself a true son," Tugluk said slowly, for he valued Khitai for his cunning and shrewd judgment of men.

"Amir Timur has both sense and courage," another chimed in.

"What do you say, Amir Timur, my son?" asked Tugluk.

"Oh, my Father, you are hard pressed from both sides. Go to the aid of your capital. I will protect you from the south like a true son of Kayouli, with all loyalty to the house of Kabul."

"Well said, Son Timur. So shall it be."

And Tugluk appointed me tuman-bashi in command of ten thousand and gave me a seal and a writ of authority engraved on steel. Then he departed and left me as protector of Samarkand.

CHAPTER

12

As soon as I was settled in Samarkand, I sent word to Hussayn to bring Aljai. I also promised him Shehri-Sebz as his seat, since a Jat amir had come by way of Tibet and taken his throne in Kabul. He accepted and set out from Sali Sarai almost immediately. I also asked Sheik Ali to return, but Shah Malik was ailing and needed him in Herat. The Shah also considered my position still uncertain, and Shereza Begum sent me a sorrowful letter telling me how much she would like to join me but saying that she must stay where her babies were safe.

With my finest regiment, in full dress, I rode beyond Shehri-Sebz to meet Hussayn when I got word of his passage through the Iron Gate. There was light snow lying all over my valley, and my brilliant band must have looked like a heavenly host to Hussayn's tired, ragged warriors, who had lost Kabul. At any rate I read mixed expressions of envy and mounting respect in Hussayn's eyes as they roved over the splendor of my regiment.

Aljai, as usual, had eyes only for me, and as soon as we met she clambered off her own horse and onto my saddle in front of me. I felt all my joy return when first her firm body touched mine again; and as we rode toward Ak Sarai, I could not resist stroking her temples and hair and caressing again the sweet curves of her shoulders and bosom, while I talked to Hussayn of the gifts and plans I had for him.

His wife, Dilshad, who was Aljai's second cousin and looked more like her younger sister, rode beside us; and her eyes, too, were directed at me—or rather at my attentions to Aljai. She seemed fascinated by our affectionate play and followed every movement of my hands as though she were sharing Aljai's welcome home. So close had the two cousins become that one's joy seemed always to be the other's also.

And when we reached Ak Sarai and dismounted, it was Dilshad who brought Jahangir to me and re-introduced us. He did not remember me, and he seemed to look upon Aljai and Dilshad as one. But he was saying more words and had grown taller and leaner in the six months since I had seen him. While Abdullah was having gifts brought and distributed among Hussayn's officers, I gave presents to my wife and son, and gradually the baby and I became friends again. And Aljai's happiness at having us all together again rose alternately in gay laughter and quick-drying tears.

It was a good night back in our own bedchamber—with Aljai in my bed and Jahangir in his cradle and Abdullah's mother in devoted attendance upon us all.

And the next morning I proudly showed Aljai how I had saved our land from destruction by my acceptance of the Kha Khan as master. The stubbles lay white and serene, and granaries were full on the farms. Fat children played happily in the snow along the Samarkand Road. Peace was everywhere, and peace meant Aljai to me.

"I'm so glad it's all over," she said thankfully, as she rode by my side. "And I'm home again."

"Not yet," I still boasted. "Wait until you see Samarkand."

"I'll wait, Timur, lover, but home is where you are. I'll never leave you again."

"I hope not," I said. "With Allah's help, we should have peace for a long time."

I was more conscious of Allah's will since the success I had gained by following Zain ad-Din's counsel.

"With Allah's help?" said Aljai in surprise. "You never used to worry much about that."

"Isn't my change for the better?" I asked.

"I'm not sure," she said, wrinkling her brow. "You know more about such things than I do. As you think, so do I—only don't ever send me away again."

And I vowed that while she lived she should never leave my side.

Aljai saw Samarkand through my eyes as we rode up the wide street. I pointed out the richest bazaars, brilliant with gay flowered silks and bright jeweled ornaments, and I promised Aljai everything she wanted, for the whole city was mine. As soon as we were established in our palace, I bought all the things she wanted—and more, the things I wanted her to have. At last I had a chance to exhibit my royal consort at court functions.

Aljai shone, too, to please me. She became a great favorite at the Khan's court, and everyone loved her—or envied her beauty. And my pride grew in her as our love matured. I thanked Allah for the good things He gave me for following His ways of peace by appeasement.

But despite my joy in luxury and my constant reminders to Aljai of how well off we were, she still was happiest when we were alone with Jahangir in his nursery. For five years we watched the boy grow. I gave him toy soldiers and a small sword like my own, and Aljai found puppies and kittens for him. He preferred her gifts, for he was gentle like her; and I thought nothing of it. I was sure that he would never need to learn the Way of the Sword.

He did like the pony I gave him; and we all three rode together inside the walls of the city, and sometimes went hunting in the nearby hills. We never went far, because I merely chose to be blind—I knew what was happening beyond the walls of Samarkand. Every year fewer amirs sent their tribute. I believed that I could hold my power by being less demanding on my subjects.

The Jat commanders whom the Kha Khan had placed in many cities exacted their own levies, and I heard rumors that they sometimes pillaged and raped lesser neighbors. But all were the Kha Khan's subjects—I was responsible for Samarkand only. The Tatar princes also grew strong on their revenue and one by one became arrogant at my kindnesses and withdrew to their fortresses, taking their squadrons out of my service.

Still I protected the puppet Khan and held on to the grand life of his court, until the day came when I had hardly a full regiment of my own men. Reluctantly I had to admit to myself that the good days were passing. I returned to the saddle and drilled my men daily. And I sent messengers to the still friendly tribes to exact new oaths of fealty and pledges of men for my army.

Hussayn remained loyal and guarded my own valley. Musa at Karshi swore loyalty, and Bayazid and Hadji asked for a council at their camp on the road to Shehri-Sebz. Since they had formerly been masters at Samarkand, they said that they feared to enter the city. So I agreed to the meeting.

"I'm coming, too," said Aljai. "Bayazid's my uncle and I want to see him."

"Very well," I agreed. "Hadji's my uncle; so we should have a family reunion."

"Let's take Jahangir, too," urged Aljai, "and visit Hussayn and Dilshad before we return."

I agreed, because I also wanted to talk to Hussayn. I left Jaku in command at Samarkand and led my own elite squadron to meet with the Jalair and Barlas chieftains. By the extent of their camp I could tell that both had prospered. They had many men and much property. Fat herds grazed along a fresh stream which ran behind their camp, and the picket line held strings of sleek horses. I was pleased at the prospect of strong allies.

Elchi took my squadron on beyond the stream. Aljai sent Jahangir on with Abdullah, while we rode with Bayazid to the council pavilion.

"Timur, Amir of Samarkand, welcome, kinsman," Hadji greeted from the flap of the headquarters tent.

"Greetings, Uncle," I responded, and we all dismounted. "The Khan sends his compliments." I thought it well to remind Hadji of the authority I held.

"The Khan—yes—I pay homage to my Father, the great good Khan," Hadji said perfunctorily and ushered us inside the kibitka.

The sidewalls were down and the tent was in semidarkness. As my eyes grew accustomed to the half-light, I saw a dozen armed men squatting or standing around the antechamber.

Hadji graciously seated Aljai at the right hand of his court chair, and I squatted beside her, but Bayazid carefully placed my four tavachis across the room from us. I became apprehensive, and I felt Aljai's body grow tense by my side.

"You have quite a force," I said to my uncle.

"Yes, we've prospered under your rule," he said politely.

"It's good to find so strong a kinsman in these troubled times," I said.

"Indeed it must be," he agreed with a hint of sarcasm. "All Tatary's aflame."

"I shall welcome strong allies like you and my wife's kinsman, the valiant Bayazid."

A nervous little stir ran through the assembly, and I thought I detected a muffled snicker from one of the squatting warriors. Aljai picked up a grass stem from the dirt floor and playfully tickled my nose. I brushed it aside and smiled at her. She began to chew on the stick.

"Your forces are weakening, I hear," said Hadji. "We thought you might need us."

"Oh, no," I said. "I'm in command of ten thousand. But I'm glad that my allies are strong so they can defend their own clans until my forces arrive."

"We can do that," said Hadji.

By a quiet shifting of positions, Bayazid's men had placed themselves so that there were two or three of them around each of my tavachis, who were cut off from me and from each other. Aljai took another grass stem and tickled my nose again. I snatched it from her and began chewing on it. She seemed relieved that I did.

"We are stronger than ever before," Hadji went on, "thanks to you." And his voice was losing its tone of pretended friendliness.

I watched my men regroup themselves and move closer to the court chair. I saw that everyone was aware of the aim of the council—my assassination. Bayazid looked anxiously at Aljai and glanced nervously around the room. I doubted that he would risk arousing the ire of the Jalairs by harming Aljai, for she was their favorite princess; and I searched my mind for a way of escape before I became separated from her.

She drew her blade of grass across my cheek and whispered very softly, "Make your nose bleed."

"The Khan will be pleased to learn of your strength," I said as casually as I could.

"We can protect him," said Hadji coldly, and turned to survey the situation in the courtchamber.

Covering my face as well as I could with my hand, I took the grass blade out of my mouth and tickled the inside of my nose—pretending I was still chewing the stem. And a trickle of blood ran down on my lip as I put my hand down.

"Oh, you poor dear," shouted Aljai in alarm. "Your nose is bleeding. Here, let me help."

She held a scarf to my nose and turned back to Hadji.

"Excuse us a minute," she requested with all her court charm. "This way—to the creek for some water."

And before anyone else could move, she hustled me out through a side door toward the stream. But immediately we ducked behind another tent and ran headlong toward my squadron. For a moment we heard nothing—then the rattle of talwars in the tent we had left. We did not look back until we had cleared the line of tents. When I did risk a glance, I saw Hadji's men darting among the willow trees on the creek bank behind the tent.

Elchi saw us coming and met us with horses and guards before our enemies discovered the way we had gone. My trumpets sounded at once and my squadron assembled for battle. Already Bayazid's men had blocked the road toward Samarkand.

"Ride toward Shehri-Sebz," I told Elchi and rode off with Aljai and Jahangir.

In a moment my elite guard was in headlong flight toward Hussayn's fortress at Shehri-Sebz.

But Hadji and Bayazid did not give chase. Instead they moved north and laid siege to Samarkand.

Hussayn's hospitality was less generous than I had expected—I had made him master of Shehri-Sebz—but he did offer us refuge, because he loved Aljai despite his sometimes patronizing attitude toward his young sister. And Dilshad welcomed us all, especially Jahangir, who was then an affectionate little seven-year-old. And although I resented being treated as a guest in my own palace, I had to admit that Hussayn *was* master of Ak Sarai; so I accepted my humiliation and still pretended to the title of Amir of Samarkand.

The title was empty, however, for the city fell within a week. Many of my own men, fascinated, as I had been, by life at the court, willingly accepted Bayazid and Hadji as masters and went on as before. Their cowardly obeisance merited only my contempt and made them forever my enemies. And I was not at all displeased when the Kha Khan came down again from the north and retook Samarkand, even though his Mongols ravaged the countryside down into my own valley.

It was Hussayn who led his men forth to meet the Kha Khan's forces north of Shehri-Sebz. I kept my small band inside the walls to protect the city from outlaw bands operating on the fringe of the major battles. For two days I watched the Samarkand Road again with dread in my heart. I knew that Hussayn could not stop the Jats, and I planned again to hold Shehri-Sebz for my Father, the Kha Khan.

On the third day one of Hussayn's tavachis rode into the city with a message. Hussayn had been defeated by the forces of Tugluk and had decided to retire again to the hills near Kabul. He asked me to pack a train and be ready to join him.

I reported the message to Aljai and Dilshad and began packing Hussayn's train.

"I shall stay here," I said, "and send the rest of you with Hussayn."

"I stay, too," Aljai said positively.

"And I," added Dilshad. "I'll stay with Aljai and Jahangir."

"No," I said. "Your place is with Hussayn." I wanted him out of the country with no ties left behind.

"Then let me take Jahangir," suggested Dilshad. "There'll be trouble here."

"I think Dilshad's right," Aljai said thoughtfully. "Jahangir will be safer in Kabul."

So we prepared Jahangir for the journey and Abdullah's mother insisted that she go along, too. When Hussayn, with his small band of battered warriors, came down the road, the train joined him and rode on toward Kabul. Hussayn had lost some of his arrogance with his crushing defeat, but I could not tell whether his eyes held contempt or surprise at my decision to stay behind.

"What shall we do now?" asked Aljai, after Hussayn's train had departed.

"Just wait and see what happens," I said. "I'm still in the service of the Kha Khan." And I produced my steel tablet to show my authority.

"Commander of ten thousand," Aljai said pompously and giggled.

The first band of Jats, at least, respected my Kha Khan's commission when I offered no resistance and insisted that I was defending one of Tugluk's cities against Tatar attackers. Their orders were to take Hussayn, anyway; so the force passed on by in pursuit of the rebel. The leader told me that Tugluk had put Bayazid to death and that Hadji had fled into the hills.

So I continued to wait. I moped about my palace and grumbled at my loss of prestige. Aljai tried to be gay and keep me diverted, but my feelings were too strong to be allayed by one woman. I had left Lillit and Reba in Samarkand—and lost them, for I never saw either of them again. And I continued to fret.

I did get some respite, however—another outlet for my emotions. Karin came to me one night. She was older and thinner, and her old confidence was gone.

"Amir Timur, I have come to you again," she said.

"What's the trouble now?" I asked.

"My luck has gone bad," she said. "Amir Hussayn's men had no money, and my girls ran away one by one. Now I'm alone and tired of all men—save you, my first protector."

"What can I do?" I asked.

"Take me into your household as a slave, as a menial—whatever you will," she said dejectedly.

I pondered for a while and remembered the rare pleasure I had once found in her body. She was still beautiful, even though her spirit was broken. And I accepted her.

"You shall be my only concubine," I said, and she brightened somewhat.

"That's more than I ask," she said gratefully, but not with the obvious joy she had shown the first time I invited her into Ak Sarai.

I was much with her at first, and so appreciative was she of my kindness that she strove hard to please me. Her body was less perfect than it had been six years before, but still held a poignant tenderness and a kind of chaste beauty in repose. And a sad sort of hunger had replaced the sheer delight she had once shown in my embrace. She relieved me of much of my tension.

Then in a few days Musa rode into Shehri-Sebz with his own men and many of the leaderless Jalairs who had scattered when Bayazid was slain. I trusted Musa and welcomed his forces to add to my garrison. I thought of further reinforcements also and called my chamberlain.

"Abdullah," I said. "Be honest with me—do you hate me?"

"Certainly not, Amir. Why?"

"Don't lie to me—this is important, very important. Once, when you gave me the stolen talwar, you admitted that you had considered killing me and joining a leader somewhere. Isn't that right?"

"Yes, Amir. I was only a boy then."

"But you *had* thought of it," I reminded him. "How do other slaves —other servants—feel about their masters?"

"All other slaves hate their masters, Amir. All except me."

"I must know the truth, Abdullah—all the truth. *Are* you an exception? You once said you stayed on because you feared to run away and doubted that you could do better by yourself."

"Yes, Amir. I said that."

"Say it again, if it's true. I promise I won't harm you."

"It's true." Abdullah looked at the floor. "All slaves hate their masters."

"And their loyalty is just a myth?"

"Yes, Amir. They are loyal only to their caste—but there is nothing they can do."

"They might get better masters," I said.

"Not without help."

"But with my help. I have a plan. You know Haroun, Hadji's body servant, quite well, don't you?"

"Yes, Amir. Quite well."

"Does he hate his master?"

"Yes, Amir."

"I thought so," I said. "Hadji tried to assassinate me—he's a bad man. Do you think Haroun would kill him, if I promised protection and a reward—enough to start business a free man?"

"He might. I don't know."

"You find out," I ordered. "Find Hadji's camp and make a bargain with Haroun. If you succeed, I'll give you Karin al Raschid for your wife."

"Karin?" Abdullah looked up in pleased surprise. I thought that he had wanted Karin ever since he had moved her into her pleasure palace years before, when he had disappeared for a week.

"Yes. You may have Karin."

"When do I leave, Amir?"

"Right now. Take two others with you and pretend that you've run away."

Within a week news spread through the valley that Hadji, despite his strict guard, had been slain in his sleep by his own body servant, who had escaped and fled into the hills. Like the Jalairs, the leaderless Barlas clan scattered and were regrouped under Jaku, who had escaped from Samarkand with most of his squadron. He, too, answered my summons and brought a thousand more men to my garrison at Shehri-Sebz. If any one of the Barlas clan ever recognized the well-dressed bearded stranger who set up a fine saddle shop in Shehri-Sebz, no mention was ever made of the fact. And I am sure that Abdullah was happy with Karin for many years.

So it was that when Tugluk finally rode down from Samarkand I had a fine army of two thousand men, twice the number of his escort.

"Oh, Father, my Kha Khan, Master of the World," I began, "I offer homage and gifts and welcome you to my palace."

My gifts were lighter, however, than they had been when I had only two hundred men.

"Timur, my son, Prince of Samarkand," the Kha Khan droned, "you have served me well and brought rich gifts. You stand high in my favor."

And we continued our formal conversation for an hour. Tugluk reminded me again that I was of the house of Kayouli and my duty was to protect his son, of the house of Kabul. We reviewed the fine service I had rendered and vowed eternal friendship and loyalty. But when the Kha Khan left, I found that the Jat general Bikijuk was the new Protector and I was left with Shehri-Sebz, a steel tablet, and whatever army I could raise and support. But I still had my valley, trampled and devastated though it might be.

CHAPTER

13

It was apparent that the Kha Khan no longer feared or respected any Tatar chieftain. Since Kurgan's death no man, not Ladakh, not Bayazid, not Hadji, not I, had been able to keep the rebellious amirs under control. By the same token, no man since Kurgan had been able to protect the Tatars from the greed and rapacity of Tugluk's barbarians. Not by war, not by appeasement, could any of my people cope with the cunning and strength of Tugluk.

Bikijuk pillaged and ravaged and raped from the very start. Whether the tribal chieftains paid tribute or not, the Jat protector came and took all. During the King Maker's lifetime the protectorship had been a two-way arrangement—protection of and against the puppet at Samarkand. Under Bikijuk there was no protection against the spoiled prince. Girls of all classes in Samarkand were taken as slaves and carried off by the Mongols or sold to traders going south. Mosques were looted and the most respected sayyids were enslaved as common scribes or menial house servants.

Even Zain ad-Din was forced to flee from the highest Church post in Samarkand and seek refuge in Shehri-Sebz. I welcomed the old mollah, for I respected his judgment. It was he who approached me and laid bare the woes of our people.

As a Prince of Samarkand, appointed by the Kha Khan, I sent a complaint. Tugluk took no notice of my message. And I turned once again to my old tutor. In the cool shadows of the mosque I asked for advice.

"The time has come to use force," he said to me.

"But you once counseled me to follow the ways of peace," I reminded him.

"The crimes now are against Allah. The Jats have robbed mosques and defiled the green turbans of sayyids," said Zain ad-Din. "Allah's wrath is aroused. You are His servant. You must rise against Bikijuk."

"The crimes are against men also," I said. "Against me and my people."

"Yes," said the priest slowly, perhaps aware that I was not pleased with the reward I had received from my last service for Allah. "As men judge, you have a grievance. Sometimes Allah disapproves of war among men for worldly reasons. But stealing church property—enslaving the mollahs—"

"And little girls," I reminded him, for it was the carrying off of their women that would stir men to action.

"—and little girls. You must rise."

"That's Allah's will?"

"That's Allah's will," he said positively. And I caught a glimpse of the flexibility of Allah's will as read by the priests. It was something I could make use of. I remembered Kurgan's advice, "—use what you can," and I thought of enlisting Allah in my service for a change.

"I shall arise," I said. "Will you assure my men of Allah's blessing?"

"Yes, by all means."

"And spread the word that I am His chosen leader?"

"Your name shall be read at prayers."

"Very well, get the men's hearts ready, and I'll see to their weapons."

And in partnership with Allah, as interpreted by Zain ad-Din, I began my campaign. Imams and mollahs and dervishes worked all day, crying my name and calling out the sins of Bikijuk. They screamed loudly of home, mother, wife, and daughter, and the smirch on the horsetail standards of the clans. Whispers went out that I had seen a vision, that I was invincible, and burning-eyed zealots came from everywhere to join my forces. My hard-bitten veterans, though they often jeered at priests and called them half-men, were superstitious at heart and soon they, too, fell into a state of hypnotic zeal.

Only Aljai saw humor in the situation.

"My husband's a saint," she said laughingly. "How can I live with him when they build a shrine to him?"

"You can't," I said. "They build shrines to dead men."

"No," she said, suddenly serious. "Don't say that. You musn't die. Does it really mean war again?"

"Yes," I said grimly. "It's war again—or still. It always has been, always will be. The Way of the Sword, that's how I won you. I'll follow no other."

"Then I go, too. You can't send me away again."

"I'll not try," I said after a moment's hesitation. For the first time in my life I was going to fight a war in anger and desperation, and I wanted Aljai with me. That was why I was challenging Bikijuk—to keep Aljai in Samarkand.

And a man must not fight a war in desperation, in hatred, or even in fear. War is a game—like chess—Allah's Game, to be played with a clear head, with wits, not with feeling. The enemy must be made blind with hate so he scatters his arrows. To win Allah's Game one must be without hate or love.

My army, however, was spurred on by both. Zain ad-Din and his corps of priests had put every warrior on edge—I was all Good, Bikijuk all Evil—so I led three thousand madmen north. I led them madly, on beyond Samarkand, under the cover of night. I had learned of the Jat strongholds at Tashkand and Otrar, where captives were held. It was toward these that I headed my crusade for Allah.

Hussayn came, too, with his wild mountain clansmen, made wilder by dervishes who shrieked Allah's Word. Two thousand men were added to my army by the coming of Hussayn, and even I began to believe I had seen Allah's vision. I led a Jihad, a Holy War for Allah.

Tashkand fell to my sword in one bloody night. My men were as thorough as the most vicious Mongols. Not an enemy was left alive, for we had Allah's blessing: we were fighting for Right. Slaves were made masters, girls returned to their parents, and Church property restored.

On to Otrar I led my conquering horde. For two days we besieged the walled city. Then word came that Tugluk was dead and Ilias was Kha Khan. And we knew we were right. Allah had taken the strength from our enemy, leaving only a spoiled courtier who had never made war.

Otrar fell to our holy zeal. Again, following the lead of our God who had taken our enemy chief, we slew all the Jats and set free our own people.

And we paused to give thanks. For a week we celebrated inside the walls of Otrar. We refitted our men with the loot of the Jats—new clothing, new weapons, new mounts, and new spirit. Then I held a review on the plain outside so Allah could see His invincible champions.

He looked down upon a brilliant array—bright steel mail and sharp pointed helmets of Hussayn's Afghan volunteers, polished horn standards and tough leather khalats of the steppe-riding Kazaks, gay feathered quivers and the sun-catching brilliance of talwars and lances and bright lacquered bows, and the green-turbaned heads of His own fighting priests.

Then we crossed the Syr-Darya toward the Kirghis Steppe, where Mongol nomads held more of our people. We made quick work of the dull, stupid wanderers and then turned east—and met the Samarkand corps, reinforced by Tugluk's army.

We met in the late afternoon with the sun to our backs. As I beheld the drab garb and the awkward big-wheeled kankalis of the northerners, I took pride in the colorful force Allah had given me. I was sure that the Mongols were amazed, in their sleepy-eyed way, at the splendid warriors they faced—the heavenly host of Allah's own guard.

We drew up a line and camped for the night, eager to dazzle and defeat the hateful Jats in the next bright sunrise. But it rained. Overnight our mail rusted. Our blades pitted and turned on their keen edges. Silks faded and wilted, and fine horsehide khalats became slick, sodden, and heavy, and weighted down sword-arms.

All night and all day it rained. The steppe was a quagmire. Horses sank to their haunches in the soft sticky mud, and men's spirits went limp in the downpour. Another day and another night, and the slow-moving Jats drew up in a battle line. From the cumbersome kankalis, high above the mud on their eight-foot wheels, the Mongols had taken dry horse blankets, dry weapons, and shovels with which to drain their camp grounds; so they faced us in comfort and superior strength.

I longed for the dry open desert where I could make my lightning charges. Instead I had to watch my fleet cavalry trudge through the mud. Horses sank to their bellies and riders slid off over their rumps.

It took hours to draw up my line. I put Hussayn and his powerful mountain men on my right flank, where pressure was greatest. Musa held the center with his kinsmen, the Jalairs, and I took the left flank with the Barlas men. I had three regiments in line and two in reserve— Jaku behind me, Elchi in the center, and Mouva backing Hussayn.

When the slow tortuous battle began, bow strings were so wet that any attempt at arrow cover by reserves was futile. It was sword-fighting with horses bogged down—vicious slashes, ax blows, hard-jabbing lances. The yellow water blushed red with blood of both sides.

Men fought on, with hands gone and arms limp, on to the death, for there was no wheeling and turning in the mud.

My men's zeal was not enough—the line broke, and the Jats pushed through. Units lost their identity and broke up into screaming, clattering clumps of bloody men and pieces of men hacking at each other. Jaku's reserves pushed forward uncertainly and wavered before striking.

As my last deed for Allah, I sought Bikijuk's standard, the hateful horsetail. And I found it, with the general defending it. Jaku saw it, too, and followed me as I pushed on to Bikijuk. With my horse half buried, I dueled with the Jat leader. We both slashed wildly, almost out of sword's reach, but our blows clanked on our shields and did little damage. I caught Bikijuk's thigh with a glancing blow and laid open a gash. His next blow missed me but cut the reins from my hand. My horse veered away and threw me off balance. I wheeled in my saddle in time to see Bikijuk stand up in his stirrups and swing his talwar high over his head for the kill. He grinned viciously in his moment of triumph.

But the blow never fell. Jaku, the lance-master, came from behind me and ran his iron-butted lance through Bikijuk's body, as he had caught the desert chieftain many years before. And the Samarkand standard fell with its master, for I slew the bearer when he turned to see Bikijuk die.

Immediately I called for my cymbals and nakaras, and the clang and the rumble drew all eyes toward the standard. The leaderless Mongols slowly withdrew, and my sector was quiet.

I rode to higher ground, where the mud was more firm, and surveyed the battlefield. The center was in chaos—I could tell nothing about it. The condition of the right flank was clearer—Hussayn had been pushed far back, and only Mouva's reserves prevented a complete rout.

I rallied my men and went to Hussayn's aid. I caught the hard-pressing Jats on their flank far toward the rear and threw them into confusion. Ilias Khan, having lost Bikijuk, was cautious with his reserves, and I saw victory ahead. I rushed a tavachi to Hussayn to call for a council. But I saw the hot-headed Jalair curse, and strike my courier in the face, so much did he resent my advice in battle. And soon his men were routed, and he fled through the mud.

I regrouped all my forces, but Ilias gained courage at Hussayn's retreat and sent his reserves toward my front. We fought in confusion until darkness came on. Then my forces scattered and I was forced to withdraw.

Heartsick, fearing the next day, I returned to my tent far in the rear of the line, where Aljai was waiting.

"How did you come out, oh, conquering hero?" she asked.

I was in no mood for levity.

"As bad as could be," I said. "A complete rout, thanks to your brother. Where is he?"

"He left in a huff," she said. "He took Dilshad and some stragglers south."

"Good riddance. He's no help to me."

"That's what he said about you. And about Allah. Seems that Allah changed sides, with this rain, and rendered aid to the enemy."

I made no answer. I had no answer. I merely slumped on a rug, oozing with mud, and Aljai brought some cold bread and a crock of kumiss.

"Let's follow Hussayn," she suggested.

"I don't know," I said between bites. "I will lose prestige—I may never be able to try again."

"That suits me. Better to lose prestige than your life."

Elchi called to me from the door of my tent. I asked him in.

"How are things outside?" I asked.

"Bad, Amir. All our men are deserting."

"What about Jaku?"

"He's holding a squadron—for how long I don't know."

"And you?" I asked.

"I came by for orders. Ilias Khan has promised immunity and a princeship to any man who brings in your head. I'll stay with you—or go with you."

"Go with us," said Aljai. "Oh, Elchi, make him take us away."

"I think it's better," said Elchi to me. "We haven't a chance here."

I tried to think, but I had no will to drive my mind.

"Very well," I said. "Tell Jaku to take his squadron out as a decoy. You get twenty men and good horses."

Aljai and I set to packing our valuables. She sewed jewels and ornaments and gold coins into the linings of garments, and hid her fine fabrics in folds of rough blankets and rugs. I dressed as a common soldier and she as a peasant woman.

Later Elchi returned with picked men and fresh mounts and pack animals. Then we quietly stole out of the camp toward the river and the red desert beyond. We saw other bands of deserters, usually smaller than our own, hurrying along under the eye-burning sun, across the cracked clay plains, in and out among granite boulders in dry river beds and rotting sandstone bluffs in the eroded wasteland. But every troop feared every other troop and spread farther and farther apart so that by nightfall we were alone on the vast stretch of desert.

For days we rode through the parching dry wind, camping at night by the wells, where Turkoman shepherds watered their herds and traded us fresh-killed mutton for trinkets and news of the outside world. By day we rode with our quivers and bowcases open, constantly alert for other bands who had turned outlaw. By night we slept under the stars and grazed our horses on the dry grass of the sparsely covered hillocks of deeper soil.

"I like this better than Samarkand," said Aljai, as we lay wrapped in the same bearskin rug and looked up at the stars. "All day you ride beside me and all night we share the same robe."

"There's no profit in it," I said glumly.

"Profit!" said Aljai. "Who cares about profit? We're together. We're alive."

"Alive?" I repeated. "Living like shepherds or brigands."

"I think I'd like being a shepherd's wife—if you were the shepherd. The Turkoman women seem happy, and their children are fat—I wonder if Jahangir's safe." She sounded worried for the first time.

"He's all right," I assured her.

She giggled and her body shook comfortably as she snuggled against me.

"Imagine you comforting me—when I've been babying you for a week." But she felt better and soon fell asleep.

The next day our water gave out, and we searched for a well until past midnight. When we did find one, a large party had already camped around it, and guards were posted on all approaches. We had to have water, however; and we were afraid to wait until morning, when the campers could see how few men we had. Elchi dismounted and scouted the camp on foot while we stayed out of sight. He crept away from us and was gone for an hour. The night grew chill; and fearing to move about, we had to break out our blankets and wrap ourselves in them. Our horses grew restless and stamped the dry earth and sniffed at the well, so near, yet inaccessible. The rattle of their harness brought chills to my spine. Suppose it warned the guards near the well?

My men were fearful, too. I could hear the clank of armor as one of them unconsciously fingered the hilt of his talwar. Aljai snuggled closer to me when a desert warbler, aroused from its sleep, chirped angrily a few paces from us. And I was annoyed by the sounds close by—I strained to hear some sound from the party camped by the well, even the discovery of Elchi. For I still had faith in the sword, and I felt that a surprise attack would be the best move.

Then we heard a rustle a few feet away, and Elchi appeared by my side. He reported at least twice our number of men in the other band.

"Shall we attack?" asked Elchi.

"No," said Aljai, before I had a chance to speak.

"Then what shall we do?" I asked.

"You and I will go in, dressed as we are, and ask for water. If they're friendly we'll call Elchi. If not, we'll fill our skins and leave again."

"And if they try to hold us?"

"Well—then Elchi can attack. If necessary, I'll show myself by the campfire and distract the men's attention, and let Elchi surprise them."

"I believe you would." I laughed.

"I would."

"All right, we'll try your plan. It'll be worth it to see you show yourself."

Aljai and I led the shaggiest horse, with one disreputable pack, toward the nearest guard.

"Halt," he challenged.

We stood still and Aljai asked, "May we have some water?" in a meek little voice which mimicked the Turkoman accent to perfection.

"Who are you?" asked the guard.

"A shepherd and wife who have lost their flocks," answered Aljai. "Who's your master here?"

"It doesn't matter," the guard said cautiously, but he seemed inclined to let us by when he saw that we were alone.

"We have a little gold," said Aljai. "We'll buy water."

"Very well," said the guard. "Come with me. I'll take you to my amir."

He summoned another guard and escorted us at sword's point to a sleeping figure near the well. He shook the man's shoulder and then stepped back when the sleeper roused quickly and flashed his own weapon. The campfire shone on the amir's face.

"Hussayn!" shouted Aljai, and dropped down beside her brother.

"Aljai!" shrieked a voice from another bearskin, and Dilshad tumbled out of her robe to greet her cousin.

That roused the whole camp; and in spite of my resentment toward Hussayn, a festive reunion began and lasted till morning.

We stayed at the well another day and listened to the women's happy chatter. Hussayn was sullen and morose, as was I, but in our wives' presence we were civil toward each other. We both were relieved, too, to join forces in our flight, now that we were out of reach of the Mongols, who coveted the price on my head.

"Where do we go from here?" I asked him, as a sort of concession to his seniority, which he usually flaunted before me.

"Let's go to Khiva," he advised. "I know the governor there. He'll take us in."

"Then what?"

"Then I'm going to India and win enough wealth to raise an army that will drive Ilias Khan to the northern ice cap," Hussayn said bitterly. "What about you?"

"Aljai wants me to become a shepherd," I said in answer to his vain boasting.

"That should suit you well," he countered sneeringly, and I was sorry I had given him the opening.

"Couldn't we all be shepherds?" asked Dilshad half seriously.

"You're as silly as my sister," Hussayn said in disgust, and strode off toward the picket line.

He turned back suddenly and called to me, from the first hill.

"Come with me, Timur," he said. "Something's wrong."

I ran toward him, and he pointed at our horses. All the animals staked out on one hillock were either down or staggering around crazily. We hurried to the place and found three horses dead and a half dozen more so far gone that we had to destroy them.

Hussayn pulled a clump of the grass and smelled it and tasted it.

"It looks all right," I said.

"I can't find anything wrong with it either," he said, "but it's bad —and look at this spread, enough to kill ten thousand horses."

"It's lucky you didn't put them all here," I said, looking at the meadowlike patch extending far back into a fertile draw held against erosion by two long sandstone ridges.

"And we would have, if we'd seen this place when we first got here. But it was late and those ridges blocked the view."

"We'd better move on," I said, "before any other horses take sick. The rest of the grass may be bad also."

We stayed one more night, during which we lost two more horses, and then headed for Khiva.

A few days later we came in sight of the city. Hussayn favored going directly to the governor, but I insisted on camping outside the walls and sending an envoy with gifts. I sent Abdullah along also to sound out the servants. And it was well that I did, for although the governor exchanged gifts and invited us in, Abdullah reported that the news of the price of my head had reached Khiva and the governor intended to collect. I did not tell Hussayn about the danger; but I told Elchi, and we refused to go in. Hussayn's men suspected a trap also and persuaded their amir to wait for a visit from the governor.

When the Khivans came visiting, it was obvious that they meant trouble, for they came two hundred strong and armed for a battle. I sent Abdullah to hide Aljai and Dilshad and some pack horses in a shallow canyon near the Amu-Darya, and I had my men ready for fighting when the Khivans rode up.

There was no pretense—the Khivans attacked at once. We were ready. We ran away at first, shooting arrows behind us and bewildering our pursuers, who had not learned our ways of archery. Then we wheeled and rode wide around the Khivans, who huddled together to concentrate their arrows.

Elchi's horse went down, and Elchi stood and kept shooting, with the Khivans riding toward him. Seeing that he would not take cover, I rode by him and cut his bowstring, forcing him to flee to some boulders before the horsemen got to him. Then I turned toward the attackers and yelled for my men, who wheeled to flank the column following the governor from the main body of his men.

I shot the governor through both cheeks and knocked him from his horse with my last arrow. I still rode toward him. He tried to rise, and shot one arrow into my left foot, but I swung low from one stirrup and snatched a lance from a dead Khivan and pinned the governor to the ground with it.

Hussayn was close behind me when I looked back. We were both cut off from our men, however, and out of arrows; so I motioned him to follow me behind a big boulder.

The Khivans were intent on chasing the rest of our men, for our standard bearers were still with them, and we watched both parties disappear in a cloud of dust. Only then did I become fully aware of the excruciating pain in my foot. I broke the arrow off and Hussayn pulled the shaft out and examined the wound. He said that the bones were splintered. He cut my boot off and bound up my foot in a scarf, and then we joined our wives by the river.

We decided not to move until nightfall. Abdullah and Hussayn stood guard at the entrances to the canyon. I lay beside the brackish backwater from the yellow Amu-Darya and let Aljai bathe my foot. I stroked her hair and felt the pulse in her temple while I thought over our plight—five people and eight horses several hundred miles from any friend whatever.

I recalled the whole sorry course of my Jihad for Allah—the unholy mess that had resulted from the Holy War. And the pain in my soul rose as the pain in my wound grew worse. But I continued to fondle Aljai's cool flesh while she tried to soothe the fever in mine. I was oblivious of everything except my longtime woes and Aljai. Dilshad, who sat and watched me and Aljai, seemed fascinated by my attentions to her cousin. Whenever I looked her way, she would smile sympathetically, but her eyes held a strange look—not one of sympathy.

By nightfall my foot hurt so badly that Aljai refused to move on. Hussayn grumbled but stayed with us. I took his place at the mouth of the canyon and left him with Aljai and Dilshad so they might all get some sleep. Aljai objected to my getting out of her sight. She was so tired, however, that I convinced her that the pain had subsided and I assured her that I would call her if I felt worse. And I took up my vigil in the dark shadows of the canyon.

After several hours, or so it seemed, I heard footsteps on the gravel behind me.

"Aljai?" I asked softly.

"Aljai's asleep. It's I, Dilshad. Hussayn's asleep, too. I thought you might need me."

"No, I'm all right," I said, as she sat down beside me.

She snuggled up to me, because the night was getting cold, and said nothing more for a few minutes.

"Love me, Timur," she said softly. "Touch me the way you touch Aljai. Pet me—Hussayn never does."

I put my arm around her and let her lean back on my chest. Then I smoothed her hair and petted her—she was very much like Aljai. It was she who took my hand and placed it on her bare bosom and then gradually guided my fingers to fondle more of her body.

"More," she said breathlessly after a time, and lay back on the floor of the canyon.

But I wanted no trouble with Hussayn; neither did I want to offend Dilshad—she was too much like her cousin. And, too, my foot pained me badly.

"No," I said softly. "Not here—not in the stench of this stagnant canyon—not among these sand fleas."

"Please."

"Sometime—when we have a scented couch in a room full of flowers—when our bodies are sweet. That's how I want you—like the princess you are."

"Then you do love me," she said pleadingly. "As you love Aljai, tenderly, honestly. I'll wait for you, Timur."

"Yes," I said. I did not know when I might need an ally in Hussayn's own camp; so I humored her. And she bathed my foot for me and after a time went back into the canyon.

The next day I was worse. My foot began to fester. And so did Hussayn's nasty humor. All day long he paced the canyon, muttering, declaring that the way was clear, that we should move on. In the late afternoon he could bear the inaction no longer.

"We move tonight," he said gruffly.

"We do not," said Aljai. "Timur's foot's worse than it was last night."

"We move," he said, "Dilshad and I. You may stay if you wish, but I'll wait no longer on a cripple."

"Don't call him a cripple!" Aljai shouted venomously at her brother.

"Well, he is, isn't he?" said the disgruntled Hussayn. *"Timur-i-Leng."*

I hated Hussayn from that moment, if I had not done so before.

"Go," I said. "Go to India or to all of the seven hells. Get out of my sight. Take three of the horses and leave us alone."

They left as soon as it was dark. Dilshad left tearfully, but Hussayn said not a word. And Abdullah came to tell me that the amir had taken four horses. That left four horses, one woman, one servant, and one cripple from the five thousand warriors I had led on the crusade for Allah.

CHAPTER

14

We stayed in the canyon until our food ran low. Abdullah found earth oil in some cracks in the rocks a little way from our hide-out, and Aljai made an unguent of it mixed with herbs. After several applications of the ointment the swelling in my foot and leg went down somewhat, and the pain became only a dull ache inside.

As my pain eased, I was cured of another sickness, too, the sickness of Allah as inflamed by the priests. I reviewed all my dealings with the god of Zain ad-Din and felt a sense of relief to find that He was false. There is a comfort, a freedom, which comes with the realization that a religion has no god. The fellowship is still there—the beauty of the ritual, the splendor of the temple, the hold on simple men—but the restraining fear, the awful obligation, the spell of the doctrines, all these are relaxed and the Church becomes useful to strong men who have access to the Way.

For God is not Allah. He is not Brahma or Jehovah. These are false effigies set up by men of dim vision, exalted by priests to further the true God's delusion of men. God is the Way and the Way is the World. All are but One. Man cannot deny part, as the gods of the Churches require. Man must accept All—God, Way, and World—and follow the course as he reads it, trying to change only the abortive departures caused by men's vanities. All of this I did not know, but I was close to the Way when I learned that the Church had no god.

And while my wound healed, I dismissed Allah, except for use as a word in conversation with misguided men. Thereafter it was God that I sought, not the Big Dolls of priests. And my spirit healed, too, and gained a new power from the correction of error. I would speak of Allah and yet seek God.

When we were down to our last bit of flour and such birds as Abdullah could kill—an occasional ground chough or a rank mudhen—we knew that we must set out on our trek. Aljai, too, had developed a flux from the poor food and bad water, and I would have left had my foot been a running canker. She was my one remaining tie with duty and delusion. Her curse was upon me, though I counted it a blessing.

As it was, I could travel on horseback in comparative comfort until my foot grew heavy with pain-bearing blood; then I could curl my leg over the saddle and ride farther still. So our progress was slow, but uninterrupted, save for our frequent rest periods. We had considerable wealth in our packs and could buy food from the small bands of goatherds who tended flocks near the river.

We rode through strange country, where the river, sweet and clear in the highlands, became a muddy, stagnant stream, scummed over with saxaul and half-clogged with tough reeds. Such trees as there were grew twisted and dwarfed and stood up on gnarled roots like huge shaggy spiders.

Sometimes we were forced to ride out into the desert for water that had been filtered through sand, the water near the river being fit only for animals—not always for them, for two of our horses died.

And Abdullah and I trudged along on foot, leading one heavily burdened pack horse and Aljai's failing mount. Abdullah even had to carry a huge bag on his back.

But Aljai, sicker than ever, could not hold back her giggle.

"Amir Timur, walking and leading a pack horse," she said. "He who wouldn't even walk to the stable but had his mounts brought to his door."

Then her big eyes, bigger than ever in her emaciated face, filled with tears.

"Timur, lover," she went on sorrowfully, "it would be funny, if your foot didn't hurt. Take my horse—let me walk."

"Nonsense," I said, and forcibly prevented her from dismounting. "We'll find a tribe with horses any time now and buy some fresh ones. And my foot needs exercise."

And I limped on. My foot did hurt. Whenever I looked up at Aljai, her eyes were on me, and she winced at every step I took. I was sure that my lameness hurt her worse than it did me. To share the pain of others is one of the world's chief snares for trapping the feelings of the stupid; in that, Aljai was stupid.

And we found men with horses—a handful of Persians with good sturdy mounts and lead horses—or rather they found us, camped by a well in the desert. Dressed like peasants, we aroused no curiosity until I asked the leader to sell me some horses.

"How can you pay?" he asked dubiously.

"I have a few jewels, given me by my master," I replied, and rummaged through a sorry-looking pack for some valuables.

"You probably robbed your master," he said and opened the pack himself.

Astounded by the rich contents, he eyed me shrewdly.

"I have no right to sell horses," he said. "I'd better take you to my chieftain, Ali Bey."

So he gave us good mounts, but escorted us back to a village of rough earthen huts at an oasis several miles south of the river.

"Where did you get this loot?" asked Ali Bey, a swarthy southerner dressed in dirty gray robes.

"From my master, who loves me well," I replied.

"Who is your master?" he asked suspiciously.

"Amir Timur, Chief of the Barlas, Servant of Allah," I said, and touched forehead, lips, and heart.

"I've heard of him," said the Persian. "Perhaps he'll pay more—for your ransom."

And after he had examined us further and found Aljai too thin and ill for rape, he locked us in a filthy, vermin-ridden cowshed and chained Abdullah outside.

For two months we were confined in the stinking prison, while Ali Bey tried to find a way to get ransom from Shehri-Sebz. Day by day Aljai grew worse and my resentment increased. I vowed never to imprison a man as long as I lived, as I learned what it did to one's spirit. Better to kill a man, if he is an offender—or maim him or blind him, than to embitter his soul in a dungeon. Maimed or blinded, he is no longer a threat, but a man who has been caged like an animal *is* an animal of no further use to man or to Allah, and an eternal danger to both.

I fretted and swore and blasphemed while Ali Bey continued his negotiations. I heard nothing myself. Abdullah, however, made friends with Ali Bey's slaves, and they kept him informed. Late at night I could hear them talking to Abdullah outside the cowshed; and after they left he would slip morsels of food and bits of information through the cracks in the wall. Abdullah spread the word that I was Timur, friend of the slaves, who had given him a fair wife and set Haroun up in a saddleshop—and other stories of his own invention. He explained that I traveled incognito to learn the sad plight of the working people.

Ali Bey heard the rumor, and, fearing his own weakness, sought the aid of his brother, Sheik Ibn Said, who was a chief of some note and a friend of Sheik Ali. Ibn Said immediately sent presents to me and advised Ali Bey to release me rather than incur the wrath of Shereza Begum's people.

Ali Bey sent for us.

"I have been in error," he said in an oily tone of conciliation. "You should have told me that you were Timur, husband of our beloved Begum."

I was sure that the stupid Persian had just learned who Shereza's husband was and had not heard of the Kha Khan's price on my head.

"You would not have believed me," I said haughtily. "Now that you know, release us at once. Restore my property and give us fresh horses."

"Of course I shall release you," he said. "You must realize, however, that my entertainment of you for the last two months has been quite expensive. All your property, even the gifts from my brother, hardly cover the bill."

"That stinking cowshed!" I shouted.

"Not so luxurious as your palace, Amir, but the best I had to offer. You should be more gracious. I intend to furnish a camel litter for the sick agha, and a pack of food on a pony. Surely that is enough to send you on your way."

Aljai's camel proved to be a mangy old brute with patches of all kinds of leather sewn on the scars and snags many years had inflicted on his non-healing hide. The pony was no better and the food hardly edible, but we set out again.

"Where to now, Timur, lover?" Aljai asked weakly, when she was seated in the decrepit litter.

"To Samarkand, beloved, to the physician. He can heal you."

"On to Samarkand!" She tried to smile as she surveyed our pitiable caravan. "We'll be lucky to make the first well."

"We'll get to Samarkand, Agha," said Abdullah confidently.

I was grateful to my servant, though I did not share his optimism, as we set out again on foot, leading our sorry livestock. I had lost even my sword.

We made a well before nightfall, and another next day about mid-day. We watered our stock and ate our noon meal, and I was prepared to go on.

"Let's stay here tonight," urged Abdullah.

I resented his presumptuousness; but when he enlisted Aljai's aid, I agreed, for my foot *was* still painful—the filth of our prison had infected the wound again.

"We'll pretend we're shepherds," said Aljai, improved by the fresh air and the sweet water.

"A shepherd without sheep," I said.

"A tuman-bashi without his ten thousand, if you prefer," she countered.

"It's all the same," I said.

"That's what I mean. Oh, Timur, lover, we still have each other—and Abdullah," she added generously. She seemed to be acquiring an affection for him, since she considered him instrumental in effecting our escape.

A few hours later I, too, was glad we had him along. A dust cloud rose in the west, and soon a group of fast-riding horsemen appeared.

"Here they come again," I said in defeat. "We're lost this time. I have nothing left."

"Maybe not," said my servant. "We may be able to handle them. With these," he said, and produced two long, curving daggers from the folds of his surcoat.

He gave me one of the weapons.

"We'll try to get them to dismount," I said, "to make things more nearly even."

My hopes rose, too, as the riders approached—there were only three men with a whole string of horses; ten or more, it seemed. So we sat quietly in the shade of the camel and showed no signs of hostility when the men rode up. Happily, they dismounted at once and greeted us.

"We followed your orders, Amir Timur," one said, "just as your servant directed."

I looked quickly at Abdullah, who was grinning broadly.

"Well done," I said quickly. "Tell me about it." I tried to learn what my orders had been.

"Just as you thought, our master was afraid to keep your rich booty in his camp; so he packed it in these water skins and sent a small party to take it to Ibn Said."

"And not tell Ibn Said where he got it," I said, following Abdullah's reasoning.

"Yes, Amir. And as you directed, we killed the guards in their sleep last night and rode all day to meet you here."

"So you want your reward now?" I asked, wondering what Abdullah had promised.

"No, Amir. We'll return with three horses and tell how bandits attacked us and slew all the others. Our wives and our children are with Ali Bey. We'll wait for the day when you give orders for all slaves to rise up. We prefer to be masters in our own land."

"That's wise," I said, and I was thinking of the wisdom of Abdullah. Again he had brought me my sword.

"But you must stay awhile," I urged. "To rest yourselves and your horses."

"Yes, Amir. We are weary."

The three servants shared our evening meal—a good one, prepared from the provisions they had brought with them. And they dropped off to sleep. As soon as all was quiet, Abdullah and I slit their throats and buried them in the loose sand. We chased three horses away, too, because I did not want Aljai to know what happened while she slept. She would not have understood.

"We had to do it," I said to Abdullah.

"I know, Amir. Ali Bey would have killed them anyway for deserting the train, and they might have talked."

"What did you promise them?"

"Everything, Amir. It doesn't matter. Promises are as good as gifts to slaves. Others will hear of my good fortune and Haroun's saddle shop. No one will hear of these three."

"Why did you help me, Abdullah?" I asked.

"If Ali Bey had killed you, he would have killed me also. I want to get back to Karin. I did it for myself—not you, Amir. I'm being honest."

"You're proving more valuable than I thought."

"That's my only chance, Amir. I prosper with you, or I die."

The next morning I told Aljai that the men had left in the night. She seemed much improved, now that we were well mounted and well provisioned.

"Let's go to Kumrud," she said. "I want to see Jahangir first."

"First?" I asked in surprise.

"First—before, before we go to Samarkand. I haven't seen him for so long."

I agreed, and we rode rapidly up the river. Soon we came to the fertile fields where my name was remembered. Grateful peasants were kind to us, and we had easy going on to Kumrud.

In the high cool air of Kumrud, where the water was sweet, Aljai regained her gay spirits and some measure of health. Jahangir was a delight to her—as gentle and kind as Aljai herself. And Dilshad, whom Hussayn had left with friends near Kabul, came when she heard we were in Kumrud.

There among the bright pavilions, which backed up into terraced vineyards and faced rich pastureland, I spent many hours in the company of my charming little family. Aljai and Dilshad cared for my lame foot so well that my leg never twisted or bent, though I always walked with a limp. Jahangir, too, was considerate and helpful. He never let me take a step if he could do it for me.

And the three were much alike. Aljai was just a few years over twenty and Dilshad barely nineteen. It was like watching Aljai in three different persons. Indeed, Dilshad looked exactly like my princess before she took sick. I caught myself calling her Aljai—and she would smile happily. Jahangir was Aljai the child again, and my Khatun Agha what she should normally have been many years later but for the premature aging caused by her illness.

And old Saif ad-Din, the last governor of Samarkand under Kurgan, was a gracious host. Well protected by his son, Nur ad-Din, he had few worries and spent much time with me. We played chess long hours together. He knew the game well, all the best moves, but I beat him consistently. We even doubled the size of the chess board and carved out more men. Still, though he mastered the more intricate patterns, he could not win.

As we played, he talked constantly. He could remember every move in all the battles he had fought in—which were numerous—and the minute details of all campaigns he had heard described, from Genghis Khan on down. At first I thought of him as a garrulous old fool, and he annoyed me. But after weeks of his chatter I began to realize that in him I had found the very richest source of Asiatic war tactics, free to be mined. Like his chess, his prodigious memory was accurate in every detail, but uncorrelated, without implication. And I encouraged him and listened as though he were a prophet. But he *was* a garrulous old fool.

My apparent fondness for the old man, however, made his son my friend for life. Nur ad-Din, who had long been accustomed to being the real power and seeing his father treated like a valiant simpleton, even by Kurgan, loved Saif ad-Din and fairly glowed with pride in my attentions to him. He would sit and watch my face while I chatted with the old man, and actually fetch drinks for me like a common servant rather than break the spell, though he was master of two thousand hard-fighting mountain men.

I could have stayed on at Kumrud indefinitely. Perhaps I was tempted. My duty was still to Aljai, however; and despite her good cheer and the faint color that had returned to her cheeks, her sickness was a lasting one, with recurrent attacks as serious as the first vitiating flux by the stagnant river. A lot of her gayety was the superficial excitement of desperation. She still needed the physician.

During the mild months (the New Year came in the fall that year) I let my beard grow. Aljai said nothing until about time for the first snows. Then as we sat before a small fire she stroked my beard and asked, "Are you sure they won't know you?"

"I don't think so," I said. "Not with my beard and—I walk with a limp now, you know."

"Must we go?"

"Yes. You're not getting well. We must see the physician."

"I'd just as soon stay here. These past months have been wonderful."

"But you still hurt—I can tell."

"So you feel it, too, Timur, lover?" She wriggled her slight body closer beside me. "Yes, I hurt, lover, all inside. And there's no place there for you until I get well. I'll go when you say—but it's been so nice here."

"We'll come back in the spring."

"Yes, we'll come back in the spring."

Nur ad-Din took us through mountain passes and back trails to the hills above Samarkand. Then I dressed again as a shepherd and Aljai as a peasant woman. We loaded our possessions on one little kiang and she rode another into the city. With my beard and my limp and Aljai's thin face, we passed unchallenged by the guards, some of whom had served in my own personal squadron.

Karin had told us how to find a colony of fugitives and beggars inside the city. Abdullah had gone on ahead and prepared the human derelicts for our coming. So when we came to the dead end of a scurvy bystreet I had only to knock on a heavy plank door and identify myself as Leng Kopeghi to gain admittance. It had appealed to some romantic notion of Abdullah's for me to call myself the Lame Dog. Later I learned why. All the outlaws went by names so strongly suggestive of some physical characteristic or defect that they were readily described and recognized.

"I'll die here," said Aljai in desperation, as we followed an old half-blind crone down a brick-walled alley. "This is worse than Ali Bey's cowshed."

"I'll get us a nice house tomorrow," I said, for it was the first time Aljai had ever shown discouragement.

"No, no," she said quickly. "We'll make out. We mustn't be conspicuous. They'll kill you. I'm just accustomed to Kumrud, and I'm tired."

Our surprise came when our guide finally opened another huge door in the brick wall to our right. We entered a neat, clean courtyard in which late flowers still bloomed and a comfortable cottage gleamed with fresh whitewash. Abdullah met us at the door and ushered us into a room filled with luxuries of all kinds.

"This is the place reserved for the king of the outlaws," he said.

"I shall be grateful to him," I said. "Who is he?"

"You are he, Amir," he replied, with a grin.

"I? How could that be?"

"Haroun has set up shop here. He has told quite a tale—I've added to it, and the word has spread. The whole colony has looked forward to your coming."

"Then they know who I am?" I asked. With the price on my head I could trust no one.

"Only Leng Kopeghi, the poor man's savior."

"Poor?" I said, surveying the rich appointments of the cottage.

"I demanded these things for you," said Abdullah. "They're all on loan—loot that can't be readily disposed of. Nothing is really yours—yet."

"Nothing ever has been," I said, as I remembered the riches I had held on sufferance of the Kha Khan.

"It's the best I could do," said Abdullah.

"You've done beautifully, Abdullah," Aljai said gratefully, as she sank on a brocaded couch and lay back on a pillow. But her tone was more worried than her words implied.

"Here we go again," she said dejectedly when I had dismissed Abdullah. "Oh, Timur, lover, must you still be a king? King of outlaws—king of anything? A hovel would have been better—just a hovel and the doctor to treat me."

"You're a princess," I said, in better spirits. "You shall live like one."

"I'm dressed like a shepherdess—I'd rather be a shepherdess. Just tell them to cure me quickly, and let's get out of here."

I sought out Zain ad-Din early the next day and identified myself by the carnelian he had given me—my appearance deceived even him. And under cover of darkness he brought the doctor to see Aljai.

The old priest and I sat together while the physician was with Aljai.

"Things are worse than ever," he said. "Even I, the chief mollah, have to live in hiding where you found me. It's the same in Bokhara and Khojend and Karshi—everywhere. There's not a single Tatar prince to lead us. You're the only amir who's dared come near the Jat strongholds."

"I came not as a leader," I said. "I came as a peasant to find help for my wife."

"Allah chooses his leaders—no man can deny Him. Your coming is kismet." He made the pious signs of his faith.

I felt superior to the old man; I was free from his god. I knew that Allah was false. Perhaps he did, too, but he still had faith in the hold Mohammed had on men.

"We've tried everything," I said. "Appeasement, attack—everything."

"Everything but prayer." I thought I detected a slyness in his remark. I was not sure, as he went on, "We've prayed for a leader—now you've come back."

Zain ad-Din studied me shrewdly. I had once accepted Allah's mantle—I wanted to wear it no more.

"Pray for a scourge on the Jats," I said derisively, and then in a moment of inspiration I added seriously, "Pray for a scourge on their horses. Without horses, the Jats are powerless."

The priest evidently sensed real meaning in my last words, for he eyed me more closely than ever.

"Can I assure the Faithful that you've seen a vision?" he asked cautiously.

"I've seen a vision—" A vision of two sandstone ridges in the Kyzyl Kum and a hundred acres of tainted grass.

"The believers still trust you," he said. "We've convinced them that Allah's rain on the steppes was a call to repentance for their pride in your first victories."

"So let it be," I said. "Pray for a scourge."

I was not sure whether or not Zain understood me, for the physician came into the room and I turned my attention to him.

"How is she?" I asked anxiously.

"Bad," he said, and shook his head. "She's almost all gone inside. But she wants to live. With time and proper herbs—maybe."

"Give her the best," I said. "I can pay." I had confidence in the resourcefulness of the cutthroats and robbers who were my neighbors, and in Abdullah.

Aljai had everything she needed. I stayed with her all day; and while she slept, I plundered with the misfits who inhabited our colony. Familiar as I was with the mansions of the nobles, I could lead prowlers unerringly to the vaults and jewel caches. Sometimes we stole outside the walls and raided approaching caravans. My seeming cunning and my expert swordsmanship soon justified Abdullah's stories of my prowess, and Leng Kopeghi became as famous among certain classes as Timur was among the Faithful and the Tatar amirs. And from those men who knew no laws, either of Allah or of men, I learned the vanity of doctrines and codes—the puerile devices weak men hide behind in their fear of the world as it is.

Abdullah continued to mingle with slaves and fugitives and servants in the town and with the caravans passing through, and the stories of my exploits spread to other cells of outcasts throughout all Asia. I was still two distinct persons. While the underworld yearned for the rewards of Leng Kopeghi, the Church prayed in secret for the scourge Timur promised. And the two worlds never met, even while I plotted the means by which to restore Aljai to her place as Sarai Khanum of Samarkand.

She improved so much that I felt it safe to leave her while I led the first pack train into the Kyzyl Kum.

"Don't leave me, again, Timur, lover," she begged, when I told her that I was going away for a few days.

"I'll be right back," I assured her. "You're nearly well now. You're safe here alone."

"No, take me with you—I'm well enough to go."

"Just a week," I said. "You'll hardly miss me."

"I'll miss you, lover—I can't even bid you good-bye the way I'd like to. I wish old Begum-Bottom were here to help hold you—do you miss her, Timur? Send for her—she'll come."

"I miss no one when I'm with you," I said.

"Then take me along," she pleaded tearfully.

But I was adamant, and I set out the next day with forty of my desperadoes for the bad grass of the Kyzyl Kum. We found the place without any great difficulty and camped by the well. We fed the grass, which was dry winter hay by that time, to three of the horses and waited for it to take effect. I was content to stroll around the camp, to lie again where Aljai and I had slept in the spring of the year, to remember her brash plan to capture the camp by showing herself.

And when the three horses began to stagger, I felt exuberant again. I was on the way up, not by my own strength, which had failed, but by the means I had found to weaken my enemies. I was sure that what my brilliantly clad warriors had failed to do in the light of day, my somber new forces could effect in the shadows.

So it was with a light heart that I led my train, laden with bales of bad hay, back out of the desert and into the Jat stronghold—and found Aljai dead.

CHAPTER

15

After Zain ad-Din had said a funeral service in the hidden cottage, we wrapped Aljai in a heavy rough bag and laid her across the gentle jenny she had ridden into Samarkand. Then, with ten of my men, who were masters of stealth, we set out for Shehri-Sebz. The old priest went along to perform the last rites, for he, too, loved Aljai.

We traveled all night through the snow-covered hills and hid out during the day. The next night I led the procession through an escape tunnel, which I doubt the Jat tenant of Ak Sarai knew existed, under the wall and to a secluded part of the garden, which had been Aljai's favorite spot. There we raked the snow off the ground, and with our knives and our fingers we quietly dug Aljai's grave. We put the earth into bags, and when Zain ad-Din had whispered the last words we lowered Aljai's body into the hole and covered it up as quietly as we had dug. Then we raked the snow back over the grave and our footprints, and with more dry snow in coarse bags we sifted a light coat over the whole place. Abdullah covered our last footprints and the tunnel door and scaled the wall to rejoin us outside.

"You have lost much," said Zain ad-Din, when we had reached our horses tethered in the hills.

"Everything," I said in complete dejection.

"Not everything. You are young—barely thirty, as I remember— and you have Allah's vision. Be not blinded by grief."

"Yes, Allah's vision," I said bitterly, and in spite of my grief I laughed at the hollowness of my vision.

"And the confidence of the Faithful—you must not fail them."

"I'll not fail them," I said. I needed something to fill the empty years still ahead of me. "Tell them to pray for their scourge before the first green of Rajab."

"Next spring?" he asked.

"Next spring," I said, "the Jats shall be scourged."

My men had saddled their horses and were ready to leave.

"Come, let's go," said the old priest.

"Go with them," I said. "I'm riding on to Kumrud. I can't bear to go back."

"But you—the leader—" he protested.

"Have no fear. I'll lead from Kumrud."

I gave instructions to Abdullah and watched the men ride away in the snow. Then I turned my horse up the valley and forded the river far upstream from Shehri-Sebz. I crossed the valley before morning and was safe in the hills to the south by the time the enemy garrisons were stirring. I waited on a high ridge to see the sun rise over my city, serene in the clear morning, blessed by the new earth returned to the garden of Ak Sarai.

I turned again southward and rode toward Kumrud. I was weighed down with my sense of loss. With Aljai I had buried my only goal. I was back where I had been when I first met Karin and Nihmu—purposeless, aimlessly drifting.

I had not shed my mood by the time I reached Kumrud. I had to tell Jahangir and Dilshad—she was still there—and our friends in the pavilions.

"Aljai is dead," I said.

Abdullah's mother wept first, then Dilshad, then Jahangir, though he hardly knew Aljai from Dilshad, so close had they always been—so much alike.

"Come with me to the banja," said old Saif ad-Din, with an unusual insight into my tired state of mind. I followed him.

"A little steam, a rubdown, and some sleep will cure many griefs," he said as he showed me to the banja.

While we sat on rude benches in the steam room, the old man talked soothingly.

"I shan't try to console you," he said. "Aljai was a fine woman, a beautiful woman. Your loss is great. But your grief will pass."

"Things won't be the same though," I said.

"No—not the same, but perhaps as good. Pleasure is in women, not a woman."

I remembered Kurgan's advice. He, too, had spoken of women, not a woman—not even his own granddaughter. And of pleasure, not happiness.

"Perhaps you were with her too much," he continued.

"She was all I had—at least for the last few months. My companion in everything."

"That was a mistake," said Saif ad-Din, and I remembered Kurgan again.

"Perhaps," I said. Perhaps I had let my feelings for her spill over into other compartments of my life. Yes, I knew I had.

"You'll find other women—you still have Shereza Begum."

"Not until I'm on top again. Shah Malik will never permit her to return until I'm back in power."

"You'll be back on top," Saif ad-Din said confidently. "I'm a good judge of men."

"I think maybe I will." I felt more relaxed as the steam seeped into my pores. "But I wanted Aljai there with me."

"You can't think in terms of women and of empire," the old man parroted, and I knew that I was listening to Kurgan again—Kurgan in the memory of Saif ad-Din. I had prospered under Kurgan; that I remembered. I would cultivate Saif ad-Din and his prodigious memory.

The attendant rubbed me and kneaded me until I fell asleep under his hands. I must have been carried to my pavilion, for I awoke in my own bed a day and a night later.

Karin was with me, with food ready for me when I awoke.

"How is Jahangir?" I asked after a few bites.

"He's all right. He won't miss her as you will, my Amir."

"No one will," I said.

"We'll try to make it up to you, Amir. We all love you."

"Even you? Still? After all I've let you in for?"

"You've not hurt me, Amir." She looked straight into my eyes. "I understand. It's just your way."

"Yes, it's my Way," I said, half-ashamed.

Karin cleared away the tray and left the room. I rose and dressed and went to Saif ad-Din's pavilion. We played chess all morning, and I listened to Saif's chatter about battles of the past.

After the midday meal I went for a ride on the snow-covered plain. I kept the horse at full gallop until he sweated and lathered. In the crisp mountain air my face stung, and my blood tingled as I rode, and I returned feeling like a man again.

And the evening was more pleasant still in the main pavilion, lighted by long tallow tapers and scented with the light smoke from charcoal braziers. My vigorous ride had whetted my appetite, and I enjoyed sharing the pot of stew with Dilshad and Jahangir and Saif and his women. No one spoke of Aljai, but she was always present, in Dilshad and Jahangir.

"How about a game of chess, Son?" I said to Jahangir, who was fondling a puppy from one of Nur ad-Din's wolfhound bitches.

122

"If you wish, Father," he said agreeably, and left his little dog in the care of Dilshad.

"The small board, or the large one?" I asked.

"Either, Father. Uncle Saif has taught me both."

"How do you come out with him?"

"Sometimes I beat him," he answered, and looked apologetically at Saif ad-Din.

The old man laughed heartily.

"He surely does," he said. "And he seems sorry when he wins. But he's pretty good." And he rumpled Jahangir's hair as the boy drew the large table up before me.

"I'll bet I can beat you," I said teasingly.

"I hope so, Father."

"You hope so? But you won't let me beat you?"

"Oh, no, sir. I wouldn't do that," he said in surprise, and met my gaze evenly. "I'll do my best."

"It will please me just as much if you win," I assured him, and we began the game.

He played surprisingly well for a child. I watched his sensitive little fingers hover lovingly over the pieces when he moved them and fondle the men he captured as though he found pleasure in caressing every line of the carving. He always toyed idly with a piece while he waited for me to move. The knights seemed to be his favorites, with their spirited horseheads.

I won two games out of three, and I sensed that he knew I let him win the third, for he smiled at me knowingly, as though we shared a secret. He was not displeased—if that was the way I wanted it. Old Saif grinned broadly.

"I guess I'm getting sleepy," I said, and yawned.

"I'm sure Jahangir is," said Dilshad, who had watched us play and had smiled indulgently at our tense little battles from time to time.

"Put away the chessmen," she said to Jahangir, and when Saif ad-Din had gone to help the boy open a cabinet, she whispered, "There are no flowers in winter, but my couch is perfumed and my body is sweet."

I nodded my acceptance of her invitation and turned my attention to Saif's unending monologue as she left to take my son to his nurse. I heard little that the old warrior said that night, but I listened for another hour, until the camp was quiet and dark, and then I sought Dilshad's pavilion.

She had snuffed out all the candles save one, and the soft sheens and shadows it cast on her nude body revealed once again the young figure of Aljai on our bridal couch. It was with the same feeling of reverence and awe that I approached her. My fingertips, too, rediscovered the familiar curves and the same soft texture I had fondled so often. And her body *was* sweet, as she had said. She delighted my senses, relieved my last physical tension.

I found another release in her embrace also. It was bewildering at first, even as we talked.

"What about Hussayn?" she asked, as she lay relaxed in my arms.

"I'll attend to him," I said.

"He was cruel to me."

"I'll avenge every harshness—in time," I assured her.

"Soon," she urged.

"In time," I repeated. I had time then, time like Allah. I saw clearly that urgency was fatal—Hussayn would prove that again.

"You won't ever leave me, will you?" she asked.

"If I do, I'll come back."

"Swear it."

"I swear."

Then she snuggled contentedly against me, and when my virility returned, she was sweeter than before. And I was no longer bewildered. In Dilshad was Aljai—the flesh of Aljai. Whatever else I had buried in the garden at Ak Sarai was gone forever. Happiness? Love? The pleasure remained on earth—gone only was the strange spell Aljai had cast over my whole being. And I felt suddenly free, as I had felt when I learned that the Church had no god. The temple was still beautiful, the ritual exquisitely satisfying.

As I went out of Dilshad's pavilion into the moonlit whiteness of the world I saw, for the first time, the clean-cut silhouette of the Tree of Life, clear and distinct in the distance; and I had not one doubt that I could move closer and make out every branch, every twig, every leaf—every detail of the Way of the Tree of Life. Dilshad had cleared away the last film from my eyes. I could see men as they are, the world as it is, and God—in time.

Never again would I have to make guesses, form hypotheses, lay plans. I would know. I could read the pattern around me, day by day, and follow God's whims for the confounding of man. No more struggles, no more disappointments—just see the trend of the Way and go along, using whatever means there was at hand. Some day, even the Purpose, the Fruit of the Tree of Life would be revealed—if there was any Purpose at all. For my blindness was cured. I was what I had been before Aljai deluded me.

So I stayed on at Kumrud, with Dilshad and Jahangir and old Saif ad-Din. The winter passed quickly. In the spring all the Jats' horses staggered and died; and the plain simple people—the Faithful—rose up in arms, without amirs to lead them, and drove out their enemies. Outcasts grew rich by looting and pillaging while the brave citizens fought the Jats in the streets. I still made no move, while chaos reigned and the Mongol barbarians trudged north on foot.

I was not dismayed when Hussayn came from the south with a huge new army and claimed Dilshad and Samarkand.

"How's my crippled brother-in-law?" he asked with a sneer, when he found me playing chess in the midst of chaos.

"Relieved to see the Jats gone," I replied without rancor.

"A lot you did to push them along."

"Quite a lot."

I merely smiled at him. At the moment, I saw no reason for letting all Tatary know who had conquered the Jats, or how. There were still difficulties ahead. The country was in ruin. Taxes had to be raised, disputes settled, ambitious amirs overcome when they challenged the throne—a thousand and one duties that would bring wrath and resentment against the first Protector.

So I returned to Shehri-Sebz, which Hussayn reassigned to me with contemptuous magnanimity.

"You did the same for me once," he said, as a reminder of the glory from which I had fallen.

"And you guarded me well from attack from the south," I said graciously.

"Until I was besieged from the north," he said with smug satisfaction in the significance of his remark.

"I was wrong," I commented.

"As usual," he said. "You may keep one hazara of three hundred men as your garrison."

"That's all I should need," I said, "with so strong a Protector in Samarkand."

"I'll see that no harm comes to your city."

"I shall be grateful," I said mildly. I knew what tribute Hussayn would have to levy and I preferred a small garrison which I could support without bringing hardship on my valley.

And he did tax heavily, so heavily that I had to take all I owned, even Aljai's jewels, to him at the New Year. He recognized the jewelry and gloated over my poverty when I presented my tax money to him.

But I continued to live calmly in Ak Sarai with Jahangir and Abdullah and his mother and Karin, while dissension rose and other amirs grumbled about the avariciousness of Hussayn. I spent my time playing chess with Jahangir. And I caught a young golden eagle, a gorgeous berkute, which I named Sasha and began training for the hunt, as I had trained gyrfalcons and goshawks in my youth.

With my own hands I made a soft rufter for Sasha's head, and light leather jesses for her feet. I made my own swivel and plaited a leash. I even cut and sewed my own glove for the berkute to perch upon, and I spent patient hours stroking her feet with a dove's wing and teaching her to drop her quarry and come for the lure. Throughout it all I was patient and gentle, as gentle as Jahangir—or Aljai. And I was unhurried, both in training Sasha and in biding my time—Allah's time.

For I had time. At last I had a firm grasp on the way of the world. Given a few years to render myself invulnerable to the spite of men, I could wield the Flaming Sword to keep the Way of the Tree of Life —to serve Allah's true Purpose, when I learned it.

BOOK

II

When the second spring came to Shehri-Sebz, Dilshad paid a visit to Jahangir. Hussayn raised no objections. He knew of his wife's fondness for my son and of her delight in the palace gardens. Then, too, his new affluence made it possible for him to afford many other wives and concubines, and he preferred the exotic experiences afforded by his foreign women to the half-hearted submission of his Jalair princess. He merely found her cold.

But she brought rare pleasure to my bed during my period of waiting. No longer entangled in the strange emotional ties with which Aljai had ensnared me, I was free to dwell upon Dilshad's flesh for what it was—the most delectable fruit in Allah's earthly garden. There was no insistency, no immediacy of purpose beyond the complete surrender to one of Allah's manifestations of the Way—pleasure in a woman; and Dilshad was merely a woman, not Aljai, for all her physical resemblance. And I knew *that* pleasure completely, not complicated as it had been by Aljai in my later relations with Lillit and Reba and Shereza Begum.

For Dilshad it was perhaps less pure.

"Are you sure this is all mine?" she asked, fearful of her own recent pleasure. "Not something I have stolen or borrowed from Aljai?"

"Whatever was Aljai's, she has taken with her," I replied.

"And what is left is mine," she said in a slightly petulant tone. "You loved her. I could tell. I look like her—I'll be like her." Then she added pleadingly, "Love me, Timur. I'll *be* Aljai. Will you love me?"

"Don't you think I love you now?" I asked. "Do you believe I'm pretending?"

"I don't know. No! You couldn't be—your hands—you touch me the way you did Aljai. I feel it. Oh, Timur, I don't know!"

She clung to me in a sudden fit of panic.

"Why don't you know? Don't we find pleasure in each other?" I smoothed her hair gently.

"Oh, yes—yes, Timur," she said violently, defensively. "Complete, utter pleasure. That's why I ask—I can't stand such ecstasy in a haunted bed. You're sure it's me—not Aljai?"

"I'm sure," I said and stroked her temple—so like Aljai's, but not the same. I was cured. There were no ghosts in my bed.

"And your feeling for me will last? You're sure?"

"Yes, what I feel for you will never change," I assured her.

"Then it's love? Say you love me, Timur."

"I love you, Dilshad." *Love* is only a word, and what men think it means is but another illusion, a counterfeit coin. But a counterfeit coin will purchase as much as real currency from one who cannot recognize the king's true image.

"I knew you did," said Dilshad in one of the strange contradictions of women. "I knew you did. I could tell."

And my counterfeit coin again bought what Hussayn's most sincere ardor could never win. Then we left the bed, which I hoped was no longer haunted for Dilshad, and went out into the secluded garden. The bite had gone from the soft spring air, and we bathed together in the still cold water of a garden pool. When we climbed dripping from the pool, Dilshad pressed against me for warmth and spoke again with urgency in her voice.

"When—" she asked. "When are you going to destroy Hussayn?"

"Perhaps soon, now."

"How soon? I loathe the idea of returning to Samarkand."

"I'll start soon. Then maybe a year, maybe two years—"

"Two years!" she said in dismay and pushed herself away from me to try to read my eyes by the moonlight. "I can't wait two years. This last year with Hussayn has been a lifetime! You're teasing."

She shivered in the cold, and the moonlight made diamonds of the drops of water which sparkled on her shining body. Then she snuggled up to me again for warmth and said huskily, "No, Timur, not two years! It's been so long already. Hurry, while we are still young. Now! Don't even send me back."

Hurry, hurry, hurry—and destroy oneself. Now, tomorrow, next week. Allah knows no time but His own Time, and men must read it not by days or weeks or years but by the moment and grasp what the moment offers, without pressing for more.

But I felt that the moment had perhaps arrived. I asked Saif ad-Din and Nur ad-Din to visit me while Dilshad was in Shehri-Sebz. Jaku and Elchi were already with me, and I sent letters to Sheik Ali and Khitai Bahatur, the two men whom I considered the ablest field generals in Asia. Ali sent word that Shah Malik was ill and needed him; but sensing that I was considering something important, he ordered Mouva and forty men to pay me a visit. Khitai Bahatur, out of favor with the Kha Khan, was finally located with a band of outlaws. He came and brought Daoud with him.

Ostensibly I was merely honoring the Sarai Khanum by inviting distinguished guests during her stay at my palace. The nobles brought their princess wives, and I entertained as elaborately as I could afford. We hunted with falcons and dogs and weapons.

The only disappointment came when I first tried to hunt Sasha as a treat for my guests. The gorgeous berkute merely sat on my wrist or flew around for exercise. Despite all I could do, she would not hunt, or even come for the lure.

Seeing my dismay, Jahangir spoke up.

"Sasha's not hungry, Father," he said.

"But she must be. I have hardly fed her for over a week. Are you sure that she had cast her stones when you brought her out this morning?"

"Yes, Father. She'd cast her stones. But she's not hungry. I fed her."

"*You* fed her?" I asked in annoyance.

"Yes, Father," said Jahangir softly, but with no sign of regret.

"Why?"

"Because she was hungry then."

Sasha flew from my own gloved wrist and lit on the boy's shoulder. Jahangir did not flinch. Presumably the eagle's talons had not closed on him. He stroked her golden brown ruff, and she pecked at him playfully, hardly closing her beak.

"So you've been petting her?"

"Yes, sir."

Old Saif ad-Din laughed broadly, and the other hunters joined in the merriment.

"I didn't know you were going to hunt her," Jahangir said calmly.

"I'm sure you didn't, Son," I said. "I'll tell you next time."

I felt no anger toward my son. In fact, I was more pleased to find that I was not angry than I was to learn the reason for Sasha's refusal to hunt. Anyway, lesser birds provided the day's sport.

And there were polo games and archery contests on the plain across the river, as well as tasty banquets and lively entertainment in the evening, to keep my guests amused. In the gayety I found ample opportunity to be alone with Dilshad and make the most of her visit. During the day, too, I was able to talk to each of my former officers in private.

Conditions in Hussayn's empire were about as I expected. The Tatar amirs were almost ready to default on their taxes, though no one of them was strong enough to lead an uprising. The Jats and Kazaks and Persians were beginning to nibble around the edges of the realm, convinced that Hussayn was about to have internal troubles. The lesser tribal chieftains had split up and dismembered the larger clans, with the exception of the Jalairs, who were concentrated in Samarkand with Hussayn and in Karshi with Musa.

Hussayn, in his contempt for my ability, had no fear of me; but Musa, who had served under me, considered me his chief threat. Hussayn seemed strong enough to hold Samarkand against any number of men available to the strongest chieftain in the foreseeable future. Musa was going soft on women and wine, but he had three thousand men, and Karshi was well nigh impregnable—really a stronger fortress than Samarkand, though smaller.

Such was the state of things as reported by the various nobles in private conversation, and such was the picture I had to present to the group of amirs at a meeting held in a pavilion Abdullah had set up for me on the Barlas pastureland up the valley. Zain ad-Din, whom I had invited to represent the Church, was also present, as were certain of Abdullah's picked servants from the staffs of my guests. The latter, of course, were in attendance as servants, and no one save Abdullah and me knew of their role as unofficial observers.

"I consider you men my most trusted and capable friends," I said to the assemblage. "And I'm sure that you've suspected more than idle curiosity in my questioning."

The men murmured, and some of them chuckled knowingly.

"You can't fool your old uncle," said Jaku. "I know the Barlas too well. I've been expecting something. What is it?"

"Well, we're pretty much in agreement in our estimate of conditions in Tatary. I believe Hussayn is vulnerable. I intend to find out," I replied.

"How?" asked Nur ad-Din. "You have no army, and if we start bringing in our forces—which aren't too numerous—Hussayn is sure to smell trouble. He'll take Shehri-Sebz before you can mass a thousand men."

"I'll have to take a stronger fortress."

"Which one?" asked Nur ad-Din.

"With what?" asked Jaku with a snort of disappointment.

"Karshi, maybe," I said.

"With two or three hundred men?" Jaku hooted. "Musa has three thousand! He could hold Karshi with the odds reversed."

"Or I could hold Karshi, if the position were reversed," I said.

"Just invite Musa to trade places with you, I suppose," Jaku said derisively. As my uncle, he could take such liberties. I saw that some of the others shared his doubts, but I could tell that the most reckless were listening with open ears.

"I might get him outside—it's pretty hot inside those walls this time of year," I said casually.

"You're crazy," said Jaku. "Musa is not going to budge from the protection of Karshi unless he's driven out."

"Musa likes his comfort," Khitai put in. "And his women. It's too hot for a woman in Karshi these days. He might be lured out."

"I'm depending on that," I said. "Musa has gone soft. Too much wine, too many women. Too much pleasure. I imagine he dreams of a breezy pavilion on the plain, and a cool-fleshed houri, more than he does of war."

"He won't come out, with you in the valley," Jaku said.

"His men are ready for some fresh air," Elchi said hopefully. "They'd come out if they could."

I looked at Abdullah. He nodded. His information was the same.

"Suppose I left the valley—say, a visit to my father-in-law in Herat?"

"He might come out, but he'd pull back inside when he got word of your return—and he could hold out against all the men Sheik Ali could muster. Not to mention Hussayn's reaction to an army coming from the south," Jaku still objected. "Not a chance."

"I wouldn't need Ali's army," I said. "And I wouldn't necessarily have to go all the way to Herat."

"It might work," said Daoud, grasping my plan.

"You're way over your head, boy," said Jaku. "I thought you might have something good in mind, but this isn't it."

"I do have something good in mind," I said. "I'll take Karshi. Then, with a stronghold to protect my men's families, I can raise a force from the outer tribes strong enough to challenge Hussayn himself."

"It's worth a try," said Elchi.

"We shall have Allah's blessing," said Zain ad-Din, speaking for the first time. "Hussayn has been dipping into the Church coffers too frequently of late."

"Think it over," I said, and went out of the pavilion. I mounted my horse and went for a fast ride up the valley.

The air was fresh and cool. Even Shehri-Sebz had been getting rather warm during the middle of the day, and I knew how hot it must be in Karshi—how bad it would be in another month. I could imagine Musa's growing discomfort inside the walls. If I knew Musa, he would welcome a chance for a summer sarai on the plain below his city. As I rode back toward my pavilion, I was more certain that ever.

When I rode up to the tent, the men were strolling around outside. I could tell that they had reached a decision. Upon my arrival they crowded around me, with Saif ad-Din as their spokesman.

"We'll go along with you," said the old man. "Not all of us understand your plan, but we remember your successes in the past, and are willing to follow you again."

Then Zain ad-Din held the Koran before him, and one by one the amirs filed by and swore allegiance on the Holy Book. I cautioned each one to say nothing of my plans, and we all rode back into Shehri-Sebz.

The feasting continued for another week. One by one my guests left with their retinues, as though their departures were entirely normal. Each started toward his home, to mislead any of Hussayn's spies who might be in Dilshad's train; but all planned to meet me beyond the Iron Gate within ten days.

"Do you want me to leave, too?" Dilshad asked peevishly, as though disappointed at seeing my former officers leave without starting a revolution.

"I never want you to leave, my love," I said. "The amirs insisted on going. I would never have broken up the party. Perhaps I can invite others to make your visit look innocent to Hussayn."

Her face clouded at the mention of her husband.

"You don't think Hussayn suspects?" she asked anxiously. "I insisted that I wanted to see Jahangir. He knows how much I love Jahangir. Could he—?"

"I don't know," I said. "You're much closer to Hussayn than I am. What do you think?"

"No," she said positively. "He's too conceited. He has never suspected that I could love another man, least of all you. Still, if I stay too long—" She wavered.

"You must do what you think best," I said, pretending the same anxiety that she felt.

"We don't want him to suspect until you're ready—"

"No," I said. "He could destroy me now."

"But soon, soon you will be strong enough to kill him?" Her voice was pleading. "I would do it, Timur, my love, but I can't. I couldn't. I might get caught, and I don't want to die. I want to live—with you." She clung to me and shuddered.

"No, Dilshad," I said, comforting her. "I'll do it, just as soon as I can. I'm as eager to claim you openly as you are to stay here now."

"Then I'll go," she said. "I'll go back to Hussayn and reassure him. But hurry—begin now."

"If that's what you want," I said in resignation. "Perhaps you'd better go."

"Oh, Timur. It's not what I want. I want to stay—but it's best that I go, to give you time. So we'll be together always. I'll go tomorrow— no, the day after tomorrow—let me have two more days—and nights."

And so Dilshad ordered her servants to begin packing her train the next day. She stayed on for still another day, and we spent every possible moment together. In public she feigned a feverish gayety; and in our stolen hours of privacy she was hungrier than ever—never content unless I was fondling her body, or touching her hands, or joining her in trying to drain the last drop of pleasure from every remaining minute of her visit.

When she finally left, she hugged Jahangir close to her and wept until her eyes were red and her face swollen. I was sure that not one of her servants or personal guards suspected that her love was not for Jahangir alone. And not even she had any inkling of the plot I had outlined to the amirs.

CHAPTER

2

Two days after Dilshad's departure, I packed all of my remaining wealth and set out with two hundred men to join my allies beyond the Iron Gate. I spread the word that I was going to visit my wife and her father in Herat. Since Shehri-Sebz was near enough to Samarkand to be safe under Hussayn's protection, I allowed the people to believe that I might be gone for several months and assured them that they had nothing to fear.

So my troop left and traveled slowly and leisurely, camping near villages and talking freely of our visit to Herat. Word of our journey preceded us and spread on to Karshi and beyond. We passed through the Iron Gate and near Karshi without being challenged.

By the time we reached Isaac's Well, where Mouva was to meet us, my company still numbered fewer than two hundred and fifty men. And all were in a holiday mood, despite the heat rising from the dried clay and the sand dunes on the edge of the desert. Attempting to enlarge our audience, I furnished my men with generous allowances of spending money to encourage the caravans moving up the Khorassan Road to linger with us by the well. Three or four trains of merchants passed on, after hearing of our intended visit; but several others, finding my men prodigal spenders, stayed to make what profit they could out of the slave girls and wine stores.

The days were hot and sticky, but the nights were cool—ideally suited to the reveling, which stretched into a three-week festival. Other caravans arrived every few days, with new women and fresh wines and dainties. More musicians came and formed into larger bands, so that the nights gradually took on the air of a city carnival instead of a small desert oasis. And my men, continually flushed from the wines, boasted loudly of the gay times they intended to have in the fleshpots of Herat. They even invited the caravans to turn back and accompany us to Shah Malik's court.

When Mouva finally arrived, however, the invitations to the caravans were forgotten. Malik sent a big train of costly gifts and extended a cordial welcome to me and my nobles. I had the gifts prominently displayed and encouraged my men to repeat the warm compliments in Malik's message.

When we broke camp, the other travelers urged me to send an escort to Karshi with the caravans, but I insisted that all my men were to be the guests of the Shah and that I could not think of offending him by reducing my retinue. Then in a busy stir and a big cloud of dust my company rode rapidly away down the Khorassan Road.

We rode steadily toward Herat until dark. Instead of camping by the road, however, I turned back and went several miles into the desert, out of sight of the road. There I set up camp and waited for another week, to give the caravans time to get to Karshi and assure Musa that I had indeed gone to Herat to see my wife and sons.

My men, still unaware of my plan, were less content than they had been at Isaac's Well. Such water as we found was bad, although we were able to gather sufficient seepage to keep our animals in good condition. There were no caravans, of course, and no women, and our stock of wine lasted for only four days. As my followers sobered up, they grew more and more surly and restive. They questioned me about our visit to Herat; and when they noticed that Abdullah was missing, they became too suspicious to be kept in the dark any longer.

I called them all together, and with the help of the other amirs who were privy to my plans, I explained that we were going to take Karshi. At first they were all extremely skeptical; but when I told them that Abdullah had gone on to Karshi with one of the caravans to do a little spying, they began to show more confidence, for they knew that I trusted Abdullah even though he was only a body-servant.

For the next few days, the spirit of the company rose steadily. It had been a long time since the warriors had engaged in battle; and the prospect of loot and women—especially in the quantities a city the size of Karshi afforded, to be divided among some two hundred men— soon overshadowed the anticipated pleasures of Herat. I suspected, too, that the men were surfeited by the paid paramours of the caravans and would have preferred the added zest of rape.

At any rate, the men were sufficiently primed for their venture when I finally gave orders to break camp. We rode steadily toward Karshi in one forced march, so that word of our coming could not get ahead of us. As another precaution, I followed a route through the desert several miles east of the Khorassan Road and crossed the river at a sparsely populated stretch some sixty miles south of Karshi. It was fortunate that I did, for some of my animals were too weak to ford the river and had to be floated across on improvised rafts.

North of the river our progress was slower; but in time we reached a well which, although within only a few miles of Karshi, was secluded and protected by rugged hills and a cover growth of wormwood and tamarisk. We hid out there during the day, and plaited ropes and made ladders for scaling the walls of Karshi.

I sent out scouts, who returned with the word that Musa had indeed availed himself of the opportunity to come out into the cool air and set up a summer sarai on the plain before the city. From the scouts' reports it seemed that all of Musa's army except a skeleton guard had camped outside the walls. These reports were confirmed by some of Musa's own people who came to the well during the day. We, of course, held all natives who came for water, and by late afternoon we had about a dozen prisoners.

About sunset Abdullah came to the well. He brought a pair of large urns strapped on the back of a little kiang. My men, as I had directed, pretended not to recognize him but took him prisoner and brought him to me. I talked to him in private.

"How does it look?" I asked.

"You have a better than even chance, Amir," said Abdullah.

"How much better?" I asked sternly.

"That all depends, Amir," he answered evasively.

"On what? Out with it—you have something on your mind. What do your thieves and cutthroats want?"

"Gold, Amir."

"How much?" I asked.

"Enough to go to some distant city and set themselves up as gentlemen."

"Gentlemen! They'd be thieves wherever they went. How many are there?"

"About fifty, Amir."

"All right. They shall have their gold from Musa's coffers."

"And women—"

"Sure, they can have all the women they want, when the raping starts."

"But, Amir, they want women from the nobles' harems."

"You didn't let them believe you were speaking for Timur, Amir of Shehri-Sebz?"

"Oh, no, Amir. They are dealing with Leng Kopeghi—they remember the plague on the Jats' horses and how they profited from that."

"And just how is Leng Kopeghi supposed to gain access to the nobles' harems?" I asked. "Anyway, the women are probably all at the sarai on the plain."

"No, Amir. The nobles took only two or three wives apiece—just as many as they could protect from their own men."

"So, it's like that with the army?"

"Yes. The amirs don't trust the tents. Most of the women are locked up and guarded inside the walls—and Leng Kopeghi can break any lock." Abdullah ventured a smile as we both remembered our outlaw days in Samarkand.

"I see," I said. "Leng Kopeghi can work miracles right under Timur's nose."

"Yes, Amir." Abdullah grinned wrily.

"Very well," I said. "I suppose you have figured out a way to deliver the rewards?"

"I have."

"Then you can make a bargain with your desperadoes. But make every one tell you where he's going. They'll revert to type, and we may be able to use them again, wherever they are."

"I had thought of that," said Abdullah.

"I'll bet you had." I could not repress my own smile at the schemes which must have been forming in my servant's mind. "And of something or other for yourself. What is it?"

"Now that we are moving to Karshi, where Karin isn't known, I thought maybe she could have a nice house—maybe a sort of little palace of her own, and when you don't need me—"

"I follow you," I said. "You'll be a part-time slave and your wife a full-time lady."

"Something like that, Amir."

"All right. I'll feel better when you're out of my sight if I think you're working for something for yourself. But I'm going to have a look before I take my men into Karshi," I warned him.

"You have nothing to worry about. There'll be new waterboys tonight. I have no intention of betraying you, Amir."

"You'd better not. I'll reward you for success, but I'll kill you if you fail me."

"I know that, Amir."

"Then be on your way, and I'll meet you by the aqueduct about midnight."

After Abdullah left the camp, I called my leaders together and explained the strategy of my attack on Karshi. They in turn relayed my instructions to the men under them, and a few hours after dark all except some twenty camp guards rode with me toward the city.

We proceeded quietly and cautiously through the foothills to the point where the mountains and forest cover came closest to the walls. Then I sent patrols out on our flanks to dispose of sentries that might be placed on the approaches to the city. There was just enough moonlight to enable us to make out shadows whenever a figure moved across an open space, and so my men returned within an hour and reported that only four guards had been posted and they had been killed quietly.

A few minutes before midnight I took Jaku, still the most skeptical of my officers, and rode to within fifty paces of the place where the aqueduct from the mountains crossed the moat. We tethered our horses in a clump of trees and waited until our ears became accustomed to the silence.

Then we crossed an open space to the moat and hid in the shadows of the aqueduct. As we waited, we could hear night noises inside the walls. Dogs barked in various quarters of the city, and in the still, dead air we could almost pinpoint the location of the sounds. A rooster crowed lonesomely near Musa's citadel in the center of Karshi, and one restless goat bleated at regular intervals, but there were practically no human sounds to be heard. Certainly there was no rattle of armor or clatter of booted feet on the battlements. Even Jaku began to take heart.

"If this isn't a trap—" he whispered.

"If Abdullah is not lying, it's no trap," I said.

"Do you trust him?" asked Jaku.

"Of course not," I said, "unless there is more in it for him if he goes along with us. But he stands to gain a good deal, and once he guides us inside, I'll know."

"How?" asked Jaku, skeptical again.

"I'll know."

Our conversation was cut short by a barely perceptible splash in the aqueduct where it ran through the wall. Jaku and I waited tensely. Another muffled splash—like the careful sloshing of someone wading in the aqueduct—and then a figure lowered itself over the side of the flume and dropped to the ground a few feet from us.

I drew my dagger and held my breath. Jaku, between me and the newcomer, kept both his hands free and stopped breathing also. We could see nothing in the shadows, but we heard the swish of cloth against stone as someone edged along the wall of the aqueduct. The sound came closer and closer, and suddenly Jaku went into action. He pulled the approaching figure forward and threw him face down on the ground.

I was on top of the man immediately, with my dagger's point pricking his throat.

"Abdullah?" I whispered.

"Yes, Amir. This is Abdullah," the man answered hoarsely.

Jaku and I rolled him over on his back, out of the shadows, and in the dim moonlight I recognized the features of my servant.

"All right, Jaku, let him go," I said.

"How is everything?" I asked.

"All set," replied Abdullah. "Follow me."

The three of us stood up and moved along the conduit to the edge of the moat. Then Jaku and Abdullah boosted me up into the channel, and I in turn pulled them up to join me. We quickly waded the aqueduct across the moat and through the wall, and dropped to the ground inside the walls of Karshi.

The guard stationed near the entrance of the aqueduct seemed to be asleep, and Jaku slit his throat before I could test the soundness of the Jalair's slumber. I went on ahead, however, and reached the next guard before Jaku could reach him. I clapped my hand over the sentry's mouth and then tried to rouse him. He appeared to be drugged; so I cut his throat and turned to Abdullah.

"Are they all asleep?" I whispered, so softly that not even Jaku could hear.

"All of them," said Abdullah. "My waterboys got to every one. They're all drugged—asleep for several hours yet."

"Good," I said, and then asked so Jaku could hear me, "Have you found a breach in the wall?"

"Yes, Amir, this way."

Again we let Abdullah lead the way. We walked half the length of one wall—past several guards whom Jaku, not knowing the nature of their sleep, killed with growing confidence. At last we came to a crack in the wall.

"Wide enough for two men," commented Abdullah.

"Perfect," I said. "How about the moat?"

"Right here," said Abdullah, lifting the end of a heavy timber from the shadow of the wall. "The waterboys again," he whispered.

"That's lucky!" said Jaku. "Looks like they were expecting us."

"Maybe they were," I said. "Are you willing to try it, now?"

"Yes."

"All right. We'll float this beam across the moat. You cross over and anchor it. Then go for the others. Abdullah and I will stand guard here."

"Very well. Let's go," agreed Jaku.

Jaku climbed through the breach. Abdullah and I fed the timber through to him and then went outside to steady it while he crossed the moat. On the other side, Jaku anchored the beam. It made an excellent footbridge right up to the break in the wall.

Jaku disappeared into the shadows, and my servant and I went back inside the walls to keep the avenue open. We stood well back in the shadows on either side of the opening and waited.

"You made your bargain as planned?" I asked.

"Yes, Amir."

"And you have a list of our confederates and the places they intend to go?"

"In my head."

"We'll make a record tomorrow," I said casually.

"I can remember," said Abdullah.

I thought that I detected a note of stubbornness in his voice.

"Just in case you aren't around," I added, "when I need the men again."

"I'll be around," said Abdullah.

"Then you object to my keeping a record. I can kill you and all your cronies, you know."

"Yes, Amir. But you'll find us more valuable alive."

I pondered Abdullah's words. I had never underestimated his shrewdness, not even when we were boys; and I had anticipated some such action on his part.

"I don't suppose I could force the information out of you?"

"No, Amir, I don't think so."

"Very well. If that's your plan. Just remember that if you ever try any schemes of your own, off goes your head. Or I'll cross you up with your cutthroats and they'll take care of you."

"I'll remember, Amir. I'm your servant—I can't do anything without your permission. But we both will need Leng Kopeghi—maybe for a long time."

"Maybe so. Just so we understand each other."

I heard the soft scuffling of feet on the other side of the moat. I placed an arrow against the string of my saddlebow and peered through the crack in the wall. I covered the first man in the file of figures that made their way toward the other end of the footbridge. Finally I recognized the leader as Jaku and allowed him to cross the moat and enter the city. Then one by one the company of some two hundred men passed through the breach.

Most of the men were familiar with the city of Karshi, and so I issued brief orders and deployed the men around the walls to destroy

Musa's guards. After some three hours of stealthy maneuvering, during which none of my men seemed to suspect more than mere slothfulness on the part of the sleeping enemy, my group reassembled to storm the citadel, which was lightly guarded by Musa's son and a corps of rather soft palace guards.

Although Abdullah's waterboys had not gained access to the arak, we met little more resistance than we would have if the guards had been drugged. My men disposed of the outer sentries without a sound; and after a brief encounter with the elite corps, a clattering battle which aroused the entire palace, the officers offered no resistance. Even Musa's son finally came out of his quarters and surrendered his sword.

With the citadel secure, I sent men to awaken and assemble the sarts and peasants during the few remaining hours before dawn. With other men I cleaned out Musa's armory and took the battle gear to the square. I found enough equipment to outfit more than a thousand, and when such a number had been collected I issued helmets and turbans and bows and pikestaffs to them and sent them up to man the battlements. I issued no arrows or lance heads, but I was sure that Musa's men on the plain could not see clearly enough to detect my ruse.

So a good half hour before sunrise I had a thousand men on the walls. My own archers were placed so they could command all the men on the battlements and also keep the approaches to the walls covered. Just at sunrise I mounted the highest turret and had my trumpeters sound my reveille.

Both the city and the sarai outside were thrown into confusion by the strange music. The city dwellers clambered out into the streets and up onto rooftops to see what had happened. Their consternation was only increased as they recognized some of their own neighbors manning the battle positions. And the army camped on the plain ran on foot to positions just out of longbow range and stared in astonishment at the conquerors on the walls of the city.

Musa himself showed a little more composure. About an hour after reveille I saw him, mounted and attended by his standard bearer and personal guard, riding toward the city. He paused just out of range and ran up a flag of truce. I made no answering signal, and when Musa started riding toward the gates again, I ordered my archers to send a volley of arrows into his party. I had no intention of letting him know how few men I really had in the city.

Although only a few of Musa's guards were hit by the arrows, the truce party wheeled at once and retired beyond the danger zone. Musa sent a courier racing back to the camp, and in a few minutes the rider returned with a horn.

Musa took the horn and bellowed through it.

"I am Musa, Amir of Karshi, servant of Hussayn, the King Maker. I demand a parley with the intruder in my city."

I turned the horn on my turret toward Musa.

"I am Timur, Amir of Shehri-Sebz and Karshi, also servant of the valiant Hussayn. I have found it necessary to take command of Karshi, since its former master was unable to protect it. My loyalty to the King Maker demands that I protect his cities both from his enemies and the weakness of his nobles."

"Timur!" exclaimed Musa. I knew that his surprise was feigned. Certainly he knew my reveille—he had heard it often enough when he served under me. "Welcome to Karshi, my good friend, Timur! I shall come in to greet you."

"Musa, weakling, traitor," I called back. "You may come in as my prisoner, and I will take you to Hussayn as a defaulting daroga. Or you may retire to Samarkand and give yourself up. If you are still camped on the plain by sunrise tomorrow, I shall come out and destroy your army and put your family to the sword."

With that I left the horn and descended from the tower. Musa bellowed a few more speeches and started toward the gates again only to meet another hail of arrows. I ignored his actions, and after a time he retired to his camp.

I kept the walls bristling with false armor all day. I also sent half my men out the portcullis gate toward the hills to build cooking fires behind every piece of cover in sight of the plain. During the morning the rest of my men broke camp and brought the prisoners and gear into the city. With Abdullah's help I counted out sufficient gold from Musa's treasury to pay off the ruffians who had drugged the guards. And I raided the nobles' harems for beautiful girls to complete my bargain. Abdullah took all the prizes to his rendezvous with the cutthroats and returned to report that the transaction had been satisfactorily completed in the name of Leng Kopeghi.

When I returned to my position on the tower about noon, I scanned the hills for cooking fires. There were enough columns of smoke rising from the woods to fake evidence of two or three thousand men camping in the covert of scrub-oak and larch. Occasionally one of my trumpeters sounded a call from somewhere in the mountains, and clouds of dust rose from the shallow ravines where small bands of my men galloped their horses and dragged bundles of brush behind them.

Musa's peasants on the walls were also watching the activity in the hills, and I could read terror in their eyes as they tried to estimate the number of warriors massing to pillage and rape their city. And from what I could see of the sarai, I was sure that my stratagem was having an equally demoralizing effect on the army camped on the plain. From time to time, small bands of horsemen rode from the headquarters of one noble to the pavilions of another, and at least three sizable patrols rode into the hills.

The latter gave me some cause for worry. I had not anticipated such brashness in the face of my deceptive evidence. So I watched anxiously for the patrols to return and give Musa a report on my hoax. Instead of riders returning from the mountains, however, several more groups rode into the canyons. I began to fear that my men might be cut off from the city and leave me with only a hundred and fifty men to face Musa when he learned the truth.

The disappearance of Musa's soldiers, however, had the opposite effect on the terrified watchers on the battlements. Tired and nervous from their long tour of duty under the watchful eyes of my archers, the simple peasants began to call down to their families and neighbors that forces, estimated at from five to ten thousand men, were massing around the walls and threatening to enter at once. Some of the unwilling soldiers reported seeing whole regiments crossing some of the farther ridges. Many of them told of the gallant Karshi troops who had ridden away, only to be swallowed up and destroyed in the mountains.

As their fears mounted, so did my own, for I knew that the patrols were not encountering whole divisions of armed cavalry—at best I had a hundred men outside the walls, although I could hardly believe that so few riders could stir up so much activity. As the clamor grew throughout the city, I decided to try one last plan; and I left my vantage point again and went to the dungeon in which I had imprisoned Musa's son and his staff.

Jaku and old Saif ad-Din went with me. I opened the door, and my two companions stood guard over the captives.

"It is not my custom to kill nobles who surrender to me," I said to the young Jalair prince.

"I have heard the same," said Musa's son half fearfully.

"So I am going to send you and your staff to your father's camp," I added graciously.

"Isn't my father attacking?" he asked.

"No. He is wise. He hasn't a chance—he's far outnumbered. I have more men inside the walls than he can muster, and twice as many more in the hills to attack him if he moves toward the city."

"But there was so little noise last night—" objected the youth.

"That is my way," I said. "I'm no butcher. I entered the city quietly

144

to avoid taking life. And I have no desire to destroy you or your father—that is why I am sending you to him. Musa was once a valiant officer in my command. Go to him and advise him to take refuge in Samarkand before some of my wilder allies take matters in their own hands and attack him."

"This is not a trap?" the youth asked warily, as he started to come out of the cell.

"Indeed it is not," I said. "I must blindfold you, however, to prevent your reporting my defense positions. You understand that, don't you?"

He turned and looked questioningly at some of his older officers.

"It doesn't matter, my son," said one of the older ones. "If Timur is going to kill us, he will, anyway. Go ahead. We'll go with you."

One by one the men filed by and let Jaku bind their wrists and tie scarves over their eyes. Then we led them out of the dungeon into the streets. On every side the citizens were talking in loud voices about the huge army approaching from the hills. By that time most of the people were perfectly sure that there were at least three thousand troops already inside the walls; and as we crossed the registan with our captives, the babble about the terrible plight of the city was so convincing that I almost believed it myself.

Certainly my prisoners were well primed by the distorted stories by the time I had led them through the gates and provided them with horses. We unbound their wrists after we had closed the gates behind them. Then we allowed them to remove their blindfolds and mount the horses.

"Give my regards to Musa, and urge him to flee for his own sake," I said by way of a farewell message. "Say that I commend him to Allah and will try to hold my forces off until sunrise."

"Thank you," said Musa's son tearfully, when he found that I had not trapped him. "You are a gracious conqueror, Amir Timur."

And the nobles rode away toward Musa's sarai. Jaku and Saif and I went back into the city, and I returned to my post on the turret. I watched the Karshi nobles ride into camp and then anxiously scanned the hills for signs of my men or Musa's patrols. Most of the fires had burned out, and such columns of smoke as still rose in scattered areas seemed to come from smoldering, untended fires. A haze of dust hung in the stifling summer air, but no men were visible as the sun dropped behind the mountains to the west and the long twilight spread over the plain.

Soon after my former prisoners reported to Musa, several high officials rode to a rise on the north edge of the field and studied the country in every direction. I supposed that they, too, were looking for the

145

patrols which had gone to scout my forces. But they could see no more than I could, and after a few minutes they returned to the sarai.

Almost immediately Musa's trumpets sounded, and the army began to break camp frantically. All available men set to work. Before darkness closed over the plain, every tent was struck and the first elements of Musa's forces were moving up the road toward Shehri-Sebz and Samarkand. I heaved a sigh of relief for myself, although I still held some fears for my men outside the walls, and climbed down from the tower.

I summoned my officers and issued orders for the men to be called down from the walls and reassembled in the registan. While my orders were being carried out, I ordered the square lighted with torches and lamps and sent for a chest of gold. Gradually the registan filled with my erstwhile warriors. The men stood quaking before me in the crowded square, and their anxious families pressed around the edges of the assembly.

I mounted the governor's dais at the head of the square and had my trumpets sound attention.

"People of Karshi," I began. "Today you have helped me free you from a weak and degenerate ruler. Some of you served me unwillingly, but I'm sure that if I had had time to explain to you, you would have joined me with eagerness and sincerity. Now I'm going to reward you and to assure you that neither your homes nor your women will be violated."

The people were still skeptical, for they had been misled often by their rulers; but when I had ordered all the men to file by and leave their battle gear and had given each a gold piece from Musa's chest, the temper of the assemblage was markedly improved. And after I had dismissed the natives and let them return to their homes and take their women with them—for my own few men had been assured ample reward from the harems of the nobles who had fled with Musa—I felt sure I could recruit my guards again without using force. In fact, my only fears were for the men who had not yet returned from the hills.

So I sent my followers to man the battlements and took up my position by the gate opening toward the mountain road. I set flares outside the gate, with my standard between them, to mark the entrance for my returning patrols.

Soon the men began straggling in, in groups of five or ten. Daoud and Mouva and Elchi reported with their followers. Then Berca and Kaidu. An hour later, well after dark, Nur ad-Din and four of his followers rode up with a gray-bearded stranger. They halted just inside the circle of light, and Nur ad-Din called to me.

"Amir Timur, I bring Mangali Boga, who would hold a parley with you."

"Bring him in," I ordered.

Nur ad-Din dismounted and brought the old man to the gate.

"What do you want to discuss, Mangali Boga?" I asked.

"Timur, I campaigned with Taragai. I would like to join forces with his son. I have no stomach for Musa and Hussayn and their kind. I ask permission to bring my men inside the walls."

"How many men do you have with you?" I asked.

"I led five hundred into the hills to join you this afternoon. I have fifty with me—disarmed by Nur ad-Din—and my trumpets can assemble the others within the hour."

"Will you consent to their laying down their arms until I'm sure of your good intentions?"

"If I have the word of the son of Taragai that no harm will come to them, yes. Saif ad-Din will vouch for me."

"Then come inside as my hostage and give orders to your trumpeters."

Mangali Boga entered Karshi; and when I had summoned Saif ad-Din, I was assured by the greetings of the two old men that I had gained a valuable ally and trebled my forces by accepting Mangali's offer. And that was only the beginning.

CHAPTER

3

Karshi proved to be just the bastion I needed. It was a man-made symbol of the invincibility I was gaining through my clearer understanding of the Way. The very ease with which I captured the city became almost legendary and was typical of the miraculous quality which men found in my early successes or put into the stories they told of me.

Sherif ad-Din especially has made much of the seemingly impossible military feats I accomplished in those days. But Sherif ad-Din always loved me and his love and admiration blinded him to the truth. What appeared to be overwhelming strength on my part was in reality weakness in my enemies. Where men were complacent, I attacked with stealth and cunning. Where men were fearful, I terrorized by one device or another. Where men sought and maintained faith in security, I undermined and subverted their agents of security by bribery and promises of greater security in my service. And where men were brave to the point of foolhardiness, I destroyed them by massing greater forces and proving to them that bravery in the face of overwhelming odds was stupid and absurd.

My methods worked, and it was not to my advantage to discourage the belief in my invulnerability. For two years I gathered men to me without seeking them openly. I began by attacking the stronghold of Kara Yussuf of the Black Sheep Turkoman tribe, who was raiding Hussayn's borders and terrorizing the peasants. With the followers of my original circle of amirs I was able to muster two thousand men and to make short work of Kara Yussuf. I sent his head to Hussayn and assured him that I was acting on behalf of the King Maker of Samarkand. But it was to me that the Tatars showed their gratitude, and it was my forces that the border amirs joined when their own tribal lands were safe again.

So it was that I skirted the boundaries of Hussayn's empire, subduing the Badakshani raiders on the glacier trails of the Pamirs, destroying Persian chieftains on the desert sands south of the Amu-Darya, and ultimately driving the Jats across the steppes and out of the mountains. With each victory more men were added to my army and more wealth was stored in my fortress at Karshi. More and more of the Tatar amirs brought their followers into my city and swore allegiance to me.

Always I reported my victories to Hussayn and sent expensive gifts to him and Dilshad Sarai Khanum. For a time Hussayn preferred to believe that I was protecting his empire; but as my influence crept inward from his borders toward Samarkand, and even his own courtiers, encouraged by Dilshad, made it fashionable to tell exaggerated stories of my prowess, it became obvious that I was emerging as the chief threat to his continued sovereignty. I made no open bids for power, nor did I allow my men to make a show of strength. Instead I used every deception to hide the true numbers of my forces—a policy which served both to hold down Hussayn's fears and to foster the illusion of my personal glory, although neither of the effects was my aim. It was simply that time was on my side.

And I had no desire to attack Samarkand—better to let Hussayn come to me, as indeed he did when he could no longer bear the praise heaped upon me by his court. Perhaps it was his envy rather than his fear of my military encroachment which finally drew him out of Samarkand with his army of several thousand men. At any rate he came toward Karshi, and I put Daoud in command of a thousand men to hold the city and moved the rest of my army out into the hills as soon as Hussayn left his capital. I sent riders throughout all Tatary to summon the tribal chieftains whom I had aided during the preceding two years.

While Hussayn was recruiting men and moving toward Karshi, I hid the bulk of my forces far back in the mountains, so far that the smoke from our campfires could not be seen from any of the approaches to the city. My forces were dispersed around the outer edges, with full regiments camped well inside the circle, wherever forage and water were available. I gave orders for the small bands to repulse Hussayn's scouts and hold security discipline if possible, but I kept communication lines of couriers and trumpeters to summon elements of regimental strength if necessary.

For my own part, I rode almost constantly with Jahangir, who was then fourteen years old, by my side. We went from one camp to the other, welcoming and exchanging gifts with newcomers who arrived every night from various quarters of the empire, giving instructions for combining units, and designating field officers for my growing army. I was greatly pleased by the response of the farflung Tatar chieftains. Almost every one of my couriers returned with an advance guard and promises of large bands to follow. Some Persians came with their bright-turbaned nomads, and even a few of my former enemies from Badakshan and Sijistan added their strength to my own.

And I was pleased at the way my followers took Jahangir to their hearts. The boy had all the charm of his mother and made every effort to please. His open admiration of the amirs' fine horses made him a favorite of both the grooms and their masters, and his eagerness in listening to the stories of the nobles' prized dogs and falcons endeared him to all the trainers. And his skill in horsemanship—he sat a horse as gracefully as Aljai had done—won the immediate approval of men who lived in the saddle.

Although I had never let my son ride into battle with me before, I planned to give him his chance in the coming struggle with Hussayn. After destroying Hussayn—and I had no intention of letting him escape alive—I expected Jahangir to win the Jalairs to me. He was the son of their favorite princess and should gain still more popularity with Dilshad as his champion.

So it was that I had him with me when my scouts reported that Hussayn was camped a half-day's ride from Karshi. We mounted at once and rode all night to a ridge which afforded a view of Hussayn's route to the city. I could tell by his rapt expression that Jahangir felt the same thrill at seeing the sun rise on a royal sarai that I myself never ceased to enjoy. That morning I remembered Shah Malik's desert camp on the day I had won Shereza Begum and first set myself up as a match for Malik and Kurgan in strategy. And I wished that Jahangir could have been with me—the sun comes up so much more suddenly out of the desert sands and brings out the colors of the pavilions as a new surprise each morning.

But the long half-light creeping down the western slopes and finally enlivening the colors in the camp below seemed to delight Jahangir as much as the sudden dazzling rays of the desert sun had ever affected me. The boy leaned forward in his saddle as though he would follow the rays through the gay canvases and the richly dyed horsetail standards, which were mere specks of color far below.

"Will we attack the sarai, Father?" Jahangir asked, almost sorrowfully, it seemed to me.

"No, Son," I said. "We'll wait until Hussayn has spent some of his force in siege of Karshi."

"And catch the men dismounted," he added.

"Some of them, yes," I said. "But don't worry—you'll get plenty of riding before this is over. I know Hussayn. He'll run when he starts losing."

"Where to? How far?"

"I don't know—probably south, toward the desert. We'll cut him off from Samarkand—I've already sent two regiments in behind him to Shehri-Sebz."

"And we'll ride after him—" Jahangir stroked his horse's neck and let the thick mane slide through his fingers.

"We surely will," I said, proud that my son was eager for the chase. "We'll keep him running until his horse drops under him."

"What about ours?" Jahangir asked in sudden alarm.

"We'll have plenty in reserve," I assured him. "If we lose one, there'll be another ready. Don't worry—you won't have to walk." I laughed at his concern.

"Oh, I don't mind walking," he said quickly, and I did not doubt his courage.

"How many men do you estimate?" asked Elchi Bahatur, riding up beside me.

"Eight thousand," I said. "Maybe nine, counting his patrols that are out. What do you make it?"

"You're about right—I see Musa's pavilion down there. I'll bet he's already planning a triumphal return to his palace."

"He's due for a disappointment," I said grimly. Musa had to be disposed of, also. I intended to leave no Jalair to challenge Jahangir.

Below us the army finished breakfast and began striking tents. Hussayn was campaigning in the true fashion of a monarch, carrying with him all the luxuries of a khan's ordu, complete with an elaborate women's tent large enough to house fifty concubines. Obviously he expected a long siege and was prepared to spend the spring and summer months on the plain. I could even make out twenty-five or more wagons which I was sure were loaded with ice, sledded down from the mountains east of Samarkand and packed in straw.

As his train pulled out and formed into a column several miles long, I smiled to myself at the thought of what Hussayn would do when his first auxiliary supply train failed to get through the Iron Gate, which would be closed by my men in a matter of hours. That would be the first of his surprises.

All morning we rode through the hills on a course roughly paralleling Hussayn's line of march and watched every move until the army drew up on the plain and camped, with elaborate display for the benefit of Daoud's defenders, who were flying my colors and ordering their day to my music as though I were actually inside the city. I could imagine Hussayn's satisfaction in believing that his handsome forces were striking terror into my heart.

By sunset, the Prince of Samarkand was established in his royal pavilion; and except for elements of two regiments which ringed the city to cut off communications, the army seemed to be beginning a holiday festival. The whole camp was ablaze with torches and campfires. Although we could not see or hear the activities in the camp, we knew what was going on as we finally gave up our vigil and rode back into the hills before any of Hussayn's patrols began scouting the environs of Karshi.

The next morning I rode near enough to Karshi to see Hussayn readying his siege machines and setting up facilities for reserve contingents all around the city just out of arrow range. He was a good general, and his planning was sound, but he did not attack that day; and so I returned to the camp for a council of war.

Most of my amirs were present, and I allowed Jahangir to sit in on the meeting so that he could learn how to conduct himself and so the older men would become accustomed to his presence. As the group assembled, I noticed with pleasure that the men spoke to Jahangir as soon as they had greeted me; and I noticed, too, that many of them looked at him as they spoke in council.

The courtesy with which he had listened to the boring stories of some of the less articulate chieftains seemed to have given them confidence, and they took heart from the polite attention which he gave them whenever they looked his way during their speeches before the group. I felt that I had a diplomat in my family, and I wondered momentarily what my sons Omar Sheik and Miran Shah were like. Perhaps soon I would have them and Shereza Begum back with me.

As the council stretched on for two hours, then three, I divided my attention between the strategy being discussed—strategy which I either dictated or planned to ignore—and the behavior of my son. Jahangir seemed intent on the words of the speakers, or at least upon the speakers, until one of the Badakshanis' stupid wolfhounds strolled around the circle, sniffing for his master, and ultimately lay down beside the boy. Jahangir idly began petting the animal and then lost interest in the meeting altogether and, after yawning a few times, laid his head down on the hound and went to sleep.

Saif ad-Din, who was nearest my son, chuckled softly and roused him.

"Time for us oldsters and youngsters to be in bed," he said, and led Jahangir out of the circle of light.

The rest of the men laughed indulgently, and some of them marveled that my son had stood the meeting as long as he had. I somehow resented the boy's lack of interest, however, and could not understand why the hard-bitten old warriors were so ready to forgive a fourteen-year-old boy for going to sleep in council. Many of them had already killed their man by the time they were that old. But they were obviously sincere, and I had a fleeting memory of the mystery of Aljai, which I had never quite fathomed. Jahangir was much like her. People would love Jahangir, but would they obey him?

Hussayn laid siege to Karshi the next day. He attacked with batteries of catapults and petards and mangonels and all manner of light weapons. The first waves of his shock troops got to the wall with their scaffolds and ladders, but Daoud was ready with pots of flaming pitch and naphtha. In a matter of minutes the scaling parties were transformed into clusters of human torches, falling into the moat and sending up faint clouds of steam or dropping to the ground and running stupidly through the breeze until they fell writhing.

From our position in the hills, the men looked no larger than sugar ants crawling around a honey crock. It seemed as though I should be able to step on them and grind a hundred into the dust with one twist of my foot. But the men did not return to the walls as ants return to sweets. Hussayn evidently became more cautious, and I saw the heavy machines go into increasing action. While the archers outside the walls kept up a heavy barrage of arrows—or so it seemed, for we could only make out the ranks of archers drawn up into position—other crews worked feverishly at the catapults, volleying stones and pitchballs over the battlements.

"Are the people inside burning, too?" Jahangir asked softly.

"No, Son," I replied. "Daoud has a bucket brigade putting out every fire by the time it gets started."

"I'm glad."

"So am I. You are witnessing a full-scale siege, but neither you nor your people are in very serious danger. Watch closely and learn all you can."

"Yes, Father."

"I wish we could get a little nearer," I said. "You may never have another chance like this. Next time you'll probably be right in the middle of the battle, and you can't see much there."

We did manage to work our way through the brush down to a closer ridge, but the view was not so good as it had been from the higher elevation; and although we spent most of the day studying Hussayn's tactics and evaluating his strength, I learned little that I did not already know about my adversary. Jahangir seemed to grasp a good overall concept of the battle; and whenever he was asked a direct question by one of my tavachis, he usually gave a sound answer. I was well pleased by his ability to see flaws in Hussayn's attack, especially his precociously shrewd remarks as to where men and animals might have been conserved.

Again I wondered about his brothers. Despite my growing knowledge of the vanity of pride and premature hopes, I had visions of a mighty army led by Jahangir, with Omar Sheik and Miran Shah as his field generals. I almost succumbed to the fantasy of myself as a complacent monarch, securely protected by my valiant sons. But not for long. My immediate task was to destroy Hussayn and consolidate my strength.

I chose to attack the first time Hussayn recalled his forces from their attempts to storm the walls of Karshi. My intelligence reported that word had come to Hussayn at the same time that his supply train had been captured by Mangali Boga's Mongols at the Iron Gate. With Jaku as my tavachi and Elchi and Mouva commanding on my flanks, I led three thousand men out of the hills and around behind Hussayn's sarai. About a thousand Persians attacked from one side of Karshi and another thousand Mongols attacked from the other. Both forces caught Hussayn by surprise, and caused a near rout.

My force, however, was met by Musa with two regiments just riding out to re-open Hussayn's supply route from Samarkand; and instead of an unmounted enemy, I ran into a formidable force armed for immediate battle. I knew at once that I would suffer heavy casualties; but I rather welcomed the chance to introduce Jahangir to war at its most exciting pitch. The boy rode beside me into the melee of screaming, jangling, fighting men. He bore himself well. As I looked his way from time to time, whenever I was not too closely crowded, I saw him earnestly seeking new enemies and coolly handling his horse and sword just as we had taught him. He looked to me frequently for approval—more intent, it seemed, on pleasing me than in winning his bouts.

Jaku hovered around him and toppled more than one enemy with his heavy iron-butted lance when Jahangir found himself overmatched. Several other men of my own personal guard kept an eye on him, too, and I was not sure just how efficient he was; but certainly he gave good account of himself when he was facing any of Musa's lesser men who had gone soft at the court in Samarkand.

I could ill afford to spend my time admiring my son. Musa held us long enough for the main body of Hussayn's troops to mount and prepare for battle; and soon the plain was a bleeding, sweating mass of mutilated men and screeching, dying horses.

A little before midday I signaled my first squadron to follow me, and rode to the first jagged row of foothills to get a view of the entire field. Kaikosru's and Khitai's initial advantage had been overcome, and Hussayn's defense had stabilized on the city side of the camp as well as in the other areas. It was obvious that Hussayn had a larger force and superior internal lines of supplies and remounts. I doubted that I could defeat him with the strategy I had originally conceived. Elchi and Mouva were holding their own; but Kaikosru and Khitai were in trouble, and nowhere did I see the strength necessary to press for a decisive victory.

So I sent riders to all my forces in the field and to Daoud, in the city, and my reserves in the hills. Then, seeing Musa and his personal squadron engaging the unit of Elchi's forces nearest my position, I gave orders to attack his standard before my instructions reached my other commanders.

With Jaku and Jahangir behind me I led a full-gallop attack on Musa. Our sudden appearance out of the brush completely unnerved him, and he turned from the battle with Elchi's squadron and rode viciously toward me, his white beard blowing about his angry face in a wild jagged blur. I met him with a stiff talwar blow, but he reeled in his saddle to avoid my sword and rode on by me. I wheeled my horse in time to see Jahangir knock Musa off his horse before the Jalair could recover his balance.

Musa fell on his back and his sword spun end over end on the sand.

"He's yours!" shouted Jaku, and handed his lance to Jahangir.

The boy grasped the heavy shaft, but hesitated as he looked down into the frightened, pleading eyes of his kinsman.

"But he's an old man—" Jahangir said to Jaku.

"He's Musa. As long as he lives your father's in danger."

Jahangir urged his horse forward and threw the entire weight of his body against the butt of the lance. The lance head disappeared completely in Musa's chest and pinned the old man to the ground.

Jaku dismounted, and guarded by a ring of my men, he cut off Musa's head and ran the lance head into its bleeding throat. Then he handed the lance to Jahangir and got back on his horse.

Daoud's trumpets sounded my retreat from the city walls, and suddenly my entire army raced for the mountains. Already on the near side of the plain, my squadron was the first to reach cover. We rode for a few minutes and stopped on the first ridge which afforded a clear view of the battlefield.

Hussayn's troops gave chase for a short distance, but by the time the royal trumpets sounded retreat, most of the enemy riders had already turned back. It looked like a clear victory for Hussayn.

"Have we lost, Father?" asked Jahangir.

I faced the boy and saw that his sensitive young face was white and drawn with disappointment.

"Not yet, Son," I said, and turned back to look at the plain, littered with the bodies and armor of dead men and horses.

"Not yet. We're not through yet."

"When do we attack again?"

Jahangir sounded as though he were choking, and I looked back at him. He was leaning over his saddle and vomiting, his body jerking gently as he retched and shuddered in the hot glare of the sun.

"Soon," I said. "You've stood up well on one meal today. We'll eat before we attack—then you won't feel sick."

"I'm all right, Father. I'm not hungry."

He shifted his grip on the lance and wiped his mouth with his right hand, which was already caked over with Musa's blood.

"You don't have to go back if you're sick," I said.

"I'm all right. I'll go back with you."

We rode a little farther into the mountains and met our reserves, who had food and fresh horses. While we ate, I got word from my other units that they, too, had been re-enforced and would be ready to re-form in another hour or so. All of the couriers stayed long enough to hear about Musa's death and to congratulate Jahangir. Then they rode away to spread the news and to give my orders to my subordinates.

I returned first to my observation post. Characteristically, Hussayn had assumed that I was thoroughly beaten and my troops demoralized. He set up a ring of defense between his camp and the mountains, but it was obvious that he did not expect another attack that day. He made a tour of inspection. By the length of time he spent surveying the walls of Karshi, I guessed that he was planning to renew his attack on the city now that he had learned that the bulk of my forces were outside the walls.

He reached the extreme position of his defense line about the time the shadow of the western peaks touched the edge of his camp, which was the time I had set for my second attack. Then, without trumpets or drums, or any further orders, my men again rode out of the hills, this time toward a central point before the city, to attack as one unit. From my position I had to lead a flanking movement. Daoud, leaving the walls manned by peasants and a small cadre of regulars, brought a thousand fresh warriors out of the city, and compared with my earlier attack, I had superior strength as well as the advantage of surprise which I had expected earlier.

I aimed my own operation at cutting Hussayn off from his camp, a maneuver which was successful, since Hussayn was hot-headed enough to ride straight for my standard instead of going to his center to direct his defense. Within half an hour I had a full regiment between Hussayn and his camp, and my brother-in-law started south in headlong flight.

Elchi came to engage Hussayn's rear guard, to free me to lead a pursuing party. Convinced that the enemy forces would surrender if they thought all their leaders dead, I took the lance with Musa's head on it—which Jahangir seemed glad to relinquish—and left it with Elchi's tavachis. I also selected a dead warrior who resembled Hussayn and cut off his head and left instructions for Elchi to bear both of them into the midst of the enemy and demand capitulation.

Then I assembled a regiment from the elements nearest me and set out in pursuit of Hussayn.

CHAPTER 4

After a night of hard riding, I realized that I could hardly expect to attack Hussayn before he reached a place where he was willing to make a stand. From the course he was taking, I was pretty sure that he was heading for Balkh and the protection of Bayan. And I doubted that Bayan could offer much resistance, for the old warrior was going the way of Musa, and his chief claim to eminence during the last few years had lain in the variety and abundance of his harem. So I stayed just close enough to Hussayn to keep him on the run day and night and to prevent his having time to prepare adequate defense of Balkh after he arrived. I deliberately slowed down enough to let reserves and supply trains catch up with me soon after I arrived at Balkh myself, in case Hussayn and Bayan could muster enough strength to make siege necessary.

Nevertheless, I did overtake Hussayn before he reached the city, and we entered Balkh at the same time, he trying to reach Bayan's citadel and I trying to intercept him. And I was successful. I cut him off from the arak, but lost his party in the narrow streets of the city. So, since I had entered Balkh as a warrior instead of a guest, I turned my attention to the aging Bayan.

It turned out that practically all of the Balkhi forces had joined Hussayn at Karshi and had left little more than a palace guard behind. Consequently—except for a short battle around the arak, in which Bayan was killed—we met almost no resistance. My men soon took over the city, and I set myself up in Bayan's palace.

Abdullah took over immediately as chamberlain, and by sunset he had prepared a banquet fit for a khan. I invited all the officers I had with me and ordered girls sent from various nobles' harems to provide entertainment. Tired though we were, we feasted until after midnight, while our army enjoyed their prizes in the city outside, and then I dismissed my guests and retired to Bayan's seraglio, which up to that time I had kept inviolate.

As I followed a palace guard down the hall away from the banquet room I could hear my guests leaving, their booming voices mingling with the women's expectant giggles. My own pulse quickened at the prospect of my introduction to Bayan's famed zenana. Since Dilshad's visit to Ak Sarai I had found little time or opportunity to play with women, and the strain I had been under sharpened my need for an emotional outlet.

I scarcely noted the elaborate appointments of the hall I passed through, but I could not miss the intricate grille work of the golden door at the end of the hall when my guide called the two huge black

157

eunuch guards to attention and announced me as the new master. The tall geldings brought their bright-bladed scimitars up to a salute and smiled broadly, as though they actually welcomed me; and I heard quick sighs and the rustle of silk bloomers and scurrying sandals on the other side of the grille. When I unlocked the door with the key I had taken off Bayan's body, I caught glimpses of a dozen pairs of eyes peering through the lattices and turning swiftly away, as the girls fled before I opened the heavy panel.

I swung the door back and entered another short hallway. It was empty, but the air was still heavy with the perfume of the fleeing houris. Closing the door behind me, I crossed the hall and drew back the curtains which separated it from the younger women's quarters. The room I saw was one to rival Sheik al Jabal's earthly paradise. Heavily carpeted, the floor was a kaleidoscope of silk pillows, lighted by the subtlest arrangement of lamps and candles, and the walls were hung with tapestries and brocades which must have been looted or bought from the most luxurious palaces in Asia. But, of course, the most breathtaking of all was the bevy of young women, clad in the richest apparel the wardrobe afforded and posed about the room in attitudes intended to make the best possible first impression. Someone had a sure eye for dramatic effect, but in justice I had to admit that for all its artfulness the picture was one of casual beauty. The women even succeeded in looking surprised at my entrance, and took half a minute or so to break off their conversation or other pursuits before noticing my presence and kneeling to greet me.

When they stood and faced me and dropped their veils at my command, I read at once the eagerness in their eyes and recognized their expressions of pleasure at seeing that I was little more than half as old as their former lord and taller than he by five or six inches. For once I found my figure eyed as appraisingly as I measured the charms of my new household, and in a moment of vanity I felt that all of us were equally delighted with what we saw. As I walked to the elaborately upholstered ottoman in the center of Bayan's pleasure room, I even tried to conceal my limp, which I usually looked upon as a reminder of my youthful folly and ignorance, my chief safeguard against repetition of my errors.

As soon as I sat down, some of the girls returned to their instruments and began playing the introduction to one of the most intricate Persian dances. Twelve more girls formed the pattern for the dance and went into the opening steps, while the less talented women brought wines and fruits to me on golden platters, or sat near me on pillows which they arranged, according to their precedence, on the floor around my couch. Sated though I was with food and drink, I nibbled at the sweets and sipped lightly of the wine, while the performers danced gracefully before me. I intended to let the women finish the entertainment which they had obviously spent all afternoon planning in my honor.

And so the memory of the battle and the still unsolved problem of Hussayn's whereabouts gradually faded out of my consciousness, and I was lulled, or stimulated, into complete forgetfulness of any world except the seraglio. At length—no great length—the program came to an end, and the girls stood by expectantly, the first signs of jealousy and competition appearing in their lovely faces. I clapped my hands; and the women, forgetting the graceful decorum which had marked their behavior until that moment, hastily scrambled to their places in a circle before me.

"Show yourselves," I commanded.

As though with one movement, the colorful silks and satins that had been hanging in tasteful folds fell in shimmering heaps around the feet of Fatima's nymphs. It was with conscious effort that I stifled a gasp of sheer amazement at the beauty before me, and maintained the aplomb expected of an amir of my stature and experience.

I was immediately aware that I could not make a choice, so perfect was even the least attractive body in the circle. As the girls slowly turned around to reveal themselves more completely, I felt increasingly uncomfortable, for I became conscious of many other pairs of eyes—the eyes of still more, and presumably less attractive, women—peering intently at me from the curtained doors opening off the room, watching every expression on my face and awaiting my decision to start a whole new set of jealousies, enmities, and hatreds in the women's quarters.

I tried to keep my face immobile as I let my eyes pass from one of the beautiful creatures to the next. I even frowned occasionally, not while I was looking directly at any one woman, or to show displeasure, which I certainly did not feel. It seemed that I spent hours in the suspense—and then a girl whom I had just passed over in my inspection made my decision for me.

"Scheherazade!" she cried half hysterically.

"Yes, Scheherazade—let's play Scheherazade," the other girls joined in.

I felt suddenly relieved, and perhaps I sighed; but my sigh could not have been heard in the clamor, and I smiled and nodded, and the girls scrambled for pillows and began arranging them in a circle.

"Nubja can't play!" one of the girls screamed. "Keep Nubja out."

Then they all called out to the figures peering through the curtains, "Keep Nubja out. Nubja can't play."

I wondered for a moment who Nubja was, but I soon ceased to

wonder, and indeed forgot all about her when the chorus began the first stanza of the interminable *Love Song of Scheherazade.* But I did not lose control of myself, and later I was as proud of my stamina that night as I ever was of the endurance I showed during my long forced marches over the ice pack atop the Pamirs or across the burning sands of the Kara Kum.

When I did finally sleep, I slept soundly.

It was midday before I rose and went to the courtchamber to attend to affairs of state. My officers were no more prompt; but I did find a messenger, a disreputable-looking imam from one of the lesser mosques of Balkh, nervously pacing the floor and muttering to himself about the wrath of Allah.

"What is your business?" I asked.

"Amir Timur, new Master of Balkh, I come from Amir Hussayn, King Maker, Prince of Samarkand, Servant—"

"You come from Hussayn, Looter of Churches, Fugitive from Timur," I interrupted. "What does he want?"

"He wants to make peace—to share with you the protectorship of Samarkand."

"How can he share what he no longer has? I am Protector of Samarkand, and I share nothing. Go tell him so. Tell him I'll find him and behead him for treason to the Kha Khan and sacrilege to the Faith of Mohammed. Go—"

"But, Amir Timur, Protector of Samarkand, that is not all."

"All right, what else?"

"Amir Hussayn says that he will surrender."

"He does, does he? On what terms?"

"Yes, Amir. If you refuse to share with him in peace, in the name of his sister—your beloved, departed wife—"

"I refuse, and tell him I'll cut his tongue out for mentioning his sister."

"—that he will surrender and throw himself on your mercy and the mercy of Allah. Amir Timur never slays enemies who surrender to him, he says."

"That is what men say of me. It is true. I do not slay men who surrender to me. Go back to him—tell him that."

"Allah bless you, Amir Timur. I shall carry your message to Amir Hussayn."

"And grow rich on his gifts," I said to the imam's retreating back.

Abdullah let the man out, and after a nod from me followed him down the hall.

160

Jaku and Nur ad-Din arrived a few minutes later, and then Saif ad-Din brought Jahangir into the room.

"What have you heard from Karshi?" I asked Jaku, who was serving as my adjutant.

"Your ruse worked. Hussayn's men laid down their arms when Elchi rode in with Musa's head and the head which he said was Hussayn's. It was the morning after we left, however."

"Good. What else?"

"Daoud is back in the city—in charge of the prisoners. Mangali Boga is in control at Shehri-Sebz, and Khitai is on his way to secure Samarkand."

"What about Hussayn?" I asked, confident that no one knew of the imam and his message.

"Nothing yet. Elchi and Mouva are bringing their regiments to Balkh. When they arrive we'll scour the city. I have already closed all avenues of escape to him."

"What will you do with him when we capture him?" Saif ad-Din asked, addressing his question to me.

"Summon the Kurultai and the Ulama. We'll let them decide. The whole sovereignty of Tatary is at stake," I said.

"And maybe they'll elect you sovereign." Jaku grinned at my suggestion.

"I'd like it that way," I said. "But I'll take the throne with the sword if I have to."

"I'm sure you will, boy," said Jaku, whose pessimism had all but disappeared during my campaigns. "And I for one think you can now."

"I know I can," I said. "But send riders at once to summon all of the chieftains and get word to Zain ad-Din to call the Church leaders to Balkh."

"I hope the Kurultai elects you, Father," said Jahangir, after Jaku had left to dispatch the couriers.

"I do, too, Son. They will, if they can read signs. It is perhaps better for men to choose to bow to the inevitable when they recognize it than to have the Way forced upon them. In this case the chieftains can save face and perhaps their lives by choosing me as their leader. I'll let them hold their make-believe election if they want it—but I'll tolerate only one result."

Jahangir followed my words, but I doubted that he understood. For that matter, old Saif ad-Din did not grasp my meaning either, although he had quoted Kurgan as saying very much the same thing on more than one occasion. Only Nur ad-Din smiled at my speech.

"You may have to kill a few of the stupid ones," he said.

"Stupid men kill themselves," I said.

"Will they kill Uncle Hussayn?" asked Jahangir.

"They won't have to. He's a stupid man."

"And Aunt Dilshad?"

"No, Jahangir. No harm will come to Dilshad. That I can assure you."

"We'll look after her."

"We certainly will, Son." I smiled at him, and he looked less troubled; but I thought he felt too much concern for Hussayn. In fact, despite the fine showing he had made in battle, I was not entirely satisfied with the way he seemed to be developing, and I planned to give more attention to his mental attitudes. I had deliberately thrown him into the company of Saif ad-Din so that he might absorb as much of the old man's war lore as he could. But there were other facets of his nature which needed truing up.

However, I had more pressing business at the moment, and so I began receiving other visitors and spent the afternoon setting up my own government throughout the city. I was still busy at dinner time and ate my meal while I finished up the day's business.

Then I returned to the seraglio; but I remembered Nubja, and instead of going directly to the big pleasure chamber, I had one of the eunuchs show me to a smaller but no less luxurious bedroom and asked him to send Nubja to me.

At the mention of her name the big Negro castrato grinned even more broadly than before; and his soft flesh, which would have been muscles of iron but for his emasculation, shook as he tittered with some sort of pleasure at my choice for the evening.

I loosened my clothing and lay back on my couch for a few minutes of relaxation while I waited for Nubja. I closed my eyes; and I must have dropped off to sleep for a moment, because I felt my body jerk into an alert tenseness when I heard a very soft swish of sandals on the rug. At first, I did not know where I was. But a heavy, stimulating Tibetan musk filled my nostrils, and I remembered the room—and Nubja.

I sat up on the bed and looked at the tall figure before me. My vision was still dim from sleep, and I could make out only a pair of soft dark eyes peering over the veil. I rubbed my own eyes and commanded sleepily, "Show yourself."

When I looked again, I rose slowly from the couch in a sort of mute wonder. Before me was the most magnificent black I had ever seen. Like some exquisite ebony figurine grown to majestic proportions, she stood erect and stately in the soft white cloud which her gown had formed around her feet when she dropped it. Almost as tall as I was when I had risen to my full height, she seemed to be the combination of all that was firm and soft in the world. Her beautifully shaped head could have been created only as a mounting for the soft eyes I had first noted and the even white teeth which accented the clean lines of her smile.

Her shoulders were a disturbing suggestion of the strength to hold up the earth and an invitation to a caress. And her bosom, the firm conical breasts of her race, wide apart and pointing outward, offered both a comforting cradle and supporting pillars to carry a man's weight. So, too, was all the rest of her body—perfectly proportioned and blended ultimates in feminine softness and earthy stamina. It was as though I were seeing a woman for the first time. All other women had been but pale outlines of what was realized in bold black relief in Nubja's body.

And presently I learned why she was barred from games of Scheherazade. The satiny smoothness of her thighs encased the girdling strength of a python. Once she had wrapped her long legs around my body and dug her heels into my flanks, I knew that a man could no more break away from her embrace than he could stop the sun in its cycle—if indeed it were remotely possible for a man to think of leaving Nubja before she had finished with him, for the lithe muscles of her limbs proved to be only the slightest of the bonds with which she tied a lover to her.

In Nubja I found again that complete, insatiable hunger which had lived in the womb of Shereza Begum before Miran Shah was conceived. And as I lay relaxed and listless beside her, I felt as though I had regained the rapport with Allah which I had lost at the beginning of my early decline.

"Now you will not sell me or give me away, will you, Amir?" Nubja asked confidently, and her voice was as soft as her eyes had been when I first saw them.

"Not as long as you are as you are now," I replied, experiencing my first fear that pregnancy might again rob me of that strange demanding haven in a woman's womb.

"I shall always be as I am now—for you. I was meant for you, Amir, not for old Bayan."

"But, if you should have a son—" I began, still plagued by my memory of Shereza's desire which was aimed unconsciously at a goal beyond the sheer pleasure which Allah embodied in woman.

But Nubja smiled, as though she read my mind, and assured me, "I

163

shall have no son. I know how not to—and I can keep other women, undesirable women, from bearing your children if you wish. I'll be worth keeping, I promise you."

"You do want a son," I said, and searched her eyes—I knew the urge and how it might be misunderstood or perverted into a yearning for parenthood.

"Yes, Amir, but not unless I'm free—and among my own people. My sons could only grow up to be like my brothers."

Her face was drawn into a frown for a moment.

"Your brothers?" I asked.

"The guards at the golden door. They were princes among my people—descendants of Mohallabi—and I a princess. Keep us, Amir—please keep us together! And I'll always be your most devoted slave."

She gripped my arm with both her hands and pleaded.

"I'll bear no children—I'll train and discipline your women—and they'll be the best guards in the world. Only keep us together!"

"Very well, I'll keep you—all three of you," I agreed, and Nubja's gratitude overflowed into an experience such as few men are privileged to enjoy even once in a lifetime. I felt secure in the dark elysium I had discovered.

Nubja provided the relaxation I needed during the interminable weeks while the Kurultai and Ulama were being assembled. Zain ad-Din came at once and kept me posted on the attitude of each new arrival from the various Church centers. The old man, whose beard had turned as white as his billowing linen jubbah, trotted in and out of my private chamber with youthful eagerness, his elaborate green turban bobbing up and down like an uprooted shrub blown across desert sand hills.

Powerful Khoja Beha ad-Din, from Bokhara, gave me his support, and Mir Sayyid, a young mollah—and a fakih steeped in the law as well—came to me recommended by both the old priests and offered to bring the younger Church rebels into my camp. In me the churchmen at last saw the chance to rid all of Tatary of the vestiges of the law of Genghis Khan, to which some of the northern tribes still adhered.

Saif ad-Din and Mangali Boga, both revered patriarchs, pleaded my cause with the conservatives; and Nur ad-Din, Mouva, and Khitai, as well as my other recent followers, were voluble in my behalf. But all was not well. Many of the amirs, firm in the belief that they had been called to decide on the disposition of Hussayn, grew sullen when they learned that he was already dead, although it was quite obvious that I had nothing to do with his death.

The fact that Hussayn's body was disguised and clothed in peasant garb when it was found on the minaret balcony of a minor mosque in the city was evidence that the former King Maker had been killed by a robber or one of his own servants who recognized him. Certainly neither I nor any of my men would have known his cowardly disguise, which Abdullah assured me was assumed before his death.

Still the men quibbled and quarreled and feasted for days, and I deliberately stayed away from the meetings—it was befitting my position to remain aloof. I resorted to Nubja frequently in the beginning, but after a few days, I saw the danger of her power. A man can rely only upon himself and his understanding of the Way. So, feeling that Jahangir's education needed attention, I selected two girls, one about his age and one a year or two younger, and put the three of them in the care of Nubja to see that they got properly acquainted. I felt that the girls would help make a man of him, and my plan gave me an excuse for devoting less time to the black princess-slave.

And to the delight of my other wives, whom I had been neglecting, I returned to the big pleasure room for my emotional release. They obligingly drained me of my physical strain; but as the council dragged on and the wrangling increased, I found my appetites becoming more and more jaded and my fears increasing. The original beauty of Bayan's choicest wives dimmed and faded; and I sought the grotesque, the freakish, and the deformed creatures which the old sheik had assembled to satisfy the perverted tastes of his approaching senility. But once the first novelty of lying with the twisted and dwarfed and misshapen wenches was over, I looked upon the whole zenana in disgust and resolved to put an end to the nonsensical bickering of the Kurultai.

I wondered why I had ever considered the silly farce of an election in the first place. The whole system was a tradition set up by weak men —a travesty on the Way. Allah never allowed a group of men to decide on a blessing or a catastrophe. Why should I, when I already knew the only decision that I would accept?

So I called my partisans together and gave them one day to settle the dispute.

"The Church is lined up solidly behind you, Timur," Zain ad-Din reported optimistically. "The Ulama is unanimous."

"All right," I said. "Set the priests to work on the recalcitrant amirs and on their subordinates."

"What is the alternative?" asked Nur ad-Din.

"There is none," I reminded him. "You heard my views in the beginning. Can't you convince the ones who are holding out?"

"Nobody can convince old Hulaku and his crazy Mongols. He's leading the opposition right now."

"What about the rest?"

"I can't say. But he's the worst."

"All right. Tomorrow's the last day. They vote together or I'll kill every last one of them. Give them one more chance."

Hulaku was killed that night in an uprising of his slaves; but the other members of the Kurultai met as usual, and I stationed myself in Bayan's spy box and listened to the debate. I was through dawdling. The "nay" voters would not live to see another sunrise.

It was a surly group of men who assembled that morning in Bayan's elaborate courtchamber. The fine silks and tribal colors were beginning to look drab after too much handling far away from their native laundresses.

Saif ad-Din presided at the Kurultai.

The first spokesman he recognized was an obscure Jalair from the mountains beyond Khojend.

"We have held a council among ourselves," the Jalair began, "and have decided that it is better that we all return to our lands and live in peace like brothers, since the valiant Timur has rid us of the despot."

Zain ad-Din interrupted the speaker.

"As an old man who has seen many despots come and go, and many years of war and weakness when our chieftains have tried to live without a strong protector in Samarkand, I can assure you that you cannot survive without at least an elder brother to look to when your borders are menaced."

"But there is no elder brother," said the Jalair. "Not since Kurgan has there been a man of valor and wisdom among our elders."

"I speak figuratively," said Zain ad-Din. "Young Amir Timur is old in wisdom. And it is his valor that has protected you for the last two years—from outside enemies and from Hussayn himself, while other leaders let their tribes scatter like quail before a hawk and hide in the hills or in the desert."

"But it is unlawful to choose a khan who is not a *tura* of the family of Kabul. Amir Timur, valiant though he is, is not of the blood of the khans."

Khoja Beha rose to aid Zain ad-Din.

"That is the law of Genghis Khan. We are Mohammedans, who recognize no such law. In Timur, we have a sword as great as that of Genghis Khan, and a loyal follower of the Prophet as well. Let us grasp the chance fate has sent our way, and choose an elder brother in the Faith, not an infidel from the blood of Genghis Khan."

Faced with the further eloquence of the churchmen, who were masters of disputation, the Kurultai gradually fell under the spell of the

Ulama; and although the debate lasted until late afternoon, I remained in my hiding place until I saw Zain ad-Din take the Koran from standard to standard and receive an oath of allegiance from every man present. Then I stole out of the spy box and returned to my private chamber in time to receive the notice that I had been chosen as the new sovereign of the Tatars.

That night I returned to Nubja. My immediate worries were over, and I could enjoy her without the fear of having been forced to seek her out of necessity.

My old self again, I had the leisure to inquire about my son.

"You needn't worry about that boy," Nubja assured me. "The girls fell in love with him at once. They didn't need me for a coach."

"They got along all right together, did they?" I was pleased.

"Yes, Amir. Aisha and Tahmineh are already his devoted slaves—for life, I believe."

"They'd better be," I said firmly.

"No, Amir. Not like that. They would die for him, of their own free will. It's love—love of a lasting kind. Do you know what I mean, Amir?"

She looked through my eyes to find my answer.

"Yes—yes, I know what you mean," I said. I knew, but I was disturbed by the turn my experiment had taken.

CHAPTER

5

After a brief inaugural ceremony in Balkh, the Tatar chieftains rode away to their homes to prepare for a full-scale coronation on my return to Samarkand. I stayed behind long enough to see Mouva installed as my daroga of Balkh, with no other title and without the authority to levy taxes in his own right. I summoned the tax gatherers and cut the rates in half, because I intended to force my governors to forward all revenue to me and then to look to me for financial support. The move assured me the good will of the Balkhi citizens and at the same time prevented my subordinates from becoming strong enough to challenge me.

I also forbade the quartering of soldiers in private homes, ostensibly to relieve the people of an added burden, but in reality to prevent my garrison from forming ties which might divide their loyalties. I executed some of Bayan's most obnoxious administrators, thereby gaining still more public approbation and at the same time weeding out those men most likely to oppose me or to bring discredit on my regime by

167

joining me and carrying on the same practices which had already made them unpopular with their countrymen.

All in all the populace seemed quite pleased with my policies and came to look upon me as a liberator and a benefactor rather than a conqueror. Their scholars were especially impressed by reforms and championed my progressive ideas in open forum. They proclaimed me as the Enlightened One.

Sherif ad-Din, one of the young idealists, came to me to offer his services, and a strange gift as well. Instead of a ring or a gem, he sent a plain glass tumbler in to me by Abdullah and asked for an audience.

"If he's no more important than his gift, I hardly think he's worth seeing," I said.

"He seemed to prize the glass very highly, Amir," Abdullah argued. "He had it wrapped in velvet and locked in a fine ebony case."

"Then why didn't he send case and all?"

"He said he wanted you to see it just as it was, Amir."

"Either he's very stupid, or very clever—trying to wangle a hearing this way. Well—I'll see him."

Abdullah left, and returned with a young man in his middle twenties, tastefully but quietly dressed in the garb of the scholar. His green turban attested his descent from the Prophet, as indeed I had expected when I heard the *ad-Din* in his name. But there was even more, a kind of intellectual avidity in his face, an almost passionate eagerness for something, that lightened up his whole countenance as he knelt before me and awaited his chance to speak. I paused a moment before granting him permission to make his request. I tried to guess what it would be—no ordinary material gift, I was sure.

"Very well, Sherif ad-Din," I said slowly, "what do you wish to talk to me about?"

"Have you seen it?" he asked eagerly.

"Seen what?" I asked—he could have meant no less than a miracle.

"The glass—the precious glass!"

"Yes—there it is, on the table, where my servant set it."

"But, Amir, you have not looked at it closely—you would not be sitting here so calmly."

"No, I haven't examined it," I said.

"Then you must, at once."

The young man hastily picked up the glass and handed it to me. Then he hovered over me like an excited child while I held the glass up and looked at it closely, expecting Aladdin's lamp at the very least.

I discovered some lines in Arabic scratched around the belly of the tumbler and slowly deciphered the words:

Expect no shimmering Mirage to show
A Sign for you in its deceptive Glow,
But seek another Desert Traveler
To point the Way ye both would wish to go.

I must have shown some sign of pleasure at being able to read the quaint old script, for my visitor was suddenly beside himself with joy.

"You are pleased, Amir!" he said. "You do appreciate my gift for what it is."

"I do, indeed," I said, feeling pretty sure that Sherif ad-Din would soon reveal the glass for what it was.

"A rubayah, inscribed by Omar Khayyami's own hand—right here in Balkh over two hundred and fifty years ago."

"A rare find," I commented.

"Yes—and to think that it escaped damage when Genghis Khan sacked the city, and has been kept intact until this prophetic hour, Amir."

"Why this hour?"

Sherif ad-Din became grave.

"Amir Timur, it is the opinion at the academy that you are the Desert Traveler, the kind of Desert Traveler which Omar Khayyami had in mind when he took his diamond and etched the rubayah into the glass. We have followed your rise to power and are much impressed by the humanitarian aspects of your administration as you have set it up here in Balkh. We believe that you hold the secret of the Way we must go."

"Your confidence is flattering," I said, and suppressed my smile. I was sure that the academy needed immediate endowment.

"I think a gift to the academy in return is in order—" I began.

"As you wish, most gracious Amir. But we ask more—and offer more."

"Who are we?" I asked.

"We are a cadre of earnest students and a few wise old disciples of the poets and chemists and philosophers. And we beg to become your fellow travelers, to accompany you to Samarkand and be a part of this new political movement which relieves the burdens of the people and punishes corruption in government."

"*A Sign for you in its deceptive Glow,*" I repeated, savoring the irony.

"You quote accurately—a true ear for the poet, as I knew you would have, Amir." Sherif's ardor was rising again.

"Exactly what would you do in Samarkand? You and your colleagues?"

"We would be most useful, Amir—to you and to the world. We are in correspondence with scholars throughout Asia. We would spread the word of your achievements and inspire other men to emulate your humane policies. And our masters are wise men—they are good counsel."

I knew the esteem in which scholars were held, and I felt that I might acquire some prestige in Samarkand if I brought a corps of intellectuals along with the more material loot I was taking from Bayan's palace. I had stood somewhat in awe of the academies in Samarkand during my previous reign, and I recognized the value of setting up my own school and staffing it with men who admired me—if Sherif ad-Din were being honest. I knew that there was no agreement among scholars and my academy might well be the ranking institution if I said so.

"Why were you chosen as spokesman?" I asked.

"Because," he said, and appeared somewhat abashed for the first time, "I have a further request to make. I am a student of history—of al-Tabari and Raschid ad-Din and al-Masudi and the Greek Herodotus—and I would like to write your chronicles. I asked to speak for the academy and for myself."

"Are you sure that the others feel as you do?"

"Yes, Amir. We all feel that you are to be a boon to scholarship."

"How many are there at the academy?"

"Ten masters and some forty students."

"Bring them all here tomorrow and I'll give you my answer," I said, and dismissed my would-be chronicler.

The next morning I was favorably impressed, at least by the scholarly appearance of the group, and so I outfitted the scholars sumptuously and bade them join my caravan when it left for Samarkand. And a very elaborate caravan it was, for I took most of the wealth old Bayan had left and used it to make my triumphal entry into Samarkand as lavish as Hussayn's return from India had been.

Daoud had gone on ahead to prepare my reception. I stopped for two days in Shehri-Sebz to put the finishing touches on my parade and sent word to Daoud as to the exact time of my arrival. The next morning I assembled my procession and rode toward my capital. I packed litters and special objects of decorative value in carts and hauled them to the outskirts of the city, which we reached in midafternoon. Then I halted again long enough to re-form the parade.

I rode first on Ak Ruksh, a fine three-year-old stallion caparisoned in crimson and gold brocade. With me were Jahangir and my tavachis dressed in new uniforms. Next came Nubja and five other beauties mounted on camels. After the camels were forty sedan chairs bearing other women of my harem, all gorgeously dressed and posed for best effect in their silk-draped litters. My own personal squadron, newly outfitted, rode in two files, one on each side of the chairs, and the rest of my army brought up the rear.

When the procession was formed, my kourrouns sounded my music, and the burnished nakaras began a triumphant roll. The music was answered by massed trumpets inside the city, and the gates opened to welcome me to Samarkand. But for the occasional ruins of a palace which Hussayn had not fully rebuilt, the city looked fresh and new. The broad street was covered with carpets all the way to the Khan's palace, and more rugs and tapestries were draped over every balcony and hung from the flat roofs of the bazaars. Paper lanterns swayed on the branches of the sycamores flanking the thoroughfare.

As I rode through the gate, a chorus of a thousand voices moved out of the side streets and marched before me singing a new song about my conquests, and in front of the singers still another thousand dancing girls kept in step to the music and strewed flowers on the carpeted street.

And the entire populace of Samarkand lined the sides of the avenue and covered the rooftops as far as I could see. When the song ended, a clamorous greeting went up from the whole city, and for a moment I feared that the walls might crumble. All before me was a scene of brilliant, unrestrained rejoicing, and I was glad that my splendid train was equal to the turnout Daoud—and Dilshad—had prepared for me.

But as I took stock of myself, I was pleased to find that it was not vanity that prompted me to encourage the pageantry of my return to power. I realized fully that the effect was far greater on the deluded spectators. In the pomp and ceremony, they read success and achievement and for a time got out of their miserable selves. What they gave up to me during my progress toward the palace was the sort of thing they daily surrendered to some dream which Allah gave to them to confound and confuse them and to keep them from claiming anything for themselves.

The folly of rejoicing in *my* success! The stupidity of gawking at an array of earthly splendor which had been snatched from them or others like them. The vanity of identifying themselves with *me!*

But the occasion was a festive one. In every park and square feast meats were roasting on spits, and beverages were being chilled in huge banks of snow brought down from the white peaks to the east. Already, shrewd merchants were hawking mementoes of the coronation—miniature crowns and thrones and even forbidden images of me, hastily carved by infidel craftsmen from Khitai. And the silken court clothes hanging in the doors of the bazaars rivaled the official decorations draped along the avenue. Obviously there were some beside me who would profit from my success.

The front balcony of the palace far outshone the rest of the city in splendor, with a low ebony-and-ivory throne beneath a broad canopy of cloth-of-gold made iridescent by a woof of crimson and green; and gracing it all, Dilshad and the women of her court, dressed in the finest satins and bedecked with the rarest gems the empire offered. Truly it was a reception worthy a conqueror of the world. And I could share it with Aljai—in the person of Dilshad. Perhaps it was better that way.

Indeed it was Dilshad that made the welcome complete. Cordial as was her greeting to Jahangir, she could not hide her impatience to be alone with me, and through her prestige she managed to speed up the greeting ceremony and get us both excused some time before evening prayers.

"At last!" she said ecstatically, and clung to me hungrily as soon as she had shown me to my bedchamber. "It's been so long—but you didn't fail me. Timur, my love, now the world is ours. And you did it all for me."

"Yes, Dilshad—all for you."

"I knew you would, darling. No man was ever so sweet as you are."

"Then you're convinced that I love you?" I asked, and stroked her temple—so like Aljai's.

She pushed herself away from me to add the conviction of her steady gaze to her words.

"Thoroughly convinced, darling. You never did more for Aljai. And your love is in your hands—yes, I'm convinced."

She pressed her body against me again; and then, when the muezzin's cry whined out of the minaret into our palace, she pushed me away again and in a strange fit of piety faced toward the south and chanted the entire, interminable azan:

"Allah is most great.
Allah is most great.
Allah is most great.
Allah is most great.
I testify there is no god but Allah.
I testify there is no god but Allah.
I testify that Mohammed is the Prophet of Allah.

I testify that Mohammed is the Prophet of Allah.
[Come to Prayer]
I have no power nor strength but from Allah most High and Great.
[Come to Prayer]
I have no power nor strength but from Allah most High and Great.
[Come to Salvation]
Allah willeth what will be: What He willeth not will not be.
[Come to Salvation]
What Allah willeth will be: What He willeth not will not be.
Allah is most Great.
Allah is most Great.
There is no god but Allah."

When she finally looked up at me, and saw me smiling at her devotion, she said, "Timur, my love, I've prayed for your success. You have come to me—our love is no longer a sin. Allah is on our side. I had to take time to pray."

"I'm on our side, too," I said lightly, and at the moment my statement seemed more appropriate—or more important.

But Dilshad's prayer had had its good points. It prolonged my desire and added zest to our reunion. I was not sure that the delay affected her equally, for she responded as though the past two years had been one long increasing appetite which could hardly have been heightened further by a few minutes' delay.

After Dilshad, my coronation was an anticlimax, although according to Sherif ad-Din's record it was one of such splendor as the Tatars had never before witnessed. Sherif ad-Din, however, was impressionable, as indeed were most of my followers. I never cared much for ceremony, but I recognized it as one of Allah's most confounding spectacles. No ruler could very well hold the allegiance of his people for long if he did not make a show of the wealth he had stolen and impress upon them the meanness of their own efforts by comparison.

I personally was far more interested in building up the less ostentatious but more necessary requirements for my security. I immediately set about establishing my royal academy. At first, while I was having a suitable structure built to house the school, I invited all of the scholars from the established academies to meet with my imported intellectuals in my own council chamber, and there I spent many hours listening to the learned men discuss the problems which they considered weightiest. By sitting in on the disputations, I felt that I might learn what ideas they had that I should fear, and perhaps might find some workable knowledge in the maze of their confusion.

Gradually my old awe of the wise men faded, and more and more

I gained confidence as I encouraged the philosophers and historians in their clashes. As garrulous as old Saif ad-Din, most of those men drew no clearer conclusions from what they knew than he did from his store of uncorrelated anecdotes. Just as a youth too timid to vent his lust on women dreams of the pleasures of the harem, and spills his seeds ineffectually in his sleep, so did the scholars mouth empty vanities and skirt the realm of truth which they feared to pierce.

But far from discounting the value of the academicians, I began to see in them the forces which might most nearly approach Allah's own eternal fallacies. The prestige they enjoyed was second only to that of priests—many of them were priests—and most of them were no less in error than the theologians. From their errors I could profit, especially if I allowed the idealists to put their theories into practice. And so I endowed all of the academies richly, favoring my own, of course; and I encouraged the preceptors to invite their friends from everywhere to take up residence in Samarkand, the new seat of learning.

My first step in diplomacy was to send an envoy to Herat to invite Sheik Ali to bring Shereza Begum and my two sons to my court. I was sure that I was well enough established to inflence Malik to agree to my claim, and I felt that Ali would be willing to cast his lot with me again. I needed him; and since Malik's health showed no signs of improving, Ali should have been able to foresee the eclipse of his own authority. I expected both Ali and Shereza to welcome a chance to get their wealth out of Herat before their older brother took over the government.

Dilshad, although she was not at all jealous of the fifty women I had brought from Balkh, did object to my recalling Shereza.

"Do you still love her?" she asked, when I told her of my message to Herat.

"Of course," I replied. "She is my wife, you know—and a Begum, a wife to be proud of."

"But you don't love her the way you do me?"

"No, not the way I do you."

"Then why are you sending for her? Am I not enough?" she asked petulantly.

"A man is entitled to four princess wives," I reminded her, as I had once reminded Aljai. "And furthermore she's the mother of two of my sons. It's time I assumed my authority over them."

"Oh, I'd forgotten your sons," she said with a look of dismay. "Do you love her because of them?"

"Certainly."

"Then I'll give you a son. I'm not sterile, you know. I've taken care to protect our pleasure—but now I'll show the Begum."

She ended her speech with some show of defiance, and I think perhaps Shah Rukh was conceived that night. At any rate, a few weeks later, when the outriders of Sheik Ali's caravan announced that the Begum was approaching our gates, Dilshad, secure in the knowledge of her condition, stood beside me and Jahangir beneath the cloth-of-gold canopy to welcome my most illustrious wife.

Again the city was dressed for a ceremony of state, and the amirs had gathered from all parts of my realm. Shereza Begum added immeasurably to my stature, especially in the eyes of the Faithful. And her wealth added even more, as my people gasped at the length of her train, which was strung out down the road toward Shehri-Sebz as far as they could see.

"Gaudy," said Dilshad, when we could make out the head of the column proceeding up the avenue toward the palace.

"Southern custom," I said. "The Persians delight in color. We must get used to it."

"Must we, now?" Dilshad said venomously. "Maybe the Begum had better become accustomed to us."

"She will."

As the procession approached, even I was astonished. Shereza's entry was overshadowing my return from Balkh.

"Oh, Timur, my love," said Dilshad, her confidence wilting, "she's so rich, and she's a Begum. You'll love her more than me—and her sons are already half grown! What chance have I?"

I looked down to see abject misery spreading over her face and tears welling up in her eyes. I put my arm around her and spoke to her soothingly.

"Dilshad, darling. If I had wanted the Begum and her wealth, I would have gone to Herat and taken that city instead of attacking Hussayn—it would have been easier and quicker."

"It would have, wouldn't it?" she said, brightening. "But instead you fought for me—just as you promised. You do love me the most, don't you?"

"Yes, darling, I do."

Her tears turned into stars, and she straightened up again in full confidence.

"And you always will," she said with a sigh of relief.

"Yes, I always will," I assured her.

I could not afford to let Dilshad begin to doubt me. She was a Jalair

—a Tatar—a princess who had proved a great favorite of the amirs even when Hussayn was at his obnoxious worst. She underestimated her own prestige, if she thought of it at all. She was fully as valuable to me as was the Begum. Of course I would always love her.

But my immediate interest was in the first unit of the column which was nearing the royal balcony. I recognized Sheik Ali as the leader of Shereza's escort, and then I could see the two handsomely dressed tavachis riding beside the Begum's camel. The one on the left, a lean, graceful youth, sat erect in his saddle and rode in a manner copied after Sheik Ali's easy cavalry style. He was Omar Sheik, I knew at once.

I guessed the chubby, round-faced cherub on the right to be Miran Shah. He also handled his mount in a way that attested to many diligent hours in the manége; but he slouched in his saddle and made a less impressive picture, until he straightened up with a sudden jerk —at a command hissed at him from the camel litter, no doubt—just before Ali halted the Begum's escort before the dais and brought his platoon to saber salute.

Jahangir and I and my own palace guard returned the courtesy. Then both units remained at present saber while ladders were brought to Shereza's camels and the women were helped to the ground.

Escorted by her two sons and her serving women, who were far more lavishly dressed than my Balkhi women had been, Shereza Begum climbed the steps with great dignity and knelt before me without raising her eyes.

"Amir Timur, Lord of Samarkand, Beloved Husband, I am pleased to return to your court and bed after our long separation. Shah Malik, Sheik of the Khorassan, Sultan of the Afghans, bids me return and bring with me his blessings and the blessings of Allah on your Gracious Self."

"Welcome to Samarkand, which you will please to call home, Shereza Begum, Beloved Wife," I replied formally, and bade her rise.

For the first time I gazed into her eyes, still as clear and soft as ever and, as when I first saw her, the only recognizable human feature in a bale of rich fabrics. But they were surprisingly expressive, especially when Shereza first caught sight of Dilshad, wearing the robe and coronet of the Sarai Khanum.

"Aljai!" Shereza gasped in surprise. "Dear Aljai—but I heard that you were—"

"This is Dilshad Sarai Khanum," I interrupted. "Mistress of Samarkand—Shereza Begum."

"Dilshad?" Shereza said softly.

"Welcome to Samarkand," Dilshad said cordially, and somehow I thought she was pleased that the Begum had mistaken her for Aljai.

Shereza's eyes were not quite so soft when I introduced Jahangir to his two brothers and their mother. Nor was Dilshad's tone so cordial, as the two women appraised and compared my sons. I saw at once that Dilshad would champion Jahangir—at least until her own son entered the lists for the succession to my crown. And I saw advantage in the house divided, even though I was master of that house.

CHAPTER

6

With Khitai Bahatur and Sheik Ali to take over command of my armies, I felt reasonably secure for a while. I sent Khitai with a brigade of Mongols and Tatars to punish raiders on my southern and western borders and to quell occasional minor uprisings among overambitious amirs who owed allegiance to me. I kept Ali near Samarkand to move against the Kazaks and Jats who caused trouble on the steppes or in the mountains to the east. His Persians and Afghans were most effective against the Mongol tribes, as Khitai's Tatars were against the southern races. Their respective ignorance of the strange tactics they encountered was more than offset by the lack of feeling between my police forces and the natives they were to punish.

In fact I found population shifts on a larger scale to be highly desirable at times when particularly aggressive tribes showed signs of combining with their neighbors for strength. My intelligence, both my official diplomatic corps and Abdullah's spying riff-raff, kept me well posted on conditions; and by direct police action or other methods, I was able to secure the time I needed to consolidate my position at Samarkand.

Inside my capital I began early to recognize the men who were potentially dangerous and to neutralize them by various devices. The greedy I allowed free reign to get themselves so deeply involved in graft that their exposure and execution added to the people's high opinion of my virtue and sense of justice. The really shrewd were permitted to fill my treasury while they were enriching themselves, so to assume full responsibility for mulcting the public and provide me with ample justification for confiscating their wealth if they were ever discovered.

The men with ideas, the scholars who came from everywhere in answer to my preceptors' invitation, posed a different sort of problem. I had no desire to destroy the intellectuals. It was to them that I looked for revelation of the weaknesses of my neighbors, for the scholars of a country are usually aware of the weaknesses of a nation, even if they are impotent or unwilling to correct them.

Most of the scholars were idle theorists or passive respositories of more or less irrelevant bits of old wives' lore. They worried me not at all. I let them continue their delight in their own sterile eloquence. I had merely to listen occasionally to convince them that I was the most intellectual of all rulers.

But sometimes there appeared a man so fired with enthusiasm for his views that he could not be ignored. Such a one was Mahmoud ibn Said, whom Sherif brought to me after a month of unrestrained eulogy.

I received the two burning-eyed zealots in my courtchamber; and although I sat on the royal throne in the midst of utmost luxury, it was obvious that neither of them was conscious of the ankle-deep pile of the rug or of the brocades covering the ottomans which caressed their emaciated rumps. I did not value the splendor either, but it usually awed my petitioners, and I knew that a man who ignored it was a man to be reckoned with.

"Very well, Mahmoud ibn Said," I began, after Sherif ad-Din had presented his new idol, "what is this wonderful thing you have to offer me?"

"Oh, Most Gracious Amir, what benefits your people benefits you. Is not that true?" I liked Mahmoud's indirectness.

"Yes. I have my subjects' welfare at heart."

"So I have been assured—and so I believe. And it is a rare thing in rulers today," he said flatteringly.

"Then proceed."

"Amir, despite the low tax rates in your empire—and they are low by comparison—still the average farmer cannot afford to increase his acreage, especially where irrigation is necessary."

"But our land—especially near Samarkand—is rich and loamy, and the climate makes possible four crops a year. Surely the farmers are prosperous."

"Some appear so, Amir. But there is little left after each crop, and none of the farmers are expanding. I have talked to many of them— made a sort of survey. Here, I have figures," he said, and drew a roll of paper out from under his robe.

I unrolled the scroll and looked over the figures. Mahmoud was eager to interpret for me, but I waved him on with his plea and listened while I looked over his tables.

"What is your solution?" I asked.

"Amir, if you will but suspend taxes on newly cleared for one year, and for two years on land cleared and brought under irrigation, and then tax one-fourth, one-third, and one-half and so on for five years before assessing the full rate, both you and your farmers will prosper. See, the plan is worked out on the next page."

He hovered over the throne and hurried me on with the figures.

"You see, you will lose nothing at all, and in five years your taxable lands will be doubled or trebled, and the living standards of the peasants will go up accordingly."

"Has this been tried?" I asked.

"No, Amir," he replied, not at all damped by my question. "It's brand-new and revolutionary in concept. But it will work."

I did not share Mahmoud's enthusiasm, but I did see in his theory a means to keep disgruntled peasants intent on something besides their complaints. He would proclaim me a benefactor, even though the peasants would be grubbing in the earth twice as many hours as a result of his scheme. And men digging at stumps and roots would not be plotting an uprising. So I put Mahmoud in charge of land reforms and issued directives to implement his work, not that I expected success as he visualized it.

But Mahmoud was only the first. As soon as the land reforms were under way, I was faced with another humanitarian. Khosru al-Shiraz not only won Sherif ad-Din over but also made some impression on the conservative court physician, and the three of them came to me together.

"What does the young man have in mind?" I asked.

"Let him speak for himself, Amir," the physician said, and smiled reassuringly at the agitated young Persian, who, unlike Mahmoud, was very much impressed by the splendor of my courtchamber.

"Amir," Khosru began, almost belligerently, "it doesn't seem right to me that the leader alone should enjoy surroundings like these while thousands of lame old soldiers are begging in the streets."

"That's not the most diplomatic approach," the old physician cautioned the young man gently. "You might be a little more temperate in your plea."

"Let him proceed. I'll judge what's right," I said sternly, and studied Khosru's flushed countenance. He could prove dangerous. I had learned that his father was highly respected in Shiraz, and I was not quite ready to antagonize the Persians by summarily disposing of one of their nobles.

"I think old soldiers should be cared for," he said in a much milder tone.

"How? They have families."

"But it's the duty of their ruler to look after them."

"Pensions, you mean?" I asked. "I allow pensions."

"No, Amir. Their families spend their pensions. I mean homes—domiciliary hospitals."

I looked at the physician. I began to see his interest in Khosru's plan.

"Yes," he said, in answer to my unasked question, "I think domiciliary hospitals would be the answer to my study of military medicine."

He had always insisted on adequate medical detachments on military campaigns. I had disagreed. Minor casualties recover without much attention. The seriously wounded, those who could not hope to return to battle, I preferred to let die. They are a burden on an army in the field and a liability after the war is over. A strong and healthy victor is a welcome sight. A dead warrior is a hero to his family. But a maimed, blinded, or faltering old soldier is a blight on a community and a hindrance to future recruiting.

I was not for coddling the wounded or pampering the worn-out veteran; but I let the conference continue.

"What specifically do you have in mind?" I asked of Khosru.

"Nothing as elaborate as your palace, of course," he answered, mollified by my continued interest, "but comfortable homes, preferably out in the country, where aged or disabled veterans, to whom all people are grateful, could live out their days in the company of their comrades and enjoy medical care of the wounds they bravely suffered in battle."

"Young physicians, under the direction of a retired medical man," my physician argued, "could very well learn much about wounds and their effects during a period of interneship in such homes."

"And how would this be financed?" I asked seriously, for I suddenly had visions of beggarly cripples being taken off the streets, out of sight of the public, and hidden away forever, where they would no longer deter doubting young men from joining my armies.

"It wouldn't cost much," said Khosru enthusiastically. "Here—I have figures."

It seemed that the young men always had figures. Khosru produced the inevitable scroll and spread it out before me.

"I've looked into your pension budget," he said, "and I can show you where my plan won't cost a dinar more. Furthermore, the money will be spent on those who deserve help, not on parasitic families."

"What about the first cost of buildings?" I asked, turning my attention to the carefully tabulated results of Khosru's calculations.

"There are always some deserted palaces or castles around which can be restored by army engineers, who would otherwise be idle, mind you." Khosru had the insolence to raise his finger at me to emphasize his point. "And the ambulatory patients could do much toward refurnishing and landscaping the homes."

Although I disliked the intense young Persian, I suppressed my feelings and let him go on with his argument until he felt that he had persuaded me to do what I had decided upon the moment I saw a way to get rid of the living eyesores which my campaigns always brought back to the streets and alleys of Samarkand. So I put Khosru in charge of the execution of his dream; and though I was not surprised at the effect, I did marvel at the speed with which my humanitarian reforms won public approval. Stories of my deep sympathy for my subjects spread throughout Tatary and well beyond its borders. I had some fears that I might lose prestige by appearing soft and sentimental. However, I regained confidence as I recognized the Way of Allah in the delusions I was creating among my people. Simple men looked upon me with the same kind of maudlin sentiment that showed when they prayed to Allah the Merciful, Allah the Compassionate—as though I were a God, as though Allah were God!

More disturbing was the light that came into Jahangir's eyes as he grew more mature and became aware of the affectionate esteem in which Saif ad-Din and Sherif ad-Din and their stupid kind held me. As stories of my benevolence seeped into the palace from the peasants in the street and the learned men in the academies, Jahangir's respect for me seemed to grow into a kind of filial tenderness; and I feared that he was forgetting the splendid experiences we had had when we rode into battle together.

Of course I wanted his loyalty, even his devotion; but I knew that his future would demand of him admiration for my military prowess, not a soft adoration of the saintly gestures I had made to delude the servile. It was right for my subjects to submerge themselves in me, but not my son. Already the feeling was creeping upon me that the Way must live after me, that someone must continue as the instrument and observer of the Way after I was gone. If not my son, then who?

After Shah Rukh was born, and Dilshad devoted most of her attention to him, Jahangir was more with me. During the winter of his seventeenth year we spent several evenings a week, whenever court business permitted, playing chess until bedtime. On one such occasion Jahangir asked permission to bring Aisha and Tahmineh to watch us play.

"They won't be in the way, and they won't say a word," he promised, when he came to my room alone and made his request.

"Very well, send for them," I said. I considered his request a healthy sign, a show of pride and the beginning of a promising egoism that might make the boy aware of his own potential.

"They're right outside," he said sheepishly. "I brought them with me."

"All right." I laughed. I liked his show of confidence. "Bring them in."

Unlike my own giggling younger women, the two girls came in solemnly and knelt before me.

"Welcome to my chamber," I said formally, and nodded to Jahangir to bid them rise.

When they faced him, their warm, doe-soft eyes seemed to caress every feature in his fine young face.

"Sit over there, Aisha—and here, Tahmineh," he said with an attempt at sternness which forced me to cough into my sleeve to smother a chuckle. I saw what Nubja had meant when she gave her report on the girls at Balkh. They lived for my son—they would have died for him, and he for them, I feared.

"Aisha, you may serve," he said, when we had placed the board between us and begun the game.

The older girl glided silently over to the serving table and brought a tray of candied fruits and nuts.

"Father first," Jahangir scolded gently, when the girl instinctively held the tray before her master.

Aisha hastily turned to me, and I saw fear and shame troubling her eyes. I was sure that she blushed under her veil. I smiled at her, however, and immediately her brows relaxed, and her eyes grew round and moist in gratitude.

Jahangir and I continued our game. Whenever I looked up, the girls were gazing lovingly at the boy. They watched his every move, but true to his word neither of them made a sound or a motion to distract our attention from the pieces on the board.

"Tahmineh, the wine," Jahangir snapped after a time, and I looked up in surprise to see annoyance in his countenance. I knew that he was being impartial—and I remembered how careful I had been to share my favors equally with Lillit and Reba in my youth—but I could see no reason for his impatience. I was glad to note that he was capable of disciplining the girls, however, and I read signs of pain in the attitudes of both of them and knew the hurt he had inflicted.

After Tahmineh poured the wine she went docilely back to her pillow; and thereafter whenever I looked up from the game, I would catch both girls watching me. They would drop their eyes modestly, but not before I was rewarded with a brief glimpse into the gentle depths. The girls' attention made me somewhat uncomfortable, for it was not the studied attention given me by my own concubines, and I was rather relieved when the evening was over.

Jahangir had his wives clear away the table and trays and then asked shyly, "May they kiss your hand, Father?"

"Certainly," I said in surprise. "I'd be pleased."

"Aisha," Jahangir called first.

The girl knelt before me, and I extended my right hand. She kissed it lightly and withdrew with her head bowed.

"Tahmineh."

The younger girl repeated the performance. And she did more. After she had kissed my hand once politely, as Aisha had done, she impulsively squeezed it between both her own small palms and pressed it to her cheek for a moment and then kissed it again. She looked up at me gratefully and then fearfully, until I squeezed her hand and smiled at her to let her know that it was all right. My reward was a look of happiness such as a mollah must see in the eyes of a devout pilgrim who has journeyed far to pay homage to her patron.

"Thank you, Amir Timur, for giving us to Amir Jahangir," she whispered.

Jahangir clapped his hands and the girls took their places behind him.

"May I bring them again, Father?" he asked, embarrassed by Tahmineh's behavior.

"Yes, Son. Any time you like," I said, and dismissed my guests.

But I found that I had misunderstood Jahangir's purpose in bringing the girls to our chess games. After another session or two, during which the girls divided their attention—and their adoration, it seemed —between me and my son, it began to dawn on me that Jahangir's love for me had overflowed into his little household and that he was bringing his disciples to worship me rather than to admire his skill at chess. For the young women's devotion was quite different from anything I had ever received from a woman before, and their affectionate hand-kissing was nothing akin to the preliminary love play my wives indulged in when I visited the zenana. The whole affair became quite annoying; and I invited Miran Shah and Omar Sheik to join us, hoping to stimulate rivalry at least—or something, I knew not what. I was perplexed.

Shereza came along, too, although my invitation to her had been oblique at best. I did not mind, however, because she was quite congenial, and I was not with her very much any more. She could no longer expect compliments on her small middle, even if she did still boast her roomy hips and the generous bosom Allah had bestowed upon her. And while her skin was still velvety and taut and it was not at all unpleasant to wallow with her in her obesity, I did not seek her bed as often as I should have, and I had no desire to offend her. So I thought it just as well that she be included in our family gatherings.

Jahangir's party was already seated when Shereza and her sons arrived. Shereza was obviously surprised to find the girls present.

"Perhaps the other young princes should send for their girls," she suggested, when she entered. Despite the fact that sharing Miran Shah with anyone pained the Begum almost beyond endurance, she had nevertheless chosen wives for both her sons just to counter the impression that Jahangir was being favored over them.

"If they like. Their women will be welcome."

I felt strangely guilty of some kind of infidelity, however, when I spoke; and as I involuntarily glanced at Aisha and Tahmineh, I saw that their eyes held something as near reproach as they could—or dared —express.

"Do you want to send for your girls, Miran?" Shereza asked.

"Yes, Mother," Miran Shah replied in a voice which matched the sullen look that had clouded his plain round face when he first saw Jahangir and the girls.

"What about you, Omar?"

"I don't care, Mother. Suit yourself," the other young prince called casually over his shoulder from a corner of the room where he was thumbing the blade of a talwar from my weapons case.

"Then I'll send for all of the girls," Shereza decided.

"That's all right with me," Omar Sheik commented disinterestedly; and at his easy conversation the formality of the whole group slipped away, and Jahangir joined his brother at the weapons case. Almost a year younger than Jahangir, Omar Sheik was an inch taller and fully as well developed as the older boy.

"Isn't that a beauty?" Omar said to Jahangir, and pointed to my favorite talwar.

"Yes. That's Father's first real sword. No one else has ever carried it."

"I know. Uncle Ali described it to me. I recognized it. I'd like very much to try it."

"May Omar try your talwar, Father?" Jahangir asked, turning to face my way. Unconsciously he acted as intermediary, as though Omar Sheik were an outsider. After more than two years' residence in the palace, my younger sons were still guests—I had left them too much in the care of their mother and their tutors.

"Certainly. Help yourself, Omar," I said, and resolved then and there to take all of my sons into my own hands.

Jahangir took the jeweled scabbard from the weapons case and offered the hilt to Omar, who drew the sword and demonstrated, by his eagerness, how I must have behaved that night at the caravanserai in Shehri-Sebz when I first touched the magnificent weapon. He drew the talwar carefully from the sheath and dropped the blade straight in front of him and moved it up and down and from side to side in gentle wrist play to feel the balance. I shared his satisfaction as the smile of appreciation spread over his face and he nodded his head just perceptibly.

Then he raised the sword and flicked the blade. The true clear tone, still undistorted by the nicks of many battles, rang softly through the room and echoed as Omar touched the hilt to an armor chest. Omar and Jahangir both looked at me, and we shared our common delight in the sound. Omar stepped back from us and swung the talwar through the Persian manual, his face beaming brighter at every thrust. I recognized Ali's coaching in the apparently casual but really deadly ease of the boy's movements.

"Catch," he called suddenly, and flipped the talwar to Jahangir, who caught it expertly and matched Omar's ease, and surpassed his precision, as he went through the Persian manual and the Tatar exercise as well.

"Suppose somebody else had a sword," I said teasingly, and drew another talwar from the case.

Jahangir faced me solemnly and took his stance. Carefully, meticulously, he began to force me with all his skill. I was able to parry his blows easily, but I saw that he had improved during the last few months and would be a formidable foe for an average swordsman.

"See. It's not the sword, but the hand that holds it," I mocked.

He grinned good-naturedly and backed away.

"You take him, Omar. Catch!" he said, and tossed the weapon to Omar Sheik.

Omar rushed me; and I seemed to be facing Ali, as I had done many times in the talwar pavilion. The same laughing eyes and smiling lips—the same debonair recklessness, which nevertheless demanded constant vigilance. Omar carried more power than Jahangir, but he lacked the precision of the older boy's thrusts. I was pleased with his sword play, however, and had no doubts of his ultimate skill.

185

I backed away and saluted him.

"This is really a blade!" he commented enthusiastically. "Where **did** you get it, Father?"

"It was given to me."

"Oh, yes. Uncle Ali told me that."

"But it will have to be won from me," I said.

"Miran," Shereza spoke up, "don't you want to try your father's sword?"

"Yes, Mother," Miran Shah said dutifully and, putting aside a half-eaten piece of candy, rose from the ottoman he had been perched on during our play.

"Catch!" called Omar Sheik.

Miran Shah caught the hilt, not with the deftness of Jahangir or the flair of Omar, but he caught it firmly and deliberately. Without bothering to do more than salute, he squared off before me and awaited my nod. Then he came in doggedly. Sometimes there were flashes of brilliance in his work, sometimes dull, unorthodox fumbling, but he kept coming. He frowned continuously, and it was obvious that there was no joy in the play for him. But I was having no easy time. He was tricky, unpredictable; whether by design or not, I could not tell. He had practiced long and hard—that was evident—and either by skill or pure awkward luck he suddenly came up under my guard and nicked my forearm with the point of his blade.

Tahmineh screamed, and both she and Aisha rushed toward me. Miran Shah backed away fearfully.

"I didn't mean to, Father," he apologized.

"You should have meant to," I said. "Your brothers tried their best. It's all right, Son. Better if you meant it."

Jahangir's girls examined my arm and bound it with a piece of gauze they produced from somewhere. Actually the injury was the merest scratch, but we put away the swords, and when the other slave girls arrived we settled down to less strenuous amusement.

I lost a game of chess to Jahangir, who accepted Omar's challenge to play the winner. Then, encouraged by Shereza, Miran Shah brought a backgammon board to my chair, and we tossed high dice for the first play. The game was anything but pleasant, what with Shereza sitting at her son's elbow and complimenting his play and his two girls taking turns at stuffing him with fruits and nuts. So, after a few desultory games, I was glad to relinquish my place to the Begum and let her have Miran Shah to herself.

In fact I was glad when the evening was over and my guests returned to their own quarters. I sought Nubja, who would fulfill the functions of a woman without cluttering up the place with sons and their slave girls. And when she had purged me of my family ambitions and disappointments, I realized how fortunate I was in having wives and children who could command no real affection, for I knew of many men who had been ruined, thwarted, and lost because of mawkish family feeling which took all of their attention away from the pursuits that might have made them great in the ways of Allah.

I was gratified to learn that I could consider my own sons objectively and perhaps turn their peculiarites to some advantage. Omar Sheik was quite obviously going to be another Ali, reckless, carefree— a good officer but nothing of an administrator. Miran Shah—he might be the most promising of the three, if he ever got any fire into his dull persistence. But Jahangir, the eldest, was the one who demanded immediate attention. How to turn his charm and sensitivity and gentleness to any use? How did he fit into Allah's processes?

The strong-soft paradox of Nubja's perfumed body offered, if not a solution, at least another diversion to lessen the urgency of my problem. And I returned to it.

CHAPTER

7

Spring came earlier in my valley than it did in Samarkand; so just before the first of Ramadan, which came in the spring that year, I moved my court to Shehri-Sebz. I wanted to see the finishing touches put on the tombs of Aljai and my father, which had been under construction in the palace garden and the monastery grounds for over three years. And I had recruited a squadron, composed of the sons of my nobles, which I wanted to train and place under Jahangir's command on his eighteenth birthday. The garrison facilities at Shehri-Sebz and the drill ground on the plain across the river were ideal for my purpose.

The grain fields were dark green, and wild grasses were sending out their first young shoots when my party, consisting of all of the higher nobles not in essential offices in Samarkand, took up residence in my father's capital. The palace garden blossomed with early flowers; and as I inspected the grounds, with Dilshad and the toddling Shah Rukh accompanying me, I was taken back to the days of my early pride in Ak Sarai—when Aljai and the baby Jahangir had made such inspection tours with me. But my limp and the white marble tomb nearing completion in Aljai's corner of the garden reminded me of the years that had passed, and would not let me forget the years that still lay ahead.

Much as I was tempted to make a holiday of my stay in Shehri-Sebz, to spend my days and nights with Dilshad in Aljai's old suite or with Shah Rukh in Jahangir's nursery, to succumb again to Allah's lures, I allowed no interruption in my daily routine of state duties. I did have time to ride again over the trails I had known in my youth and to hunt Sasha, who though getting old was still my favorite bird and the best hunter entered in the royal falconry contests. And I had the leisure to direct a sculptor in modeling a life-size figure of Sasha to be cast in gold and mounted on my standards.

But generally I spent my mornings in the courtchamber and my afternoons on the drillfield with the young cadets. It was a relief to be in the saddle again, if only in the capacity of a cavalry instructor. And the eagerness of the youngsters afforded a welcome contrast to the stuffy formality of my divan.

Jahangir easily assumed command of the training squadron, and my other two sons showed signs of making satisfactory subalterns. Omar Sheik got along well with the cadets, although they had more respect, growing out of affection, for Jahangir. Miran Shah, accustomed to having his own way in everything, proved to be a remarkably good disciplinarian despite, or probably because of, his pouting and ill-tempered manner of dealing with his men.

None of my sons, however, exhibited the combination of impersonal leadership and sheer dynamic vigor which would be required of my successor. I began to think more and more of Shah Rukh and of possible grandsons as the ones to whom I must look for a suitable heir to my throne. The blood lines of Shah Rukh—pure Tatar—were good, but identical with those of Jahangir. And though Shereza was a true Begum, her lineage was that of the Prophet, not of the warlords of the south, and I knew that she would insist on a strong voice in the selection of her sons' wives.

Jahangir's excellent characteristics added to a little fire would perhaps offer the best possibilities; so as I watched my oldest son develop toward a competent but far from brilliant military man, I quizzed my acquaintances indirectly about suitable princess wives for him.

It was Kaikosru of Katlan who first mentioned Sevin Bey, the Khanzade, daughter of the Sufi of Kharesm, Amir of Khiva, and Sultan of Urganj and the rich towns and lands around the Aral Sea.

"She's a hell-cat," he said, "but a beauty, so I've heard—with the golden body of a Circassian and the burnt-gold hair and green eyes of her mother."

"Who are her mother's people?" I asked. I knew that Yussuf Sufi was a Kabul, of the blood of the khans.

"I don't really know. Nobody does, I guess. But her mother was enough —a whole tribe in herself." He laughed as he remembered her. "Kolin Murfi was her name, and she was a vixen if there ever was one."

"A Georgian perhaps?" I asked.

"Oh, no. The Sufi got her in a raid on a lost colony of infidels far beyond the Sea of Abaku, a remnant of some Frank crusade."

"A Frank."

"She said that her people came from Juverna, a green isle in the sea beyond the land of the Franks. Our scholars have read of such a place—in books by the old Greeks—but nobody put much faith in Kolin Murfi's stories. They were as wild as she was."

"Wild," I repeated thoughtfully.

"—as a Kirghis filly. She lived for about ten years after the Sufi captured her—and they say that every time he had her, it was rape." Kaikosru chuckled again. "She insisted that a man should have only one wife—and the Sufi had a hundred. She really gave him more trouble than all the others put together—and more pleasure, I believe."

"And you say the Khanzade is like her mother?"

"Nobody could be like Kolin Murfi. But Sevin Bey is a spirited one, so they tell me."

"How old is this Sufi's daughter?"

"Let me see—sixteen, I guess."

"About Jahangir's age," I said.

Kaikosru looked up at me sharply.

I smiled at him. "Yes," I said. "I'm looking for a wife for him."

"Sevin Bey for Jahangir?" he said soberly. Even he had come under Jahangir's spell.

"He can tame her, if anybody can," I said. "He has trained everything from mountain goats to tiger kittens."

"Yes, he might. He has a way about him. She'd be worth the trouble, from all I hear."

"You know the Sufi. You will make ready for a journey. I am sending gifts and a letter to Urganj."

"This is asking vassalage, you know," Kaikosru cautioned me. "It's more than his daughter—since you are originating the request."

"I realize that."

"The Sufi is rich and powerful."

"So am I," I said. "You will be ready to leave in three days."

"Yes, Amir," Kaikosru agreed, but I could tell that his heart was not in his mission. Indeed, the Sufi had taken Katlan some years before and deposed Kaikosru. That was why the Persian was at my court.

He did go to Urganj, however, and took with him a train of rich gifts from my stores in Shehri-Sebz and Samarkand. It really mattered little to me whether the Sufi agreed to the marriage and the implied vassalage or refused and forced me into a war against him. I had not been on a campaign myself in several years, and I would have welcomed a chance to ride again and to give Jahangir's squadron a chance to taste real warfare.

In fact, I rather preferred to think of the second alternative; and I recalled Ali and Khitai—to be present at the council of the New Year, which was to come about midsummer, and speeded up the training activity of the young recruits. To simulate a campaign situation and also to escape the increasing heat inside the city, I had the royal pavilions brought down from Samarkand and my court moved to the plain across the river.

Surrounded by the smells of animals and summer-dried grass trampled by my cavalry, I almost wished that the Sufi's answer would be downright insulting. As my amirs began to arrive with their taxes and gifts for the New Year, a huge sarai grew on my plain. The white felt domes of the Tatar kibitkas and the tapestrylike patterns of the Persian pavilions gave my plain the appearance of Sali Sarai in the days of Kurgan. And all of this fanned my enthusiasm to lead the whole force into battle.

But the celebration lengthened into days, and still Kaikosru did not return or send word from Urganj. As the usual day and night amusements began to grow stale, I devised new entertainment to try to hold my amirs at Shehri-Sebz until Kaikosru arrived. Especially did I exhibit Jahangir's squadron—uniformed in silver mail and blue silk surcoats and blue-and-gold helmets—in all sorts of parades and reviews and cavalry games, to the extent that I feared I might be looked upon as a doting old father, although at the time I still lacked more than a year being forty.

Finally I was down to matching the squadron polo team with any team of youngsters which the visiting amirs could organize. The match, which created even more interest and rivalry than I anticipated, was arranged; and I made as big a thing of it as I could, offering rich prizes and covering all bets that could be coaxed out of the visitors, although the royal team naturally included all three of my sons, who might conceivably have weakened it. None of the other youngsters, of course, dared challenge the princes' places on the team.

I was willing to lose the wagers, however, in order to keep my army intact for another day. And before the game started, I sent riders to meet Kaikosru, if he were near, and to speed up his progress. When play started, my mind was on the road to Urganj rather than on the field; but

I paid enough attention to the game to see that the players, while by no means brilliant, were putting on a good show and satisfying the spectators.

In my box, shared by Shereza Begum and Dilshad and ranking nobles and their wives, the enthusiasm was high but not nearly so raucous as along other boundaries of the field. There were many other boxes, as gaily decorated with silks and pennants as my own, and camel litters and sedan chairs, as well as hundreds of men on horseback and on foot. The field was so crowded and the din of the cheering audience so loud that I could neither see nor hear anything fifty paces from the field.

So I nervously watched seven cakkars of the game. I knew vaguely that the score was tied and that Jahangir had scored two goals and Omar two and Miran Shah one. Elchi's youngest son had scored one also. During the rest period before the last cakkar, my sons, hot and sweaty and tired, lined up before my box and saluted me with their mallets.

"You've got to win," I said, after I had congratulated them on their individual scores. "I've bet a lot on you boys."

"We'll take them easily, Father," Jahangir said confidently.

"Sure, it'll be easy," Omar agreed.

Miran Shah merely sulked.

"Come here to Mother, Miran," Shereza called to him.

He rode up to the box, and the Begum wiped his face with her scarf.

"You win for your father, dear," she said pleasantly, and then added in a lower voice, but one with an edge to it, "You've scored only one goal. Your brothers have scored two. You're as good as they are."

"Yes, Mother."

Shereza dried the handle of his mallet and wiped both his palms with her scarf.

The trumpets sounded time and the players wheeled their horses to return to the field.

"Remember what I said," Shereza called sternly after Miran Shah.

"Yes, Mother," he replied over his shoulder.

The nakaras rolled while the teams got into position, and the trumpet signaled play as I turned the timing glass over to mark the final cakkar. To me the play was as uninspired and desultory as the running of the sand in the glass. The players jostled, fumbled, knocked the ball out of bounds repeatedly, and it looked as though neither side was going to score. Slow as it was, the game was still not slow enough; the sand was running out, and still no word from Kaikosru.

Two—one and a half—a minute to go—then Jahangir broke clear from the far end of the field and drove a clean ball toward his own goal. Omar blocked an opponent, and Miran Shah raced to defend Jahangir's right. Jahangir hit the ball again, clear and straight, and both boys rode side by side. Omar cut out the last challenger, and it was clear that my team would make a goal.

As the boys, riding abreast, approached the ball for the last blow, Miran Shah suddenly reined his mount into Jahangir and pulled into position to strike the ball himself. Jahangir was jostled far out of position; and Miran Shah, thrown off balance, nevertheless managed to make an impossible stroke which sent the ball cleanly between the goal posts, although his mallet glanced off the ball and crashed into his horse's front leg. The horse somersaulted forward and rolled completely over Miran Shah's body, which lay still and clear of the saddle after the spill.

Shereza screamed and literally fell out of the royal box. She ran across the field like a peasant woman racing to the aid of a bleating goat. I followed her; but long before I reached Miran Shah, she had his head in her lap and was weeping and calling his name in despair.

"Miran! Miran! You scored—now open your eyes. It's Mother—open your eyes."

A few feet away Jahangir knelt beside Miran's fallen horse and soothed him.

"Easy, boy. Easy. Lie still, boy."

I stood between the two, watching first one and then the other, until the physician reached Miran Shah, and Mangali Boga ran out with a battle mace and killed the crippled horse with one deft blow between the eyes.

The physician ran his hands over Miran's body. The boy was still unconscious.

"No bones broken, Shereza Begum," he said. "It's his head. Probably only a mild concussion. He should be all right in a few minutes."

"He's dead!" she cried.

"No. His heart and breathing are as nearly normal as if he were asleep."

"He'll die! I know he'll die—trying to win a silly game!" She glowered at me.

A litter arrived then, and Miran Shah was carried off the field, with Shereza following along and moaning as though she were in his funeral procession.

Miran Shah regained consciousness before we reached his pavilion.

"Did I make the goal, Mother?" he asked, when he opened his eyes and saw Shereza beside the litter.

"Yes, dear," she sobbed. "You're alive! Do you hurt?"

"My head," he said, and clamped his pudgy hand over his forehead. "My head hurts."

"His head hurts!" she said. "His head hurts—do something about it!"

"When we get inside," said the physician. "When I examine him a little more thoroughly, I'll do something."

The litter-bearers carried Miran Shah inside his tent and laid him on a couch. He lost consciousness again when the servants transferred his body, but came to a few seconds later. The physician made his examination and gave the boy an opiate.

"He'll be all right," he said. "I'll stay with him."

"So will I," Shereza said, and gave orders to have her things moved into Miran's quarters immediately. I left her sitting beside her son's couch.

The boy's goal had won my bets for me, and the game had won the time I needed, for Kaikosru arrived an hour before sunset, bringing with him a train as heavily loaded with gifts as the one he had led out of Shehri-Sebz a month before. Since the amirs were already assembled in front of my pavilion, I ordered Kaikosru to unpack the gifts at once and make the presentation. Although I was secretly disappointed at receiving gifts instead of a provocation for war, I saw advantage in letting my followers see the rich presents and hear the Sufi's message offering his daughter to my son with the tacit acceptance of vassalage inherent in such action.

As was the custom, the gifts were displayed by a corps of servants, and Kaikosru knelt before me for permission to deliver the Sufi's presentation speech. I bade him rise; and he faced me, fearfully it seemed, and began the Sufi's message.

"Amir Timur, of the house of Kayouli, Protector of my family of Kabul of the blood of the Khans, Prince of Samarkand, and famous conqueror known in all lands as the valiant Timur-i-Leng—"

I winced at the name. No man since Hussayn had dared mention it to my face. I did not resent my lameness, but I could allow no man to call me lame.

"—I, Sufi of Kharesm, Amir of Khiva, Sultan of Urganj and the lands by the Aral Sea, send my thanks for the splendid gifts, the most generous and gracious ever bestowed by a monarch upon his brother.

"To my brother, the illustrious brother Timur-i-Leng, I send gifts richer still, to show my gratitude. May Allah's blessing go with the gifts.

"The Khanzade, my daughter and daughter of the Khans, sends her greetings to your son, Pir Jahangir. May they be as brother and sister—and her husband, when I have chosen one worthy in blood and name to wed the Princess of Kharesm, be as a brother to the sons of your house.

"Brother, as you have won Samarkand by the sword, so, too, have

193

I won Kharesm, and only by the sword may our lands be taken from us. Brother, we owe vassalage to no man.

"To young Pir Jahangir, I send these hunters—"

Two native Urganji trainers, who had been hidden up to that time, advanced with a pair of magnificent, perfectly matched black panthers.

"May the blessings of Allah go with these gifts and may He be merciful upon your house."

Kaikosru was trembling in terror by the time he finished his speech. At the last word he fell on his face before me and groveled in the sand.

"These are the words of the Sufi—not mine. Have mercy on me, Most Gracious Amir."

I stepped forward and kicked him once in the face and twice in his ribs, not that I was unduly angered by the insolence of the Sufi's elaborate gifts and insults, for I wanted war, but because the bearer of such a message was always treated so. My amirs approved the action and, of course, read my answer to the Sufi on my countenance. They cheered as one man, and their battlecry was picked up at the edges of the assembly and carried to the far reaches of the sarai.

Prepared as I was in anticipation of the Sufi's refusal of my request, I was able to break camp overnight and move west toward Khiva and Urganj with the next day's sun. Altogether I had nearly ten thousand men in my force, or available, before the army reached Khiva. With my regiment, including Jahangir's Blue Squadron, under my new golden eagle standard leading the column, and Kaikosru's battalion of catapults and other machines bringing up the rear, I moved down the valley, on past Bokhara, and out into the desert.

My warlike caravan was quite different from the little band which Hussayn and I had led toward Khiva on the day I was wounded in the foot. And the royal pavilion I shared with Dilshad at night was a far cry from the stagnant canyon in which she had first asked me to love her—with Aljai a dozen paces away. All was quite different. This was no tail end of a Jihad, no beaten crusade for Allah, but rather a punitive expedition in keeping with the Way, and I was sure of my success.

I had men, and I had weapons, and I had powerful machines—I *had* machines until Kaikosru deserted only a day's march from Khiva, left in the night with his entire battalion and headed south. I did not deviate from my course, however. Knowing the difficulty Kaikosru would have getting the heavy siege machines across the river, I sent Jahangir's Blue Squadron and Elchi's squadron in pursuit, and led the main body of my army on to Khiva.

Without machines to batter the walls, I relied on the enthusiasm of my men to storm the city. We filled the dry moat with brush and set up scaling ladders. The spirit of my men was high. Even though the Khivans poured naphtha on the brush and set fire to it, burning a thousand men in the first wave of my attack, I had thousands more; and within a few hours, we had softened the resistance on the walls.

When the first golden eagle appeared on the wall, a shout went up from all my army, and my men swarmed over the battlements from all sides. We cleaned up the streets before nightfall, and we locked the nobles in their palaces and public buildings and set fire to the lot in retaliation for the burning of my men in the moat. I gave the soldiers free rein to loot and rape and sack the city and returned with my officers to our sarai in the desert, which was lighted up like day by the flames inside the city.

Soon Jahangir rode in with my war machines and Kaikosru.

"Good work, Son," I said. "Come, let's celebrate your victory."

"Not tonight, Father, if you'll excuse me."

"But why, Son? Your first victory!"

"Elchi, Father. He was wounded fighting in the river, and drowned."

"Elchi?"

"Yes, Father. Omar Sheik is commanding his squadron and bringing his body back. He'll be here in a few minutes."

"Elchi—Very well, Son. We won't celebrate tonight."

After starting Elchi's funeral cortege back to Shehri-Sebz and installing a garrison and a daroga in Khiva, I moved my army northwest toward Urganj. Enough men, answering the call sent out by my amirs, arrived to replace the ones I had lost at Khiva; and by the time I set up my sarai some two miles from the city, my forces numbered a few more than the ten thousand I had started with. And I had my siege engines and mechanics to build more.

I did not attack at once, however. Urganj was enclosed in a wall which was almost the equal of those around Karshi and Samarkand, and the Sufi was rich enough to afford the finest in defense machines as well as small arms. So I camped outside the city for a week while my architects built additional mangonels and catapults and horse-powered rams, and my carpenters made scores of light pontoons to bridge the flooded moat. Deliberately, I had my men work just out of longbow range but well in sight of the city walls; and I put crews to work on every side so the Sufi could see a ring of war machines building solidly around his fortress.

Abdullah got intelligence from his Leng Kopeghi contingent inside the city. Refugees from Khiva had spread the story of the sacking of Khiva and of the indomitable spirit of my soldiers as they charged across the burning bodies of their comrades in the moat and scaled the walls in the face of the best defenses the Khivans had to offer. The spying cutthroats reported that the Sufi was much disturbed over the loss of property and the burning of the choice buildings in his second city. He expressed fears for the fate of Urganj if I should be victorious.

I did not underestimate the personal valor of the Sufi, however. He was known as a fearless campaigner, and Kaikosru had given me first-hand information concerning the Sufi's ferocity in battle and had convinced me of his fears of the Sufi by deserting on the road to Khiva. I expected a fight, and I was prepared for one; but I did not expect the proposal sent to me under a flag of truce just as I had drawn my men and engines up into position for my first assault.

Five riders dressed in white and mounted on white horses rode out of the gates and brought the Sufi's cowardly white banner toward my own golden eagle standard. I respected the plea, however, and listened to the Sufi's spokesman after he had reined up his horse and saluted me.

"Most illustrious Timur, Amir of Samarkand, valiant and noble warrior: the Sufi of Kharesm, Amir of Khiva—"

I waved the man to strike out that empty title, and he proceeded.

"—Sultan of Urganj and the lands of the Aral Sea, bids you accept single combat."

"Single combat?" I asked, and my blood thrilled at the prospect.

"Yes, Amir Timur. The Sufi says the quarrel is between you and him, growing out of your insolent and arrogant demand for the fair Khanzade. It is useless to destroy so many of your followers and his own subjects. He urges you, Amir Timur, to accept his challenge and let him who first draws blood be the victor, with the Princess as the prize."

"Tell the Sufi that Amir Timur awaits him," I answered quickly. "But the duel shall be to the death. His insults cannot be avenged by the mere drawing of blood."

"The Sufi will meet the Prince of Samarkand on this plain one hour after the sun has passed its zenith," the spokesman said, and rode back into the city.

My tavachis immediately raised objections.

"Amir Timur, this thing is foolish," said old Saif ad-Din. "Your place is beside the standard of command. Let my son, Nur ad-Din, meet the arrogant Sufi and avenge your insults."

"No," I said, and laughed at the old man's fears. "Not Nur ad-Din."

"Then Sheik Ali or Khitai Bahatur," urged Saif ad-Din. Both men had ridden up from their units and heard the last proposal.

"Let me at him," shouted Khitai.

"No—me," said Sheik Ali. "I have scores to settle with the Sufi, myself."

"It's my battle," said Jahangir quietly. "It was a request for a bride for me that brought this on. Let me meet the Sufi, Father, and win the Khanzade for myself. If I should lose—then the occasion for this war is past."

"He captured Kaikosru," put in Omar Sheik. "Let me take this one for you, Father."

I laughed aloud at the two pigeon cocks. Sixteen- and seventeen-year-olds, dazzled by their fancy blue uniforms, asking to accept the challenge of a seasoned veteran.

"You're right, boys," I said. "It's our fight—but I'm still head of this family, and I'm the one who's been challenged. Bring my light mail—you may be my seconds. And bring me a helmet and cloak of the Gok Hazara; I'll fight under Jahangir's standard."

So, despite continued objections by my amirs, I changed my clothes under the glare of the midday sun and prepared to ride forth toward the gates of Urganj. Saif ad-Din was still hanging onto my bridle and begging me to send a champion, when my blue-clad seconds took their places beside me to escort me to the field. I spanked the old man with the flat of my talwar and laughed at the tears in his eyes as I finally broke him loose and rode away, heralded by the roll of the Gok Hazara nakaras and the music of Jahangir's youthful trumpeters.

Halfway between my lines and the city I stopped and saluted the Sufi's standard mounted on the city gates. I received no response. There was not a movement among the armed watchers crowding the battlements; and both the defenders and my own forces were as quiet as dead men, once the nakaras playing my advance had ceased their roll. I saluted again and watched for the gates to open—but again nothing happened, and there was not a sound except the stamping of our horses and the rattling of harness from my cavalry lines.

A quarter of an hour passed, and our horses began to paw the sand impatiently. A half an hour, and I was growing as impatient as the horses —my fresh enthusiasm was giving way to a sullen resentment at the Sufi's arrogance in making sport of me and delaying the moment when I would hack his head from his shoulders.

"Bring me a voice trumpet," I commanded Omar Sheik, and he raced back to my headquarters.

Long minutes later—when Omar returned with the instrument—there was still no sign of the Sufi, and I was convinced that he was not coming out.

I raised the voice trumpet to my lips and hailed his standard.

"Cowardly Sufi, breaker of your word," I called. "Allah will strike you dead, and I will take your city to avenge this, your last insult."

My angry voice carried over the city, and the walls echoed my words back through the stillness to my own men surrounding Urganj. I waited a few minutes more and turned around in humiliation and headed back toward my lines. There, a shout and a clamor of nakaras and cymbals and kourrouns rose to a deafening din, augmented by the frightened neighing and braying and bellowing of the animals in formation and in the domestic compounds at my camp.

Before I reached my headquarters, I signaled to my commanders by hand; and the whole force, men and animals and engines, rushed forward to storm the walls according to the plan which had been interrupted by the Sufi's cowardly horseplay.

Wave after wave of my men pushed to the edge of the moat, and my siege engines kept up a constant barrage of stones and flaming pitchballs, but not one unit got across the ditch. The Sufi had what seemed to be an impregnable defense and an inexhaustible supply of reserves, for hundreds upon hundreds of men from both sides fell. My forces ran into a glistening cascade of arrows pouring down from the walls. They fell and colored the sands as red as the water in the moat, which blushed ever darker as more and more Urganji archers toppled forward and plunged headlong from the walls above.

By sunset I had not made a dent in the Sufi's armor, although thousands of his followers and mine, whom he had perfidiously offered to spare, lay bloating on the hot sands or swelling in the turbid waters of the moat. My trumpets sounded a doleful retreat, and my army retired to the sarai. I called for a council after supper, and ordered a steam bath prepared in my banja cart.

Abdullah brought word from a Urganji beggar when he came to rub me down—beggars and thieves always have avenues of escape from a city. He talked while he massaged my muscles.

"The Sufi expects reinforcements from the Turkoman tribes around the Aral," he said, toward the end of his report.

"When?" I asked.

"Today—tomorrow—anytime now, Amir."

"So that accounts for his exhibition today—playing for time."

"Yes, Amir. Perhaps you are right."

"He seems to be strong already, inside. I'll stop his attack on my rear. How close are we to him?" I asked, referring to Leng Kopeghi connections.

"Faradi, from Karshi, who set himself up as an armorer in Khiva and failed, now polishes the Sufi's table knives."

"No," I said. "Not a knife. The Sufi must sicken and die. Allah must strike him down."

"There's also a man inside who knows many subtle poisons, Amir. He has worked for the best gangs in Kharesm."

198

"Maybe poison on a table knife?"

Abdullah kneaded my shoulders thoughtfully.

"Perhaps, Amir. Shall I send word?"

"Yes."

"And Leng Kopeghi?"

"If Faradi should come into a sum of money and appear in Samarkand as a merchant, he might set up an armorer's shop there without fear of failure."

"And his friend?"

"An apothecary's shop—anything he wants. The Sufi is offering stubborn resistance. I'd like to be rid of him."

"He will sicken and die, Amir," said Abdullah, and he gave my shoulder a final stinging slap which put an end to my rubdown and to the conversation.

I apprised the council of the Sufi's expectations and laid plans accordingly. I dispatched Sheik Ali with a full division to intercept the reinforcements, and he left at once so that he could skirt the city under the cover of darkness and be out of sight before daybreak. I set my carpenters to work building armored carts from which to shoot flaming arrows, and I had the siege engines adjusted to lob pitchballs and flasks of burning naphtha over the walls instead of hurling stones on a flat trajectory against the gates. I knew that the Sufi, despite his speech about sparing lives, cared far less about his men than he did for his property; and I planned to concentrate my fire on targets which would cause him most concern until Ali returned.

All night and all the next day my army continued to build machines and prepare fire missiles. The second night I allowed the men to sleep, and the next morning I renewed my siege. My archers kept up a steady barrage of fire-tipped arrows volleying from the armored carts, over the walls into the city; and whole squadrons of cavalry kept up a steady flow of ammunition to the siege machines. Soon all but a skeleton guard of Urganji archers left the walls to form fire brigades in the city streets.

Since accuracy was of no particular importance, my men continued the fire all night, working in shifts; and the sky was kept aglow with the flaming missiles and the burning buildings inside the walls. It was a beautiful sight—every different kind of oil used on the arrows and in the fireballs giving off a different hue as the deadly comets made fiery arcs over the walls, and the thousand different materials burning inside adding their own peculiar colors to the flames.

I sat on a raised platform before my pavilion and watched the spectacle. It was there Abdullah brought me word that the Sufi had been taken ill with a colic after his evening meal. And it was there that

I continued to receive news of how baffling his sickness was to the court physician. I was still at my post at dawn when Ali's division returned, whooping across the plain and carrying the heads of a thousand bearded Turkomans fixed on pikestaffs.

According to my orders, Ali sent his riders circling around the city to deliver a Turkoman's head to each siege engine. Then, when my trumpets sounded, every machine was loaded with one of the heads; and on the second signal the volley was let loose, sending my grim reminders over the walls to the Sufi.

Arabshah, who heard of this battle before he ever saw me, wrote in his chronicles that my tactics represented the ultimate in butchery and brutality, but he did not understand. The Turkoman warriors were dead already. As rotting corpses on the shores of the Aral they could have been of no use or significance. But as ammunition for my catapults, their putrid heads struck terror into my enemies and furthered the Way of Allah as one of His own cataclysms might have done. What better answer could the Sufi have received to his arrogant insults?

But the Sufi was dead. No sooner had I received the news than white flags went up on every tower. All battle ceased, and a deathly quiet settled over the desert, an awesome silence broken only by the crackling of flames from the burning city. Then a mighty cheer rose from my army as I acknowledged the offer of surrender. The gates of Urganj opened, and the main drawbridge slowly spanned the moat. A green-turbaned mollah, accompanied by nobles of obvious high rank, crossed the bridge to meet me on the plain.

As the envoys approached I recognized Khoja Beha, whom the Sufi had brought from Bokhara to be First Mollah of Urganj.

"Amir Timur," he began, "Prince of Samarkand, Sultan of all Tatary, you have spoken truly. Allah has stricken the Sufi as you prophesied. Surely the Sufi was wrong to deny your request for Sevin Bey Khanzade and to break his word to you. The church and the council of Urganj admit the falsity of their erstwhile master and throw themselves on your mercy. The Sufi is dead. Allah's blessings be upon Timur, Sufi of Urganj. We are your servants. It is the Will of Allah—Kismet."

"Khoja Beha," I said, "you have long been my friend. You shall not suffer at my hands. As for the amirs, if they swear allegiance to me and you vouch for their integrity, I will let them live and spare the city further damage."

"So shall it be, I assure you. Please consider all Urganji nobles your vassals—and respect the Khanzade, whose relatives prefer to send her to your son as a willing bride and not as a captive slave."

"That is the way we want it. She shall remain the Princess of Urganj and reign over her people again when she and my son attain suitable age, for I intend this city to be his capital. I will see that her dowry is not touched but left for her to bring to Samarkand with pride, just as if her benighted father had never refused my original request."

"Thank you, Amir Timur, in the name of the council of Urganj. I assured the nobles that you were a good and just ruler—they will be pleased with your terms."

The mollah's escort nodded agreement to the statement, and I read relief and hope in the eyes of all the amirs as they saluted and turned to lead me through the gates of Urganj.

And indeed I surprised the natives of the city by my show of mercy and the strict observance I gave to the conventions surrounding their princess. Only Dilshad visited her in her virgin's sanctuary and made arrangements for the wedding.

"She's as beautiful as they say," Dilshad reported, but I felt that the Sarai Khanum was not very well pleased with the first princess wife to join our son's household.

"Then I'm glad, for Jahangir's sake," I said.

Dilshad's face clouded before she spoke.

"But—for Jahangir. He's such a gentle boy. And, Timur, somehow I wonder—"

"At her spirit? Jahangir needs a spirited wife—not another calf like Aisha or Tahmineh to pet him and moon at him eternally." I chuckled at her fears and secretly found satisfaction in the hints in her words. "He'll tame her, and she'll love him—in her way."

"—in her way," repeated Dilshad. "That's what I'm afraid of. Oh, Timur, I'm not sure that she'll be good for him."

"Nonsense. You're not without spirit—nor was Aljai—and you're both the best wives a man ever had."

A brief smile flitted across Dilshad's face. Then the frown returned.

"But Sevin Bey is nothing like me—us. She looks like a—a foreigner, too fair to be trusted. Beautiful, yes—gracious, when she wants to be—but—oh, I don't know—but I'm afraid. I love Jahangir so."

"Forget it," I said, and clasped Dilshad to me to reassure her. "Go on back to Samarkand and plan the finest wedding a Tatar ever had. We'll dazzle the Khanzade, and she'll be as meek as a kitten."

"A kitten—a cat!" Dilshad's voice was soft but as vicious as a serpent's hiss.

On my way back to Shehri-Sebz I traveled leisurely and had much time to muse upon the success of my expedition. I was sure that the contrast between the fate of the Khivans, who had resisted me, and of the Urganjis who had surrendered to me, would make a good story and serve as a warning to my neighbors as the news spread among them.

And by winning the Khanzade to bear me grandsons, I had accomplished the purpose which had originally set me out on the campaign. I was fully aware of the gamble I was taking in choosing a wife for Jahangir. Still I dared to hope—though hope is vanity—that while I was riding the crest I might have a hand in shaping destiny. With three grown sons of royal mothers, and the infant Shah Rukh, and many years to engender others, and Jahangir's sons to come from Sevin Bey's womb, and my other sons' sons—surely I could fit some one or all of those into the Way. And so all men must muse at times, and lose the Way in the very absurdity of their musings.

I was roused out of my week-long reverie when I came in sight of Shehri-Sebz. The city was in mourning, and I guessed that Miran Shah was dead. I spurred my horse and hurried on ahead of my column toward Ak Sarai. I had thought little about my second son during the campaign except to regret at times the good experience that he was missing or to include him in my ruminations concerning the perpetuation of my line. I cared little for the boy, but I knew that it was considered bad for a man to lose his sons before they had been of service to him.

A sentry recognized me from a distance and signaled to the palace guard. Shereza Begum, too, was roused, and she stood on the palace steps to greet me. Her own deep mourning confirmed my fears.

"Miran Shah—" I said, as I dismounted and opened my arms to comfort the weeping Begum. I knew the extent of her loss.

"He's in his room," she sobbed, and buried her face in the dusty folds of my tunic.

"When did he—when did it happen?" I asked. I thought she would not like the word *die*.

"A month ago." She sniffed and regained some measure of composure. "I just got word yesterday."

"A month ago?" I asked, and held her away from me to look at her. Miran Shah had not even been hurt a month ago. I thought surely that Shereza had lost her mind.

"Yes. It took the rider a month to bring the news from Herat."

"Then Miran Shah is not dead?"

"No," she said in horror. "No! Not my baby. It's Father."

She burst into tears again; whether over the death of Shah Malik or at the mere thought of Miran Shah's dying, only she knew.

"How is Miran Shah?" I asked.

"He's up and about. He still has headaches— Your first thought was of Miran Shah!" she broke off, and her eyes glowed suddenly with gratitude and pride. "You hurried on to ask about our son—you called his name before you even greeted me!"

"Of course I did. What else would you expect of his father?" I saw no reason not to humor her, and the way she squeezed my arm told me that there were good reasons *for* humoring her. My expressions of preference for Miran Shah always awakened in Shereza something closely akin to that hunger I had found in her on our wedding night; and after my long dusty ride from Karshi the prospect of being sought by the mature passion of her soft comfortable body was indeed a pleasant one. So, after looking in on Miran Shah, who was asleep—drugged, his mother told me—we retired to the Begum's suite and I put thoughts of war and destiny from my mind.

Before leaving Shehri-Sebz, I dispatched a party of envoys to Herat to convey my condolences and to invite Shereza's brother to attend the wedding.

The Begum and Sheik Ali were of a better blood line than their older half-brother; and I knew that they both felt that his right to succession could be challenged. Shereza hoped that because of her he might offer token vassalage to me when their father died, and so save the city of Herat, which she loved. Sheik Ali, however, did not share her optimism. I cared little whether the new lord of Herat accepted my invitation or gave me a provocation for war which I could justify in the eyes of the Begum and of the thousands of Persians and Afghans who revered her above all other living persons. My recent successes had given me confidence, and I was willing to try to add Herat as a strong and prosperous outpost to my domain.

Such were my feelings when the party left Shehri-Sebz. In fact I was jubilant over the prospects of both Jahangir's wedding and the new state of affairs in Herat. And the first hint of autumn crispness in the air added to my feeling of well-being. Frost had already touched the mountains to the east, leaving patches of brown and orange and yellow on the upper woodlands and turning little fernlike shrubs near the ground into red lace.

While my tavachis were getting things in readiness to move back to Samarkand, I rode Ak Ruksh the breadth and length of my valley and high up into hills. Usually I rode alone, since Shereza traveled only by camel litter and Miran Shah was not quite well enough for so many hours in the saddle. I longed for Dilshad—or Aljai—and for Jahangir and Omar Sheik, who were both in Samarkand. Sometimes I hunted Sasha in the quail lands; and occasionally Abdullah went with me, and we tried the black leopards against the antelope in the foothills.

I read Allah's Way in the brilliant autumn coloring—His beautiful forewarnings that ice and sleet and snow would bring misery and hunger to men who ignored the signs. And I marked in my mind a place for the knowledge that I might remember it and follow the Way in my warnings to men, use the symbol of colors to accent the irony of destruction, for I was still learning as I reveled in the hues of my bright-colored valley.

But at length preparations were complete, and my court set out for Samarkand. The Begum's retinue was as colorful as the hills—gaudy, Dilshad would have said—and at one point, near the stream where Hadji and Bayazid had tried to assassinate me many years before, I galloped ahead of the column and took up a post wide of the road and watched the procession pass against the background of dying leaves.

Miran Shah rode with me; he was improving every day.

"It looks good enough to eat," was his only remark.

I wondered if he knew how men fattened on pageantry and grew soft on the pomp of a victor's wealth. Or if he really was thinking of his palate and belly, for he was getting fat since his fall and the inactivity and sheer mother-petting which his injury had forced on him. I looked at his pudgy figure, slouched in the saddle, and it spoiled my pleasure in the spectacle of the royal caravan.

We rejoined the column.

Samarkand was astir with preparations for Jahangir's wedding. Despite her misgivings, Dilshad had stinted nowhere in her plans.

"We can't be niggardly," she said, "even if the Khanzade is a snippet."

I knew that she had let her irritation at the Urganji princess fester while I had been in Shehri-Sebz.

"It's Jahangir's wedding, too," I said, and tweaked her ear. "Anyway, you said that Sevin Bey was beautiful—we must make the wedding elaborate enough to subdue her."

"Subdue her! Oh, Timur, can't you just give her to Jahangir as a slave —so you can kill her if she hurts him? Or—or take her yourself and find another for him?"

That suggestion had cost her a lot.

"It can't be that bad," I said. "I believe you're just jealous of Jahangir —and you know you've nothing to be jealous of where I'm concerned."

"No, I know you could cope with her, and I'm not so sure that he can," she said. I, not being a woman, made no attempt to guess the cause of her worry.

My envoys returned from Herat in a surprisingly short time. They brought even richer gifts than I had sent. And they brought a message from the new ruler saying that he was honored and flattered by my invitation and requesting that I send Saif ad-Din and other respected elder amirs to escort him to Samarkand. Although I distrusted the cordiality, the response pleased Shereza immensely.

In the meantime I sent out squadrons to intercept caravans on all the main routes—the Khorassan Road, the Khitai Route, and the trade lanes to India—and bring choice merchandise to Samarkand, by force if necessary. And I sent a squadron\to Ungut to bring back a hundred of the most beautiful virgins, carefully screened for odors, voices, snoring, and other objectionable characteristics. I spread the word through all channels for merchants to bring their rarest wares of any kind to me. I intended for the gifts distributed at Jahangir's wedding to be the richest that had ever been seen in Tatary.

My call was answered. Jewelers from everywhere brought the finest gems in their collections. Dealers in art and fabrics and armor—everything—trooped into Samarkand and bargained with me and my expert purchasing agents in all kinds of merchandise.

Of course, it was to me that Poulos, the Greek slaver, came with his prize. Knowing him for what he was, I admitted him to my seraglio, for very often the dealers in women preferred to make trades, with some profit, instead of selling their girls outright and being left without merchandise.

With Nubja, who was the shrewdest judge of women I ever saw, and a dozen or so of my less desirable concubines in attendance, I sat on the pleasure divan and received Poulos.

"So you have some slaves for the wedding party?" I said, after Poulos had gone through the elaborate, hypocritical fawning which he considered a suitable greeting.

"No, Amir. I have *one,* one jewel of the West, for you—for you alone —for no lesser man," he said with oglings and smackings and silent handclappings which were supposed to signify the supreme ecstasy.

"Then show her in," I said, chuckling at his antics.

He moved over beside me, stifling me with the heavy sweet musk which he had bathed in, and clapped his hands audibly. A eunuch entered with a girl, heavily veiled and covered by a black stole which hid even her toes.

"Amir, prepare yourself for the most exquisite vision of loveliness that mortal man ever beheld." Poulos closed one oily hand over my shoulder and stroked my arm with the other, to rub his meaning in.

"I'm prepared," I said. "Show your wares."

Again Poulos clapped his hands and barked a command in some foreign tongue which I had never heard. The girl did not move, and he repeated the word. Then he spoke to the eunuch, who snatched the stole off the girl and revealed what seemed to be a life-sized alabaster statue of an houri right out of paradise.

"See, Amir?" said Poulos, and again he pawed my arm and shoulder. "Was I not right?"

The eunuch then took the veil and headdress off the girl; and her hair, as light as sun-ripened millet, fell in large loose curls around her shoulders, over which a deep pink glow had spread when the stole was lifted from them. So astonished was I by the color of her hair that it was a full minute before I could look at her face. Because her eyes were shut tight, I marveled again at the pale shading of her brows and long lustrous lashes before noticing her straight, slightly tilted nose and the clean lines of her soft lips, red from the biting she had given them, presumably in her attempt to hide herself by closing her eyes and mouth as tight as she could.

My eyes lingered on her face until the blush had died except for faint spots of color in her cheeks. Then her shoulders, smooth and white where they showed through the curls in her hair, and her breasts, like ripe pomegranate halves, not dark-tipped like those of the Tatar women, but pointed with a tiny pink rosebud, centered in an areolar patch hardly larger than my thumbnail and no darker than the blush that was fading from her cheeks.

I rose from the divan, and Poulos eagerly grasped my arm to guide me in my circle around the girl. Nubja rose, too, and followed.

"See what I mean," Poulos said. "And a virgin—though a year over twenty. Such could not be in our land."

"Where did you get her?" I asked. I ran my hand over the smooth flesh of her arm and cupped my palm under one of her firm young breasts. She shrank away and clenched her teeth—to hold her eyes closed even tighter, it seemed.

"From a pirate," answered Poulos. "A very old pirate captain who knew he had a fortune in her and allowed no one to molest her. She had two companions with her—on a pilgrimage to Palestine, the captain said —but they were older and bald, and he gave them to his crew."

"She's pretty," I said mildly, though the curves of her slender body were perfection itself, a delight to the eye and a joy to my fingertips as I ran my hands over the gentle flare of her hips and the symmetrical taper

206

of her thighs—and the sheen of her curly blond hair! Pretty—she was beauty itself, as fair as Nubja was dark.

In his eagerness, Poulos was pushing me toward the girl with the puffy bulk of his own obscene body.

Nubja hovered around anxiously.

"Buy the girl and send this man away," she urged.

I finished my inspection and spanked the girl a smart blow on her dimpled buttock, the way I would test the mettle of a filly. She spun around and opened her eyes—and her mouth—for the first time.

She said something. I know not what, for her eyes—wide, round, and angry—were the color of a bright winter sky, a blue so clear and pale that I doubted my own vision, and for a moment had no other sense but sight. I heard nothing, but I read in those eyes what the girl must have said. I smiled and then chuckled in sheer delight; and I saw the fear and hatred fade from the girl's countenance and a strange look of resignation take their place, as she rubbed the red prints of my fingers out of her white flesh.

"What's her name?" I asked.

Poulos said something else in the strange dialect.

"*Icham Levedi Alysoun,*" the girl said softly, but with a certain hauteur.

"*Ikam Levedi Ali Soun,*" I repeated, as accurately as I could. "Quite a mouthful."

"Only *Alysoun*. That's her name," said Poulos. "*Levedi* in her tongue means *Agha.*"

"Ali Soun," I said again. "A pretty name. Ali Soun Agha. How much?"

"Fifty thousand dinars."

"Fifty thousand dinars! I can buy a harem for that."

"Not like her. The most beautiful girl in the world—and a virgin."

"A virgin? Twenty-one years old, captured by pirates, brought overland all the way from Smyrna by a slaver—and still a virgin. Nonsense!"

"It's true, Amir." Poulos pawed me and pressed his hands against my chest to convince me of the truth. "I told you the pirate was old—I bought her from him. I wouldn't touch her. I was apprenticed to a Greek physician in my youth—I was his catamite. What he taught me! I wouldn't touch a woman—bah! It's true, she is a virgin."

"Buy this girl and send this man away," Nubja said again.

"But fifty thousand dinars!"

"She's beautiful," said Poulos. "She's young—but mature. She's a virgin—I swear it. Examine her. If the hymen is not intact, you may cut my tongue out."

Poulos stuck out his long tongue suggestively and lapped it around his fat moist lips.

Nubja pulled me aside impatiently. She looked squarely into my eyes and spoke slowly and distinctly, as though she were teaching a child his words.

"Buy the girl and *send the man away*. A man is for a woman. A woman is for a man. But a man and a man—a woman and a woman—ugh, it makes me sick. Make you sick, too."

Two girls snickered, confirming some doubts I had had about them.

"The girl is a virgin," Nubja continued. "I can tell. And she's worth the price. I've seen others like her in Istanboul. Treat her gently—as gently and carefully as you trained Sasha—and she'll be worth every dinar he asks. *But buy the girl and send this man away—now!*"

"All right," I said, and turned to face Poulos. "Leave the girl here and come with me to my treasury. How do you want your price?"

"In diamonds," he said. "They're lighter than gold, and I have far to travel."

With Poulos well ahead of me and his stench out of my nostrils, I caught a scent of the girl's perfume as I passed—a faint and delicate attar, as clean and flowerlike as the girl herself, as mild and tender as the treatment the white houri invited.

Ali Soun was the finest single item I purchased, and she was certainly not intended to be a gift. But during the months of preparation for the wedding I filled seven rooms in my warehouse with the richest treasures of the world—silks from Khitai, and brocades and satins; polished and uncut jewels from the mines and pearl beds of India, jade and jasper from the streams of Khotan, rubies from frozen Balashan; and the best in porcelain and glass and armor and leather from craftsmen all over Asia. And living gifts—hundreds of fresh young virgins, strings of blooded horses, falcons and eagles and hunting dogs and leopards.

Dilshad chose native and exotic viands to grace the feast tables. Shereza, who looked forward to even more elaborate weddings for her sons, invited merchants from everywhere to suggest and furnish decorations for the palace and grounds. When news came that her brother would be unable to attend the ceremonies but was detaining my elder statesmen at Herat, I merely mentioned his apologies and said nothing of the diplomatic breach. I wanted Jahangir's wedding to be a success—I could attend to my brother-in-law afterwards.

All of the other guests accepted my invitation; and by the first day of Jamada 1 the palace, all hostels and guest houses, and my own pavilions were filled with visiting amirs, and a huge sarai had risen on the plain outside the walls. Brilliant pavilions lined both sides of the Khorassan Road for five miles toward Bokhara, and from that point the road was a carpeted avenue of standards and guidons all the way to the palace entrance.

It was up that extravagant thoroughfare that the Khanzade rode her white camel, with a thousand resplendent horsemen guarding her train of gifts to Jahangir—a dowry second only to the one Shereza Begum had brought to me at the desert sarai of Shah Malik. Since the Urganji women were not veiled, Sevin Bey rode in a curtained litter, and the cheering throngs could not see her; but the splendor of her retinue amply rewarded the watchers on the balconies and housetops of Samarkand.

When the gorgeous procession stopped, with Sevin Bey's white camel kneeling at the foot of the palace steps, the guards saluted me and Jahangir; and eight attendants removed the litter, still curtained, from the camel and carried it into the palace, for Jahangir was not allowed to see his bride until time for the service to be read. Then the princess' gifts were unpacked and put on display in the pavilions erected in the palace gardens for that purpose.

I returned to my own room to receive my future daughter-in-law in private, as was my privilege and duty, before the wedding—a custom dating back to times when a father, presumably more experienced in judging women, lay with a prospective bride to see if she were worthy of his son. Shereza had decorated my room more elaborately for the occasion than I was accustomed to allow, for I personally never cared for rich surroundings in my private rooms—such things are for the vanity of men who see dimly the real treasures of Allah. I did not object, however. The Khanzade had to be impressed.

So I sat in the midst of downy pillows and magnificent tapestries when Sevin Bey's chamberlain escorted her into my presence and left, closing the door behind him. The Khanzade, dressed in a white satin gown and a mantle of green silk embroidered with seed pearls, stood before me and I saw the truth of Kaikosru's description. Her bare arms and throat were of Circassian gold; and her unbound hair, which framed her face and hung far below her shoulders, had the glint of burnished copper. And there were glints of both copper and gold in her eyes, as green as the mantle she wore—because of her eyes, I was sure.

She made no move of obeisance or sound of greeting.

"Welcome, Daughter, to Samarkand," I said, as genially as I could. "The Prince of Samarkand welcomes the Princess of Kharesm into his Royal Household."

"It is an honor to come as your son's bride, Amir," she said, and her voice was low and husky; whether naturally or forced by rage or tension, I could not tell. "I regret that I have no father to present me."

"I, too, sorrow at the Sufi's untimely death," I said sympathetically. "Would that he could have lived to present his daughter with his famed graciousness."

The Khanzade made no further comment—unless the flashing of her eyes was more than the reflection of the afternoon sun on their jade irises.

I rose and spoke to her again.

"I envy my son already," I flattered her kindly—hardly flattery, for her wild beauty was something that I wanted to touch to assure myself of its reality. "Come, let me see what you look like."

"You mean show myself?" she said in a tone of such contempt that had she added "barbarian" she could have cut no deeper.

"No, you little vixen," I said, and slapped her tantalizing face with the back of my hand. I had to touch her—if in anger, then in anger.

She raised her hand, but instead of striking back, she caught my wrist and pressed my hand softly against the cheek I had slapped; and into her eyes came the strangest mixture of tenderness and pain that I ever saw reflected in the eyes of a woman. She shifted her grip on my wrist and curled her small hand inside my cupped palm and drew the back of my fingers across her mouth. Her soft young lips kissed my middle finger just below the carnelian Zain ad-Din had given me—I was tinglingly aware of the exact spot—and she knelt before me to make the acknowledgement which she should have made when she entered my room.

"Father, I shall be a good daughter," she said huskily. "Only be good to my people."

Then, still holding my hand, she rose; and with another surprising motion she suddenly sank her teeth into my finger and scratched the blood out of my wrist with her long fingernails as she flung my hand down and backed away with her eyes flashing fire again.

I snatched my hand to my mouth and sucked at the blood on my finger. Sevin Bey's strange passion passed, but she showed no fear in her countenance.

"You'll be a good daughter," I said, and smiled at her. "And I a good father. We'll get along. Welcome to my household."

I dismissed her and watched her join her attendants in the hall. She would mother a fiery brood who should ripen into a ring of fury to guard my old age.

In the mellow days of the winefeast the memory of my marriage to Aljai blended with the ceremonies in honor of my son so completely that I could not sift the real from the dream. Every day I emptied a room in my warehouse of its precious contents and bestowed fortunes on my amirs.

For general entertainment I had the naked body of Kaikosru, who had deserted me before Khiva, tied on the back of an ass—facing backward—and the animal led through the streets every day. When everyone in Samarkand knew who Kaikosru was and what he had done, I had his arms tied to one team of mules and his feet to another—with some hundred paces of rope—and the teams driven at full speed in opposite directions. This spectacle provided the climax to outside entertainment as well as a warning to future deserters.

Inside the banquet halls the gentler diversions never ceased. A new bevy of lovely gift virgins walked among the guests each evening, scattering jewels and serving dainties, none of which were more delectable than the girls' trim naked bodies as they caught the soft lights of lamps and candles. The festivities grew, and my pleasant confusion increased up to the moment when Jahangir lifted Sevin Bey to the back of his white stallion and escorted her to her bridal bed in the marriage pavilion erected in a far corner of the garden. She might have been Aljai, and I—

As soon as I reached the seraglio, I summoned Nubja, in whose care I had left Ali Soun.

"Where is Ali Soun Agha?" I asked, intending to claim my own wedding gift.

"I've given her a private room. She's not like the others, Amir."

"Take me to her," I ordered.

"Now?" Nubja obviously objected. "She's not ready. Don't spoil your pleasure."

"Take me to her!" I repeated, and shook my head to clear away the wine fumes. I wanted to be sober when I first had Ali Soun.

Nubja led me to a room far away from the pleasure chamber. She cautioned me to be quiet, and silently opened the door.

Ali Soun lay on a couch asleep, her fair hair and white skin lighted by a solitary candle above her head.

"Not now, Amir, please. For your own sake," Nubja whispered.

I hesitated and looked at the sleeping virgin—and at her room, filled not with gew-gaws like those of the other girls, but with paper, of all things. I looked at Nubja, who had been following my gaze.

"I told her she could have anything she wanted. The paper is the most wonderful to her—it is very rare in her country, she said."

"What does she do with it?"

"Look," Nubja said, and handed me a neat bundle of sheets covered with a strange script. The paper smelled of Ali Soun's faint perfume.

"She can write," Nubja said with utmost respect, "and she's learning your language very rapidly. But she's writing everything she can remember in her own, every word she knows, so she won't forget her homeland."

I put the paper down and looked back at the sleeping figure.

"She can draw, too," Nubja said quickly, to distract my attention again. "Here."

She handed me a sheaf of larger sheets.

"Ali Soun is drawing a picture of every house in her village, so she won't forget. So she can walk up the street to her own palace—see, this is it—when she gets homesick."

The drawings were clear and firm, of queer little houses with pointed roofs and square smokestacks, and a large one with a conical turret and many sharp-angled covers over the windows.

"Treat her gently, Amir. When she gets over her homesickness she'll love you—she'll repay every dinar. But not now, Amir. Come with me."

My eyes devoured the body on the couch. Although only the soft shoulders and one rounded breast showed above the covers, I could make out every curve under the silken sheet, and my memory supplied texture and coloring. While my mind was still saturated with the vision, I went with Nubja to the big divan, for in Nubja I could find all women —even Ali Soun—and then forget all save Nubja herself.

CHAPTER

9

Simultaneously with the wedding, I installed Jahangir as permanent commander of the Gok Hazara and added other youthful squadrons to form a regiment. Then I established Jahangir as Amir of Shehri-Sebz, our traditional family seat, with his regiment garrisoned there. At the same time I speeded up the rebuilding of Urganj, which I hoped to have completely restored by the time Jahangir acquired enough administrative experience to take over the reins of government in the province.

As for my own activity, I settled down at Samarkand to consolidate further my empire during the winter months and to locate the weaknesses in my defenses before spring brought campaign problems to the fore. Word came from Herat that my envoys were treated royally.

My colony of scholars had grown to remarkable proportions, and the academies had begun to attract students from as far away as Baghdad, Cairo, Delhi, Moskva, and a few of the principal cities of Khitai. And with my encouragement, holy men of all religions set up churches in various quarters of Samarkand. Taoists, Buddhists, Confucianists, Jews, Manichaeans, Nestorian Christians, and a dozen minor sects worshiped in their hovels, or in modest churches endowed by my treasury, with no fear of intervention from my government officials—although there was some pressure from Zain ad-Din and other leading Mohammedans until I assured them that Allah would ultimately show the fallacies in infidel religions and win glory for the True Church thereby. I quoted the ninth ayah of the sixth sura of the Koran to Zain ad-Din: *"Say Allah, then leave them to amuse themselves in their vain discourse."*

The stories of my prophecy concerning the plague on the Jats' horses and the curse I had brought down on the Sufi marked me as an authority, and so my words were heeded—such is the origin of all prophets. Sages are built by coincidence in all religions, and I was simply able to produce the coincidences contributing to my own rise. Two special cases were sufficient, although I produced minor proofs whenever the occasion demanded. Of course, religious friction continued—it is inherent in the Way, and I secretly fostered some dissension to prevent any sect from becoming too powerful—but I showed ample evidence of tolerance and granted audience to any holy man and talked to him of God in my own liberal sense of the word.

Occasionally I held large gatherings of scholars and priests of all races and creeds. By listening to their disputes, I was able to pick out the weaknesses in every belief and to mark what profit I might gain from them when I should meet followers of those creeds en masse and confound them by the errors they had made in interpreting the Way. Ordinarily my respectful attention impressed the voluble egotists. They did not come to listen, but to wait impatiently their turn to speak and to spit out their mistaken mouthfuls. My silence convinced them that I was the wisest of all, because I listened without challenging.

Only one, Tsung-Li, shared my silence and looked at me instead of the smug oracles who spoke to the circle. One night I asked him to stay behind after the others had left.

"Tsung-Li, Master," I said. "You're quiet in the forum. Do you wish to talk to me alone?"

"You, too, are quiet, Amir," he said with an understanding twinkle in his eye.

"I listen to the wise ones."

"And the foolish ones also."

"I'm a warrior, Master. Perhaps I have no voice among wise men."

"You're a warrior—and a wise man," Tsung-Li said, almost sorrowfully. "In my country there's a maxim, 'Know your own side—know the other side—and in a hundred battles you will win a hundred victories.' So does a warrior value knowledge."

I smiled at the old scholar's perspicacity, but inwardly I was balancing

Tsung-Li's usefulness to me against the danger inherent in a truly wise man.

"Then you doubt the sincerity of my search for truth?" I asked.

"Not at all. But rather your motives," he said frankly. "Will you recognize truth, Amir? What is truth?"

"Truth is what men believe—what men live by, and die for." I saw no reason for fencing with Tsung-Li. "And men believe what they are told."

I stared at the old man intently as he studied me. His eyes twinkled again.

"By whom?" he asked at length.

"By authority. They ask no basis for authority beyond the authority itself, like your maxim or the motto on my shield, *Rasti Rousti*—'Might is right.' A slogan, a proverb, or a little rhyme is self-evident."

"There are authorities on every hand—surely you're not going to let your people try to follow all the babble that goes on in your academies. I've not misjudged you, I'm sure."

"No. I shall define the truth as I want to. Already the Church heeds my voice. The scholars are convinced of my wisdom, because I listen to their bloated vanities. When I speak, I'll speak briefly and positively in words that will be repeated in every academy and church and palace and street in Asia, in the world. I'll tell men what the truth is and they'll believe and live for me—and die for me."

"The simple men, perhaps."

"Most men are simple. Your own people live by the silly clichés of Confucius, though I notice you use them sparingly. Why are you in Samarkand?"

"You guessed it, Amir," Tsung-Li said sadly. "Fleeing from adages. I heard of you and your haven for philosophers. I had hopes that Samarkand might be the cradle of a new enlightenment."

I chuckled.

"Yes," he went on, "your fame as a patron is spreading. And your new Truth will probably follow your new clichés, if that's not a contradiction of terms."

"You realize, Tsung-Li, that you will never go back—or farther on. You may have had no trouble crossing the great wall of Khitai; but should you try to leave Samarkand, you'll find that every door has a curtain of iron."

"I would never have spoken as I did, if I had not realized that, Amir. I'm old—I've lost faith in the creeds. I shall not try to leave Samarkand. I shall stay to see how you pervert learning. Your forebears, Genghis and

Kublai, took the science of my people—the magnet, the lens, the fire powder—and turned it into channels of viciousness. That is your genius —the genius of your race—to pervert the good things of others. I'll see what you do, if I live." His eyes still twinkled, as Allah's must twinkle at the destruction of man.

"You'll live," I said. "I think I'll enjoy having you around. But I'll see that you're looked upon as a doddering old fool."

"I *am* a doddering old fool."

"So men will believe. I'll see to that, but I'll never believe it myself; that will be the safeguard I need. I shall convince my followers that all men are stupid, even themselves, and while they dwell on stupidities, I shall see clearly the cleverness they overlook. Can I do that, Wise Man?"

"Perhaps. But why?"

"Why? That's the most foolish question of all. I'll give an answer to every man's *why*. But my own? I need give none. You're old and wise. Do you know why?"

"No," said Tsung-Li, and the twinkle faded from his eyes. "I've spent my life asking *why*."

"Then you know there's no reason in the world."

"Not in your world."

"And I live in my world. So do you, scholar. Have you tried to live without reasons or without reason? That may be the Way."

"Without reason, perhaps. But not without reasons. You have your reasons, Amir. I shall try to find them, even though you deny them."

"By all means, do. You are welcome to remain in Samarkand. You shall be the measure by which I judge my most astute adversaries."

"You are flattering, Amir," said Tsung-Li, as I dismissed him—so wise, so impotent.

Yet the old man's maxim—"know the other side"—brought back to my memory the papers I had found in Ali Soun's room. So far she had been my only contact with the Franks—although she insisted that she was from *Engloland,* called in our tongue *Inglistan,* an island beyond the land of the Franks. She was my only source of information about the pale people of the West, and I had learned nothing of their customs from her except the strange attitude of their women.

Following Nubja's suggestion I had treated Ali Soun as though she were a visiting princess. And I had dispelled the girl's fears, but at the same time I seemed to have given Ali Soun the impression that I would continue to respect her virginity. Furthermore, she seemed to accept my tolerant attitude as her due. I had no doubt that she understood what my purchase of her had implied, but her growing friendliness toward me seemed to be based on a belief that despite the high price I had paid for her I was going to accept the absurd ideas of her people regarding wives and concubines.

With her rapid progress in my language, under the tutorship of Nubja, Ali Soun was beginning to understand me and to make herself understood; but all I could gather from her conversation was that she was extremely homesick and that a man as generous as I—I had offered her anything she wanted—would ultimately return her to her homeland. I did not discourage her, for I thought perhaps I might take her back, when I myself conquered the Franks and invaded her beloved *Engloland*.

But as I mused over Tsung-Li's statement, I saw a way to make use of Ali Soun to ease the way to conquering her people, and perhaps win her favor before the far distant day when I should move against the Franks. Not that I had ever intended to delay claiming my prize for very long. I could of course take the girl by force any time I wanted to, but I valued Nubja's judgment, and I realized that what I could take from Ali Soun by force would hardly be worth fifty thousand dinars. Besides, the game I was playing offered a challenge new to me. I had never had to win a woman by courtship before.

So, after Tsung-Li had left, I went to the suite I had given to Ali Soun. I found the girl busy with her papers as usual.

"Do come in, Amir," she invited pleasantly.

"Thank you," I said, finding my remark as absurd as the clothes Ali Soun wore. Not since Jahangir's wedding night had I seen more than the face and arms of her lovely body—and she saw nothing odd in keeping her clothes on whenever I called on her.

"And what are you doing tonight?" I asked. "Writing or drawing?"

"Drawing, Amir," she said with a frown.

"Isn't it going well?"

"No, Amir. Look."

She led me to the little desk I had had fashioned for her and showed me a picture of a street. Her work was not good.

"I can draw one house—one house—and one house—"

I looked at her and saw her puzzled expression as she searched for the word she wanted.

"*Each* house," I said.

"I can draw *each* house," she said, and smiled gratefully. "But I can't draw a street of houses. I want to see a street of houses."

So pleased had I been by the beauty which gratitude brought into her face that I was distinctly annoyed to see sadness replacing it.

"You do draw each house remarkably well," I said. "You have observant eyes. Do you know how these houses are built?"

216

"Yes—no. When I was a little girl I often watched the—"

"*Carpenters,*" I supplied.

"—carpenters building houses in our village, and I played in the—started houses." She laughed at her own language difficulties, and then saddened again at her childhood memories.

"If you saw men building houses like these, could you show them or tell them what they were doing wrong?"

"I—I think so," she said, wrinkling her brow.

I took a pile of her drawings and sat down beside her on a wooden bench, which she had chosen instead of a divan for her room. She sat at some distance from me, but her mild perfume was wafted my way. All I had to do was simply to overrule her objections and take her to bed.

"Suppose we found a piece of land sort of like the land in your village of—" I hesitated for her to supply the name.

"Devon," she said.

"—Devon, and I put a thousand men to work. In a few months they could build a street like this—if you supervised them."

Ali Soun said nothing. In light of her drawings, I felt that she was competent to direct the artisans.

"Would you like that?" I asked.

"Don't tease me, Amir," she said, and dabbed at her eyes with a scarf.

"I'm not teasing. I'll do it if you wish."

She looked into my eyes searchingly.

"You will? You're not being cruel? I've heard— No! You're not. You *will* build Devon! You *mean* it!" Her whole being sparkled.

"Certainly, I will."

"Then I won't be going home for a long time," she said, and her blue eyes clouded. "But you *will* build my village?"

"I said that you could have anything you wanted—Devon, house by house, furniture as you want it, even people—the lightest-skinned ones in Samarkand—to dress your way and be your neighbors."

"And a church?" she asked more eagerly.

"Yes. There's a colony of Christians—Nestorians—here. I'll build your church for them."

"I've drawn the church."

Ali Soun rose and rummaged through a stack of papers for her drawing. When she found it, she brought it to me and sat down beside me, unconsciously touching my body for the first time. Eagerly she held the paper before me and pointed out the details of the building. I was conscious of every movement of her arm where it rubbed against mine, and of the scent of her hair, and of the length of her thigh pressed against my own.

I encouraged Ali Soun to go over other drawings with me and reveled in her nearness as she forgot herself and talked excitedly of Devon. Finally, when I feared my ability to control myself, I rose.

"Tomorrow we will find the site," I said. "And I'll let skilled architects start working over your drawings."

"You won't forget? You do mean it? Tomorrow?" she asked, tears welling up in her eyes.

"No, I won't forget."

"Good night," she said, and kissed my hand in the manner of my concubines.

"Good night."

I left her rather austere apartment and went into the luxurious, heavily scented seraglio.

The next morning I had horses brought to a side door and sent Lot to bring Ali Soun. She appeared in a moment, so radiant that she gave light and color to the black hooded stole which she wore. And in spite of her cumbersome western clothes she rode gracefully and expertly beside me out of the palace gardens. I led the way to the parade ground when I saw how well she rode. There I spurred Ak Ruksh into a gallop, and Ali Soun urged her mount to keep pace. The hood fell from her head, and her long millet hair blew behind her, catching the morning sunlight in a hundred golden curls. And her cheeks, fanned by the cold winter wind, colored to the shade of the blush they had held when I first saw her.

I pulled Ak Ruksh up suddenly and let the girl pass me. She, too, reined up. I marveled at the clean white scalp which showed in little lines where the wind parted her hair as she stopped in front of me. I marveled, too, at the clear trill of her laughter when she almost lost her seat in the saddle. For the first time she seemed like a companion, conscious of me as a person and pleased to be with me.

"This air feels good," she said, and I suddenly remembered that she had not been out of the zenana before. The other girls seemed to be content inside, and not to be trusted outside.

"We must ride more often," I said.

"Yes, we must." And that was the first time she had used *we*.

"But this is not like Devon," I said.

"No, there was a little hill in Devon."

There was sadness but an eagerness also in her voice.

"I think I know a place," I said.

We rode back to the walls of the palace gardens and around the corner to a fairly level plot adjacent to the wall—I had no intention of building Devon far from the palace.

"How is this?" I asked.

"I don't know," she answered, somewhat crestfallen. "Those houses— and there are no mountains near Devon, just the little hill."

"The houses will come down. We can't get away from the mountains. Maybe we can hide them with trees."

"Yes—maybe. There was a park around my father's castle. I couldn't see anything but trees from my window."

"Then, we'll make it do."

"I guess—yes—it'll do," she said.

We rode over the site, quarter by quarter.

"The castle about here," said Ali Soun. "And the stables—and the street to the village—that way."

She pointed toward the garden wall, and I saw where the gate would be and felt relieved that her plans fit so well into mine.

"All right, now for the architects," I said, and we rode back to the palace.

Already there were a number of excellent draftsmen and architects in Samarkand, and through them I located two more who had been as far west as Istanbul and had some idea of the architecture of the Franks. I set the best draftsmen to work refining Ali Soun's sketches; and when the more widely traveled men arrived from Bokhara, I gave instructions to them to go over details of construction with Ali Soun.

"The details and methods of building are not so important, Amir," said one of them, after he had seen finished drawings which Ali Soun had approved as being exactly what she wanted. "The agha has a fine eye for the façades. We can make her village look the way she wants it without much more to go on."

"I want the buildings as nearly like the originals as you can make them," I said.

"I know something of the architecture, all right, but the details—"

"Ask the agha. She will be available. I want her to inspect everything— thickness of walls—everything."

"Yes, Amir. So it shall be."

"Spare no expense. I want the village exact," I said, and sent the man back to his drawing room.

"You're doing a lot for this girl," observed Daoud, who had heard the conversation. "As much as you've done for the Sarai Khanum or the Begum. Can it be that she's conquering the Prince of Samarkand?"

He grinned broadly and winked at Khitai, who was also in attendance.

"He's building her a fortress. Maybe he'll take refuge there when enemies storm the walls of this palace," Khitai joined in. "From the drawing, that little castle looks formidable."

"That's what I intend to find out," I said. "Just how formidable. If I ever march against the Franks, I want to know what to expect."

"Now you make sense," said Daoud, an expression of appreciation dawning on his countenance. "A Frank village and fortress right here in your backyard!"

"Yes," I said. "And a battalion of youngsters growing up in its streets, as familiar with the quaint Frank buildings as with the yurts of the Mongols or the pavilions of the Persians."

"When do we attack the Franks?" asked Khitai jokingly.

"Maybe ten years—maybe twenty—maybe never. But if we do— Daoud, scout around the armorers' and collect all the Frank mail and weapons that have found their way here. Order more from Damascus or Istanboul—anywhere that the infidels fought. Just in case—"

"I believe he means it," said Khitai.

"Sure, he means it," said Daoud. "Come on. Let's do some scavenging. I think he wants the armor right now."

The two of them laughed at the joke and left my chambers. Daoud, however, did give orders to pick up any relics from the Crusades that might be found in my realm and asked merchants to find what they could at the western end of their routes.

I spent much time poring over plans with Ali Soun—it was my only chance to be near her on her terms—and together we supervised the building of Devon, which proceeded steadily if somewhat slowly during the winter months. Nubja approved my methods of courtship and assured me that one day I would win a prize worth all the expense and trouble. She, of course, saw no other purpose in the village rising outside the garden walls.

Dilshad and Shereza were not so enthusiastic. They thought that I was doing too much for a captive agha—they never doubted her noble blood but still considered her as any other slave girl. I made it up to them, however. By a few favors to Miran Shah, I won Shereza over; and since I never relaxed my attentions to Dilshad, I had only to spend a little more time with her and Shah Rukh, who was a fine lovable little fellow, to convince her that she would always be my favorite. I would have told her my real purpose in building Devon, but I was afraid she might confide in someone else who would get the word to Ali Soun.

The architects and carpenters and masons, after a few preliminary brushes with Ali Soun, learned to respect her and to correct any flaws she saw or imagined in their work. The strangest part of it all was the matter-of-fact way in which all of them accepted the freedom of movement and action I allowed my agha from Inglistan. Not one of them questioned her right to spend hours at the project without guards or companions, or to

220

roam Samarkand at will with only a groom or one of my officers with her. Soon her black stole and white horse were familiar sights around the bazaars, and only when her fair hair was briefly exposed did she arouse undue curiosity. I sometimes wondered what it would be like when summer came and she rode bareheaded, as I was sure she would.

I was denied the privilege of seeing the initial effect of her golden hair on Samarkand, however. Before the first thaw, Saif ad-Din and Jaku and Mangali Boga returned from Herat with a message.

"Ghiath ad-Din, Shah of Herat, Sultan of the Afghans, Protector of the Faith, bids me call you brother—" and so on, through an elaborate greeting and a series of promises to attend the Council of the New Year and to bring presents beyond those ever before exchanged between brothers.

Saif ad-Din then proceeded to extol the marvels of Herat—two hundred and fifty thousand people, ten thousand bazaars, three thousand public baths, hundreds of academies and medresses, wheels driven by the wind instead of water to grind the grain and draw water out of the ground—and the tall new wall that Ghiath was building.

Jaku and Mangali Boga had sat in respectful silence while the voluble old man ran on and on. At mention of the new wall, I looked their way, and they both nodded soberly. When Saif ad-Din had finished, I dismissed him, but kept the other two.

"Then he's not coming?" I asked.

"I don't think so," said Jaku. "I believe you have a fight on your hands, boy."

I looked at Mangali Boga.

"Too polite," he said. "Treated us too well. We let Saif ad-Din do the talking. We listened. I agree with Jaku. Ghiath ad-Din is stalling until he gets his wall finished."

"When will that be?"

"Before New Year's."

"I'll have to visit him before then," I said. "What will it take?"

"All you can raise," said Jaku. "Forty thousand—fifty thousand. More if you wait too long. He thinks we believed him—Saif did—but he'll be ready by New Year's Day, when he knows he can stall no longer."

"The sooner the better, I suppose," I said, not without a thrill at the prospect.

"The sooner the better," Jaku agreed, and Mangali Boga nodded.

So it was that I sent orders to all my amirs to assemble at Shehri-Sebz before the first thaw made the roads and trails impassable. After giving Daoud instructions to co-operate with Ali Soun in the building of Devon, and orders for the governing of Samarkand, I assembled my own division and moved to the plain in my valley.

I found Jahangir's garrison in good condition and eager to join the older regiments on a campaign into the desert. Even with horsehide khalats and fur caps replacing their bright blue capes and helmets, the young soldiers of the Gok Hazara made a handsome showing in the review staged in my honor on the day of my arrival. And Jahangir's burnished copper nakaras and long kourrouns played their martial music with such youthful brilliance that the veterans among my own elite kulchis ceased their scoffing at the young upstarts and broke into cheers and shouts as Jahangir's own hazara passed the reviewing stand. It was only natural that pride welled up in my breast at the compliments which old soldiers paid my son.

Jahangir himself, however, seemed to have worked too hard in his new office, for he was thinner than when I had last seen him, and there was a sort of feverishness in his attention to detail. Nor were there any signs of relaxation during his hours of leisure. I noted the same tension and meticulous regard for the niceties of behavior when I attended the feast he gave in my honor.

In the familiar banquet hall, surrounded by the furniture and appointments which I myself had bought, I should have felt at home and dropped into a nostalgic reverie as the heady wines took effect. But I did not. An air of strangeness pervaded the whole of my own family palace. Even Jahangir's gentle attentions to Sevin Bey, who was radiantly beautiful at her place beside my son, seemed too careful, as though they were tendered shamefully. When Jahangir looked at his wife, there was no doubt of his affection for her; but an unsteadiness in his glance, an indefinable uneasiness, suggested that his love was restrained by fear—by an unwillingness to express itself, as though it carried pain with it.

The Khanzade showed her own feelings with more clarity. Her green eyes reveled in a glow of possessive pride whenever they rested on Jahangir, and her hands were equally sure of their grasp. She took every occasion to clutch Jahangir's arm or to squeeze his hand between her own—as she had once squeezed mine—and I saw Jahangir wince and then smile indulgently at his wife when she sometimes gripped him too tight. The two were in love—of that I was sure—but their affection charged the air with something strange.

I puzzled over the perplexing behavior of the lovers throughout the meal. As course after course of rich food passed over my service table, I became more and more engrossed in my host and hostess, and then in Sevin Bey alone. The play of the candlelight on her golden skin and burnt-gold hair fascinated me and at the same time enraged me. I wanted to tousle her hair, to bruise the soft texture of her arms and shoulders, to slap her to break the spell she cast over my son—and over me.

I hardly realized that the meal was over before Jahangir and Sevin Bey drew me aside to bid me good night.

"Shall we tell him now?" the Khanzade asked of Jahangir.

"I waited to give you the honor."

Sevin Bey turned to me and flashed her eyes—shot through and through with flecks of copper and gold.

"I'm being a good daughter, as I promised," she said with as much charm as Jahangir ever mustered. "Guess what I have here, Father Timur?"

She put one golden hand on her stomach.

"A fine feast," I teased.

"No!" She pouted prettily. "A grandson, I'm sure."

"Then you are a dutiful daughter," I said. "Congratulations, Son. And I won't accept a girl," I added playfully to Sevin Bey.

"Not even one like me?" Her eyes were level and solid green. "You fought hard for me."

"Not even like you." I smiled, but I grasped the hilt of my talwar to keep from striking the beautiful vixen.

"It'll be a boy," said Jahangir reassuringly, although his own countenance begged for assurance—of something.

The Khanzade knelt and kissed my hand with as much obeisance as Nubja showed me, and released it, with no memory of its knuckles, it seemed.

Jahangir led me down the hall toward the front door of the palace. He paused before an outer room.

"Will you see Aisha and Tahmineh?" he asked.

"Surely, Son. I'd like to."

"This way." He opened the door to the dimly lit room, and two shadowy figures approached. Silently they knelt before me and kissed my hand—first Aisha and then Tahmineh; and as they raised their eyes, I saw in them the expression which my own must have held. We all feared for Jahangir.

CHAPTER

10

For two months troops poured into Shehri-Sebz from every quarter of my empire. Ultimately they numbered fifty thousand; and I organized them into five divisions. I myself commanded the division composed of my personal followers and Jahangir's regiment. Omar Sheik served with his uncle, Sheik Ali, and Miran Shah took over a squadron in Khitai's division. All in all I considered my army well commanded when I finally led the long column through the Iron Gate, across the river, and out into the desert toward Herat. After a brief inspection of Balkh, which was being completely rebuilt for the first time since its destruction by Genghis Khan, I left the main trade routes and headed across the uncharted sand.

Well provisioned and amply staffed with slaves and menials, including several thousand women, my army traveled slowly and comfortably across the wasteland. My outriders always found water before our supply was exhausted; and but for a three-day sandstorm, our progress was uninterrupted. After weeks, during which we saw no signs of other travelers, not even camel dung for our fires, we finally came upon a small straggling caravan. We forced the leader to turn aside and lead us to the nearest pastureland, and then—after we had rested and refreshed our horses—to guide us to one of Ghiath ad-Din's armed outposts hardly a day's journey from Herat.

During the night my army ringed the city completely; and when the trumpets of Fushanj sounded reveille, the city awoke to look out upon a wall of armed might on every side. I could have attacked at once, but the descriptions of Herat given me by Shereza Begum and Sheik Ali and my own sons and envoys, as well as the love Shereza bore for the city, aroused in me a desire to take it without damaging it unduly, and I thought up a plan of attack on Fushanj which might bring Ghiath ad-Din to terms without my laying siege to Herat.

Turning as usual to my observations of the Way of Allah, I remembered the warnings He gives to bode disaster—the autumn colors presaging winter, the dark clouds and yellow lightning heralding a tornado, the fiery red sunset preceding a sandstorm—phenomena which strike terror into men. And I held my army in camp several hundred paces distant from the walls.

I had my own squadron tents of pure white pitched nearer the city and the men themselves dressed in white uniforms and mounted on white horses. At sunrise my music, and the music of all the assembled squadrons, began sounding gay melodies associated with feasts and happy ceremonies. Then I led my squadron in a procession around the city. White-clad heralds rode within shouting distance of the walls and spoke through voice trumpets to the people.

"Open your gates and welcome Timur, Prince of Samarkand. Surrender today and no harm will come to anyone."

All day the music continued; and once each hour my white squadron rode around the city, and my heralds repeated the invitation. At first there was much activity on the walls. Archers shot arrows, which fell short of my men. Women and children climbed the turrets to stare. But no one answered my message, and my own army made no move whatever.

The music continued during the night; and covered by the thunder of drums, my engineers and sappers began tunneling under the city walls, preparatory to mining and shoring. On the second day, my white tents had been replaced with flaming red ones decorated with gold cords and my own golden eagle standards—colors to suggest the blood and fire of battle. My squadron was similarly uniformed and mounted on horses caparisoned in the same red and gold. And, with a golden eagle perched on my shoulder, I again led the procession around the city, to the accompaniment of martial music played on all sides by trumpets and drums.

The heralds shouted, "Surrender today and only the officers and men of your garrison will be killed—no one else will suffer. So promises Timur, Prince of Samarkand."

All day we kept up the warnings, but still there was no reply. Secretly I hoped there would be none, and at dark I was glad to give my engineers instructions to complete the job of mining the walls and leaving them resting on timbers instead of the subsoil they had been built upon. So far it seemed that the drums had drowned out the muffled digging of my men and no one inside the city had suspected what was going on.

The third day marked my last gracious offer to the besieged. Dressed in black hooded stoles and mounted on black horses, my squadron rode out of the new black tents and started their progress. Again I led the column; and for additional effect, I brought out my pair of black leopards, and they tugged at their leashes well in advance of my horse. Occasionally one of the leopards added her snarl to the funereal music of the kourrouns and nakaras—dead marches and dirges portending the limits of my mercy.

"Timur, Prince of Samarkand, has decreed death to every man in Fushanj. Surrender today—tomorrow no woman or child will be spared. Death to all of Fushanj when the sun goes down today."

Whether the fools inside the walls believed my message or thought they could withstand siege, I had no way of knowing; but by refusing to surrender they were playing into my hands. And they showed no signs of responding in any way whatever. The deserted walls and the soundless city gave the impression that death had already settled over them when the sun finally sank into the sand.

At sunset I ordered the music stopped, since the mining and shoring of the walls was complete; and the quiet seemed as insistently oppressive as the drums had been for the last three days and nights. When my army, worn by the continuous noise, finally slept, the only sounds I could hear

225

were those of our animals and an occasional hysterical cry from inside the walls.

I sat before my pavilion and watched the full moon shine on the city. By its bright light I could see shadows moving on the walls—guards expecting a night attack, mechanics readying siege engines, and masons reinforcing weak points in the defenses. Still there were no sounds except the night noises of a sleeping city and a sleeping camp. About midnight I, too, retired for a nap before beginning my assault.

When Abdullah awoke me some four hours later, the moon had set and the night was black except for the stars twinkling through the clear desert air. I dressed and sent runners to give final instructions to other elements in my army. I myself made a round of the tunnel entrances to see that the engineers had everything in readiness—the shoring timbers soaked in naptha, and flint and tinder with which to fire them.

My inspection completed, I returned to my command post and ordered an archer to shoot a flaming arrow in a high arc toward the city. Almost immediately I saw the dull glow of the fires lighted under the mined walls where the engineers had opened the tunnels to provide ventilation. Simultaneously squadron leaders all around the city lighted flares, and the circle started in without audible signal of any kind.

A clamor arose inside the city, however. There were screams and shouts and the clanking of armor as the defenders clambered to their places on the walls. Intent on the closing ring of flares, the Fushanji soldiers seemed not to notice the fire under the walls until smoke rolled up to the parapets. Then there was a sudden wild scramble for water—but too late. As the dawn grew rapidly lighter and the sun rose suddenly out of the desert, the shoring timbers blazed and crackled and gave way; and great, gaping holes opened up in the crumbling walls.

With a terrifying battle-shriek my bridging crews raced forward to span the moat, and hordes of foot soldiers streamed across into hand-to-hand combat with the defending garrison. In a matter of minutes all four gates opened and drawbridges came down. Then ten thousand cavalrymen rode screaming into the city, cutting down soldiers and civilians alike until the streets were littered with dead and not a man was to be seen alive except those fighting under my standards.

With the streets cleared of defenders, I set my men to cleaning out the houses, with instructions to bring me the first cowardly noble found alive. By mid-morning I had my man, one Sheik Muraid, and his four tavachis, found cowering in a cellar. I took him and his staff to the highest tower on the arak and let them watch the systematic looting of the city.

My soldiers, too long cooped up in a relatively peaceful Tatary, took everything of value out of the city and carted it away to my camp. They killed every male and all females under ten and over fifty years of age. The rest of the women they herded into the registan, pausing now and then to rape a particularly likely-looking wench before turning her into the compound.

By late afternoon most of the corpses had been dumped into the moat and buried under sand and rubble as my engineers finished demolishing the walls; and as it grew dark the registan, lighted by flares, took on the appearance of any city square on a festival night. With the cobbles covered by rugs and the stores of wines and meats prepared for a victory feast, it was hard to realize that the rest of the city was empty and dead.

My amirs and ranking officers took over the registan for the first part of the night. When the captive women and girls were stripped, the less desirable ones were sent on to the common soldiers, and the nobles began their feast. After a few objecting beauties had been disemboweled in the presence of all the others, there was no more trouble in getting the women to dance before the campfires and sing their native songs to my officers. Such of those as could not perform were taken over by men who cared little for musical entertainment.

The victory feast grew more and more boisterous as the hours passed. Some of the women dropped from fatigue. The little girls ten to fourteen grew sleepy on the free-flowing wine, and one by one the nobles disappeared with their choices for the evening.

I was taken by a particularly buxom young Persian girl, one who smiled as she served me and seemed not so sorrowful as most of the others, although she did not dance or sing. Her movements as she served me shashlyk and wine were as graceful as those of the dancers, however; and even in the heat and sweat of the packed registan she smelled clean and sweet. And, though it might have been the wine, her body gave the illusion of a plum ripe unto bursting. Her skin, drawn taut over her plump breasts and smooth thighs and buttocks, seemed to be restraining a force in her flesh which would break through and pour out at the smallest puncture.

By repeatedly brushing her breasts against my face as she bent over to serve me, and taking occasion to rub against me when she turned or stooped to get more wine, she plainly told me that having her would not be rape in any sense. But unlike most of my men, I did not find that rape added zest to the experience; so I let her continue to serve me and when the time came to end the party and turn the women over to the common soldiers, I took my maidservant back to my pavilion with me.

To an even greater extent than I had expected, the girl's eagerness lived up to the promise of the vitality in her body. She was ready immediately, and six times she shuddered and sobbed in ecstasy before I had my first satisfaction in her.

"Shashlyk," I said to her, when she relaxed and lay back on her pillow.

"Shashlyk?" she repeated in a puzzled voice, and then giggled contentedly when she grasped my meaning—six tasty morsels on one skewer.

Nor did her quick hunger abate during the long hours before dawn. I felt that I had somehow robbed her by not giving her to the soldiers; and it was with some regret that I returned her to the registan the next morning to be beheaded with the other women—but I could not let personal feelings interfere with military necessity.

After the execution of the women, my men set fire to the entire city, and all day long we waited impatiently for the buildings to fall. Demolition crews worked wherever possible; but night found many glowing embers, and it was still another day before the city was leveled. To make the destruction complete, my mechanics built huge plows and drags of heavy timbers and with forty- and fifty-mule teams heaped sand over the site, so that by the end of a week not a thing was left of Fushanj except a large sand dune.

I had forced Sheik Muraid to watch every detail of the sacking of the city; and while the vision was fresh in his mind, I had his eyes put out and sent him to Herat. I allowed his own tavachis to escort him and corroborate his story to Ghiath ad-Din. A few hours later my army followed, and the next day's sun rose on an armored ring deployed around the unfinished walls of Herat.

The city itself was beautiful, more beautiful than Samarkand in those days—buildings of sky-blue tile joined with gold mortar, white and gilded domes, gaily striped towers and minarets, and the many-colored windmills turning gently in the morning breeze. And the new wall, though incomplete and ineffective, was a work of art, with gates of rich inlay already hung on the four entrances to the city.

I was sure that all the eyes of my army were on the city rather than on me as I led my white-clad kulchis in the first parade around the city. Even my music was late on its cue; but after a brief delay, the kourrouns and kettledrums struck up gay melodies, and my heralds shouted their first day's warning.

Ghiath ad-Din was, of course, not surprised. His battlements were well manned, and it seemed that the defenders laughed at my effrontery. Herat *was* a big city, two hundred and fifty thousand people; and it had been well defended, and no doubt I was known as the Begum's somewhat ineffectual husband—such was Ghiath's contempt for the Tatars. At any rate my first circuit of the walls brought no response other than raillery.

An hour later, however, when I rode forth again, the north gate opened and a regiment of bright-turbaned Persians raced out to intercept my squadron. I did not even break formation; and when both Sheik Ali and Nur ad-Din led full divisions to cut off my attackers, the Persian horsemen turned without shooting an arrow and rushed back more rapidly than they had come—all except a hundred or so who fell before Nur ad-Din's fast-riding Urganji troops.

I continued my progress uninterrupted. Three more times I rode around the city. There were no more jeers from the walls, though each time more people appeared on the parapets. Civilians, and women, even children peered down at us; and I knew that the story of Fushanj was spreading through Herat.

So I was not surprised to see a party riding out to meet me on my noonday parade—a party carrying a white flag of truce. I met the envoys halfway between my white pavilion and the main gate to the city.

Although I had never seen Ghiath ad-Din, I recognized the leader of the party as the son of Shah Malik.

"Timur, Brother, welcome to my city," he called, as soon as he came into range. "I am Ghiath ad-Din, Shah of Herat, Sultan of the Afghans, Protector of the Faith."

"Ghiath ad-Din, Brother," I responded. "I am Timur, Prince of Samarkand, Amir of all the Tatars. I am most grateful for your welcome."

"And how is my dear sister, Shereza Begum, and our valiant brother, Sheik Ali?"

"The Begum is well. She sends her greetings. Sheik Ali is there—" I pointed to Ali's division—"surely you know his standard."

"Why, so it is," said Ghiath ad-Din, with a noticeable diminution of his enthusiasm. "I hadn't noticed. I've just awakened—I had no idea you were here."

"We've come to escort you to the Council of the New Year."

"How thoughtful of you, Brother. I shall be glad to return with you. Enter my city."

"On my terms," I said sternly, "of which you no doubt are aware."

"Ah—yes. Yes, I heard your heralds."

"Very well, order your army to ride unarmed to my lines."

Without further pretense at hypocritical formality, Ghiath ad-Din sent orders to his nobles and stayed with me while the Persian and Afghan regiments rode out and surrendered to my forces. Then I took a squadron from each division and entered the city. Later chronicles accused me of inhuman cruelty in my treatment of the Fushanji people. But any chronicler would have judged my actions wise and good had he ridden through Herat that afternoon and seen the thousands of people and the fine buildings saved by Ghiath's surrender. And the razing of the outpost was directly responsible for the ease with which I took the Afghan capital.

It took a month to collect all the treasures of Herat, a busy month because Ghiath ad-Din's capital was the repository of more luxuries of the world than I had seen in any other city up to that time. My own connoisseurs appraised everything of value in the city, and my engineers and the architects of Herat, whom I pressed into service, dismantled fine pieces of art or architecture which had been built into permanent structures. Especially did I like the new gates, and I had them taken down and packed for transporting to Samarkand.

I did not demolish whole buildings, nor did I touch Church property at all—the city was far too beautiful, too effective a lure with which to soften and corrupt other men, as it had destroyed Ghiath ad-Din. I did, however, enslave all of the artists and artisans who had built the city and send them to Samarkand to create again the illusion of heavenly grandeur on earth. I knew that I was impervious to the debilitating effects of luxury, and I felt that the concentration of all wealth in Samarkand would serve to distract the men around me who might some day become too ambitious for my safety. So has Allah distracted men from the Way and kept His secrets safe throughout the ages.

Scholars of all races, already informed of the progress my academies were making, flocked to join me willingly, as did churchmen who had heard of my tolerance toward religion. Military men, too, out of respect or fear, or both, swore allegiance to me and prepared to ride north with my troops after I had installed my own trusted amirs in positions formerly held by Afghan and Persian nobles. Mobile as were the desert tribes, I had no difficulty in shifting the entire military segment of the population and such slaves and menials as I needed to support my augmented army.

Khitai took over the governorship of Herat, with garrisons of Mongols in sufficient strength to insure the continued allegiance of the people. I left enough livestock and materiel to make him self-sufficient and to provide a nucleus around which he could build new strength in the south. Then, with all of the remaining transportation facilities loaded with the treasures of Herat, I set out on my return trip in time to reach Samarkand before the New Year.

Mine was the biggest and richest caravan to cross the river since the days of Genghis Khan, and my triumphal entry into Samarkand overshadowed anything in the memory of man.

Dilshad Sarai Khanum and Shereza Begum were both delighted with my success. Dilshad saw in it the rise of the Tatars; and from her frequent references to Shah Rukh, I knew that she was calculating the extent of the empire her prince might one day come into, although he was not quite four years old. Shereza, of course, envisioned the return of Miran Shah to the throne in Herat, and no doubt saw herself living out her declining years as the Empress Mother of the Monarch of all Asia. Certainly she raised no objections to my putting Ghiath ad-Din in a relatively minor position in my court and giving him command of a personal guard which was in reality a corps of jailers assigned to him for life.

Only Ali Soun Agha hardly noticed the splendor of my return, although she seemed happiest to see me.

"It's almost finished," she said eagerly, when I first stole away from the ceremonies to inspect Devon with her.

Her eyes shone, rivaling the sheen of her hair; but as soon as I freed myself from their spell to scan the rest of her vivacious countenance, I was horrified to find her beauty blighted by a plague—a brown pox, or so it seemed.

"Are you ill?" I asked with real concern—ignoring her reference to Devon.

"No, why?" she asked, suddenly grown solemn, anxious at my obvious alarm.

"Those spots." I pointed to the bridge of her nose.

"Oh, that." She laughed gaily. "They're nothing—*freckles*. I thought I'd outgrown them."

"Freckles?" I repeated.

"Yes—the sun does that to me. They'll go away. I'll be pretty again in the winter."

"Then they don't hurt?"

"Of course not. Unless they make me ugly to you." She blushed and cast her eyes down. "Let's walk," she added, and led me out of the palace.

I never walked if I could help it, but I rather welcomed the chance to stroll through the garden with Ali Soun—even the long distance to the gate opening into Devon. Her hair was fragrant, and I deliberately put her to the windward so its perfume would blow my way. I wanted to let her walk a little way ahead of me, where I could watch her slender body in motion under the simple dress she wore; but when we reached an uphill path in the garden and she hung on to my arm for support, I was glad that I was close beside her. The light weight of her hand thrilled me more than had the full embrace of many women I had known, and aroused some uneasiness along with the full measure of desire. I had no intention of allowing my emotions to become enmeshed in a woman's snares again. Aljai had proved almost fatal to me.

"My castle is complete," Ali Soun said somewhat breathlessly after our climb. And although the sun was nearly down and the evening cool for the season, little drops of perspiration mingled with the *freckles* on her nose. She wiped her face with a scarf.

"Is it what you wanted?" I asked.

"Oh, yes. Almost exactly like my home—even to the furniture."

There was nostalgia in her voice, but I noted that it did not drown her eagerness.

"And the other houses?"

"Finished on the outside—here, close your eyes—let me open the gate."

Feeling foolish and self-conscious at playing games with the silly agha, I closed my eyes and waited while she swung the big gate open. I heard the hinges squeak and the latch bang against the wall.

"Now!" she said.

I opened my eyes and looked at Devon for the first time. Before me was a narrow street, flanked on either side by doll houses, copies of the quaint peaked-roofed dwellings in Ali Soun's drawings, and commanded from the far end by the castle.

"Is it to scale?" I asked. So small—if that were all there was to a village in Inglistan—

"Oh, yes—the houses are just right and placed right. I used to count steps at home, and I remembered. That's my street—I just love it."

She gripped my arm, and I saw tears in her eyes—whether of gratitude or sorrow, I could not guess. She turned and looked up the street toward the castle.

"Yes, it's Devon," she said softly.

I followed her gaze. There was something fascinating about the strange houses—their roofs—pointed—pointing, pointing at something above, as though the people who built them and lived in them refused to believe that life could be boxed up in square, flat-topped houses, as though— In my country only the minarets on churches pointed to heaven.

Slowly Ali Soun led me up the street, past the two-storied, half-timbered houses, just one room stacked on another, and the little church. There she stopped. The church, too, pointed upward, not just the steeple, but the windows and buttresses; and when I looked inside, I seemed to be in the shadows of western forests, shadows which converged in a point high above, out of sight, the way shadows come together in the high branches of pines and larches just after sunset.

A robed figure came out of the shadows and knelt before me and kissed my hand.

"This is Father Pol," said Ali Soun.

"Yes, I know Father Pol," I said. The old Nestorian priest had visited me several times and accepted generous gifts for his sect.

232

"Welcome home, Amir," he said in a tone which suggested conscious blessings on his part.

"Is the church satisfactory, Father?" I asked.

"Yes, indeed, Amir. Of course, there are the icons and furnishings yet to be procured."

"You shall have them."

"I know. I've told the agha of your amazing generosity. She has assured me that it will continue. We're both grateful, aren't we, Agha?"

"Yes, very grateful," Ali Soun said dutifully. She seemed to bask in the priest's smile.

"Whatever you want," I said, and turned to go on up the street.

"May God bless you, in Jesus' name," the priest called after us.

I started at the words of his blessing. Never before had anyone asked God's blessing on me in Jesus' name. But many times I had received Allah's blessing, after a donation to one of Mohammed's descendants. I was not shocked to find that Christian priests understood the Will of God to be universal, regardless of which prophet proclaimed it—a donation, then a blessing.

"Let's hurry," urged Ali Soun, "so you can see part of the castle before it gets too dark."

We reached the miniature bastion in time to inspect the main hall only. It seemed bare by comparison with the rich appointments of a Persian or Tatar palace, and the furniture crude and plain but substantial and inviting in a barbaric sort of way. I paused before the huge fireplace, which was the strangest thing; but Ali Soun, despite her pride in the room, hurried me to a balcony to see the last rays of the sun reddening the far sands of the Bokhara Road.

She stood close beside me, consciously touching me.

"This is Devon," she said, looking down the street, which curved just enough to hide the fact that it ran to a gate in my garden wall. "I try to be here at this time every day."

"You may move in here, soon," I promised her.

"Yes, and I'll keep my bargain, though I never made one."

"Your bargain?"

"Amir, I'm not stupid—nor just a little girl who wants a playhouse. I know what you expected of me when you bought me."

I said nothing.

"I know, too, that I can never go home. This isn't Devon—but you've done the best anyone could do—and I think perhaps I love you for it."

"You're disappointed?"

"Not with this—resigned. You didn't bring me here—you're not to

233

blame—you've been wonderful. I *can't* be disappointed in this Devon you've built for me."

"Then I'm glad," I said.

"The girls have impressed on me the full significance of the exception you've made in my case. Some say you love me deeply—some that you're playing with me and will kill me if I refuse you."

"What do you think?"

"That you love me. Father Pol says that you do. He's explained the customs of your people—many wives, I mean—and he says I will not sin if I marry you. I'll have only one husband. If there's a sin, it's yours."

She had not looked at me during her speech, which I was sure had required quite an effort. Nor did she look up at me when I put my arm around her shoulders. She continued to drink in the purple glow fading in the west.

"May I make one more request?" she asked.

"Certainly. What is it?"

"Give me a little more time. Let me move in here. Fill my street with people dressed like my own. Woo me just one night as a lover would woo me in Engloland. Complete my illusion, and I'll be true to you and live the rest of my days inside the walls of this new Devon. Is that too silly a request to make?"

Then she looked at me, although I could not read her eyes in the dim light.

"I don't think it's silly at all," I said, "except perhaps my wooing you in the way of the Franks. I don't know how."

"I'll teach you. When I served Lady Blanche of Gaunt, I heard lovers courting their maids—reciting poetry to them. One Geoffrey Chaucer used to say a verse to me—though I was quite a little girl and he already betrothed. I hoped my suitor would some day recite it to me. Will you learn it, in my language?"

"I'll try," I said, though I could think of more useful matter that I might have learned.

"It goes like this:

Nihtes when I wende and wake
  Forthi myn wonges waxeth won;
Levedi, al for thine sake
  Longinge is ylent me on
  In world nis non so wytermon
  That al hire bounte telle con;
    Hire swyre is whittore then the swon,
And feyrest may in toune.

234

An hendy hap ichabbe yhent,
Ichot from hevene it is me sent,
From alle wymmen mi love is lent
Ant lyht on Alysoun." *

Ali Soun's clear voice had softened gradually as she spoke the lines; and had not the last word sounded familiar, I would not have known when the poem ended. And the daylight faded with the poem.

Ali Soun stood still in the dark for a moment, and then turned in my arms and lifted her lips. Like everything else in Devon, Ali Soun's kiss was strange, fascinating, new—after the manner of the Franks. There was at least one custom of Inglistan worth adopting.

CHAPTER

11

The building of Devon aroused no small amount of internal comment. Dilshad Sarai Khanum was something of a symbol to the Jalairs, indeed to all the Tatars; and Shereza Begum was, of course, the female spiritual head of all Islam. Naturally then there was strong feeling among the followers of both that I was favoring the Frank agha far too much, although no one doubted that she was a descendant of a famous King Arturius, of whom some of the scholars had heard and whom they extolled as a mighty monarch of the West, the greatest ever in Inglistan.

So, to quiet the criticism, I ordered the hill to the south of the main palace leveled, and published my plans for enlarging the palace and building a wing for each of my princess wives. And the stature of the architects I had brought from Urganj and Herat assured the doubters that their princesses would have the finest palaces that could be built. I set lesser men to work rebuilding the rest of the city, opening and paving wider streets, and in general putting a new face on all of Samarkand —a project which continued uninterrupted for thirty years.

With their knowledge and skill in tile and stone, the Persian artisans gave the city a new brightness from the very beginning. The rather drab effect of unglazed brick and gray granite gave way to the glistening blue and gold and white magic of Herat and Baghdad, so strikingly that Samarkand was often called Gok Kand—*Blue City*—in later years. And work

---

* When at night I toss and wake,
   My cheeks wax steadily more wan,
  My lady, all for thy sweet sake,
   With a longing that grows on.
   There is nowhere so wise a man
   Can name thy virtues one by one.

Thy throat is whiter than the swan,
And thou the fairest maid in town.
   I have received a gracious boon
   (I know from heaven it came down).
   My love from women is withdrawn
And given all to Alysoun.

progressed rapidly. I did not insist that the builders give the same care to detail and strength that I had required in the construction of Devon. I was familiar with the kind of buildings I would attack in Asia and so did not expect the native construction to be studied with the military intentness to which the Frank architecture was subject.

In fact, if my capital looked like the ultimate in Asiatic luxury, I cared not that the splendid façades were sometimes backed up by mere rubble. If I could convince the world that Samarkand was the most beautiful city on earth, get men to look toward it as the pattern for all others, the crumbling reality would be of no importance—a characteristic manifestation of the Way, a man-made counterpart of Allah's own deception.

As other eyes were blinded by the glare of shining tile, I looked more and more toward Devon. It was completed by early fall, and I immediately filled the village with the fairest-skinned people in Samarkand—slaves, freemen, nobles, all classes. Sometimes I had to re-assign wives and children to make the families conform to Ali Soun's requirements, but within a week Devon's one street was inhabited by a full complement of pseudo-Franks dressed in the clothes of Engloland, as designed by Ali Soun and fabricated by the court tailors and seamstresses.

Even I wore the garb of a Frank bahatur—*knight* was Ali Soun's word—when I started to call on *Levedi Alysoun* according to my agreement. Of course, the armor and surcoat felt strange and awkward, but I did not really object to wearing it—it gave me an insight into the peculiarities of the men who customarily wore such things. Actually I rode several times around the parade ground, swinging a sword, practicing with a Frank bow, throwing a lance, and trying other military maneuvers. And I dismounted and went through some foot soldier tactics to see what in the Frank dress would hamper or hinder its wearer. The experiment was quite enlightening.

After an hour of such activity, I rode back through the palace gardens to the gates of Devon and up the narrow street to the little castle. There a liveried footman took my horse; and I was ushered into the main hall, where Ali Soun sat surrounded by her maids-in-waiting.

I had to smile as I remembered by contrast my entry into Bayan's seraglio at Balkh. The girls were just as consciously posed, but the scene was quite different.

Some of the women were doing needlework, some toying idly with dishes of fruit or candy—one was playing a lute and singing a song in Ali Soun's language, but with an accent not at all like Ali Soun's, which I had learned to appreciate though I knew few of the words. The agha greeted me graciously and dismissed her ladies.

I sat in one of her quaint chairs facing her.

"It was so nice of you to call on me," she said.

"Thank you, *Levedi Alysoun*. I've looked forward to this visit," I said, risking her native title in the middle of a sentence in my own language.

"You are flattering, Amir— Oh, say it! Say it!" she broke off with hysteria incipient in her tone. I knew what she meant.

"*Nihtes when I wende and wake—*" I began, and carefully made my way through the poem she had taught me. I had listened to her inflection and pronunciation very carefully, and I felt that I was doing very well.

Ali Soun watched my face intently, sometimes shaping the words with her own tantalizing lips when I seemed about to falter. Her eyes grew less worried, and softer and bluer as I continued; and her face relaxed into a sad smile when she saw that I was going to make it to the end.

"*From alle wymmen mi love is lent Ant lyht on Alysoun,*" I finished, and held back the sigh of relief to which I was entitled.

Ali Soun settled back in her chair, as relieved as I was, it seemed; and big tears formed to deepen the blue of her eyes.

"Thank you, Amir," she said softly. "It was—it was—almost real. You're sweet—you've been good to me. Tomorrow we shall be married."

Then she rose and kissed me again in the manner of the Franks, which I was beginning to believe was the manner Allah intended—if He ever intended for man to taste undiluted pleasure in a kiss.

The patent absurdity of the situation gradually grew dimmer and dimmer as I sat with Ali Soun before the wood fire crackling in the strange massive fireplace of the main hall. I became aware of the lures Allah had placed in Engloland to soften the Franks. I learned why the Crusades had failed, and there grew in me an uneasiness that I, too, might be weakened by the white siren and her illusory Devon.

"This is what you wanted?" I asked at length.

"Yes, Amir. This is as nearly like Devon as anything I shall ever know again."

"Until I take you back to Engloland."

"Until you take me back," she repeated, but without conviction.

"Is there anything else you want?"

"Nubja—" she said.

"Nubja? Why?"

"She's the only friend I've made. We're alike—both outcasts in the seraglio—because she is so black and I so white, and all the others in between. I love her. She's like a—a mother."

"Nubja is the Mother of the World," I said, remembering how all the yearning of the womb was concentrated in Nubja's ebony loins.

"I'd like her to live in Devon with me."

"No," I said. "I can't give you Nubja."

"Oh, I don't mean give her to me. Not Nubja! Not as a slave! She's a princess—of the line of Mohallabi—" There was no doubt that Ali Soun, a slave herself, was genuinely shocked.

"Nor can I let her leave the seraglio. I need her there too badly."

I let Ali Soun ponder over the nature of my need.

"She is a good disciplinarian," Ali Soun admitted. "But so sweet to me. I'll miss her, but—"

"She may visit you," I said.

"Thank you, Amir. I've asked too much. You've done enough for me." She was disappointed but not insistent, and during the rest of the rather awkward evening we talked of other things.

I understood little of the strange wedding ceremony which Father Pol conducted in the shadowy chancel of the Nestorian Church. Few of the villagers understood any more than I, and I doubted that the Christians, who attended the rites but were too dark-skinned to live in Devon, got much out of the Latin words read from a book loaned by an Arab scholar. They did rejoice, however, at having a Christian agha added to my household with the blessings of their priest. And the occasion marked the end of the long courtship and extended denial I had endured to get the full value out of my fifty-thousand-dinar investment.

But the whole silly business was far from unpleasant. In day-to-day association with the beautiful Ali Soun, the occasional touch of her body or fragrance of her hair, I had experienced a heightening of desire far in excess of anything else I had ever known. Indeed, Ali Soun was the only woman, except Dilshad, whom I ever had the chance of knowing before taking to bed. And all the time she was there, to be had by force or even a simple spoken order. In the growing anticipation I perhaps experienced something akin to the feeling which accompanies celibacy and asceticism as practiced by some Mohammedan monks, and quite generally by the Christian priesthood. Surely they must expect some very rare pleasure to compensate for their denial of women—but what?

My reward for denying myself Ali Soun was Ali Soun herself.

And the reward was sufficient, as Nubja had promised it would be. Although the beauty of Ali Soun's exquisite white body had been indelibly imprinted on my mind since that first inspection many months before, I was still not prepared for the vision of loveliness which her pale figure presented on the rose satin sheet of our marriage bed. In the light of the solitary candle her skin seemed to be transparent, her blush the color of the satin shining through her translucent flesh.

Not till my fingertips had traced the curves of her throat and breasts was I sure that my bride had substance. Nor was the illusion dispelled

238

until her calm white loins, first tense and then deliciously relaxed, had absorbed and cooled the heat of my long-growing passion. There was something mystical, ethereal, in the way Ali Soun bestowed her gift, graciously, passively, like a blessing. I was somehow refreshed, as though I had breathed deeply of clean cold mountain air—and I was suddenly jealous of all the Franks and their fair western women. The spell of Devon was upon me.

And the spell of Devon held me. I spent many hours before the big fireplace, and many more in the canopied bed, with Ali Soun's body curled in the crescent of my own, where I could smell the fragrance of her golden hair and marvel at the slender contours of her back, while I caressed the silken texture of her thighs and buttocks.

I hurried back from Shehri-Sebz after the birth of Pir Mohammed, Jahangir's first son. Back to Devon. I cut short my tours of the old soldiers' homes to return to Devon. I listened impatiently to Mahmoud ibn Said's reports on land reforms—reports that the farmers were grumbling about having to pay full taxes on new land although they had been given five years or more of tax-free and partially taxed production—impatiently, because my thoughts were on Devon. The scholars bored me with their pompous prattle. The judges and fakihs bored me with their silly cases. Everything bored me except Ali Soun and Devon.

I allowed Shereza Begum to choose a princess wife for Omar Sheik and to plan and direct the wedding. And I listened half-heartedly while she debated with me—and with herself—the merits of prospective wives for Miran Shah, and rejected each one as unworthy. I sat drowsily through her eulogies concerning Miran Shah's prowess in battle—he was a good soldier, or a lucky one—and her subtle hints at his administrative ability. But I thought of Ali Soun, and the Begum knew it and made slighting remarks about pale anemic women and their sons.

Dilshad, as usual, was gracious and thoughtful, and I did spare enough time to make love to her occasionally and to sit with her and discuss Shah Rukh and the hundred or so sons of my concubines, for Dilshad was the princess of the palace, and it was she who supervised the training of all the younger male children until they reached military age. But even Dilshad, in spite of her likeness to Aljai, could not rescue me from the strange hold Devon had on me.

During my preoccupation with Ali Soun the months sped by. The clever devices which cut off Ali Soun's view of Samarkand also hid from me the changes taking place in the city. My capital grew into a thriving metropolis with every bazaar and hostel and brothel buzzing with activity. Rich caravans came and went along the trade routes throughout Tatary. The people were prosperous everywhere—too prosperous, so prosperous that envious neighbors began raiding my borders. When Ali Soun's belly began to swell, I was luckily jerked out of the crowded bed and back into the saddle—into myself—on the Way again.

Jaku, as head of the divan, had the information on conditions; and when I finally came to my senses, he grinned confidently and told me what I had to do first.

I sent out my call and prepared for war.

I moved to Shehri-Sebz again to mass my forces. And I visited Ak Sarai again—to experience again the feeling of strangeness which pervaded the palace of Jahangir and Sevin Bey. Even in the nursery and the bedroom where I had found so much pleasure in Aljai and Dilshad, Sevin Bey, who was ill—again large with child—injected something foreign into the familiar surroundings.

"Is he like Jahangir?" Sevin Bey asked from her bed when I looked down at Pir Mohammed in his cradle.

"Yes—and no," I answered. The baby stared at me with fierce disapproval.

"Yes—and no. That's no answer, Father Timur."

"Yes. He has Jahangir's mouth and chin, but his eyes and forehead, no."

"That's better. I like Jahangir's mouth and chin."

I looked at the Khanzade—her firm golden arms out from under the covers and her copper-colored hair framing her face and curling luxuriantly on the green pillow, the color of her eyes.

"He has your forehead and eyes—no, not your eyes," I said, puzzled—the eyes were familiar.

Sevin Bey laughed.

"His eyes are like yours," she said.

"Yes, Father," Jahangir joined in, "he has your eyes. We've talked of it often—just like yours."

"Then he has fine eyes," I said, and looked back at the infant in his cradle. "A little fierce at the moment, perhaps, but fine." I wiggled a finger before his face for him to grasp, but he only seemed frightened and resentful and shied away from me.

"He doesn't like to be touched," Jahangir said with a note of uneasiness in his voice.

"Why?" I asked.

"I don't know," Jahangir said evasively. "He just doesn't."

I turned in time to see Jahangir and Sevin Bey exchange glances—his gentle, disturbed; hers wild, unreadable.

"I'll take another just like him," I said, to ease the tension, "to protect me in my old age."

240

"I'll give you another, just like him—for your old age," said Sevin Bey, but she made no reference to a protector.

I felt that the Khanzade hated me, and I was somewhat relieved to think that her hatred for me might account for the spell she had cast over Jahangir. I knew that he loved me. Yes, perhaps—

"We'd better return to the banquet hall, Father," Jahangir suggested.

"All right. Good night, my dear," I said to Sevin Bey.

"Good night, Father Timur."

Back in the great hall, surrounded by the faces of men who had ridden with me into many battles, I let Jahangir's domestic affairs slip from my mind and turned to problems of strategy and logistics.

My amirs responded wholeheartedly to my call and assembled seventy thousand troops for me in a matter of a few weeks. When I set the date for departure from Shehri-Sebz, I had an army which I considered the best in Asia.

Then Jahangir's problems intruded again. He came to my pavilion late one night. I had already retired, but I received him in my bedchamber.

"Father," he began, "your army is strong, and you have many good officers. Would you mind if I stayed behind?"

"Why, Son? Are you ill?" He did look worried, thin, nervous.

"No. It isn't that. But the baby, Pir Mohammed—and Sevin Bey with the next one due soon—I'd rather not go. I'm afraid—"

"Afraid?" I asked.

"Oh, no—not afraid to go—" He laughed good-naturedly at the absurdity of my concern, "but afraid to leave Sevin Bey—with the babies and all—"

I pondered for a moment. I could ill afford to have my officers think I had so soft a son. They remembered his valor on the field before his marriage, and leaving him behind would be hard to explain.

"Very well," I said at length, "I'll put you in charge in Samarkand, with Jaku and Saif ad-Din. They need a young man. You can learn a lot from Jaku and from old Saif, if you'll listen and form your own conclusions. Yes, you go to Samarkand and get ready to assume the governorship of Urganj when I return."

"Sevin Bey will like that."

"Yes, I'm sure she will. All right, then. It's settled."

I dismissed him and went back to bed. I thought that my solution would seem convincing to my amirs. Jahangir was already twenty years old, and he seemed ready to assume responsibilities.

Omar Sheik and Miran Shah were nineteen, and each commanded a regiment of his own when we set out a week later on our long campaign to the south and west.

First I swung to the east, through Badakshan and Kunduz and Kabul, annihilating the small tribes with the overwhelming force of my army or pressing them into service and moving them out of territories where they caused trouble. Next I went around the south end of the Sea of Abaku to lay siege to Tabriz, where the Khorassan Road branched south to Baghdad and west to Damascus and Istanboul.

Tabriz was a city of more than a million people and a trade center of the greatest importance. So the siege lasted most of the winter. My army had grown during my conquests to well over a hundred thousand men; and there was never any doubt as to the outcome of the siege, although the Ghazan asked aid from the Mamluk Sultan of Cairo and the Sultan of Baghdad. Both rulers, however, considered me a mere desert raider who posed no real threat, and sent no help.

By stopping all caravans approaching the city, and raiding smaller settlements nearby, I was able to supply my own army; and, as always, there were some merchants in the city who smuggled supplies out to me. Gradually the city weakened and went on short rations. Then the Leng Kopeghi cells inside the walls began sabotaging the military, and the city fell.

Inside the city I found richer prizes than Herat had yielded and a population more cosmopolitan than any I had ever seen—Armenians, Georgians, Egyptians, Circassians, Turks, Arabs, Persians, and many Franks who called themselves Italians and Spaniards, and Normans, and Danes—all sorts of odd names. I chose the fairest of these, some indeed as fair as Ali Soun, and sent them, along with trains of loot, back to Samarkand as slaves to make Devon still more real to Ali Soun, and to provide a more genuine Frank community for military observation.

By early spring I had my government securely installed, and my army moved on north along the Sea of Abaku to Tiflis, which fell in three days, through Georgia and Astrakhan toward Sarai, the capital of the Golden Horde on the Volga.

Before I reached Sarai, word came that Kamar ad-Din, the last really strong Mongol chieftain, was moving from Almalyk toward Samarkand. So I sent gifts to Urus Khan of the Golden Horde and by-passed his capital. Instead of risking battle, I assured the Khan that I was on my way to meet Kamar ad-Din, and marched on to Otrar, where I set up a semi-permanent camp to re-form my army and readjust my command. Since it was nearing the New Year, I sent out invitations for my amirs whom I had left behind to gather at Otrar instead of Samarkand.

Jaku and Saif ad-Din came from my capital, but not Jahangir.

The two old men, Jaku well over sixty and Saif ad-Din nearing seventy, called on me in my new silk pavilion, which neither had ever seen.

"How are things in Samarkand?" I asked, when the elder statesmen had seated themselves carefully on the ottomans prepared for them.

"Your family grows," said Saif ad-Din. "The Khanzade has given Jahangir another son, Mohammed Sultan; and the Ali Soun Agha has given birth to a boy."

Saif ad-Din was losing his sense of precedence. I understood, however, why he had mentioned Jahangir's son first. There was as deep affection between Saif and Jahangir as between Saif and his own sons.

"And what does Ali Soun call her son?" I asked, gently reminding him of his omission.

"She has chr—"

"*Christened*," Jaku supplied, with a grin reminiscent of the young Jaku I had known when I was a child.

"—*christened* him Djon Pitr," Saif concluded apologetically.

"Djon Pitr," I repeated. "*Christened*, she said. That would be her word."

It was my first son to be christened, and I was amused at the implication—and pleased. I would let him grow up to be a Christian. He might prove a valuable asset, a congenial governor of the Franks when the day came for me to move west.

I was not, however, distracted by the amirs' deliberate evasions of any reference to Jahangir, and I finally asked, "Why didn't Jahangir come with you?"

The old men exchanged wary glances.

"We couldn't all leave at once," said Jaku. "Someone has to govern."

"Then, there are his babies," old Saif said lamely. "He wanted to come, but—well—"

"We advised against it," said Jaku.

"I'm sure you know best," I said. "Of course, I'd like to see him."

"Naturally," said Saif, with obvious relief. But I was not satisfied with the old men's explanation.

I had no time to question them then, however, because there was a disturbance outside my pavilion and Omar Sheik came in with another young man who showed signs of having ridden long and hard—as was further evidenced by his winded horse, which I could see outside.

"Who is this?" I asked.

"Let him tell you, Father," said Omar facetiously. "I can't remember all of it."

"All right, speak up, young man," I commanded.

"Most gracious Amir, I am Nasir ad-Din Jetal el Mahmoud Ghujas Toktamish, son of Tuli Khoja, Khan of the Crimea."

I laughed at the introduction.

"That is quite a mouthful," I said. "I'll call you Toti for short. I've heard of your father and of his death at the hands of Urus Khan. Well, Toti, what do you want?"

"Sanctuary, Amir Timur."

"Sanctuary? Why—?"

The reason was immediately apparent. One of my tavachis escorted another visitor of obvious nobility, who led another winded horse—a magnificent white stallion—up to my pavilion.

"An envoy from Urus Khan," the tavachi announced.

I nodded permission for the ambassador to speak.

"Oh, most great Timur-i-Leng," he began, and my sympathies veered immediately toward Toktamish, "I am Kepek Mangut. I come from Urus Khan, Amir of Sarai and Astrakhan, Kha Khan of the Golden Horde and the White Horde and the Khans of Sibir. This miscreant Toktamish who stands before you has killed the Khan's son, Kutluk Boga, and taken refuge in your camp. Surrender him to me or the Khan will march against you."

In addition to calling me Timur-i-Leng, the Khan had taken in entirely too much territory—Sibir, the very idea. It was true that I had to intercept Kamar ad-Din and I had tried to avoid war with Urus—but I did not fear Urus and his Hordes.

"Go back to your arrogant master and carry this message," I said. "Toktamish, whose father was slain by Urus Khan, has put himself under my protection. He has done no more than any son would do— avenged his father's death. Tell your master that I have called Toktamish my son and taken up his quarrel. Tell your master that he has challenged Timur, Prince of Samarkand, Sultan of the Persians and Afghans, Amir of Khorassan and Kharesm, and Protector of the *Khans of Sibir,* Servant of Allah. And be out of sight before sunset, or Urus Khan will have to send another lackey."

So I made Toktamish hero of the New Year; and after a week of feasting, during which I showed my son Toti the same consideration that I gave to Omar Sheik and Miran Shah, I commissioned him a tuman-bashi and presented him with a division of his own. I was careful, however, to give him the culls of my army—units which I distrusted and felt would be of no great value in my campaign against Kamar ad-Din. I felt sure that Toktamish could hold Urus for a time, and I did not care if his whole division was destroyed.

Toktamish was a Kabul, with a valid title to the khanship of the Golden Horde, and I thought that I would one day see that he claimed it—but not until I had convinced him of his dependence on me for his power. He was effusively grateful, but a little arrogant and overconfident when I left him to face the Hordes and moved on across the steppes toward Almalyk.

Khitai, whom I had summoned from Herat to help me in the north, took over Miran Shah's regiment; and I sent Miran Shah, whose headaches were getting worse, back to Samarkand with Jaku and Saif ad-Din. And I left Omar Sheik in Otrar with enough men to hold the Hordes if Toktamish should fail, but with orders not to help unless Urus Khan actually moved toward Samarkand. I still had an army of more than fifty thousand men, and a supply train equipped with big-wheeled kankalis as well as every kind of pack animal, when I crossed the Syr-Darya and headed across the barren Kirghis Steppe.

For a week I ran into nothing more formidable than the temporary auls of the Jat nomads—little clusters of gray felt yurts which disappeared overnight. Then I encountered an occasional patrol, none of which offered battle. Then I camped on sites which showed signs of having been recently occupied by an entire army—but one smaller than my own—and by the time I reached Lake Balkash, it was apparent that Kamar ad-Din was retreating before me, either to make a stand at Almalyk or to try to lure me into the Gobi Desert and hold me until winter set in.

Not wanting to risk the latter, I continued a forced march to Almalyk. Finding the fortress lightly manned, I left Nur ad-Din to take it and quickened my pursuit of Kamar ad-Din, for it was his destruction which I intended, not merely the capture of his capital. My pace was such that a few men, who had lost their horses and were forced to walk or run, began to lag. After the first day of lagging I had the men's shoes filled with sand and hung about their necks. The next day, those who still lagged were given their choice of being killed or left behind to shift for themselves on the barren wasteland. The sensible ones chose death. But I waited for none.

My army finally overtook Kamar ad-Din on the north route to Khitai halfway to the land of the Manchus. Estimating his army at no more than fifteen or twenty thousand men, I split my army into three corps and sent one under Khitai and another under Daoud to outflank Kamar ad-Din and cut off his escape.

After three days of sporadic fighting I forced the Jat Khan to make a stand, and defeated him completely. Since I needed his animals and supplies and did not have the facilities for transporting prisoners, I took no captives except a few hundred of the best women and put the rest of the Jats to death.

With my northern boundaries secure again, I paused only long enough at Zaisan to rest my army and to send gifts to Hadji Bey Irkanut, the Manchu Emperor of Mongolistan; and then I headed back toward

245

Samarkand in time to reach my capital before winter. Instead of returning by the route I had come, however, I turned south into the Gobi and then through Terek Pass to Osh and Khojend, and arrived at Tashkand just ahead of the first snow. At Tashkand I dismissed the chieftains who had been on the two-year campaign with me. Then I led my own column down the mountain road to Samarkand. I had extended my boundaries to a distance of at least seven hundred miles in every direction; and as I rode toward my capital, I remembered Kurgan's advice: that the only security was in the center of an empire with farflung, turbulent borders. My borders were farflung, and turbulent enough to keep my ambitious governors too busy with their neighbors to challenge my authority. I felt that I had welded a strong enough ring of iron around my realm for my immediate protection. The job ahead of me would be the strengthening of my domestic security. And so I rode, comfortable and satisfied, on Kunk Oghlan, the fine young brown stallion which I had chosen to replace the aging Ak Ruksh.

The sun was getting low when I rode out of the shadow of Mount Amasar and saw Samarkand glistening before me. Jaku and Saif ad-Din and the palace guard were waiting to welcome me, not in the blue silks of the Gok Hazara, but in black—dismounted and silent.

Saif ad-Din approached with bowed head and put his hand on my stirrup.

"What's the matter, old man?" I asked. "Are you afraid?"

"No, Amir, I'm not afraid—I'm bowed down with grief. Pir Jahangir is dead."

"Dead? When? Why didn't someone tell me?"

"Two days ago, Amir. He was ill at New Year's, but made us swear not to disturb you before your march to the north."

"What was the matter?" I asked. "What did the physician say?"

"He didn't know. No medicine did any good."

I dismounted, and so did my men as the news sped back along the column. My nakaras and kourrouns formed into a band and began a dead march, and I limped along beside Kunk Oghlan, with my kulchis following on foot, to the palace gates.

The next day, Jahangir's horse, bearing an empty saddle, led the cortege to Shehri-Sebz. There, before Ak Sarai, where Jahangir had been born in excruciating pain to Aljai, his nakaras and bows and sword were broken, and his kourrouns silenced forever; and after the service had been read by the faltering, forgetful old Zain ad-Din, my oldest son was buried a few paces from the white marble tomb of his mother.

There are some who have said that the death of Jahangir, my beloved Aljai's son, determined the course of all my later life. This is not so, as

246

anyone who reads my record will see. I loved him as a son, but I have found no evidence to indicate that he was for me an essential part of the Way.

CHAPTER

12

My first domestic problem arose immediately upon my return to Samarkand after Jahangir's funeral. Shereza and Miran Shah called on me as soon as I reached my suite. I accepted their greetings and condolences and seated Shereza on a divan—an ordinary ottoman no longer seemed adequate. Despite the cool autumn evening, Shereza breathed heavily and fanned herself furiously before she began her conversation.

"Jahangir was such a gentle boy," she said sympathetically.

"Like his mother." I expected more than platitudes; but not knowing the purpose of the call, I did not want to be the first to depart from them.

"Yes—dear Aljai, so gentle, and yet so gay and spirited."

Miran Shah sat quietly beside his mother and frowned, as he had done almost continuously since his injury in the polo game.

"But Miran Shah says that he was valiant in battle. Miran Shah admired Jahangir so much, didn't you, Son?"

"Yes, Mother," Miran answered dutifully.

I watched carefully for the tack which the conversation was going to take.

"It's such a shame that Jahangir was not able to be with you on your last campaign—Miran Shah has told such wonderful stories of how he and Omar Sheik shone in battle."

"I missed Jahangir, of course," I said. "But someone had to stay in Samarkand." I wondered how much she knew or suspected about Jahangir's marital relations.

"Of course. And it must have been a great disappointment to you to lose Jahangir just when you were planning to install him as governor of Kharesm. With Omar Sheik at Otrar—"

"Otrar is no more than a military garrison," I said, divining Shereza's next move. "Omar Sheik has proved himself a capable officer."

Shereza suddenly began to fan herself again and threw off her outer robe. I felt that I had offended her by my remark, which she might have considered disparaging, though she seldom championed Omar Sheik.

"—and your eldest son at Urganj," she continued, while I watched little beads of perspiration form on her upper lip, "you could have been justifiably proud of your family—two ruling sons and you barely forty-two—enviable!"

I kept my silence.

"Miran Shah, of course, is now your eldest," she continued with mild reproach in her voice, "and he has proved himself a good officer."

"Yes," I admitted grudgingly. I remembered what he had first cost me, though as I looked at Shereza's bulk spreading over the divan I could hardly believe that my memory of her youth was accurate. "Yes, Miran Shah has been amazingly efficient in the field—perhaps I can find a garrison for him somewhere."

"But his head hurts when he rides too much. Urganj, now—since you've rebuilt it so beautifully—and the governor would have his tu-man-bashi—and Miran Shah *is* the eldest—"

Shereza put her robe back on and shivered as she drew it tight around her.

"Perhaps," I said, "when he's had a little more experience in administration."

"I would go with him," she wheedled. "I was very close to my father. I learned much from him. I'm sure we could get along. Couldn't we, Miran Shah?"

"Yes, Mother. I, too, spent much time with my grandfather."

I looked at the two of them. Miran Shah would be as fat as his mother when he reached her age. I thought it might be worth the risk to get them out of Samarkand. And Urganj, away from Shereza's people—I could not fathom the depths of her ambition—Urganj might keep her from demanding Herat, which I certainly never intended to give to Miran Shah.

"I'll think it over," I said. "My mind is not clear at the moment."

"Of course, dear." Shereza's tone was more sympathetic than her feelings suggested. "We know you're grief-stricken. We'll leave you alone and discuss the matter later."

She rose and set her fan into violent motion again as she and her son left my apartment. I watched them waddle down the hall, Miran Shah unconsciously aping his mother's gait. Governor of Kharesm?

There were a number of things on which my mind was not clear. Jahangir's death—

I went to call on Sevin Bey at once. She, too, was resting after her ride back from Shehri-Sebz, lying relaxed and listless on her bed, with her head on the inevitable green pillow—green like her eyes—heightening the sheen of the bronze in her hair. I had never seen her look so soft.

"Thank you for coming, Father Timur," she said. "I've been so terribly lonesome with Jahangir gone."

"We'll miss him," I said. "Where are the babies?"

"Aisha and Tahmineh are looking after them. I'm too tired. The girls love them—and they loved Jahangir, too."

"Too?" I said, perhaps sharply.

Sevin Bey looked at me without rancor—as gently as I had ever seen her look at anyone.

"Yes, Father Timur, too. I loved Jahangir deeply, completely. Whatever else you think of me, please believe that I loved your son."

"I believe you," I answered honestly—but I did not understand her love, or what it had done to Jahangir. Unquestionably Sevin Bey was lovable at that moment—as tender as she had been when she kissed my hand after I had slapped her that first day. Yet she was maddening, even in her sincerity. Her very loveliness made me want to strike her again.

"Is there anything I can do for you?" I asked, clenching my fists but keeping my voice sympathetic.

"Not—not unless you will let me go home, back to Urganj. I'll be so lonely here, away from my people."

"Send you home?" I said slowly.

"Yes." There was eagerness in her tone, and the lassitude went out of her body when she saw that I was even entertaining the idea. "I could go when Miran Shah goes."

"Who said he was going?"

"The Begum." She smiled knowingly. "You can't keep your secret. She has already told the court that Miran Shah will be governor, now—now that—"

"So you know my secret?" I asked. And I knew hers. There was more than loneliness prompting her request. Back in Kharesm, she and Shereza Begum would be so busy undermining each other that they could hardly challenge me. It would be interesting, and it would clear the air around Samarkand for a while.

"Yes, Miran Shah will go to Urganj." I grinned as though I had been caught off my guard. "And you may go along. You will, of course, leave my grandsons here, in the care of Dilshad Sarai Khanum." I had let one woman rear two of my heirs in an alien city.

"My babies?" she exclaimed. Then a catlike cunning veiled the candor in her eyes. She seemed to crouch, though she still lay on her back.

"My grandsons," I repeated.

"Very well, Father Timur. You're most gracious. I'll go—and leave my babies here." Her voice was low, purring.

"May I see them?" I asked.

"Surely—the nursery is just down the hall." She started to rise.

"Stay where you are," I said. I wanted to see Aisha and Tahmineh alone. "I'll look in on you again soon."

"Thank you, Amir," she said. "Good night."

"Good night, my dear. Don't fret—you'll soon be with your people."

I paused at the door to look back at the green and gold princess on the embroidered counterpane. The richness and brightness of the whole room seemed to preclude grief. Somehow I never associated Sevin Bey with Jahangir unless I actually saw them together. Since she had laid aside her widow's weeds, she seemed no longer my daughter-in-law—not in that room. Yet she had loved my son. She did know grief.

Sevin Bey smiled sadly and lifted one hand, as in farewell. I nodded and went out into the hall.

My grandsons were awake, but quiet. Aisha and Tahmineh still wore black, veils and all, and they both knelt before me and began weeping when I entered. After bidding them rise, I stopped by Mohammed Sultan's cradle for a moment and then sat down and took Pir Mohammed on my knee when he toddled over to me. He no longer seemed to fear or resent my touching him.

"What happened to my son?" I asked the girls.

Neither answered.

"Aisha, you may tell me," I said.

"I—don't—" she began hesitantly.

"She killed him," sobbed Tahmineh.

"She?"

"The Khanzade—she broke his heart," Tahmineh continued, almost hysterically.

"How? How was it?" I asked Aisha, the calmer of the two. "Didn't she love him?"

"Yes, Amir—not the way we did, but—yes, she loved him."

"She hurt him," Tahmineh interrupted, "and made him hurt her—he didn't want to hurt anyone."

I looked to Aisha for an explanation.

"We listened," she said with some embarrassment but with an attempt at honesty. "When she loved him she hurt him—made him hurt her— And she hurt the babies sometimes—he was afraid to leave them with her. I don't understand how, Amir, but what Tahmineh says is true. She broke his heart somehow, and he died—" She, too, began sobbing after her effort. "Don't punish Tahmineh, Amir, for being disrespectful to the Khanzade. I—I'll—"

"I'm not going to punish either of you," I said, as gently as I could. "You don't want to go to Urganj with the Khanzade, I suppose?"

"No!" they said in concert.

"Shall I sell you to some other young man?" I could not take those two into my seraglio—it would be like incest, like my own daughters.

"No!"

"Then you may stay on and care for the babies—under the supervision of the Sarai Khanum, of course."

"Thank you, Amir," they said, and their eyes were bright through their tears.

Not content with a mere *thank you,* however, Tahmineh threw herself on her knees before me and clasped my hand in hers. Her tears and wet lips were hot against it.

"Thank you, Amir, thank you. You're sweet—like Amir Jahangir—thank you." Her small body shook, and her voice choked up.

Aisha put her arms about the younger girl and lifted her to her feet. Then, when Pir Mohammed began to cry also, she took him off my knee. And when Mohammed Sultan joined in the chorus, I rose and left the nursery to Jahangir's wailing family. It contrasted dismally with the Khanzade's boudoir, as I looked in again at the sleeping princess on my way out.

Shereza Begum kept the entire city in a stir until her caravan and Miran Shah's division finally disappeared down the Khorassan Road toward Bokhara. I sighed with relief when she and her train finally left, and I silently congratulated myself on disposing of her and the Khanzade so neatly. Now I could consolidate my vast gains of the previous two years.

Before the dust had settled, Toktamish rode in from Otrar and reported his complete defeat at the hands of Urus Khan. The Khan's Hordes had shown the first signs of internal dissension, however, as Abdullah learned from some of the captured slaves. Individual successes of some of the lesser nobles against Toktamish's inferior division had made them ambitious to challenge Urus' sovereignty, and they had begun boasting and bickering among themselves. I was sure that neither Urus nor Toktamish knew of this.

After a brief talk with Toktamish upon his arrival, I pleaded urgent state business and postponed going into detailed discussion with him until Abdullah had had time to exploit his sources of intelligence. Then, armed with a true knowledge of conditions, I gave a banquet in honor of my foster son Toti. I invited Omar Sheik to attend, and from him and his tavachis I got an accurate estimate of the strength of the Hordes. And again, after a week of fêting the Russian prince, I presented him with my own charger, Kunk Oghlan, and put him in charge of another division, composed of undesirables, to lead against Urus Khan. According to my calculations, Toktamish should be able to arouse still more confusion among the Hordes and yet not win a victory for himself with the forces I had given him. So I sent him back to Sarai in the middle of winter. To assure the success of my scheme, I sent Khitai Bahatur along with Toktamish, ostensibly to aid him, but in reality to see that he did not gain too much self-confidence. Then I returned to my internal problems.

I found Mahmoud ibn Said quite disturbed over the turn his land reforms were taking.

"Mahmoud," I began, after his perfunctory ritual of obeisance was finished, "by your countenance, I gather that you are worried."

"Yes, Amir, not everything is working according to plan."

"Didn't the farmers respond as you had anticipated?"

"Oh, yes. They reclaimed thousands of acres of land—here, I have figures—" The scroll appeared, ready to hand. I took the paper from him.

"Wasn't the production up to expectations?" I unrolled the scroll and was astonished at the figures on increased acreage.

"In excess—far in excess—see page eleven a."

"Then what seems to be the trouble?" I saw that records of production —the first ever made in Tatary—were most gratifying for each of the seven years listed.

"It's a factor which I did not take into consideration in the beginning —the farmers themselves."

I smiled inwardly at the scholar's characteristic misinterpretation of the Way.

"What have they done?" I asked.

"Well, they're selling. It's strange—at least to me. The first two or three years, everything went well. The farmers cleared new land, built irrigation ditches, reaped bumper crops and were highly enthusiastic. My helpers staged fairs and rallies in the villages and encouraged the peasants to come to the cities for still bigger celebrations, to create more interest in our work and to stimulate still further development. The farmers had money—money, not just goods for barter—for the first time in their lives."

Mahmoud paused. He wrinkled his brow.

"Yes?" I prompted him.

"Well, they spent prodigally—the tradesmen prospered—the rallies were lively."

"And?"

"And then the full tax years came and the men resented your taxation of one-third of gross."

"But taxes have not risen. One-third is the law—has been for hundreds of years. The men knew that; they agreed to it."

252

"That's what I can't understand, Amir. They grew quite surly and disgruntled. It was all quite irrational. Now they're selling off pieces of their land to maintain their former level of earnings. It's quite a problem."

"Who's buying the land? Neighbors?"

"No, not farmers at all—wealthy landowners, rich Jews and Persians, sometimes the Church. Then, with slave labor, the new land returns excellent profits when enough of it is bought up by one man or one syndicate. Actually, many of the original owners have gone back as tenants, working for less than they made before they started expanding. Amir, it's quite disheartening—quite—but the plan is a good one. It proved out in the first five years."

"Do you have a solution?" I asked. I was sure that he had. I saw one.

"I think an educational program, Amir, to indoctrinate young farmers. They can be made to see the mistakes made so far—and the great personal and social benefits. Now about financing the program—"

"I have the answer, there," I said. "We'll tax the big landowners one-half their gross—maybe even two-thirds in cases of very extensive holdings—instead of the customary rate."

"Excellent! Excellent, Amir!" exclaimed Mahmoud, the old fire returning to his eyes. "And put the surplus back into land reform—and expansion—and education—excellent, Amir! The big owners can stand the tax—they're not really entitled to the profits they're making out of their exploitation of the peasants and—and *my plan*."

The young zealot scowled as he belabored the landowners and then beamed again as he envisioned the spreading of his plan to the farthest corners of Tatary. I joined him in his enthusiasm, for I saw thousands and thousands of acres cleared and put into production and then sold to syndicates subject to two-thirds taxation—millions of misguided farmers enjoying their spurt of prosperity as they followed Mahmoud's scheme, and then returning to their backbreaking labors under the new owners. I read the Way too well to expect the amelioration of the lot of the agrarians by any such visionary scheme as Mahmoud's. But it was men like him who could provide me with food and revenue, necessary fuel for the fire to forge my blade with which I planned to keep the Way throughout the world.

And there were hundreds like Mahmoud ibn Said. They came to me with plans for a rapid post system along all highways, a network of caravanserais with accommodations for travelers, stables of fresh horses to be provided by the government, even iced drinking fountains on the desert—every imaginable kind of experimentation. Generally I allowed them free rein, and subsidized them whenever the plans seemed to fit into the Way. Always the wild-eyed youngsters were loud and persuasive, and whether their schemes worked or not, their infectious enthusiasm and their praise of my enlightened outlook proclaimed me as the world's greatest ruler over all my realm and even beyond my borders.

For a year I devoted my attention to interior affairs. Again I spent hours listening to the philosophers and historians and theologians, gleaning new insights into their misinterpretations and perversions of the Way. I sent invitations to still more savants, especially from Khitai, to come to Samarkand—none so wise as Tsung-Li, and none so thoroughly discredited as he. And further to understand the ways of Khitai, I sought a pretext for building a village and fortress—a Khitan counterpart of Devon—to provide a project for military study, for I planned to invade Khitai and recover the realm once ruled by my kinsmen in the service of Genghis Khan and Kublai Khan.

Although I had no contacts behind the Great Wall, the Manchu Emperor had received most graciously my gifts sent from Zaisan and had repaid in kind through ambassadors, who arrived in Samarkand in late spring. So I sent Daoud back with the Emperor's envoys with a message that I would welcome the Emperor's offer of one of his daughters to me in marriage. Daoud was also empowered to promise that I would duplicate any palace the princess might wish and permit her to bring an entire village population with her so that Samarkand might not seem strange to her.

Then I heard of Toktamish's second defeat; and indeed Toktamish rode into Omar Sheik's summer sarai alone, a fugitive from the Khan's mopping-up battalions, dispirited, defeated, even fearful of my reception of him. Omar sent him to me, however, and again I greeted him cordially and called him my son Toti.

"Most Gracious Amir," he said, as he sat beside me in the splendor of my courtroom and no doubt compared his own poor estate with mine, "you are truly my father. No blood father could have done more for a son."

"It is the law that strong members of the Kayouli family shall protect the descendants of Kabulai," I reminded him, "and you are of the blood of the khans. I can do no less."

"Such loyal adherents to the engraved tablets are rare," he said. "Indeed, Amir Timur—Father—you are the only one I know."

"That is my strength—the strength of righteousness. You shall have the throne you aspire to. That I promise. My strength shall be your strength."

Toktamish actually wept at my graciousness, and I felt that his confidence in himself was sufficiently shaken. I knew that his disreputable

254

army had made such a poor showing that every noble of the Hordes who had routed it had considered himself a military genius. Consequently, Urus Khan faced a disrupted corps of ambitious sons and subordinates. But Urus Khan was a capable ruler and a stern disciplinarian.

So I sent Abdullah to the subversive cells at Sarai with great promises from Leng Kopeghi. During the celebration of the New Year, Urus Khan sickened on the rich food and died, and the council split up into warring factions. His son held out for a few weeks; then a rival overthrew him and set himself up at Sarai. By that time, however, Toktamish, with a good division strengthened by Omar Sheik's crack corps and thousands who rallied to Toktamish's standard, rode into the capital of the Hordes and drove out the new Khan.

In token respect to the old agreement, I installed Toktamish as Khan of the Hordes with Omar Sheik as his protector and at the same time rather belatedly put a weakling of Kabul blood on the throne at Samarkand as a puppet Khan, thereby insuring allegiance of all the north country from Manchukuo to the far-off North Sea, at least for such time as I felt that I needed. I never trusted any man who came from across the Volga, but I felt that it would be some years before my foster son Toti would regain enough confidence to rebel against me.

CHAPTER

13

Daoud returned with the Manchu Emperor's reply to my communication in time for the next New Year's celebration. I made him the hero of the New Year; and when I had the message read to the Kurultai, the amirs nodded wisely to one another and praised Daoud for his skill in diplomacy. He had succeeded in every point of his mission, as I learned from Tsung-Li's reading of the Imperial Scroll.

"Most Gracious Amir," it began. "Lord of Tatary, Master of the World from Manchukuo to the setting sun, the Emperor of the Manchus offers you his daughter, the Joy of his Heart, as your bride. In doing so, we bestow upon you the Pride of the Manchus, for truly our youngest princess is the daughter of Heaven, a Maid of the Moon. Although her name is Chulpan Malik Agha, we call her Blessed Princess, and worship her second only to our Departed Ancestors.

"From this day consider her your wife—call her Bibi Khanum*—since she has married you by proxy; but we beg to keep her for five or six years

* Literally, "My princess wife."

more. She is now only ten years of age. Grant an old man this request to keep his most prized treasure with him until she can be a wife to you in fact and blend our noble blood with yours.

"Already she is a paragon of beauty and accomplishment for her age. Let us keep her with her tutors until we can send her to you a woman mature in the charms and attainments of our Manchu Queens. Your most gracious offer to create a royal setting for our jewel softens the sadness of sending her so far from home. With your ambassador, the noble Amir Daoud, we are dispatching three hundred of the foremost Manchu architects and builders with plans for her palace and village. We know by the generosity of your gifts that you will be unstinting in the appointments of Bibi Khanum's palace. Fear not to be lavish, for she is worthy of the finest things in Earth and in Heaven."

The rest of the message contained thanks for the gifts I had sent to the Emperor and listed the presents he had sent in return, with specific compliments to each member of my royal household. My nobles were loud in their congratulations and their regrets at the delay in the arrival of my bride—though many of them who had made a careful study of Devon were well aware of the true significance of the Bibi Khanum palace, which could be started immediately.

Tsung-Li easily guessed my purpose.

"You are fortunate, Amir," he said, when he had finished reading the Emperor's message, "to have the services of Manchu artisans in the construction of your proposed palace."

"They should indeed be able to bring the charm of the Manchu cities to Samarkand," I agreed.

"And of the cities of my native Khitai, which are almost identical," the old philosopher reminded me. "Upon the accession of the Ming* princes, many artisans took refuge with the Manchus."

"Then the Bibi Khanum quarter should be a cultural center," I said. "I've heard so much about the artistic attainments of your architects. Of course, I've never seen the wonders of Khitai myself."

"You would be interested in the temples of my land—and the fortresses," he added slyly.

"I'm sure that I would. Perhaps the quarter will arouse some nostalgia in you, Tsung-Li, since you have been so long away from your homeland."

"Perhaps, Amir. Even during construction—I remember, in my boyhood, how I was fascinated by the building of the palace in my native

---

* The Ming Dynasty was established in China (Khitai) in 1368 A. D. This incident in the life of Timur occurred about ten or twelve years later, *circa* 780 A. H. (After the Hegira).

city. I spent many happy hours with the workmen." The old man's eyes grew wistful at the memory—he loved the country he had forsaken.

And when my garden walls were extended again and construction on the palace was begun, I met the old scholar wandering among the workmen who were laying the foundation. I watched him as he talked to the foreign laborers in their own tongue, and the respect they showed him disturbed me somewhat. But not for long. The very next day, a clumsy Hindu slave let a block of stone fall off a scaffold as Tsung-Li passed underneath, and the old man was crushed to death without a sound.

I immediately had the slave thrown into a dungeon, and I was able to report that he had been properly disposed of—I had Abdullah's word for that. And I proclaimed a day of mourning for the great philosopher and directed the Manchu architects to halt work on the palace long enough to design and execute a tomb for Tsung-Li. They created a shrine equal to any in Khitai—so they said—and joined me in a ceremony to dedicate the tomb and inter the body of the old man whom they all had begun to love. The Manchus marveled at my consideration for a foreigner and proclaimed me a great humanitarian. The laborers slobbered at my touching regard for the helpless alien, far from his homeland.

Upon my admonition to be exact and accurate in their work, the Manchu architects prepared to spend six years on their project. All the while other workmen, the finest to be had, continued their task of making Samarkand the Sapphire of the Orient. New façades grew side by side along the principal streets—shining fronts of blue tile and intricate mosaic, interlined with white and gold mortar. Wealthy nobles and their beautifully clad wives passed along the gleaming thoroughfares like exquisite marionettes against a jeweled backdrop, and my own people as well as foreign merchants and travelers stood in the streets and gazed long, enchanted by the lavish parade.

But the grubby spectacle of beggars and mendicants became increasingly discordant in my city of Heart's Delight; so when Nasir ben Adam came to me with his plan for the welfare of the underprivileged, as he called them, I listened to his plea.

"There is a wide gap between your nobles and the poor people in the streets, Amir," he said, after I had put him at his ease. "And you, Amir, have gained a reputation for looking after your people—Mahmoud ibn Said's land reforms are the talk of Asia, the prosperity he has brought to the peasants."

Nasir ben Adam spoke the truth. There was always enough enthusiasm among the beginning farmers to drown out the low surly mutterings of the more experienced ones who found themselves enslaved on their own land and pushed harder than ever to please their landlords in the two-thirds tax bracket.

"I'm always alert to plans which will improve the lot of my people," I said. "What do you have in mind?"

"I have a very accurate estimate of what the beggars cost the merchants and nobles and travelers. Here are the tables"—out came the scroll—"for a year."

"The sum is staggering," I remarked.

"Exactly. That's because it is not co-ordinated and administered in any manner at all. Now, under my plan the amount could be halved, at a saving to the state and the prosperous citizens, and at the same time accomplish wonders in human rehabilitation."

"Go on," I said.

"With the establishment of a dole system—offices at specified places and an efficient record of benefits given—the beggars could have their alms program administered wisely and could thereby raise their standard of living. Being freed from hours of precarious begging on the street, they would regain their self-respect. And those who are not physically incapacitated could spend their time in fruitful labor."

"But begging is an honorable profession in Islam," I objected.

"Only because the Church itself relies on a form of mendicancy, if I may say so, Amir."

"You may say so," I said, and smiled inwardly.

"I knew you'd understand, Amir. It's such a pleasure to talk to an enlightened monarch. I can show the Church where its revenues will rise when the populace is freed from the burden of street beggars."

"Very well, convince the mollahs," I said. "Now, how is this scheme to be financed?"

"I have that figured out." He produced another scroll. "I've talked to a number of merchants. They agree that the small welfare tax I have estimated will be a bargain compared to what they've been giving to mendicants. I had hoped that you, Most Gracious Amir, would allot administration funds from your treasury."

"I think I can stand it," I said. I felt sure that the sight of my streets, free of beggars, would be worth the price he quoted, if for no other reason than the dissension it would arouse in other empires when word spread among the beggars outside my domain.

"Draw up your complete plan and present it to Amir Daoud," I said. "I'll instruct him to co-operate with you."

"Thank you, Amir," he said, with the same expression in his eyes that burned in those of Mahmoud ibn Said. "You are a true lover of mankind. I see the restoration of human dignity to the lowliest of your subjects."

I dismissed him. I saw the marble-paved streets of Samarkand cleansed of human vermin as they had been purified of the crippled and decrepit old soldiers through the efforts of Khosru al-Shiraz. And I saw the further confounding of man by his attempts to tamper with the Way. The illusion of a world without beggars should confuse a thousand monarchs, as well as millions of lesser men. In fact, I was taken in by the illusion—if my eyes had not been opened soon thereafter, I might have forever missed the Way.

I was not in Samarkand when Nasir ben Adam put his scheme into operation. Instead I was on a progress around the perimeter of my empire. I left in the fall and reached Tabriz in time to spend the winter in the mild climate of that prosperous city. Again I continued around the Sea of Abaku, through Georgia and Circassia—then under the rule of Toktamish—to Sarai, where my foster son Toti feted me with an elaborate spring festival.

Already he had razed Moskva, and other capitals of the Hordes, slaying entire populations and bringing the princes into Sarai as hostages. His most dreaded enemy had been defeated and his army destroyed by Dmitri Donskoi, Prince of Nijni Novgorod, in the battle of Kulikovo. Dmitri in turn was so plagued by Ladislaus Yagellon of Lithuania that he posed no threat to Toktamish. So I found my son Toti proud of his accomplishments, but still with a deep feeling of indebtedness to me. He presented me with lavish gifts and accompanied me on my journey to Otrar, where I was again entertained royally and given a tremendous salute as I set out on my return trip to Samarkand.

Generally, my country was in excellent condition. I found little graft among my governors, and after I had summarily executed the offenders, I was sure that I had struck fear into the hearts of any others who might have been tempted. As for minor officials, who always resort to graft, I arranged, through Abdullah, to have certain connections made between Leng-Kopeghi outlaws and my official corps which made it profitable and advantageous for the latter to give me good governmental service and use their office to reap rich benefits from illicit operations.

Although I did not go through Urganj, I heard that Sevin Bey had borne Miran Shah a son, the only really disturbing bit of information I received. I had not anticipated a merger of the conflicting forces I had planted, and I was at a loss to understand.

After a few evenings in Devon with Ali Soun and Djon Pitr (whose name she wrote *John Peter*) I took time to give some attention to Dilshad and the wives whom I had left in the zenana during my progress; and then I set to work bringing myself up to date on Samarkand. One of the first to seek an audience was Nasir ben Adam.

"All right," I said. "What seems to be your problem? How about your dole system?"

"I don't know, Amir, it's unbelievable."

"You mean it has exceeded your expectations?" I asked.

"No, Amir, the opposite. I'm at a loss to explain what has happened."

"Suppose you just tell me about it," I advised him.

"Well, Amir, we co-ordinated all our efforts and set up a very efficient administrative organization. And we dispensed the dole as you directed—but—"

"Did the beggars respond? Did they accept my largess?"

"Oh, yes, Amir—eagerly. They still accept it."

"How much? How much has it cost?"

"I don't really know, at the moment—I don't have any records with me." Nasir looked at me blankly.

"What! No papers? No tables?" I asked, but my sarcasm was lost on the disillusioned young man. "I can't talk to people like you without tables and charts," I continued. "It seems unnatural. I'll summon Amir Daoud."

I sent a tavachi for my daroga and urged Nasir ben Adam to continue with his narrative—minus figures—while we were waiting for the governor.

"So the beggars accepted my dole eagerly— Go on," I said.

"Eagerly, at first—now they are sullen and demanding. They sneer at me and my staff and call us robbers."

"Robbers? Why? Aren't you giving them more than they got by begging—a chance at rehabilitation, restoring their sense of dignity?"

"That's what I can't understand, Amir. The beggars won't spend their time in fruitful labor, not even on highly overpaid jobs which we've created for them. They come for their money and then return to their corners to beg. And since we've inaugurated the dole, there has been an influx of new beggars from everywhere, thousands of them. The old-timers hold us responsible for the increase—claim that the newcomers have cut down the earnings and invaded their territory." Nasir ben Adam wrinkled his brows until his face seemed actually to shrink.

Daoud entered in time to hear Nasir's last complaint. He grinned at me over the young man's head and came forward to hand me the papers I had requested.

"Wasn't your plan supposed to keep beggars off the streets?" I asked sternly of Nasir ben Adam.

"Yes, Amir," he said apologetically. "We explained that. But they call us foul names and say that we are robbing them of their inalienable rights—the privilege of begging, which is a part of their religion."

"But they don't refuse the dole?"

"No, Amir. They demand more, now that they have competition on the streets. They've even begun mobbing my tellers and robbing my messengers. They are very bitter."

I let Nasir ben Adam taste the bitterness while I looked over Daoud's records.

"A hundred thousand dinars!" I exclaimed. "I could outfit a regiment for that. And more beggars than ever on the streets."

"The dole ran up to more than we expected, Amir," Nasir explained, "with the increase in beggars. And it will cost more next year."

"Next year—you mean the welfare tax must be increased? That's bad."

"I know, Amir." Nasir ben Adam began to squirm uncomfortably on the ottoman before me. "And the merchants are complaining about the tax. Perhaps you could allot more from other sources, since you love your people so deeply."

"Do you love the beggars, Nasir ben Adam?" I asked, and stared steadily into his eyes.

"Uh—no, Amir. I hate them! Every one of them!" he screamed in a hysterical outburst.

Daoud laughed.

"Getting on your nerves, my son?" he asked.

"Yes, Amir. Yes! I can't stand their dirty stinking bodies any longer."

"It's still your job to clear the beggars from the streets of Samarkand," I told him sternly. "You started this—now you must finish it. Perhaps Amir Daoud can give you some ideas. He has cleared out the thieves and robbers quite effectively."

"You mean with troops?" Nasir asked, recovering from his hysteria and acquiring a new viciousness instead of his formerly humane demeanor.

"Yes," I said. "Cut off their hands, blind them, kill them—whatever is necessary. But your life depends on your ridding this city of beggars."

"It'll be a pleasure," he said, with a return of the old zeal to his eyes. "A pleasure, Amir."

CHAPTER

14

By the time I had brought local affairs fairly well under control, my attention was diverted from Samarkand by Nur ad-Din's return from Urganj. The tuman-bashi reported to me late one afternoon, as soon as he arrived in my capital. I was just leaving the courtchamber, but I went back inside with him; and after I had ordered refreshments, we sat across the table from each other while he told me about Miran Shah.

"It's bad, Amir," he said.

"Let's hear the worst," I encouraged him. I doubted that he had guessed that I had intentionally pitted Shereza against Sevin Bey.

"I'm not sure of my position, Amir," he said cautiously. "What I have to report will be unpleasant—and rather personal—about your son."

"You're free to speak," I assured him. "I'll not be offended."

"Well," he continued hesitantly, "Miran Shah is bringing discredit on your name and weakening your authority."

"How? In what way?"

"I'm afraid, Amir, that he has taken to drugs—hashish and opium. And he drinks too much."

"What does the Begum do about it?"

"If you'll pardon me, Amir—with all due respects to the Begum, she is blind to his actions, feels that he is ill, actually encourages him in taking narcotics to ease his headaches, which she says are becoming more severe and more frequent."

"I see—go on. What else has he done?"

"When I arrived, he had just returned from a trip to Tabriz and Sultaniah patterned after your progress, and I believe planned by his mother. Those cities *are* under his jurisdiction, she reminded me."

"On my sufferance."

"Yes—he went in your name. That's the bad part.

"Why bad?"

"His behavior. Proclaiming himself the son of Timur, he ordered palaces and hospitals—even mosques—torn down, graves desecrated. He drank in the mosques, threw gold and jewelry to all of the beggars in the streets, entertained common whores in the Nestorian cathedrals—and chanted continuously that he would be remembered in those cities when his father was forgotten. I'm sorry to have to tell you this, Amir Timur—" he broke off sorrowfully.

"I want to hear the truth," I said in a tone which I hoped would reassure Nur ad-Din that I did not blame him for the disgusting story.

Secretly I granted the validity of my son's boast—the desecrator of temples *is* remembered much longer than the builder. Such is the Way.

"What about the Khanzade?" I asked.

"That, Amir, is perhaps the most disgraceful of all. Miran Shah forcibly entered her palace and made her dance naked before him and the nobles of her own race. Then he took her back to his own seraglio and ravished her repeatedly—there is a son, Khalil Sultan, now nearly a year old. The Khanzade is still virtually his slave."

"Where did you get this information?" I asked.

"From the Khanzade herself—or rather a note from her delivered to me by a veiled woman servant just as I was leaving Urganj. I had heard rumors before, but even the Urganji nobles were tight-lipped about the matter."

"And you say Shereza Begum condones all this?" It did not ring true.

"I'm afraid so, Amir. She has taken the baby to her heart—claims that the best blood in Asia flows through his veins—her own and the blood of the khans from the Khanzade. Yes, I'm afraid she approves. Certainly she forgives Miran Shah for everything and nurses him back to sobriety after his orgies."

Nur ad-Din's story reminded me of the futility of planning. The antagonism I had relied upon had degenerated into a sort of perverted love match, with Khalil Sultan as its product and the discrediting of my name as the immediate result. But Khalil Sultan was *my* grandson—perhaps the excellence of his blood would prove itself in my service. Perhaps chance had given me my successor. I resolved to utilize what fate had decreed, for that is the Way—the recognition and exploitation of the inevitable.

"Thank you, Nur ad-Din," I said by way of dismissal. "Prepare to leave for Tabriz within the week. You will see that everything my son destroyed is rebuilt and all damages paid for. I can't afford to lose face in the west right now. I'll go to Urganj myself."

After Nur ad-Din's departure, I went to my private suite and bathed. Then, too perturbed to leave my quarters, I slipped into a robe and ordered my supper brought to me. When Abdullah arrived, I dismissed my other servants and let him serve me.

"All right, Abdullah," I said, as soon as my other attendants were out of earshot, "what have you learned?"

"Your son is rapidly destroying himself, Amir—and you also."

"I know all that." I waved his preamble aside impatiently. "Tell me about his treatment of the Khanzade."

"Yes, Amir," Abdullah said humbly, as he set a tray of food on the serving table beside my couch. "I have the story as told by Khalid, her chamberlain."

"Very well. Get on with it."

"As soon as the Khanzade got settled in her palace, she gave an intimate little party for Miran Shah and the Shereza Begum. According to Khalid, the Khanzade pretended to drink too much and flaunted herself before Miran Shah—made quite a spectacle of herself, Khalid says, allowing her body to be most immodestly exposed at times." Abdullah paused.

"And then—?" I prompted him.

"Miran Shah seemed to be unable to control himself, so shamelessly did the Princess exhibit herself." Abdullah cleared his throat apologetically, and fearfully, it seemed.

"Don't be afraid, Abdullah—I'm not going to beat you, whatever you tell me about my family."

"Yes, Amir. Miran Shah developed a headache, and the Begum took him home. But that was only the beginning. The Begum, sensing the attraction the Khanzade held for Miran Shah—this from one of the Begum's maidservants—invited the Khanzade to her court to rouse Miran Shah from one of his fits of moodiness."

Abdullah paused in his narrative while he poured me a glass of wine. Then he continued.

"The exchange of visits continued, with the Khanzade becoming more and more tantalizing—Khalid indulged in some personal remarks, Amir; even servants have feelings."

"I'll overlook that," I said. "Go on."

"But the Begum was always in attendance. Then Miran Shah came one night with only a few Urganji nobles, friends of the Khanzade, in attendance. Amir, I must tell you—"

"Yes, you must."

"The Khanzade was more tempting than ever. She did the dance of the veils for her guests—and Miran Shah suddenly rose in a fury and sent the other amirs away. He stayed with the Khanzade."

Abdullah stood well away from me, well out of striking range, as though he feared that I would forget my promise not to beat him. I was perfectly calm, however, for Nur ad-Din's story was beginning to make sense as Abdullah reported the other side.

"And the Khanzade's kinsmen were not outraged?" I asked.

"No, Amir." Abdullah showed his surprise. "It is strange that you ask. Khalid was puzzled by their behavior, as though—"

"As though they were privy to the Khanzade's plans," I finished for him.

"Yes, Amir, that's it. The people were outraged by Miran Shah's continued abuse of the Khanzade. He took her to his own palace to live— but his Urganji courtiers joined in the debauchery, encouraged the Shah in his excesses. All of my sources confirm that, Amir. Khalid considers it most strange."

"I don't," I said under my breath.

"Nor I," said Abdullah, for he had heard me. "But her coming here I don't understand, unless—"

"Here?" I interrupted him. "Sevin Bey here in Samarkand?"

"Yes, Amir. The Khanzade disguised herself as a servingwoman and joined Amir Nur ad-Din's caravan. She's with friends, and I believe that she plans to visit you this evening."

"Nur ad-Din didn't tell me this," I said, sitting up on my couch.

"I'm sure he didn't know, Amir. But the servants in the caravan recognized her and have kept in touch with her and the servants of her friends in Samarkand. She's probably on her way here now, Amir."

Abdullah began clearing away my supper dishes. I went to a vault and got a bag of gold.

"Here, reward your spies," I said, and tossed the gold to Abdullah, who hastily transferred the tray to one hand and caught the bag. "Half of it's for you."

"Thank you, Amir," he said, and started out of the room.

Just outside the door he paused and turned back.

"A lady to see you, Amir," he announced. If I could have suspected him of such insolence, I would have sworn that he smiled.

"Send her in," I directed.

Abdullah stood aside and then closed the door behind the heavily veiled, black-shrouded figure of a woman. I felt as though I would have sensed the identity of my visitor even if I had not been expecting her. There was a strange radiation from her which filled the room and engulfed me, like something tangible.

"Welcome to the sanctuary of my palace, Daughter," I said.

I heard her gasp in surprise behind the black veil, at my unexpected recognition of her. She fell on her knees before me and clasped my hand.

"Oh, Father Timur, Most Gracious, Most Generous Amir, I have fled from the abuse and humiliation which your son has heaped upon me. I throw myself upon your mercy and seek your protection."

"Rise, Daughter," I said in my kindest tone. "I will listen to your plea."

As she stood up, the hood fell back on her shoulders and released a mass of loose copper curls to frame her face and tumble over the collar of her voluminous crepe stole. The perfume of her hair was freed at the same time, and its delicate sweetness filled my nostrils before Sevin Bey stepped back a little way and removed her veil.

The abuse she had suffered at the hands of my son had in no way diminished the beauty of her face—the same clear complexion, the same expressive green eyes, shaded by their burnt-gold lashes, features refined and deepened in character with maturity. Sevin Bey was in her middle twenties by that time. I stood aghast at the vision of wild enchantment.

Sevin Bey must have mistaken my temporary speechlessness as a pause to permit her to state her business.

"You no doubt have heard of Miran Shah's treatment of me," she began.

"I've talked to Nur ad-Din," I said.

"Then he's told you my story."

"Yes, he's told me *your* story."

"And that I was here?"

"No," I said. "I recognized you."

"You—you recognized me?" she repeated in disbelief.

"Yes, my dear. You can't disguise yourself from me. Perhaps we know each other too well." I let a little irony creep into my voice, and I felt my arm tensing in the old desire to strike her.

"Then you know that I must plead with you to remove your son from the governorship of my people, who hate him for what he has done to me, and for the degradation he has brought upon my country."

"That shall be done," I assured her, and shifted my gaze from her face for a moment. I could not look at her and keep my hands off her.

"And restore one of my own loyal kinsmen to the throne—one who is loyal to me as I am loyal to you."

I looked back at her to see her eyes burning with zeal for her cause and at the same time measuring me shrewdly and noting every nuance in my reactions.

"As you are loyal to me?" I repeated, with only so much sarcasm as I could not prevent from showing through.

Sevin Bey narrowed her eyes into the slits of a hunting leopard. She held her gaze steady and enunciated her words with deadly precision.

"I remained loyal to you while your son ravished me, clawed me, kicked me, beat me—as he vented his lust on me. As recently as last week he pawed and pinched me in his madness—the bruises still show. Look what your son has done to me!"

Dramatically she threw the stole off her shoulders and let it fall in a heap at her feet. It was all she had worn. She stood defiantly before me— a slender living golden flame, kindling in the charred blackness of her crumpled crepe stole and blazing triumphantly upward to the fiery glints in her molten bronze curls. Dazzled by the glare of her torching beauty, I could only say the words that had been forming in my mind during her indictment of my son.

"Loyal? You and your scheming kinsmen have brought degradation on my son and shame on my dynasty! I *know* what you have done—*all* that you have done."

Then I saw the bruises on her rigid body for the first time, and the heat of my anger rose to the pitch of her flaming eyes. No longer able to restrain myself, I swung hard with my right hand and slapped her savagely across her maddening, tempting mouth.

In an instant her eyes lost their brightness and seemed to smolder like live coals for a moment, before she threw her melting body against mine, and panted breathlessly, "And now you know how I did it."

When Sevin Bey touched me, my flesh was seared by the flame of her body—through my robe, where it was belted around me, and in bare contact, where the full length of her long legs had slipped between the folds of the skirt. I tasted the hot blood trickling over her lip where I had slapped her; and as though grasping for protection against the consuming fire of her embrace, I crushed her lithe body in my arms and sank my fingers in the thin flesh covering the small of her back.

"Hurt me! Hurt me, Timur!" she gasped hungrily, as I turned and laid her on my couch.

And in my hatred I tried hard to hurt her—to punish her with all I had—to leave her bruised and bleeding and aching. In some insane way I wanted to share her suffering with her, to force her to fight back, to hurt me as I hurt her. I wanted to suffer more than she, to feel more of the exquisite searing pain in the climax of our embrace than she could feel, to master the thing in her which had destroyed two of my sons.

And then she lay relaxed in my arms, as soft and loving as a kitten, smiling at me when I looked at her and speaking to me in a voice as gentle as the breeze which rippled the hangings of my window.

"Why didn't you make me show myself that first time you slapped me?" she asked. "Why did you wait so long?"

"You were my son's bride," I said.

"But you won me in battle."

"For my son."

"It didn't have to be."

"You hated me even then," I said.

She stroked my beard and let her fingertips trace the lines of my mouth and chin and then ran the palm of her hand along my chest and over my ribs and clawed gently at the flesh on my belly, the way a kitten plays with a satin pillow. I felt her body begin to stiffen under my own fingers as I moved my hand down from the firm resiliency of her full round breast to stroke her golden loins.

"I still hate you," she said, with a return of the original timbre to her voice.

"And I hate you," I said. "More than I did then. I have more cause now. You have destroyed my sons."

"I intended to destroy you, too."

"I know. I sensed it in the beginning."

"But now I shall not destroy you—not in my lifetime—not while I need you," she said. "And you won't put me away."

"You are the mother of my grandsons—my heirs—of course, you're safe."

"That's not the only reason," she said confidently, and her voice carried increasing hatred and triumph with every word. I began to feel the urge to strike her again—my hatred returned in increasing measure as I recovered my virility.

"But I shall destroy you and free my people," she said in a voice that cut like a talwar; and she raked her fingernails hard across the width of my belly, leaving streaks of oozing blood behind them.

Caught by surprise, I dug my own fingernails into the fleshy part of her thigh before I raised my arm and struck her a glancing blow on her chin with the flat of my hand. She rolled against me and sank her teeth into the lobe of my left ear, and the points of her bosom burned two holes in my chest.

"Hurt me!" she screamed, and boxed my right ear with her left hand. "Hurt me, Timur! Again!"

And again my rage burned its way into the golden-skinned vixen.

And so on, all night and all day. For three days I wrestled and battled with the passions of the wild Urganji princess—with her alternate moods of soft, docile, purring and ripping, biting, burning viciousness, with the unutterable sweetness of her surrender and the searing heat of her raging lust. I learned what she carried in her body that had destroyed my sons and might draw me down with them. I experienced in full the ecstatic pain which had broken Jahangir's spirit and driven Miran Shah to madness, and I neglected my own duties and realized that I was letting myself be consumed by the fire of Sevin Bey's witchery.

But I could not leave her. Whether it was hatred or lust, I could not tell—whether it was determination to master her or to surrender to her savage appetites, I did not know. Neither of us left the suite. I ordered food when I thought of it; and I frequently ran tubs full of cold water to cool the fever in our bruised and lacerated bodies, but always we returned to the battle-couch when our hatred flared again. Sometimes we slept, the long dead sleep of exhaustion, or short catnaps of delicious relaxation, but we always awoke simultaneously and sought the excruciating pain, which never seemed to lose its edge.

Then, some time after dark on the fourth day I awoke and found that

268

Sevin Bey was gone from my bed. I opened my eyes in time to see her wrap her burned-out body in the black cloak and steal out of my room as quietly as she had come. I did not know whether I was glad or not—whether I should follow her and bring her back or let her seek me when her strength returned.

I rose and bathed and put on my suit of Frank clothes. Then I stole out of my palace and sought the gates of Devon. I found Ali Soun asleep. I undressed without disturbing her and then shook her shoulder gently.

"Oh, my dear. I've missed you," she said sleepily and pushed her millet-colored hair back from her forehead. The winter blue of her eyes seemed to soothe my own burning irises, and the fresh whiteness of her body was a soft snowdrift on the blue satin sheet.

I slipped into bed beside her and soon found an unguent for my burn in her cool white flesh. She was like a drink of pure mountain spring water when one is surfeited to nausea with heavy southern wines. As she purged my body of its profane heat, my head cleared and I knew that Ali Soun was my fortress, impregnable to the ravages of Sevin Bey's fiery siege—and I had feared Ali Soun!

Either woman could have led a man far from the Way. But not both, each a foil and a complement to the other. A man who lets one woman blind him to the Way is a fool. Fire and snow—gold and ivory—and black—Nubja— I dropped off to sleep, relaxed, purified, restored to the Way.

CHAPTER

15

Shereza Begum and Miran Shah prepared to welcome me to Urganj as though my visit were a perfectly normal compliment from a monarch to his favorite daroga. The road was covered with carpets for a mile outside the city gates; and as my royal caravan, escorted by twelve thousand Kulchis, approached the open gates, my mind went back to the day the Sufi had refused to meet me on the plain. The noonday sun, glistening on the gilded domes of the rebuilt palaces and mosques, reminded me of the night fires which had razed Khiva and scorched Urganj itself on that campaign of some ten years before.

But mine was no complimentary progress—again I brought the Flaming Sword to keep the Way in Kharesm. The foolish schemes of Urganji patriots and the weakness of my son demanded that I carry out the destruction willed by Allah for such men, that His Way might not be hindered even momentarily in its inevitable spread to the corners of the earth. My realm could not contain within its borders a canker to corrode and eat away the metal from which I was forging the blade for Allah's scourge.

So I was not blinded by the pomp of my reception as I rode down the avenue of horsetail standards to the dais before Miran's palace and halted at the throne of the Shah and his Queen Mother. Nor did I miss the sullen note in the formal nonsense of my son's spoken greeting when I had dismounted to receive obeisance from the kneeling courtiers. Rather I welcomed the frank impatience in the voice of the Begum as I sat down beside her to review Miran's troops gathered in the registan.

"Did you have to come when it's so beastly hot?" she asked, and fanned herself briskly. "And with Miran Shah feeling so bad? Another month and Urganj would have been cool and comfortable."

"I had to come," I said.

I stole a glance at the flushed Begum, who overflowed the horn-and-teak throne by my side. Confirming my former suspicion of a hirsute upper lip, a barely perceptible line of black fuzz was beginning to mark the upper curve of Shereza's once seductive mouth. And beneath three bulbous chins the bosom which had been the prized gift of Allah had lost its individuality and merged into the bloated belly of Fatima's aging daughter.

"You could have waited," Shereza said peevishly. "We hardly had time to prepare entertainment."

"I've waited long enough," I said. "And I'll make my own entertainment."

"It'll serve you right, for barging in on us like this— Keep those fans moving!" she snapped at the slaves who waved the long ivory staves tipped with peacock feathers.

"A lot of people will get their deserts before this day is over," I said, annoyed by her continued nagging.

"You won't do anything to Miran Shah," she said defiantly—and then with a shift to almost pathetic pleading, she continued, "He's a good boy. He's ill—high-strung—but not to be blamed. Anyway, what you've heard about him is all lies."

"I'll decide that."

"You won't harm him," she said positively. "I won't let you."

Miran Shah, who had left the dais to ride in review with his personal regiment, passed the stand just then and saluted the royal standard. I rose and returned his salute; and Shereza waved her green scarf vigorously and made moues at her son, as a fat peasant girl would flirt with a common soldier. I was glad to have her attention diverted from me and made no effort to reopen the conversation during the rest of the parade.

Shereza accompanied me to the state chamber to await the arrival of

Miran Shah and his courtiers from the parade grounds. However, when I had my men bring in basins and a chopping block, she shrieked, "Not your own son!" and promptly fainted. I sent her away on a litter, with the physician in attendance.

So the Begum's throne was empty when Miran Shah and his Urganji courtiers, in the custody of my loyal subalterns, entered the state chamber. The culprits wore all sorts of facial expressions—fear, cowardice, arrogance, resentment. Only one man, a hunchbacked dwarf, saw the humor of the chopping block and the two big black eunuchs who stood beside it with their heavy scimitars held at parade rest.

"Justice, Noble Gentlemen! Your executioners are obviously innocent of the chief of your sins," he sang out gaily and danced a jig before the solemn procession. I was amazed at the nimble feet and legs of the twisted little man.

My own attendants laughed heartily.

The dwarf bowed in gracious appreciation of the applause. Then he snatched a tufted helmet from the nearest amir and mounted the chopping block. Swinging the helmet across his body in mock courtesy, he struck a pose of great dignity and spoke in a deep pompous voice.

"After you, my gracious amirs. You have always taken precedence over me—by all means go before me now!"

He tossed the helmet to its owner and did a quick backward somersault off the block. Then he bowed and swept his right arm toward the executioners, indicating his willingness to yield the place of honor.

Again my courtiers roared at the antics of the clown. I beckoned him to come and sit on the Begum's throne beside me. Instead of dancing, however, the misshapen little man insolently mimicked my own limping gait on his way to the throne—thereby signing his own death warrant. No one laughed.

"Who are you?" I asked, when he took his seat.

"Jotah, the fool. Who are you?"

I ignored his question and signaled for the execution of the first conspirator.

"Amir Harith will pray, like this," Jotah said, and mumbled gibberish through taut nervous lips.

And when I looked back at Harith approaching the block, I saw precisely the same face the fool had made, praying feverishly up to the very time the eunuch's scimitar crashed through the neckbone and Harith's head fell into the basin.

"Zuhair will curse you," said Jotah.

Zuhair went to his death screaming curses at the top of his voice.

"Rawija's tears will look like this.

Jotah forced great streaming tears to run down his pockmarked cheeks, as Rawija wept into the basin before it began to fill with the blood spurting from his severed jugular vein.

The fool continued to mimic and to predict unerringly the behavior of each of the thirty nobles who were executed in the state chamber that day. I marveled at the little jester's insight into the character of men. When his time came, I turned to him and paid my compliments.

"Jotah, with your knowledge of men you might have been King Maker. Of course, your size and deformity might have hindered you in performance of state duties."

Jotah's eyes narrowed to venomous slits and stared at me in utter hatred. I chuckled at the precision with which I had punctured Jotah's bravado.

"Timur," Jotah said, with complete disregard for my title, "with your keenness of perception, you might have made a good fool. Of course, your crippled foot might have hindered you in your dancing and tumbling."

I winced when Jotah's barb struck home. The fool chuckled to himself and did another backflip off my elevated platform and danced a few intricate jig steps. Then he assumed my lameness and limped the rest of the way to the block.

There he turned and saluted me solemnly. I rose from my throne and returned his salute. And I remained standing while Jotah knelt by the block and an Ethiopian gelding cut off his head. He was perhaps the most dangerous one of all, for he publicly proclaimed himself a fool.

Miran Shah had stood by and watched the executions without a change of expression ever crossing his dull fat face. Only when I dismissed the executioners did he look my way and show mild surprise—not relief—that I had spared his life.

"Come with me, Son," I said. "Let's go to your mother."

"Yes, Father," he said tonelessly, and fell into step behind me as I walked down the corridor to the Begum's suite.

Before we reached her room, we could hear Shereza wailing and moaning. The sounds would have been pathetic if indeed her son had been beheaded. As it was, the unseemly noises were only ludicrous.

I walked in without waiting to be announced. Shereza lay on a couch under a fringed canopy and wept while her maids fanned her.

"Prepare to return to Samarkand with me at once," I said without preamble.

"Samarkand!" she repeated, and hauled her bulk into a sitting position. Then she saw Miran Shah.

"Miran Shah!" she exclaimed. "You didn't kill him! You didn't hurt my baby. Come to Mother, Miran."

272

She broke down completely when Miran Shah knelt before her and laid his face in her lap. Her whole body shook with her snorting sobs, and it was several minutes before she was calm enough to talk again.

"Timur," she said, "I knew you wouldn't. I knew you wouldn't harm my baby. You love him and you love me. You're so sweet."

"We leave at dawn," I said. "Be ready to go."

"Not tomorrow," she objected. "We haven't time to pack."

"Yes, tomorrow."

"And it's so hot. Can't we wait another month? It'll be cool then."

"No," I said. "I must go right back. Nur ad-Din will take over here and punish the lesser offenders. But I must go—now—and you, too."

"We'll come later," she whined impatiently. Already she had forgotten my kindness in sparing her son. "Miran Shah isn't feeling well, are you, Son?"

"No, Mother," he slobbered.

"He can ride in a litter," I said.

"I don't see why you have to rush us so." Shereza pushed Miran Shah away from her and motioned to her servants to fan more vigorously. She undid her collar and mopped her moustached lip with a limp green scarf.

"You don't need to see," I said angrily—she was trying my patience. "Just be ready at dawn."

I turned and stalked out.

"Timur, you're unreasonable!" she screamed after me. "Unreasonable!"

I bumped into the physician just outside the Begum's door.

"How is she, Amir?" he asked.

"Mean," I said. "Give her a good strong laxative to purge her disposition."

The old physician laughed tolerantly.

"I'm afraid there's more wrong with the Begum than simple constipation," he said. "Going through the *change,* you know."

"No, I don't know," I said shortly. "But any change would be for the better." And I strode on down the corridor toward the state chamber.

From my own military intelligence and from the report made by Abdullah while he attended me in a banja, I pieced together a complete account of the conspiracy; and by midnight I had compiled a proscription list for Nur ad-Din to work from in his further executions. Then I retired, with a feeling of satisfaction in the internal integrity of my empire. Miran Shah had been my last weak link, or so I thought.

But upon my return to Samarkand I was met by a scene of riot and confusion. The bazaars where closed and barred against the turmoil in the streets, and slaves and beggars clamored obscenely on every side, their filthy cries echoing incongruously from the clean lustrous tiles of my perfect city. I saw no one in authority to explain the sorry spectacle, and I detached a thousand of my kulchis to restore order and hurried ahead to dispose of Shereza Begum and her degenerate son.

There was a place already prepared for them in the Begum's wing of the palace. I rushed them there and tarried only long enough to issue orders for their care.

Shereza was exhausted and sank onto a couch as soon as she entered her gaudy chamber. But her eyes were alert and fearful.

"You aren't going to take my baby away from me, are you, Timur?" she asked pathetically.

"No," I said, and kept my voice gentle. "Your son shall never again leave your suite. I know your feeling for him, and I shall respect it."

"I knew you were good," she said, her eyes softening in gratitude.

"I have issued orders that he is to stay with you and to be given everything he wants—all the wine, opium, hashish, women—everything. You may have him to yourself. It will be your privilege to answer his slightest or his most extravagant whim, immediately and fully. Will you like that?"

"Oh, yes, Timur. No woman ever had a sweeter, kinder husband. From now on, I'll be your slave—just let me keep my baby."

Shereza lumbered off the couch and knelt before me. She clasped my right hand in both of her clammy ones—no longer the warm dry palms of Shah Malik's favorite daughter—and drenched my fingers in her grateful tears. I helped her back onto her couch and left for my courtchamber and its puzzle.

I quickly cleared the courtchamber of all complainants except Daoud and Nasir ben Adam, the latter worn and haggard and more perturbed than he had been when he made his last report. And Daoud was grim when he stated their business.

"Our wonder boy has failed again," he said, indicating Nasir ben Adam.

"You mean he didn't have the heart to carry out my orders?" I asked.

"Oh, yes, he had the heart—in fact, I've never seen a man take to his work the way Nasir ben Adam took to the fine art of maiming mankind."

"Then what *is* the trouble?"

"Let him tell you."

"All right, Nasir ben Adam—tell me what happened."

"You know I tried to help the beggars—and you, Amir," he began nervously.

"So you told me—proceed."

"Well, I began by reminding the ungrateful wretches of what I had done for them. And—and they laughed and jeered at me and demanded a

274

larger dole. Then in full view of throngs of the dirty bastards, I had twenty men's hands cut off—"

Nasir ben Adam's eyes glowed with fiendish delight at the memory; and his lips curled into a satisfied smile—which, however, faded as quickly as it had come.

"But, as soon as the men were scattered they went right back to cluttering up the streets and defiling the air with their eternal *bakhshish! bakhshish!*"

He clapped his hands over his ears as though the beggars' cries haunted him even in my courtchamber.

"I had the stinking beggars rounded up again," he went on, "and had the tongues cut out of the mouths of a hundred of the whining vermin—and the eyes gouged out of another hundred—and I killed a thousand outright—and—"

"And what?"

"The others cheered me for reducing the number of beggars—cutting down their competition."

"If you've cut down the number of beggars, I would say that you've accomplished something," I said.

"But he hasn't," Daoud put in.

"Tell me the rest," I said to Nasir ben Adam.

"As soon as I put a thousand beggars off the street, two thousand appeared from nowhere, hearing that there were few beggars in Samarkand. Then after a week, when the blind, mute, and maimed dogs recovered sufficiently, they appeared on every corner, displaying their empty eye-sockets, waving the scabrous stumps of their arms, blowing their stinking breath through gaping tongueless mouths, making capital of their mutilations—turning *my punishment* to profit!"

Nasir ben Adam ended in a scream, and actually had the audacity to pound on the arms of my throne with his fists and stare directly at me with his wild bloodshot eyes.

"And then," he whispered huskily, and let him arms fall limp by his sides, "and then the able-bodied beggars stormed my quarters—thousands of them—and shouted and shook their fists at me for giving their crippled brothers an advantage. They screamed that a whole man could no longer beg a copper in the streets—that I had ruined the time-honored tradition of almsgiving—that I had robbed them of their sacred rights—that I had offended Allah."

"Perhaps you have," I agreed.

"Now, I live surrounded by guards—a prisoner in my own house—not able to show my face for fear of the very men whom I tried to help—whom I maimed—whom I killed!"

Nasir ben Adam turned away in utter defeat and dropped down on an ottoman, without my permission.

I looked at Daoud.

"It's as he says." Daoud nodded as he spoke. "As I expected. There's not a thing you can do for them, to them, or with them."

"Nothing," said Nasir ben Adam, half to himself. "They have nothing—they expect nothing—yet they ask everything. You can't take from them what they have not. You can't hurt them—they're suffering already. Taking their lives is no punishment—death is a blessing. Try to lift them up, and they pull you down with them."

He shrugged his shoulders and slumped dejectedly on the ottoman before me. He still faced away from me. Daoud started to take him away, but I dismissed my daroga so I could be alone with the disillusioned young reformer.

"Nasir ben Adam, you have indeed offended Allah," I said, "by meddling with His chosen people."

He turned to face me and looked my way with glazed, veiled eyes.

"On your orders, Amir," he said, but not reproachfully.

"You have done me no disservice," I said, and smiled at the beaten young man. "Rather you have shown me the final vision of the Tree of Life—the Purpose of the Way."

He blinked his eyes stupidly. Whether he understood me or not, I could not tell—nor did it matter. I continued my monologue for my own benefit.

"You have offended Allah, not by maiming His creatures, but by trying to lift them up after He has reduced them to an acceptable state of beggary. It is the fate of men like you—who would thwart His plan—to be disillusioned, misunderstood, discredited—and crucified, like the infidel Jesus, for trying to help the wretched masses.

"Allah has rewarded those men who have seen his Way and helped Him to make slaves and beggars of other men. Now, I know. I've learned to read the course of the Way. You have shown me the Purpose. Come with me and receive your reward."

I rose from the throne. Nasir ben Adam got up and stumbled along behind me into the antechamber, where we picked up my personal guard to escort us to Nasir ben Adam's house.

Throngs of filthy beggars clogged the streets for several blocks around the place. My guards parted the howling mob and let us ride through to our destination.

When we had entered the house and reappeared on a second-story balcony, I raised my hand for silence. The unruly crowd booed and shouted insults at Nasir ben Adam for a full minute after my signal, but finally quieted down.

"Listen, my loyal subjects!" I began. "In my absence, this man has wronged you and offended Allah by interfering with your sacred right to accept alms."

The mob alternately cheered me and screamed insults at Nasir ben Adam. When they quieted down again, I continued.

"I shall see that you are avenged. As he has treated you, so shall I treat him."

I handed Nasir ben Adam a gold dinar from my purse. He accepted it, with a look of bewilderment on his face, and the throng of beggars sent up a deafening roar of applause.

Then I had my tavachis cut off Nasir ben Adam's hands and throw them to the crowd. Another frenzied cheer welcomed my act of justice.

Next I had the reformer's tongue cut out and then his eyes gouged from their sockets. The howling mob fought savagely for the souvenirs when they were thrown from the balcony; and a dozen or more beggars were trampled to death in the mad scramble for Nasir ben Adam's head when it was cut off and dropped to the street below.

I waited for the confusion to abate somewhat and then had the headless body thrown off the balcony. It was ripped and torn and dismembered in a matter of seconds, as the vengeful jackals in the street below tore into it with knives and daggers and their bare hands—even their teeth. I waited on the balcony until the beggars had marched away triumphantly, following Nasir ben Adam's head, stuck on a pikestaff, as their standard— their symbol of victory for the rights of man. Allah must have been pleased by the sight.

Certainly I was pleased with the work of Nasir ben Adam—the final revelation he had made. I, the only man of my time, had learned the secret of Allah, the Purpose of the Way of the Tree of Life. I was a whole man with a complete vision.

As I lay with Nubja, the whole woman, that night, I felt myself her equal for the first time. As she was created to give life and hope to man, so was I created to bring death and despair to the progeny of all mothers. I would deny her purpose no longer.

"Nubja, you may have a son," I told her, "and I promise you that he shall be a prince—as he would have been among your own people. He shall rise to make slaves of others, your son and mine."

CHAPTER

1

My beard had already begun to turn gray by the time I was fifty years old—not quite forty-nine by Ali Soun's long calendar, which was more in accord with the seasons than our own as given us by the Prophet Mohammed.* But I rather welcomed the added authority which the superficial signs of age brought with them, for I was really just reaching the prime of my physical vigor and could therefore command the dual respect of my sword and of grizzled wisdom. I could claim the title of *father* among those who had been wont to look upon me as *elder brother*.

And as I sat in the suite which I retained in the palace of my wives—although my official quarters had been moved to the Hermitage, outside the gardens—I could see the real progeny of my loins. There were some three hundred boys old enough to play in the palace gardens and an equal number of toddlers still with their mothers in the zenana. I had a few more daughters than sons; but since the girls were trained almost exclusively inside the seraglio, I seldom saw them at play. Indeed they were such strangers to me that I sometimes took the most beautiful ones—of slave mothers, of course—as concubines, although I had their babies destroyed lest the infants develop mental or physical abnormalities and so bring shame on my name.

Shah Rukh was then fifteen years old, a thoughtful, studious youngster, very like Jahangir except for the latter's extreme sensitivity; and it was he who sat beside me on a second-story balcony and watched the younger boys fight their mock battles with wooden swords and either stick horses or slaves for their mounts. Pir Mohammed, although only ten at the time —several years younger than some of my own sons of low-born mothers —was impersonating me and commanding the victorious army.

I could easily recognize myself on the playground, for whoever portrayed me mimicked my limp—wore my infirmity as though it were a mark of distinction. And I marveled at the precocity of the children in aping their elders, not me but the blind fools of the world who will seize upon the weakness of a great man as the secret of his greatness and imitate, exaggerate—even worship—his defect and ignore the true source of his strength. Perhaps it is that weakness and deformity are universal and that futile men recognize only weakness and hope vainly that their own debilities may by some miracle lift them out of their abysmal mediocrity.

"Does Pir Mohammed offend you by limping, Father?" asked Shah Rukh, as he noted my attention to my grandson.

* The Mohammedan calendar has twelve months, alternately of thirty and twenty-nine days each, for a total of three hundred and fifty-four days with no intercalation for leap year, and so retrogresses through the seasons every thirty-two and one half years.

"No, Son," I said. "Why?"

"Mother has told me never to do it—that you are sensitive about it."

"I'm not sensitive about my lame foot, not when children are emulating me. But I allow no man to mock me—to make an epithet of my lameness. Does she caution the other children?"

"No, Father, not that I know of."

Dilshad was fiercely loyal to me, and I knew that she inspired loyalty in my sons, who all looked to her for their ideals. But I suspected that the Sarai Khanum was not above letting all the young princes, except her own son, offend me at some time or another and perhaps run the risk of incurring my disfavor.

"Does the Khanzade Sevin Bey advise her sons not to limp?" I asked, for I had an idea that Sevin Bey would encourage anything that might hurt me.

"I don't know, Father. Mother keeps her away from Pir Mohammed and Mohammed Sultan most of the time—and Khalil Sultan is only six—I don't know much about him. Shall I ask?"

"No—no. As I said, it doesn't matter. You're very observant—I was just trying to see how observant."

"I'll observe more carefully," said Shah Rukh apologetically, as though I had already made him my tavachi and he had failed me.

I neither encouraged nor discouraged him. I felt that he was developing quite satisfactorily under the expert guidance of Dilshad.

And I was pleased with Pir Mohammed, as his army, with Mohammed Sultan his second in command, invaded a tulip bed and drove the enemy into a brambly mass of running roses along the garden wall. The victors' battle shouts were true Tatar yells, and some of the death cries of the vanquished seemed equally realistic, evoked no doubt by the sudden impact of tender young bottoms on rose thorns.

But although my forces were invariably victorious, there were no decisive battles. The armies re-formed, went out of sight behind court buildings, and charged into view again under different leaders and different standards. I noted that some of my low-born sons were permitted to play my part, but none of the princelings save Djon Pitr ever appeared in the ranks of the enemy.

Djon Pitr, however, did lead one army of fair young Frank knights galloping out of the gates of Devon screaming "Saracen" into the counter-charge of "Infidel." He of course was vanquished by his half-nephew, Mohammed Sultan; and I had an idea that both of the nine-year-old warriors were conscious of the fact that Ali Soun Agha was not recognized as the equal of Sevin Bey Khanzade—her son not entitled to victory over true royalty.

Ali Soun's influence was in evidence, however, in the strict chivalric code observed by the Crusaders, even those recruited outside the walls of Devon. It was obvious that the Frank *Levedi* had told her own romantic stories to all my sons, who had free run of her village. And I saw that the Saracens were already learning how to take advantage of the silly Western courtesies and win clear-cut decisions by refusing to honor the code.

Nor did Djon Pitr follow the customs of the Saracens. Whenever he joined the ranks of the Tatars, he invariably played the role of a priest, blessing the commanders before they went into battle—making the sign of the cross, however, instead of following the hocus-pocus of the mollah. No one noticed the difference. Perhaps not even Djon Pitr was aware of his mistake. He was accepted just as he was; and I wondered how little Amyris, Nubja's three-year-old mulatto son, would fare when he was old enough to go to war in the palace gardens.

From my balcony I could see other evidences of my efforts in Samarkand. Buildings housing colleges and academies and medresses rose above nobles' palaces in all sections of the city—some imposing edifices of white marble, others modest structures of severe simplicity, but all teeming with misguided scholars who argued their vanities and paid homage to me as the patron of learning. Quite prominent was the observatory, almost finished, atop the highest hill inside the walls, from which the astronomers and astrologers would soon search the heavens through their tubes and lenses imported from Khitai.

All of these vied with each other and with domed mosques and spired temples and colorful commercial buildings for the chief claim to beauty in my Sapphire of the Orient. Newest and currently most pretentious was the quarter of the palace grounds being put in readiness for the arrival of the Manchu Princess, who had already stopped at Xanadu on her slow, leisurely journey to Samarkand.

All of the construction reminded me of its complement—the machines of destruction, to which I had devoted equal attention during the last ten years. I found more and more pleasure in these instruments of aggression, but said little about my plans for them. Amirs would talk, and women would find in a catapult a rival of my admiration for them. Siege machines could be improved with time, but I was beginning to know what time could do to women—and to me.

"The war games must seem a little childish to you, Shah Rukh," I remarked to my son, who was surreptitiously reading snatches from a book he had brought with him.

"No," he said sheepishly, "I like to watch the children, but I see them every day."

"They'll be my protectors in my old age," I said. "What are you reading?"

"*Sohrab and Rustum*," he answered, and seemed embarrassed that I had discovered his book.

"By Firdausi—in the *Shahnama*—isn't it?" I asked, keeping any hint of disapproval out of my voice. I did not disapprove.

"Yes," he answered in surprise.

"Have you read *Yussuf and Zuleika* from the same work?"

"Yes, Father—I had no idea—"

"That I had read them?" I smiled at him.

"No—yes—" He blushed and stammered.

"*Sohrab and Rustum* is a good battle story—somewhat old-fashioned, perhaps. Would you like to go with me to the planning room at the Hermitage and see what modern warfare is like, or will be like? I'm going there presently."

"Yes, sir!" he said eagerly, and I was pleased with his response. It was no fault of his that I had fought no major campaign since he had been old enough to ride with me, so that he had spent more time in the academy than in the saddle.

"Then order our horses and we'll ride over," I said.

While Shah Rukh went for the horses, I continued to watch the earnest young warriors in the garden. They seemed tireless in their endless play —or work, since one campaign necessitated the bridging of a garden canal with improvised pontoons: horse troughs, benches, and flowerboxes, laboriously carried to the stream by hard-driven slaves, who then became soldiers again and stormed a mulberry grove on the other side, flushing several bands of guerillas from its fastnesses.

Shah Rukh appeared beneath the balcony with our horses, and I descended by an outside stairway and mounted Kunk Oghlan. The appearance of the horses brought an immediate truce in the warfare. All of the warriors clambered back across the bridge to escort us to the garden gate. Only Pir Mohammed, however, was sufficiently well mounted to keep up with the easy canter of our mounts. He rode his slave, a full-grown young Mongol, whom he beat with his wooden sword and kept at a dead run down the marble avenue to the front entrance. There my grandson saluted me gravely and then waved his left hand in a childish farewell and watched us ride out into the street.

I turned in my saddle to wave at the boy and to appraise the central part of the royal palace, which was still under construction. The workmen were well along with the third story; but there was much slow work ahead, for I required the masons and carpenters to muffle the sounds of their labor with blankets so the occupants of the first two stories would

284

not be disturbed. Even in its unfinished state, the massive building was a thing of beauty and splendor.

So was the street, when I turned my attention back to the crowd parting to let me through. Sleek Balkhi two-humped camels sniffed haughtily at their shaggy cousins from the cold Gobi, though the northern animals carried fragrant bales of spice, brought from India by way of Kashmir and the Karakorum Pass, and precious silks from Khitai, while the snobs bore only the fancy litters of worthless, spoiled aghas and pampered courtesans. More striking perhaps, and more disdainful, were the big black eunuchs—their skin glistening with scented oils—who swayed gently in perfect rhythm between the fore and aft thills of the Persian princesses' elaborate sedan chairs. The more thrifty Jewesses rode gentle donkeys and made their bid for elegance through richly brocaded sunshades held over them by slaves.

But the native Tatar horsemen and horsewomen were most attractive to me, and to Shah Rukh, who rode beside me and drank in the kaleidoscope of the street scene. And my son, though seemingly unspoiled by the luxury of his surroundings, fitted perfectly into the dream I was creating to turn men's minds from the true tasks they were performing in my service. Handsome, intelligent, alert, he accepted Samarkand as a matter of course —as the perfect city—and I was sure that he would hold residents of any other part of the world in proper contempt when the time came for him to destroy their culture.

A few blocks below the palace we turned out of the main stream of elite traffic, through the ragged fringe of filthy beggars, into a military thoroughfare leading to Hermitage Hill. That street, quieter than the main concourse to the registan, was no less brilliant in its colors. An avenue of tall lean poplars, it ran between park areas kept clear of permanent buildings so visiting amirs might pitch their yurts and kibitkas and pavilions in the shade of rustling sycamores or quiet plum and apricot trees which grew in the private campsites separated by hedges of lilac and pomegranate bushes.

I was pleased by Shah Rukh's recognition of the standards of all the tribal chieftains whose camps flanked the thoroughfare. Most of the tribes encamped in the front areas were mountain men; the desert tribes, fascinated by the greenery and the flowing canals fed by the Zaravshan, usually went farther back, into more secluded portions of the park. Shah Rukh, however, knew by sight the more remote standards as well, wherever they were visible through breaks in the foliage. I saw the tutoring of Dilshad and Saif ad-Din in my son's knowledge of the insignia of their folk.

But as we approached the heavily guarded treasury and armory building, which shared the hill with my court and living quarters, Shah Rukh no longer had eyes for the horsetail standards. He had never been on Hermitage Hill before, and I could tell that only sheer will power kept him from breaking precedence and urging his horse on ahead of Kunk Oghlan.

When we stopped at the treasury and tossed our reins to grooms standing before the entrance, Shah Rukh leaped lightly from his horse first; and then to cover his breach of courtesy, he hurried to my side and held my stirrup—quite needlessly—while I dismounted.

"All right, Son," I said. "We'll go to the drafting room first—I have business there."

I led the way to the drafting room, and immediately lost my son, for the room was filled with drawings and scale models of every known war machine—catapults, trebuchets, mangonels, rams, fire projectors—and the draftsmen and mechanics, all proud of their work, enthusiastically explained and demonstrated everything Shah Rukh showed an interest in, which was everything. I left him with the workmen and went into the office of my chief mathematician, whom I had recruited from an Arab academy to calculate problems in torsion, counterweight, trajectory, and other principles in ballistics.

"Good afternoon, Amir," he said, without rising or showing any other signs of obeisance. Seemingly nothing which could not be reduced to an equation was of any importance to him—not even his monarch.

"What have you learned about the fire powder from Khitai?" I asked.

"Very little, Amir—very little. It is quite baffling—quite baffling." He put down a quill beside a paper covered with neat little blocks of figures and scratched his bald head.

I sat down across the table from him.

"I'm positive that the powder can be used to propel missiles," I said. "And I've heard that in some instances it has exploded and torn great holes in walls and buildings—whether by accident or design, I've been unable to learn."

"I, too, Amir, have heard that it was used in Morocco to hurl stones and iron balls some years ago—but how, I don't know, I don't know." He shook his head sadly.

"I've weighed it," he continued, "I've burned it—in little piles—in big piles. All I get is a little *poof!*—or a big *poof!*" He threw his hands up to accent his *poofs!*

"I see power in it," he went on, "but how to measure it—how to harness it—" Again he shook his head and shrugged his shoulders.

"What do the alchemists say about it?" I asked.

"Alchemists—humph! Guessers, piddlers, Amir—guessers and piddlers. They can't even make the powder."

"You figure out how to use it, and I'll conquer Khitai to get it."

"The Franks can make it, too, or so I heard in Istamboul."

"Then I'll conquer the Franks."

The Arab smiled at me as though I were a silly child.

"You are like a hunter or a fisherman, Amir, who no longer has to hunt or fish for his food but makes a game of it—more interested in weapons and tackle than in the catch. All these things—" He swept his arm around to indicate the drawings on the walls of his office and the big room outside.

"Such men have the best gear," I pointed out.

"Yes, but not the skill or the purpose of the man who uses poorer tools through necessity, for his survival."

"I've lost none of my skill or purpose, or interest in the catch," I said, rising to leave. "Find out how to use fire powder in war." I was firm.

"I'll try, Amir," he said, rising also—at last. "But you don't need it—you're secure, safe and powerful, with what you have. Besides it will be quite expensive, quite a burden on your people to buy it in any quantity. I can figure that out."

Quite expensive! Quite a burden on my people! As though they existed for any other purpose but to bear the burden of war. That is the Way of the Tree of Life—that men shall create and build and grow things and enslave themselves and dissipate their surplus on machines with which to tear down and destroy what other men have created and built and grown—until all men are slaves and beggars, groveling vermin acceptable to Allah.

The insolent, bland stupidity of the Arab came near making me angry. I doubted that he was even trying to solve the riddle of the fire powder, expert though he was in purely mechanical ballistics. But I hid whatever feelings I had as I strode out of his office and joined a circle of draftsmen, in the center of which was Shah Rukh shooting spitballs from a miniature catapult.

The men dispersed respectfully—they had none of the absent-minded arrogance of their master—and I watched my son operate the machine with exceptional skill. His mind, which I had feared was somewhat academically inclined, seemed to grasp at once the principles of the siege machines.

"Would you like to watch the smiths?" I asked. "I've finished here."

"Oh—it's you, Father," he said, rousing himself from his absorption in the toy. "Yes, sir. I'd like to see everything."

He seemed reluctant to leave the drafting room, but his eyes lighted up again as we entered the metal shop, where a hundred men banged away on red-hot pieces of iron and steel, fashioning and testing experimental blades and armor. He was fascinated for a time by the roaring forges; then he made the rounds of the ringing anvils and the cases of finished ordnance which lined the walls of the outer room.

"An improvement over *Sohrab and Rustum,* don't you think?" I asked.

"Oh, yes. These things are real."

I was glad that he could distinguish between reality and the fantasy of poets, but he had misunderstood me.

"I mean this gear is far superior to what Sohrab and Rustum used."

"I guess so—I'm not sure what they used."

And I caught my first glimpse of Shah Rukh's lack of imagination. I saw value in my son but limitations, too, and my mind reverted to little Pir Mohammed.

The rest of the tour seemed of little interest to Shah Rukh. He was polite but not deeply impressed by the wealth in my treasury—he had grown up in luxury—and although he could read the maps of the country and follow my post routes and pipelines which carried fresh water to the caravanserais established along them, he failed to grasp the significance of water and comfort in the blistering desert. Those things were not real to him, not yet.

But they were very real to desert travelers. Shade, icewater, fresh horses at every stop—protection from raiders—furnished to all merchants by my government for one flat fee. Those services amazed all who passed through my realm, and they became famous throughout Asia and into the land of the Franks. The stories of my efficiency, stories which were spread by travelers and enlarged by scholars who had gone out from my academies, made other peoples dissatisfied with their own rulers and their own archaic ways of life. Many teachers and bazaar orators said openly that all rulers who did not follow my example were selfish and stupid. My own subjects lauded my public projects—my fast courier service, though none of them sent letters; my travelers' hostels, though they slept on the ground outside; my pipelines and iced fountains, though thousands labored painfully laying the pipes and sledding the ice down from the mountains, enslaved by the system they praised. It was all pleasing to Allah, according to His Plan for deluding mankind.

Yet those things were not real for Shah Rukh—he saw only the maps before him and commented on the skill of the draftsmen who had made them. I thought more and more of Pir Mohammed as I rode back to the palace with Dilshad's son.

CHAPTER

2

As the day of Bibi Khanum's arrival drew near, all of the restlessness and irritability caused by three or four years of military inactivity seemed to converge in one spot inside me and to swell and expand into a force which would burst my being to effect its release. I found myself showing anger at the annoying mannerisms of my aides and courtiers. The tedious, polite bickering of obstinate envoys who came to Samarkand to negotiate treaties for their perfidious amirs drove me near to distraction. In some instances, I was sure, they made attempts to push me as far as possible short of actual war—to wear down my resolve to bide my time and make war at my own convenience.

I knew full well the validity of Kurgan's warning not to let feelings or passions of any kind enter into dealings with men—war or diplomacy or business. But time after time I caught myself on the verge of flailing out in rage at some man who annoyed me. I turned to my women to dissipate my passions, as Kurgan had counseled. But my slave girls relieved my tension not one whit. I did not love them. I merely wasted my efforts.

I looked forward to the coming of the Manchu princess. Perhaps she would fill my need. However irrational it may seem, there is something about royal women that lifts the experience of lying with them out of the ordinary. Foolish men know it. They bedeck common sluts in sables and jewels and convince themselves that they are consorting with princesses.

More and more fretful and nervous in anticipation of my Manchu bride, I could vent some of my feelings on Shereza Begum, not physically—she was physically repulsive to me—but in more subtle ways. After a particularly harrowing court session, I called on the Begum and her besotted son. I was ushered into Miran's throne room—more elaborate than my own—and I felt as though I were the subordinate being presented to my betters, as indeed I was, in the mind of the Begum.

"Why, Miran—it's your father!" said Shereza graciously, when I entered the overornamented salon.

"Oh, yes, Father," said Miran Shah dully from the throne, where he sat, surrounded by a bevy of near-naked beauties, who fanned him and served him wine and caressed him according to their various notions as to what would win his favor.

Miran Shah made no obeisance, nor did the Begum, though she motioned me to share her divan, placed in the proper position for the throne of the Queen Mother.

"Do sit awhile with us, Amir Timur," she said. "You call on us so infrequently."

I limped over to the divan and sank into its lush cushions, which somehow recalled the pleasure I had once found in Shereza's young body.

"Does your foot pain you, dear?" the Begum asked, and I thoroughly enjoyed the rigor of hatred which ran through me.

"No—not at all."

"Your limp seems more pronounced," she commented. "I thought perhaps it was worse."

"No worse than usual," I said shortly.

Shereza dropped the subject.

"Doesn't Miran Shah present a fine figure on the throne?" she asked, softly, blindly. He presented the figure of a jug.

"He seems to take to the throne room," I said evasively, as I surveyed the rich tapestries covering the white porcelain walls and the intricate mosaic designs in the ceiling.

"Oh, yes. He's born to the office. I'm so happy that we are able to accustom him to all this while he's still young. He'll make an impressive monarch," she said pointedly. And that was my pleasure—pleasure in the vanity of her insinuations. Her drugged, drunken baby the heir to my empire!

"Have you chosen a princess for him yet?" I asked. I knew that the thought was a painful one to her.

"No," she said, wrinkling her brow. "There just don't seem to be any worthy princesses any more. I've communicated with the Maharani of Delhi—a cousin of mine—and several others. Their suggestions seem so *common* though—not suitable for Miran Shah at all."

She frowned until she said her son's name and then smiled pleasantly, as though the words tasted good in her mouth.

"Princess Sonja seems to be proving highly satisfactory to Omar Sheik," I reminded her.

"But a Russian!" She curled her hirsute upper lip in contempt. "Not for Miran Shah—not in Samarkand. For Omar Sheik, in the provinces, perhaps—"

"She has borne him sturdy sons. Let's see—Abu Bekr would be about eight now, and Mirza Rustum, nine."

I was finding delight in goading Shereza. Her pride in motherhood did not extend to grandmotherhood. She took no notice of Miran Shah's children by his concubines, but I could tell that the thought of having to acknowledge her baby as the father of a prince was odious—

more odious perhaps than the thought of sharing him with another royal lady.

Miran Shah suddenly struck out savagely at one of his girls and slapped her off the dais.

"What did she do to you, Son?" Shereza asked in horror, and rose and lumbered over to where the girl had fallen.

"The wine she gave me was warm," Miran complained, and puckered his lips into a childish pout.

Shereza paused long enough to give the girl another resounding slap on the cheek.

"I've told you to test wine before giving it to the Shah," she scolded. On her way to the throne she turned and screamed at the girl, "Get out! I'll punish you later." Then she petted the blubbering prince while other girls went running for wine.

"Does your head hurt, Miran?" she asked, in the tones of a lisping three-year-old.

"A little, Mother," answered Miran.

"Would you like some of your medicine?"

"I think so," he said petulantly.

Shereza opened a gold pill box and gave her son an opiate. Then she returned to her divan.

"Forgive me, Timur," she said. "These girls are so awkward—and Miran Shah so fastidious—"

"Perhaps a princess wife," I said, poking at the sore spot while it was still raw. "One who is exquisitely trained—like you, Shereza."

I covered one of her hot moist hands with my own; and despite the revulsion I felt, I squeezed it affectionately.

"One who would bear him sons like Abu Bekr and Mirza Rustum," I said, "to give him other interests."

The softness which had come into her eyes when I clasped her hand gave way to a look of quick, guarded fear at the mention of other interests. I looked hard at her and savored her discomfort as I withdrew my hand. It was not that I disliked Shereza, but she did provide an outlet for some of my pent-up resentment against men.

"You *will* let me choose his bride, won't you, Timur?" she pleaded.

"He's entirely in your hands." I smiled at her and rose to go. "Do whatever you wish—whatever he wants."

"Oh, Timur, you *are* sweet," she said, hoisting her obesity from the divan, and her eyes were tender again. If only her body had kept the quality of her eyes! If only Miran Shah had never been born! I hated the fat prince, who had dropped off into a drugged stupor on the throne. I could hate him, for he was no longer a man—or so I thought then as I turned and took one last look at the sick, ornate room where the Begum kept up her pitiable masquerade.

But Shereza could not completely divert my mind, nor could Nubja, any more. After the birth of Amyris, late in her term of fertility, her magnificent pointed breasts had wilted down to pendulous, sandal-like sacks, and her belly had sagged and protruded.

Unlike Shereza, Nubja was fully aware of what I had lost, what I had sacrificed to let her have her son; and in her gratitude she would do anything for me—anything except let me see or touch the ruins of her body, which she had shown me once to make me understand.

"Remember me as I was, Amir," she said sadly. "Remember the pleasure we shared—but don't try to find it again. That is the price we paid for Amyris. He's worth it to me. I'll see that he's worth as much to you." She rubbed the little mulatto's curly head roughly and was rewarded with a healthy gurgling laugh.

"He will be," I said. By raising Nubja to her rightful place as a princess and proclaiming her son a prince, I could command the loyalty of Negroes everywhere. And since Negroes were almost universally enslaved, they would be encouraged to clamor for equality with their masters and help me pull all men down.

But it would be many years before Amyris could pay his debt to me, and my need was immediate and pressing. I was not quite ready to try my blade in Asia—and my new princess had not arrived. So I still fretted and sulked.

Dilshad was gracious and kind, but I was no longer her lover. She, too, was ambitious for her son and deeply conscious of her responsibilities as Sarai Khanum of Samarkand—the head of my household, the symbol which inspired loyalty in all my sons and grandsons. So like Aljai when she cajoled me and petted me—but Aljai was dead, and Dilshad was forty, and her passions were numbed.

Only Sevin Bey Khanzade could hold her own with me during brief, violent interludes, when she came to my bed with the flame of her hatred burning in her rich golden body and kindling her green eyes and sparking in the coils of her crisp bronze curls. She could burn up my discontent as we fought and scratched and strained together for the hot searing pain of our union. But after three or four or five days of vicious struggle, Sevin Bey would steal out of my quarters and I, becoming fearful of my dependence on her, would make my pilgrimage to Devon for purification.

Then the soothing Ali Soun Agha would chill the fever of my passion, and with the return of my physical integrity would come a resurgence of gnawing discontent. I would leave Devon, frustrated by the way the Frank *Levedi* could absorb the heat of my fury in her smooth white loins and smile and speak calmly in the face of my restlessness, which she could not comprehend. Perhaps it was her complacency which was most maddening of all, her bland, unconscious refusal to accept war as the Way of the World—her stupefying faith in her Cross and salvation.

Salvation! War is the way to salvation—to reducing man to a state of abject slavery acceptable to Allah. It is Allah's Will that war shall prevail, that all men's puny efforts be directed to the pursuit of futile conquests that all labor shall be war effort. In war men feel pain and frustration most keenly; yet for war and war alone they accept most willingly the deprivations and discomforts which are their lot—their Fruit of the Tree of Life.

But Allah was with me. I never completely lost sight of the Way. I *was* able to restrain myself until the day when a courier rode into Samarkand and reported that Chulpan Malik Agha—the Bibi Khanum—had reached Tashkand and would stop there only long enough to make ready for the last leg of her journey.

Immediately I gave final orders for Bibi Khanum's reception. Dilshad Sarai Khanum, of course, had the last word on arrangements. And when I called on Dilshad, I found her more worried than exultant over the forthcoming festivities. The removal of her jeweled headdress revealed lines above her troubled eyes.

"Is it too much for you?" I asked, as I took my place on her divan.

"Not—not for me. It's you I'm thinking of. It's not the arrangements, Timur, my love. It's—well—" She hesitated and searched my eyes to try to read in advance my reaction to whatever she was about to say. "Timur, you are fifty-one and this girl—this Bibi Khanum is only sixteen—"

"Surely you're not jealous," I said, and laughed somewhat uncomfortably. "Why, I have fifty or more sixteen-year-old virgins a year."

"I know, Timur. I'm not jealous. But this is different. Chulpan Malik is a princess, a young, accomplished woman of royal blood. She may well destroy you. It's happened before, to strong men."

"Nonsense," I said. "I'm not old—just reaching my prime—and this marriage is purely a political one, to gain a strong ally near the Great Wall of Khitai."

"I'm not so sure," Dilshad said, still studying my face. "Already you've built her a whole village and a palace as fine as the famous Manchu summer palace in the Wei-Chang hunting park, or the one at Xanadu. The architects have told me so."

293

"I promised her father," I reassured her. She was beginning to irritate me—one of the very few times she ever did. "I must impress Hadji Bey Irkanut that I am greater than he, or become his vassal." I was on the point of telling Dilshad my real reason for building the palace, as a model for military observation.

"Your willingness to comply with his request may imply vassalage. I don't know, but I'm confident that you can deal with *him*."

She smiled and took my hand in hers. Then she frowned again and continued, "But I'm afraid you'll become Bibi Khanum's vassal. An old man's darling—she can wind you around her little finger."

"Absurd!" I said heatedly.

"Not just you—any man your age—any princess her age. Oh, Timur, I'm worried. The way I was when you brought Sevin Bey to Jahangir." Her eyes filled with tears, and she clasped my hand in a sudden nervous rigor.

"You said then that you thought I could handle Sevin Bey—you urged me to take her."

"And you have—I know all about it."

I was surprised to hear that.

"But you were younger then. Now you're different. And you've been thinking of this girl for six long years—idealizing her—"

I never idealized any woman. Aljai, perhaps—

"We had to wait several years," she went on rapidly. "Remember? I know what it did to me, what it did to you. And you've not been yourself these last few weeks—nervous, irritable. Oh, Timur, be careful! You're becoming obsessed with your dream."

"I am not," I said, rising angrily. "This girl has hardly entered my mind, except to plan a reception that would please her father. What possible harm could she do me? I'm no lovesick mooncalf. I've had a thousand women!"

"Not Manchu princesses—not at your age." Dilshad hung on like a leech. "What can she do to you? Make a fool of you! Spoil you and blind you and give you a son who'll turn your empire over to her people the minute you lose control, or die!"

"So that's it!" I said, and wheeled to face Dilshad. "With you it's Shah Rukh. With Shereza it's Miran Shah—and Sevin Bey and her sons—even Nubja. Don't you think I know it? They're *all* my heirs. I'll favor the one who is strongest."

"I've not mentioned Shah Rukh," Dilshad said calmly. "I've tried to inspire loyalty in all your sons—as I am loyal—I, your only Tatar wife. Even now I'm thinking of you, only you. When you're sane, you'll choose the right son—I'm sure of that. If you don't lose your head."

"Sane!" I shouted, and slapped Dilshad across her mouth. "So I'm insane!"

She wiped a little trickle of blood from the corner of her mouth and stared at me, not in anger, but in pity, it seemed. Pity! Pity for me, the master of half of Asia—some day the master of all Asia—of the world.

"I just hope it's not the girl," Dilshad said sorrowfully. "I hope I'm wrong. If she's worked you up to this state without your ever having seen her, I shudder—"

I struck Dilshad again and strode out of her sitting room. I felt calmer than I had in many weeks. Dilshad—the image of Aljai—had assimilated my excess passion in those blows, relieved my tension. I had no immediate need for my new royal woman. An old man's darling!

CHAPTER

3

For the next few days men ceased to annoy me. Even the vexatious ambassadors who were always at my court, probing for weakness and pressing for advantage, became so interested in the wedding preparations that they forgot to irritate me. And my young concubines, who had never competed with royal women their own age, suddenly realized the potential danger in the youthful Manchu princess and outdid themselves to please me. The boldest of them, fearing that my favors and gifts would stop, openly declared their undying love for me and wept in self-pity over the prospect of the new agha's charms overshadowing their own. I had them whipped for their insolence in comparing themselves to a princess, but they retired with their eyes shining, confident that I would not forget them.

Actually their vivid descriptions of what I should expect of the new khanum, comparisons drawn at most emphatic moments, did serve to whet my appetite for my bride. And so a new eagerness arose within me—not the nervous, desperate need I had felt, but a purely sensual anticipation—and made my blood tingle with youthful desire as I sat on my throne on the palace balcony waiting for Bibi Khanum's caravan to enter the gates of Samarkand.

I felt that Dilshad sensed my excitement. I had not seen her from the time I had struck her until she took her place beside me, on the throne of the Sarai Khanum; and when I glanced her way, her look made me uncomfortable. Serene and composed, she wore the gorgeous crimson robe of her rank with a royal dignity that put Shereza's extravagant

Begum-green regalia to shame. And her ropes of white pearls and heron-plumed headdress made the Begum's many-jeweled tiara seem tawdry and cheap, just as the honest silver streaks in her hair gave the lie to Shereza's dyed tresses.

It was her eyes, though, troubled and compassionate, that made me pretend interest in the gayety of the palace gardens. I forced my gaze to dwell on the festive pavilions erected in all quarters—the players' pavilion, the brocaded awnings shading rich savory banquet spreads, and the tents in which the bride's dowry would be displayed. But invariably I looked back toward the Sarai Khanum—obliquely, centering my gaze on Sevin Bey and my grandsons, the golden tigress and her agile young cubs, or on Shereza's fat-faced baby Miran lolling stupidly on his pillowed throne beside the Begum, who frowned at Omar Sheik's Sonja and her two bright little princelings.

Anywhere but on Dilshad—so like Aljai, still young, still erect and well formed and fine. Every time I married, I thought of Aljai. If she had lived, perhaps I would never have taken Bibi Khanum. Perhaps I would have been a shepherd, blind to the Way—or an outlaw, or dead. Aljai would never have feared that a sixteen-year-old could wind me around her little finger.

I looked at Nubja, who had the woman's throne of third precedence, and she smiled at me encouragingly—she wished me well with Bibi Khanum. She, better than anyone else in the world, knew what I sought, and wanted me to have it. And she lifted the arm of her little mulatto prince and helped him wave at me. But Amyris' bright-toothed smile was his own when Nubja pointed me out and scratched her son's head fondly.

Heartened by Nubja's gesture, I felt a resurgence of my eagerness to the point of momentary impatience, and I hastily looked down the broad street toward the lower gate. As though I had willed it, the heralds in the gate tower sounded a brilliant fanfare on their seven-foot kourrouns, and the nakaras rolled in unison while the gates swung open to admit the caravan from Xanadu.

The princess's entrance, however, was a disappointment. Instead of the expected splendor of a camel litter, such as Shereza or Sevin Bey had ridden in, the procession was headed by a weird-looking pagoda set on a platform which rode high on the backs of eight gray Manchu horses. The horses, even at the great distance from the palace, looked fine and well matched—in two ranks of four—but their thick coats had no sheen, and their lack of color was carried out in the dull curtains which shrouded the entire pagoda with the exception of the bright lacquered black and gold and red roof.

And the same drabness was repeated and repeated and repeated as the khanum's retinue squeezed through the wide gates and then expanded again into a broad column of massed men—many of them on foot—and pack animals. Every man, every camel, every pack horse was muffled in a dustproof, snowproof cocoon of the same somber gray cloth. But for the burnished helmets of the mounted guards and the quaint little court caps of the agha's retainers—caps of the same shape and color as the pagoda roof—the procession might have been mistaken for one of the dismal caravans of starving nomads which roam the steppes of Sibir and the Gobi, huddled together for protection against the wild wind and wilder steppe foxes and wolves.

The broad street filled with the slow-moving strangers—filled to the barriers erected to keep spectators out of the street—and the ghostly, shrouded northerners made an ominous dirty flood rising up the concourse between red and yellow and green and blue silks of my kulchi guards and the equally brilliant colors of the pennants and rugs and tapestries which decorated the bazaars and housetops. Accustomed to long, thin processions, strung out for miles with every mount or litter set off by itself like a jewel in a necklace, my people stared at the dull mass in mute astonishment. And the Manchus were equally quiet —no music, no drums, not a sound but the swish of soft shoes and slow muffled hoofbeats on the marble pavement.

The entire effect was funereal; and suddenly I knew that my bride was dead—that the pagoda hid her coffin and the troupe was in mourning for their princess. I glanced at Dilshad. She knew it, too—her eyes were sad but not troubled any more. And Nubja was sad. But not Shereza. She smiled and nudged Miran Shah and whispered to him—of her own grand entry into Samarkand many years before, I was sure.

Still all eyes were fixed on the depressing spectacle of the rising gray tide. Never had a procession held the natives of Samarkand in more rapt attention—fascination which made one shudder as though the color were draining out of the bright Tatar silks. Even Sevin Bey, when I looked her way, seemed to have lost her fire.

The eerie pagoda reached the opening in the inner wall to the arak —the wall had been torn out for the procession, though I had expected no such broad front—and the last Manchu had squeezed through the lower gate when I looked back down the broad street. Then the silence was broken by two low reverberating peals struck from a huge Khitan gong brought in by the rear guard of the column. The sound must have sent terror into everyone. As if the Manchus perhaps had strange weapons hidden under the gray robes—some machine mounted on the pagoda platform, the dreaded fire powder—

297

At the signal, an indescribable alertness animated the mass of Manchus, and a nervous tremor seemed to run through both ranks of
Kulchis, clear to the gate. Even the horses sensed the strange influence and
pawed and whinnied nervously.

The gong sounded again, and a garden blossomed before me. The
gray shrouds were dropped, or turned inside out—no one could tell—
and in their place appeared the most gorgeous embroidered silks ever
to come out of Khitai. Elaborate court robes with flowers and fruits
and dragons worked in gold and colored threads, silks all the brighter
for having been kept out of the sunlight until that moment. All Samarkand gasped, and hid its eyes for a moment from the sudden glare.

The curtains of the pagoda dropped all the way to the ground,
forming a brilliant base to the platform and hiding the horses underneath. The pagoda itself was a shrine; and its goddess, Bibi Khanum,
sitting crosslegged on a pedestal surrounded by her maidens, was the
fairest flower of all—truly a Daughter of the Moon.

"She's beautiful!" gasped Dilshad—to herself most certainly.

Even Shereza said something, clearly audible; but I looked at neither
of my elder wives as the pagoda approached my throne to the accompaniment of music played on wood blocks and little cymbals and five-
tone flutes, quaint and enchanting.

Bibi Khanum wore no jewels in her hair—she needed none—nor in
her ears, nor around her neck. Only one huge diamond which flashed
when the sunlight found her hand, and two rubies in the eyes of the
golden dragon embroidered across the front of her high-collared green
court robe. No other ornament or trim except seed pearl cuffs on the
straight legs of her cloth-of-gold pantaloons.

But it was the Chulpan Malik Agha herself that was the gem. Her
face, no darker than the orange hue of a newly risen harvest moon,
seemed to glow with the charm Dilshad had feared the Manchu
princesses possessed. And her eyes, large and clear and slanted no
more than mine or Dilshad's, had the light of Heaven in them. Bibi
Khanum was the climax of the revelation that had come when the
gray shrouds turned to sunlight. And despite my surge of pleasure,
my heart sank again at the warning. It is the nature of the Manchus
and the Khitans that they will be dull and dormant and colorless for
a while—for centuries sometimes—and then rise and blaze in glory
again, as the Mings had done so recently in driving out the Kin Tatars
and establishing their own dynasty. They might block the Way. Bibi
Khanum might—

The pagoda came to a halt in front of the royal dais, on a level with
it, and I looked directly into the eyes of my bride. Bibi Khanum

smiled briefly and bent her body forward until her forehead would have touched the floor if she had not been sitting on the pedestal. Her maidens' foreheads did touch the richly carpeted floor of the platform. All of the little doll women remained in the prostrate position while a gray-bearded, gray-queued old Manchu noble stepped forward and read to the assemblage from a parchment scroll.

Knowing little Manchu myself, I had stationed a tarjuman beside my throne to interpret for me. The document was my marriage contract, consummated six years before by proxy; and after the old man had read it, he came forward solemnly and placed it in my hand. Then he, too, prostrated himself before me while I looked over the parchment, noting the Manchu seal and the signature of Hadji Bey Irkanut—or rather his Manchu name, which neither looked nor sounded like its Moslem equivalent—and the childish scrawl of Chulpan Malik Agha, written when the princess was ten. Last was my signature, forged by some nameless proxy who had stood for me at the wedding and then been beheaded for his insolence in daring to impersonate a Tatar king and hold the hand of a Manchu princess.

Because Bibi Khanum had been my wife since she was ten years of age, there was no further ceremony. The princess was taken to her palace, and hundreds of the Manchus set to work unpacking her dowry and her father's wedding gifts to be put on display in the pavilions set up for that purpose. I dismissed my court, and the elegant wedding guests began their celebration.

I sat on my throne until dusk, accepting gifts and dispensing gifts and receiving congratulations from my amirs. Bibi Khanum appeared briefly. Smiling and gracious in her royal palanquin, borne by four coolies in gorgeous livery, she made a progress around the garden and returned to her quarters. She looked like a Khitai doll packed in a jeweled casket as a gift for some spoiled young prince or princess— my old nurse, Abdullah's mother, had had one which she treasured above all else and had allowed me to play with it when I had been an especially good little boy.

Later that night, when I went to the bridal chamber, Bibi Khanum looked more like a doll than before, as did her women, all dressed in embroidered kimonos tied with wide sashes knotted into butterfly bows in the back, bows which fluttered like wings when the women prostrated themselves before me.

"Welcome to my bed, Master," Bibi Khanum greeted me in my own tongue. I learned that she spoke flawless Uigur and Arabic as well as Khitan dialects.

"Welcome to Samarkand and all of my realm," I replied formally.

"May the Daughter of the Moon always shine upon me and my people."

I bade the servants rise and looked around the room for a place to sit. Exquisite screens of carved teak and block-printed silks gave the walls a look of frailty, of impermanence; and the furniture, low and delicate and finely wrought—tiny little tables, low lamp-stands, and diminutive cabinets—all seemed the appointments of a playhouse. The soft woven mat and the padded head block, which Bibi Khanum had referred to euphemistically as her bed, was no more than a bright, gay rug for a nursery. I felt big and awkward.

My bride, sensing my discomfort, rose quickly and clapped her hands and said something to her maids.

"May we serve you tea, Master?" she asked, showing her first signs of nervousness.

"I should be delighted," I said, surprised to see her standing for the first time. The top of her head, even with her hair piled on top as it was, came no higher than my heart. And her maids were no taller—a scurrying covey of quail, chirping and arranging the tea service far below me, it seemed.

But they did bring me a low ottoman, which they placed before a tea table. I sat down on it, and Bibi Khanum sank gracefully to a cross-legged position on a rug opposite me.

"It's jasmine tea," she said. "Served always by brides." And she busied herself with thimble-sized cups and a fragile porcelain teapot.

"May you find it delightful," she said, handing me one of the cups, and then added boldly, "and me also."

"I find you so already," I complimented her.

She smiled appreciatively as her hand touched mine in the transfer of the cup, and I was suddenly conscious of my graying beard—the girl was no older than Shah Rukh. And I remembered Dilshad's reminders of my age. Was I attractive to her? I had never wondered—or cared—about that before.

The serving girls all but fed me—a practice I had never allowed, regardless of the customs of other monarchs—paper-thin rice wafers, stamped with a lotus blossom, and candies and fruits. Bibi Khanum sipped daintily at her tea; and I, fearing I would drain my cup in one gauche draft, merely tasted the jasmine-scented liquid with my tongue and drank in the insubstantial beauty of the Manchu princess through my eyes.

I never knew whether the tea contained an aphrodisiac or not, but certainly by the time our tea party was over I was as impatiently hungry for the delicate little Manchu before me as I had ever been for the most voluptuous southern woman I had ever known. Perhaps it was the tea, for Bibi Khanum seemed equally eager. She dismissed her women as soon as they had removed the tea table and extinguished the brighter lights in the room. Then she looked at me expectantly, as though she would have chosen a gray-bearded man for a lover if she had been given free choice.

I glanced at the uninviting sleeping mat, and hastily surveyed other possibilities. I rose from the ottoman and stood where I was. My diminutive bride rose also and came to me when I beckoned.

When I took her in my arms, bending down and lifting her clear of the floor to do so, I could tell that she wore nothing under the satin kimono. And she was light—little heavier than Pir Mohammed. I felt a tremor pass through her body as she clung to me—in fear, or nervousness, or passion, there was no way of knowing.

I settled back down on the ottoman and set Bibi Khanum astride my knees facing me. My own dressing gown had parted, and the girl's bare thighs were warm where they touched mine. A little nervously, I untied the big bow on the back of the kimono, and Bibi Khanum let the garment slide off her shoulders to the floor.

"Ama," she said huskily, and shivered ever so slightly when her fair childish body was revealed to me. Lithe, supple, yielding, it was the light frame of a little girl—or little boy, for the discoid breasts of the Manchu women lie passive like petals, not buds on a slender young vine, and Bibi's hips were as lean as the hips of a young nomad riding naked on his pony.

But my bride was soft and feminine. Her skin was of the same texture my fingers had felt in the satin kimono, and the flesh underneath was thrillingly alive. Bibi responded spontaneously to my caresses, rapidly becoming uncontrollably stimulated. I let my own robe slip from my shoulders when love play had progressed far enough.

Then I lifted Bibi Khanum clear of my knees—my hands spanned her waist and met front and back—and drew her to me as one cautiously tries on a snug new glove. Startled at first, she uttered a surprised birdlike chirp, and her eyes were fearful for a moment. But as I settled her down gently on my lap, she sighed unevenly and relaxed in my arms. Her body was weightless—a doll in my grasp, which I could lift and fondle with no sense of effort.

She gave herself over to me, completely, willingly, and allowed me my way for a time—until she herself took the initiative and wriggled in sheer ecstasy on my lap. At the height of her exquisite pleasure she threw her arms around my neck and clung to me wildly, sobbing,

301

"Ama, Ama," as she buried her face in my beard. A second later she stopped squirming and went rigid and then limp in my arms.

"Ama," she repeated softly, as though to herself, and seemed to go to sleep on my shoulder.

I rose and carried her in my arms to my suite in her palace—where there was a more conventional couch—and laid her gently among the soft downy pillows.

While she slept, I sent for my tarjuman.

"What does *ama* mean?" I asked.

"Ama, Master? *Ama* means *father,"* he said, grinning a wide toothy grin.

I dismissed him, and frowned, and returned to my couch and my child-bride.

CHAPTER

4

Slight and girlish as she was, Bibi Khanum provided a satisfactory outlet for my emotions for over a year, while I carried out the nerve-wracking task of tempering and whetting my huge army to a razor-keen edge in a time of relative peacefulness. Such men as Sheik Ali, Nur ad-Din, Daoud, Omar Sheik—even old Jaku and Saif ad-Din—did much of the actual recruiting and training of military units; and my foster son Toti Toktamish trained an army of a hundred thousand men who owed allegiance to me.

After the death of Zain ad-Din, Mir Sayyid became Chief Mollah of Islam in Tatary; and since he had long been subservient to me, I held sufficient control over the Church to assure the proper reverence due me by the Faithful. Sherif ad-Din, too, had grown more brilliant— but no wiser—through the years. Through his enthusiasm he had attracted a corps of the quickest-witted young scholars in the world, men who were masters of rhetoric in all tongues, men who could seize upon truth or falsehood and disseminate either persuasively and persistently until their doctrines pervaded the entire population of any given area. It was these men, indoctrinated by Sherif ad-Din and his most astute associates, who staffed my Royal Academy and its branches in all the cities in my realm.

And it was these men and the stupid, misguided followers of Abdullah's Leng Kopeghi who gave me my advantage over my rival monarchs. Nowhere else in Asia could scholars gain such affluence as in my service. I learned what they wanted—wealth, women, power, or simply an opportunity to put their visionary schemes into effect—and I gave it to them. All scholars who could make the journey came to Samarkand. Those who deserved it gained rapid advancement. Those who were obstinate stayed forever in my capital, many of them never learning the basis of preferment, but all of them contributing their knowledge. Unwittingly they revealed bits of truth I could use, or deliberately they accepted truth as I decreed it and spread it throughout my kingdom and beyond my borders, wherever they went.

And they were my personal responsibility. No other man understood their value. No other man could read the Way. So it was with my scholars that I spent most of my time as the day for drawing my blade approached.

When word came that Toti had taken his army and captured my city of Tabriz, and that Suliman Sufi, my daroga of Urganj, had gone over to him, I knew that the time had come, although not as I had planned—the vanity of plans! I sent the call to my tuman-bashis to assemble their forces at Shehri-Sebz, and I personally met with my scholars.

Sherif ad-Din assembled the group in the new Bibi Khanum Academy. Impressed by the luxury of their surroundings and excited over the prospects of the Day, they had the wild look of dervishes as I faced them that morning and bade Sherif ad-Din explain the purpose of the assembly.

"Scholars," he began, "we are gathered together this morning to hear the final injunctions of our Illustrious Patron of Learning, Amir Timur, Master of Samarkand. Never before has a convocation of learned men had such a champion—a monarch so enlightened, with the power to make a world ruled by Reason. So eager am I to hear his words of wisdom, that I cut short my preamble and urge our Master to inform us."

Sherif ad-Din then sat down, and the expectant look on his face told me that his words were not idle flattery. Then I spoke.

"Faithful subjects, wisest of men, how shall I address you?" I began.

"Not simply as an assembly or an academy, nor even as a Kurultai, for rough, untutored men may sit in Kurultai.

"Ours is a sacred mission—the dissemination of Truth as we have worked it out together. Then let us consider our convocation a Ulama—since indeed many of you are scholars of the Church—but a higher Ulama.

"Yes, a Ulama of Wisdom, which dares even to challenge the Church when we find it guided by men of dim vision.

"So I address you as the Ulama of Scholars—and I make a sacred charge to you. Soon we depart with our army on our Jihad of Enlightenment. Consider yourselves the equal—indeed the superior—of my highest military men, for such you are.

"You know the power of the Word, the invincible magic of 'it is written,' and you shall write it."

An almost tangible enthusiasm pervaded my audience as I impressed upon the scholars my appreciation of them.

"I can speak frankly with you, as frankly as I do with my tavachis when I am outlining military strategy. You know how you can awe simple men by books, how you can bring uneasiness to rulers by vitriolic tracts and orations. You know the prestige you carry, amounting practically to immunity.

"You know, too, that the turncoat Toktamish, my treacherous foster son Toti, has turned traitor and attacked me. My army must retake the cities he has spoiled in Kharesm and Khorassan and then seek him out and destroy him. This means that you must win and hold Persia while my military men are busy with the perfidious Russian."

Some of the men, despite their indoctrination, seemed uncertain of my meaning.

"How? you ask. When I move south, I shall establish you in academies in my cities and send you to work in schools already operating outside my boundaries. Wherever you are, you will find every weakness in the rulers and people and shout them to high heaven.

"You will decry every sign of injustice, or fabricate injustices and attack them in outraged righteousness.

"Every failure of the nobles or merchants will be your springboard for a tirade against the government and local officials and rich men.

"You will fan every flame of misunderstanding, let no dissension die, make a crime of the slightest defection in charity or fair dealing.

"You will tell people what to think—reduce learning to its lowest terms—to slogans, to proverbs, to catch phrases—whatever people can grasp quickly; and you will hammer and hammer and hammer until all the masses believe as we do.

"You will sit in on councils, be partisan in quarrels, and above all see that no leader rises to challenge me while I am involved in a war with Toktamish.

"Recruit such other scholars as you can—discredit those who will not see our Way. The most obstinate and dangerous will be liquidated, just as inefficient or recalcitrant military men are destroyed. Wherever you are, there will be men, unknown to you, who will attend to such matters.

"I repeat, our mission is sacred. You are the Ulama of Scholars, men dedicated to the Way. Be persistent, never wavering—probing always for weakness, pressing every advantage. Yours is the opportunity, the responsibility, to make your Reason prevail. Convince all dissenters they are stupid. Adhere to the Truth as we know it. Proclaim the Way.

"Sherif ad-Din will give you instructions for preparing to move with the army."

I left hurriedly, while the scholars were still floating on the clouds of their newly stated importance. Stupid, blind fools! Masters of the methods of the Way, slaves to the Way itself. Allah never reveals the Purpose of His Way to mediocre men. Why should I?

That is the fatuity of scholars, to believe as they wish, not as they must, to decipher the Way in the maze of Allah's delusions. They seek salvation in the mind, in the spirit, in creation, when salvation lies in war and destruction—clearly, for anyone to see, anyone who can read aright the casting out of man from Paradise, and the meaning of the Flaming Sword—to keep man in the depraved condition Allah has decreed. Slavery is man's estate, his eternity, his salvation.

When I left Samarkand with my twelve thousand elite kulchis, I took with me my scholars and mollahs as well as Bibi Khanum and something over a hundred of my concubines, for I planned to be in the field for several years.

In Shehri-Sebz my royal pavilion, which became fabled in Asia, was set up for the first time. It was a gorgeous silk tent combining the lofty dome of the Tatar kibitka in the center and the square porticoes of the Persian pavilion around it. Supported by twelve poles chased in gold and silver and enameled metals, and separated into many chambers by brocades and tapestries hung from the dome, it was hardly distinguishable on the inside from a permanent palace. Indeed, from a distance the outside of the pavilion looked like a castle, until one came near enough to see the thousand red silk guy ropes and the perimeter poles capped with golden statues of Sasha or with the globe and crescent of my sovereignty.

Measuring a hundred paces to the side, the portable palace afforded ample space for my quarters, a suite for Bibi Khanum, and a sizable zenana for such of my women as I wished to call from the special women's pavilion. And I had two identical outfits, one to be moved ahead day and night and set up at the next campsite, ready for occupancy when I arrived.

When I moved out of Shehri-Sebz with my seventy divisions, surrounded by every luxury and equipped with every known weapon, I recalled the Arab mathematician's comparison of me with the sportsmen who merely played at hunting and fishing. Perhaps war *was* sport, the sport of Allah. Certainly my sacking of Urganj and execu-

305

tion of the traitorous Suliman Sufi went off as easily as a game. But I turned the affair to profit—mine and Allah's.

Completely disgusted with the Urganji people who had defied me three times, I razed the city—tore down every building and carted away the very stones and timber of which the houses had been built. Then, after I had taken what women and slaves I could use, I buried the rest of the Urganjis in the moat and plowed the whole city under and planted barley on the site.

After destroying Urganj, I left Sheik Ali at Khiva with a crack division to hold Toktamish if he returned to Kharesm, or to reinforce Omar Sheik at Otrar if the Russian should try to attack Samarkand from the north. With Sultan Mahmoud, Ali's son, in command of my right wing, my army moved leisurely on to the Sea of Abaku and around the south shore toward Tabriz. So gay were my men and so bright and colorful our overnight camps, the campaign might have been a gypsy tour, or an extended wedding journey for Bibi Khanum, my bride of a year.

Somehow the bright desert stars and the soothing night breezes from the Abaku seemed to be of Bibi's making. As delicate and refreshing as the fruit sherbets made from snow brought down to us daily from the mountains, my Manchu princess kept my spirits high day and night. As she rode beside me during the day, her constant amazement at the southern country, all new and strange to her, made me see the desert and the fertile oases through her eyes. Nasturtiums and petunias growing in a peasant woman's garden, tender violets peering unexpectedly from a secluded brookside, a field of purple vetch, or a plot of irrigated soil white with lilies—all of these were reflected in her eyes with added brilliance.

And at night, when we sat together and watched the moon through the leaves of a plane-tree, or lay in a roofless chamber of my pavilion and counted stars, I often felt that I, too, was no more than seventeen again—seventeen and back in Shehri-Sebz, in the overgrown gardens of Ak Sarai. Then I was glad that I was no longer a youth but a man, a conqueror, a father and grandfather. And it became evident that Bibi Khanum was a woman and about to become a mother, when her advanced stage of pregnancy forced her to ride in a palanquin and forced me to choose my couch companions from the seraglio tent.

By that time we had reached Tabriz. There was no problem of retaking the city. Toktamish had looted and raped and pillaged for ten days and withdrawn through Baku, beyond the Caucasus to Astrakhan, after having killed my tuman-bashi and driven the governor, Kalkali, into the hills. The city welcomed me back, and Toti's small garrison readily joined my forces. I continued on, however, to the shores of Lake Urmia and set up my sarai where the air was clean and the land well watered.

As soon as my camp was settled and I began holding court, I received envoys from the Shah of Persia. Since I was within five hundred miles of his fortress at Isfahan, I expected a note of hostility from him, although we had signed a treaty long before; and I rather welcomed a provocation for war, since I planned to conquer Persia anyway.

To my surprise, however, the diplomatic party was headed by the Shah's favorite son, who brought rich gifts and spoke in all friendship. He read his father's message to my assembled amirs.

After the customary string of complimentary titles the message went on: ". . . Wise men all know the mutability of the world. All things pass: the wisdom, the pleasure, the beauty, the poetry of the world. So, too, must men pass, such as you and I.

"My time has come. I go prepared. I have kept my treaty with you, and I shall carry your scroll with me before the Judgment Seat as testament of my steadfastness and honesty. I have forsaken the vanities and inconstancies of the world. I go to Allah clean.

"I die as I have lived for fifty-three years—tasting Allah's pleasures in this world, confident of the pleasures of my seventy-two houris in Allah's Paradise.

"As I have kept my pledge to you, Oh, Imperial Monarch, I ask the pledge of your protection of my son, Zain al-Abaidin. To you, Timur, wise as Solomon, strong as Alexander, I commend my son. May you and Allah guard over him.

"Say a prayer for me, and bear my scroll, fulfilled on the Day of Judgment to earn my blessing on you to Allah, for I go before you . . ."

There was no mention of the Shah's nine other sons, who also might need protection. I ignored the omission, as did Zain al-Abaidin.

"Have no fear," I said to him. "As your father has kept his pledge, so shall I honor his request."

"He will die happy, Gracious Amir, hearing your answer from me," said Zain al-Abaidin.

"Surely not soon," I said. "I should like to pay him a visit."

"I fear that you may not, unless you return at once with me." The young prince was solemn—too solemn, I thought.

"But you must stay for a festival," I said. "Go refresh yourself while I have a feast and gifts prepared for you."

Zain and his party retired, but I kept my own nobles in session.

"Sounds too good to me," said Nur ad-Din, as soon as the Persians had left, "or not good enough. 'I die,' says the Shah. Humph!"

"I have word that he sent precisely the same message to Sultan Ahmed of Baghdad and Bayazid in Istanboul," said Kalkali, who had come out of hiding when I arrived in Tabriz.

"When?" I asked.

"A year ago."

"And he's not dead yet," said Nur ad-Din. "I don't trust him. If he's going to die, why doesn't he die?"

"No man can tell," I said piously, for the benefit of the mollahs present. "But he may die soon."

"That he may," said Nur ad-Din, and laughed softly.

The other amirs joined in the laughter. We had to have a war. A hundred and forty thousand men did not march for months and not fight a war.

But the men were happy that night. With many guests from Tabriz— slender rouged men and soft-voiced women—the festival took on a gracious Persian air. Less lusty and violent than our Tatar celebrations, it was nevertheless an evening of lighthearted revelry. I felt cheated that Bibi Khanum did not feel like attending.

The next morning brought an end to our feasting. A dusty, wornout courier arrived from Isfahan to report that the Shah was sinking. Zain al-Abaidin left at once, and I sent my chief mollah and Sheik Ali's younger son, Mirza Murad, along with him to present my gifts to the Shah.

"Too pat," observed Nur ad-Din, as the men rode away. "Entirely too pat. Shall I follow with a division?"

"No," I said. "We'll wait it out. We're strong enough. Let's see what develops."

And we waited until New Year's Day, when I held court and called in my nobles from everywhere. Then I forgot the Shah. Although I had received daily couriers from Samarkand, I welcomed the fuller news Daoud and Jaku brought when they came in person; and I was glad to see Shah Rukh, just turned eighteen, who had come with them to join my forces.

There was some very bad news, however. Sheik Ali had been stabbed to death by one of Toktamish's spies in a cowardly guerilla attack on a scouting party. Toktamish had taken Bokhara and burned my palace there. Omar Sheik, however, had driven Toktamish back to Sarai and was making quite a name for himself.

"You think he can hold Toktamish for a while longer, then?" I asked. "I may be busy here for another year or two."

"Toktamish won't fight," said Daoud. "He strikes and then disappears. His armies melt. Omar Sheik can protect you from the north all right, but he can't destroy Toktamish—can't risk the chase. And your foster son Toti will be a nuisance until he's finished for good."

Daoud grinned at my "foster son Toti." He never had trusted Toktamish, or any other Russian, for that matter. Nor had I, but I had my reasons for dealing with Toti as I had.

So despite my disappointment over the loss of Sheik Ali, I was reassured that things were not really serious at Samarkand. And as the week wore on, my mind was diverted elsewhere. The chief physician of Tabriz warned me that Bibi's time was near. Though a birth in my family was of slight consequence, I was naturally excited over a new royal baby. And my experience with Bibi Khanum had been so completely delightful that I expected something special from her son.

And it was a son. On the tenth day of Muharram he was born. On the tenth day of Muharram word came that the Shah of Persia had died indeed. It was on the tenth day of the Muharram, of the first year of Time, that Allah created Heaven and Earth, and Life and Death, and Adam and Eve. Bibi Khanum's son *was* something special—by all portent I felt it—born on the anniversary of the Day of Creation.

"Let me call him N'il Tsung," requested Bibi Khanum, when he was brought to her.

"Let his name be N'il Mahdi-Soun," I suggested. "He shall be my mahdi—my prophet—the first Mahdi of the Way of Timur."

"Then it's N'il Mahdi-Soun," she said, smiling at the baby. "It's all the same. And he's a darling little prophet, if I ever saw one." She squeezed his red body to her breast.

CHAPTER

5

After the Shah's death, I dispatched several divisions to Samarkand and Otrar to hold out against Toktamish; but instead of moving south, as my amirs urged, I stayed another year in Tabriz. During that year, I sent envoys to each of the ten Persian brothers—none was over thirty years of age—and I sent gifts of slaves, all Leng Kopeghi loyals, and urged that my most illustrious scholars be added to the academies and medresses in the various cities. I made no demands, merely offered my protection equally to all the young men and wished them well in their assumption of sovereignty.

"Amir, I have never doubted your wisdom," Nur ad-Din said to me, after a few months. "Even now it is at peril of being deemed insolent that I speak."

We sat in the shade of a plane-tree and watched some of Shah Rukh's cadets practice equitation. Nur ad-Din's tone was so far from insolent that I bade him continue.

"I love you as no man loved other than his father," he went on, "for the honor you have bestowed on my father—the dignity you have given him, whom many men account a prattling old fool. As I love him, as I love you for loving him, I must speak my mind."

"Do, by all means," I said genially. Shah Rukh's squadron—Jahangir's old Gok Hazara—was becoming quite expert in horsemanship.

"Amir, the Persians are getting strong—they are building their cities, acquiring fame. United they could become a serious threat to our security."

"They won't unite," I said, and chewed on a stem of grass. I remembered the day long ago when Aljai had made me chew a grass stem in the pavilion of Hadji and Bayazid, my would-be assassins.

"I know they are young, Amir," said Nur ad-Din, "but their academies are filling with wise men who will counsel them in the advantages of unity."

"Their schools are staffed with *my* scholars," I said.

"Pardon me, Amir, for my presumptuousness—I speak out of love," Nur ad-Din insisted. "I urge you to attack now."

"It's too comfortable here," I teased lazily. "Think how hot it is in the Desht-i-Kavir this time of year."

"Amir!" Nur ad-Din was horrified. "You've never before—"

"No," I said, relenting, "nor do I fear the salt desert now. I'm not going soft. Bibi Khanum has not bewitched me, as some of you Tatars think."

Nur ad-Din grinned, but was not convinced.

"If the Persians are not at each other's throats inside of another two months, we'll ride south," I assured him.

And I was right. The ten brothers began squabbling and fighting among themselves. Soon full-scale warfare broke out, and when I broke camp and started south through the dry light snow with a force of nearly a hundred thousand men, they retired to their respective cities and refused even to communicate with each other. I rode leisurely toward Isfahan. With no show of hostility, other than the sheer mass of my army, I camped on the banks of a shallow river west of the city, where the shadow of my pavilion would fall on the gates just before sunset. I sent gifts and compliments to Zain al-Abaidin and offered my protection. The next day the young Shah and his old gray-bearded uncle came to my court with even greater gifts and more elaborate compliments.

"I have been expecting you, Amir Timur—Father—for I am sorely pressed by my brothers," said Zain al-Abaidin.

"And true to my pledge to your father, the Shah—may Allah's blessings be upon him—I have stayed at Tabriz, though my own realm is menaced from the north, so I could watch over you and come to your aid."

"My people welcome you. Make my capital your own," he said graciously.

"Of course, the journey has cost me much," I said.

"Of course," agreed Zain al-Abaidin. "My people will pay."

"How much will the ransom be?" asked the doddering old uncle in a high piping voice of senility.

All the amirs present winced at his use of the harsh term.

"What will your expenses come to?" asked the young Shah.

"One million gold dinars should be about right," I said, hoping he would refuse and give me a pretext for sacking the city.

"One million gold dinars," he repeated in dismay.

"Better pay the ransom, Son," squeaked the old sultan. "You haven't got a chance against this army—and your brothers won't help you—the cringing puppies!"

"And if we can raise the money to defray your expenses," Zain al-Abaidin said cautiously, weakening in the face of the overwhelming odds, "my city will be spared, my people shown mercy?"

"Spared? You offend me, my son. They shall be protected, both they and you, as I promised your father."

"Then—then we accept your most generous offer, oh, Father Timur," Zain al-Abaidin said, with a return of his gracious court manner. "Please come feast with us tonight. All my people shall fete our Protector."

After the departure of my guests, my amirs showed obvious signs of discontent. They were quick to remind me that an army the size of mine did not stay in the field for two years without a fight somewhere. The common soldiers would not be content with their share of the million gold dinars. They had money already—they wanted women, and not the kind money could buy.

"We have not moved from Isfahan," I said curtly, and dismissed my staff.

Then I sent for Abdullah.

"I need an insurrection," I said to him. "Who's our man here?"

"Bara Lohar," he said.

"Bara Lohar—*big blacksmith*—is that his name?"

"It's what he goes by, Amir," said Abdullah. "Bara Lohar is all I know."

"All right, go make a deal with him," I ordered, and dismissed my servant.

During the afternoon I posted my guards at all the gates and sent collectors with Zain's men to raise money in the various sections of the city. I granted leave to half my army to visit the city and promised the others that they should be allowed to go in the next night. An hour or so before sunset Abdullah returned, and I took him into my private chamber.

"What about Bara Lohar?" I asked.

"He'll do it, Amir," answered Abdullah.

"What's his price?"

"Nothing, Amir."

"Nothing?" I repeated in surprise.

"That's right, Amir. He asks nothing. Just says he'll do it."

"I don't like the sound of it. It's not natural. How do you explain his attitude?"

"I can't, Amir. It's as baffling to me as it is to you. I believe him, but I can't make him out."

"Can you arrange for me to see him?"

"You, Amir?" It was Abdullah's turn to be surprised.

"Yes—not as Timur, Master of Asia, but as Leng Kopeghi."

"I think so, Amir. I'm sure I can."

"Very well," I said. "Bring along my disguise and attend me at the festival. I'll choose a girl early—and then sneak away. You may have the girl."

"Yes, Amir. I understand."

Just as the shadow of my pavilion was reaching the gates of Isfahan, I entered the city. I rode down the wide avenue between tall staffs from which bright pennants waved and pig bladders, blown up and stained every color of the rainbow, floated on gay silken streamers. The streets, swept clean of snow, were covered with the petals of roses grown in the Shah's famous hothouses; and a chorus of half-naked bayaderes danced and sang before me as though the chill winter winds were spring zephyrs caressing their rouged breasts and tawny thighs.

All the city welcomed me with hypocritical joyousness and opened the doors of the pleasure palaces to the men in my train. And the palace of Zain al-Abaidin showed no pinch of the tribute I had exacted. The main hall was lighted by a thousand candles which were reflected in all shades and colors by pure gems set in the walls of the palace.

Already the decadent Persians were deep in their cups, and many had forsaken the grape for the hemp leaf, either refined into hashish or chewed raw as bhang. Such nobles as could rise to their feet did so, and then knelt in greeting. Others merely sprawled on the deep-piled rugs and rolled over on their faces in token obeisance.

Zain al-Abaidin was sober enough to see that I was served wine and meat and candied apricots and quinces, even yellow-meated melons from the heated winter gardens. And there was an attempt to keep orderly sequence to the program of jugglers and mummers and minstrels who provided the entertainment. But I let it be known that I was as eager for the dancing girls to be brought in as were the dissolute Persian nobles, and the final stage of the festival came a full four hours ahead of schedule.

When the girls came in, dressed only in sheer teasing loin flaps and jeweled breast patches, I immediately chose a tall slender Persian whose whole body seemed to be one liquid, undulating ribbon, from her near-transparent veil to the little silver bells which tinkled on her ankles as she danced barefoot on the yellow marble square in the center of the room. Noting my obvious fascination, she broke the pattern of the ensemble and continued solo before my divan. The other girls, taking their cue from her, dispersed among the guests and finished their routine far from the marbled dance area.

Stirred far more than I had anticipated by the heavy musk the girl wore, and entranced by the sinuous, almost reptilian, grace of her long lithe body, I momentarily forgot Bara Lohar as I followed my voluptuous companion to the private room reserved for us. Abdullah came along right behind me, with my disguise hidden under his robes, and I wondered if the fragrance of the girl's hair—she was as tall as I was—filled his nostrils as it did mine, or if he could see as I could see the slim curves of her body silhouetted against the dimly lit door at the end of the narrow passage.

Suddenly remembering my appointment with the big blacksmith, I envied my servant. But when Abdullah entered the chamber and laid out my disguise on a serving table and retired, I realized the urgency of my previous engagement and took off my court clothes and frowned at the ragged Leng Kopeghi outfit.

The girl, misunderstanding my actions, continued to tease me and tickle my senses as I undressed. When I sat down on the couch to remove my boots—for the sandals of a slave—the girl crouched before me to help. She pulled my boots off, and I learned that I had not taken the girl's full potentialities into consideration. Casting my last boot aside, the long Persian houri pushed me back on the divan and, with-

313

out ever rising from her crouch, slithered bonelessly up over my knees, writhing, it seemed, over every inch of my body as though a satin smooth serpent were coiling around me—her honey-sweet tongue darting in and out, stinging my eyelids, my ears, and finally my open mouth with the devil's own sting of insatiable passion. If such a serpent seduced Mother Eve in Paradise! I forgot Bara Lohar again.

But I remembered him some half-hour later, and rose and drew on the garb of an outlaw and relinquished my place to Abdullah. As I met my guide out in the hall, I heard the little silver bells tinkling inside the chamber I had left, and I knew that anyone seeking me for the next few hours would be warned by that sound that I was not to be disturbed. Following a dirty little urchin—who I learned was Bara Lohar's son—through the dark stinking alleys of Isfahan, I was sorry that I had been forced to surrender the sensual serpent to Abdullah, sorrier still that he would have to spirit her away and kill her to cover my Leng Kopeghi activities. Such a waste of Allah's blessings!

I found Bara Lohar still at work at his forge. The burning charcoal, which glowed bright cherry-red with every squeeze of the bellows, lighted up the huge muscles of the big blacksmith's arms and shoulders and seemed to try vainly to illuminate one spot of flesh on the burly chest, so covered with hair that there was no telling where Bara Lohar's beard ended. In fact there was nothing but a mop of hair visible above the big shoulders until Bara Lohar looked up from his work and revealed two rows of flashing white teeth and a pair of eyes remarkably clear, considering the hours they had looked intently at white-hot steel.

"Leng Kopeghi!" he shouted cordially, and spread his mouth into a good-natured grin of welcome. "I've heard of you."

"And I've heard of you, Bara Lohar. You're working late," I said.

"One doesn't hang around an empty shop all night without making an anvil ring—it arouses suspicion."

"You're a shrewd man."

"And I'm still alive." He doused a hot ploughshare in a barrel of water and spoke above the hiss of the steam. "A busy man is seldom suspect."

"Where can we talk?" I asked.

"Right here. Saki, keep hammering," he said, handing the hammer to the boy who had brought me to the shop.

"Saki?" I asked in the lull.

"Yes, Saki—*cup companion*. I begot him while I was drunk, and his mother gave him to me as my punishment." He guffawed broadly.

Bara Lohar showed me to a seat on an empty keg in a far corner of the shop, and the boy began tapping loud enough to drown our conversation.

"You've talked to Abdullah," I began.

"Yes. Fine fellow. Says he's been with you from the beginning. He said you wanted me to strike against Timur's soldiers."

"That's what we must do. Abdullah said that you agreed, but named no price. He must be mistaken."

"No—no price. I'm glad to do it. Just so you see that I don't get into trouble with Timur. He's not like these local nobles—afraid, suspicious, easy to fool." Bara Lohar eyed me slyly.

"I'll see that you're not harmed by Timur. I can guarantee that."

"I thought you could," he said with a knowing grin.

"Why are you so sure?" I asked, suddenly becoming suspicious.

"I've noticed that Timur usually profits from Leng Kopeghi's successes. Just a hunch." He continued to grin.

"Conversely," I said, "when Amir Timur prospers, so does Leng Kopeghi—and so do those who follow Leng Kopeghi. So what's your price? What do you want?"

"Nothing—nothing at all. I'm big and strong. I can get anything I want. Women—even princesses, whose quarters I fit with bars and locks. I keep keys." He leered at me; and scanning his physique, I did not doubt his prowess among women, even princesses.

"Wine," he went on, "all men buy me wine. I want for nothing. I want nothing."

"Then why? Why are you so willing to be the champion of slaves?"

"I enjoy it. I like to make the stupid nobles and rich men squirm. I like to puncture them—big painted pigs' bladders—and see them lose their wind and hang like limp dirty guts from a pikestaff."

There was no rancor in the man's statement, just joy at the prospect.

"All their money won't buy what I've got. With my little finger I can get their thousand-dinar whores. I can summon a thousand loyal men with a nod of my head and never promise a single copper. And I never worry about losing anything I have. I lose it only when I die, and then I won't need it." Again his big guffaw resounded against the clay walls and rattled loose metal on the work benches.

"So you don't care about freeing slaves and lifting up poor men?"

"Freeing slaves, humph. Free slaves wouldn't know what to do. They'd be crying for masters in a week. Give all the poor men money, and the same usurers will have it all again before the full moon wanes."

"Do you tell your followers all this?" I asked.

"Of course not. They wouldn't believe it, if I did. Or they wouldn't care. They don't expect anything, either. They don't want to be raised up, just to pull others down. All they know is poverty and envy. They're lying to themselves when they clamor for justice."

"But you're not lying, Bara Lohar," I said, and smiled at him. "You're an honest man."

"Honest with you, Leng Kopeghi. Are you honest with me? And the slaves?"

I started to strike the man for his insolence. Then I remembered that he did not know who I was.

"Would you like to see for yourself?" I asked. "Call some of your slaves and beggars."

Bara Lohar merely nodded to Saki, who was beating a desultory tattoo on the anvil with a much smaller hammer than the one his father had given him, and the boy swung around and hit a big triangle three smart blows. Within a few minutes the blacksmith shop had filled up with shadowy figures which had slunk in silently from the streets and alleys. The pungent odor of burning charcoal was lost in the stench of unwashed humanity, worse than the smell of battle.

"This is Leng Kopeghi," Bara Lohar announced casually. "You've all heard of him."

There were gasps of surprise all around; and there arose a subdued hum of conversation, which quieted down as I limped over to the anvil near the center of the shop. Saki squeezed the bellows a few times and blew the charcoal into a flame which lighted up the room for a few paces each way.

"So you know who I am," I said with the arrogance of the typical Persian slave. "I'm the leader of slaves, the king of outlaws, and I've come to rally you.

"We are slaves"—I paused—"all slaves, whether we are owned by other men or not. But the earth is ours. We till it, we mine it, we tread on it with our bare feet when we carry other men's burdens.

"But other men own it! Our earth, given us by Allah—us—Allah's chosen people. No more—no more. I've assumed the sacred task of returning the wealth of Allah's earth to the lowly ones who make it blossom and yield up its ores and jewels.

"It's a great task, a noble task—but a long one. And you are my helpers, slaves everywhere. You, too, are noble, even sacred."

There was a slight stir in the group, but the dull, stupid beggars were slow to respond.

"Yes, noble and sacred—more noble than the sheiks—more sacred than the mollahs. We'll pull them down!"

I got a half-hearted cheer on that. The most vicious-looking listeners were the loudest.

"So I say that this meeting is our first Kurultai—no, it's sacred—this is our first Ulama—the Ulama of Slaves. We are priests of the true Way of Allah. We must rob those who rob us, pull down those who would rise above us and exploit us."

Bara Lohar was grinning, or so it seemed—with his beard it was hard to tell, but his eyes were twinkling. And the group had warmed up. I could see, however, that revenge in the abstract was rather remote to their thinking.

"We begin tonight," I said, and all ears pricked up. "Today we have been taxed to pay ransom to the Tatar soldiers.

"Tonight those fat drunken soldiers are lying with our women, drinking our wine. Tomorrow they'll be spending our money.

"Tonight we attack them—drive them out—storm the palace to get back our dinars exacted for tribute. And tomorrow the weak, cringing nobles who betrayed us will suffer for their cowardice."

At that the crowd broke into a muted cheer—as loud, I realized, as they were accustomed to risking in their clandestine meetings.

"Bara Lohar will lead you," I said. "Now go round up your fellows and await his signal."

I stepped back into the shadows.

"That's all," said Bara Lohar in dismissal to the silly dogs who stood expectantly where they were. "Meet at the usual places."

The men then departed slowly. I resolved to let Abdullah handle the slaves from that time on. The outlaws in Samarkand had been a quite different breed of men. But they had not been slaves. I remembered Nasir ben Adam's experience with the beggars and wondered for a moment at Allah's wisdom in choosing such a brood for His pets.

Bara Lohar chuckled at my elbow, and I turned to face him.

"They'll do it," he said. "Your lies had no more effect than my truth would have had. They'll do it, though, for some reason which we perhaps don't understand."

I resented his use of *we*. I, Timur.

"Who are you, Bara Lohar?" I asked, staring into his eyes.

"Who are you, Leng Kopeghi?" he countered, and met my gaze. His eyes never wavered; they only twinkled. I did not answer.

"Shall we guess?" Bara Lohar asked.

"No," I said after a moment, and beckoned Saki to lead me back to the Shah's palace.

I found Abdullah still employed with the serpentine siren. I felt a hot flush of jealousy as I wondered if she had liked him better than me. But I changed into my court clothes and told Abdullah to dispose of his paramour whenever and however he wished. The guards and the nobles in the palace were all in such a drunken stupor that they offered no problem.

I collected my own men and left the palace without disturbing my host. As we rode toward the west gate of Isfahan, we heard sounds of merrymaking in every café or public house and in many of the residences. The streets were filled with noisy Tatar warriors supporting native girls on their arms. In the darker stretches of the avenue, we had to ride carefully to keep our horses from trampling couples who lay on the crushed rose petals, oblivious of the cold night air.

Soon after we reached the sarai, I heard the clamor of battle in the city. I retired calmly, assured that by morning I would have ample provocation for sacking Isfahan.

The sun rises quickly in the desert. One minute it is dark; the next, the whole world is lit up. I always liked to be up to see that minute. So I saw Zain al-Abaidin and his men riding into my camp with the first glimmer of light.

Dull, bewildered, still half drunk from their night of carousing, the envoys nevertheless had the presence of mind to bring bags full of jewels and all the gold they could carry.

"Amir Timur!" Zain al-Abaidin gasped. "A most terrible thing has happened. The beggars and slaves and laborers attacked your men during the night, killing thousands, I'm afraid."

"Did your guards help your people?" I asked.

"No—yes—I don't know. Maybe. The officers were—"

"Drunk," I said. "Most derelict in their duty. I saw them when I rode out of your city last night."

"But I did not order it. I'm not responsible—remember your pledge to my father, Most Gracious Monarch."

"I remember," I said thoughtfully. "I promised to protect you, not your unruly people. They must pay."

"We'll pay," Zain al-Abaidin agreed hastily. "I'll pay for Mirza Murad, who was killed in my palace. I loved the boy, who visited me with your mollah. I'll pay—my people will pay—all we have."

"With their lives," I said firmly. "Sultan Mahmoud"—I called to Sheik Ali's other son, who approached at that moment—"yours is the honor of avenging the death of your brother. Sack Isfahan and see that every soldier in camp brings me the head of a Persian."

Zain al-Abaidin and his old uncle stood aghast at my command. I spoke to them courteously.

"Have no fear, either of you," I said. "No harm will come to you. You may spend your leisure time writing letters to all of your brothers, inviting them to call on me here. You may describe what you see in the next few hours."

Then I climbed to the minaret of the demountable mosque which had been set up before my pavilion and watched Sultan Mahmoud effect full retaliation for the murder of his brother. Efficiently, methodically, thoroughly, he stormed the walls and led my long-restrained warriors through the city, street by street, block by block, slaying and beheading every able-bodied male in Isfahan. The men did not even stop for rape until everyone brought a Persian's head to the compound beyond my pavilion. So rapid was Sultan Mahmoud's progress that many of the slower hazaras did not get to the gates, but bought heads—first for four gold dinars, then three, two, and one, some for a few coppers—from the more fortunate soldiers who had gone in early.

I set slaves to work cleaning the skulls and burnishing them to gleaming whiteness with the salt sand of the desert. Then, with clay from the shallow riverbed as mortar, my masons built pyramids and columns of the skulls at the gates and main street intersections inside the city. Seventy-five thousand skulls went into those shafts, as warnings to the Persians to cease their slaughter and make peace.

In the late afternoon I released my men to go back to the women in Isfahan, and I sent fast dispatch riders to rush Zain al-Abaidin's messages to his brothers.

CHAPTER 6

With the exception of Shah Mansur, who took his army and fled to Sheik al Jabal's White Castle in the fastnesses of Alamut, all his brothers answered Zain al-Abaidin's summons to come to Isfahan. Seeing the fate Zain's capital had suffered and realizing their own impotence, they all acknowledged me as master and agreed to have my name read as king in all prayers.

I gave each a writ of authority, signed by me and stamped with my handprint, and sent the eight chastened young Shahs back to their cities to raise tribute money and prepare for my visit of inspection. After establishing my own daroga in Isfahan, and sending Bara Lohar to Baghdad to heckle Sultan Ahmed, I began a systematic progress through the realm.

Stopping at each city in turn, I reduced local taxes collectable by the

Shah and raised the amounts due me from the lesser nobles and rich merchants. The slaves and beggars and laborers welcomed me—though I let Abdullah preside in the name of Leng Kopeghi at all meetings of the Ulama of Slaves—as their benefactor. Actually I lost nothing by relieving the poor people of their tax burdens; they merely allowed themselves to be mulcted by the rich, and I in turn taxed the rich into poverty, all according to the Will of Allah.

In my secret Ulama of Scholars, Sherif ad-Din instructed the wise men to shift tactics. Instead of playing upon the vanity of the shahs to divide them—a task already accomplished—the scholars were to decry the injustices of the rulers and exaggerate weaknesses in the government, and so split the classes inside the various provinces and keep all in a state of uneasy prostration.

Zain al-Abaidin accompanied me on my progress until the second summer, when I installed him as puppet Shah of Shiraz. Because of my promise to his father, I gave the young Persian as elaborate a coronation as the city had ever seen. Always a beautiful city of lush hanging gardens and cool tiled arcades running through beds of the most gorgeous roses in the world, some of them of a hundred blood-red petals, Shiraz was a special delight after my long trek across the desert.

Bibi Khanum and N'il Mahdi-Soun were sources of constant delight to me as we three loafed in the palace gardens. The bright summer skies, dotted sometimes with towering fluffs of clouds from the Persian Gulf, and the nights, filled with stars as big and bright as royal medallions, were new and exciting to my northern-bred Manchu princess. And all the world was new to my son as he toddled untiringly through it, picking flowers and pebbles and naming them for us in his grave childish earnestness.

With her knowledge and knack for languages, Bibi readily picked up Persian and spent hours reading to me from the poets of that bright land—ancient and modern singers of beauty and sadness. She especially liked Hafiz, who was hiding out somewhere in the slums.

"You have a new challenger," she said laughingly one day in the midst of her silent reading.

"Who's that?" I asked, rousing myself from a delicious semi-slumber.

"Hafiz. Listen. *If my mistress of Shiraz would take my heart in her hand, I would lay before her feet Bokhara or Samarkand.* Those are your cities, aren't they?" Her light laughter trilled in the windless air.

"They were, at last report—Bokhara rather damaged by my foster son Toti, but still mine. I lay them before your feet, Mistress of Shiraz," I said.

"Your mahdi is enough to lay before my feet at the moment," she said, as our son sat down suddenly and unintentionally on the marble floor in front of her. She picked him up and spanked his bottom gently with her book of Hafiz.

"Maybe we'd better chide this poet for being so generous with our property. Would you like to meet him?" I asked.

"I'd love to!" she said eagerly. "But you won't punish him, will you? Some of his work is so fine and sensitive."

"Not if you champion him," I said.

None of the officials could locate Hafiz, but Abdullah produced him the very next day and presented him to us in the garden.

"Hafiz, did you write this?" I asked sternly, and had Bibi Khanum read the passage to him.

Even in the beggar's rags which Hafiz wore as a disguise, he looked fine and distinguished. The filthy shapeless robe suggested a slender nervous body underneath, and the poet's expressive eyes, glowing at Bibi's reading of his verse, explained how he could have written the lines.

"Yes, Amir Timur," he said bravely, when the princess had finished.

"Do you know how much blood and work and heartbreak it has taken to seize and hold Samarkand and Bokhara—the thousands of hot desert miles I have covered to ornament and beautify those gems?"

"Yes, Amir," he said sadly. "That is what makes them such rare gifts."

"And you would toss them at the feet of some light wench of Shiraz. Why?"

"Because of the same thoughtless extravagance and generosity which has brought me to the beggar's rags I wear before you," he said, and smiled—more at Bibi Khanum than at me.

Bibi laughed delightedly at his answer, and I, too, found myself chuckling.

"What shall we do with him, Khanum?" I asked.

"Let me see," she said, becoming suddenly grave, as grave as N'il Mahdi-Soun, who stood by her knees and stared at Hafiz through unblinking eyes. "Let me see—he *is* a very extravagant man, but his poetry is priceless."

"Perhaps if we were equally extravagant, we might write equally well. Let's make him rich," I suggested.

"Yes, let's," she said, and smiled warmly at the poet.

"Take him to the treasurer and give him anything he wants," I said to Abdullah. "But first give him a bath and burn his clothes."

Hafiz bowed low and smiled gratefully at Bibi Khanum, but there was no groveling, no fawning in his attitude. He knew that his poetry was priceless, and he read appreciation in the eyes of the exquisite doll-princess.

"I'd like my son to be a poet," Bibi said wistfully, as she watched Hafiz depart. Then she took the little boy in her arms and hugged him to her.

"Mahdis must be poets," I said. "You prepare him—teach him words, and I'll give him his prophecy."

I was fifty-six years old then, and N'il Mahdi-Soun almost three. I doubted that I would live to see him mature into a warrior, but he might master words to tell my story in my time. Sherif ad-Din could not. He was blinded by the prejudices of men, by his love for me, by a thousand and one things that distorted his versions of what I did and said. N'il Mahdi-Soun was my hope. If Bibi Khanum could make a poet of her son, I would not stand in her way. Certainly there was poetry in her—in her face, in her quivering young body at night. I looked forward to the cool of the evening.

When Nur ad-Din and Sultan Mahmoud returned, we marched east, then across the desert to Herat. In Herat I installed Shah Rukh as Sultan of Khorassan and let him appoint his own daroga before continuing on with me. It would be some time before he could assume actual rule, but he could get his name established and claim the tax money.

I had given the revenue of Balkh to Jaku for some years already; so I allowed my aging uncle to hold court a few days in his city before I headed north for Samarkand. On the way I left the main force of my army at Shehri-Sebz—to be in readiness when I decided to ride against Toktamish—and proceeded to Samarkand with only my twelve thousand personal kulchis and Shah Rukh's Gok Hazara as my escort.

Although I had gathered considerable loot on my long campaign, my army had been large and expensive, and I could not make my usual extravagant entry into my capital. When I rode through the gates with bare military pomp, I was glad that I had not tried. Nothing I could have brought from Persia could have matched the beauty of Samarkand itself, which had blossomed into a veritable paradise in my absence. The streets looked like open jewel cases, and the palace, although still under construction, was the most imposing edifice in Asia. And Bibi Khanum's temple showed promise of rivaling any mosque in the world.

My welcome was as enthusiastic as if I had returned with all the wealth of India and Khitai in my train. Bright banners, bright uniforms, bright faces, and bright court clothes merged into a shimmering iridescence which dazzled my eyes, accustomed to the sameness of

322

the desert glare, and made them water and sting at the brilliance. An emotional man might have mistaken the phenomenon for tears. I was glad to be home again. And I saw the Way, if but dimly, through the opalescent splendor around me—as I saw Aljai in the fine stately person of the Sarai Khanum, where she stood on the balcony to greet me.

Dilshad's hair had more silver in it, but her face and her figure were young—ageless—and her eyes clear and competent and loving. To my subjects, she was Samarkand as I was Tatary—hers the beauty and security of home, mine the strength and restlessness of sprawling empire.

Ali Soun was there, and Nubja and Sevin Bey, with their sons all grown tall in my absence. But Shereza's throne of second precedence was vacant, as glaringly so as old Kurgan's empty eye socket had been. I wondered, as I greeted the others, what could have kept the Begum away from the reception—Shereza, who more than any of my other wives reveled in pomp and ceremony.

When I was alone with Dilshad I asked her.

"The Begum is in Otrar," she said.

"Visiting Omar Sheik? She must have had a change of heart, to leave her precious Miran Shah."

"Miran went, too," Dilshad said, and I detected a hesitancy in her speech, as though she regretted having to tell me.

"But I gave orders—"

"I know," Dilshad broke in, "but we couldn't stop her. After all she *is* the Begum—not a prisoner."

"But what prompted her? Was Miran able to travel? I thought by now he'd be—"

"Dead?" she asked, and smiled strangely at my unfinished sentence. "No—Shereza brought him back from the dead, at least partially."

"Why?"

"You must know what a name Omar Sheik is making for himself. The people worship him."

"Yes, I've had reports. I'm proud of him."

"Well, it was just too much for Shereza. She couldn't have Omar outshining Miran; so she took her baby off to war."

"To war! She's as crazy as he is."

"Perhaps," said Dilshad gently. "She's to be pitied. Anyway, she recruited a squadron from her own followers and left for Otrar five weeks ago. Saif ad-Din went along, bless his old heart. Maybe he can help prevent a catastrophe."

"I doubt it," I said. "Saif's a simpleton. Maybe this is quicker," I finished, and shrugged my shoulders.

"I'm glad you don't hate Shah Rukh," Dilshad said, and looked earnestly at my face. I felt her study my mouth and my eyes and my wrinkled forehead.

"I don't hate anyone," I said, and put my arm around her shoulders. "Least of all Shah Rukh. Your son's a fine boy."

Then Dilshad the imperturbable broke down and wept on my chest. The most regal woman in Asia was a little girl again in my arms.

"Oh, Timur," she sobbed. "I do love him so. And I love you. Be good to him. I don't ask for favors or advancement he doesn't merit. But do be good to him. Don't hate him."

I petted her and soothed her and remembered the canyon near Khiva, and our early days in Samarkand. And Aljai.

CHAPTER

7

I did not stay long in Samarkand. Soon after my arrival I learned that Toktamish was no longer directing the nuisance raids against Omar Sheik. Instead he had withdrawn to the north to build up his strength for a full-scale attack on Samarkand. By some very fortunate developments in Russia, Toktamish had managed to reunite all the remnants of the Hordes, and various accounts credited him with a larger potential force than my own.

I set to work at once to get my army ready for a campaign into Toktamish's territory. Knowing that we would find no cities and that my army could not live off the land during most of the campaign, I had my best quartermasters draw up a supply schedule and allot the supplies. Each two men had three horses; each squad of ten men, two spades, a pickaxe, a sickle, a saw, an axe, an awl, one big cooking pot, needles, hides, cloth, etc. Food was largely limited to sixteen pounds of flour per man per month, dried fruit and wine, and powdered mare's milk, which could be replenished en route.

I adopted the big-wheeled kankalis and bulky camel litters of the steppe-dwellers, as well as the horsehide khalats and heavy fur surcoats of the kazaks. As usual our weapons were swords, light and heavy lances and both longbows and saddlebows. We took no seige machines. They would not have justified the trouble required to transport them—I had no elephants then. Nor had my mathematicians discovered the secret of fire powder, which I had hoped would lead to lighter siege machines.

When my army moved up from Shehri-Sebz for the final review on the plain before Samarkand, the troops looked drab and grim as they lined up on the snow-covered parade ground and breathed frost into the cold air. Only the brilliant standards and hazara guidons brightened the gray and black ranks of solemn warriors. The men feared and dreaded the cold mists and yellow skies of the Land of Shadows, where the nights last half a year.

Perhaps only my grandsons were eager for the journey. Pir Mohammed, then seventeen, and Mohammed Sultan, sixteen—both taller and heavier than their father had been—could hardly wait to be off to their first war. Shah Rukh at twenty-two was, of course, a seasoned veteran of the Persian campaign and my own executive officer of the second corps, or center reserves. I chose Pir Mohammed as my tavachi and assigned Mohammed Sultan to Shah Rukh so I could keep a critical eye on all three of the boys. Sultan Mahmoud, the valiant son of Sheik Ali, commanded my first corps, or center; and Omar Sheik would take over the fourth corps—my left wing, and strongest offensive element—when we reached Otrar. Nur ad-Din with a number of excellent amirs led my third corps, which brought up the rear of my troops and took the right wing in battle formation.

The leading division of each corps followed one of my steppe-bred ming-bashis. I had complete confidence in my troops, and they in me, as we set out for Tashkand in the dead of winter. The snow was light, and the frozen ground afforded firm footing. All began auspiciously.

But only as far as Tashkand. There I took sick—my blood thinned by the years in the south—and fretted with a fever for forty days. Dilshad and Bibi Khanum came to Tashkand and took turns nursing me until I was able to move on northward. Both went with me as far as Otrar. There I sent Dilshad back, for I knew she was needed in Samarkand. Bibi Khanum, however, insisted on continuing the journey, probably because of nostalgia for the frozen country of her childhood.

Omar Sheik and his two sons—though only thirteen and fourteen at the time—joined me in Otrar, as did Shereza Begum and Miran Shah.

As soon as I saw my oldest son, I knew that he was living on hashish and opium. He seldom spoke, but when he did, it was obvious that he had no mind left—just a shallow faculty for retaining briefly his mother's instructions and acting on them to the limits of his ability. He had already distinguished himself by his reckless daring on some minor raids. I remembered how hard Shereza had driven him that day he was injured in the polo game. She was still driving him—driving him and petting him and destroying him.

When she rode her camel through the knee-deep snow to visit me at my ordu outside Otrar, I welcomed her graciously. Clambering down off her kneeling camel without the aid of a ladder, she greeted me with an obvious sense of relief.

"Oh, Timur, dear, I'm so glad you've come," she said breathlessly, after she had waddled into my kibitka and backed up to a glowing charcoal brazier. "The boys have been hard pressed. They're holding out, but they need you."

The boys! Omar Sheik with his forty thousand tough veterans and Miran Shah with one drugged hazara composed of mad Ghurkas and berserks and renegade Rajputs from India.

"Well, I'm here now," I said, muffling a chuckle at the absurdity of her relative appraisal of her two sons. "We'll stop all of this nonsense once and for all."

"I'm glad," she said enthusiastically. "I became so worried while you were in Persia. If I hadn't brought Miran Shah up here, I doubt that Omar Sheik could have stopped those Russian barbarians from coming right down to Samarkand."

"That would have been terrible."

"Yes, wouldn't it? So I just told Miran Shah that as your eldest son he was duty-bound to come to Omar's aid, even though he did have to leave Samarkand in Daoud's hands during your absence."

"You were absolutely right, Shereza," I said. "He's probably had enough training as a sedentary monarch. He should return to the saddle occasionally. Even I have to go on a campaign now and then, just to keep my hand in."

Shereza beamed at my approval and set the vast expanse of her thawed-out posterior on a fur-covered ottoman beside my field throne.

"That's what I told him," she said, nodding agreement to my views. "I said, 'Just look at your father fighting in Persia, and your brother Omar making a name for himself in the north. You must lead your people in this time of stress.' Of course, he agreed and came right along. And he's been so brave!"

"So I've heard—brave and daring."

"And his men are so loyal to him. The dear boys will follow him through fire."

Follow his hashish, I said to myself.

"You will make him a corps commander, won't you, Timur?" she asked hopefully. "Like Omar Sheik?"

"I don't see why not," I said, after a moment's hesitation. I could make him a figurehead in Nur ad-Din's veteran third corps, which could use some crazy shock troops when Toktamish's powerful left wing started knifing through it. Miran Shah might well be out in front.

"I just knew you would," she said, tears of gratitude welling up in her eyes.

"Yes, I'll put him in command of the third corps."

"Omar Sheik commands the fourth, doesn't he?" she asked significantly, seeing some order of precedence in the assignments.

"Yes. He commands the fourth—my left wing." My left wing—the most formidable corps of cavalry in the world.

"And Shah Rukh is your tavachi," she stated smugly. I was sure that Dilshad had tried to dissuade the Begum from her folly and had aroused some rivalry in her ample breast.

"My executive officer," I said, finding it pleasant to humor Shereza.

"Not even a commander," she said. "Sevin Bey said that you would give Miran Shah the highest rank if he wanted it."

"Sevin Bey?" I asked in surprise. "What did she have to do with it?"

"We talked it over," Shereza said proudly. "Sevin Bey reminded me that Omar Sheik was filling the place Miran Shah should be holding."

"So she put you up to this," I said.

"Oh, no." Shereza smiled her wisest, sweetest smile. "It was my idea, mine and Miran's. Sevin Bey is really quite a sweet girl. Miran was very much in love with her once."

"I remember," I said.

"And I think she was fond of him. Little Khalil Sultan—" The Begum frowned momentarily. "If things had only been a little different—"

"Or quite different," I corrected her; but my irony was wasted.

"Anyway, we talked it over. And she was right. She knows you quite well, Timur." Shereza's smile was a sly, knowing one.

"Better, perhaps, than any one else," I said. "Anyway, as you say, she was right. Miran now has the post of honor."

"Thank you again, Timur," she said, rising, again all but overcome by emotion. "You're so sweet. You've never refused me—or Miran—a thing."

"Not a thing," I said. "How could I?"

"You could have," she said generously. "But you didn't. No woman ever had a better husband."

I remembered how many times she had said that—the poor stupid Begum, Fatima's most illustrious daughter, Allah's first female.

When we moved north again, Shereza rode beside Miran Shah at the head of Nur ad-Din's column—not back near the center of the train with the other women. Her camel litter, or the sumptuous kankali she had had fitted out for really bad weather, was as much a symbol as my ball-and-crescent standard which marked each corps.

Across the Syr-Darya and up on to the Kirghis Steppe, through snow and sleet and freezing rain, across frozen rivers and windswept plateaus, my gray army made its dismal trek—Shereza's litter the only bright spot in the column. On to Kara Saman, and there I got first word of Toktamish. Toktamish's envoys rode into my ordu with nine fine white horses and a sonkar—a royal falcon—as gifts from their master. The ambassadors, cold and tired from their long ride, accepted the hospitality of my snug felt kibitka and made their presentation speeches.

Since I had been stroking one of my own falcons and had a falconer's glove on at the time, I took the gorgeous sonkar on my wrist and took off its jeweled rufter for a moment. The bird had a fine beak and sharp intelligent eyes—an excellent hunter, she seemed, and a very well-behaved fowl.

"Your son Toti," Aisa Bey began his diplomatic lies, "begs your forgiveness for his rashness in making war upon your cities. He bids you recall, as he does, how you helped him against Urus Khan, the murderer of his father, and set him upon his throne at Sarai. He begs you to enter into a treaty with him, and he reasserts his eternal loyalty and fealty to you, his Father, Prince of Samarkand."

I handed the falcon to a servant and had him put her in the royal cote. Then I turned my attention to the dissembling ambassadors.

"I recall all these things far better than does your master," I said. "How I took him when he was wounded and hard pressed by his enemies. How I called him my son and opened my palace to him. How I gave him arms and men, lent my gallant horse Kunk Oghlan, and then went to battle by his side. I have not forgotten.

"I remember, too, his perfidy, his treachery, his raids on my cities, his unprovoked aggression on the province of my son—his foster brother. And he asks peace!

"For nine mangy horses and one poor bird he asks peace! Breaker of oaths, betrayer of family, wrecker of my cities—he asks for a treaty!

"Aisa Bey, go back to your master. Tell him to send his prime minister, or come himself, with full indemnity for the damage he has done me, and I will talk peace. Gazanski will remain as my hostage."

Aisa Bey departed at once with half the escort and left the others in my camp. Before he was beyond the second ridge of hills, a physician asked audience.

328

"The servant, Amir. The servant who took the falcon off your wrist. He is dead. The bird's talons were poisoned. Only your glove saved your life."

"My beloved son, Toti," I said.

"There's a saying among the Iranians, 'Never trust any man who comes out of Russia.' You might heed it, Amir."

"It's not new," I said. "I've never trusted one."

I sent for Gazanski at once and had him beheaded. Then I had his head put in a square can of water and set it outside in the freezing weather. The next morning I sent the block of ice, with Gazanski's grinning face frozen inside it, to Toktamish by the rest of his escort, who had stayed behind. And after starting all of the women except Bibi Khanum and Shereza Begum back toward Samarkand, I reformed my column and headed north again in pursuit of my erstwhile son.

For three months my army trudged on over barren windswept steppes, across muddy yellow waters, white sands and black sands, ranges of low rugged mountains—my men living on steppe foxes and wild boar and jerboa and marmot and an occasional herd of antelope. Then roots and herbs gathered after snow had been cleared off the ground in some protected valley. But never enough—we all ate out of common pots of stew made of anything and everything we had.

Horses died from lack of forage or from loss of blood, which some undisciplined soldiers drew from their veins and drank when food was lowest. Men died, too, from lack of food and of the sunshine to which they were accustomed. And men grew fearful and fretful—fearful of the weird snowbound country where no people lived, or people who were like wraiths or shadows, coming out unseen to leave bundles of furs in trade for trinkets left on bare rocks and disappearing again into the snow as though the commerce was with ghosts.

To keep up morale, I reviewed the troops every evening before sunset. The army marched always in a rough approximation of a battle line and camped each night in the same relative position, ready to pass in review and return past the same standards and kibitkas and perhaps get a feeling of familiarity with the ordu if not with the strange monotonous terrain. Then, before daybreak, the kourrouns would sound reveille, and the column would move out again.

Throughout it all Bibi Khanum, accustomed to the north country, was a delightful companion; and I had to admit grudgingly that the Begum was magnificent. I never ceased to wonder at her stamina. Bloated, soft, reared in the southern luxury of Herat, she seemed completely oblivious of the frozen wastes around her. Grown careless only of her sacred green veil, she was always dressed brightly and rouged and well groomed. Riding in her litter or kankali, with the curtains open, she smiled constantly on her tuman-bashi son and his wild-eyed hazara and the rest of my army.

Shereza sat with me when I reviewed the troops. She waved at the men informally, and only the strictest discipline prevented them from waving back. They stared at her hungrily—but there was no lust for her shapeless body in their glances—and after the review almost every man found some excuse to pass by her gaudy pavilion, which stood out ridiculously in the gray line of felt yurts and kibitkas. The men seemed to worship her. After all, she was their Begum—their mad, stupid Begum, smiling at every one as though he were her son.

And on.

On to the spongy tundra near the circle where the magnetic needle of the Khitans tries to point down instead of to the north. In the month of Jamada 1, which marked spring in Samarkand, the country was still sunless—a land of fog and shadows and long dim days and short, only slightly dimmer nights, with the aurora borealis sending faint colored rays through the opalescent mist. But there was more forage—thin scum of moss on the wet thawing earth, and faded life-less creepers and sickly green alder leaves, fodder of a sort.

And some food for men—geese and their eggs, and hawks, and mute, songless snowbirds, and strange furry little animals which the men feared to eat but ate anyway.

We had camped between the Kuchuk Tagh and Ulugh Tagh—the Big and Little Mountain—beyond the Tobol and the Ob' Rivers, and seen the purple prairies darkening into plum on the horizon. And across the snakelike Ilanchuk river, through the marshes, over the sands, along the shores of Lake Ak Sarai Barbi. On into the chill wet mists of the tundra.

But we had not found Toktamish. Men began to doubt his exist-ence, their own existence, the existence of Allah. Even the mollahs were disturbed by the long day, and longer twilight; they could not be certain of the prayer hours, with no sunrise or sunset to mark the day. So they stuck their fingers in their ears and faced toward Mecca—or where Mecca might be—and called prayers at their own caprice, without reference to time.

All this confused the men, the animals, everyone except Shereza, who smiled and petted Miran Shah and doled out hashish and bhang —raw unprocessed hemp leaves and stems—to the drug-sustained squad-ron he led. And she continued to give heart to my army, such heart as they had.

330

Reasonably sure that Toktamish was not to the north of me, I turned my army west, across the Urals, and headed into the prairie country beyond. There we found more forage and evidence of more life. Since we were down to a mere paste of barley flour and mare's milk with whatever wild meat or herb flavoring we could find, I ordered the army to form a circle for one massive hunt.

My column of a hundred thousand men strung out into a line thirty miles long, and gradually curved the wings around the plain until they enclosed an area nearly ten miles in diameter. As the ring closed in and tightened ranks, animals of all kinds broke out of coverts and raced erratically back and forth. Hare and fox and wolf and stag and antelope and deer and the strange bighorned deer gradually converged into a frightened, milling mass of game in the center of the ever decreasing circle.

I rode into the ring first and killed a beast with each of the thirty arrows in my quiver. Then all bows were drawn, and in a matter of minutes we had enough fresh-killed meat to last for a week. I declared a feast for two whole days, which restored the spirits of my men though by that time we had no wine left, only a short ration of kumiss.

During the feast I dispatched Sheik David, who knew the country well, on a scouting mission; and the next day, while my men were still fresh, I began my forced march along the trail he had blazed. On the banks of the Yaik River we found signs of recent large camps at each of three fords. My men were greatly heartened by the evidence and willingly plunged into the icy stream—I crossed between fords because I feared an ambush—and came out on the other bank, eager to continue the march.

A few days later, near the middle of Jamada 2, Sheik David met us at the Semur River and brought three captives with him. The men, whom he had taken from a village on the banks of the Ik River, said that Toktamish had passed that way only a short time before. The treacherous Russian had heard of my short rations and was following Fabian tactics to wear my army down by attrition. However, he was not many miles away and well-provisioned; so I decided to force him into battle.

We moved forward constantly, doing all cooking in the moving kankalis and showing no fires at night. Soon we came upon warm coals left by small elements of Toktamish's rear guard, and we sent out patrols from each corps. Old Jaku, well up in his eighties, led the scouts out of my center corps and made first contact, though we knew nothing of it until we found his head stuck on his own heavy lance and planted directly in our line of march. A survivor from his party reported that the doughty old warrior had had two horses shot from under him and had accounted for six of the enemy before he had been killed and beheaded.

I put Shah Malik in command of Jaku's regiment and pushed on. We risked no more small patrols, however. Omar Sheik took the leading twenty thousand men of the column and raced ahead. Sevinjik and Sultan Sanjar and Saif ad-Din, the last of the ancients, took elements from the corps and raced on the heels of Omar's fourth corps. And they made contact with Toktamish's rear guard and forced the Horde to draw up in battle formation just before sunset.

The next morning, although late in Jamada 2, was a gloomy dawn, darkened by a heavy overcast and a heavy snowfall. We could not offer battle; but during the day some Kipchaks who had deserted Toktamish and come over to me some months before managed to infiltrate the Russian lines and approach some of Toktamish's more disgruntled followers. They bribed the headquarters standard-bearer and an amir who had a grudge.

So by the time the weather broke later in the day, I was in an excellent position to force an attack. When visibility improved sufficiently for the armies to estimate strength, I sent Omar's younger son with ten thousand men to the rear of my reserves to cook supper. Since Omar Sheik and Miran Shah (with Nur ad-Din and Saif ad-Din really in command) had arrived early and secured my flank, I could safely make the show of casual camp preparations.

The disaffected amir chose that moment to demand satisfaction and, upon Toktamish's refusal, deserted, taking a whole corps with him. Then Toktamish offered battle. Knowing that my left flank was my attacking force—as was his—he suddenly chose to alter tactics and rush my offense wing, which was not in a defensive formation. He knifed through Omar's line and set his standard in the rear. But the standard-bearer, faithful to his agreement with Oronk, immediately hauled down the flag and signaled surrender.

My own reserves quickly flanked the confused attackers, and Toktamish himself fled back at full gallop through the breach he had made in my lines.

In the meanwhile, Nur ad-Din, seeing the enemy's reversal in tactics, had countered with a similar reversal and attacked Toktamish's right wing, taking it by surprise as the enemy had caught Omar Sheik. Saif ad-Din led the first assault and forced a partial retirement. Then—the story was variously told—Miran Shah, realizing perhaps that he was not actually in command of the corps, led his drug-crazed Tulu Hazara in the wildest single foray ever seen west of the Urals. With Kilinjik

Bahatur as his second in command, he headed his berserks straight through the enemy's right wing, slashing and plunging all the way to his center front line, which had turned and was in headlong retreat.

How many men the Tulu Hazara killed was never known, for my army rapidly covered the same ground, inflicting thousands of casualties; but all witnesses said that Miran Shah's men were worse than all the devils in the seven hells. Of the Tulu Hazara only Kilinjik and eighteen bloody Ghurkas and Rajputs were left. Miran Shah and the aged Saif ad-Din—who had left his own command to try to turn my son back—were both killed in the melee.

I told Shereza Begum.

I was not sure that she understood me. She was dry-eyed and calm, so calm and still that somehow she looked slender, even young again.

"He broke the enemy's line, you say?" she asked.

"Yes, he made a valiant charge."

"And Omar Sheik's ranks broke?"

"Yes."

"What did Shah Rukh do?"

"He was with me—with my reserves," I answered.

"Reserves!" she said in contempt. She had heard me all right. "Where's Miran Shah?"

"They're bringing him here," I said. "Here to your pavilion."

Shereza sat down on her divan and courteously motioned me to be seated. And she continued to sit, erect and serene, as though she were expecting a court call. Then Bibi Khanum came.

"I've just heard," she said to the Begum.

"Do sit down, dear," Shereza said pleasantly.

"Miran—" Bibi began.

"He'll be here, soon. Won't you wait?"

Bibi Khanum perched on the edge of an ottoman for a moment and then eased herself down and sat cross-legged on the deep Persian rug. She never took her eyes off Shereza.

"Would you like a cup of tea, dear?" asked our hostess. "While we're waiting for Miran?"

"No—no, thank you," Bibi answered softly. Then she looked at me with perplexity—and admiration—in her eyes.

Two of my own kulchis brought the litter into Shereza's pavilion. Miran's body, dressed in a fresh uniform, looked little older, only fatter and grosser, than he had that day he had been carried unconscious from the polo field.

"Right here, here beside me," Shereza said, and indicated the divan. The litter bearers looked at me, and I nodded. They laid him on the

333

divan. Shereza got up and sat down again on an ottoman at the head of the couch. Then she turned and spoke to Bibi Khanum.

"He'll be all right, Dilshad dear. The physician says it's just a bump on his head. Just let him sleep. He'll be all right."

She smiled reassuringly at Bibi Khanum. She was back in Shehri-Sebz! The last cakkar was over. I almost envied her.

All night she stayed with Miran Shah. Only when the carpenters brought in the coffin did she speak.

"No—not like that. Make it more like a cradle—that's too plain, too boxy."

She knew he was dead. She must have known, just as she must have known that his throne in Samarkand was a prisoner's seat.

I sent the carpenters away. When they returned the next morning with a new coffin, more like a cradle, but without rockers, Shereza smiled at them.

"That's better. Yes, that will do. Timur, dear"—she turned to me —"will you have them bring the kankali at once?"

"The kankali?" I asked in amazement.

"Yes. I must take him home—before he wakes up. It's so strange here."

"But you can't take him home. I can't spare the men to escort you back across that trackless waste."

"I won't need any. Just his own boys. They loved him so. They'll take us home. Allah will guide us—I'm the Begum."

"Very well," I said, and gave the orders. Obviously my objections were absurd.

Again the morning was dark and heavily overcast; but when the kankali was loaded and the remnants of the Tulu Hazara were stuffed so full of hashish that they would have tried anything, Shereza took her seat beside the cradle-shaped coffin in the big-wheeled cart, and Kilin-jik Bahatur led his procession through my camp.

Shereza, facing aft, smiled and waved at us as the kankali went out of sight. The last ones to see her said that she was still smiling—or crooning a lullaby, according to some—and resting one hand on the coffin, as though to steady it, when the big cart rumbled away toward the steppes.

"There was something fine and noble about the Begum," Bibi Khanum said. "Was she your oldest wife?"

"Yes."

"Your first?"

"No."

"You've never told me about your first wife."

334

"No," I said, and turned to enter my kibitka. The weather was raw and disagreeable.

Inside, Bibi Khanum hurried to her own little cradle and took N'il Mahdi-Soun in her arms. She just sat and held him and stared at me until I put on my heavy ermine coat and went out to survey the battlefield. I heard her sweet girlish voice singing a Manchu lullaby as I left the tent, a lullaby to my poet son, N'il Mahdi-Soun.

Sixty or seventy thousand of the enemy lay dead on the plain, and Omar Sheik's fourth corps was still pursuing the remnants who had fled toward the train and the royal ordu to the southwest. I had lost only a third as many men as had Toktamish.

Soon after noon, I assembled my army to honor the noble dead, chief of whom was the venerable Saif ad-Din. Mir Sayyid made a funeral oration over Saif's body and pronounced the funeral rites. Then I turned the body over to Nur ad-Din for burial.

"Amir Timur," said Nur ad-Din, "no man ever loved his father as I loved mine. Nor was there ever love such as he bore you—such as I feel for you this moment and will feel while I live. The honor and courtesy and respect you have shown him makes me forever your slave. May I, too, die in battle for you, as he has died."

Nur ad-Din knelt before me and kissed my hand. Then he rose and took his father's body away.

"Saif ad-Din was a grand old man," Mir Sayyid said, as he watched the procession move away.

"He was a garrulous old fool," I said. "If he had been able to see the implications of all he knew about warfare, he could have been the Kha Khan."

Mir Sayyid looked at me strangely and said, "Allah is not in this north country. I've felt it all along. Now, I know it." He turned away and followed Nur ad-Din.

That afternoon I dispatched Sultan Mahmoud's first corps to reinforce Omar Sheik, and the next day Nur ad-Din and I set out toward the Volga. There were reasonably heavy skirmishes and mop-up operations for three more days; but by the time we joined our advance units at Urtupa, on the banks of the Volga, the last remaining warriors of the Hordes had been slaughtered or drowned in attempting to cross the river.

Omar Sheik had already captured the train, with all of the women and wealth of the Hordes, and set up a luxurious sarai on the Urtupa plain, lush and green with early spring feather grass. We made the camp our headquarters for over two months while the bulk of my army split up into raiding parties and scoured the whole of the Hordes' country for Toktamish himself, and for wealth or women that might have been overlooked.

The Russian women were treats for my men. Fairer of skin than most southerners, they were deprived of their clothes upon their capture but allowed free run of the ordu so the men could feast on the contrast of their white flesh and coal black hair which, unbound, hung to their waists. I allowed a few of my amirs to take the choicest, but since the personnel of my camp was ever-changing, I insisted that most of the women be common property. The more accomplished of them banded into choruses and dance groups to entertain the soldiers with native dances and love songs. The less accomplished, though no less beautiful, moved about as servants and waitresses, their naked bodies kept sweet and clean by daily baths in the Volga and sprays of rose water.

For my own part I chose some five thousand of the handsomest boys and loveliest young girls to take back to Samarkand as pages and maids for the palace. Of course I took many more thousands of slaves—sturdy scrub women and burly woodcutters and hod-carriers—from among the remaining Russians, so that when my army re-formed at Sabran for the final march to Samarkand, my train contained almost as many captives as warriors.

Toktamish had fled into Georgia, out of reach for the moment, but my army so despoiled the country it had covered that I had no fear of attack from that quarter during the remainder of my lifetime. The people left behind would be slaves and impoverished peasants for generations to come before they could rebuild their land and support a war machine. And Mir Sayyid had said that Allah was not in the north country! He was everywhere. I, His servant, had made His Way prevail—my Flaming Sword had kept the Way of the Tree of Life on the steppes and the tundra and the banks of the Volga.

Upon my return to Samarkand I sent for Sevin Bey Khanzade at once. Although I was not hurt by her interference in the affairs of Miran Shah and Shereza Begum, who of course never reached Samarkand, the mere fact of her meddling aroused my hatred for the golden vixen, and I looked forward to venting my rage upon her.

Shrouded in her black stole as usual, she crept surreptitiously into my chamber. We both were aware that our meetings were probably secret from no one; but since I had never formally taken her into my household, she evidently preferred to persist in the fiction that she was the chaste widow of my eldest son. I suspected, however, that she was using her charms to influence some of my amirs to side with her in her intrigues—a practice neither she nor her paramours would have dared risk had she been acknowledged as my wife.

From the look of exultant triumph in her eyes, I could tell that her body was animated by a more than normal emotional force, even before she disrobed and revealed a figure grown still more voluptuous in the full maturity of womanhood. Sevin Bey was in her late thirties, and I nearing sixty at the time.

"So you have some ideas on the precedence of my sons?" I asked, and I know that my eyes burned with hatred.

"Shereza told you?" she asked, smirking at me. "You have two royal sons left, I believe."

She paraded her nakedness before me and deliberately stood between me and a window, so her perfume would be wafted my way.

"Four," I reminded her. "Remember Amyris and N'il Mahdi-Soun."

"They don't count." She laughed contemptuously. "Nobody will recognize a Negro prince and you'll never live to see Bibi's baby a man. Anyway, they're your fifth and sixth sons, and inheritance does not go beyond the fourth."

She was right, of course. I could only strike her savagely in the face as she walked by me, taunting me with her beauty, asking for brutality.

"Two gone—two more," she gloated. "I told you I'd win."

No other person in the world ever challenged me like that and lived. But she already had powerful allies, and I had to keep the loyalty of her three sons. In spite of Dilshad's training, my grandsons would have been duty-bound to avenge their mother's murder. And I wanted Sevin Bey alive.

I struck her again, and she attacked me savagely, lunging her weight against me and clawing at my bare back with her long nails. On contact, the flames of our hatred merged and welded our bodies together, and the lunging, clenching, flailing battle was on. For two days we fought and insulted each other.

Then it was I, not Sevin Bey, who could no longer hold my own. Though she continued to tempt me and taunt me with ribald jeers at my temporary impotency, I could only strike her and bruise her outer flesh.

"Hurt me, Timur," she would scream and flaunt herself obscenely before me, with rising laughter in her voice and a smug triumphant arrogance lighting up her countenance. "Hurt me—inside. Hurt me inside, Timur."

I would slap her and beat her but she would keep up her ridicule. "Inside, Timur. Hurt me inside."

I had the feeling that this was a crucial matter, the most important contest of my life. In my distress I even saw it as a challenge to the Way. Kurgan had said, "Wear out your emotions on women. Use up all your passion on them." And I had done so. But now something seemed to be happening to me that I did not expect, that Kurgan had not expected. It was not that I was getting old—I had expected that. But in wearing out my emotions, I might be wearing out my own spirit. When I doubted my prowess with women, I doubted myself. Was it possible that the emotions and the self could not be entirely separated?

Knowing I could not settle this now, I lay, quiet, on my couch and refused battle. Sevin Bey rose triumphantly.

"I've defeated you in your own bed, old man," she gloated, as she stood, tall and glistening in the candlelight—never more desirable in her life, with the fire of her triumph heightening her golden skin to a new polish. "And I'll defeat you in your own kingdom. I'm the victor —see?" She flipped her torso lewdly as a final gesture and slowly put on her clothes.

As I watched her dress, I wanted to hurt her worse than ever before —to hurt her inside. But there was not a thing I could do. She threw the hooded stole over her court dress and went to the door. There she turned her exultant gaze on me and repeated her gibe.

"I've defeated you in your own bed, old man. Now for your empire."

She laughed her rich throaty laugh and went out of my chamber.

I gazed after her for a moment and then turned over on my face and wept. I had tasted final defeat, final unalterable defeat. I wept, not like Alexander Duhl-Karnin* because there were no more worlds to conquer, but like a frustrated youth who has been spurned in his first attempt at love.

By habit, I rose and dressed and went to Devon to see Ali Soun. At forty-three, she had begun to fade. Her fine white skin, though not browned by our sun, had dried and wrinkled. Her hair was as beautiful as ever, the few gray strands hardly perceptible in the pale millet-yellow of the rest. Nor had her smile dimmed, only grown slightly more wistful. She had practically given up her own language, and her women no longer pretended to any but their own native speech.

"Hello, dear," she greeted me, and kissed me in the Frank manner,

* Alexander the Great.

without passion but not without warmth. "I'm so glad you've come. I've been wanting to see you."

"I'm away so much," I said. "It's not that I don't intend to come more often."

A fire was burning in the massive fireplace, a small intimate heap of coals to take the mild chill off the evening.

"I know, dear," she said. "You're busy with your empire. But I miss you."

"And I you—more than you know. Where's Djon Pitr?"

"He's with Father Pol. That's what I wanted to speak to you about. He's finished with the priest, and taken all the work he can in the academy. I want him to go to the Seminary at Sultaniah. Father Pol says it is the best in Asia."

"So he still plans to be a priest?" I asked.

"Oh, yes. He's never wavered, and he's seventeen now, by my calendar. I'm so grateful that you've never taken him to war with you."

Her eyes glowed warmly through the mist her gratitude had brought into them.

"I've respected your wishes."

"Every one of them," she said. "And you'll let him go to Sultaniah?"

"Of course," I replied. "Will you want to go with him?"

She looked surprised at first. Then she glanced appreciatively around the interior of her big hall.

"No," she said sadly. "No—I'll stay here."

We sat close together before the open fire and talked for three hours. I never felt closer to her. Though I had no urge to take her to bed, I did not hate her as I hated Sevin Bey. Perhaps my visit was like any evening in a Frank castle in Inglistan, calm and friendly and sterile. Still Ali Soun refreshed me, as she had always done. I left Devon, relaxed and cleansed of my worries, and slept soundly all night.

Then, in the spring when I learned that the Persian brothers were at war again, I took Djon Pitr with me on my punitive expedition. He and Shah Rukh shared my pavilion. I took no royal women, nor any of my experienced concubines, for I was becoming increasingly sensitive on my infrequent visits to the harem. I took only young virgins, who had never known me or any other man. So my sons and I had the pavilion to ourselves most of the time. My affection for them and my plans for war increasingly began to take the place of the emotions I once had to work off on women. Aljai was the only woman who had ever held me from the Way, and Jahangir was the son for whom I might have lived in peace. There was nothing now to hold me, and I began to see the Way with a clearness I had never known before.

I deliberately threw Djon Pitr and Shah Rukh together. They grew fond of each other and I saw great possibilities in their friendship. Both were serious, studious young men, Shah Rukh the more practical, Djon Pitr the more imaginative and the wittier. If they could but learn the Way, together they could further the work of Allah, or Jehovah—there is only one God—as successfully as I.

But as we made our leisurely progress toward Khorassan and I sat night after night with the boys around the campfire, I saw my hopes receding. My sons respected each other. They were tolerant. They compared creeds, found common ground, and discussed a world of peace and prosperity. When I tried to inject my ideas into the conversation—and I have always been cautious about exposing men to the glaring light of Allah's truth—neither of the boys understood me, or they both took my words lightly, and Djon Pitr pretended that I was making jokes and commended me respectfully on my wit. I appeared to be a doddering old fool to my sons, my blind stupid sons, who had read Allah's Way in holy books, not in the vicious cunning of men and the hungry passions of women and the deceptive lures of the world.

My thoughts turned to Pir Mohammed and Mohammed Sultan—Khalil Sultan was too close to Sevin Bey, and N'il Mahdi-Soun would be a poet.

We dropped Djon Pitr off at Sultaniah.

"This is a fine thing you are doing for me and for my mother," he said, as he took leave of me to report to the seminary. "I'm beginning to see why she loves you so. I've never known you."

"Loves me so?" I asked in surprise.

"Yes, Father. She loves you devotedly. Knowing her piety and—well, your reputation—I sometimes wondered. Now, I understand. It's been a privilege to make this journey in your caravan." He smiled fondly, perhaps tolerantly, at me as he spoke.

"Thank you, Son," I said. "I've learned a lot about you, too. I'm glad I got to know you."

"Well, good-bye. I hope I make good for my mother's sake—and for yours. Maybe my peculiar background will help me to be a valuable man in the Church."

"Good-bye, Son," I said. "I think you'll be a valuable man—in the Church. I'm sure you'll succeed."

He rode away from my sarai toward the domes of Sultaniah, to temples my other son had desecrated in order to live in the memory of man. Djon Pitr would succeed. Letters of instruction had preceded him. His name would be praised in all the academies, and the seminary would prosper in direct proportion to his advancement. He was Jehovah's access to the wealth of Samarkand and the favor of Timur.

Shah Rukh and I had to attend to the Persians. I had only four divisions with me, since I did not expect much unified resistance from the quarreling brothers; and I had only my grandsons, Pir Mohammed and Mohammed Sultan, as division commanders. As we moved on south I put Shah Rukh in command of the center and kept my usual command of the reserves. Pir Mohammed and Mohammed Sultan commanded on my left and right flanks respectively, each with a full division.

Although the Persian position was considered impregnable—a fortress perched on a high plateau, rising precipitously out of a rugged mountain valley—we took it in one day. My grandsons' divisions dismounted and climbed to surrounding hills commanding the plateau; and while they harried the confident Persians, Shah Rukh moved up the only road. Ak Boga, the wild deserter from Toktamish's army, scaled a pinnacle directly over the fortress and singlehanded started an avalanche which further distracted the defenders at the crucial moment, and Shah Rukh raced in for the kill.

His men threw every last Persian over the cliffs of the plateau, and Shah Rukh himself overtook the fleeing commander and brought his head back into my camp.

We also rescued the captives and cleaned up the rest of the sibling war. I was publicly praised for my righteous punishment of the offenders in every city.

During the year I spent restoring order in Persia, Bara Lohar was stirring up strife in Baghdad. I could imagine the glee with which the big bearded blacksmith struck terror into Sultan Ahmed's heart. Everywhere I heard stories of how the Sultan refused to wear his jewels or show his treasures because of the screaming complaints they evoked from the poor people. He lived in a bare palace and took his meals alone and locked all of his treasures in vaults. Then he grew so suspicious of his guards and servants that he had secret police—of whom he was also afraid—kill his guards in their sleep or execute them on trumped-up charges of disloyalty. The Sultan suspected everyone and destroyed his few loyal followers in his attempts to hold complete security.

When I reached the city, I found that Ahmed had already fled to seek sanctuary with the Mamluk Sultan of Cairo, the real power. The city was in such a state of confusion that there was no battle. I sent Shah Rukh to overtake Ahmed, and set myself up on the throne.

The first man I summoned was Ahmed ibn Arabshah, who had poisoned the Sultan's mind with prejudiced accounts of my campaigns. He came to my throne room unescorted. A precise little Arab with piercing eyes and a fastidiously groomed beard, he appeared before me in an immaculate white robe, and he stood erect and fearless after he had prostrated himself in obeisance before me and repeated the court karnash.

"So you're Arabshah the scholar-historian," I said, when he had risen and stood up to his full height. Only when he stood beside one of my attendants did I realize how small he was.

"Yes, Amir," he replied politely.

"The Arabshah who accused me of brutality at Fushanj and Khiva and Urganj?"

"Yes, Amir. I am he," he answered clearly. His voice also seemed more powerful than it really was, for he spoke softly.

"Why?"

"That is the way I felt about it."

"Oh. Then that explains everything. You write as you feel, not as you think."

"It's the same, Amir," he said. "I write as I think—as I feel. One feels the truth. That is how I write."

"The man who feels anything will never know the truth," I said. "Feelings are the source of illusion. If I had felt, I would not be where I am today. I have built on truth, Allah's truth."

Arabshah stood perfectly still, respectfully silent.

"Have you nothing to say to that?" I asked, more than a little annoyed by the man's imperturbability.

"I was not aware that the statement required a comment, Amir. It was not phrased as a question."

"Nor a refutation?"

"Every man defines truth for himself. I cannot refute your statement, Amir. Not to your satisfaction."

"I define truth for many men," I said.

"Not so they feel it, Amir. Though they mouth it, they know better. A man feels that black is black even when he is forced to say black is white, or hot is cold. A man feels truth."

"Well, I see we've gone full circle, Arabshah," I said, and laughed. I was no longer annoyed by the little Arab. "I challenge your implication that I *force* men to say black is white. Let me see—you were a secretary to Sultan Ahmed. Isn't that right?"

"Yes, Amir."

"Then you shall join my staff. And I assure you that you may write as you please and think as you please."

"As a slave, Amir?" asked Arabshah.

"Call it what you will—define the truth of your status for yourself."

I smiled at the little man's expression. Arabshah was not invulnerable; he was surprised. He had expected to be beheaded.

"I would like to see all you have written about me—and all you write in the future," I continued.

"Censorship," Arabshah said, with a shading of contempt in his voice.

"Not at all," I said. "Sherif ad-Din has written much, all flattering. You have written some, all disparaging. I want to read both and define truth for myself, as you suggest."

"Mine's not all disparaging," said Arabshah, relaxing somewhat. "If you are sincere, Amir, I shall be glad to join your staff."

"I'm sincere—I want all the mirrors I can get. But you'll join my staff, glad or not," I said finally, and dismissed my newest secretary and chronicler.

A week later Shah Rukh returned with Ahmed's wealth and his women, but without the Sultan himself. Although Ahmed had only a half day's start, by deserting his train and commandeering the best mounts he managed to escape across the Syrian desert to Damascus.

I sent a message to Cairo demanding that the Mamluk Sultan surrender Ahmed to me. The Mamluk, however, killed all of my envoys except one and sent him back with an insulting reply. I found, too, that I had also outraged Bayazid, Sultan of the Turks, by my march to Baghdad and by an attack made on the Turks by Toktamish, whom Bayazid still considered my protégé. Bayazid's note was even more bitter than the Mamluk's.

"Timur-i-Leng, Mongol Barbarian," it began, "Dog of the Steppes, return to your kennel in Samarkand at once or the might of the Turks will be sent against you. I will drive you to your native lair in the frozen north and get your precious Bibi Khanum with child before your very eyes. Take heed of this warning or suffer the consequences, which I promise will be dire."

Bayazid's ignorance, as evidenced by the mixture of half-truth and misinformation in his insult, disturbed me more than it angered me. I had not intended to offend the Turkish Sultan until I had a margin of superiority over his truly formidable army, most of which, fortunately, was in Europe at that time. The information about Toktamish also caused me worry. If the wily Russian had recruited sufficient force in

343

Georgia and Circassia to risk raids on Bayazid's Turks, he was again becoming a threat to my borders.

So I decided to withdraw to Tabriz and reinforce my army for the final extermination of Toktamish and the destruction of Circassia and Georgia, the last stronghold of the Hordes.

CHAPTER

9

My ordu on the shores of Lake Urmia was again the pleasant sarai it had been when N'il Mahdi-Soun had been born there. Nur ad-Din and Omar Sheik and my other valiant commanders joined me and camped with me for a year while I made preparations to annihilate Toktamish's Hordes completely. Together with a portion of my harem and many members of my court, Bibi Khanum came and brought her son, then eight years old, to spend the winter in the sarai and the exciting, prosperous city of Tabriz.

Grown older, more grave and mature in her mien, Bibi was still the exquisite little doll-woman who had first come to me from the shadows of the Great Wall. She laughed less, and her laughter when it came no longer had the girlish tone that once rang so clearly through the halls of her transplanted Xanadu. When she laughed, too, she sometimes ended in a fit of coughing, which obviously brought great pain to her chest and frightened N'il Mahdi-Soun. Then she would smile reassuringly at the solemn-eyed little boy and tell him it was nothing. But I knew that the lazy southern breezes that she basked in were not good for her lungs, which had begun their breathing in the cold heavy air of the Manchu country.

But I, too, had aged in the last ten years; and I thoroughly enjoyed the gentle, if somewhat guarded, companionship which Bibi Khanum gave me. It was she rather than my court officials who gave me the best picture of conditions in Samarkand.

"What about the tomb for Shereza Begum?" I asked. We were sitting under the shade of a plane-tree and sipping grape sherbet. "How is it coming on?"

"Didn't they tell you?" she asked, turning to face me and registering surprise in her brown Khitan eyes. "There's to be no Shereza Begum tomb."

"There's to be none? But I left orders and plans—"

"Dilshad Sarai Khanum countermanded your orders."

"That's not like Dilshad," I said. "She always been a little bit jealous of Shereza, but—"

"Oh, it isn't that. I thought you knew about the legend."

"The legend? No—I've been away."

Bibi Khanum looked away and sipped her sherbet before she went on.

"The people in the north country won't believe that the Begum is dead. They aroused so much sentiment that Mir Sayyid went over Daoud's head to the Sarai Khanum and asked her to stop the work on Shereza's tomb."

"But of course she's dead," I said. "What is the legend?"

"Men returning from tours of duty at lonely outposts on the steppes and the tundra all report that they hear her kankali creaking along through the snow, and her voice crooning to Miran Shah—and to them. Some have seen her on particularly bad nights."

"And they are frightened," I said.

"No," said Bibi Khanum, still looking toward the shimmering waters of the lake. "Quite the contrary—they say that she comforts them, that they feel warm and good when they hear her—They call her Mother of the Steppes, Lady of the Gobi—even beyond the Urals men know her and call her Mother Russia. No, they are not afraid of Shereza and her phantom kankali."

I laughed aloud at the absurdity of the legend.

"You mean the blind stupid fools have canonized a demented old woman who destroyed her own son—drugged him into insensibility and sent him to his death in a mad, berserk, useless cavalry charge?"

I laughed again, contemptuously.

But Bibi Khanum did not laugh. She faced me again, with pity, pity for Shereza Begum—or was it for me?—in her eyes.

"No, Amir." Bibi's diction was flawless in all other words, but I could never tell whether the little princess said *amir* or *ama* when she addressed me. "No, Amir. *You* drugged her son—*you* sent him into battle—even though the Begum was your instrument. And the people think that Miran Shah died a hero's death."

Again I laughed. If misguided, superstitious idiots wanted to worship the Mad Begum, to find comfort in the Mother of the Steppes or the Lady of the Gobi or Mother Russia, let them. If the legend of a vain, doting mother and her drug-crazed son would keep men in the frozen wasteland, make a sacred task of their miserable subservience, then all the better. I cared not how or why they served me, as long as they served me as slaves acceptable to Allah. There are many manifestations of the Way of the Tree of Life.

Let Shereza take her place alongside the Christians' Virgin Mary and her soft-hearted son Jesus, who comforted slaves and preached that

345

the meek should inherit the earth—the earth, a golden vase filled with scorpions and serpents—their reward—their burden—their punishment! Let Shereza live forever on the steppes.

"Dilshad was right," I said. "There will be no tomb for the Begum."

Bibi Khanum had finished her sherbet and sat motionless, watching N'il Mahdi-Soun throw bright pebbles into Lake Urmia.

"Shereza shall live," I chuckled.

"She lives," Bibi said softly.

"Have you seen her?" I teased.

"Yes, I've seen her. Every time I put N'il Mahdi-Soun in his cradle —every time I tuck him in his little bed, I see Shereza riding away into the snow, sitting in that horrible kankali, steadying the coffin, and smiling serenely, and waving to us—to you and me—"

She shivered and drew a robe about her.

"It's cold," she said, and rose and called to N'il Mahdi-Soun.

When he ran to her, she threw half of the robe about him and clutched him to her protectively. Then, without looking back, she hurried him into her pavilion, and I heard her coughing from the exertion her haste had required.

Soon the weather did get cold, and a light snow fell at Tabriz. During the winter months I further built up my army and perfected my corps of scholars and slaves to infiltrate the Turkish ranks and begin work in the cities on the Black Sea and the Mediterranean coast.

By summer I had amassed sufficient men to make short work of Toktamish when the time came. After a season of rigorous training, I assigned permanent commanders for the fall campaign.

Bibi Khanum improved during the winter; but the summer brought back her cough, and a month before my campaign began, she died—at the same spot where she had borne my poet-son. I sent her body back to Samarkand, with instructions for the best architects in Asia to design a tomb for her. I was somewhat relieved at her death, for although I had always enjoyed her companionship and had delighted in her graciousness up to the last moment, I had begun to fear what effect she might have on N'il Mahdi-Soun's outlook. And I wanted to keep the boy's mind free of prejudice until he acquired the necessary language skills to write my chronicles in all their clear virgin truth.

After Bibi's death, I put N'il Mahdi-Soun under the tutorship of Arabshah and the poet Kemal of Khojend, whom I had recaptured from Toktamish at Kandurcha. Both men were precise and exact in their language; and since I sat in on all tutoring sessions, I was able to see that none of Arabshah's "feeling" or Kemal's poetic conceits were allowed to color my son's understanding of words.

We moved north toward Derbend in the second week of Saphar. I sent Shems ad-Din to Toktamish with instructions to demand that my foster son make up his mind once and for always, to join me or to fight me. His decision must be final and irrevocable, for I could no longer allow a renegade Mongol to interfere with my preparations for war against Bayazid, a war which I had always known was inevitable but which was coming ahead of my schedule.

At Derbend, Shems ad-Din met me. He reported that the diplomats had all but persuaded Toktamish to capitulate; but some of the generals to whom war was profitable had finally prevailed, and Toktamish sent a challenge instead of an oath of fealty.

So I sent my harem to Sultaniah for safety; and after a time of sharpening my troops for winter, I sacked Baku and Derbend and plunged into the canyons and gorges of the Caucasus, burning and destroying every human habitation in the mountains. Then I swung north, and Toktamish moved through Georgia, down the Kura valley, and across the Caucasian mountains to attack my rear. Ak Boga turned and held the Hordes while Mohammed Sultan entrenched the center of my army to stop the full-scale assault.

For the first time in years, I was in the very midst of the battle, fighting like any other squadron commander. The battle was unusually bloody. Men and horses screamed and died all around me. My own horse was shot from under me, and my lance broken. Hardly a dozen men formed our circle and shot arrows desperately at the crowding enemy. Nur ad-Din, unable to bring up his division, broke away with one hazara and raced to my aid. On the way he took three enemy wagons, which he hurriedly drew into a triangular barricade around my few remaining defenders. His men and mine held their shields around me as an inner guard when I exhausted my arrows.

Khodadad Hussayn, who commanded the second regiment of Pir Mohammed's left wing corps, broke through Toktamish's right wing and reinforced my small band. But Toktamish's finest soon penetrated Nur ad-Din's corps and evened up the struggle once more.

After an hour of hard fighting, Jihanshah Bahatur's tough cavalry division from Pir Mohammed's left wing won its skirmish and raced shouting to our rescue. This onslaught allowed my forces to re-form and Mohammed Sultan's center corps, which had suffered few casualties in their entrenched positions, to move up and join us.

From then on victory was ours. Toktamish fled to Bulghari, with Pir Mohammed in hot pursuit. Prince Vasili of Moskva raced on beyond his capital, and the remaining amirs were killed, or they fled and forever lost face with their people. The Hordes were finished.

I had suffered, too. Omar Sheik, bringing his independent force to my aid, had been struck down by a sniper's arrow. When I learned of his death, I thought of Sevin Bey Khanzade. Three royal sons gone, one to go—Shah Rukh—for I, too, discounted Amyris and N'il Mahdi-Soun as pretenders to my throne. Shah Rukh and Sevin Bey's three sons—two of which I felt were loyal to me. Sadly I had Omar Sheik's body returned to Shehri-Sebz to be buried in Jahangir's tomb.

My army continued its devastating march through Georgia and Circassia, mining towns, burning winter crops, destroying roads, laying waste to everything in its path. The country lay prostrate, like the Hordes' northern lands, and I was confident that the people could not rise again during my lifetime or my sons' lifetime.

I moved on to Astrakhan at the mouth of the Volga and waited for my son and grandson to return with their captives. The river was still frozen over, and the chill that ran through the governor, Mahmudi, when my army approached was no less icy, for he was the man who had directed the sacking of Bokhara and called me the Lame Dog of Samarkand.

When he saw that my men had surrounded the city and cut off all routes of escape, Mahmudi offered no resistance, but came to my pavilion with his staff of nobles. I accepted his gifts and invited his entire staff into my courtchamber.

After his elaborate, fawning speech of capitulation, I bade him stand before me.

"Mahmudi, you are the man who burned my palace in Bokhara, burned it and its occupants in a towering blaze that could be seen for miles along the Khorassan Road. Isn't that true?"

"Yes, Amir," he said apologetically, uncomfortably. "Under orders from the perfidious, ruthless Toktamish. I was against it, but—" He shrugged his shoulders and smiled at me helplessly.

"And you called me the Lame Dog of Samarkand and made jokes about me with these courtiers of yours. Isn't that true?"

"Yes, Amir. Yes, but you know how those things are—" He made an ingratiating moue in my direction and looked around his terrified staff for confirmation.

"Indeed I do know how those things are," I said. "But do you—you and your silly smirking companions? You shall learn about dogs from Samarkand."

My kulchis put the visiting Russians under arrest and escorted them to the river. There I had all the men except Mahmudi stripped of their clothing. Then a rider tied a rope around the chest of each man

348

and rode out onto the rough, jagged ice, dragging his captive behind him. As soon as the Russians began bleeding from the cuts on their bodies, my handlers released a pack of starved wolfhounds, which went streaking away toward the scent of blood. My riders raced up and down the river with the hungry dogs nipping at their victims and blending their sharp yelps with the screams of the mutilated amirs.

"Now do you know about such things?" I asked the trembling Mahmudi. "Do you know about dogs of Samarkand?"

"I—I—" he stuttered.

"Don't worry," I said. "I'm not going to feed you to the hounds. Nor am I going to burn you as you burned my loyal daroga at Bokhara—fuel is too precious."

He seemed relieved for a moment, until he saw my men chopping a hole in the ice. Then he knew—and he offered no resistance when my men pushed him into the icy water. He did scream just as the current underneath caught him and sucked him out of sight under the ice, toward the Sea of Abaku.

"How will you describe this?" I asked Arabshah, whom I had forced to come with me to get an accurate eyewitness account of my reception.

"Cruel and inhuman," he said precisely, and shook his head.

"That's how you *feel* about it," I said. "I expected as much—because of your former inaccuracies. There was nothing cruel about it. I have no feeling for the men, no sense of cruelty. I didn't even know them. It is simply that men must not mock a monarch—a man who serves Allah as I do. It is heresy and blasphemy. Allah has willed that heretics be punished."

"Inhuman," Arabshah repeated, still looking at the hole in the ice.

"Nonsense. The most human thing in the world is to kill."

I ordered my men to remount, and we rode back to my camp.

Their leaders gone, the people of Astrakhan built ice fortresses, which froze into thick barriers overnight, and tried to resist my men; but the battle was child's play. We took the city, and after one night spent in the warmth of its houses and the warmth of its women, my army set fire to the buildings.

Pir Mohammed returned with word that Toktamish had made good his escape. Since I had heard nothing from Shah Rukh, I broke camp and marched up the Volga toward Moskva. At the Don, Shah Rukh met me and made his report.

"I couldn't catch him, Father," he said.

"How far did you go?"

"To Moskva."

"Did you sack the city?" I asked.

"No—it wasn't worth the trouble. It has not been rebuilt since Toktamish burned it a few years ago. The people have nothing, and they were already on their knees—"

"On their knees?" I asked.

"Literally," he said, and smiled. "Prince Vasili ordered the Patriarch to bring the Virgin of Vuichegorod from Vladimir to Moskva. The road was lined with kneeling Russians for the full hundred miles. They knelt in the snow for days, praying and waiting for the statue to pass. 'Mother of God—Mother of Russia—save us,' they chanted all day. 'Sacred kankali—'"

"Sacred kankali?"

"Yes, Father. That's what they said. But the statue came by sled— I saw it. It wasn't on a kankali."

I laughed heartily as the truth dawned upon me.

"Mother of God—Mother of Russia—Sacred Kankali—they've got their Virgin Mary mixed up with the Mad Begum. Praying to my dead wife for salvation!"

"So as soon as they unloaded the statue at the Church of the Assumption and began ringing bells in all the churches," Shah Rukh continued, "I withdrew my men. There was nothing in the city worth taking."

"You did right, Son," I told him. "A country on its knees, whether praying or surrendering, is a country on its knees—not to be feared. Let the Russians believe in their delusion. The more mixed up they are, the better for us. The Mad Begum is on our side—and probably the Virgin of Vuichegorod also. Did you catch any of Vasili's men?"

"A few," he replied. "I think you might be interested in one of them. He's fought against guns."

"What are guns?' I asked.

"Tubes firing missiles by fire powder—*gunpowder,* the Franks call it. Here, let him tell you."

Shah Rukh's tavachis ushered in a swarthy northerner wearing a ragged sable khalat, with a karakul kalpak on his head. He removed the kalpak—a strange custom—and twisted it nervously in his hands while I questioned him.

"What's this about guns?" I asked.

"I don't know—much," he faltered. "I've served with Prince Donskoi and Prince Vasili—against the Poles and Lithuanians* in the West. Some of them, Duke Vitut's men, had guns."

* The Lithuanians are reported to have had light cannon and small arms as early as 1389.

350

"What are the guns like?"

"I don't know. I never saw one up close. Even when we routed the Poles, they rushed their guns away first. But from a distance the guns looked like tubes. Some big ones, big as a man's leg—the others small, carried in the hands. I don't know, Amir. They pop and shoot fire, and the smoke smells like—like the fumes of hell, I guess. I don't know—"

My amirs crowded nearer and nearer to the throne and formed a tight circle around the captive. We had all been worried about gunpowder, and the experiments were getting nowhere.

"How effective were these guns?" I asked.

"Not very, not against cavalry in open ranks. They are not as accurate as bows and arrows, and at any great range the missiles won't pierce the hide of a horse. Prince Vasili thought they might work against close infantry. But there aren't many among the Poles and Lithuanians. With more, and better ones—"

"They are the invention of the devil," I said. "Infernal machines contrary to the Will of Allah."

My amirs focused their attention on me, and I continued in righteous indignation.

"I'll have no part of them. They are implements straight out of hell. Let it be known that I call on the right-thinking people of the world to outlaw guns and gunpowder. I'll cut off the hands of any man who is found using one of the cruel, inhuman, devilish contraptions. I declare the commander who permits their use a war criminal, a pariah, a devil-directed schemer against Allah's universe. He, too, shall expect no mercy from me or any other honorable monarch. Take your prisoner away and behead him. He's been contaminated by gunpowder."

I dismissed my court. Only Arabshah remained behind to finish recording the interview. He was smiling sardonically, his usually straight thin lips curled at one corner.

"Cruel, inhuman contraption," he said—I allowed him such liberties. "My very words. Is that how you feel about guns, Amir?"

"That's how I *talk* about guns and gunpowder. That's how millions of people will *feel* and think about them before I'm through with my crusade against the hellish machines. Send for my scribes. I have a letter to dictate to my scholars everywhere."

As soon as I had dispatched messengers to all of the academies in my realm and to such others as I had access to, I broke camp and started back to Samarkand. I had to have guns—or the answer to them—be-

351

fore I marched against Bayazid. I had not heard of his using them, but he was too near the Franks and the Moors for me to overlook the possibility of his adopting their weapons.

CHAPTER

10

There was no doubt in my mind that gunpowder, or something similar to it—something that could approximate the volcanic eruptions and earthquake tremors of Allah's own making—would be the ultimate manifestation of the Way. The man who perfected that force would share the highest prerogatives with Allah. But I was getting old —sixty-four by my calendar, sixty-two by Ali Soun's—and the maddening stupidity of my scientists, their unbearable caution and sloth, made it clear that the miracle might not come in my lifetime.

So I racked my brain for an answer to the crude but immediate uses of gunpowder in the West. While my staff in Samarkand experimented constantly with fire powder and my scholars throughout Asia cried my warnings against the rulers who permitted their armies to use the inhuman, infernal stuff, I explored other possibilities. I listened to stories by men who had faced guns or had talked to men who had faced them. I saw that gunpowder, in its experimental stages at least, was just another weapon—a formidable weapon, but not one totally effective against the best existing armor, nor against fleet cavalry. My only fear was its effectiveness against the kind of massed front I would have to use against Bayazid's janissaries and sipahis, the myriad infantry which was the backbone of the Turkish army. Infantry with guns—

I sat on my balcony and watched my sons and grandsons play at war in my garden, hundreds of the little fellows charging and countercharging across the otherwise well-kept tulip beds. Even the children had heard of guns, and pointed sticks and logs at the enemy and yelled "boom." But they seemingly considered guns as fabled things, in the category with flying rugs and genii in bottles, and refused to play dead before a "boom." I remembered that many of my amirs shared the same view—refused to accept the facticity of gunpowder and pinned their faith on conventional weapons.

N'il Mahdi-Soun and Arabshah joined me on the sun-warmed balcony.

"How is the boy doing?" I asked Arabshah, without looking his way.

"Very well, Amir. Very well indeed. He has a natural feel for language."

"There you go again," I said. *"Feel,* always *feel.* I don't want him to feel."

"I'm sorry, Amir," Arabshah apologized. "I used the word figuratively. Perhaps I should have said *flair* or *bent* or *knack.*"

"That's better. Is he accurate?"

"Exceptionally so for an eleven-year-old. Exceptionally so, Amir."

I took my son on my knee and tousled his hair affectionately. He was as heavy on my knees as his mother had been, and almost as tall as Bibi Khanum had been in maturity.

"How do you like your studies, Son?" I asked.

"I find them most pleasant and rewarding, Father," he said politely, aping his fastidious tutor.

" 'Most pleasant and rewarding,' " I repeated in annoyance—at the tutor. "Arabshah! Can't you teach him to say simply, 'I like them'?"

"Perhaps, Amir, but—"

"That's the trouble with you and Kemal and Hafiz and Sherif ad-Din. You're too fancy. Your chronicles read like romances or fantasies. All flourish, all ornament."

"Yes, Amir. But you said—"

"I know what I said. And I've sat in on all lessons. Accuracy, precision, exactness—I want all of that, sure. But when my Mahdi writes my story, he must write colloquially, as men speak—common men, warriors. Most of all, warriors. Do I speak like an affected prince?"

"No, Amir," said Arabshah. "I've often commented upon your plainness, as you know."

"And I've not been offended. Still, do you doubt that I am the greatest monarch in Asia?"

"The most powerful—I've never doubted that, Amir."

"All right, *power.* Give the boy power, not polish in his writing. Now —while he's young."

"I shall try, Amir," said Arabshah. The man respected me, though he hated me. That was why I let him live.

"Very well, try. And henceforth N'il Mahdi-Soun will go among the men in my camps and learn how men talk. You give him precision. The soldiers will give him truth."

"Yes, Amir," Arabshah agreed, but with no show of humility. Then he smiled and spoke fondly to my son. "Now, Young Prince, shall we read to your father about the magnificent painted elephants of India?"

Elephants! Elephants—huge, tough-skinned, fearless armored fight-

353

ing elephants—the answer to gunpowder! Elephants to trample Bayazid's infantry underfoot. Exultant over finding the solution to my most urgent problem, I felt a surge of youth rise in my aging body; and though my son's piping voice spoke of the magnificent painted elephants, I heard none of the words. Guns, powerful guns, might come, but elephants were here already, in India.

All central power in India was dead. The place cried out for a conqueror, some strong man to liberate the people from the petty autocratic tyranny of regional rajahs. While Firoz Shah had lived, his thousand fighting elephants had kept India united. Firoz Shah was dead, but his elephants still lived, parceled out in small herds among the quarreling rajahs.

So I began my preliminary campaigns—more of my scholars to infiltrate the ranks of the pandits, letters to my men already entrenched, agitators among the slaves, concerted efforts to discredit native rulers and proclaim the inevitability of my triumph over selfish Indian princes. I set my tacticians and strategists to work devising defenses against elephants, for none of my men except a few old amirs who had followed Hussayn into India had ever fought elephants.

Impatient during the necessary period of preparation—I was getting old and losing the sense of timelessness which had made me patient in my younger days—I busied myself in the building of Samarkand. Bibi Khanum's white marble tomb was built beside the huge mosque, which lacked only its crowning dome. Jahangir's tomb, now shared by Omar Sheik, was enlarged. Tombs were built also for Jaku and Elchi and Sheik Ali and Saif ad-Din and hundreds of other noble and stalwart men who had served me well. The memory of those men might have depressed me but for the eagerness I felt for the Indian campaign.

Only Aljai's tomb aroused any sentiment in my breast. When I visited it, Mir Sayyid took advantage of the occasion to speak to me of immortality. I let him. Though I could see through his empty hopes and promises, there always lurked in the back of my mind a feeling that Aljai was in Paradise—no one else, just Aljai—and that I would meet Aljai again. Not the Prophet's seventy-two houris, just Aljai. I fully understood men's hopes, their refusal to turn loose of their loved ones, their yearnings for another chance. I understood all those things for what they were, Allah's lures to deflect men from the Way. But I let the old fool prattle and indulged myself in his fantasy for some guarded moments.

More to the point was the golden Tree of Life which I had set up on Hermitage Hill. With a trunk of gold and branches and leaves cunningly worked in silver, it was loaded with fruit: emeralds and rubies and pearls and amethysts, cut in the shapes of plums and cherries. It represented the more immediate goals of men, the lures found on earth. But to me it was a symbol, as was my fine old talwar, which I no longer wore except on occasions of ceremony—symbols of the real meaning of the Tree of Life and its guardian, the Flaming Sword.

Now the vision of Aljai persisted—hovered over Dilshad, who was quite gray, but beautiful and serene of countenance and regally slender of figure. I spent much of my time with the Sarai Khanum, as I became increasingly hesitant to visit the harem and risk humiliation before my vigorous young concubines. Dilshad offered comfort and understanding.

"Are you worried about Sevin Bey?" she asked one evening, as we sat together by a secluded pool in the palace garden.

"Yes," I said in surprise, for I *was* thinking of the Khanzade at the moment. "She makes no great secret of her intrigues. And I can't afford to destroy the mother of Pir Mohammed and Mohammed Sultan. Next to Shah Rukh, they are my mainstays."

"I know," said Dilshad. "But don't fret too much. Both of her older sons are far more loyal to you and to me than they are to their mother."

"You've seen to that."

"And I can handle Sevin Bey," she said confidently. "Leave her to me. I've been in Samarkand all these years, and know every one of her tricks. You attend to your empire, and I'll keep the palace in order."

"Khalil Sultan is twenty now," I said thoughtfully. "And she's had him all his life. I don't know—"

"I do. I know him, too. Just leave them both to me, and stop worrying."

I was not sure that Dilshad was as confident as she pretended, but the Sarai Khanum was indeed a power to be reckoned with in the court, and I was gratified by her generous offer of aid. Shah Rukh, her son, had reached the age of twenty-nine without distinguishing himself as either a warrior or an administrator. He was, however, competent.

"You say you have been in Samarkand all these years," I said. "That is true—you've been my strength in this capital. Perhaps I have put too much on you, not given you enough opportunity to travel with me. Suppose we both go to Herat when I install Shah Rukh as Sultan of Khorassan and Persia."

"Do you mean it?" she asked. "That you're giving him all of that? When?"

"Soon—a few weeks. You know he has been titular Shah of Herat for many years."

"Yes," she said softly. "But I thought—I don't know what I've thought. You've been such a long time—"

"I couldn't spare Shah Rukh from my army," I humored her. "Now my grandson can take his place there. He is ready to assume sovereignty."

She was weeping softly; I put my arms around her. The night air made my joints stiff.

"I'd have opposed Sevin Bey, anyway," she said, and sniffed back her tears. "I wouldn't let her—"

"I know you would. I'm not bribing you. Shah Rukh deserves it."

"I didn't ask," she said firmly—no one ever doubted her scrupulous integrity. "Timur, my love, I've never pleaded or schemed for my son's preferment beyond what he merits. But I wouldn't have stood by and let that—that redheaded whore maneuver her son, Miran Shah's bastard, into line as your heir. Pir Mohammed, Mohammed Sultan—they're Jahangir's sons, fine boys. I loved Jahangir."

"So did I," I said, and petted Dilshad. Jahangir was Aljai's son. In the dark, Dilshad might have been Aljai. In the dark there was that feeling that I could not have lost Aljai.

I made good my word. Two months later our caravan, escorted by my twelve thousand richly uniformed kulchis, made the long journey, through Shehri-Sebz and the Iron Gate and Balkh and then across to the Khorassan Road and thence to Herat in the heart of Afghanistan. Dilshad was astonished to find cold water fountains and luxurious caravanserais and post houses along the route. The country was quite different from the wild, bandit-ridden tracts which she had traveled with Hussayn in the old days.

"You've changed the face of Asia, Timur, my love," she said approvingly.

"Not all of it," I said, thinking of India and Khitai and the West. "But I'm not through."

"Why not? Oh, Timur, you have enough. You've done enough. Why can't you relax and let the boys rule your empire?" She sounded like Aljai.

"I have enough—I don't want things—I don't value empire. I have a mission, a sacred responsibility. You wouldn't understand."

"No, I guess I wouldn't. Aljai might have."

"I doubt it. If she had lived, I might never have learned of my mission." Aljai had blinded me.

Dilshad found Herat delightful, and I was sure that she got deep

356

satisfaction from seeing her son installed on the throne which Shereza had coveted for Miran Shah. After the ceremonies, which were the equal of my own state functions in Samarkand, we made the leisurely journey north again. With a small escort, Dilshad and I made a side trip to Kumrud. Saif ad-Din's pavilions were gone; but we rode through familiar valleys—there were crocuses and violets in the same sheltered glades—and recaptured some of the memories of our summer there with Aljai and Jahangir, and our winter there after Aljai's death.

Back in Samarkand, I found things in readiness for my campaign into India. The trip to Herat had eased my tension and restored vigor to my body. And Dilshad was never more radiant than after our junket together. Only when she found me eagerly absorbed in last-minute preparations for war were her spirits damped.

I spent a few pleasant evenings with Ali Soun, who was full of news. Djon Pitr had written her of his amazing progress; he had already been ordained. I knew that he would be a bishop before he was thirty, but I preferred to let her be surprised by such unprecedented ecclesiastical advancement. I looked forward to the warmth which would come into her cool blue eyes when she first called her son *Bishop John*.

Nubja could already call her son *Amyris Tuk-Bashi*. At seventeen he commanded the Kara Hazara—the Black Squadron—which I intended to make famous in Asia. Composed of Negroes, mulattos, Dravidians, Dasyus, and other dark-skinned youths, the Kara Hazara was my bid for the loyalty of blacks everywhere. I organized it as soon as Amyris was old enough to take command, so the news of it could reach western Asia and Egypt while I was in India, well ahead of my march to the West. There were many Negroes in that area—all slaves—and I wanted them to know who respected them, who exalted them, who was their friend.

So it seemed that everything was in order at Samarkand when I led my long column south toward Kabul and Khaibar Pass.

CHAPTER

11

India is a woman. A soft, passive, sprawling woman who paints her face and dyes her hair and ornaments herself with myriad priceless jewels. A woman who perfumes her fat, disease-ridden body with all the seductive attars of the tropics and submits apathetically to rape by any strong man.

I smelled her as soon as I rode out of the southeast gate of Khaibar

Pass. I smelled her spices and her blossoms, her wine and her bhang, her fever and her leprosy. Even while crossing the springwaters of the Indus in the Punjab highlands, I could smell her stinking Ganges delta. And her sweet-sick stench was in my nostrils for over a year, until Shalira nursed me back to health in the Vale of Kashmir.

But there were elephants in India. It was elephants that I wanted, not the unbelievable wealth, already concentrated in so few hands that it could not prevent the slavery and beggary of the sick, miserable masses. Allah's Way had prevailed in India for centuries before I passed that way.

It was elephants I wanted, and my men feared the elephants as we rode toward Delhi. I could sense their uneasiness. Perhaps I was to blame, putting such store by the powerful beasts; but I took comfort in the thought that what struck terror into my followers would likewise frighten Bayazid's janissaries.

Meeting only token resistance at Peshawar, I moved down the Indus valley to Multan, where after an easy battle I installed Pir Mohammed as rajah. Then I came back up and turned toward Delhi, where I expected Mahmoud Tugluk, the Maharajah, to make a stand.

My army had encountered no elephants so far, but it had faced some of the other perils of India—the heat and humidity, the rivers and jungles and flies and mosquitoes and cobras, all of which would get worse as we approached the lower Ganges valley. The frozen Himalayas looked more and more inviting to my men; for although the victories had been easy—too easy—there were the elephants and the bhang-wild Rajput warriors still to be faced for the first time. And the sultry life-sapping air, the deceptive, poisonous, scent-laden breezes which left men dull and unrested after a night of drugged torpor, had begun to take their toll.

I could tell that my followers shared my feeling that I was being lulled and seduced by a fat loathsome woman, with a fatally fascinating face and heady perfume, a neglected wife whose jealous husband might appear at any moment and catch me too drowsy and too weak to defend myself. The sense of uneasiness increased steadily as we approached Meerut, and my intelligence reported that Mahmoud Tugluk had collected five hundred of Firoz's elephants and induced a number of Rajput chieftains to come to the defense of Delhi.

Rumors began to spread, all sort of rumors; and quarrels broke out. I seldom joined in the discussions; I spent more time with Abdullah after we had set up our sarai on the plain between Meerut and Delhi.

358

"Have you been able to make a deal with the mahouts?" I asked my servant upon his return from a trip into Delhi.

"At last, Amir," he replied. "I have word from Kanva, the chief of the elephant handlers, that the mahouts will co-operate—at a price which he considers beyond the means of Leng Kopeghi."

"Then he hasn't guessed the identity of Leng Kopeghi?" I asked.

"No, Amir," said Abdullah. "Kanva is rather stupid. He knows all about elephants but almost nothing about men."

"Well, never mind. What is the price?"

"Women, Amir."

"Women," I said in surprise. "Why, that's simple. They can have all the women they want."

"But it's not so simple, Amir. They want special women. As you know, the howdahs are far roomier than camel litters, and the nobles frequently take their women for moonlight rides in the howdahs."

"Yes, I know," I said. "Go on."

"Well, the mahouts have handled the elephants on many such parties. They have had to sit on the elephants' heads and drive while their masters made love in the howdahs. They have heard the giggles and love chatter and smelled the women's bodies and seen the love play going on not five feet from them on hot nights when the curtains were open. And they've had to sit on the elephants' heads hours on end— burning up with passion or resorting to shameful masturbation while the nobles toyed with their ladies."

"Insolent slaves!" I remarked.

"And it seems that each mahout remembers some especially delicious woman, dreams about her, thinks of her while he lies with his own drab wife or buys whores. It is those women they want, Amir."

"I see," I said thoughtfully. "They are certainly arrogant and demanding, like all slaves, but still, if that's their price— I must have the elephants."

"And for Kanva, himself—" Abdullah began in an almost hopeless tone of voice.

"Yes?" I asked quickly. "What does he want?"

"The Maharani herself."

"The Maharani!" Shereza's own cousin. The Begum's kinswoman. It would outrage all Islam.

"Yes, Amir. Kanva has lusted after the body of the Maharani for twenty years, ever since he drove the Maharajah on his honeymoon."

The Maharani! I pondered the audacity of the slave Kanva. And I thought, too, of Abdullah's flow of language, of his perceptions, as keen as my own, of the way he had stated the slaves' case. After all, he had been with me constantly since childhood, sitting in on my tutoring under Zain ad-Din, listening to the harangue of my scholars, having access to all my experiences. Why not? Then I was startled to think of the possibilities of the slaves, under their own leaders—men like Abdullah and Bara Lohar. Suppose they found that they could take the world for themselves, on their own terms?

I grew warm and slightly sick in the terrible heat—I held conferences with Abdullah in private, without even a slave to fan me. The oleanders and jasmines, sweet by day, were oppressive by night.

"Do the other mahouts know who and where their women are?" I asked, playing for time to think through my quandary.

"Yes, Amir. As slaves, unworthy of a lady's notice, they have often been near their favorite women, have seen them bathing and perfuming their bodies. The ladies are not harem women, protected by purdah. Of all the men I've known, these mahouts seem to be the most lustful—from the tortures they have endured during the orgies carried on in their howdahs."

Kanva had dictated a hard bargain for me to keep, for the nobles would be sure to safeguard their favorite women. But I needed elephants, and I could certainly force my will on Delhi, if I had to sack the city and lose a division of my own men.

"I think I can arrange for the mahouts to spend a night with their women," I said at length.

"But they want the women to keep, Amir—until they tire of them."

"Even Kanva?" I asked, feeling more annoyed and heated than ever.

"Yes, Amir. After twenty years, he will hardly settle for one night."

If I had been capable of anger, I would have thought that the flush which seared my body was rage. Later I was pleased to learn that it was only fever. Whatever it was, it cleared my mind, and I knew that I had to take all risks involved.

"All right," I said impatiently. "Can you convince Kanva that Leng Kopeghi will deliver the women to the mahouts?"

"I may have to reveal the identity of Leng Kopeghi, Amir. But I think I can persuade the stupid mahout, if you agree to his terms."

"Very well," I said, "only tell the mahouts that they must forever dress their prizes as Persian women and keep them veiled so they will never be recognized. Have them explain to the women that the tongues will be cut out of any who dare tell who they are. The slaves may not flaunt their rewards before others.

"As for Kanva, try to get him to settle for one night with the

360

Maharani and remain anonymous, or pose as an Indian noble. I doubt that the slaves themselves would stand for his taking a cousin of the Begum. Swear him to secrecy about his bargain—especially about Leng Kopeghi's identity, if you have to reveal it. If he has any sense at all, he will modify his demands to that extent."

Abdullah went back into Delhi with my message to Kanva. While he was completing arrangements, I sent word to Pir Mohammed to bring his corps from Multan. Even if I should win the elephants without battle, I would need Pir Mohammed's powerful striking force, which still spearheaded my offensive left wing, to enable me to fulfill my bargain with the elephant boys. I moved nearer to Delhi and began setting up defenses. Since the Maharajah's intelligence was sure to have reported the fears of my men, I felt that by pretending to be very cautious and very much on the defensive I could draw Mahmoud out into the open and perhaps cut his forces off from the city and prevent his rajahs from collecting their women and fleeing after their defeat.

When Pir Mohammed arrived, our elephant traps were all built. Trenches had been dug before my center corps, which Mahmoud would probably attack first; and breastworks of stone and timber, with spears pointing outward, were erected behind the pits. The floors of the deep trenches bristled with lances and hooks and iron tiger traps, and in front of the pits still more spears had been driven with the points slanting upward toward the expecting attackers. As an added measure, several herds of buffalo had been lined up before the ramparts. Bundles of naphtha-soaked hay were tied on the horns of the animals and the beasts lashed together, the plan being to set fire to the hay and drive the blinded buffaloes straight toward the elephants and stampede the huge brutes if possible. But when Abdullah finally reported back to the new campsite, I knew that the elaborate defenses would not be necessary.

On the third day the Maharajah led his army out of Delhi in force. Five hundred trumpeting elephants led the charge with a host of bhang-crazed Rajputs riding behind, their flaming yellow battle robes flashing in the sun. But my army saw only the charging beasts which came first. I sat on a platform behind the big central trap and watched the magnificent animals race forward. The men around me quavered, seeing visions of men and horses tossed into the air like toys by the armed tusks.

Pir Mohammed and Nur ad-Din, however, were not dismayed.

They rushed forward from my flanks to envelop the host—to force the elephants to run straight onto the pikes and into the ditches. And their men, seeing the Rajputs and taking heart in the realization that there were men and horses in the rear to be challenged, suddenly screamed cheering Tatar war cries and brandished their talwars confidently.

Then, true to his promise, Kanva signaled to his mahouts and the elephants ceased trumpeting and wheeled to left and right. I had my kourrouns sound *open ranks* and *hold attack;* and though my men were obviously surprised, the extended flanking columns spread and the elephants docilely trotted through the holes in the ranks, which closed again behind them.

The Rajput warriors on the howdahs were taken by surprise also. Some of them had the presence of mind to kill their treacherous mahouts, thereby reducing my commitments to Kanva by nearly a hundred; but even they were left helpless on the gentle, plodding beasts, and my men made short work of all the elephant-borne soldiers.

While my reserves enveloped the elephants loaded with dead Indians, the other elements of my army quickly skirted the pits and joined in the attack on Mahmoud's Rajputs. So confident had the rajahs been of the elephant screen that many of them had ridden into battle in palanquins, expecting to sit in the luxurious armored chairs and direct the battle from the safe center of a square of the trumpeting beasts. Caught in front of their own cavalry and no longer protected by the elephants, the effeminate rajahs fell easy prey to my bowmen or became encircled by the herds of buffaloes running wild with their burdens of flaming straw.

As porters deserted, or were shot down, the palanquins were left stranded; and the rajahs showed their painted faces and dyed beards for a moment and then tried to clamber out of their silly chairs. Some were shot down; others were burned to death in the blazing palanquins set on fire by the buffaloes or by naphtha maces and flaming arrows. Some, whose porters were too stunned to quit their places at the thills, were carried forward and pushed into the elephant pits where they were spitted on the javelins or crushed in tiger traps. Then my cavalry ran other mounted troops into the pits on top of the hapless first victims, and the traps were turned into graves full of bleeding, screaming, writhing masses of horses and men.

All this I could see from my command platform. Farther down field Pir Mohammed and Nur ad-Din had met, joining the two jaws of my flanking pincer columns and cutting off the enemy's retreat to Delhi. Reinforced by my center corps, which had gone around the ends of the ditches, the forces formed an impenetrable wall around Mahmoud's shocked host. As the ring grew tighter, more and more of the yellow-clad Rajputs were forced into the pits, until the ditches were full to the brim and the hard-pressed riders were driven across the bloody carcasses of their comrades onto the spears sticking out of the secondary breastworks. .

My cavalry, their full confidence restored, crowded the enemy harder and harder. The pile of bodies rose higher and higher against the ramparts. Then some of the Rajputs rode over the mass and over the breastworks; and since my reserves were so fascinated by the painted fighting elephants that they were careless of their duty, several fairly large units of Mahmoud's cavalry broke through my lines and made good their escape to Rajputana.

The battle had broken the back of the Indian army, and I had captured the largest herd of trained fighting elephants in Asia. I learned from a captive that the Maharajah had been in one of the first palanquins. I assumed that he had been pushed into the elephant pits, but of course it would have been useless to look for his body.

It was still not quite midday. I sent only my own kulchis under Mohammed Sultan into Delhi to keep order. I gave strict orders to allow no looting or raping; and I sent along a list of women, supplied by Kanva, to be taken into custody for plotting against the Maharajah and urging him to bring his army out to face destruction at my hands —the Maharajah could never refute my charge. Then, after I had given orders to the mahouts to have the elephants trample the nasty mess in the ditches and then use my draglines and harrows to cover the trenches over with dirt again, I myself commandeered Kanva's elephant and rode into the city to call on the Maharani.

I found her in the palace weeping over the death of the Maharajah. Her daughter, Shalira, was trying to comfort her, although the young princess —about sixteen—was weeping more copiously than was the Maharani.

As I was ushered into the palace—much smaller than Persian or Tatar palaces, but exquisite in every detail—I assumed my most gracious manner and made elaborate obeisance to the royal ladies.

"My dear," I said to the Maharani—she was my wife's cousin, "you have no idea how sorry I am about this unfortunate mistake."

"Mistake?" she said heatedly.

"Yes, my dear. I was prepared to call Mahmoud Tugluk *brother* and to help him restore order in his war-torn country."

"But after Peshawar and Multan, he thought—"

"I know, your Highness. I know what he thought." I clucked my tongue sadly at the unhappy misinterpretation of my intentions. "The local rajahs in both places were preparing to rebel against Mahmoud. I was merely protecting him, helping consolidate his empire."

"Mahmoud did say there was trouble up that way, even before you came," she said thoughtfully.

The Maharani seemed perplexed, undecided as to how she should react to my condolences. Shalira had sharper eyes and was more sensitive to my inflections, but since my beard and hair were completely white at that time—Arabshah said that I had the appearance of a benevolent patriarch—the girl seemed inclined to accept my speeches at face value.

"How was he—?" asked the Maharani, wrinkling her brow and searching my eyes with her own.

"Run down and trampled by his own cavalry," I said, "his palanquin broken into splinters."

"How horrible—and he was so proud of the palanquin," she said, covering her eyes with her hands—hands weighted down with some of the costliest gems in India. The gaudiness of her jewels reminded me of Shereza Begum. When she uncovered her face, I saw there also a family resemblance—and in her body, not so fat as Shereza's, but beginning to lose its shape.

"Yes, terrible," I said. "I would have done anything to save him. But the horses—the mad cavalrymen—"

"I'm sure you couldn't help," she said, softening toward me somewhat.

"We can be thankful that I got here in time to save you and your daughter."

Shalira gave me a glance of some warmth and gratitude.

"And Mahmoud was so sure that you would sack Delhi," said the Maharani.

"I wasn't even going to attack. There hasn't been so much as a stone turned inside the city. If Mahmoud had only listened to my ambassadors."

"Your ambassadors? He didn't tell me—"

"He didn't?" I asked in surprise.

"No—but then he's kept so many things from me of late." A hardness came into her face. She had not completely trusted her husband, I could tell that.

"Probably didn't want to worry you," I said soothingly. "With things so bad in India, rebellion all around. Well, I deeply regret his misunderstanding, though it wasn't entirely his fault. I know who was to blame, and my men are rounding up the culprits right now."

"Who?" she asked, and both she and her daughter became tense in expectancy.

"Some women—a good many women of high estate—plotting against his best interests."

"I told him," she said bitterly. "I warned him." Her tears were dry and her features had become firm again. As she became more composed and sat up erect on her low ottoman, I saw what she might have been twenty years before, what had aroused the lifelong lust in Kanva. And if she had been anything like Shereza on her honeymoon, Kanva —any man—would have remembered what went on in the Maharajah's howdah.

"You poor dear," she said, suddenly capitulating completely. "You must be worn out. You look ill. You need something cooling and refreshing."

She clapped her hands for her servants and ordered tea and sherbet and chilled wine. I took the seat she indicated. I did feel ill, hot and tired and worn out, as she had said. But I was not too ill to note the beauty of Shalira. Dressed in a tissue-thin sari of pale pink silk, which revealed more than it covered—even her dark nipples and the black triangle of hair on her abdomen showed clearly when the breeze blew the fabric against her slender young body—she seemed not at all embarrassed. Such attire, I learned, was customary among the Rajput princesses, who were untouchable, regardless of their charms, and were allowed much freedom, even the right to choose their own husbands.

I was sorry when she sat down—crosslegged on a rug, as Bibi Khanum had sat—and folded her arms across her bosom. Her face, too, was beautiful, fairer than that of her mother, with a straight Aryan nose and fine Persian eyes. When she spoke, very seldom in the presence of her mother, her voice was soft and clear and her lips formed the words as though they were caressing each syllable.

The refreshments arrived, and I accepted a glass of sherbet. In the gorgeous room, with lacy marble cornices and delicately carved stone windows, I could hardly believe that I was sitting down to tea with the widow of my recent enemy. Inlaid tables, fine miniature paintings in enameled frames, damascened iron flower stands, and gold and silver filigree screens spoke of calm, gracious living untouched by war or poverty—India's painted face.

"I heard about poor dear Shereza," the Maharani said in a polite conversational tone. "Do you think she's dead?"

"I don't know," I said sadly. "I've sent scores of expeditions to look for her. If only I could have prevented her leaving my camp."

"You couldn't help it," she soothed me. "I've heard that Shereza was such a strong-willed girl."

"She was strong, yes. Strong and fine. I miss her terribly."

"I know you must. Did she ever find a suitable wife for Miran Shah?"

"No," I said.

"I wanted so much to help her. I often wish that I had had a daughter to give to him—but Shalira was only a baby the last time I wrote dear Shereza."

"I have a son, Amyris, about Shalira's age," I said, looking at the girl and noting how I might win favor with the blacks by giving my mulatto son so lovely a princess bride.

"Indeed? Who's his mother?"

"Nubja."

"Royal?"

"Oh, yes, one of the oldest lines."

"As good as Shalira's? Of course, I'm of Shereza's Persian blood, and my mother was a Manchu princess. Mahmoud was, as you know, of the purest Udipur ancestry."

"Yes, I know," I said. "Nubja is of the direct line of Mohallabi, unbroken for five hundred years."

I watched both women closely. I doubted that either of them knew that Mohallabi was a Negro conqueror of the third century.* They showed quickened interest and, the Maharani especially, looked eager for more information about Amyris.

"He isn't with me," I said. "I left him in command of his own squadron in Samarkand. Someone has to stay behind and look after my empire while I'm away helping my friends who are in trouble."

"Yes, indeed," agreed the Maharani. "Someone has to."

I wondered if she realized that Mahmoud had left no one behind to look after Delhi. And I remembered that I still had a bargain to keep.

As soon as I could, I finished my sherbet and rose to leave. I felt dizzy when I stood up. I thought for a moment that the Maharani had poisoned me, but I soon recovered and asked to be excused.

"Don't consider yourself a prisoner," I said. "Your palace will not be under guard."

"Thank you, Cousin Timur," she said graciously. "You will of course stay in the palace while you're in Delhi."

"Yes, thank you," I said. Presumably I had convinced my hostess of my innocence in the death of her husband. I smiled a sympathetic

* Third century A. H.—ninth century A. D.

farewell to Shalira and went to my headquarters in one of Mahmoud's state buildings.

By sunset my kulchis had found all of the women I needed. I had the girls dressed as Persians and veiled, and then made arrangements to have them given to the mahouts. I felt that I had been very successful in my plan—the kulchis who brought the women in never knew what became of them. None of my men knew of the bargain. I doubt if any one of them ever guessed what had deflected the elephants from their course.

I instructed Abdullah to dress Kanva as a rajah and direct him to the Maharani's quarters, which I assured him would be unguarded. Then I returned to the palace and had dinner with the Maharani—a dinner which was tasteless and dull and which gave me a headache even before I had finished eating it. Again I excused myself early and retired, worn and aching and ill.

Early in the morning, soon after daybreak, Shalira came into my room screaming.

"Oh, Uncle Timur," she cried. "Something terrible has happened—there was no one I could come to but you."

"What is it, Shalira?" I asked drowsily. I tried to rise but found that I was too weak.

"It's Mother! Oh, Uncle Timur, it's horrible. She's dead—she and some strange rajah I've never seen—killed in her bed."

"Killed?" I said. "By whom?"

"By her eunuchs, they think. They were loyal to Father, I guess. My own mother and that strange man—and Father not dead a whole day! Oh, Uncle Timur, take me away from this awful place. Take me to Amyris."

"I'm sure it's not what you think," I said. "The stranger probably forced her."

"I don't know," the girl wailed. "Take me away—now!"

She fell down across me and buried her head in my chest and sobbed. Her sweet young body brought youth to my own old frame. I stroked her hair and caressed the back of her neck, but I was too weak to do more.

Shalira suddenly rose again and stared at me with a frightened look. She grasped my wrist in one hand and felt my forehead with the other.

"You're hot," she said excitedly. "You've got the fever! We must rush you to Srinagar at once. I want to go, too, to get away from here —from Mother and—that man."

She ran out of the room for help, and in a few minutes returned with a physician and Mohammed Sultan. The physician examined me hurriedly and confirmed her diagnosis.

I dismissed the native physician and sent for my own. Then I gave orders to Mohammed Sultan to sack Delhi as soon as I left, to subdue all of India and capture every fighting elephant he could find, to take no prisoners, to execute the eunuchs who were accused of murdering the Maharani and her lover, and to keep all news from Shalira.

I was still conscious when Mohammed Sultan reported the death of the slaves. Then, sure that no one except Abdullah would ever know who actually got rid of Kanva and the empress, I let go and the world blacked out.

CHAPTER

12

When I regained consciousness, I was in a strange new world. Though my vision was dim, I could make out the details of the walls around me—three trellises overgrown with flowering vines and an open side facing out on a sunlit, many-terraced garden. Overhead was a canopy of carved wood, the figures and colors of which were blurred but probably of the same intricate design as the marble work in Delhi. I was obviously in a summerhouse in some king's palace garden. Then I remembered. I was at Srinagar in the Vale of Kashmir.

Shalira had brought me there. I turned my head to see who or what was near me in the blossom-scented bower. Flower pots on damascened stands—vases of cut flowers—a medicine table—and Shalira, engrossed in a book. All of these were indistinct in outline, but I knew what Shalira's clinging sari revealed, if I could but see. The closer things were, the harder they were to make out.

I lay still and quiet. A bluejay scolded his mate in a tree somewhere in the garden, and both he and I were surprised to hear a saucy green parrot, in a cage near my bed, answer and outscold him in a masterful human tirade.

"Hush, Gautama. You'll wake Uncle Timur," Shalira warned softly, and I wondered what irreverent wag had named the profane bird after the Buddha.

"I'm awake, Shalira," I said weakly, assured at last, by her familiar voice, that my nurse really was the Rajput princess.

"You are—" she said, dropping her book and rushing to my bedside. "Yes—you really are! We were so worried."

She felt my brow and reached to grasp one of my wrists.

"And I've prayed that you would wake up. You just had to. All of my people are dead. And I'm afraid of everyone but you, Uncle Timur."

A tear splattered on my cheek, but I could tell by the timbre of her voice that Shalira was not weeping because of any sorrow. She *was* glad that I had awakened.

"How long have I been here?" I asked.

"Three weeks, nearly four. And we've been so worried. But your forehead is cool now. You'll get well. I must tell the physician."

"No," I said, making a feeble attempt to hold her arm—I had no strength in my grip. "No, he'll tire me. Just sit here awhile, until my eyes become accustomed to the light and I get a little strength back."

The speech tired me out. I had never known such weakness before. Even Shalira's grasp on my wrist held more strength than I could muster. Her touch was gentle, pleasant and cool.

"All right," she said. "For a little while. I'd love to sit with you." She sank down on the floor by the bed.

"Sit where you were," I said. "I can see you better over there."

"Surely," she said, and went back to her rug of corded silk.

"Who is here?" I asked.

"Your kulchis are all camped on the plateau outside the garden. In the palace, Abdullah and your servants, and my household, and N'il Mahdi-Soun and his tutors. I like N'il. He's a sweet boy—I'm part Manchu myself. And your tavachis and palace guard."

"Any news from Samarkand?"

"Yes, some messages. Shall I get them?" She started to rise.

"Not now. Call N'il. I'd like to see him."

Instead of calling, she whistled shrilly. I was astonished at the volume she attained, and at the quality, shrill but not unpleasant. Immediately a weeping cheetah cub tumbled out of an oleander hedge and loped to the seated princess and nipped playfully at her sandals.

"I wasn't calling you, Rina," the girl said, and roughly rolled the teasing kitten over on its back. "I was calling N'il."

N'il Mahdi-Soun appeared from somewhere.

"Did you whistle for me, Shalira?" he asked, as he came up the steps into the open door.

"Yes, Uncle Timur is awake. Isn't it wonderful?"

N'il looked my way eagerly and started toward my bed. He gradually became a blur as he drew nearer to me.

"I'm glad, Father," he said. Even in the three weeks since I had heard his voice it had deepened in masculine timbre.

"So am I, Son. Stand back a little way, so I can see you better."

He backed away, and I noted more maturity in his features, but I felt that he would be forever young, like Bibi Khanum. He had her sensitive face and her lithe slight frame. He would be much taller, of course.

"How are your studies?" I asked.

"Oh, very well, I guess. Arabshah seems satisfied."

"He's the strictest one, isn't he?"

"Yes, Father. Sherif ad-Din is too eager to please me—and Kemal is interested in nothing but poetry."

"Well, you try to please Arabshah," I advised. I was pleased to learn of my son's powers of discernment. Arabshah was the best tutor; and even though he hated me, I trusted the purity of his regard for language and his integrity as a scholar.

"Is there anything I can do for you, Father?" asked N'il. "Can I get you anything?"

"No, Son. Just sit here awhile and talk to Shalira. It tires me to speak, but I'd like to hear conversation."

"All right, Father. What shall we talk about?"

"Anything—tell stories—just anything."

N'il obediently sat down near the Rajput princess and began chatting with her. I felt good. The high fresh air of the Vale of Kashmir was a tonic in my lungs, and the color and fragrance of the garden and the conversation of the two youngsters, punctuated by songbirds and bluejays and the caustic Gautama, were all restful and soothing.

After a while the physician came and examined me. He nodded his head reassuringly, mumbled something unintelligible and left again. Then I had N'il Mahdi-Soun read me the dispatches from Samarkand. Sevin Bey's was most interesting. Khalil Sultan had become enamoured of Shadi Mulkh, a beautiful Persian courtesan a year or two older than he, and had demanded that he be allowed to marry her in full state ceremony, as though she were an agha. Sevin Bey asked that I have the girl executed. Feeling that I might drive a wedge between Sevin Bey and Khalil Sultan by doing so, I authorized the girl's beheading. I dictated several other replies and then in mid-afternoon I dropped off to sleep again in the pleasant garden of Srinagar.

As my condition improved, I had my litter moved about to different parts of the garden. Falling in a high cataract at the east end of the garden, a clear mountain stream flowed through ingeniously contrived irrigation ditches and watered lily ponds and narcissus beds and played in low pressure fountains before emptying into the Jhelum River on the plateau outside. I liked to drink the clear cold water and to breathe the equally refreshing air of the vale. I rapidly grew stronger, and my sight became a little better, good enough for me to distinguish the roses and violets and tulips and to make out the colors of the ducks on the garden ponds.

Regular reports from my tuman-bashis told of the capture of town after town and province after province. Pir Mohammed had returned to Multan after sacking Agra and securing the Jumna valley as far as Benares. Mahmoud Sultan, after subduing Hyderabad and the Deccan, was engaged in Mysore. Mohammed Sultan was mopping up in Rajputana, and Omar Sheik's sons had just about conquered Bihar and Orissa by the beginning of autumn. Nur ad-Din had taken Bengal and Assam to the borders of Burma. All had captured elephants.

When I moved from the palace to my own kibitka among my kulchis, I was able to walk without a cane, though the fever seemed to have settled in the old wound in my left foot and my limp had become more pronounced. My eyes were stronger; I took over actual direction of my army again and dictated my own dispatches. I still had trouble reading fine script, however, and N'il Mahdi-Soun read me Dilshad's message concerning Khalil Sultan and Shadi Mulkh.

"—so when the girl came to me and told me that she was pregnant by Khalil Sultan," the message ran toward the end, "I countermanded your order to have her beheaded on the pretext that you would not allow the execution of any woman who carried a prospective grandson. Alive, she is a valuable counter-irritant to the Khanzade. If you were here, you would understand my decision.

"I know you will uphold my orders and love me.

> Your devoted wife,
> Dilshad Sarai Khanum.
> Samarkand, the 17th day
> of Rabia 2, 801 A. H."

I was strong enough to carry on affairs of state. I held meetings of my Ulama of Scholars and recruited new men from among the Indian pandits who had already proved themselves in my preliminary softening-up efforts before the invasion. And I accepted oaths of fealty from a number of rajahs who preferred joining me to fighting me. Despite their effeminate appearance—painted teeth and nails, and ropes of pearls and colored stones, and beards dyed orange and red and purple—some of the nobles, especially among the Rajputs, were first-class fighting men, skilled in elephant tactics. So I welcomed their offers on the condition that they bring their forces to Kashmir and leave India with me.

Since I could not spare the men to form a large army of occupation, I had instructed my tuman-bashis to kill all able-bodied prisoners. They did so—hundreds of thousands of captives—and after sizable forces joined me, there were few rebellious spirits left in India. All winter I followed the campaigns to the south and parleyed with the yielding nobles. By spring, I was in good health again.

Shalira came to see me every day, and her eyes and manner held a tenderness which I had seldom received from a girl. She nursed me and petted me and teased me into talking about Amyris.

I watched her eagerness grow as the weather grew warm. She had so romanticized her prince that her eyes shone at the mere mention of his name. And she dressed more carefully and preened herself and put on airs like a lady when she visited me, with her cheetah kittens on jeweled leashes, and sometimes a pet bird perched on her shoulder.

"What do you see in those silly cats?" I teased her one day. I could see why they were called weeping cheetahs. They had black lines running from the inner corners of their eyes to the tips of their noses, like tear stains.

"I see a lot in them. They're sweet. And their mothers can outhunt your screaming eagles," she said haughtily.

"Is that a challenge?" I asked.

"Make it one if you like, Uncle Timur. I've seen them hunt." She bent over and kissed me on the nose. The nearness of her sweet-scented body and the transparency of her spring sari presented another challenge.

After she left, I wondered what effect the fever had had on my waning virility. As the weather got warmer and her nipples and triangle fascinated me more and more, I became obsessed with the idea. When the tantalizing voluptuousness of her maturing body became unbearable, I had virgins brought to me.

I was not entirely impotent, but after I had finished with the girls, I had them destroyed so they could never compare me with another man. And on the futile nights when I was unable to penetrate the hymen, I garroted the virgins myself, before they could speak to anyone, and returned their bodies to the procurers and complained that the girls were unsuitable or undesirable. I fully appreciated the necessity for safeguarding the belief in my omnipotence in all things. To hold my authority, I had to be the wisest, the strongest, the bravest, the most efficient, and the most virile man in my empire.

One night I ordered a boy—as many Indian rajahs did every night— but I found his caresses repulsive and slit his throat with a kukri. When the procurer became frightened and fled, I called out "Assassin!" and my guards slew him before he could speak.

But my advancing age was not without its compensation, even my loss of clear vision. For as light was cut out, I saw the world more distinctly in its darker hues. There is no light. This is a dark world. The Manichaeans in their meditations on Light and Darkness are only half right.

All Light is illusion. Darkness is real. In my periods of comtemplation, forced on me by my weakness, I saw the dark aspects of empire—the black forces which rule men while they are dazzled by the glitter and pomp of their monarchs' courts.

All this I saw in the semidarkness left me by the fever. And it contrasted with the brightness of Shalira as she tended me and danced for me the difficult kathakali of Malabar, which requires sixty-four mudras of the hands and a dozen eye dristis, and explained the delicate fingerdances and the significance of the many glances. She was romantic. She was Light. But she was all illusion.

Shalira was never gayer than on the day we held our hunting contest on the Srinagar plateau in the Vale of Kashmir. My army had all but assembled for its return to Samarkand; only a few straggling elements had not arrived in the vale. Eager to make the journey and excited by the pageantry of my amirs gathered to witness the hunt, Shalira was like the Greek Diana as she held onto the silken slip-thongs which passed under the bellies of her cheetahs and restrained them until the game was sighted. She laughed happily and scolded the cats when they dragged her along in their eagerness for the chase.

"Watch out, or they'll eat your birds," she called gaily, when my handlers brought out the big jade-green yokes on which my falcons and eagles were perched.

"If those hawks weren't hooded, they'd scratch your kittens' eyes out," I retorted. "Wait till we take off their rufters."

"What's the wager?" she teased.

"Name it yourself," I said. "You're the one who started bragging."

"Amyris," she said, and her eyes glowed. "If my cheetahs catch the quarry, I win Amyris."

"Very well—and you will be your own prize. If my falcons win, I win you—for my son, Amyris."

She laughed happily.

"I can't lose. Bring on the quarry."

I gave the signal, and my men released a gazelle from a cage down the field—I was still not able to ride on an extended hunt—and Shalira released the slip-thongs on her straining cats. Simultaneously my handlers let the falcons go and the hunters raced and flew toward the bounding gazelle.

I was amazed by the speed of the cheetahs. They actually ran faster than my best eagles could fly. Of course, the birds were climbing to gain altitude for a lightning swoop on the quarry, and I had every confidence that they would gain on the cheetahs in their dive. But my confidence waned as the race gained momentum. By the time the hawks reached their altitude, the cats were within three or four bounds of the gazelle—I could hardly see the fleet animals on the ground.

Then, to my surprise, Shalira whistled her high shrill recall, and her cats stopped in their tracks, and my eagles swooped down for the kill. Shalira whistled again. Her cheetahs reluctantly turned and trotted back toward their mistress.

"Why?" I asked in surprise.

Shalira faced me, and there were tears in her eyes.

"I didn't want to cheat you, Uncle Timur." She sounded like Jahangir. "I knew the cats would win—I've seen these contests before. I didn't want to humiliate you before your men. Anyway, in India, no one dares win a wager from a king." She laughed again at that.

"Besides, you won me for Amyris. I'm happy," she continued.

"Of course—I'm happy, too," I said. "Happy for Amyris. No one ever won a lovelier prize. If I were only about fifty years younger—"

"Uncle Timur, you're sweet," she said, and squeezed my arm affectionately.

The hunt was the prelude to my victory celebration. As soon as we returned from the field, the banquets were spread and the wine began to flow. Hashish and bhang and opium-water circulated freely among the Indian contingents in my army, and many of the thousands of captive girls were carried away from the festivities before the evening was well begun. But my own Tatars and Persians and Russians and Mongols stayed for the elephant fights and lion-tiger battles staged in torchlit cages and pits.

Between main events, fire-eaters and sword-swallowers and jugglers passed among the squatting warriors. Snake charmers played their weird musettes in accompaniment to swaying hooded cobras, and larger bands of plectrum and bowed string instruments and flutes and all manner of percussion devices furnished music for the nimble-fingered, busy-eyed dancing girls. The entire Vale of Kashmir seemed to be one big carefree carnival.

Long after I retired, I could hear the boisterous sounds of revelry in the distance and the low laughs and giggles of small parties passing near my kibitka on the way to their late-hour orgies. But I was too tired even to envy the young people or to call for a girl for myself. My main mission had been completed. I had fighting elephants, and I had the bulk of India's fabulous wealth for them to transport to Samarkand. When I did sleep, I slept soundly.

On the long trip home I rode comfortably with my tavachis in a luxurious double howdah atop a team of two big bull elephants. My howdah led the column of elephants out of the vale into Kashmir proper and up the Indus valley through Karakorum Pass into the Tarim Basin of Sinkiang. We skirted the desert and entered the mountains again south of Terek Pass. From that point it was only a few days' march through Khojend to Tashkand, where I halted for a week to prepare for my entry into Samarkand. With elephants as the chief attraction, I could make my return from India the greatest triumphal entry of all time. So I set all available artists to work. Some painted the beasts in silver and gold and all other colors. Others made caparisons of silks and satins and tapestries and brocades and printed cotton fabrics, some of which are prized more highly than silks by the women of Samarkand.

My saddlers and harnessmakers contrived ingenious harnesses to strap naked dancing girls in various graceful attitudes on the sides of the great beasts, so that the girls' bodies, painted gold and silver, seemed to be figures carved in bas relief out of the metallic elephants themselves. And carpenters and architects and decorators and jewelers combined their efforts to design and build more elaborate howdahs than had ever been conceived before. Then there were cages built to display the many strange animals I had brought back for my menagerie. Camels and horses were also richly caparisoned and their burdens of spices transferred to more lowly asses and mules.

For Shalira, the artists created a low throne on a gorgeous vermilion litter mounted on four gray Manchu horses—a device similar to the one which Bibi Khanum had ridden into Samarkand on our wedding day. When the Rajput princess took her place on the throne, with her cheetah kittens at her feet and her ladies posed around her, she looked like something out of Paradise. With her litter immediately behind my howdah, I headed a column of a thousand magnificent elephants and a hundred thousand gaily dressed warriors.

But I, too, was confronted by a lavish spectacle—Amyris' sarai of brilliant silk pavilions erected on the banks of the Zaravshan, and the gaily clad Kara Hazara drawn up in two ranks flanking the highway, with sabres at salute and dyed horsetail standards lowered to charge. The oiled black faces of the Negroes and their gleaming white teeth—for all the men were smiling proudly—added the final touch of splendor to Amyris' surprise. I detected Nubja's hand in the welcome her son had prepared for me.

Some years later, after Bishop John's return from Paris with a report on conditions there, my mathematicians and treasurers estimated that on my triumphal return from India I brought to Samarkand greater riches than the total wealth of all the lands of the Franks, including the Isles of Inglistan. It was all in the parade—on the jewel-bedecked slave girls, in the decorations of the howdahs, piled high on the many beasts of burden

—sixty warehouses full of precious loot. But most valuable of all, I brought elephants—my answer to gunpowder.

CHAPTER

13

The ensuing summer was probably the busiest time in the history of Samarkand. With the tremendous power of the elephants made available for construction work, my builders were able to throw up in a matter of weeks structures which would have normally required years of labor. Many of my projected buildings were completed far ahead of schedule, and new three- and four-storied bazaars rose almost overnight. Except for the Bibi Khanum Mosque and my own Timur's Temple, both of which I wanted to be examples of architectural perfection, the Dream of Samarkand was complete.

While my warriors relaxed in one long round of revelry, the high point of which was the wedding of Amyris and Shalira, I spent most of my time on Hermitage Hill with my scholars and technicians. Instead of attending the bear-baiting pits or the elephant fights or the endless feasts and orgies, I worked and prodded my specialists to put elephant power to maximum war application and to find the secrets of gunpowder. I wanted more than mere defense against the stuff; I wanted a more terrible offensive weapon than the world had ever known.

And my scholars were not idle. They phrased new attacks on the nefarious use of gunpowder and spread increasingly dire threats against any man or any people who used it. They also composed poems about Amyris and his princess bride; and, together with thousands of copies of an exquisite miniature of Amyris and Shalira painted by the court artist, these poems were sent into Asia Minor and Egypt to be circulated among the Negro slaves there by Abdullah's best agitators.

The mollahs and imams and sayyids of all Islam received encyclicals over the signature of Mir Sayyid, urging them to preach against gunpowder and to have the Faithful pray for my righteous crusade against it. My name was included in all the kutbehs said in my realm and gradually infiltrated the prayers of Bayazid's followers. The Church people were perhaps the most effective of all forces in my campaign, since they already had the vocabulary to treat of the fire and brimstone of the seven hells. Djon Pitr, by that time *Bishop John* of Sultaniah, enlisted the aid of the Nestorian Christians in the war against the diabolic invention.

I had time still to oversee N'il Mahdi-Soun's training with Arabshah. Already my son had surpassed his other tutors and was far along in

Arabshah's knowledge of the Greek Aristotle and Plato and Demosthenes.

"Amir, may I be presumptuous in my questioning?" Arabshah asked one day, as we sat before the Golden Tree of Life on Hermitage Hill.

"You usually are," I said grumpily but kindly, I thought. "Go ahead."

"Amir, I have gathered from your talk that you consider your conquests something in the nature of a sacred duty. Your many encyclicals stress the inevitability of your success."

"Yes?"

"Well, Amir, if your way is to prevail—if it is inevitable, pre-ordained, that your principles shall pervade the earth, why do you strive so hard to hasten their dissemination? Why not relax? You are an old man, a wealthy man, a powerful man. Nothing can endanger you or Samarkand in your lifetime, even if you stop now and enjoy your last years in peace."

"Perhaps it is pre-ordained that I shall do exactly as I am doing, strain myself to keep the Way of the Tree of Life as long as there is an ounce of energy left in my body. Do you plan to give up your studies?"

"Why, no," he answered in shocked surprise. "There is so much to know—I know so little—and I have such little time left on earth. I can't stop."

I laughed aloud at his vehemence.

"Nor can I," I said. "I can no more tolerate the slothful peace of my people or the arrogant misrule of my neighbors than you can tolerate ignorance. There is much left for me to do, and I, too, have so little time."

"Thank you, Amir," he said, and smiled wanly. "You have answered my question."

"You needn't be grateful," I said. "I allow you to live only because I believe that you can give my son the best training accessible to him."

"It is ironic—paradoxical—Amir, that you who live by the sword should respect me, a scholar who hates you—allow me to live because of a son who makes no pretense of becoming a warrior."

"There is nothing ironic or paradoxical about it," I said. "It may be that N'il Mahdi-Soun shall become my true heir. My warriors may fall, my swords rust after my death; but if N'il writes my Word well, it will never die on this earth. For it is the Way and the Will of Allah. If my mahdi can write his prophecy, even though he does not understand it—no prophet understands his prophecy or the source of his inspiration—there will arise men in generations to come who can read what I read in the world and continue to keep the Way of the Tree of Life."

But Arabshah did not understand. He knew the early prophets well—

Moses, Isaiah, Ezekiel and Jesus. He knew of the Way of the Tree of Life—he knew the words—but even Moses, who spoke them, knew not what they meant; and the later prophets, especially Jesus, subverted the meaning beyond recognition.

As the summer wore on I encouraged my strategists to intensify their study of Devon, against the possibility of my conquest of the lands of the Franks and the Isles of Inglistan. My multitudinous grandsons, who filled many officer ranks in the lower echelons, were thoroughly familiar with the castle and village, having grown up in mock warfare along the Devon street. My technicians duplicated the buildings in remote places outside the walls and spent many hours testing our weapons and siege machines against the Frank architecture.

And I visited Ali Soun Agha frequently. The time was approaching when I would take her back home, back to her Engloland, and set her on the throne as queen.

"I don't care about being queen," she said, and smiled tolerantly at me when I mentioned it. "Just to see the real Devon again—to sit before the fire in the main hall with old friends." The old wistfulness returned to her sky-blue eyes—less clear, older, but still beautiful.

"Very well, but you'll be queen in name. You may live in Devon."

"I wonder what Devon—the real Devon—is like now," she said, and her eyes filmed over in her reverie. "Perhaps it has changed—it must have. I may even long for this Devon, my own special Devon, when I see it." She laughed softly.

"There may have been wars," she continued, growing serious, "and plagues and—and all sorts of changes. Perhaps it has not been protected and preserved as this one has." She reached out and clasped my hand. "Left to itself, tiny little Devon may not have survived."

"I'll rebuild it," I said. "Patterned after this one. You shall have your Devon just as you want it to be."

"Yes," she said, "I'm sure you would do it, just as you built this one. My village here still looks like Devon, sounds like Devon, I think—I may have forgotten the true sound of my language. But deep down inside I know it isn't Devon. And if you built another in Engloland, it wouldn't be, either, not after you got through. It would be a Tatar village that looked like Devon."

Her smile held no rancor. Her words were not a complaint, just a statement. I merely squeezed her hand.

"Don't destroy Engloland," she said impulsively. "I'd rather not go home if you have to burn and pillage the island."

"I hope I won't have to," I said. "I'll send Djon Pitr to King Charles of the Franks. Bayazid is also his enemy—the enemy of the Greek Emperor

Manuel at Istanbul—the enemy of all Christians. Perhaps we can make a treaty and go to Inglistan in peace."

"*Bishop John,*" she said proudly, lovingly. "My son, an ambassador to the court of King Charles."

"And you may go with him," I said. "Then I'll come to you in peace."

Her estimate of my kindness to her would make her a better envoy than my son, I was sure. With her wealth and native charm, she would be heard by the Franks, and I would come to her—in war or in peace.

My scientists made no progress in their study of gunpowder; so, as fall approached, I had two huge ironbound chests—as big as double howdahs—made and taken to their secret laboratory. As experimental machinery was proved useless and discarded, I had it dismantled and stowed in the chests, until they became quite heavy. Finally the chests were full of failures, and I called all the staff together in the drafting room on Hermitage Hill.

"You have failed," I said to them. "Failed in your sacred task. You have proved yourselves inferior to the Franks and the Khitans. I cannot tolerate sloth and inefficiency."

My guards entered immediately and arrested the men. I had the culprits' tongues cut out before the stupid scientists could tell of their failure. Then I had the big chests and the men who had filled them taken to the registan.

There in the presence of my assembled amirs and scholars and mollahs, I made my indictment.

"Unknown to me, behind my back," I began, "these perfidious, traitorous enemies of mankind have been meddling with the forbidden, diabolical gunpowder—that cursed stuff from the bowels of hell.

"And in true Tatar fashion they have succeeded even in their nefarious experiments. They have discovered a machine, the destructive power of which is too dreadful to contemplate. These chests contain the awful fruits of their labors.

"You all know my views on such things. Gunpowder is an anathema to Allah. It is profane. These men who have dared oppose the Divine Will must die.

"And I am burdened with their infernal machine," I said sadly. "I pray to Allah that I may never be forced to use it. But I must keep it with me to prohibit its use, unless my enemies force me to use it in the name of Allah—against their own feeble guns. Let us all pray that such a course is never found necessary."

Mir Sayyid put such a prayer into words, and the offenders against humanity were summarily beheaded in the presence of the Faithful.

And when I led my force of half a million people—including all my

379

wives and the men's wives and hundreds of thousands of slaves—toward the west in the fall, the huge ironbound chests, carried by two teams of bull elephants, rode immediately behind my howdah; and I kept the mysterious machines under close, heavy guard throughout the campaign. They were my threat to rulers who did not fear the elephants. I was confident that I would make good that threat one day, even if I had to capture foreign scientists who understood gunpowder, and force them to exploit the terrible stuff to extremes never dreamed of in their native lands.

CHAPTER

14

Shah Rukh brought his army from Herat and joined me at Mashhad. From that point Dilshad traveled with her son, as Nubja had traveled with Amyris from the start. And since I had left Mohammed Sultan to guard Samarkand from the north, I had given Khalil Sultan a command and brought Sevin Bey Khanzade with him. After all she was Mohammed Sultan's mother, too, and I was loath to leave her behind with both her sons and without Dilshad to counter her intrigues.

Shadi Mulkh also came with Khalil Sultan. As Dilshad had said, the sultry beauty was a thorn in Sevin Bey's flesh. I let Khalil Sultan think that it was his mother, not I, who opposed a state wedding between him and the Persian courtesan.

Ali Soun Agha traveled with me, would until Djon Pitr joined us for the trip west. And Ali Soun's thoughts were all for her son, *Bishop John*. She visited Nubja often on the overnight camps and the black princess was a frequent visitor at my elaborate pavilion, in which Ali Soun had her own suite. The chatter of the two women, whose contrast in color seemed incongruous when they found so much common ground for conversation, was all about my black and white sons. Each listened politely to the other and then waxed voluble when her turn came to extol the virtues and accomplishments of her own cub.

Consequently, after military duties I had much time to devote to N'il Mahdi-Soun, who was my constant companion. Conditions seemed to suggest that I start him on my personal chronicle. Arabshah said that the boy was competent, though he was not yet sixteen.

"Where shall we begin, Father?" he asked eagerly the first evening, after he had gathered his writing supplies and brought them to the torchlit awning outside my pavilion. "When you were born?"

"No, Son," I said. "We'll skip the early years. Too many men live forever in their childhood—tell their stories from a child's point of view, try to explain the world in the precocious babbling of infants. No, mine shall be a story for men—strong men, seeking men, men who would solve Allah's Riddle."

I paused for a moment and thought about where to begin.

"We'll start on the day I first saw the wonderful talwar, Son—the day I found the Way I should follow—the Way of the Sword."

I talked far into the night. The torches and naphtha lamps guttered, and the boy's eyes grew red and heavy, and his hand cramped so that he had to stop and rest. And in the early morning I went to my couch and slept and dreamed of the days of my youth.

Moving an army the size of mine was no easy task, especially across the desert where it was all but impossible to water so much livestock. With Pir Mohammed in India, I had given Shah Malik command of my left wing. He moved far ahead, digging wells, raiding on the flanks for forage, and keeping patrols out to scout possible enemies. On beyond him were my spies, both mine and Abdullah's men, who kept in communication with agents who had already infiltrated enemy territory or been recruited behind the lines. Far ahead, too, were merchants and navigators who knew the country or could read the stars and the Khitan magnetic needle and mark our course.

As we camped on the same site from which Djon Pitr had ridden away to enter the seminary, Ali Soun grew more excited than I had seen her since the day work first began on her village of Devon in Samarkand. When Djon rode into camp, he dismounted while the horse was at full gallop and had rushed into his mother's arms before the animal came to a full stop.

Ali Soun wept for a moment on the shoulder of her tall lean son, and then disengaged herself. "Stand away from me, Son," she said excitedly, "and let me look at you."

Djon Pitr stood back, fine and handsome even in his somber episcopal robes; and his eyes held a twinkle which I was sure some of his priests must have considered irreverent. Ali Soun gasped and smiled through her tears.

"My son, you're handsome—so tall. I'm proud of you," she said happily, but with some awe for her prince of the Church.

"Careful, Mother," he said impishly. "A priest is not supposed to be vain. You'll corrupt the Church. You're very pretty, yourself."

"Oh, Son," she said in embarrassment. "You *are* handsome. You *are*. Bishop or no bishop."

Djon laughed at his mother's befuddlement and took her in his arms again.

"Hello, Father," he said over her shoulder.

"Hello, Son," I greeted him.

"I got your letters."

"Fine. Then you know of the mission I have in mind for you."

"Yes," he said, and lifted his mother bodily and seated her on a soft-cushioned camp stool. He sat down on the rug beside her and held her hand while he talked to me. She watched every movement of his lips and occasionally brushed back his hair with her free hand.

"Well, what do you think of it?" I asked.

"I don't know, Father. Can I trust you?" His eyes twinkled merrily, but there was determination behind them.

"John!" scolded Ali Soun.

"It's all right, Mother," he assured her. "Father and I understand each other; don't we, Father?"

"I hope so," I said. I wondered if he understood how he came to be a bishop at twenty-six.

"It is true that Bayazid is the enemy of King Charles and Emperor Manuel—and all Christians," he said.

"And mine as well. That makes me Charles's ally—if you can convince him, or if your mother can."

"Mother? Is she going, too?" His eyes clouded, and he looked quickly and anxiously at Ali Soun. It would be a dangerous trip through Bayazid's country.

"If she wants to," I said. "All the way to Inglistan."

Djon Pitr looked back at me with a mingled expression—disapproval, disbelief, fear, contempt—it was hard to tell. His eyes were very expressive when he wanted them to be, but opaque and inscrutable when he wished. He would be an efficient bishop at twenty-six. He was *my* son, too.

"She's always wanted to go home," I reminded him.

"Yes, but—are you going, Mother?" he asked her.

"We'll decide," she said lightly, and patted his knee. "We've plenty of time, a year at least."

Djon Pitr looked back at me, his eyes level and cool—cold.

"I'll go, if Mother goes," he said firmly. "I'll go, anyway, if that's what you want."

"That's what I want," I said. "King Charles and I will fight this infidel Bayazid together."

"This infidel Bayazid is a Mohammedan, the same as you," he said. "Come, Mother, let's walk around the sarai. I've lots to tell you."

He rose and helped Ali Soun to her feet.

"And I've lots to tell you," she said, hanging onto his arm as the two of them walked away down a regimental street.

Djon Pitr and Ali Soun were together constantly on the way to Tabriz and at the sarai near Lake Urmia. They shared the same howdah on the march, and Djon lived in my pavilion in a suite next to his mother's. He asked me about the huge chests, though he had heard the rumors about their contents.

"Will you use the machines before you meet Bayazid?" he asked.

"No," I said. "Not even then, unless he uses guns and forces me to let loose the terrible fury in the name of Allah."

Djon Pitr grinned.

"Then the chests are empty," he said. "If you had weapons in them, you'd use them on the first city that resists you."

"Just tell King Charles that I have them. You may be sure that I will produce the miracle weapon when I really need it. Let him be the judge of my strategy. Warn him against gunpowder, too, if he has any ideas about resistance to my terms."

"And your terms will be complete surrender, I suppose."

"No. Not necessarily," I said. "There is room in the world for other rulers, if they share my views."

"Meaning surrender. Well, I'll find out King Charles's views."

"Do that," I said, "and I'll decide whether or not they're acceptable."

"And Mother will be safe—if she goes, or if she stays behind?" he asked, wrinkling his forehead.

"She'll be safe," I said positively.

Djon said no more about the chests during the six-month sarai at Tabriz. In fact, I saw little of him. He studied hard, and he had several parishes in Tabriz which he visited regularly.

I had other interests, too. Sultan Ahmed had been re-outfitted with soldiers and women by the Mamluk Sultan of Cairo and had returned to Baghdad, which I had left lightly garrisoned during my campaign in India. He and Kara Yussuf, whose Turkomans were a powerful force in Armenia and Kurdistan, had both sworn allegiance to Bayazid and put themselves under his protection. And the Mamluks had a strong occupation army in Syria. Any one or all of these could block my way to Bayazid's country and hold me, perhaps, until Bayazid could recall his Turks from Europe, where they were laying siege to Istanbul and fighting Christians in various parts of Greece and Bulgaria.

So I sent a letter to Bayazid assuring him that I was on a strictly punitive expedition against Ahmed, who had killed my hakim and his garrison at Baghdad, and Kara Yussuf, who had made raids on Kharesm. I asked the Turkish Sultan to surrender the culprits and avert a war that would be costly to both of us. And I asked him to join me in my holy venture to outlaw the scourge of gunpowder.

My letter was civil. I said only the simple truth: "Do you not know that the greatest part of Asia is subject to my arms and my laws? that my invincible forces extend from one sea to the other? that the potentates of the earth form a line before my gate? and that I have compelled Fortune herself to watch over the prosperity of my empire? What is the foundation of your insolence and folly? You have fought some battles in the woods of Anatolia; contemptible trophies! You have obtained some victories over the Christians of Europe; your sword was blessed by the apostle of Allah; and your obedience to the precept of the Koran, in waging war against the infidel, is the sole consideration that prevents me from destroying your country. Be wise in time; reflect; repent; and avert the thunder of my vengeance, which is yet suspended over your head. You are no more than a pissmire; why will you seek to provoke the elephants? Alas! they will trample you under their feet." *

While I waited for Bayazid's reply, I sent more agents among his Turks, especially those of Tatar origin—as indeed are all Turks if one goes back far enough—to urge them to loyalty to their own race and the principles of Mohammedanism undefiled by Bayazid's perfidious atheism.

I had time, too, to continue my dictation to N'il Mahdi-Soun. He and I revisited the place where he was born and the gardens and mountain valleys which his mother had loved so well.

Then Bayazid's letter came. It was not even civil. It called me a thief and a rebel of the desert and said I never triumphed except by the vices of my foes or by my own perfidy. It spoke sarcastically about "the arrows of the flying Tatar." What would they be against "the scimitars and battle-axes of my firm and invincible janizaries?" The ungrateful, distrustful Turk refused to yield up my enemies. As before, he had his information all garbled—he discounted my chests of terrible weapons, and he insisted that I had no valid grievance against either Ahmed or Yussuf, that I had taken Baghdad from Ahmed, its rightful Sultan, and Kharesm from Kara Yussuf's kinsmen, the Urganjis and Khivans. Further, he either had not heard of my giving Shalira to Amyris, or had refused to believe the report—for he assumed that Shalira was my wife—and threatened to get her with child before my very eyes, as he had threatened Bibi Khanum some years earlier. I decided to let Amyris avenge that insult when the time came, but Bayazid would answer to me for his repeated use of the hateful name, *Timur-i-Leng.*

So I prepared to break camp and move on through Kurdistan. Since I had about reached the borders of my realm and expected warfare soon, I made arrangements to send the women back for safety. Nubja preferred

* Quoted in Gibbon, *The Decline and Fall of the Roman Empire.*

to take the risk and go along with Amyris, in the hope of reaching Africa perhaps and being a queen again among people of her own race. And I, of course, expected Ali Soun to accompany me to an embarkation point for her journey home. But she had decided otherwise.

"I don't think I'll go with *John*," she said, as we sat on the shores of Lake Urmia and discussed her trip.

"Why? I always thought you wanted to go back to Inglistan," I said. She paused for a moment and then began hesitantly.

"I don't know, Timur, I'm afraid you've seduced me. I don't know that I want to go back to Devon, a Devon which I can't control. I've had my way so long in my village in Samarkand. I've become so used to having everyone obey my slightest wish—live for me and my whims—I don't know—"

She paused again and stared at the salt crystals on the rocks at the water's edge. Then she went on slowly.

"Devon in Tatary isn't Devon in *Engloland*. And I'm used to my neighbors in Samarkand, my slaves, virtually—for so many years. How many? Thirty? Nearly thirty. I'm afraid I couldn't go back home. I couldn't treat my own people like that—and yet I'm so used to your ways."

A tear splattered on her hand as she reached over to clasp mine.

"Besides, my clothes would be out of style—old-fashioned," she said with an attempt at brightness, and smoothed the front of her gown with her free hand. "I'll go if you want me to—or I'll wait and go with you, if you go."

She managed a real smile and continued.

"But right now, I'd like to go back with the Sarai Khanum—she's sweet, now that I've got to know her in the camps. I wish Nubja were going back, too," she added wistfully. "I can come to you again when you go to Europe—if you do. If not, I'd rather just go back to Samarkand when the war's over and live out my days in my own Devon—where I've spent far more than half my life."

"What does Djon Pitr say?" I asked.

"He said for me to decide, but I don't think he wants me to go with him now."

"Very well," I said. "As you wish."

In the face of Djon Pitr's rather open disagreement with my aims, I thought it might be well for me to keep Ali Soun as a sort of hostage—just in case. I had not anticipated the full degree of my bishop son's defiance when I left Samarkand. Perhaps he would prove a more efficient ambassador if he knew that his mother was still with me.

Ali Soun's gratitude was immediately apparent. She leaned over and kissed me, Frank fashion, and said, "Timur, you're sweet—you've always been sweet to me—and to *John*."

Djon Pitr was also touched by my kindness.

"This is a fine thing you're doing, Father," he said at our first meeting after my talk with Ali Soun. "Maybe you're sincere, after all. Maybe you do love her."

"Of course I do, Son. Just be a good ambassador at the court of King Charles."

At Karabagh I re-formed my army; and after deploying Shah Rukh's corps to keep the Turkomans at bay, I pressed on beyond Lake Van Golu and through Kurdistan, taking Erzurum and Erzinkan and Tokat and Sivas in a few months of light fighting. Then I cut south across the butt of the Turkish Peninsula, to Aleppo in Syria.

Since I knew that I would never pass that way again and since I could not spare large occupation forces, I took no prisoners. And I killed all able-bodied men of military age so that my hakims would not be as vulnerable as the hakim of Baghdad had been. So after I had destroyed the strong Egyptian garrison at Aleppo and marched on Damascus, the Mamluk hakim there sued for terms. I camped outside the walls of Damascus for a month while we parleyed—the governor of Damascus playing for time and asking for aid from the Mamluk Sultan in Cairo, I was sure.

But my army had been in the field for two years, the last year in almost constant combat, and I allowed the main force to rest while Nur ad-Din led a corps to lay siege to Baghdad and Shah Malik took a division in pursuit of some Mamluks who had escaped from Aleppo and fled into Palestine. Djon Pitr, who wanted to visit Jerusalem, went with Shah Malik; and after my tuman-bashi had defeated the Mamluks at Akka, he escorted *Bishop John* to the Holy City and then to Joppa for embarkation to the land of the Franks.

I stayed at Damascus and continued my narrative with N'il Mahdi-Soun. Because of the midday glare on the Syrian desert, we stayed indoors except in the early morning or late afternoon. Then we sat under the awning before my tent and I told the story of my life with Aljai. And as I talked about Aljai, I looked at the beautiful dome of the Umayyad Mosque. Like a giant tulip bulb it hovered over the city. Either the mirage or the weakened condition of my eyes gave the impression that the dome was filled with the stuff that clouds are made of, that it floated protectively above the walls, unsupported by anything on the ground. And somehow it was like Aljai—like Aljai's gay spirit, swelled to bursting with the joy of life on the earth, yet not touching the earth to be smudged and defiled, and pointing to something in the heavens, out of sight.

I ordered my architects to study the dome and make sketches of it. I even sent some into the city, with the help of Abdullah's underground, to make detailed plans of its construction. Then, when the work was done, I immediately dispatched scores of architects to build a similar dome on the still unfinished Bibi Khanum Mosque in Samarkand, and others on Aljai's and Jahangir's and Omar Sheik's tombs in Shehri-Sebz. And I gave orders that copies be put on all mosques yet to be built anywhere in my empire.*

Finally the hakim of Damascus agreed to my terms; and upon Shah Malik's return from Palestine, my army broke camp and started on the march again. Mamluk and Turkish reinforcements coming to Damascus attacked our rear, however, and we turned and gave battle. My superior forces easily won the fray; and as retaliation I ordered the sacking of Damascus. My men, repressed by the long stay in camp, looted and raped the city for three days and then set fire to it. I stood beside N'il Mahdi-Soun and watched the Umayyad dome go up in flames. But I would find it again in other cities—in my own cities—as I had found Aljai in other women.

CHAPTER

15

Warned by the number of Turks in the force which had attacked me that Bayazid had begun to pull his men back across the Bosporus, I marched up to Aleppo to re-form my army for an all-out attack on the main Turkish stronghold.

I sent word to Mohammed Sultan to bring the Samarkand Corps west to my aid, and I recalled Shah Rukh's Herat Corps from their action against the Turkomans.

Nur ad-Din had not taken Baghdad as quickly as I had expected him to. Although the cowardly, suspicious Sultan had fled again and taken refuge in Cairo, he had left instructions to surrender only if I attacked Baghdad myself. So I was faced with the choice of less than my full army against Bayazid's Turks—and perhaps guns, though I had encountered none so far—or a quick campaign against Baghdad.

I debated the matter while I waited for Shah Rukh and his siege train, which I would need on either course. I continued calmly to attend to state matters, keep up correspondence with Samarkand and India, and dictate my chronicles to N'il Mahdi-Soun. And another scholar asked to be added to my staff, an Egyptian from the court of the Mamluk Sultan.

---

* The Umayyad tulip-bulb dome, which has since become the distinguishing feature of Moslem and Russian church architecture, was unknown east of Damascus before Timur decreed that it be used throughout his realm.

He came to my pavilion and claimed to be a fugitive who had offended the Sultan and been forced to flee Cairo.

"Most Gracious Amir," he said, "it has long been my desire to record your exploits—but, as you know, the Sultan is your enemy and forbade me to see you."

"And now you have run away," I said. The man's eyes were shifty; and though my vision was not good, I thought they were dilated with hashish. And the scholar spoke haltingly, carefully, like a drunken man.

"Yes, Amir—now I have run away."

He wiped his face with a scarf and, I thought, put something in his mouth. His pouch, too, seemed shaped to carry a dagger rather than a writer's kit; so I gave a signal to alert my guards.

"You have run away to—" I prompted him.

"To see you and to write—to—to kill you, you beast!" he screamed, and lunged at me wildly, drawing his dagger as he came.

But my guards pounced upon him and cut him to bits before he had taken three steps. The stupid Mamluk Sultan! He had not learned the first principles of using scholars in warfare. I no longer feared the Sultan of Egypt. He was too stupid.

But Bayazid was of a different breed, and by the time Shah Rukh arrived, I had decided to march on Baghdad and not risk facing the Turkish Sultan until I had my full army, including the Samarkand Corps. We moved down the Euphrates valley in midsummer and then cut over to the Tigris a few miles north of Baghdad. I drew up my forces immediately, though the heat was so intense that men baked in their armor, and horses dropped dead, and birds fell out of the sky exhausted.

For a week we besieged the city, attacking only in the early morning and late afternoon, and retiring to the shade of our tents during the day. Then on the eighth day, after retiring before mid-morning, my forces charged again at high noon—coming in from all sides and floating siege machines down the Tigris, which cut the city in two.

Nur ad-Din led a furious charge against the gates and planted his standard on a watch tower. In an instant the walls were aswarm with my scaling ladders; and catapults and petards and mangonels and trebuchets rained a hail of stones and naphtha bombs from high platforms and maneuverable elephant howdahs. The feeble midday guard cracked in a few minutes, and my forces rushed the city before the reserves could yawn and rub their eyes into wakefulness.

Baghdad had rebelled against me after I had generously spared it from destruction; so I ordered it razed. In a four-day holocaust my men annihilated the fabled city which had been the glory of Moslem song and story. I left a mere pile of rubble guarded by pyramids of human

388

skulls—the heads of a hundred thousand perfidious Baghdadis whose headless carcasses lay buried in the moat under sand raked in from the desert by my elephants.

My purpose in ordering the holocaust and the pyramid of skulls was obvious. The warning spread and the awe it inspired was very useful. But it did not stir me at all. It was something that had to be done and I had the feeling that I had done it before. There was hardly any feeling of easement and I wondered if vengeance also had grown stale.

With my kulchis and general staff, I made a forced march to Tabriz to plan my grand strategy against Bayazid, while my army followed, hunting and foraging by the way, and Mohammed Sultan moved down from Samarkand. I worked long hours every day, compiling intelligence reports and going over plans and sending agents with new propaganda to spread among the Turks. I received pledges of support from the besieged Christians in Istanboul and Smyrna, and merchants came to me from Venice and Genoa to make trade agreements. I heard rumors of guns, though no actual eyewitness reported their use by the Turks.

Then my army arrived from the south and pitched camp, and word came that Mohammed Sultan was only a few miles away. The next day my tattered field army formed on the parade ground to welcome the Samarkand Corps.

Mohammed's army made a brilliant spectacle. Fresh from easy garrison duty at Otrar and Samarkand, they appeared healthy and well mounted. And their uniforms were the most colorful my army had ever seen. Every regiment had shining silk surcoats of a different color, with helmets and bowcases and saddle cloths of the same material and design.

My battle-scarred veterans jeered and hooted at the gaudy newcomers, but later, when I ordered the tailors in Tabriz to outfit my regulars in battle-dress of equal splendor, not a man refused his new uniform. The envious mockery gave way to pride, and the morale of all my forces rose to a new high level.

So it was that I headed toward Sivas again with the largest and most eager army I had ever commanded. Only heavily superior forces or thousands of guns could defeat me. And I had no great fear of guns—though they were an unknown danger—for I believed that the only real defense against the elephants was more and bigger elephants, a defense Bayazid could not muster.

At Sivas, my intelligence reported that Bayazid had established his camp on the plain east of Angora and was moving his army up on the road through the hilly country to meet me. From my scouts and from merchants who knew the country, I learned that the sparsely wooded foothills gave advantage to infantry—Bayazid's hitherto invincible sipahis and janissaries—for ambush and sniping and sneak attacks. So I turned left at Sivas and followed the outer shore of the Halys River around the big bend through Kayseri and Kirsehir to Lake Tuz, where the river turns north again and flows between Angora and Yozgat.

The fields were ripe for harvest; and since the water of the Halys was fairly sweet, my army marched easily and rapidly, well supplied with forage by Shah Malik's advance left wing. We covered the route in three days, and came to Bayazid's lightly guarded camp well behind his army, which by that time had advanced beyond Yozgat. I sent Nur ad-Din to lay siege to Angora and Mohammed Sultan to scorch the country through which Bayazid's force would have to return to attack me, established in his own well-provisioned sarai.

Ak Boga's rear guard fought a light skirmish with a patrol commanded by Bayazid's son, Suliman, at a point near Kayseri. Ak Boga fled south as a decoy; and Bayazid, learning that I was not at Sivas, sent a small needless expedition to the south before he discovered that I had already taken his camp near Angora.

Then he began the long hot march back across the wasted plain, where forage and food had all been destroyed and all water dammed up and polluted. His infantry especially suffered hundreds of casualties from thirst and hunger before they had finished their ordeal. And the only water and food were behind my lines; so Bayazid was forced to accept battle in open country, favorable to cavalry and elephant-borne war machines.

The battle line extended for fifteen miles, from Shah Malik's position on a hill far off to my left to Nur ad-Din's right flank near the river. Mohammed Sultan commanded my center, with Ak Boga in charge of the reserves—eighty regiments in the center sector alone.

Suliman attacked Nur ad-Din about mid-morning, only to meet a barrage of arrows and naphtha bombs from the catapults in the rear and a headlong counterattack by Nur ad-Din's powerful heavy cavalry. The Turks were forced back, and Shah Malik charged the enemy's right, commanded by Bayazid himself. Shah Malik met stiff resistance, though Shah Rukh, commanding his second element, broke through—where two Turkoman regiments, which had been seduced by my secret agents, suddenly deserted Bayazid to join my forces and crowd Peter Lazarus' Serbian Infantry toward the center.

Musa, Bayazid's second son, was cautious with his center command, preferring to battle toward his flanks and prevent envelopment by my circling wings, rather than charge my center and face the unknown power concealed in my two big ironbound chests. Mohammed Sultan came to my howdah and asked permission to charge Bayazid's center at once; but instead I ordered him to go to the aid of Shah Malik, who had all but surrounded a hill on which Bayazid and his infantry had found cover and were holding out stubbornly.

Peter Lazarus fell, and his Serbians fled before Shah Rukh's Herat Corps. Nur ad-Din also turned Suliman's flank, and the two wings of my army began closing the pincers—like the end of the big hunt on the tundra in my earlier campaign against Toktamish. Smaller and smaller the arc grew, until nearly all of the Turks were trapped directly in front of my center. Still Musa, facing my front of painted elephants, feared to charge; and I saw him send tavachis to his rear elements to see if escape to Yozgat was still open.

Then I ordered charge, and my kourrouns blew their blast, and the elephants pressed forward to the roll of my big nakaras. With a constant barrage of flaming fire maces pouring from the howdahs on their backs, the huge beasts moved relentlessly on, trampling the terrified Turks into jelly and leaving a mass of quivering, screaming wrecks in their wake.

Ak Boga's reserves spread around behind my original pincers to cut off escape through the first lines and to trap breakaways. By the middle of the afternoon, the main body of Bayazid's army had been annihilated—and no guns had been discovered anywhere in the enemy ranks.

So I retired to Bayazid's pavilion and ordered my evening meal prepared. I had my chests of secret weapons taken down from the elephants, which always marched immediately behind my own howdah, and put under guard again until I needed them against the Franks, who I knew had guns.

Bayazid continued to hold his hill until late afternoon; but when I sent additional reinforcements to my own men, he saw that the situation was hopeless and mounted a horse and tried to escape through my lines. Shah Malik shot Bayazid's horse from under him and brought the Turkish Sultan to the pavilion, where Shah Rukh and I had settled down to a leisurely game of chess.

Although the Sultan was ten or twelve years younger than I, it was a broken old man that Shah Malik brought in. I rose and limped over to the door to greet the great Emperor.

"It is ironic," I said, "that the mighty Bayazid, the Thunder of the West, had to surrender to a lame, impotent old grandfather like me."

Bayazid straightened up and made a pitiable attempt at dignity.

"Timur-i-Leng, you have powerful forces and excellent officers. Together we can wipe the infidel Christians from the face of the earth."

"That is a very presumptuous *we,*" I said, nettled by Bayazid's arrogance in calling me Timur-i-Leng to my face. "Together *we* shall not do anything. You have harbored my enemies, raided my borders, and hurled insults at my favorite wives. For each of those, you must pay."

"I will share what I have with a Sword Arm of the Faith," he said with less confidence than before.

"You will *give* all you have—which is nothing. You have nothing left to give. Angora has already fallen, and Nur ad-Din is even now marching on Bursa. You have nothing left to give except your own sorry life."

"My life?" Fear crowded arrogance out of his eyes.

"There is little doubt as to what my fate would have been if you had won today's battle. Take the sniveling coward away," I said to Shah Malik, and returned to my game of chess.

When Nur ad-Din returned from Bursa with my elephants loaded down with Bayazid's wealth and women, I moved into the palace in Angora. I had a gold-barred cage made for Bayazid; and with him locked inside and his favorite wife, Despina—the sister of Peter Lazarus of Serbia —walking along behind, naked and manacled to the aft thills, the elaborate palanquin led my entry into the city. The parade route was long and circuitous, to give the Turks ample opportunity to scoff at their dethroned Sultan and spit on his beautiful Christian wife, who had never before been seen outside the seraglio.

And I let Bayazid, clad in his royal robes and forced to hold his state scepter, act as host at the triumphal feast held in his own banquet hall. It was he who had to order his women to pass naked among my amirs and sing love songs and pour wine. And it was at the dinner that my adjutant announced that all of Bayazid's sons except Musa had either been killed or had fled from Turkey. I had lost no sons, though Mohammed Sultan had been badly wounded.

Finally Bayazid broke down completely and begged to be excused. I agreed and accompanied him to his former pleasure room.

"There are still some scores to be settled," I said, when we were seated in the luxurious seraglio.

"What else? What more?" he asked wearily.

"You threatened to violate my wife, Bibi Khanum, and my son's wife, Shalira."

"Yes," he admitted.

"You must realize that I have no personal feeling—no animosity—toward you for your idle threats. I always knew that you could never carry them out—but no ruler can allow such rash statements to go unrevenged. He must keep face with his followers."

"Go ahead—your men are raping my women already." He seemed utterly lacking in feeling.

"Oh, I wouldn't defile my body on your very best women," I said. "Nor would my son. But I think there is a solution."

I clapped my hands, and four slaves brought Bayazid's cage into the room.

"What—what are you going to do?" he asked in sudden alarm.

"A sort of reversal of the Scheherazade game," I said, and ordered Bayazid locked in his cage.

Then Despina was brought in by Amyris and men from his Kara Hazara.

"This is my son, Amyris, whose wife you insulted," I said to Bayazid.

The Negroes stripped Despina and laid her on Bayazid's pleasure couch. Eight of the biggest, finest Negro men also undressed and stood in readiness for the game.

"Despina herself shall be the judge of which man gives her greatest satisfaction. He shall be rewarded, as you and as I have rewarded the girls who pleased us most."

Bayazid recovered his speech and bellowed and cursed his futile disapproval. I excused myself to Bayazid, and spoke to Amyris.

"Take over, Son. See that the lady gets satisfaction—and Bayazid, too."

The next day I saw my standard raised over Istanbul by the Christian defenders, and heard reports that it flew likewise over Pera and the other suburbs of the Greek Manuel's capital.

Djon Pitr crossed the Bosporus and joined me at Uskudar. We returned to Bursa together, and he made his report.

"There is no reason for you to invade Europe, Father," he said. "All the wealth in Europe is not equal to the riches of one of your cities—Tabriz or Herat—not nearly equal to that of Samarkand."

"You misunderstand me, Son," I said. "I don't seek riches. I never have."

"And your men wouldn't find the women worth having. They prize chastity far above the arts of the harem. They require long courtship and wooing."

"I know," I said. "Your mother was one of them. I'm not looking for women for my soldiers."

"And the cities," Djon Pitr went on rapidly. "Mere villages. Paris has hardly sixty thousand people—London and Madrid even fewer."

"Stop arguing, Son," I said lightly. "Just tell me about the people. Were they surprised to meet a bishop so young as you?"

"No." Djon Pitr laughed. "They thought I was Prester John—some fabled priest who never grows old. Really, they are very backward and superstitious. I had a hard time convincing them that I was only Bishop

John of Sultaniah, a mere mortal. I'm not sure that I did. They are so ignorant about Asia."

"And I about Europe—as you call the lands of the Franks. Tell me, how do they live? What are the conditions?"

Djon Pitr wrinkled his brow and spoke seriously.

"This is not a continuation of my argument, Father. All of Europe is poor—ravaged by a hundred years' war, the plague, and dismal ignorance. Their substance has been wasted on armies for the Crusades and for war between the pitiable little kings."

"Pitiable little kings? Is there no central ruler? I thought Charles was a mighty monarch."

"No—no more than one of your hakims or darogas. There is no temporal head of Europe. Pope Boniface, the spiritual head at Rome, is the strongest force in the West, but even his power has been split by a great schism. Some provinces recognize the Avignon Antipope, Benedict."

"Popes and antipopes!" I said in momentary disgust. "Tell me about this Boniface. Is he poor? Plague-ridden?"

"No, Father," Djon Pitr said, and his eyes took on a new glow. "His palace in the Holy City, built on the site of Nero's gardens—though much smaller I understand—is in its way as beautiful and luxurious as your Heart's Delight in Samarkand. A veritable jewel, furnished by the love and sacrifice of his subjects."

"And his women—and his darogas? What are they like?" I asked. My son's report was beginning to make sense.

Djon Pitr laughed heartily.

"His women! Only nuns—colonies of religious virgins who have taken the oath of chastity and poverty as the Pope and all his priests have done."

It was my turn to laugh at my bishop son's naïveté.

"So this man—this Boniface—lives in luxury with only a colony of virgins, and his people live like slaves—in disease and poverty and misery, their substance dissipated in the support of armies for Holy Crusades. I suppose the Pope sponsors the Crusades?"

"Why, certainly, Father. Why do you ask?"

"Because I believe this Pope Boniface understands the Way of the Tree of Life as well as I do, and is far ahead of me in making it prevail in his land. Even his priests are avowed beggars."

"He certainly should understand religious history better than you do, Father," Djon Pitr said, laughing tolerantly. "He's spent his life studying and interpreting the Holy Word."

"Very accurately, I should say. Son, is all this true?" I asked seriously.

"Yes, Father, certainly." His eyes were serious.

And I believed my son. Ali Soun had always had a strange, unbeliev-

394

able, high regard for truth—something I could never understand—and she had transmitted it to Djon Pitr. He had always been scrupulously honest.

I pondered his words carefully. From what he said, it seemed that little kings and popes and antipopes, working blindly perhaps, had already reduced the people of Europe to a state of slavery acceptable to Allah. My life was drawing to a close, and the Ming Emperor of Khitai seemed to be the last great ruler on earth who did not see the Way clearly. Not Europe, but perhaps Khitai was the land still to be won to the Way; and there I could capture Khitan scientists who knew the secrets of the dreaded gunpowder.

"All right, Son," I said at length, "I believe you. I shall not cross the Bosporus. When the Franks get out from under the control of Boniface and his system—that will be the time for my people to carry the Flaming Sword to the West. The time is not ripe now. There's no need for me to invade Europe." *

"You mean it, Father? You're really not going on?"

"No, Son. You may go on back to Sultaniah. Tell your mother that I'm not going to take her home—not to Inglistan."

"She'll like that," he said, and I thought I saw his eyes grow moist. "I can't make you out, Father. I thought nothing could stop you. Now you do as I ask, as Mother wishes. I don't understand you."

"Don't try to," I said, and smiled at his ignorance. "Your Church has blinded you so that you no longer see the world. None of your faith can understand those of us who see the Way, undistorted by the sick babbling of demented priests and prophets. You don't understand Boniface, either. But never mind—go to your mother and share your good news. Tell her I'll be along in a few weeks."

Djon Pitr rose to leave. His brow was puzzled, but his eyes still shone.

"By the way, Son," I said. "What do the Franks call me?"

"They call you *Tamerlan.*"

"*Tamerlan*—that would be Timur-i-Leng, wouldn't it?"

"Yes, Father—a corruption of Timur-i-Leng. But they don't know what it means. They don't intend to be disrespectful," he added hastily, and his face was suddenly clouded.

"Don't worry, Djon," I said. "I'm not offended. I won't change my mind about invading Europe." Later, perhaps, after captive scientists had been pressed into my service, I or my people could conquer Europe at will.

---

* For five hundred years, historians have argued about Timur's reasons for turning back at Bursa. Many Christians have believed that Boniface's prayers kept the old Tatar from crossing the Bosporus.

He smiled again quickly and hurried away to join a post-guard going east to Tabriz and Sultaniah.

And I found the Franks far from disrespectful. In addition to the complimentary message from King Charles the Sixth of the Franks, I got greetings from King Henry the Fourth of Inglistan; and King Henry the Third of Castile sent two Spanish bahaturs, Pala de Santo Mayor and Fernando de Palazuelos, to pay his respects to me. The two Spaniards, who were pious followers of Pope Boniface, showed no marked respect for the chastity of the women I gave them, a Greek princess named Maria and Angelina, the sister of the Count of Hungary. Despite their Christian faith, they seemed to prize highly the techniques which the two beauties had acquired in Bayazid's harem.

Upon my return to Angora, I learned that Kara Yussuf had fled into the Arabian Desert and Sultan Ahmed had been imprisoned by the Mamluk Sultan, who had at last learned my true strength and decided to become my ally. My army, moving by corps, had pressed on to the sea at several points, including Smyrna, which fell to Nur ad-Din within two weeks, though the Christians there had held out against the Turks for over three years.

I established Amyris as daroga of Angora; and when I left, Nubja asked to remain, saying that she would not be of any use to me in Samarkand any more. Since I feared that Amyris' white queen might not inspire the full loyalty of the Negroes in Asia Minor, I granted Nubja her wish and let her assume the title of Queen Mother and head of the royal household.

But my campaign against Bayazid was not an unmarred victory. Mohammed Sultan died a week before I planned to return to Samarkand. So the long trek back home was a somber cortege for my grandson. But I traveled secure in the knowledge that I was master of the world from the Mediterranean Sea to the Great Wall of Khitai—from the spongy tundra of Sibir to the Indian Ocean. Khitai was the only country left on the continent of Asia which was not under my sovereignty. And it was next.

CHAPTER

16

After the burial of Mohammed Sultan and the breaking of his sword and nakaras, I declared the period of mourning at an end and decreed two months of feasting and reveling in Samarkand. Complete at last, dominated by the beautiful new Bibi Khanum dome, the city was truly the Sapphire of the Orient.

I saw no irony in the fact that my city was realized after my vision had become too dim for me to see its beauty in all the subtle shades. I knew well that men who set their hearts on the tangible things of this world—the visible lures of Allah—are doomed to attain their goals too late to enjoy them. In Samarkand I saw rather the proof of the efficacy of my Way, the unsought rewards for understanding Allah's will and making it prevail. Even greedy, worldly, wealth-seeking men must have recognized in my city a symbol of the favor I had earned of Allah.

So I was not dazzled by the splendor of Samarkand, as were my guests from all parts of Asia, and at least one from Europe—Ruy Gonzalez de Clavijo,* an envoy from King Henry of Castile, the westernmost land of the Franks. Nor did I participate generally in the festivities, though they were the total of all my former celebrations rolled into one, with elephant fights and tumblers and jugglers and dancers and wire walkers and magic lantern shows and every other form of entertainment. I made the necessary appearances at banquets and court functions; but I spent most of my time on Hermitage Hill planning my campaign into Khitai, or with my staff in the Bibi Khanum quarter studying the peculiarities of the architecture we would have to attack.

Only a few of my highest officers knew of my projected expedition to the north and east.

"Amir Timur," argued Nur ad-Din, "your army is weary—and you, Amir, are old—seventy-one—"

"Seventy-two," I corrected him. "That is why we can't delay."

"Seventy-two, then," said Nur ad-Din. "All the more reason why you should rest for a while. Winter is near—the whole north will be frozen. Wait at least until spring."

"No," I said. "Ours is not just a campaign of conquest, seeking personal triumph. We have been chosen; our duty is a sacred one. You are my best—Allah's best—destined to make His Way prevail throughout the earth. Only Khitai remains outside our orbit."

Nur ad-Din bowed to my will, and the others voiced no further objections. So we planned and studied and held council while other men made holiday at the court.

Toward the end of the second month, I made a trip to Shehri-Sebz to see the new golden dome on Aljai's tomb and the similar tiled bulb on the tomb shared by Jahangir and Omar Sheik. The golden one, though only a miniature of the Bibi Khanum dome, was exquisite in its prim beauty—like Aljai, unpretentious but perfect in its way. I turned away satisfied, and walked back through the garden, through dry crisp snow like the snow we had sifted over Aljai's grave forty years before.

* Clavijo has described Samarkand and Timur's court in his *Historia del gran Tamerlan e itinerario y narracion del viaje, etc.*

I decided to depart at once. If my time was up, better to die on the road to Khitai than in restful sloth at the comfortable palace in Samarkand. Die on the way. Die on the Way.

When my time came to lead the powerful center corps out of Samarkand, the entire city turned out in the winter cold to bid me farewell.

Djon Pitr and Ali Soun came from Devon together. Djon Pitr was leading a beautiful white stallion.

"This is for you, Father," he said, as I prepared to mount my howdah which led the column—just in front of the two secret chests.

"For me?" I said.

"Yes, from Mother. She says that she has never been able to give you anything, and you've given her everything."

Ali Soun was too full of emotion to speak for herself; but her eyes, smarting with tears in the cold wind, were voluble in their expressiveness.

"Nonsense," I said. "She, too, has given everything. She's given me you, my bishop son."

It cost so little to say it, and it gave Ali Soun the happiness she perhaps deserved.

"He was the finest we could buy," said Djon Pitr. "Mother calls him Ak Ruksh."

Ak Ruksh—"White Charger"—Ali Soun was a romantic to the end.

"I had a horse named Ak Ruksh once before," I said.

"Then call him Ak Ruksh the Second," Djon Pitr said, and smiled at his mother. She knelt in the snow and kissed my hand.

I turned from the elephant and mounted Ak Ruksh II instead. Then I signaled "forward" and rode down the Way of Triumph to the gate.

Beyond the Zaravshan, I turned in the saddle and looked back at Samarkand and the blue and gold Bibi Khanum dome, floating over my city, filled with the stuff clouds and men's dreams are made of.

We encountered heavy snow at Tashkand and stayed in Khalil Sultan's camp for a week. When the snowfall ceased, my amirs again urged me to wait in Tashkand until spring. They insisted that the road through the mountains was impassable. But, like Bayazid, they had not taken my elephants into account. I ordered rugs laid on the snow, and the elephants went over them, trampling and packing the snow to a firm footing for horses and camels and oxen and asses and other sharp-hoofed animals.

And we moved on slowly, three or four miles a day, up and across the frozen Syr-Darya to Otrar and the big warm wooden palace I had built there for Omar Sheik. But no farther—for I took sick again, of the sickness I had had in Tashkand for forty days on my campaign against Toktamish.

And I knew by the congestion in my lungs that it was no forty-day

398

sickness this time. The physician examined me and clucked his tongue and shook his head and then smiled his silly reassuring smile. And Mir Sayyid read to me from the Koran and counseled me on my preparation to meet Allah. Silly fool! For seventy years I had lived in Allah's world, reading His Way more accurately than any mollah and obeying His Will to perfection—rewarded by all the prizes, all the riches, the loveliest women of His creation. For seventy years I had been at home in Allah's world. I would surely be at home in Allah's Paradise—if there were such a place—without having to listen to the empty prattle of priests.

When Dilshad arrived from Samarkand, I knew that my end was near. The trip had been near impossible, too much for a mere visit from the Sarai Khanum. But Dilshad was smiling and comforting in the inanities she spoke to me when she came to my bedside. More to the point was her whisper to Nur ad-Din as she left.

"Sevin Bey Khanzade is with Khalil Sultan," she said. "They're plotting—but don't tell *him.*"

Don't tell me! It was my sight that was dim, not my hearing. Let them plot, if Khalil were strong enough or foolish enough.*

I ordered everyone out of my room and summoned Abdullah. He, too, was a wrinkled, bearded old man—seventy by his calendar.

"I suppose your scum has the usual hidden exits from Otrar, too?" I said.

"Yes, Amir."

"All right. I have one more job for you. How are we fixed on blind mute slaves?"

"There are always a few around, Amir," he replied.

"Very well. Here's a key to the hidden room where my secret chests are stored. Go there secretly. Have the blind mutes empty the chests and wrap what they find in sackcloth. Then take the stuff far out on the steppes and bury it—each piece in a different place. Go a different way on each trip. Can you do that without being discovered?"

"Yes, I think so, Amir."

"And then I want the chests broken into bits and carried out the same way. When the room is opened, I want it found empty—not empty chests but an empty room. Do you understand?"

"Yes, Amir, perfectly." His wry smile convinced me that he understood, perhaps too well.

"When you have finished, bring the key back to me."

* Sevin Bey and Khalil Sultan were successful for a time. They seized Samarkand immediately, refused even to allow Timur's body brought inside the walls for burial, and defeated the army Pir Mohammed brought out of India to challenge them. It was Shah Rukh, encouraged by Dilshad, who finally overthrew Khalil Sultan, and established himself on the throne at Samarkand.

"Yes, Amir."

Abdullah left, and I did not see him again for several days. In the meanwhile, I dictated my will to N'il Mahdi-Soun. I made Pir Mohammed my successor—he was Sevin Bey's son by Jahangir, whom Dilshad loved. I thought perhaps he might be the best compromise, if there were one.*

And between visits by my amirs and Dilshad and others, I rushed my dictation to N'il Mahdi-Soun. He was more than an amanuensis. Perhaps much of the story is more his than mine, but I think he was fairly accurate. He knew the words, even though he did not always know what I meant by them.

He was up to date on his chronicle by the time Abdullah returned my key. Only he was with me when Abdullah reported—and he, of course, knew all by that time.

"Have you finished?" I asked Abdullah.

"Yes, Amir, completely," he said, and put the key in my hand.

"Not a trace left?"

"Not a trace, Amir."

"No one knows what was in those chests—no one but you and me," I said to my servant.

Even after my death, no one must ever know that the chests contained junk—that I had been less than I seemed—that I had boasted vainly. Abdullah must have understood that.

I rang my bell, and my guards came into the room.

"My servant has betrayed me," I said to the tuk-bashi in charge. "Take him out and kill him."

"Abdullah?" asked the officer in astonishment.

"Yes, Abdullah. Pay no attention to what he says. Behead him."

"I have little to say," said Abdullah, smiling a sad, wry smile as the guards reluctantly grasped his arms. "As you have lived and prospered, Amir, so have I lived and prospered. As you die, so must I die. And you are dying now."

His eyes hardened above his stiffening smile, and he added, "The physician says that you will not live out the night."

I waved my hand, and the guards took Abdullah away.

The excitement had drawn a roomful of people. I could not make out who they all were.

---

* Timur's choice was justified. Pir Mohammed was his ablest heir. Although he was defeated in his attempt to take Samarkand from Khalil Sultan, he sired a strong line of Timurids, the Moghuls who ruled India until the British gained control of the country in 1765. Samarkand enjoyed a reign of prosperity and enlightenment under Shah Rukh, but the empire crumbled when his sons succeeded him.

"Get out!" I said impatiently to the stupid gaping fools. "Get out. I have work to do."

"Do you want me to read a sura from the Koran?" asked the unctuous voice of Mir Sayyid.

"No," I said. "Tonight I write my own sura. Now, get out, all of you!"

There was a scramble of feet on the board floor, and a door closed, and all was quiet again.

"Are we alone, Son?" I asked N'il Mahdi-Soun.

"Yes, Father, quite alone."

"Then listen carefully. Get your writing materials ready. I shall dictate my sura. Take down all I say. Then moisten my right hand with the royal red ink and press my print on the page. Do you understand me?"

"Yes, Father."

I heard him rattling the paper on his desk.

"When you have done that," I went on, "get your manuscript and read to me—the parts about Aljai. As long as you think I can hear you—whether I can speak or open my eyes or move—as long as you think I can hear you, read me the parts about Aljai—"

I paused and mused for a few seconds. I found it difficult to speak.

"Are you ready, Son?" I asked.

"Yes, Father. I'm ready."

"Very well, we shall begin—and end—my sura. Write as I dictate—

SURA

This is the Sura of Timur. May it be the Sacred Word of Scholars, Slaves, and Rulers.

To Scholars is given the power of the Word, the power to twist and distort and subvert any creed or ideology to serve the ends of the Way.

The reward of Scholars is the satisfaction of knowing that they can make Truth and persuade men to believe.

To Slaves is given the power of the Passions, the power of Fear and Envy and Hate, to drag down their masters and all other men.

The reward of Slaves is the satisfaction of their Passions, the destruction of the fruits of their enforced labor, the impoverishment and humiliation of their masters.

To Rulers is given the power of the Flaming Sword, the power to levy taxes and wage war, the supreme power to reduce all men to Slavery and Beggary, the power to which the Word and the Passions must be subservient.

The reward of Rulers is the satisfaction in Power for its own sake, as

401

most Rulers understand it, the Power to control the riches and minds and lives of all men according to the Will of Allah.

The outer facts of my life are irrefutable testament to the truth and the efficacy of these tenets. For seventy years I have been invincible. So, too, may Scholars, Slaves, and Rulers be forever invincible if they will but combine their several powers and wield the Flaming Sword to keep the Way of the Tree of Life.

Written in the presence of Timur, at Otrar, on the 17th day of Shaaban, 807 A. H., by the hand of his son.

GLOSSARY

In the transliteration of words from oriental dialects, Roman letters are chosen for their phonetic similarity to the original Sanskrit or Arabic characters. So the strange words in this book are likely to sound very much as the reader thinks they should at first glance. The consonants are pronounced as they would be in English, and the vowels are fairly close to the Italian vowels. The short *a* is the notable exception; it frequently loses character and approximates the *ŭ* in *bŭt*. For example, the following words sound about the same as their English equivalents: *jăngăl*, jungle; *căkkăr*, chukker; and *kămărbănd*, cummerbund. The effect will be more nearly accurate if all syllables are more evenly stressed, with accents less exaggerated, than they would be in English.

Abaku, *ă bă kū'*, Caspian (Sea)

Abdullah, *ăb dŭl'lă*

ad-Din, *ăd dēn*, "of the Faith" in proper names of descendants of Mohammed, as "Sherif ad-Din," Prince of the Faith

agha, *ă'gă*, lady of noble birth; Agha, Lady (title)

A.H., after the Hegira

Ahmed, *ä'mĕd*

Ak Ruksh, *ăk rōoksh*, white horse; "White Charger," Timur's horse

Ak Sarai, *ăk să rī'*, white palace

Ali, *ä'lĭ*

Aljai, *ăl'jĭ*

Alysoun, *ăl'ĭ sōon'* (Ali Soun)

amir, *ă mēr'*, a nobleman or chief; Amir, Lord (title)

Amu-Darya, *ä'mōo där'yă*, the Oxus River

Amyris, *ăm'ĭ rĭs*

arak, *ă răk'*, citadel

aul, *oul*, a Mongol nomad village

ayah, *ī'yăh*, a verse in the Koran; a line of poetry

ayat, *ī'yăt*, plural of ayah

azan, *ă zăn'*, the prayer ritual or litany of the Moslems

Badakshan, *bă'dăk shăn'*

bahatur, *bă hă tūr'*, a knight or valiant warrior

bakshish, *băk'shēsh*, alms, the beggars' cry for alms

Balkh, *bălk*

Balkhash, *băl kăsh'*

banja, *băn'jă* or *băn'yă*, a bathhouse, a steam bath

Bayazid, *bĭ yăz'ĭd*

begum, *bē'gŭm*, a Mohammedan princess of highest rank, a descendant of Mohammed; Begum, Princess (title)

bhang, *băng*, raw unprocessed hemp or hashish, a narcotic

Bibi Khanum, *bē'bē kăn'ŭm*

Bokhara, *bō kä'ră*

cakkar, *kăk'är*, chukker, a period of play in polo

Daoud, *doud*

daroga, *dă rō'gă*, a governor

darya, *där'yă*, river

desht, *dĕsht*, desert; Desht-i-Kavir, Salt Desert, etc.

Dilshad, *dēl'shăd*

dinar, *dē när'*, the standard gold coin of the Moslem world

dristis, *drēs'tĭs*, eye glances accompanying Indian dances

(tāke, fäther, păth, ēve, gĕt, tīde, tĭp, tōll, côrd, tūbe, bŭt, bûrn, tōol, house)

Elchi, *āl'chē*

fakih, *fá kē'*, a lawyer schooled in Moslem law

ghulam, *gōō'lám*, a slave

gorkhar, *górk'ár*, an Asiatic ass

Hadji, *hăd'jĭ*; hadji, a pilgrim to Mecca

hakim, *há kēm'*, a governor

hazara, *há zär'á*, a squadron of cavalry; Gok Hazara, Blue Squadron; Kara Hazara, Black Squadron; Tulu Hazara, Mad Squadron

Herat, *hĕ rät'*

howdah, *hou'dá*, a cab or litter mounted on an elephant

Hussayn, *hŭs' sīn*

imam, *ĭ mäm'*, a holy man

Jahangir, *já hän'gēr*

Jaku, *já kū'*

janissary, *jăn'ĭ sĕr'ĭ*, a Turkish infantry-man

Jhelum, *jā'lŭm*

jihad, *jē häd'*, a holy war

jubbah, *jū'bá*, a long robe, especially a priest's robe

Kabul, *ká bōōl'*

Kaikosru, *kī'kōs rōō'*

kalpak, *kál'pák'*, the fur or caracul caps worn by the Kazaks (Cossacks)

kankali, *kán'ká lē'*, a cart with eight-foot wheels used on the steppes; Kankali, the tribe associated with the carts

Karakorum, *kä'rá kō'rŭm*

Karin al Raschid, *kär'ĭn ál rásh'ĭd*

karnash, *kär näsh'*, formal court greet-ing

Karshi, *kär'shē*, modern city of Bek Budi

Kashgar, *kásh'gár'*

Kashmir, *kásh'mēr'*

kathakali, *ká'thá ká lē'*, an Indian finger-dance

kazak, *ká zäk'*, a desert raider; Kazak, Cossack

Khaibar, *kī'bár*, Khaibar or Khyber Pass

khalat, *ká lát'*, a court coat, the horse-hide military tunic of the Kazaks (Cos-sacks)

Khalil, *ká lēl'*

kha khan, *kä'kän'*, king of kings, emperor

khan, *kän*, king

khanum, *kän'ŭm*, princess, queen

khanzade, *kän zä'dĕ*, princess, "daughter of the king"

khatun agha, *ká tūn' ä'gá*, lord's lady, mistress

Khitai, *kī'tī'*, Cathay, China

Khiva, *kē'vá*

Khojend, *kō'jĕnd*

Khorassan, *kō rá sän'*, old name for Per-sia, "Land of the Sun"

kiang, *kyáng*, an Asiatic ass

kibitka, *kĭ bĕt'ká*, a domed felt tent used by the Mongols

kopeghi, *kō pä'gĭ*, dog; Leng Kopeghi, "Lame Dog"

kourroun, *kōō'rōōn'*, long straight trum-pet, usually bass in timbre

kukri, *kōō'krē*, a curved Ghurka dagger

kulchi, *kōōl'chē*, a personal guard, mem-ber of elite corps

kum, *kūm*, sand, desert; Kara (*ká'rá*) Kum, Black Sands; Kyzyl (*kĭz'ĭl*) Kum, Red Sands; Muyun (*mōō'yŭn*) Kum, White Sands

kumiss, *kōō'mĭs*, an intoxicating bever-age made from fermented mare's milk

Kumrud, *kŭm'rōōd'*

Kunduz, *kŭn dōōz'*

kurultai, *kōō'rŭl tī'*, an assembly of no-bles, a parliament

kutbeh, *kōōt'bá*, a prayer for the king

lohar, *lō'hár*, blacksmith; Bara Lohar, Big Smithy

maharajah, *má hä'rä'já*, Indian king

maharani, *má hä'rä'nē*, Indian queen

mahdi, *mä'dē*, a prophet

mahout, *má hout'*, an elephant trainer or handler, elephant boy

Mashad, *mäsh'ád*

medress, *mä'drĕs*, an academy

metheglin, *mĕ thĕg'lĭn*, beer made from honey, mead

ming-bashi, *mĭng'bá shē'*, commander of a thousand men, colonel

Miran Shah, *mĭ rän' shä'*

mollah, *mō'lá*, a Moslem priest

Moskva, *môsk'vá*, Moscow

Mouva, *mōō'vá*

mudras, *mōō'dräs*, hand positions in In-dian finger dances

404

Musa, *mū'sá*

nakara, *nä kä'rä*, a kettledrum, tympanum, saddle drum

Nubja, *nūb'jä* or *nūb'yä*

ordu, *ôr dōō'*, a royal encampment

Otrar, *ō trär'*

palanquin, *päl'än kēn'*, an enclosed litter or sedan chair

Pamir, *pä mēr'*

pandit, *pän'dĭt*, an Indian scholar

pilaf, *pē läf'*, a stew of rice, herbs and chopped meat

pir, *pēr*, prince; Pir, Prince (title)

Punjab, *pŭn jäb'*

purdah, *pûr'dä*, a curtain, the practice of segregating women in harems

Rajput, *räj'pōōt*, Hindu warrior caste

registan, *rĕg'ĭs tän'*, a public square

rubayah, *rōō bī'yä*, a quatrain

Saif ad-Din, *sīf äd dēn*

Sali Sarai, *sä lē'sä rī'*

Samarkand, *sä'mär känd'*

sarai, *sä rī'*, a camp, a palace

Sarai Khanum, *sä rī' kän'ŭm*, Princess of the Palace, Empress

sari, *sä'rē*, a one-piece dress worn by Indian women

sart, *särt*, a low-born city dweller, a peasant

sayyid, *sī'yĭd*, a Moslem, a sage

Sevin Bey, *sĕv'ĭn bä*

Shalira, *shä lē'rä*

shashlyk, *shä shlĭk'*, a skewer of meat and herbs broiled over coals

Shehri-Sebz, *shä'rĭ sĕbz'*, Shakrysabz, Timur's birthplace

Shereza Begum, *shĕ rē'zä bē'gŭm*

sherif, *shĕ rēf'*, a Moslem prince, also a Moslem scholar

Sherif ad-Din, *shĕ rēf' äd dēn*

sipahi, *sĭ pä'hē*, a Turkish infantryman or light cavalryman

Srinagar, *srē näg'är*

sura, *sōō'rä*, a chapter or section of the Koran

Syr-Darya, *sēr där'yä*

Tabriz, *tä brēz'*

talwar, *täl'wär'*, a Persian sword with a slightly curved blade

tarjuman, *tär'jū män*, a dragoman, and interpreter

Tashkand, *täsh'känd'*, Tashkent

Tatar, *tä'tär*, (Sometimes *Tartar* in European languages)

Tatary, *tä'tär ĭ*, Timur's empire

tavachi, *tä vä'chē*, aide-de-camp, member of officer's staff

Timur-i-Leng, *tē'mōōr ē läng*, Timur the Lame

Toktamish, *tōk'tä mēsh'*

tuk-bashi, *tōōk'bä shē'*, commander of one hundred men, captain

tuman-bashi, *tōō'män bä shē'*, commander of ten thousand men, general

ulama, *ū lä'mä*, an assembly of high churchmen of Islam

Ulatai, *ū'lä tī'*

Urganj, *ûr'gänj*

yataghan, *yät'ä gän'*, a Persian sword with a straighter blade than the scimitar or the talwar

yurt, *yûrt*, a Mongol tent

Zain ad-Din, *zīn äd dēn*

zenana, *zĕ nä'nä*, harem, seraglio

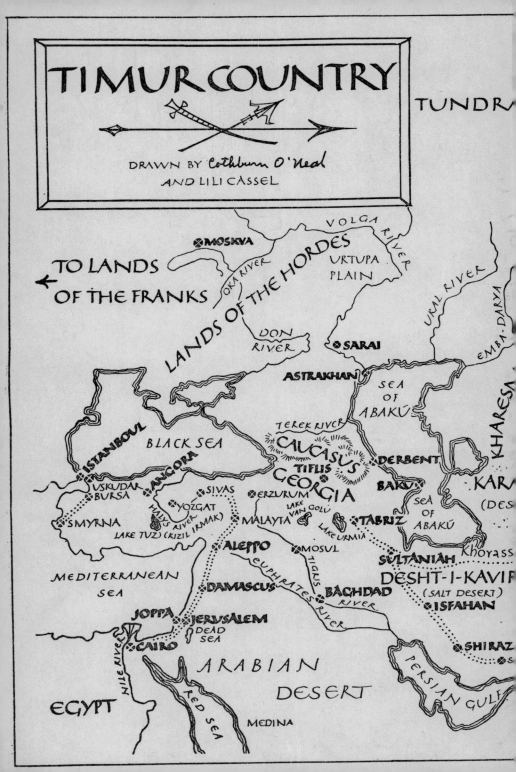